The woman they loved

Many men needed Elizabeth. Some, for her beauty and fame. Others, for her indomitable courage.

ALAN—The storybook romance transformed into a nightmare . . .

QUIGLEY—Could her great strength save him from his own destruction?

ADAM—Over the years, he taught her all there was to know about passion, joy—and heartbreak . . .

TONY—The impossible affair, the greatest love . . .

Fawcett Popular Library Books
by Helen Van Slyke

ALWAYS IS NOT FOREVER	04271	$2.25
THE BEST PEOPLE	08456	$2.50
THE BEST PLACE TO BE	04024	$2.50
THE HEART LISTENS	08520	$2.75
A NECESSARY WOMAN	04544	$2.75
SISTERS AND STRANGERS	04445	$2.50

THE HEART LISTENS

Helen Van Slyke

FAWCETT POPULAR LIBRARY ◆ NEW YORK

For the dear friends
who lightened this labor of love.

THE HEART LISTENS

Published by Fawcett Popular Library Books, a unit of CBS
Publications, the Consumer Publishing Division of CBS Inc.,
by arrangement with Doubleday & Company, Inc.

PRINTED IN THE UNITED STATES OF AMERICA

First Fawcett Popular Library printing: September 1975

32   31   30   29   28   27   26   25   24

introduction

CALIFORNIA 1972

The hands were soft and thin now. Almost birdlike as they rested lightly on the arms of the chair. She pretended that they belonged to someone else, some woman other than Elizabeth Quigly. It was a game she enjoyed playing, fantasizing that she was some chance acquaintance meeting and making a quick assessment of herself. What would a stranger have thought of those neat, idle hands with their oval-shaped, unpolished nails, the beginnings of the faint swelling of arthritis at the joints? He would not have seen a bruise or a callus to betray all the years of hard work. There was not even a nicotine stain to commemorate the hundreds of thousands of cigarettes which hadn't killed her yet, though the doctors kept saying they would. Just as they said that the martinis she loved would be the death of her.

Elizabeth smiled. Poor, dumb stranger. He would have pegged her as a pampered old lady, rolling gently into her sixty-eighth year, her days spent in serene contemplation of the picture-postcard scenery outside her window. A surface analysis. Deceptive, as most are. It had been nearly fifty years since anyone had pampered Elizabeth. Many had loved her. Not a few had used her. Some, she liked to think, had benefited by knowing her. But none had pampered her. It was not a word one used in thinking of this handsome, white-haired woman with the alert blue eyes, the quick humor, the sturdy, competent air. "Elizabeth is so incredibly self-sufficient," they said. As though she never needed a shoulder to weep on, arms to shield her, quiet words to gentle away the hurts and fears. "Elizabeth can take care of herself," they said. And so she had.

Nor, dear stranger, was she serene. The quality mistaken for serenity is control, self-discipline. And, most of all, pride. She had built the myth of capability, fostered it. In a strange way, she supposed, even enjoyed it. Now she was stuck with it. Her still clear gaze took in the great stretch of beach below her, the restless Pacific assaulting the great black rocks, the stretch of arrogant, unassailable Monterey pines scattered like an army of memories across her line of vision. She sat quietly. And inside she laughed at herself. And at the giant joke that calls itself life.

part I

BOSTON 1905-1933

Chapter 1

Ann Treadwell Quigly was the first of her friends or family to have a baby in a hospital. In 1905 it was considered suitable to give birth at home, preferably in the same bed in which the mother and her mother and her mother's mother had been born. A bed that had come to America from England or Ireland and been handed down, reverently, through the generations to receive each succeeding infant. Ann would have none of it. This was her fourth pregnancy but her first child. And after three miscarriages, she was far less interested in tradition than in safely producing the son that Charles so desperately wanted. "New England antiques are fine for tea parties," she said crisply, "but with my history of nonreproduction I'd much rather look at sterile instruments in a delivery room than at Great-aunt Charlotte's dauntless old face staring at me from the foot of my bed."

Her adoring Charles agreed in this, as he did in the case of nearly everything Ann made up her mind to do. He was a gentle, loving man, soft-spoken and devoted to this woman whose mind was as strong as her body was delicate. He did, indeed, want children. And his disappointment at their failure to have them was as great as Ann's, though he took pains to

11

keep that fact well hidden. "We have each other, Annie," he reassured her when she raged against her inability to go full term in her pregnancies.

"Nonsense," she said. "You, Mr. Quigly, are going to have a fine, strapping son if I have to die trying."

The words turned out to be frighteningly ominous but only partially true. Ann Quigly did die trying. And though she produced a healthy, nine-pound baby, it was not the son she had predicted but a beautiful little girl whom a heart-broken Charles named Elizabeth. His family and his wife's pleaded with him to name the baby after Ann, but he refused. "There is only one Ann," he said. "Always was. Always will be for me." Out of courtesy to the relatives, he compromised by giving his daughter her mother's name as a middle name, but aside from her baptismal certificate, it was never used. "Ann and I were both fascinated by Elizabeth the First," he explained. "Such a proud yet loving queen. She had compassion with strength of purpose. A woman of tender fire. I want this child to have dignity and courage. As her mother had."

He never discussed it again. She was Elizabeth Quigly. Never Beth. Or Betty. Or Liz. Or Liza. Elizabeth suited her, for she did indeed, from infancy, have a kind of regal bearing that went with her name. She was a solemn baby, almost as though she knew what was expected of her. As a child, it was evident that she had her mother's high spirits and determination, as well as Ann's beautiful face. And she had, as well, the good mind, the humor, and the soft understanding of Charles Quigly.

"It's God's blessing," Ann's mother said. "She's everything that my own dear daughter was, and more. There's much of the good of you in Elizabeth, too. What a great joy she is, Charles. And how happy Ann must be, knowing that she has left you such a precious living memory."

The bereaved husband could never quite look at it that way. He was still a young man, yet the thought of remarriage did not occur to him. He knew that a life built around a "living memory" was an incomplete existence, yet he was incapable of giving of himself to another woman in any permanent sense. His life was almost monastic. He sought forgetfulness in his work as a professor at Harvard, happiness in the company of his lively daughter. And he waited, without real hope, for grief to subside. Amazingly, he did not spoil Elizabeth. He tried to be both mother and father to her, thankful that he was sufficiently advanced in the knowledge of psychology not to blame her, even subsconsciously, for the loss of the woman who never could be replaced. Occasionally he cheerlessly paid for the physical relief afforded by some prostitute who would never be seen again. And on these rare occasions he turned to the house in Cambridge therapeutically restored, drained and untouched as though he had endured some boring but necessary exercise. He lived, not entirely for Elizabeth, but for the sense of security he could bring her. He did all he could to compensate for her "lopsided life." And Elizabeth understood and adored him.

She grew up as her own person. Sometimes a puzzling one. Beneath the circumspect, predictable exterior of the well-bred Boston girl there was another, unconventional Elizabeth, full of curiosity and a strange kind of hunger for life. She accepted, gracefully, the "outer trappings," the comfortable, middle-class house near the university. The daily maid-cook. The seemingly endless supply of aunts and cousins and grandmothers always ready with advice about the preparation of meals, the intricacies of needlework and, later, the delicate facts of emerging womanhood. She did not go away to school. Charles urged it, but with Annlike determination she saw no need to leave the home or the father she loved. She had many friends, went to and gave parties, and indicated that she fully expected to marry a Bostonian and spend her life in the city of her birth.

That was the Elizabeth on public view. The other one was known only to herself and only glimpsed, briefly and disquietingly, by Charles. At sixteen, this pent-up Elizabeth was beginning to hammer ever so lightly at the bars of her comfortable cage. She arrived home at eleven o'clock one night from a party to which she had been escorted by a young man Charles knew and liked. Charles was reading in the library and Elizabeth came in and curled up on the floor beside his chair. She sighed deeply. Her father lowered his book.

"That sounded as though it had great significance," he said lightly. "What's the matter, baby? The party all that dull?"

She patted him lightly on the knee. "Parties aren't dull, Professor. People are dull. At least the people I know are dull."

"Thanks very much."

"Not you, silly. People my age. They don't care about anything important. My Lord, you'd think the world began and ended in Boston!"

Charles frowned. "And what do you think?"

Elizabeth's chin went up in the determined gesture that was to stay with her through her life. "I think there's a whole magic universe out there. Full of exciting places to go. Wonderful things to see. Danger, maybe, but that's part of the gloriousness of it. There must be so many things to change. So much to do for other people. I'd like to reach out and scoop up experiences with both hands. But the people I know are only interested in getting through school and getting married and having babies and letting their whole lives go by without doing anything more exciting than belonging to the PTA! I wish I'd been a man and could have gone to Europe with the army! At least I'd have felt that I was helping to change something!"

Charles smiled. "My dear Elizabeth, I doubt that General Pershing would have accepted a twelve-year-old infantryman. Even one as high-spirited as you."

She laughed. "Don't tease, Father. You know what I mean. People are so self-centered. All they care about is their own well-being. Nice, safe, selfish lives. They'll die and nobody will know they ever lived. I can't bear that idea. My life is going by and I want it to mean something!"

"For heaven's sake, child, you're only sixteen."

"Sixteen, sixty, what's the difference? People are so stupid. So lacking in curiosity. Haven't you ever wanted to accomplish great, exciting things, Father?"

He shook his head. "I guess I'm one of those without curiosity. All I ever wanted was my work. And you. And your mother."

She felt ashamed. "I know. I'm sorry."

"Don't be," Charles said. "If the world didn't have people like you, Elizabeth, it would be a very dull place indeed. Like one gigantic library, I suppose. All dark and hushed and somber. Living would be a terribly pedestrian business without the impatient ones. The seekers. Always searching for something new, something relevant to leave their mark on. Always on tiptoe, anticipating discovery. Such people find change as necessary as the air they breathe."

"Is that a bad way to be?"

"No," he said, "but it can be dangerous. Or heartbreaking. Or both."

She looked puzzled.

"What I mean is, my dear, that when you plunge into such ambitious waters, you can drown in a sea of disappointment. You yourself become vulnerable. People can disappoint you cruelly. Sometimes, the more you try to help, the more harm you do, to yourself and others. Helping others can be a thankless task. I don't mean helping in the sense of church or charity. I mean taking a hand in other people's destinies. Giving of yourself, your knowledge, your understanding, is a wonderful thing, Elizabeth, as long as you keep it in perspective. Sometimes, you know, it's possible to confuse crusading with ego. You've got to remember that you're not God. He helps but He never meddles. He doesn't need that kind of self-gratification."

"I don't understand," Elizabeth said.

"Nor should you. Even if my philosophy were a little less obscure, you're a bit young to understand. And perhaps I am misconstruing simple youthful restlessness as exaggerated zeal. Let me give you one example, though, before we drop the subject. Do you remember your cousin Natalie?"

"The one who lives in New York?"

"That's the one. Your second cousin, really. She was your mother's cousin. Anyway, Natalie was a seeker. Anyone with a hard-luck story headed straight for Natalie. And if they didn't, she went looking for them. Your mother used to say that Natalie surrounded herself with the 'waifs and strays'—people with money problems or romantic problems or job problems. Your cousin counseled them and mothered them and tried to sort out their lives and took their troubles on her shoulders. She was so busy saving the world that she never thought about the course of her own life."

"What's wrong with that?" Elizabeth asked.

"Nothing. Except that one day Natalie realized why she was doing it. I'll never know what brought her to the realization. Somebody kicked her in the teeth pretty hard, I guess. Anyway, she finally faced a cold, hard fact. She wasn't really selflessly trying to help these people. At least, that wasn't her primary motivation. The real impetus was that appearing all-wise and indispensable gave *her* more satisfaction than it gave help to the people whose lives she literally took over. She was subconsciously bolstering her own ego. Playing God, if you will. The only way she could feel important to herself was by seeming to be a very superior person in relation to a lot of very inadequate people. She thought she was changing the world. Or a small part of it. But what she was doing was using weaklings to strengthen her own very insecure opinion of herself. She couldn't compete with competent folk, so she made herself high priestess of a bunch of parasites. Does that make any sense to you whatsoever?"

"I'm not sure," Elizabeth said slowly. "I guess what you're saying is that if you do things for the right reason—or at least if you understand why you're doing them—it's okay to help people. Otherwise you're just fooling yourself. Is that it?"

Charles kissed her on the forehead. "More or less. Close enough for now. Anyway, the main point is, don't start worrying about conquering the world just yet. When you're needed, the right people will find you. And not necessarily the waifs and strays, please God."

Elizabeth stood up. "By the way, did Cousin Natalie ever end up doing anything important?"

"You bet she did. She married a nice, solid stockbroker without a neurosis to his name. They have three kids and live in Greenwich, Connecticut. Isn't that important?"

"I'm not sure," Elizabeth repeated.

The midnight conversation with her father troubled and rather disappointed Elizabeth. For the first time she felt that he did not understand her. All that rigmarole about Cousin Natalie's waifs and strays seemed pointless. Elizabeth did not admire weak people. On the contrary, she had something closely approaching impatience with them. The people she knew now were weak, she thought. That's why they bored her. If she had her way she'd give them all a good shaking. "Wake up!" she'd say. "Life is out there waiting to be lived!" But that was different from trying to solve their problems for them. She didn't want to change their limited outlook. She simply refused to accept it for herself. She was amazed that Charles Quigly did not grasp that. She would never be a Natalie with a self-deluding early life and a stereotyped middle age. Never. Nor would she wait for the right people to come to her when she was needed. It was too early now, but in a few years she would find the answers to all her unformed questions. She would not die as her mother had, knowing nothing but the mundane satisfaction of producing a child. And then not even truly knowing the full joy of that.

In bed, she opened her Bible, as she'd been trained all her life to do. Wouldn't it be funny, she thought, if I accidentally picked the passage that said, "Seek and ye shall find." She chose a page at random. She'd missed it by a mile.

Three years later, Charles brought home a guest for dinner. He had phoned earlier to say that the son of an old school friend had come to see him and Charles had invited him to take potluck that evening. "Sorry to give you such short notice," he said, "but he seemed so lonely that I couldn't resist."

Elizabeth was completely unruffled. She had long since learned to manage the house and preside graciously on the rare occasions when Charles invited guests—usually other professors and their wives—for an evening at the Quiglys'. It was no problem to have Delia set another place. The roast chicken would easily feed one more and there were vegetables and dessert enough to accommodate the unexpected addition.

"Sounds fine," she assured Charles. "Is he madly handsome?"

"Madly."

"New in town?"

"Just arrived yesterday," Charles said. "Which undoubtedly accounts for his eager acceptance of my invitation. He looks as forlorn as a beagle. Desperate enough to dine with a crotchety professor of his father's vintage."

"You mean you didn't mention your beautiful young daughter?"

"Now that you mention it, no. Must have slipped my mind."

"Fa-ther!"

Charles laughed. "Actually, I thought the boy could use a pleasant surprise, so look your prettiest."

"I'll be the cat's pajamas."

She could imagine his frown at the other end of the phone. "Really, Elizabeth, your language! And don't tell me it's nineteen twenty-four. I am thoroughly aware of the calendar and it has no effect at all on the ultimate desecration of the language."

"As you have no doubt just finished explaining to your class in English lit," Elizabeth teased.

"Precisely. See you at six."

As she dressed, Elizabeth wondered about the "forlorn beagle." At least the prospect of a new man in town was something to look forward to. Or was it a new man? Charles had referred to the "boy." Perhaps he was only a student, all stammers and acne and bifocals.

Alan Whitman was not only a man; he was, as Charles had promised, "madly handsome," with the kind of muscular, stocky, compact physique that Elizabeth found particularly attractive. The blue eyes exuded easy confidence and the smile he gave Elizabeth left no doubt that this was, indeed, a pleasant surprise.

Charles introduced him. "Elizabeth, this is Alan Whitman. Alan, this is my irrepressible daughter. Try not to be surprised at anything she says."

"How do you do," Elizabeth said. "We're delighted to have you. Are you married?"

Her father shook his head in despair. "See what I mean? I

should have said 'my unmannerly daughter.' You must forgive her, Alan. She has a terrible problem. Nineteen years
old and still a spinster."

"I have a worse problem," Alan said. "Thirty-two years
old and still a bachelor." He and Elizabeth exchanged
amused glances. Alan was overwhelmed to find Charles
Quigly's daughter such a knockout. She's a raving beauty, he
thought. A really exciting girl. Maybe Cambridge won't be so
dreary after all.

In slightly altered terms, Elizabeth's thoughts matched his
own. Alan was the best-looking man she'd ever seen. All the
more interesting for being thirteen years her senior. He's going to be important to my life, she thought. I don't know why
I know. I just know.

Over dinner, in her role as hostess, Elizabeth led the conversation. "Where is your home, Mr. Whitman?"

"Here, now, I hope. And it's Alan, please. My parents are
no longer living, but I grew up in Chicago. I've been working
for Moreford Aviation outside Baltimore for the last five
years. They just transferred me to their plant in Weymouth.
It seems as though I'm becoming a gypsy. First the Midwest,
then the semi-South and now New England. Not that I mind.
I transplant easily."

"How exciting to be seeing the world," Elizabeth said.

Charles gave her a knowing look. "With all due respect,
my dear, the world is a bit bigger than that. Of course, in
Alan's kind of work I suppose there's no telling where he may
end up. He's in at the beginning of a great new field, commercial aviation. And Moreford's one of the biggest."

"What do you do for Moreford, Alan?"

"I'm an aeronautical engineer," he told her. "One of
those crazy fellows who design commercial airplanes. Military
ones, too, for that matter."

"So Father's right. You might be sent anywhere in the
world."

"It's possible," he said. "But I'll be around here for a long
while. We've just gotten a big government contract with a
ten-year completion date."

Elizabeth looked horrified. "Ten years! That's a lifetime!"

"That's the way it seems when you're nineteen," Charles
said. "Wait until you're my age. Ten years go by like ten
minutes."

"Even I'm beginning to find that out," Alan agreed. "Of
course, I may not stay the full time, though that's the present
plan. I must say, Elizabeth, that I'm a little disappointed by

your reaction," he teased. "I'd hoped you'd like the idea of
having me underfoot for the next decade."

To her surprise, Elizabeth found herself blushing. "I didn't
mean that the way it sounded," she said. "It's just that it's
such a long commitment to one place. I mean, ten years
is—"

"More than half of *your* lifetime," Charles said pointedly.
The implication did not escape Alan. "How wonderful to
be so young," he said innocently. "Think of all that Elizabeth has to look forward to."

For the next six months, the pursuit of Elizabeth by Alan
was the talk of half of Cambridge. The other half, less
charitably inclined, referred to it as the pursuit of Alan by
Elizabeth. Neither pursued nor pursuer cared in the least.
They were gloriously, deliriously, laughingly in love with each
other. Or perhaps with the idea of each other. In Elizabeth,
Alan saw youth, beauty, spontaneity, and a circumspectly
restrained but unmistakable sensuousness, a challenging, un-
awakened sexual urge. In Alan, Elizabeth believed she'd
found the man who could bring her all the things she sought.
She, too, felt the strong physical pull. But beyond it, she
was captivated with this handsome, sophisticated older man
who lived an exciting present and promised a dazzling future.
It was a joyous period in time for them both, as though they
were waiting for the curtain to go up on a spectacular
performance.

Charles Quigly's reactions to this galloping romance were,
at best, mixed. He liked Alan. It was almost impossible not to.
But he had reservations about the man who seemed destined
to be the son he'd always wanted. Alan was too perfect,
Charles reflected. And then ridiculed himself for such an
absurd assessment. Still, it was true. Every move of Alan's
was so right that it seemed almost rehearsed. As though he
had studied his part well and was performing it flawlessly.
His gaiety, his manners, and his protective attitude toward
Elizabeth were a study in charm. His solid future in aviation was real. Charles had carefully and quietly checked it
through friends at Moreford. With the exception of the age
difference, there was no fault that a father could find with
his only child's choice. And the deciding factor was that
Elizabeth was so wholeheartedly, happily committed to sharing her life with Alan Whitman. "My dream man, Daddy,"
she said contentedly. "Alan is all my dreams come true."
Charles prayed that she was right and that his instinctive,
out-of-character hesitancy was no more than the normal

reluctance of a father to let his beloved daughter go. May he be your dream man, my darling Elizabeth, he answered silently. Dear God, make this dream as real as she believes it to be.

When they finally told him that they wanted to be married, an unsurprised Charles gave them his blessing and publicly assumed the attitude of the delighted father of the bride. He joined in all the parties and dinners that were given for them, and not until the night before the wedding did he voice to Elizabeth even a hint of the intangible fears that haunted him. He begged off from Alan's bachelor dinner, apologizing that it was his last evening alone with his "hostess." Typically, Alan assured him that he understood. "We'll miss you, sir," he said, "but I can appreciate how you feel. Of course, we'll be living nearby, but I know it isn't the same. And I imagine that Elizabeth would like this evening alone with you, too." Alan paused. "I know it sounds ridiculously Victorian, but I want to thank you for giving her to me. And I want you to know that I'll never intentionally cause her a moment's unhappiness."

Charles nodded. "If I didn't believe that, Alan, I'd never let her go." The stiffness of the exchange, the very patness of it, rekindled Charles's misgivings. Then again, he was impatient with himself. What an ass I am, he thought. What would you have Elizabeth marry—some raccoon-coated, flask-carrying, flaming youth? Count your blessings, Quigly. Your girl is getting a fine man.

That evening he gave Elizabeth his wedding present to her —a delicate gold pendant entwined with diamonds and sapphires. "It was my gift to your mother when we married," he explained. "She wore it on her wedding day, as I hope you will on yours."

Elizabeth thanked him tearfully. "It's beautiful. It's the most wonderful thing I've ever owned. Oh, darling, I couldn't leave you for anyone in the world except Alan."

He hugged her. "I wouldn't let you leave me except for a man like Alan." There was a long pause. Finally, feeling his way cautiously, Charles spoke. "Remember the conversation we had about three years ago, sweetheart? The one in which you spoke so violently about wanting to gobble up life, to change things and people?"

Elizabeth looked at him curiously. "Yes, I remember. Why?"

"Nothing special," Charles said, "except that I'm glad you don't feel that way any more. I wouldn't want you to go into a marriage expecting Alan to be your airborne knight in armor. Living with another person, no matter how much you love him, is the hardest job in the world, Elizabeth. It isn't a ticket to glamour. Nor an escape hatch from boredom. It's sometimes very tedious and trying. I keep remembering your rebellion against dullness. This euphoria you're in now won't last forever, my dear. If Alan is not quite the carefree play-mate of your courtship, don't try to make him over. He'll have his problems, just as you'll have yours. But don't try to solve them for him. Help him. But don't take charge. Okay?"

Elizabeth smiled mischievously. "Why, Professor Quigly, I do believe you're feeling called upon to give the proverbial fatherly advice!" Then she sobered. "But you're right, of course. I guess at heart I'm still something of that sixteen-year-old seeker. But not so much any more. That was teen-age romanticism. A phase. I've learned a lot. From you and from Alan. I love him and I mean to make him a good wife and have a beautiful home and a raft of babies and never, never try to carry the world on my shoulders. Honest Injun. Please don't worry, darling. I'm like Cousin Natalie. At last I know what's important. And believe me, I've found it." She fingered the pendant draped around her slim throat. "And if I forget, this will remind me."

The next day she wore the jewel proudly down the aisle of the little church in Cambridge. On Charles's arm she looked as serene as Ann had looked twenty-five years before when Charles stood waiting to receive his bride as Alan waited now.

Charles prayed that their happiness would not be as short lived as his own.

They spent their honeymoon in Saratoga Springs. In August 1925, this New York state spa was at the height of its fame as an expensive health resort. It was more than a resort, really. Though it originally had become famous for its health-giving waters available at public fountains up and down the main street, its greatest lure in August was the racing season which attracted the rich horse owners and their friends, as well as the professional gamblers, the hangers-on, and the socially ambitious. It was an exotic world and Elizabeth felt as though she had been born into it. She loved the monstrous old Grand Union Hotel with its wide veranda which afforded a day-and-night view of the panorama of elegant strollers. She crowed with delight over the impressive room she and Alan occupied, a room jammed with heavy Victorian furniture yet filled with incredible summer light which danced through the sheer white curtains. She was amused by the quaintness of a hotel which still had heavy ropes coiled beneath the bedroom windows, the only possible mode of escape in case of fire.

But most of all, she loved the worldliness and affluence of the August visitors. She made it a point to be in the lobby every evening to watch the parade of famous women take out of the hotel's vault the jewels they would wear that night. And in the dining room, she stared incredulously as names she'd only read about appeared in their diamond and ruby necklaces, their massive emerald bracelets and brooches, a different set, it seemed to her, for every evening of the four weeks they spent in this sophisticated wonderland. She was dazzled by such wealth but not envious of it. Her mother's necklace and the discreet diamond engagement ring and wedding band she wore were as pleasing to her as the king's ransom of precious stones the others flaunted so casually. She was as happy in her simple dinner dresses bought "off the peg" at Filene's as the rich were in their beaded and feathered knee-length creations from the Paris houses of Chanel and Lanvin. She did not dream of possessing such things. She simply loved to be around them.

It was in Saratoga that Elizabeth learned to smoke cigarettes, a practice in which an amused Alan encouraged her. She had never seen women smoking in public before and she first took up the habit for the novelty of it, the illusion of slight wickedness and liberation it gave her. She soon learned to enjoy it, particularly the companionable feeling it gave her to have a cigarette after dinner while Alan lit up one of his slim cigars. For the first time, too, she discovered cocktails, discreetly served in teacups. There had been table wine at home, but never hard liquor. Now, in the nightclubs of Saratoga's gambling houses, she was introduced to Prohibition gin and to those monstrous drinks of the twenties, called Pink Ladies or Clover Clubs.

It was all part of the ritual. Just as going to the racetrack every afternoon was a required part of the daily routine. It seemed to her that Alan bet too recklessly, rooted too intensely for his horses, took his losses in an angry, ungentlemanly way and his successes in over-boastful, gloating triumph. He was conpulsive about gambling, elated when he won, resentful when he lost. Once Elizabeth made the mistake of chiding him gently about being a poor loser. His rage was startling.

"I detest losers!" he stormed. "There is no such thing as a 'good loser.' It means you've been wrong, stupid, careless.

That you've tackled something you can't handle and it's defeated you!"

She was appalled. "Darling, isn't that a little exaggerated?
Nobody wins all the time. Betting on the horses or at the
roulette table is just a game, isn't it? There's no shame in
losing at a game."

"Nothing is a game," Alan said. "Not anything in life. Life
is just one endless competition. Winner take all."

From the ignorance of her twenty years, Elizabeth kept
quiet. She did not understand this sudden transformation
from the gentle, loving man she'd married to this bitter,
angry compulsive gambler. The moment passed, but it spoiled
the idyllic pattern of this wedding trip. Obviously regretting
his outburst, Alan tried to control his reactions in the few
final days of their stay. But Elizabeth could not entirely shake
off the feeling that there was some resentment deep within
him which had broken through in that unguarded moment.
She could not help but compare Alan's unreasonable rationale
about losers to Charles Quigly's sympathy and tolerance for
all human failings. Alan's uncontrolled fury was the first disquieting note in their relationship. It filled her with bewilderment and an undismissable anxiety.

She was happy to get back to Cambridge and the small
house they had rented across town from Charles. Though she
had run the household for her father, these were her first
very own four walls and she filled them lovingly and taste-
fully with what she always referred to as her "lares and
penates." Though she did not know it then, it was to be the
first of many homes she would make in many places, each of
them different, yet each reflecting the love she felt for beautiful things. She had a talent for making any room warm, inviting, and intensely personal, and this first "honeymoon house"
was as full of joy as the young woman who arranged and
cared for it.

She had plenty of time to lavish on the house. Almost too
much time. Alan returned to his work at Moreford with almost fanatic zeal. He stayed late at the plant two or three
nights a week, complaining that it was obscene how much
had piled up in his absence. Elizabeth felt sorry that he was
burdened with work, but she filled her evenings with visits
to her father and to her aunts and cousins and friends, re-
galing them with amusing stories about the incredible people and the foreign way of life at Saratoga. Many evenings
she stayed at home quietly. She was an omnivorous reader
and a dedicated needlepoint expert and she could pass the
hours happily, anticipating Alan's return. She always hoped

that he would be full of love and desire for her after these "long separations." But more often he simply fell exhausted into bed, apparently done in by his grueling fourteen-hour day at the office.

Even after they had been home for two months, the night work continued. Elizabeth praised him for his ambition, admired his genius, and begged him not to work so hard. He would only smile and kiss her.

"I'm a man with responsibilities," he said half seriously. "No more carefree bachelor I. Now I have a wife to care for and a full-fledged household to maintain, to say nothing of a career to pursue. What do a couple of nights' work a week matter, darling, when there are five others to make love to you?"

Laughingly, she agreed that she was, perhaps, being selfish. And one evening, five months after their marriage, she conceded, mock-solemnly, that she supposed five nights a week was enough.

"I'm not sure I really like that admission now that I've succeeded in getting you to make it," Alan said. "Sounds a little like you're getting bored with me already."

Elizabeth curled up in his lap. "I'm not bored, dearest. I simply realize that I *am* well loved. So much so that I'm pregnant. Two whole months' worth. We'll have a first anniversary and a first baby next August. I'm so very, very happy, Alan."

She waited for his reply. It seemed a long time coming. Elizabeth felt a touch of panic. They had never discussed a family. She had simply assumed that, like herself, Alan would want children. Several of them, hopefully. They themselves were both only children. He must know how lonely a state that is. Perhaps, she thought suddenly, he's concerned about me, knowing how often my mother tried to have a baby and what happened when she finally did. She hastened to reassure him.

"Darling, if you're worrying about me, there's no need. Dr. Franklin says I'm healthy as a horse and that I should have no trouble at all. I'm a big, strong type, in case you haven't noticed. I inherit that from Dad. You're not going to fret, are you? I mean, you are happy about it, aren't you?"

He stroked her hair. "Of course I'm happy. I guess I'm overwhelmed, if you want to know the truth. Funny. I hadn't really thought much about children. Subconsciously I suppose I knew we'd have them in time. You just took me off guard, darling. Now that I've recovered, I make a motion that we have a drink on it. What say?"

She still felt uneasy. "You're really glad, Alan? You're not sorry it's so soon?"

"Glad? My love, I am ecstatic! What shall we have, a boy or a girl?"

"What would you like?"

This time there was no hesitation. "Oh, a girl, definitely. One just like you."

"You are an unorthodox man," Elizabeth laughed. "I thought all prospective fathers yearned for a son and heir."

"Not me. I identify better with women. Now how about that drink?"

The pattern of her life did not change drastically throughout Elizabeth's pregnancy. As the doctor had predicted, it went well, with no complications. Unlike her delicate mother, she was a tall, sturdy young woman, "born for breeding," Dr. Franklin said with satisfaction. He did advise her, rather firmly, to cut down on both cigarettes and cocktails, but that was a difficult demand. On the nights he wasn't working, Alan liked to have her entertain at small dinner parties, usually for one of his bosses and their wives. Or they joined other young couples at the theater and late supper. Alan hated it when she refused a drink or a cigarette.

"Must you act like Mother Earth?" he said petulantly one evening when she had declined both. "Good God, let's not make a fetish out of a simple pregnancy."

She tried not to let the others see how his words hurt her. And she was embarrassed by his churlishness in front of their friends. "Doctor's orders," she said lightly. "Only temporary. Wait till September. I'll go on the biggest bender in history!"

The others laughed, the tenseness dispelled. But Elizabeth was both wounded and angry. How dare he make me look like such a fool, she thought. Especially in public. When they were alone, she faced him angrily.

"What made you speak to me that way tonight, Alan? It was uncalled for. You know very well that I'm not supposed to be smoking and drinking with the baby only six weeks away!"

He poured himself another drink. "Just setting up the ground rules for the future," he said casually.

"Meaning?"

"Meaning that having children is fine, but if there's one thing I can't stand it's those women who suddenly think they're sacred because they're performing their natural functions of reproduction. If you're starting to get so holier-than-thou at this point, what in God's name will you be like when you have real living, breathing proof of your ability to populate the world?"

It was as though he had struck her. She tried to keep her voice calm. "Have I really been behaving that way?"

Immediately, Alan underwent one of his meteoric changes of personality. "No. Of course not. I'm sorry. I don't know why I acted the way I did. Or said what I just said. I apologize. Chalk it up to too many drinks."

Elizabeth took a deep breath. "Perhaps," she said slowly, "this is as good a time as any to say something that's been on my mind for the past few months. You have too many drinks all the time, Alan. And you're home less and less. I'm worried. About you. About us."

He did not, as she'd feared, revert to his cutting sarcasm. He was almost gentle.

"Nothing to worry about. Usually I know my limit on the booze. As for the working, I'm afraid you can't expect less of that, my dear. If anything, we'll have to accept the fact that there'll be more. We'll have, as the saying goes, another mouth to feed, and I'm bucking for a substantial raise. This is the time. The economy is good and so is business. And so," he said tenderly, "is this marriage. I love you very much, Elizabeth. You might be the only woman in the world who could understand and put up with me, but at least I know it. And I'm grateful."

She was instantly enchanted, disarmed. Now it was her turn to be apologetic. She went to him, pressing her big bulk against him. "I'm sorry. I guess I'm just supersensitive these days. I know it isn't easy on you either. But it will be over soon. We'll be just as we were in the beginning. And I swear to you that I won't come all over maternalistic. You come first. Always have. Always will. No matter how many children we have."

Alan's expression was quizzical. "How *many?*" he repeated. "Do you have a plan for that? If so, you might let me in on the secret."

"Just so it's more than one," Elizabeth said. "I know how lonely it is to be an only child. You must, too. Didn't you ever want brothers and sisters, Alan?"

"Frankly, no. Never. I thought it was just fine being the king of the hill." Then, seeing the disappointment in her face, he relented. "But there's time to talk about that, isn't there? Good Lord, we haven't even got the first one born yet!"

"Of course there's time," she said. "There is all the time in the world."

Ann Treadwell Whitman was fiercely determined to get into this world and lost no time about it. Elizabeth delivered her speedily and almost effortlessly on a blistering morning in August of 1926 and then lay back in exhausted triumph, thinking how pleased Alan would be to have the daughter he had "ordered." It had already been decided that if the child turned out to be a girl she would be named for the mother whom Elizabeth never had known. This time, Charles Quigly had no objection. Twenty-one years had understandably softened his adamant stance that there never could be another Ann. In his sorrow, he could not have given away his dead wife's name, even to her daughter. But now, a touched and grateful grandfather, he was delighted that another Ann had come into his life.

"Mark my words, she's going to be exactly like her grandmother," he pronounced, looking affectionately at the hours-old baby. "See that resolute jawline? Just like Ann's. She'll know exactly what she wants from life, that child."

Elizabeth smiled at him affectionately. "As opposed to her mother, I suppose? Good thing you finally got your hands on a female with some sense, Professor. But isn't it just a little early for such positive predictions? She might turn out to be a silly dreamer like me. Or," Elizabeth added wryly, "a volatile and unpredictable charmer like her father."

Charles gave his daughter a searching look. It was the first overt reference she'd made to the fact that Alan Whitman was a difficult man to live with. Not that the suggestion came as a surprise. On the surface, Elizabeth appeared gay, enthusiastic and contented, and Alan was apparently the same devoted, well-mannered man he'd been since the first evening he came to the Quiglys'. But Charles was uniquely sensitive to everything that affected Elizabeth. He had been suspicious that her marriage was not the perfect thing she led the world to believe. Only he recognized the occasional nearly indiscernible signs of strain. A slight tightening of the mouth. Faint lines of fatigue around the eyes. An unusual sharpness in the normally composed and gentle voice. He was determined to mind his own business and keep his worries to himself. Even now he did not pursue the opening Elizabeth had given him. He made no comment, and her relief was obvious. She hadn't meant to blurt out even this veiled criti-

cism of Alan. For one thing, she reasoned that it was up to
her to solve her own problems. And, even more importantly,
the last thing in the world she wanted was to worry Charles.
Particularly now. She loved him deeply, and lately she worried a great deal about him. He had not looked well in the
past few months. And although he assured her that he was
in good shape, she was sure he hadn't gone to the doctor
for the checkup he'd promised to have. She had asked him
to do so once, a few weeks before, and he'd agreed, making
light of her anxiety. Since then, they had not discussed it.
This seemed an easy time to bring up the matter again.

"Since you're now an all-important grandfather," she said,
"I hope you're ready to take on a whole new set of responsibilities. Like baby-sitting, for one. Feeling up to it these
days?"

Charles smiled. "You're as transparent as that pretty
negligee you're wearing. Darling, will you please stop cluck-
ing over me like a mother hen? I told you I'd see the doctor.
It's nothing. I just have a little cough, that's all. Come on,
Elizabeth. You don't think your old man is going to pop off
at fifty, do you? No chance. I'm here to stay for a long, long
time. Especially now that Ann has joined us. Nothing could
keep me from sticking around just to prove that my predictions about her are one hundred per cent accurate."

Elizabeth allowed herself to believe and be comforted. Life
without Charles was unthinkable. He represented all that
was solid and good and unchanging. Maybe that's why I'm
so often intolerant of Alan, so supercritical of him, she
thought. I expect him to be all the things that this man is.
And no one ever could be. She made herself a promise to
stop comparing her husband to her father. It was immature
and unhealthy. They're both wonderful, she told herself.
Each in his own way. I'm the luckiest of women. Glancing
down at the baby at her breast, she felt content. When she
answered Charles, her voice was tender.

"I'm so happy you think she's like Mother," Elizabeth said.
"She'll never receive a higher compliment. Nor will I."

Charles kissed her gently on the forehead. His smile said
everything.

Alan's reaction to his firstborn only strengthened Elizabeth's determination to stop comparing the two men. He
took Ann's arrival as a personal achievement, as though his
offspring confirmed his manhood and virility. He couldn't
keep his eyes off of her.

"Will you just look at her, Elizabeth?" he crowed. "A

perfect specimen. She's going to be an absolute tearing beauty."

"Dad says she looks exactly like Mother."

Charles frowned. "Really? Well, maybe so. But to me she's unmistakably Whitman. Remind me to find some of my baby pictures to show you, darling. You'll be amazed at the resemblance. Anyway, they say that a girl who looks like her father is born for good luck, don't they?"

"Yes, I think they do." Elizabeth was amused by his pride. "Anyway, dear, you got the little girl you wanted."

"Never doubted it for a moment," he said smugly. "My little princess. Anything she wants is hers. She's Daddy's pet."

"Alan, you must promise not to spoil her rotten!"

He kissed his wife. "Promise no such thing," he teased. "She was born to be spoiled. You can tell that already."

"No child is born to be spoiled," Elizabeth remonstrated. "It's the parents who do that awful thing to them. We mustn't make that mistake with Ann."

He refused to be discouraged. "What are little girls for except to be adored by their fathers? You certainly had your share of it. Charles thinks the sun rises and sets in you." A note of resentment crept into Alan's voice. "Anything you do is perfect in the eyes of Professor Quigly. Even up to and including marrying me."

The peace Elizabeth had felt earlier began to leave her. They were already on the verge of another senseless quarrel. It was ridiculous the way they kept building nuances into major conflicts. She would not let it happen. She had chosen her life with Alan. And if, occasionally, he was quixotic and unreasonable, it was a small price to pay for a brilliant and successful husband whom she really loved. She'd just have to work that much harder to keep the marriage on an even keel. He would spoil Ann unbearably, she knew. And not so much for Ann's sake as for the pleasure it would give him. Elizabeth's role would be the unpopular one. She foresaw clearly that any discipline would have to come from her if this little girl were to grow up an attractive, well-rounded human being. It was as plain as the tiny, upturned nose on Ann Treadwell Whitman's face. And one other thing was clear as well. She must not be allowed to be an only child, with all the interest and adoration focused on her. While she was still in the hospital with Ann, Elizabeth was already planning another baby. This one, she told herself, would be a boy. And he would be named Quigly Alan Whitman. This was her secret. For the time being, she would keep it. Even from the man who would father her second child.

Chapter 2

In the year that followed, Ann flourished and lived up to the promise of becoming exquisite. She was small-boned and delicate-looking as her grandmother had been, yet she was well formed and healthy, a good baby with signs, even at that early age, of having a will of her own.

Her parents and grandfather adored her for the same reasons they had from the moment she was born. Ann's presence brought a new kind of harmony into the Whitmans' life and Elizabeth was grateful for that as well. Alan still worked late one or two nights a week, but on the whole he seemed to have found a new contentment in his marriage. Even his lovemaking with Elizabeth was rekindled, almost to the ardent pitch of their honeymoon. It was as though the arrival of a child had bolstered Alan's self-confidence and paid off in other directions as well. He received two promotions at Moreford in rapid succession, with compensation to match. His name began to appear regularly in the Boston newspapers, in interviews about the fast-growing aviation industry and in reports of the speeches he made at banquets and seminars attended by aeronautical experts from around the world.

Elizabeth was proud of him. Only a shade less proud, perhaps, than he was of himself. He was riding the crest of recognition and had a somewhat unattractive tendency to believe his own publicity, to be just a little condescending to his co-workers and friends. He also continued to drink immoderately. He never appeared drunk in public nor missed a day at the office. But it was on the way to becoming excessive and it was the one dark cloud on Elizabeth's horizon. Not that she was against drinking. She thoroughly enjoyed her two martinis before dinner with Alan. It relaxed them both, made conversation flow more easily, brought on a gentle, artificial glow that was pleasantly companionable. Unfortunately, Alan did not stop with two. He would have four, sometimes five martinis before dinner. His capacity was formidable and the more liquor he found he could handle, the more he stepped up the intake. Still, Elizabeth forced herself not to dwell upon it too much, nor to mention it often. She had tried to cajole him into more "social" drinking habits like her own. She had, on one or two occasions, tried to talk seriously with him about his growing problem, trying to handle it deftly, to avoid sounding like a nagging wife. Neither approach had any effect. The first was ignored, the second summarily dismissed with the defensive, and apparently still true, rationale that he knew exactly how much liquor he could consume without getting drunk.

Fifteen months after Ann was born, Elizabeth made two simultaneous discoveries. Dr. Franklin confirmed that she was pregnant again, and Alice Baldwin, the wife of one of Alan's co-workers, confided, with apparent reluctance, that Alan was having an affair with one of the secretaries at Moreford.

The joy she'd felt at the first piece of news was wiped out by the horror of the second. Over the luncheon table at Filene's Restaurant, Elizabeth stared with disbelief at her friend. Alice squirmed uncomfortably. "I've debated for months whether or not to tell you, Elizabeth," she said. "Fred said to shut up. That it was none of my business. But everybody's talking about it, and I can't stand for you to be made such a fool of. Oh, God, don't look like that! I wish now I hadn't said a word! I should have listened to Fred."

Elizabeth shook her head numbly. "No. You were right to tell me. Really you were, Alice. I know you only meant to be a good friend."

As she lit a cigarette, Alice's hands were trembling more than Elizabeth's. "I don't know," she said. "Perhaps it was wrong of me. I just thought I'd want somebody to tell me

if I were in your place. So I could take some kind of action,
I mean. What are you going to do?"

Elizabeth gave a bitter little laugh. "I'm not sure. Talk to
Alan, I suppose." She sensed Alice's nervousness. "Don't worry. I won't tell him how I found out. I know Fred would
kill you. But you see, it's even more complicated than you
realize. I went to Dr. Franklin this morning. I'm two months
pregnant."

Alice ground out her cigarette angrily. "That bastard! As
if it wasn't bad enough before Ann—" She stopped abruptly,
dismayed by the further disclosure she'd made.

Elizabeth didn't answer. She was busily occupied in finding
the billfold in her purse. Perhaps she didn't hear me,
Alice thought hopefully. But of course she had. She had
just wrapped herself in that goddamn dignity of hers.

As though nothing had occurred, they split the luncheon
check and went their separate ways, parting in front of the
store, promising to get together soon. Alice watched the
straight-backed figure of her friend disappearing down the
street. She would have found out sooner or later, Alice consoled herself. Men. If Fred Baldwin ever did that to me I'd
cut his heart out. Elizabeth's different. She'll cut her own
heart out. And nobody will ever know.

The heaviness in Elizabeth's chest felt like a giant stone.
She was literally gasping for breath when she let herself into
the house in Cambridge, and instead of going straight to the
baby's room as she normally did, she slumped into a hall
chair, breathing hard. In a few minutes, the housekeeper-
nurse appeared. Elizabeth's ashen face and spasmodic panting
terrified her.

"Are you all right, Mrs. Whitman? I heard the door, but
when you didn't come up to the nursery, I thought I'd better
see where you were. Are you ill? Is there something I can
get you?"

Elizabeth managed to sit up straight. "I'm perfectly all
right, Beulah," she said. "I guess I just got worn out shopping. How's Ann?"

"Fine as always. I have a hard time keeping her in her
crib. She's dead set on getting out and toddling around. She's
a determined one, that child."

"I know. A mind of her own."

"Yes, ma'am. Nothing's going to stop that young lady when
she decides to do it. All energy. Just like Mr. Whitman."

You'll never know how true those words are, Elizabeth
said silently. Nothing will stop Mr. Whitman when he de-

cides to do something. Whether it's to marry me or have a series of affairs. She had not missed Alice Baldwin's final, uncompleted sentence. The current involvement obviously was not the first. Probably, she thought cynically, there had never been a legitimate "late working night" in their whole marriage. Not since the beginning. Strangely, though she wanted to cry, she could not. She was beyond tears. Beyond anything but the search for the best, most sensible resolution of this problem. Alice was right in that she hated being the proverbial "last to know." But that was not the most important thing now. That, like her feeling of rejection and wounded pride, was secondary to reality. Should she leave Alan or could she live with this? What was the intelligent thing to do for the sake of her children? And what drove her husband to this? Where, she wondered, had she failed?

Wearily, she dragged herself to her bedroom and lay down. We have to talk like civilized human beings. All the blame is never on one side. I must find out where I'm lacking, what needs in Alan I don't fulfill. I should have known, she thought. The strange hostility, the heavy drinking, the need for constant reassurance of his brilliance. Even the attitude he took about Ann, as though she was a single-handed accomplishment. Weariness overcame her. There were so many things she didn't understand about this complex man she had married. She closed her eyes. In a moment she was in a heavy sleep of forgetfulness.

Hours later, Alan woke her from this drugged oblivion. She awakened slowly, reluctantly, trying to focus on the face which looked down on her, the mouth that was forming some undecipherable message. Unwillingly, she came back to life, forced herself to hear what her husband was saying.

"Elizabeth! Are you all right? I've been shaking you for five minutes! Beulah says you've been asleep for hours. What's the matter? Are you ill?"

She half sat up on the bed, running her hands through her close-cropped hair. For a hopeful moment, she thought that perhaps her conversation with Alice Baldwin had been only a bad dream. But then, as though with the gesture she had pushed her scrambled wits back together, she knew that this nightmare was real.

"What time is it?"

"Past seven. Beulah says you've been in here since before three. She says you seemed funny when you came in. What's wrong?"

She wasn't yet ready to put the horror into words. "Why

don't you go down and have a drink, Alan? I'll shower and pull myself together and join you in a few minutes. We have some things to talk about."

"Are you crazy? We're due at the Sloans' for dnnner at seven-thirty! I'll have a drink while I change. Do you want one while you're dressing?"

"No," Elizabeth said. "I don't want one. And I'm not dressing. We won't be going to the Sloans' tonight."

"Then you *are* ill."

"Not really. Not in the way you mean."

He looked annoyed now. "For Christ's sake, Elizabeth, what is going on here? If you're not ill, we can't call the Sloans at the last minute and tell them we're not coming. He's my executive vice president! He'll be mad as hell if we cancel like this. And if you're feeling all right, there's no *reason* for us to cancel!"

"We're not going," Elizabeth said wearily. "We are staying home to talk. Now, will you call or shall I?"

There was no mistaking the cold determination in her voice. Angrily, Alan turned away. "I could go alone," he said.

"No."

"Since when are you giving the orders around here?"

Elizabeth smiled grimly. "Since, I would say, about two o'clock this afternoon. The approximate hour at which I found out that our marriage is falling apart."

Alan fell silent. It was not difficult to guess what she had discovered. It was only surprising that she had not heard about it sooner. He had tried to be discreet, of course. But he'd always known that one day she'd hear about his "little flings," as he thought of them. He was not especially upset or repentant. Only faintly annoyed that there would be a scene. He hated scenes unless he provoked them.

"I don't know what you're talking about," he bluffed, "but if you're so dead set on staying home then *you* call Trudi Sloan and lie your way out of it. Don't expect me to put myself in the awkward position of trying to explain your erratic behavior."

"I'll call her," Elizabeth said calmly. "Please go down-stairs, Alan. I'll be with you in a few minutes."

He started out of the room, stopped at the doorway. "What about dinner? Am I also supposed to skip my evening meal because you've decided to stage some great accusatory scene at home?"

His last words were a giveaway. He knows exactly what this is all about, Elizabeth thought. I suppose he's been expecting it. Even so, she could not summon up anger. Only bewilderment and hurt. She looked at him dispassionately.

"What makes you think I'm going to stage some great scene?"

He hesitated. "Well, God knows you've set the stage for it! Anyway, what about my dinner?"

"Ask Beulah to heat up some stew for you. There's a little left over in the refrigerator. It's enough for one."

"What about you?"

"I don't seem to have much appetite. Besides, I had a big lunch. I'll just have some coffee."

In twenty minutes she joined Alan in the living room.

"What happened with Trudi?" he asked. "What did you tell her?"

"The truth," Elizabeth said. "Part of it anyway. I told her I'd been to the doctor today and that I wasn't up to going out. She was very understanding. Trudi knows how one feels in the early stages of a pregnancy." She waited, almost curiously, to see the effect of the bomb she had deliberately dropped. Alan's face was a study in relief, but only for a moment. For a split second, he thought that her puzzling behavior was only her whimsical way of telling him she wanted to be alone with him on the night she announced the conception of their second child. Then, immediately, he remembered the almost offhand reference to their marriage falling apart. Of course, he couldn't be certain of what, or how much, she knew of the other matter. Until he did, he'd have to keep up the charade.

"Early stages of a pregnancy?" he repeated. "Is it true? Is that what this is all about? Oh, darling, I'm so happy! When did you find out? Today? When is the baby due?"

"In June," Elizabeth said flatly. "Seven months from now. Are you really pleased? I seem to remember that you used to be in favor of the only-child marriage."

He laughed indulgently. "That was before I knew the joys of fatherhood. You just give me another little girl like Ann and I'll encourage you to procreate like a rabbit!" His voice became serious, low, almost seductive. "You make a wonderful wife and mother, Elizabeth. You're so—I don't know— perfect in those roles. So warm and proud and competent."

"Am I?" Elizabeth asked quietly. "But that isn't enough, is it? I must lack other qualities that you require in a woman. Or women. Otherwise you'd have no reason to go looking for them elsewhere, would you? The way you've been doing for God knows how long. You must have figured out by now that I've finally heard what everybody else seems to know; that you're having an affair with some girl at the office. And that it isn't the first. I'd like to know about them, Alan. I'd like to know what these women can give you that I cannot."

Her reasonableness only infuriated him. "Jesus Christ, you are the professor's daughter, aren't you? All logic and scientific curiosity! For God's sake, Elizabeth, what kind of paragon are you? Yes, I've been unfaithful. Six, seven, eight affairs. I don't know. There's always been somebody. Right from the beginning. Somebody who expects nothing of me but the ability to be a good stud. A night in the hay and no questions asked. 'So long' until the next time I can sneak away. Somebody I don't have to measure up to, who doesn't care that I know the right people and get the right promotions and am intellectually and socially brilliant. What I need occasionally, Elizabeth, is a tart. The unpaid kind, but a tart. Someone I don't feel inferior to. A dame whose underwear is occasionally dirty. Does that shock you? Do you think I'm sick? What the hell difference does it make to you? I've never failed you, have I? In bed or out of it? You're the mistress of my house, the mother of my children, the legal bearer of my name. In my own way, I love you. But in a terrible way I'm afraid of you. Afraid I'm not good enough for the well-organized, tolerant, understanding Elizabeth Quigly. Does that answer your question? If not, let me spell it out for you. What you can't give me is a feeling of superiority. No matter how shallow that is, I need it. And you can't give it."

Elizabeth was stunned. She didn't know what she had expected. Lies, perhaps. Or confession and pleas for forgiveness. But not this outburst of resentment against her and condemnation of himself that had poured forth in a torrent of ugly accusation. His hostility was frightening. She felt defenseless against it. All her background and training told her that she should be outraged by his almost defiant admission of guilt and the arrogance of laying the blame for it at her feet. Instead, she felt only sorrow that his ego was so fragile, his manliness so questionable that he had to seek reassurance from women who were far beneath him. He was a dark world of insecurity. How strange that she could have ignored all the signs that pointed to its terrifying depths. She would not defend the kind of woman she was. She saw no need to. Strangely, with all that he had done to her, she still loved him. And above all else, she wanted to help him. That was not to say that she was undisturbed by his unfaithfulness. It wounded her deeply. Her own ego was bruised, her own confidence shaken. Yet she felt pity for him. It was a sickness over which he had no control. She was sure he had not wanted to hurt her. Just as she was sure that now the problem was out in the open she could help him. It seemed like hours rather than seconds before she answered him. When she did, there was no recrimination in her voice. Simply matter-of-fact acceptance. Her question seemed anticlimactic.

"Where do we go from here?"

Alan looked at her curiously. "Isn't that up to you? I presume you'll want a divorce, now that you know all about me. All the legal and moral rights are on your side."

"Is that what you want? A divorce?"

He was calm now. He shook his head wonderingly. "No, I don't want a divorce, but I think you should get one. I told you that in my own way I love you. I love my home, my child. But I'm not prepared to live with an accusatory saint. I don't want to see reproach in your eyes when you look at me. I don't want you to stay with me out of a sense of duty or even a misguided belief that people should live together for the sake of their children. I can't believe, Elizabeth, that even you could live happily ever after with a man who has insulted you. I can tell you that I'll try to change. And I will try. But there's no money-back guarantee. I don't think either of us can become different people overnight. I think the sensible thing would be for you to leave me. And to discuss a therapeutic abortion with Dr. Franklin. I'm sure it can be arranged. After all this, another baby would certainly jeopardize your mental health. And," he said cynically, "one unstable member of the family seems quite enough."

Her eyes filled with tears. "I don't want a divorce, Alan. It's not as though you'd fallen in love with someone else. I know these women don't matter to you. This is a strange, disturbing part of your mind we're dealing with. Maybe together we can fight it more successfully than you can alone."

He started to protest, but she stopped him. "The only thing I can contribute is love and admiration. And I have them both for you. I don't promise to forget. Maybe not even to entirely forgive. But the martyr role doesn't suit me. You need have no worries on that score. You've given me quite an insight into me, believe it or not. I'll have to do some changing too, if this marriage is to work. But it will work if we both try. I want to try, Alan. Do you?"

"More than anything in the world," he said. "But I don't really hold out much hope, Elizabeth. Sooner or later you'll

walk away from me. It might be better if it were now, while
you're still young and desirable. In any case, I think you
should talk to Dr. Franklin. Tell him everything, if you like.
I think in this probationary period he will agree that we
should not add another child to our problems."

She stubbornly refused. "I will not see Dr. Franklin and
I will not think in such ridiculous terms as 'probation.'
Marriage isn't a sentence, it's a voluntary commitment.
There's no parole, any more than there's a term to be
served. We're not playing accused and prosecuting attorney.
We're just two people trying to work out our problems. And
we will if we try. I'm sure of it. Let's try to start all over,
Alan. Without telling anyone."

"Not even your father?"

"No," Elizabeth said. "Least of all my father."

All through the winter, Elizabeth lived in a state of acute
watchfulness. She searched Charles Quigly's face for signs
of illness and was relieved to see that his color seemed
better, his energy higher. And despite her promises, she saw
in every unusual act of Alan's some indication that he had
slipped back into his old ways. She was careful to disguise her
uneasiness and, in fact, Alan was on his good behavior. He
was trying hard to overcome his deep-seated sense of in-
feriority, and Elizabeth made every effort to help him.
She resigned from the charity committees in which she'd
previously been active and which had brought her a certain
amount of recognition and satisfaction, and she politely declined any further civic participation which could put her in
the limelight. Her way of keeping her bargain was to slip
into the background, to do nothing that would threaten
her husband's role as the superior member of the family.

It was, of course, against everything in her nature. She
was inherently a doer. And it was not easy to stifle the
gift for organization and management which made people
seek her leadership. But it was worth it if such self-efface-
ment bolstered Alan's fragile belief in himself. In any case,
her self-imposed retirement seemed to be working. Her husband appeared happier and more content. She was reasonably sure that since the night of their frank talk he had
broken off his latest illicit relationship and had not formed a
new one. They did not refer to it again. This, of course, was,
in itself, unhealthy. It was like a guarded truce. Elizabeth
wished they could have talked more about their problems
but she hesitated to approach the subject. It was better to
leave well enough alone. Her pregnancy could not have

come at a better time, since it gave her the excuse she needed to withdraw from her former prominence in the community. And impending fatherhood also seemed to give Alan the ego lift he required.

By spring, she allowed herself to relax a little. In June of 1928 she gave birth to Quigly Alan Whitman, the son she had secretly planned for almost two years before. This time, Alan's reaction was suitably enthusiastic but without the exuberant delight he had shown at the time of his daughter's arrival. In fact, after admiring the baby and visiting briefly with Elizabeth in the hospital, he seemed almost impatient to get back to Ann. Elizabeth was puzzled and a little hurt by his almost indifferent attitude toward his son. For the first time in months, she allowed herself to be cross with Alan.

"I don't understand you," she said. "Most men would be overjoyed to have a son. Aren't you pleased that there's someone to carry on your name?"

"He's a nice little boy," Alan said, "and I'm delighted with him. But I've never been concerned with immortality, particularly my own. I guess I'm not that anxious to envision an endless stream of reproductions of me. Probably because I don't really think I'm the species that should be perpetuated, even in name."

Disappointment gave Elizabeth's voice a cutting edge. "You were pleased enough about Ann. You're still fatuous about that child. Even now you can't wait to get home to her."

"You're quite right," Alan agreed. "I don't know why you still refuse to accept me as I am, Elizabeth. I told you before Ann was born that I preferred girls."

"So I noticed," Elizabeth snapped. Instantly, she would have given anything to take back the words. For a few moments, silence lay heavily between them. Finally, Elizabeth apologized. "I'm sorry," she said, "I didn't mean that the way it came out."

"Didn't you?"

Alan rose to leave. At the foot of her bed, he stood quietly looking at her. "I am trying to decide whether to tell you the truth," he said. "It would be easy to say that I'm concerned about Ann because I don't want us to be faced with sibling rivalry. She's nearly two years old. She's been the center of the world up to now. My world, particularly. It's almost inevitable that she's going to resent this intruder who will take our attention away from her. I could tell you that I want to be with her to assure her that she's as important as ever, that no one will ever take her place in our lives.

"That," he continued, "would be an intelligent, acceptable explanation of my concern for Ann. It would also be only a partial truth. The rest of the story—the more telling part —is that no matter how many children we have, Ann will always be my favorite. I know that good parents aren't supposed to have favorites, but that's sentimental slop. If we're lucky, maybe we'll even out the score. I'll favor Ann and you'll be partial to Quigly. That will keep the whole family in nice mathematical balance, provided you don't go and get yourself pregnant again."

Elizabeth was stung by his cynical words. "You're punishing me, aren't you, Alan?"

He looked surprised. "Punishing you? For what?"

"I don't know. Maybe for the tactless thing I said a few moments ago. Maybe for just being alive and in your way."

He would not be taunted. "My, my, how melodramatic we are today! You've always prided yourself on your ability to understand me, Elizabeth, so why not get down to the real root of the problem now? Even an amateur psychiatrist should recognize the real reason I'm not excited about our son: I don't like masculine competition in any form. Okay? Now, will you excuse me? I'm sure you need your rest."

She turned her face away from him on the pillow. As the door closed she wept bitterly. This time she planned no more children.

As her strength returned, so did her perspective. After Quigly's birth, things went relatively smoothly for the Whitmans, as they seemed to have after Ann's. Alan continued to "behave," as far as she knew, though their physical reunions were far less passionate and far less frequent than they had been in the short-lived period of delight following Ann's arrival. Still, it was not an unhappy time. Alan took a mild interest in the baby, but his devotion to Ann was defiantly apparent. Elizabeth tried to share her love. She did not, as Alan had suggested, "even the score" by becoming partial to Quigly. She gave both children all the affection and security she knew how to offer. If anything, she was unusually careful to avoid even the slightest show of favoritism. When visitors came to admire her son, she made it a point to bring Ann in, to praise her and make reference to her daughter's beauty and brains. Quigly was still an infant, with little awareness, but she held him and cradled him and hoped that subconsciously he felt his mother's love and protection. He was very unlike what Ann had been as an infant. She had been all smiles and appealing gurgles, flirtatious almost from birth. Quigly was a quiet, solemn baby with an expression that, in an older human, would very nearly be described as sullen. Looking from one to another, Elizabeth speculated how their characters would eventually form. What kind of people will they be in twenty years? For that matter, what kind of person will I be?

Every day it became more clear to her that she could not live her retiring role indefinitely. She was bursting with energy, eager to get back into the swim of things. It was becoming harder and harder to say no to the charity committees and the various local enterprises that sought her help. She was bored with lack of activity. Beulah took good care of the house and saw to the children. During the day, there was nothing to do but read and sew, sometimes work a little in the tiny garden, have lunch with friends at the country club or go in to downtown Boston for some listless shopping.

Even the activities of the evenings did little to relieve her feeling of boredom. She was tired of the dinners they gave and went to, weary of the same cast of characters at each, most of them Alan's business associates and their wives who, she imagined, looked at the Whitmans with silent curiosity about the state of their marriage. She decorated and redecorated the house until Alan wryly commented that he thought he'd have all the furniture put on tracks so she could just sit and pull switches to move it around more easily. She laughed, but she knew it was all part of her restlessness. Still, she hesitated to resume any degree of prominence in the community, fearing that she might once again be cast into a "competitive" role in her husband's eyes.

It took the Wall Street crash of 1929 to move her back into some kind of satisfying action. Fortunately, the Whitmans were not personally affected. There were cutbacks at Moreford, but Alan was not among those who suddenly found themselves jobless and frightened. He was much too valuable and important, a key man in helping the company ride out the Depression. Nor was Professor Quigly touched. He owned no stocks, was involved in no speculation, and lived, as he always had, on his modest but adequate academic salary. Elizabeth was conscious of their blessings. She was also acutely aware of the poverty of many in the Boston area. Their need finally loomed larger than her own fears about returning to some kind of public involvement. She had, in the past, served on several committees appointed by the mayor, and she was delighted when she was approached by His Honor himself, asking her to form a Women's Relief Committee to do what she could for the unemployed and their families. But before accepting, she discussed it with Alan.

"Why should I object?" he asked calmly when she explained it to him. "God knows those poor devils need all the help they can get. What will you do for them, you and your committee of Lady Bountifuls?"

"I'm not sure," Elizabeth said. "I suppose we'll try to raise money for food and shelter and clothing, mostly. Perhaps donate things to wear. Maybe set up soup kitchens in some of the worst parts of town."

"I don't see how it can do any harm. Anyway, I've been expecting you to get into something. You're like a hen on a hot griddle. Probably do you good to start flexing your muscles again. I must say you've been a model of restraint. It was almost beginning to get on my nerves, this shy little wife act you've been working so hard at."

His reaction made Elizabeth uneasy. She tried to make light of the project. "It really isn't all that big and important," she said. "You're still the one in this family with the brains and the responsibility."

"Oh, for Christ's sake, cut out that sugar-coated crap! It insults my intelligence. I know exactly what's in your mind. You're afraid I'll start feeling threatened again, aren't you? Well, maybe I will and maybe I won't. But there's no point in living out this farce forever. You are the way you are. You can't make a career out of helping me feel superior. Or trying to. It's never been anything more than a ridiculous pretense anyway. If you didn't do anything more than sit on your butt for the rest of your life, I'd probably never get over the feeling that I'm inadequate. Not only in comparison to you. In comparison to the world."

She protested. "But you're not inadequate, Alan. You prove that every day. Look how far you've come in your work, how respected you are in the whole industry."

"I don't want to go into all that again," he said. "I'm bloody tired of your not-so-subtle efforts to build me up by playing yourself down. We'll either make it or we won't as far as this marriage is concerned. And there's not a goddamned thing either of us can do about it. Let it alone, Elizabeth. Let our lives alone before you ruin them with your misguided ministrations!"

She lay awake half the night wondering what the best course would be. Toward dawn she accepted Alan's cold-blooded analysis. He's right, she thought fatalistically. I can't juggle our lives the way I can move a group of pictures on a wall. We'll have to take our chances the way all married people do.

Next morning she called and accepted the assignment. By twelve o'clock the Boston papers were photographing her at City Hall, shaking hands with the mayor. The pictures, head-lined "Mrs. Alan Whitman Accepts Important Local Post," appeared in the press the next morning. The next evening Mr. Alan Whitman "worked late at the office."

The old pattern started again, but this time Elizabeth did not need an Alice Baldwin to bring her the unhappy news. Helplessly, she watched the return of Alan's heavy drinking, his frequent absences in the evening, his barely hid-den hostility whenever her activities were reported in the papers or on the radio. When the phone rang after dinner, it was as though he were deaf. He knew that it would be some matter concerning the Women's Relief Committee, and that Elizabeth would be summoned to take the call, even though she tried to discourage these after-hours questions and conferences.

For her part she accepted the slow but steady disintegra-tion of their relationship with sadness and a feeling of utter frustration. She knew now that she could not change Alan, any more than she could control her own need to be useful and constructive. There was no more talk of divorce but there was, equally, no more pretense of a happy marriage. Alan was discreet about his affairs but Elizabeth knew that their intimates were aware of them. She left it at that, stub-bornly keeping her own counsel, successfully putting a good face on the whole matter.

Their only mutual bond was the children. By 1932, Ann was a beautiful six-year-old, openly adoring of her father and shamelessly aware of her ability to twist him around her little finger. Quigly was a well-made, chunky little boy built like his father, with the same unpredictable temper and the same penchant for stubborn rebellion. He showed no great affection for either of his parents. He was much more at-tached to Beulah, who was the only one who could cope with his tantrums and keep even a loose rein on his willfulness.

Elizabeth pronounced herself a failure as a mother. Her attempts to establish a closeness with Ann never seemed to come off. Just when she felt she was reaching her daughter, Alan would almost magically appear and the two of them would run off to examine some new toy he'd brought her, or to sit cozily together, Ann in his lap, and exchange giggling secrets. Quigly was too young for meaningful communication. Most of the time he accepted her affection with indifference, as though it was his due, and as though whether she existed or not was a matter of supreme indifference to him.

Early on, Elizabeth tried to instill in her children a love of beauty and culture. She stole time from her continuing city activities to take them to the museum, to children's theater, to Boston Common, where she tried to teach them the names of trees and of birds. They were bored and restless during these expeditions. Nonetheless, she persisted. She persisted, too, in her efforts at discipline, even when her orders to Ann often were countermanded by an indulgent Alan. In spite of him, she insisted that Ann learn to keep her room tidy, that Quigly learn to dress and feed himself. As she had known she would be, she was the unpopular authoritarian figure in Ann's life. To Quigly, she supposed, she was simply another adult to be tolerated.

Her work stimulated her, and her father was a tower of strength. Although she did not discuss with him her problems with Alan and the children, she knew that he was aware of them and that the knowledge was as painful as the symptoms of ill health which seemed to be increasing. One day when she arrived for a visit, Charles was barely able to rise from his chair. He looked frail and gray, but as always he smiled at the sight of her. His affectionate greeting was interrupted by a violent attack of coughing. Elizabeth could not conceal her alarm.

"Dad, what is it? Please tell me!"

Gasping for breath, unable to speak, he simply waved his hand at her in a reassuring gesture. When the spasm was over, he sank weakly into his chair, his face pinched and drawn but his composure once more complete.

"Sweetheart, it isn't serious," he said. "Damned irritating, I'll admit, but not fatal."

Elizabeth did not believe him. "What does the doctor say? What kind of treatment is he giving you?"

"There really isn't anything to treat," Charles said. "It's just a chest weakness. Best thing is plenty of rest and fresh air. Nothing for you to worry about. Take my word. Have I ever lied to you?"

She would not be put off. "I think there's something you're not telling me. You should see a specialist. Why don't we get you into Massachusetts General for a real going-over? I'd feel such better about it."

"Honey, I tell you you're making too much of this. I have

these little spells from time to time, but they pass. Now, let's forget it. Tell me about yourself. How are the children? What have you been up to for the betterment of our town?"

She noticed that he did not inquire for Alan. He never did lately. She told him about Ann's new interest, swimming lessons, and Quigly's progress in nursery school. She chattered about a project in which she was intensely interested, help for retarded children. "It's a heart-breaking subject," she said, "but such an important one. We're forming a committee in the hope of getting the public interested. We need financial support, and the city just can't handle it. We're looking for private funds."

"And I suppose you'll add that chairmanship to all your other work?"

"No, I won't chair it. Just work on it. It makes me so sad to see those handicapped babies. And so selfishly grateful that mine are healthy, difficult as those little brats sometimes are."

He nodded. "Give you a little trouble, do they?"

Elizabeth laughed. "To quote you, 'Damned irritating but not fatal.' I'm afraid our Ann is impossibly spoiled. If she keeps on at this rate, she'll grow up smug and arrogant. Quigly is a mystery to me, I confess. Sometimes I think he lives in a world all his own, which I know is a very odd thing to say about a four-year-old, but it's the only way I know to put it." She shrugged philosophically. "Anyway, they're physically strong kids, thank God, and probably they'll outgrow these quirks that irritate me so. Meantime, all I can do is love them and try to give them some appreciation of the good things of this world. Lord knows they seem to have little enough interest in the latter."

"Perhaps you expect too much of them, Elizabeth. They're only babies."

"I know. I keep trying to remember that." She looked at him impishly. "No, you don't have to say it, Professor. I haven't forgotten my wedding-eve lecture. I'm not trying to change anybody. Not even my own children."

Charles sighed. "There's a difference between change and guidance. As a mother you have an obligation to provide the latter. If you do it well, the former should happen without your pushing it. Keep exposing them to the solid things of life, the beautiful things. Sooner or later all these impressions will sink in."

She glanced at her watch. "Oops! Where on earth did the time go? I have to run, dear. Will you come for dinner soon?"

"Yes, of course."

"And will you think about that checkup?"

"I'll think about it," Charles said, "on one condition."

"What's that?"

"That *you* don't. You have enough real problems. Don't add an imaginary one."

She smiled at him wistfully. "All right, I'll try. But you know I couldn't stand it if anything happened to you."

"It's an eventuality you must ultimately accept, my dear."

"No," Elizabeth said. "I won't even think about it."

"That," Charles replied, "is precisely the idea."

In 1932, Elizabeth did indeed have enough problems, many of them personal, but not a few resulting from the chaotic state of the country. This was the year in which Franklin Delano Roosevelt was elected president with promises of a New Deal to bring the nation out of its long Depression. Things were at their worst. The breadlines filled Elizabeth with pity. So did the news of mortgage foreclosures, widespread joblessness, and acute poverty which seemed to be destroying her country. Always a stanch Democrat, she looked to the strong, compelling new president for rescue, and she selfishly thanked God that the plight of so many others did not materially touch her or her family.

If anything, by an almost embarrassing chain of events, the Whitmans' fortunes improved. Alan's work was getting more and more attention from the administration in Washington, an administration prone to favor bright, forward-thinking young men. The famous "One Hundred Days" of legislation which brought about such dramatic measures as the Civilian Conservation Corps, the National Industrial Recovery Act, and the Tennessee Valley Authority also brought changes in various areas of the aviation world. The New Deal was hunting scandals of the Hoover administration, and that year the Black Committee, headed by Senator Hugo L. Black, would open hearings on what were supposed to be subsidies paid for over-ocean airmail routes. These hearings quickly turned to the domestic airmail situation, with charges that the big airlines had improperly been awarded airmail contracts. In 1934, FDR would cancel all contracts and turn the carrying of the mail over to the army for a short period of time, with disastrous results.

In 1933, government participation lay in two areas: The Post Office, which controlled airmail, and the Bureau of Air Commerce, which was responsible for technical regulations involving pilots, aircraft, air traffic, and the like. This latter area, under the Department of Commerce, was the one into which Alan Whitman was called. He was appointed assistant to the head of the BAC and ordered to Washington.

Elizabeth was jubilant.

"Oh, Alan, I'm so proud of you! Number two man in the Bureau of Air Commerce! We'll be really important in Washington, won't we?"

"Slow down," he advised. "I haven't been made Secretary of State. It's not a top job, but it's important. I hope to Christ I can handle it."

"Of course you can handle it! And I'll help any way I can. You wait and see. We'll be the most popular couple in Washington!"

"Franklin and Eleanor will be surprised to hear that," Alan said. There was no mirth in his voice. "Anyway, we have a lot in common. I understand their private life is as much of a mockery as ours."

"Perhaps," Elizabeth said quietly, "a change of scenery will help that part of our lives, too."

He seemed determined to be unusually cruel. "Anything's possible, I suppose. But you do know, don't you, that there are five women to every man in Washington?"

Exasperation took over. "My God, is there no way to reach you? It's as though you're determined to fail, not only at your marriage but at your job as well!"

"Not determined. Destined."

"Then turn down the damned job," Elizabeth said angrily. "Stay here in Boston with your safe berth at Moreford and your stable of oversexed secretaries! You turn your back on every gesture of affection I make. You reject any encouragement I offer. Well, fine! I've had to make a life for myself these last five years. I can keep on doing it, without any help from you. I don't need Washington, Alan. *You* do. But if you're simply going to transfer your pattern of fear and self-deprecation from one city to another, then forget it! Your big hope for advancement is being offered on a silver platter and you 'only hope you can handle it'! We get one more chance to find what we've lost and you quote statistics about the proportion of males to females! You're through before you start, aren't you? You abdicated responsibility long ago. It's all an idiotic, childish game, so why bother?"

He looked at her steadily. "They expect us there within sixty days," he said. "You'd better go down next week and start looking for a place to live."

Without another word he left the house. She heard his car start. She knew she would not see him again that night.

By the time she visited Charles the next day to tell him the news, her surface excitement and happiness had returned. He was looking much better again and he was obviously pleased and impressed.

"It's wonderful, kitten," he said. "Great recognition for Alan. And well deserved, I'm sure. I admit that I'll miss you, but Washington isn't that far away. We'll still be able to see something of each other, I hope."

"But of course! I wouldn't go if it meant a big separation from you."

Charles looked at her curiously. "I hope you don't mean that," he said. "I'd prefer to think that Alan comes first. That you'd follow him anywhere in the world, regardless of what it meant to us."

Elizabeth didn't answer. Nor did she look directly at him.

"What about it, Elizabeth? Isn't this a good time for us to have that long overdue talk? I'm not exactly blind, you know. You may be able to fool most of the world, but where you're concerned I'm more sensitive than most. The last few years have been very difficult, haven't they?"

She nodded. "Very." Almost matter-of-factly she told him the story, including the conversation of the night before. She was in control now, able to discuss her marriage as clinically as she might have analyzed the problems of some other woman. It struck Charles that she was too composed, too unemotional about it. He knew now that he'd been right about Alan from the beginning. His charm was all a façade, a defensive cover-up for some ugly torment. It was incredible that Elizabeth could detail her husband's infidelities, his hostility, with such cool acceptance. Perhaps, Charles thought, it comes from having too much responsibility too early. From being mistress of a motherless house and wife of a man more than a decade her senior. Part of it, he supposed, was an inheritance from the original Ann, who also had this steady determination to keep her troubles to herself and run her life in an orderly fashion, as she had until the uncontrollable end. While these things went through his mind, Elizabeth finished her story. Suddenly she smiled at him.

"Darling, you do get me to blurt out the most unexpected things!" she said. "I had no intention of ever telling you all this. It's not your problem. I can handle it, and you are not to worry. Now that's an order! This Washington thing is fortuitous. I just know it. It's going to be all right. Truly. I promise." Once again she was the Elizabeth the world knew —gay, unruffled, competent. But he knew that this was not the real Elizabeth. The real one was frightened and insecure and pleading for help that he did not know how to give. She was not the model of self-sufficiency that this glass-smooth exterior indicated.

"Do you want to leave him?" Even to himself, Charles's words sounded stupidly inadequate. "You know that you and the children can come here."

"Leave him?" Elizabeth made the two words sound preposterous. "No. I don't want to leave him. If I'd wanted to, I'd have done it long ago. He needs me, Father, whether he knows it or not. And I suppose in a strange way I need him, too. Please, please try to forget what I've told you. I'm going to work it out. You'll see. Alan isn't the first husband to stray and I won't be the first wife to get him back on the track. Good Lord, this isn't the Victorian era. I'm not about to take to my bed with grief and smelling salts. This is 1933. An emancipated age. We females fight our problems. We don't run away from them like some abandoned young woman, appearing on the family doorstep in a blizzard with a baby in her arms, moaning, 'He done me wrong.' Now will you stop being a darling old-fashioned fuss-budget and leave it alone? I only need one thing from you: *you*. So take care of yourself, will you? And I'll take care of me. Word of honor."

He nodded in mute agreement. There was nothing to say. Nothing to do but hope.

part II

GEORGETOWN
1933-1935

Chapter 3

Much later, when she could be more objective, Elizabeth realized that her marriage to Alan had been like a ride on a roller coaster. It started quickly but evenly, with the knowledge of thrills and moderate risks ahead. It proceeded in long swoops of pleasure, rose to heart-stopping heights of ecstasy and peaks of breathless joy, and plunged rapidly to terrifying depths. Like any carnival ride it ultimately came to a halt on the ground, where the passengers got off shaken and relieved to be released from their terror. During the ride, she had never been able to ease her fears with shrieks and screams. She had sat frozen with a kind of desperate fright that she would not allow anyone to see. She had made the trip in silent agony, anticipating the upward climb, knowing that it led inevitably to the downward plunge and bracing herself every moment for the gut-wrenching uncertainty of it all.

No wonder people never go alone on a roller coaster. Like marriage, it is a trip on which one needs a strong seatmate, someone to cling to, to clutch frantically when the long, perilous descents begin and to laugh with when the car climbs safely up again. Up and down. Down and up. And never sure what is around the next bend.

This kind of dispassionate analysis was, of course, far from Elizabeth's mind as she flew from Boston to Washington to find the Whitmans a place to live. She was excited about the trip. In 1933 commercial aviation was still a novelty and, for most people, flying was considered avant garde and dangerous. Elizabeth adored it, just as she loved being on a train or a boat, as long as she did not have to be the "pilot." She even detested driving a car. It was strangely out of character. In any other situation, she felt safest when the controls were in her own hands. Transportation was the only exception—an incongruity which even she recognized. She was infinitely more at ease in the care of a competent pilot or engineer, sea captain or chauffeur than she was when she guided her own destiny. Her admittedly egotistical conviction that she was more capable than others seemed not to hold for moving vehicles. It was an odd admission of inadequacy, she thought ruefully. Perhaps life would be better if she could concede her weaknesses in other, more meaningful areas.

For now, though, the business at hand was to find a house in this strange and beautiful new city. Nearby though it was, she did not know Washington, and driving into it at dusk from the Virginia airport, she was caught by its pure, untouched beauty. She breathed a sigh of delight at her first glimpse of the Lincoln Memorial. She looked with wonder at the broad, sweeping, tree-lined avenues and marveled at the cleanness of it. She had never seen Paris, but she could believe that the architect who planned Washington had modeled it after the French capital. The city seemed to have vitality and chic combined with an unexpected small-town peacefulness. Incredible, she thought, that the destiny of the world was being shaped behind this friendly, unassuming exterior.

The cab drew up to the Carlton Hotel, just across a small park from the White House itself. A smiling bellboy took her bag and indicated the reservations desk, where she identified herself. The clerk had a slight southern accent which she would come to know as typical of the Washington speech pattern.

"Room four twenty-two, ma'am," he said. "Hope you enjoy yoah stay with us."

Elizabeth settled herself in her room, hung up a few clothes, and placed a call to Cambridge to let them know of her safe arrival. Alan was not there, Beulah told her, but the children were fine and she was not to worry about them. Yes, Beulah would call Professor Quigly and report that she'd had a good trip. And she was not to worry. Just hurry home. "We miss you already," Beulah said.

"I miss you, too," Elizabeth answered truthfully. It was the first time she'd been away from the children. The first time, for that matter, that she'd ever traveled anywhere alone. It was strangely exciting to realize that she was anonymous in a big city. No one knew exactly where she was at the moment. She felt suddenly free and lighthearted. So much so that she decided to go to the cocktail lounge and have a drink before dinner.

With the very recent repeal of Prohibition, the cocktail lounge assumed a new importance in the life of the big-city dweller, and the Carlton Lounge was the most popular gathering spot in Washington. From five o'clock on, the dimly lit room, done in strange pseudo-Moorish decor, was the mecca for natives and visitors alike. More correctly, one should have said "residents and visitors." Washington had very few natives, and those who existed—the "cliff dwellers"—rarely frequented public bars or restaurants. The capital was a town of home entertaining. It had only a handful of passable restaurants, most of them in great hotels like the Shoreham and the Mayflower, with only one or two well-known eating places like the Occidental on Pennsylvania Avenue or Harvey's Seafood House on Connecticut Avenue.

At this point, Elizabeth was unaware of the fine line of distinction between the "outsiders," who drank and ate in public places, and the established Washingtonians, who received guests or were entertained in Georgetown or Chevy Chase homes or found their entertainment in the lavish parties given in the great diplomatic mansions of "Embassy Row" on Massachusetts Avenue. She only knew that she was in the midst of the most cosmopolitan atmosphere she'd ever encountered. Even more impressive and far more solid than the opulent, make-believe world of Saratoga.

She ordered a very dry martini and sat back contentedly to drink in her first sight of Washington at play. Her eyes had become used to the murky room now, and she was delighted to discover several well-known faces, politicians and columnists, whom she recognized from their newspaper photographs. She ate a quiet dinner in the hotel dining room and returned to 422 to go over the listings of real estate agents in the telephone book. It was a hit-or-miss business. She was staggered by the number of rental firms listed, and none of the names were familiar to her. She finally chose a firm with offices near the hotel and jotted down the number to call first thing in the morning. Then she bathed and climbed into the strange bed in the strange room in the strange city. Life suddenly seemed remarkably undemanding. Probably, she thought, it was because I didn't have to exert myself in a moment of conversation beyond ordering a drink and dinner. How restful it was. And what a basically selfish beast I must really be.

If she was selfish, she was also inordinately lucky. She called the real estate office next morning and fell into the capable hands of a cheerful middle-aged southern woman, Mrs. Chapman, who offered to pick her up at the hotel at eleven o'clock and show her "some mighty fine properties." Elizabeth accepted eagerly. And for the next three hours she followed Mrs. Chapman's energetic little figure in and out of houses. When they got to the eighth one, in Georgetown, Elizabeth knew she'd found it. She stopped right there, though Genevieve Chapman wanted to show her even more.

"Now you might just find one you like even better, honey," she said. "Don't be in such an all-fired rush to take the first one. My goodness, I thought you-all were such cautious folk up there in New England! Seems to me I never had such an easy client!"

Elizabeth laughed. "Don't believe everything you hear about Yankee traders. Not this one, at least. I fall in love fast."

Mrs. Chapman sniffed. "Might be just infatuation, you know." Then, seeing Elizabeth's determined look, she gracefully acceded. "Well, if you're that certain, Miz Whitman, I guess we can say this is it. Unless, of course, you want your husband to see it too."

"He'll come down and sign the lease," Elizabeth said, "but the choice is up to me. And I've made it. Isn't it an angel of a house?"

Looking at the graceful Georgian house with its old brick front, its small but well-proportioned rooms rising in three narrow stories, Mrs. Chapman had to admit that it was one of the more charming residences on the cobblestoned street. It seemed to have everything the Whitmans needed: a decent-sized drawing room and dining room on the first floor; a master bedroom, bath, and family sitting room on the second; three bedrooms and two baths on the third for the children and a nurse. The kitchen and utility quarters were at the basement level, accessible from the street by a separate flight of stairs. There even was an enclosed garden in the rear, ideal for Ann and Quigly to play in. Elizabeth couldn't believe her good fortune. She was glad now that she had allowed Mrs. Chapman to show her so many available rentals. In contrast to the new houses in Chevy Chase and Shepherd Park with their imitation stucco walls and faux Castilian archways, this eighteenth-century treasure was a perfect little jewel. She loved everything about it, including its location on a quiet street with delicate trees and authentic gas lamps. It was to be many years before Georgetown would fall prey to "Kennedy chic" with pretentious little French restaurants and overpriced, hideously fashionable boutiques. Georgetown, in that period, was like a better Cambridge, an untouched town within a town.

She gave Mrs. Chapman a deposit on the house and hurried back to Boston. Alan listened to her glowing description with mild interest, almost indifference.

"The price is right," was his only comment. "Sounds okay. I'll go down and sign the lease next week. Not for more than two years, though."

Elizabeth looked surprised. "I think they want three years. Probably they base it on the term of the administration."

"That's too bad," Alan said, "but they're not renting to FDR. He's safe until 1936, but that's not to say that I am. I don't know how long I'll last in this job. I'd be a damned fool to tie myself up in a long lease. If you want to know the truth, I'd feel a helluva lot more comfortable renting on a month-to-month basis."

She made no comment. She had learned that the tough talk was simply a cover-up for his nervousness.

"It would be a shame to lose this house for the sake of one year's difference in terms," she said gently. "Maybe they'll give us a sublet clause if we sign for three. Wouldn't that solve it?"

Grudgingly, he admitted that it probably would. "Assuming we could unload it if we had to." He hated it when Elizabeth came up with a logical solution to a problem, shooting holes in one of his unreasonable, arbitrary pronouncements. He did not understand why he felt so competitive with her. She was not a militant, overbearing woman. Yet he went into every discussion with her as though it were a battle and winning was the most important thing in the world. Her quiet understanding of him was intolerable. He would have preferred it if she had met his irritating objections with emotional protestations, even hysterical tears, rather than with this cool and indisputable counterattack.

Their relationship left Elizabeth equally at sea. She had

been brought up in a house where quiet reason prevailed. If anything, she had been the volatile, unpredictable member of the family and Charles the steady voice of equanimity. In this stage of her life, the rules within her own house were reversed. It was Alan who created the storms and she who tried to calm them. She was learning that it was useless to engage in long arguments with him. Better to try to make her point quickly and hope that his inherent intelligence would prevail over his deliberate attempts to be difficult. The ridiculous discussion over the Georgetown house was only one of the almost daily arguments they had.

She thought of Charles's offer of shelter for her and the children. Undoubtedly it would have been the realistic, sensible thing to do: leave Alan now before the situation deteriorated beyond repair. But for reasons she did not fully understand, she couldn't do it. She was not sure that she'd been entirely truthful when she told her father that she and Alan needed each other. Perhaps it was the masochistic streak in both of them that kept them locked together in this insane struggle. Perhaps neither was willing to admit failure, which was the way Elizabeth thought of divorce. She confessed only to herself that it might simply be stiff-necked pride that kept her tied to this flimsy marriage. Just as, perhaps, Alan's weakness was the thing that bound him to the relationship.

In a strange way, she felt sorry for him. The starry-eyed adoration had long since turned to compassion. And while pity is a very shaky foundation for marriage, she was not the first woman who stayed because she believed that without her a frightened man's destruction would be rapid and complete. The saddest thing was that he had become more child than husband. She felt almost protective and maternal about him. Regrettably, it was not a feeling that engendered respect. And without respect, mature love is not possible.

To her credit, she did not let her pity show. If anything, she disguised it so carefully that Alan mistook it for arrogance. Goddamn her, he thought. All she cares about is saving face. How long will those well-bred rules she lives by be enough for her? He knew how often he had hurt her and often many times more he would humiliate her in the future. He knew that his cruelty was only a symptom of his mental sickness. But he knew with deadly certainty that he would strike out at her time and time and time again. She was the handy target for his own self-hatred. He would torture himself by torturing her until one day he would achieve the ultimate viciousness which would end it once and for all. It might be tomorrow or ten years from tomorrow. But he never doubted that it would happen. His own deliberate self-destruction was his goal. He accepted that fact. If Elizabeth chose to go along, that was her affair.

Had they been able to communicate, there might have been a ray of hope. But to Elizabeth, arguing with Alan was like trying to reason with a drunk, even when he was not literally in that condition. And to Alan, talking to his wife was like crawling to the feet of some self-appointed oracle who would condescend to speak her calm but unintelligible words of wisdom. He had abandoned hope of success in either his professional or his personal life. He was simply marking time in both areas, helpless to change his course. And though she accused him of abandoning responsibility, she refused to face the facts emotionally even while she accepted them intel-lectually.

In this limbo, then, was where they stood in 1933 after eight turbulent years of marriage. Elizabeth saw Washington as yet another straw to grasp at, another hope for a change in Alan which might come through greater business ac-complishment. Alan saw it only as a temporary reprieve from eventual oblivion.

Yet, despite his gloomy outlook, even Alan was caught up in the excitement of Washington in the early days of the Roosevelt administration. There was a supercharged atmo-sphere which emanated from the suave chief of state with his sophisticated charm, his bold plans of action, even his spell-binding Fireside Chats which kept millions of Americans glued to their radios. Alan found his job fascinating. He liked his new power over the giants of the aeronautics in-dustry and visibly bloomed under the shower of praise and publicity he received. These days, he did not overtly fault Elizabeth's performance. She had turned out to be one of the most popular of the young Washington hostesses, giving elegant little dinners in the charming Georgetown house or looking beautiful on Alan's arm at the receptions and parties to which they were invited almost every night. He did not resent the compliments other men paid him about his wife. Suddenly, the perfection she radiated seemed, in his con-fused mind, evidence of his cleverness in selecting the perfect mate. The Whitmans were much sought after, much admired. And for the first time, Alan felt that it was he who set the pace. He was the star. In this new flush of success, he saw Elizabeth as no more than an unthreatening and becoming satellite.

Ironically, it was Elizabeth's restless attitude that began to threaten the first harmonious period they had had in years. Pleased as she was with Alan's cheerful new outlook, and delighted as she was with his apparent new-found confidence, Elizabeth began to weary of the endless, empty social activities of prewar Washington. The girl who had hungered for a cosmopolitan, glamorous life was the first to tire of it. One evening, after they'd been out for ten consecutive nights, she tried to explain her feeling to Alan. At the dressing table, putting on the light makeup she wore, she sighed deeply. Alan looked at her in the mirror where he was adjusting his black tie.

"Would you care to translate that for me?" he asked.

She looked at him seriously. "The sigh? It just means I'd give my soul for a quiet evening at home. No small talk. No New Deal gossip. Just us by ourselves. Do you realize we haven't been home one night in the last ten, Alan? And before that we gave three dinner parties in a row. It's been almost two weeks since we've had a moment to just relax."

He frowned. "I don't get it. You were the one who thought this was the most exciting life in the world. There wouldn't have been much point to moving here if we were going to lock ourselves in the house every night."

"No. But there is such a thing as a happy medium."

"Sure there is. Her name's Mrs. McClaren. She reads fortunes. They say she used to be President Harding's spiritual adviser. And you know how well *he* did."

"I'm not making a bad joke, Alan. Our life is getting way out of balance. We never have a chance to talk to each other or just stay home and recharge our batteries. It worries me that I see so little of the children, too. I know what it means to be deprived of a mother."

"Oh, for Christ's sake, Elizabeth, don't be so dramatic. Mary is a jewel," he said, referring to Mary Jackson, the black nurse Elizabeth had found when Beulah was unable to come with them to Washington. "Besides, you have all day to see the kids if you want to."

"Do I indeed?" Elizabeth asked. She tossed her engagement book at him. "Well you might just look at this." Every page was crammed with appointments, luncheons, teas, fashion shows, all the pastimes that the ladies of official Washington engaged in, not only for social reasons but as part of the business of keeping the right contacts which might help their husbands in their jobs.

Alan threw the book back. "I haven't asked you to do these things," he said defensively. "Hell, you can stay home and make mud pies as far as I'm concerned. I'm doing okay at the job. I don't need any help from you. Those daytime hen parties don't mean a damn anyhow. But," he continued, "the evening things do. That's where I get to talk informally with men who are important. It's a big part of operating in this town. You may not like it, but it comes with the territory."

She fell silent. Suddenly Alan was very angry.

"What are you going to do now? Sulk all through the evening?"

"Do I ever sulk?" Elizabeth asked reasonably.

His tone was sarcastic. "Of course not. You're never anything but the perfect lady. The professor's daughter. You and your lousy good manners."

She tried once more. "Alan, don't fly off the handle so quickly. All I'm trying to say is that if I don't have some quiet time I'm going to go mad. I feel like we've been delivered into the hands of the New Deal. That we're no more than a couple of puppets dancing to this insane tune. It's fun most of the time, I'll grant you that. But anything is bad in excess, and for months we've been on an absolute merry-go-round. All I'm asking is that we try to temper it a little. Refuse a few of the less important invitations. Plan a couple of nights at home every week. Is that too much to ask?"

"Yes," he said harshly. "That is too much to ask. We don't make up the rules here. You were the one who was so goddamned sure I would make good in this job. Now you want me to make good only if the method suits your convenience. Well, if the way the game is played doesn't suit you, Your Highness, you can go sit on the sidelines. But you'll sit there by yourself!"

How does it always happen like this? Elizabeth wondered. Why can we never have a normal, reasonable conversation about a problem? Because, a voice inside her answered, you do not live with a normal, reasonable man. She tried to see it from his point of view. In a way he was right. She had been excited and hopeful that this job would work some kind of magic in Alan. Now that that dream seemed to be coming true, it was unfair of her to be troublesome. Alan had a point. She would start cutting down on the daytime activities and accept the fact that life in Washington never gave its ambitious inhabitants a night off.

Gracefully she tried to apologize. "You're right. I'm sorry. I suppose I'm just overtired. Too tired to get through this evening, though. Would you mind terribly, dear, making my excuses? I'm sure the French Ambassadress will understand if you say I have a touch of flu. Besides, it will be such a big crush nobody will miss me."

He was not about to match her graciousness. "You're right," he said pointedly. "Nobody will miss you."

He left without another word. When the door closed, Elizabeth began to tremble all over. She had been afraid that this recent amiable coexistence would sooner or later run into trouble. But she had not imagined that she would be the one to set off a new set of problems. She hoped that if she adjusted again, Alan would get over his bad temper and go back to being as reasonable as he'd been these past few months. Unfortunately, she didn't really have faith in her hope. She knew him too well.

She was right. The stupid little spat was the excuse that Alan, probably subconsciously, had been looking for. The outward signs of his renewed hostility were the same old ones: increased drinking and undisguised disdain toward her. At least, Elizabeth thought, he can't have resumed his philandering. He got home every night around seven, as he had since they'd moved to Washington, just in time to change before they went out or received guests. Docilely, she made no further protest about the excessive social life. Instead, she spent more time at home in the afternoon, playing with the children when they returned from school, trying, with discouragingly little success, to get closer to them. Ann lived only for the moment when her daddy came home. And Quigly had transferred whatever affection he could give to Mary Jackson, who was as good with him as Beulah had been.

Elizabeth's relief about her husband's faithfulness was, unfortunately, only the naïve thinking of a woman who had not been long enough in Washington to understand the sophistication of the people who were stationed there. She was aware that a good deal of innocent flirting went on among the high-ranking officials and the worldly diplomats. It was harmless diversion that relieved the monotony of big parties. She even noticed that Alan was openly attentive to many of the beautiful women they saw at these gatherings. She did feel a twinge of anxiety over the special attention he paid to the young wife of an elderly Austrian industrialist, but she dismissed her fears. After all, the Whitmans were together every evening. Even if Alan had thought of getting involved, where would he find the time? It was not like the old Cambridge days when he "worked late" several nights a week. Luckily for Alan, Elizabeth was too conventional to realize that the daylight hours offered quite ample op-

portunity for clandestine meetings. She was yet to discover
that a quiet lunch on the Washington Hotel Roof was often
the prelude to two discreet hours in a nearby Virginia motel.
Or that in a city inhabited by so many chic Europeans, the
"cinq-à-sept" rendezvous was accepted practice between elegant women and their lovers. It never occurred to her to
wonder why, although government offices closed at four
o'clock, Alan did not get home until seven. She did not think
to question those three unexplained hours until he came in
one evening to change rapidly and she, already dressed, sat
idly on the bed watching him. He got out of his business suit
and threw it, along with the shirt, on the chair beside her.
She picked up the shirt to toss it into the laundry hamper. It
smelled heavily of perfume. The kind the industrialist's wife
wore. And on the collar there was, of course, the classic
badge of a hurried assignation: a faint smear of lipstick.

She said nothing. Somehow she got through the evening
with a smile pasted on her lips. Suddenly she was aware that
the Austrian woman and Alan now studiously avoided each
other, their greetings only casually, correctly polite. How
could I have been such a fool again? Elizabeth wondered.
She should have known that his heavy drinking and his
aloofness would not be enough punishment for her. It had to
have this added thrust to be complete.

When they returned home at midnight, Alan stripped
quickly, yawned hugely, and was in his own twin bed before
she was out of her dress. "Jesus, I'm beat," he said, his
voice muffled by the pillow. "These goddamn nights are
killing me."

At another time, Elizabeth might have been almost amused
by this unwitting admission that the constant social rounds
were also beginning to tire Alan. But tonight there was no
humor in her.

"Funny," she said in response, "I would have thought it
was your *days* that were doing you in."

He chose to misunderstand. "Job's tough," he mumbled,
half asleep, "but so far I can handle it."

"Damn you, Alan, stop trying to make a fool of me!"

He was awake now, lying on his back, looking at her coldly.

"How long has it been going on?" Elizabeth demanded.
"Who is she? No, you needn't answer. It's that cheap Austrian tramp, isn't it? Her perfume was all over your shirt
when you came home this evening. My God, you really were
clever this time, weren't you? You haven't been missing from
home a single night since we've been here. I was stupid
enough to think you'd given up your sordid little adventures.

Obviously I'm no match for you. It never occurred to me that you were spending your daytime hours so romantically."

He watched her steadily. Almost, it seemed, with enjoyment. His silence only increased her frustration. "How dare you do this?" Elizabeth demanded. "If you don't care anything for your children or me, what makes you fool enough to risk a public scandal in your position? Don't you know what this could do to your career?"

"I don't give a damn what it does to my career," he said quietly. "I'm bound to louse it up anyway. Just as I'm hellbent on ruining myself. That shouldn't come as news to you. You've lived with it long enough."

"Living with it is one thing," Elizabeth said. "Understanding it is another. I've accepted the fact that you haven't loved me for a long time. Perhaps you never loved me. But what have I ever done to you to make you humiliate me so? Where is your pride, Alan? Doesn't your own vulgarity embarrass you, the way it embarrasses me?"

He got out of bed slowly and put on his robe. "I think I'll have a drink," he said.

"That's your answer to everything, isn't it?"

"Do you have a better one?"

Suddenly she felt defeated. Anger gave way to pleading. "Please don't run away from this talk, Alan. Don't have another drink. You've had so many this evening. It's the same every evening."

"So it is," he agreed. "How fortunate that you don't know how many I have during the day. Or do you? You seem to be turning into a remarkably good detective. But I wouldn't want your dossier on me to be incomplete. Do you know I keep a bottle in my desk drawer? Very important for midmorning pickups when you have my kind of monumental hangovers. And then, of course, there are the very legitimate three martinis at lunch. As for the cocktail hour, which is the most convenient time to lay the lady in question—"

"Stop it!" Elizabeth screamed. "I don't want to hear any more!"

"But you asked for explanations, didn't you?" he queried mildly. "I seem to remember your saying you couldn't understand why I humiliate you so, why I jeopardize my big, wonderful job. Isn't that right, Elizabeth? So I am going to tell you, my dear. It's very simple. I humiliate you because I whore around. And I whore around because I drink. And I drink because . . . Well now that's really the key question, isn't it? I suspect that I drink because I am basically a very insecure man who has been exceptionally shrewd or lucky. I

have managed to fool everybody about my ability. Or lack
of it. My employers, and even my wife, think I'm brilliant. A
real powerhouse, that's me. I've been very clever, you see,
but only because ninety-nine per cent of the world is so
stupid. Nobody has caught on to the fact that I'm made of
papier-mâché. A one-dimensional, hollow man who's bluffed
his way into jobs that are too big for him and a wife who's
too far above him. And since only I know the truth, I keep
postponing the inevitable day of discovery by bolstering my
ego with hard liquor and soft bodies. Now that's really not so
hard to understand, is it? I have nothing to lose. Because,
you see, I really have nothing."

Elizabeth was bewildered. "It's not true," she said. "You're
inventing excuses for your fears. You can't fool the world,
Alan. You *are* brilliant. You would have been found out
long ago if you weren't. You were already on the way to
success when we met. And you didn't drink like this. It must
have something to do with marriage and with me. Somehow I must have failed you, tied you down too quickly with
the responsibilities of a family. That must be why you drink
and do these terrible things. To escape from the pressures
at home."

His voice became gentle. "No. You haven't done this to
me. On the contrary, I'm the one who's done terrible things
to you. In my own sick, tortured way, I love you and the
children. You are the only people in the world who have
any meaning for me. The rest is like a terrible compulsion.
The drinking. The cruelty. The womanizing. I don't want to
do any of that, but I have no control. I told you all this
before. Face it, Elizabeth, I'm a weak, frightened man. You
deserve better. Whatever is eating me won't go away. It will
only get worse. I know it as surely as I know my own name.
I'll get more scared. More alcoholic. More indiscreet. I can't
beat it but *you* can. If you're smart, you'll leave me now
while I'm still rational enough to understand why. Get the
divorce I asked you to years ago. My mind is going a little
more every day. I don't want to hurt you more than I already have. But I will if you stay, my dear. I surely will."

It was, Elizabeth thought, a cry for help. Help she did not
know how to give. She was dealing with a sick man. One who,
incredibly, she still cared for. She was frightened for them all.
But mostly, she was filled with pity for him. As she had before, she tried to reach him.

"Alan, you *must* see a doctor. A psychiatrist. Neither of us
can understand this, but there has to be an explanation hidden away, deep down somewhere inside you. Our only hope

is to get to the bottom of your fears. I believe that you are frightened. But you're not weak. Please, darling, let's get help for you. Let's not throw away something important. Analysis may take a long time, but it's our only hope."

He shook his head. "Forget it. It's been tried. I spent two years with a head doctor before I met you. It didn't help."

"Perhaps he was not the right man for you. We'll find the right one."

"No."

She was close to tears. At the same time, to her amazement, she felt her passion rising. The intensely emotional scene they had lived through excited her. Suddenly she wanted him to make love to her. Wordlessly she stepped out of her clothes and stood before him.

"Then let me help," she said. "Let me be all the things you need—wife, mistress, friend. Let me show you how much faith I have in you. Take your strength from me." She held out her arms. Almost reluctantly he came to her.

"It won't work," he said.

"We'll make it work."

That night Charlene Margaret Whitman was conceived in a kind of desperate, last gasp of ecstasy.

Elizabeth always felt well when she was pregnant, and carrying this new baby seemed to evoke a special kind of joy. Even to herself, her happiness was incongruous. The night that the seed which was to be Charlene Whitman entered her body was one of the most devastating of Elizabeth's life. The rapture that ended that evening was almost an animal thing. Yet she felt elated. It was, perhaps, a kind of self-hypnosis, a desperate belief that this latest "confession" of Alan's was the ultimate purge. Stubborn optimist that she was, she convinced herself that the sickness within her husband was, at long last, on the wane. Her letters to Charles reflected this new peace of mind. They were chatty, carefree notes, mostly full of news about the children.

"Ann is such a grown-up eight-year-old," she wrote. "She makes *me* feel awkward! Where on earth do you think she got such poise?" Quigly, she reported, was a miniature Alan, with all his father's brooding good looks. "I do feel sorry for the women he'll meet in this life. That face and body will leave a trail of broken hearts among the debutantes of 1950!" It was an unconsciously revealing comment, Charles thought. Without realizing it, she was saying that Quigly had his father's cruelty as well as his father's physical appeal.

Elizabeth spoke happily of the new baby. "As we say in

the airplane business, we don't have her E.T.A. yet, but the approximate time is early July. I'll be glad to have one not born under the sign of Leo. They're so strong and outgoing. Achievers. I must confess that I don't need another little 'lion' like Ann. Two fierce cubs in one family might be too much for me! You see that I speak of the new baby as 'she,' Father. I know it will be a girl and I've already decided to name her Charlene after the most wonderful grandfather a child ever had."

She made no mention of her problems with Alan, and Charles forced himself to believe that this meant all was well between them. Since the conversation in Cambridge, Elizabeth had said no more about the difficulties of her marriage, and Charles was not one to pry, even though he suspected that there was much she was not telling him in these light-hearted letters.

If that is so, Charles thought ruefully, then we're even. His letters to her were equally upbeat and serene. He told her of his daily activities, conveyed amusing bits of Cambridge gossip and omitted the one tragic piece of news he'd received from his doctor. There was no point in burdening Elizabeth with the knowledge that her father had, at best, a year to live. The persistent cough, the increasing weakness which he had self-diagnosed as bronchitis had now been confirmed as tuberculosis. He had delayed too long seeing Dr. Samson, his longtime friend and physician. By the time he got around to it, the disease was far gone. It had increased with deadly slowness, though no one could be sure exactly how long Professor Quigly had had his fatal illness, nor at what point his minor "chest complaint" had become a killer.

When they gave him the terrible news, Charles's first thought was for others. "Could I have communicated it to Elizabeth and her children?" he asked anxiously.

"Possible but not probable," Dr. Samson said. "If you have passed it on, we'd have seen some symptoms in the family by now."

"Thank God."

"Of course, it might be wise for them to have tests anyway."

Charles frowned. "I'd rather they didn't know, unless you think it absolutely necessary."

Dr. Samson regarded him compassionately. "I wish we knew more about the disease, Charles. Someday we'll have miraculous drugs, but right now—well, it's just a matter of rest and, if possible, a better climate than Boston. You should move to a high altitude like Denver. Or a warm, dry climate like Arizona."

"Would that cure me?"

"Maybe not cure," the doctor said, "but it undoubtedly would prolong your life. For how long, of course, no one can say with certainty."

"But if I moved, Elizabeth would have to know why."

Dr. Samson did not answer. "We could try a lung operation," he said finally. "With no guarantees, of course."

"And if I do nothing," Charles persisted, "how long do you give me?"

"Hard to say. Six months. A year, maybe. But with an operation and a move to another climate you might live many years, Charles. Don't be foolish, man. Elizabeth would rather have you alive, even if she worried about you. She's a strong woman and a sensible one. You know what her choice would be. Good Lord, you're not yet sixty years old! You conceivably could have another ten, maybe fifteen years under the right conditions. You owe it to Elizabeth, even if you don't think you owe it to yourself."

Charles shook his head. "I'm no more anxious to die than the next one, make no mistake about that. But I'm not willing to live knowing that every breath I take is the cause of anxiety for the people I love. Elizabeth will grieve when I go. But a few months of unhappiness is better than years of tortured watching and waiting. It would be different, Ed, if I had something curable. Something that caused her only a few weeks or months of worry. But you've just said that this could drag on for years. I know her. She'd be torn between her desire to be with me and her proper place with her family. I can't do that to her. Her life is just beginning. Mine holds no more promise tomorrow than it does today. No, Elizabeth must not be told anything. I'll stay right here, put my affairs in order, such as they are, and hope I last to see my new grandchild."

Dr. Samson tried once more. "That's drivel and you know it. The self-sacrificing role doesn't suit you very well, my friend. For a logical man, you're acting like the hero in a soap opera!"

Charles Quigly smiled. "I don't feel very heroic," he said. "I'm scared to death."

Samson knew when he was beaten. "I still believe you should give some serious thought to moving away," he said half-heartedly.

"All right, I will," Charles lied. "Remember, though, this

is a doctor-patient relationship. Privileged information. No one must know."

"You should tell someone. For obvious reasons."

"All right," Charles said, "I'll tell my sister, Beatrice. When the time comes she can call Elizabeth. And not a moment before." The old worry returned. "I'd like to visit Washington before I get too bad, but I suppose that would be out of the question."

"Completely. At this stage you're highly contagious. No direct contact with anyone. Even the dishes you use shouldn't be used by anyone else. I'm sorry, Charles, but you can't go near Elizabeth and the children. You should be hospitalized, but I suppose you won't agree to that, either, since you want this all kept so secret."

"No hospitals," Charles said. "By the way, how does one get TB?"

"It's a germ. Not a very discriminating one. It hits young and old, rich and poor, men, women and children."

"But it's not inherited."

"No," Dr. Samson said kindly, "it is not inherited."

Quietly, Charles went about arranging his "estate." It was a ridiculous term for the pitifully little he had to leave. He wished now that he'd been more of a businessman and less of a scholar. He had no investments, not even life insurance. Such things had been of no interest to his academic mind. All that he had to leave Elizabeth was the small, not very valuable house in Cambridge and a good but modest collection of antique furniture, china, and silver which had belonged to her mother. Even these, he thought bitterly, were nearly worthless. In good times the house would not bring much of a price. And in this era of economic chaos, Elizabeth would be fortunate to realize even a few thousand dollars from it, provided she could sell it at all.

As for the antiques, though they might be worth something to collectors, they would bring little in the current market. The china and silver were service for twenty-four. Good God, he thought, only millionaires entertain on such a grand scale these days. But he doubted that Elizabeth would sell her mother's things in any case. She would love the beautiful pieces and cherish them as a precious legacy. She might even find use for them, since she seemed to do so much entertaining in Washington. He drew up a simple will, leaving her all his worldly goods except his beloved books, which he directed be given to the university library. It was a small return for all the years of happiness and livelihood his profession had given him.

At the last moment, late in December, he begged off from spending Christmas and New Year's with the Whitmans in Georgetown. Elizabeth was hurt. It was the first holiday he had not been with them. He tried to make his excuse sound reasonable, pleading that he had gotten so far behind in his work that he needed the peace and quiet of the Christmas vacation to catch up and be ready for his classes when they resumed in the new year. The truth was he was wretchedly ill now, going nowhere, seeing no one. The snow and cold went right to the marrow of his bones and he shivered from morning until night. The medication Dr. Samson had started him on didn't seem to help his cough, not that either of them thought it would. In any case, he would not let Elizabeth see him like this. On the phone, he managed to sound sprightly and cheerful.

"I know you're disappointed," he said. "Probably not half as much as I. But if I don't use this period to catch up, I'll be hopelessly snowed under with work. Besides, darling, I've always had a yen to see Washington in the spring. Are those Japanese cherry trees really as beautiful as I've heard? Could you stand the old man for Easter vacation? It would give me something marvelous to look forward to."

Elizabeth tried to be understanding. She hated to think of him alone in Cambridge working, but she felt that it must be important to him. It did not occur to her to be suspicious. Wrapped in the natural self-involvement of her newly discovered pregnancy, her world was peaceful.

"We'll miss you terribly, Dad," she said, "but you know what's best. I'll try not to be infantile about it. After all, we have a lot of Christmases ahead. Next year you'll have three little brats to play Santa Claus for!"

He tried to sound natural, at ease. "So we'll talk again on Christmas Eve and we'll plan the Easter visit, okay?"

"It seems forever," Elizabeth said, "but okay. Father?"

"Yes, dear?"

"Love you."

"I love you, too," he said.

When Charles made excuses about coming to Washington at Easter, Elizabeth began to get suspicious.

"I don't understand," she said when he called. "We've been counting on it, and there's no earthly reason why you can't come down while school's closed for vacation. There's something you're not telling me, Father. You're sick. That's what it is, isn't it? You don't want me to see you looking ill."

"Still my little girl with the vivid imagination, aren't you?" Charles laughed. "No, my darling, I'm not sick. Unless you count being sick of thick-headed college students. Okay, I'll confess. I'm being selfish. Arthur Cabot has arranged a fishing trip to his camp in Maine. He's invited me and four of our other professor friends, and if you don't mind terribly, sweetheart, I'd really like to go. I could do with a good rest, and even though I'm *not* sick, I have a hunch that all that fresh air and relaxation would do me good. It kills me not to be with you and the kids, but I'll be seeing you in July for sure. Nothing in this world could keep me from being on hand to greet my third grandchild!"

She was not easily convinced. It was impossible to believe that he would opt for a male outing instead of a chance to be with her.

"I'm not sure I believe that story, Professor. I still think you're keeping something from me."

"Have you and I ever had any secrets?"

"But we were so looking forward to it!" It was almost a childish wail. "You didn't come at Christmas, and you haven't seen Ann and Quigly in months, and I want to show you the house! Besides, I miss you."

She was making it almost unbearable, but he knew what he had to do.

"Elizabeth, dear, you know how much I love you and the children, but indulge your old man just this once, won't you? It was a hard choice, but it's not as though I won't be seeing you within a very few months. Look, honey, I told you I was being selfish. Right now, I'm just more in the mood for rough male companionship than I am for the childish demands made on a grandfather. It's been a tough winter, sweetheart. Much as I want to see you, I don't quite feel in shape for a round of Washington social life or a week of playing catch with Quigly."

She tried to understand. She told herself that he was entitled to some fun and freedom. For twenty years his every thought and act had been with her in mind. He'd never taken a vacation away from her, never indulged in the masculine outings that other men with wives were able to enjoy. Now that she was married with a whole different life of her own, why shouldn't he do some of the things that men of his age enjoyed? Still, the sense that something was wrong just wouldn't go away.

"Have you seen Dr. Samson lately?"

Charles sighed in mock despair. "You're worse than a nagging wife," he said. "Yes, I saw Ed last week. And if it will make you feel better, he said that some good, clean air was just what the doctor would order. He thought the Maine trip was a great idea. He gives me hell all the time for overworking, you know that. You'd have thought he'd won the Nobel Prize for medicine when I told him I was finally going to take a real vacation!"

She had to be satisfied with the explanation. When he'd first said that he wasn't going to come to Washington for Easter, Elizabeth had thought she'd bring the children to see him in Boston. But his proposed trip eliminated that possibility. Besides, she was almost six months pregnant, and the idea of lugging her bulky self and two small children on even such a short trip seemed more than she could cope with. She managed to change her tone to one of pleasure for him.

"Well, I can't say I'm not disappointed because I am," she said, "but for once in my life maybe I can stop wanting everything my way. I do understand, darling. It's not the kind of Easter I'd planned, but it won't kill me to let you do something *you'd* like to do for once. I hope you have a marvelous time and get a good rest. It's crazy the way you work. I agree with Dr. Samson. You don't take enough time for yourself."

He did not tell her that he had quietly resigned his teaching duties, asking the dean to make no public announcement that Elizabeth might hear about.

"You're both right," he said. "From now on I'll be the local goof-off. Make you and Ed Samson happy. Wait and see. This may just be the beginning of the new Charles Quigly. Next thing you know, I'll be taking a cruise and meeting up with a lot of rich widows. Serve you both right for encouraging me to become a playboy."

They were laughing when they said goodbye, content that they were doing the right thing for each other. Both were, in different ways, relieved. Elizabeth had feared that in the loving company of her father she might be tempted to tell him about the Austrian woman and the frightening dual personality of Alan. In truth, she had almost managed to block out the first matter, which had brought on such an erotic culmination. And with her eternal optimism, she had nearly convinced herself that Alan really had changed in these past five months. There had not been an evening when he came home later than six o'clock, and sometimes it was as early as four-thirty or five. Frequently he brought work home with him, digging into a bulging briefcase of papers and working on them at the living-room desk while Elizabeth sat quietly reading or sewing.

Her pregnancy gave them a perfect excuse to decline many of the boring invitations that they once had felt compelled to accept. Now they went only where it was really important for Alan to be seen, or where they actually wanted to go. Their only disagreements, these days, were over some matters of the children's training. Alan thought she was far too strict, especially where Ann was concerned. And Elizabeth tried to convince him that discipline was necessary.

"They're darlings, but they're just little people, complete with faults," she said one evening when he'd become angry about her scolding Ann for some minor offense. "We can't let them think they're perfect and privileged, because they'll learn soon enough that they're not. The world isn't going to be as permissive as their parents. We're wrong, Alan, if we don't prepare them for the fact that they won't always be allowed to do exactly as they please."

"I still think you overdo it," he'd said. "Such clinical analysis is not exactly in keeping with the maternal instinct."

Elizabeth would not be drawn into a serious argument. "Maybe you're right," she smiled. "I don't seem to be blinded by fatuous motherly love to the point where I can ignore their shortcomings. Maybe I'm better as a pregnant woman than as a parent. Probably I should just give birth and then offer them up for adoption."

"That's not funny, Elizabeth."

"I'm sorry, darling. It was a bad joke. But I'm serious about our helping them keep themselves in perspective. Next thing they'll be wondering why their pictures aren't always in the paper, like FDR's grandchildren."

Even Alan had to smile at the comparison. "Well, just take it a little easy, will you? You're not winning any popularity contests at the moment."

"Believe it or not, I don't consider popularity a requisite for good parenthood. I want my kids to love me now. But even more, I'd prefer that they like me later in life."

That was as close as they came to a fight these days, and compared to the past it seemed normal and untroublesome. In her letters to her father, Elizabeth continued to sound a note of contentment, and nothing could have been more welcome to a dying Charles Quigly.

He did not leave the house at all now. Only his sister Beatrice, his housekeeper, and Ed Samson knew how desperately ill he was. His one regret was that he knew he would never see Elizabeth again, unless it was on his deathbed. He was relieved that she'd accepted the hunting-trip story. He'd feared that she might try to check further, perhaps call her aunt Beatrice and wangle the truth out of that worried woman. But apparently she had believed both the story and his later fictionalized account of the trip when he called her upon his "return." If he could just sustain the deception until the end, he'd be grateful.

God was good, Charles thought. Elizabeth had become the woman he wanted her to be, beautiful, gay, intelligent, and fulfilled. He was not foolish enough to want her life to be endlessly placid and unruffled. No life could, or should, be. People needed moments of trial to savor the sweet parts when they came. He rejoiced that things seemed to have come into some kind of balance for her. One could not protect a child from a certain amount of trouble in life. All a parent really could do was provide love, realistic and unswerving. Elizabeth had had all of his. And she had developed her own brand of tolerance and determination, mixed with the delicious sense of the ridiculous which was a gift from her Irish ancestors.

Charles was content. These, he thought, were the parts of Elizabeth's inheritance that really mattered. These were riches. Most men died leaving much less.

Chapter 4

In the sixth month of Elizabeth's pregnancy, Charles Quigly died. As she had promised, Aunt Beatrice waited until he was hospitalized and very near death before she called and told his daughter everything. Elizabeth's shock was profound. In a daze she threw a few clothes into a bag and prepared to catch the next plane, reassured by Mary that the children would be well taken care of and by Alan that he could be there in a matter of hours when needed.

"I'd come with you now," he said gently, "but there's so much going on at the office that I really should be here unless you think I can do some good in Boston."

Elizabeth shook her head. "There's nothing any of us can do now. I don't even know whether he'll recognize me. But I have to be there. I want to be. I love him very much." She looked puzzled and forlorn. "He never said a word. He must have known, but he never said a word. Why didn't he let me help him? Why did he close me out when he needed me most?"

"He didn't close you out," Alan said, almost harshly. "He wanted to save you just that much more suffering. My God,

75

Elizabeth, can't you see how brave it was of him not to let you know?"

She refused to accept this. "But we still might have been able to do something," she said stubbornly. "We could have seen other doctors. Maybe found new treatments. I begged him years ago to get other opinions, but he had such faith in Ed Samson. People don't have to die of TB these days. They go away to places where they can be treated. Why didn't he tell me, Alan?"

He tried to be patient. "Because he knew how you'd react. Just like you're reacting now. Charles knew that you'd drive yourself crazy with worry about him. If he'd thought you could have helped, Elizabeth, you know he'd have reached out to you. Now you must stop this! Think about the baby. I'm sure Charles was thinking of that, as well as of you."

It was the first thing that made sense to her. The baby. It was true. Charles, who knew her better than anyone in the world, knew how she would take the news of his illness. Probably he feared she might even miscarry. It was an old nightmare of his, born of his early, disappointing years with his wife. She sighed with hopeless acceptance.

"It seems unreal to me. I can't think of a world that doesn't have him in it." With effort, she turned her mind to practical matters. "I don't know how long I'll be gone," she said. "Aunt Bea says he's very bad. Oh, God, Alan, suppose I don't get there in time."

"You will," he reassured her. "And you don't have to worry about things here. Mary will take care of the house and the children. And I'll call you every evening."

"No, I'll call you. I don't know how much time they'll let me spend with him, but I'll be at the hospital every minute I can. It will be better if I phone when I get back to Dad's house."

Alan smiled cynically. Was that the real reason or did the old pattern of distrust continue? Perhaps she was thinking that he could always call her from somewhere else, but if she telephoned him at home she'd be sure he was there, behaving himself. When the cat's away, he thought. But he did not voice his own suspicions.

"Perhaps you're right," he said. "That does make more sense. Take care of yourself. We don't want any premature arrivals. And give my love to Charles."

The hospital vigil was a horror that lasted for two weeks. Elizabeth spent as much time at her father's side as the doctors would permit; not enough to suit her, but more than they normally would have permitted a young woman going into her seventh month of pregnancy. It was as though she had to store up a reserve of courage to use in the years ahead. She sat beside him for hours, unable to read or even work on her needlepoint, just gazing at the strong but gentle face of this man who meant so much to her. Most of the time he lay in a drugged sleep. But once in a while he opened his eyes and even managed to smile at her, as though to say, "It's all right. I'm content. You be that way, too."

Toward the very end, as deeply as she wished him to live, Elizabeth willed him to die. This helpless person in the narrow hospital bed was not Charles Quigly. He became, to Elizabeth, someone silently begging for release. To this end she allowed them to continue administering the pain-killing drugs, but ordered all the vitamins and other life-prolonging aids discontinued. Her control was remarkable, her suffering so deep that it could not be seen. She did not cry or pray or give way to hysterics. She simply sat and silently poured out her love to him.

Aunt Bea strongly disapproved of her orders to discontinue the medication. "You have no right," she told Elizabeth. "You are shortening his life."

"Yes," Elizabeth said, "but I know that's what he wants. Who else should do him this last act of kindness?"

During those two weeks, she arrived at the hospital early in the morning and stayed well into the night until the nurses ordered her to leave. Then she would stumble, drunk with strain and fatigue, to her father's house, have a cup of soup, and telephone Alan before she fell exhausted into bed. She was ashamed to realize that a tiny period of anxiety preceded every call and a wave of relief came over her when she heard his voice. In this period, he never failed to be there. And she was never completely confident that he would be.

When Charles died, Alan flew up immediately to help with the arrangements and be at her side. She was dry-eyed and gaunt. Except for the huge belly, she was a skeleton. Alan was horrified.

"My God," he said, "you've lost pounds! Are you all right? Have you checked with the doctors here?"

His concern comforted her. "I'm all right," she said. "I just want to get home and see the children." Neither she nor Alan approved of exposing children to the barbaric ritual of death. She would explain to them later that their grandfather had died. But she would not tolerate the idea of their remembering Charles as a cold, artificial figure in a coffin.

For that matter, Elizabeth would have none of it for herself or for others. Contrary to custom, she ordered the casket closed. There would be no morbid viewing of her father in death. Nor would she go along with the accepted practice of having his body lie in the living room of his home. Like the first Ann, who chose to give birth in a hospital rather than in her traditional bed, Elizabeth now opted to have Charles repose in the funeral home until the services. She would not be moved from this decision, even by Aunt Bea and the rest of the family, who were scandalized by this unorthodox procedure. Aunt Bea was gentle with her, but unmistakably opposed.

"It seems so impersonal, Elizabeth," she said. "Charles should be buried from his own house. And the people who loved him should be allowed to see him there one last time."

Elizabeth stood firm. "I'm sorry, Aunt Bea, but I don't look at it that way. Dad left his house for the last time alive. Returning him to it now is meaningless for him and too painful for me. As for seeing him, I'll see him always. As he was. Gentle and sweet and full of life. I'd like to think that's the way everyone will remember him."

After the simple, moving church service, the Whitmans returned to Washington almost immediately, leaving the lawyers to sell the house and settle the estate.

"Not that there's much to settle," Alan said. "I'm afraid Charles left you very little."

Elizabeth managed a half smile. "By your reckoning, perhaps," she said. "Not by mine."

The children were uncharacteristically excited to see her. Ann, the reserved and dignified Ann, covered her with kisses. And even Quigly clung to her with an unusual display of affection. It was Elizabeth's first moment of joy in weeks and it surprised her. She examined that fact curiously. "How odd that I should be surprised by joy," she thought. "Is it possible that I've come to expect so little?"

Despite her grief, she found a great sense of peace in being home again. Mary hovered over her solicitously, finally convincing the children to go outside and play. "We got to let your mama rest," she told them. "No need to worry. She's home now. Isn't that wonderful?"

"Wonderful, wonderful, wonderful," Elizabeth agreed.

"Yes, Mrs. Whitman. In many ways."

There was a peculiar nuance in Mary's reply. As though there was something on her mind that she would not, or could not, say. Why is it wonderful "in many ways" that I'm home? Elizabeth wondered. Something must have happened while I was gone. Her thoughts immediately flew to Alan. Did Mary know something that she could not report? There was no question that the housekeeper's emphasis on the last three words was deliberate. She was hinting at something that, Elizabeth reasoned, was not "her place" to say outright. It could only have to do with Alan. No small household problem or minor troubles with the children would be cause for that undeniably ominous inflection. She tried to think of a tactful way to draw out Mary, but her mind was blank. Maybe I'm just imagining the whole thing, she told herself. I'm so bone-weary that nothing makes sense. She put it out of her mind. Whatever it was, she would probably know soon enough.

In the two months that followed, things seemed so idyllic that Elizabeth gave only an occasional passing thought to the warning—if such it was—that Mary had tried to give her. She sometimes wept for her father. But they were healing tears and she felt better for them. Gradually, the comfortably undemanding day-by-day activities of the household absorbed her again. She rested and felt her strength returning. Washington was unbearably hot, but the Whitmans followed the "survival pattern" of those who had to spend the summer in the city. First thing in the morning, all the shades in the house were drawn down, keeping out the blistering sun and leaving the rooms dim and as cool as possible. Electric fans whirred in every room. From lunchtime until four o'clock the children, called in from their play, were placed, naked and rebellious, on their beds for an afternoon nap. Georgetown was quiet. Most families had already left for one of the nearby Eastern Shore resorts, Rehoboth Beach or Cape May. The more social had repaired to Newport or the South of France.

Elizabeth's condition kept them in town, but they didn't mind. It was wonderfully relaxing. The frenzied round of parties would not resume until after Labor Day. The summer hiatus reached even the government ("Hell," Alan said, "even FDR's in Hyde Park!"), but Alan's work load did not lessen. The departure of his superior for an extended vacation put more responsibility on his shoulders. Elizabeth was pleased to see that he was apparently handling it well, even thriving on his temporary added duties. He continued to behave as he had since their latest reconciliation, coming home early, drinking little, giving her no reason for worry. She was lulled into a sense of security, eagerly awaiting the arrival of the baby. They had agreed that the name would be either

Charles or Charlene, one life for another, the warmest tribute they could pay Charles Quigly.

Since her father's death, Elizabeth had changed her mind about wanting a girl. Now she hoped for another boy so that there would be, literally, another Charles Quigly. Her wishes were not granted. On the Fourth of July, 1935, Charlene Margaret Whitman announced her arrival with a healthy yell. One look at the impish little face and all Elizabeth's disappointment vanished. She somehow knew—and was secretly ashamed of the fact—that she had given birth to her favorite child.

"Let's give her your mother's name for her middle name," she said to Alan. "It suddenly occurs to me that I've been downright selfish. The other two have been dubbed for my side of the family. Since I wasn't lucky enough to ever meet my in-laws, I'd like to have at least one of our children partially named for them."

Alan shrugged. "It doesn't matter to me, really. I hardly remember my mother and father. They both died very young. We Whitmans are great exponents of 'a short life but a merry one.'"

"Try not to espouse that cause, will you?" Elizabeth was her old, gay self.

Alan reacted strangely, almost defensively, to her light-hearted banter. "I do espouse it," he snapped. "I want to have one helluva good time while I'm here. And I don't want to hang around long enough to get old and sick and ugly."

Elizabeth did not answer. She had learned to let such unexpected flare-ups go by unpursued. With someone else, she would have tried to discuss this overreaction. With Alan it might only lead to still another irrational argument.

She brought Charlene home from the hospital a week later, to Ann's reluctant, jealous acceptance and Quigly's typical lack of interest. She had anticipated both reactions and they did not mar her happiness. Charlene was an enchanting baby who did not look like her parents or her brother or sister. Elizabeth could almost swear that even when she was a month old Charlene fairly bubbled with lively curiosity.

This new child captured her as the others never had. She supposed it might have something to do with the period of turmoil that preceded her birth. The death of Charles. Even the unique moments of terrible-joyful lust on the night of her conception. Whatever the reasons, Charlene seemed more hers than the other two ever had. She spent hours simply sitting and admiring the baby, to the point where Alan commented on it.

"Don't ever accuse me of favoritism again," he said one evening when he came in to find her gazing lovingly into Charlene's crib. "If you think, to use your own words, that I'm 'fatuous' about Ann, you should see yourself when you're looking at this one."

Elizabeth flushed. "Don't be silly. I love them all."

"Don't *you* be silly. Poor old Quigly. He'll have to find his adoration somewhere else, won't he? You and I have made our choices."

The very idea shocked Elizabeth. "Alan! What a terrible thing to say! It's not true."

"Of course it's true. We won't turn him out in the snow to sell newspapers, but when it comes to parental affection, Quig gets the short end of the stick. Well, that's the breaks, right? Just proves again that nobody can order the world the way he wants it. Not Quigly. Not me. Not even you."

She had not heard that tone in his voice for a year, but she recognized it for what it was: the return of the defensive, hostile Alan. As she led the way out of the room they had improvised for Charlene, she felt her knees begin to shake. Alan went to the bar in the living room and made two drinks.

"Join me?" he asked.

"Yes. Thank you." She took a sip of the ice-cold martini. "Alan, what's wrong?"

"What makes you think something's wrong?"

She tried to keep control. "The tone of your voice. The strange things you said in the baby's room. I've lived with you for ten years, you know. I think I can sense when something is bothering you."

"Do you? Then you must sense how bloody bored I am."

Her voice was full of surprise. "Bored? No, I didn't realize that. I really thought you were enjoying this quiet summer as much as I. Well, the boredom will soon be over. Labor Day is just around the corner. All the fun and games will soon be starting."

"That isn't the main part of the problem," he said. "If you must know, I'm fed to the teeth with the job."

Her surprise turned to utter astonishment. "You're joking! How could you possibly be bored with your job? Why, every day you're becoming more important, more respected! I thought it was the most exciting thing in your life."

"It's a pile of garbage." He made himself another drink.

Elizabeth was alert now. There was much more to this than Alan was saying. It couldn't be true that he was fed up with his work. He was backing away from something, making excuses to himself for something he couldn't face. She tried to think what it could be. "Has something gone wrong at the office?" she asked. "Is there some kind of problem? Couldn't we talk about whatever it is that's really bothering you?"

"God damn it, I told you. I'm bored, bored, bored! For Christ's sake, Elizabeth, shut up and stop nagging me!"

She was more bewildered than hurt, more anxious than angry. Wisely, she kept silent. The stillness hung between them as Alan had five martinis in rapid succession, not even offering her another. It persisted through a tense dinner in which he barely touched his food. After the meal, he settled into a chair, turned the radio up to ear-splitting volume, and put a bottle of brandy and a glass beside him. By nine o'clock the raucous noise of the baseball game had given her a pounding headache.

"I'm going to bed," she said. "Good night."

Alan did not answer. She lay awake until one o'clock when he came unsteadily into the room and fell heavily into his bed. Tears ran slowly down Elizabeth's face. It was beginning again. And she knew, with dreadful certainty, that whatever had set him off this time was the worst of all. She knew, too, that they would not survive it.

In the weeks that followed, as though he was tired of playing the role of devoted husband, Alan's behavior became flagrantly impossible. His drinking was prodigious, his absences from home more frequent and more prolonged. One night when he did not come home at all, Elizabeth demanded angrily to know where he'd been. He told her to mind her own goddamned business. She wavered between trying to ride out this storm or finally admit defeat. There were the children to think of. Charlene was only three months old, for one thing. And there was the simple practicality of the situation. If she left Alan, how would she live and take care of all of them? She had never earned a living, wouldn't know how to begin. And as important as any of the materialistic problems was her terrible sense of failure. Why hadn't she been able to make this marriage succeed? Alan was treading a thin line of rationality, perhaps paranoia. This she knew—had known, really, since the first year. Still, there must have been something she could have done. She felt an unreasonable burden of guilt. I should insist that he get medical help, she told herself, knowing all the while that there was no way she could force him to do so. Her frustration and futility were obsessive. How could she abandon him, in spite of everything he'd done to her? But how could she continue to live with a man who was so consumed with self-hatred and fear?

In these days, Alan was totally unreachable. Their life together was a mockery. In public, they gave an impeccable performance. Privately they lived like sworn enemies. And still Elizabeth did not know what had triggered this most recent and most terrible change in her husband. She learned the reason for it at last, not from Alan but from an innocent and well-meaning friend, George Stanlowski, one of the men who worked with Alan. They were at a cocktail party hosted by the Secretary of Commerce when George cornered her.

"Terrific about Alan, isn't it?" he said. "Couldn't happen to a nicer guy."

She tried to look as though she knew what he was talking about. "Yes, indeed. Terrific." She waited for him to go on.

"We've all expected it, you know," George continued. "When the chief took three months off this summer we knew damned well that he was getting ready to bow out. And Alan's the logical choice for the top spot. Of course, it isn't official until they make the announcement, but I imagine that'll be any day now, don't you?"

She was dimly aware that he was going on about Alan's capabilities and that she was smiling and nodding and hopefully looking proud and excited. In fact, she was not hearing another word Stanlowski was saying. All she heard was her own voice inside her head. So this is what it's all about, the voice said. This is the ultimate threat, the one he's been fearing and courting at the same time. The big job that he's afraid he can't handle. The one that might finally show him up for what he actually believes he is—an incompetent impostor. Now she understood it. The anger, the alcoholism, the need for reassurance that somehow, no matter how hard she tried, she never could give.

"Excuse me," she said to George, "I have a fearful headache. I think I'd better find Alan and have him take me home." She laughed inanely. "Maybe it's all the excitement. You're kind to say such nice things about Alan. I know he appreciates your support."

She threaded her way through the crowd to where her husband stood talking to an attractive blonde. "May I see you a moment, dear?" She smiled brightly at the woman. "Please forgive us."

The blonde waved her glass good-naturedly and turned away.

"Take me home, will you, Alan? I'm not feeling well."

"What's the matter with you?"

"Nothing serious. Just an awful headache. Anyway, I'd like to leave now."

Alan took a sip of his drink. "Then leave," he said matter-of-factly.

She couldn't believe it. Was he going to abandon even the last pretense of harmony between them? "Alone?" Her tone was incredulous. "Isn't that going to look a little peculiar?"

He shrugged. "Maybe you can find somebody to escort you. Or you can take the car. Here are the keys. I'll get a cab."

"Alan, I told you I'm not feeling well. I can't stay here another minute, and I'm not going to be embarrassed in front of all these people by leaving this party without you."

"Your choice," he said. "I'm having a good time. No intention of leaving now. So you can hang around and try not to be such a wet blanket or go home by yourself."

She chose to leave, offering some lame excuse to the hostess about one of the children not being well. "I've insisted to Alan that he stay and enjoy himself," Elizabeth said. "It's such a beautiful party! No reason for us both to miss out on all the fun!"

She got her coat and tried to slip unobtrusively out of the front door. No one seemed to notice. Except George Stanlowski, who watched her departure with a thoughtful frown.

It was only eight o'clock when she let herself into the house, but it was middle-of-the-night quiet. The children had been put to bed and Mary had retired to her own room. Elizabeth made herself a cup of tea and sat down in the living room, still fully dressed, to await Alan's return. As though she were taking a last inventory, she looked carefully at each piece of furniture, each cherished object in the room. It was like looking at the sum total of her life. The pictures of her parents; the things that had belonged to her mother; the carefully chosen furniture she had sought out in antique shops; even the needlepoint rug and pillows she had slowly and painstakingly made since she was old enough to master the art. It was like a lovely stage setting in which the third and last act of a drama would begin.

While she waited for Alan, she thought again of the news that George had so innocently revealed. She hoped, for the sake of whatever dignity was left, that her expression had not given her away. It was unthinkable that Alan had given her no hint of what a hundred people probably already knew. Then she amended her own thought. It was not unthinkable at all. She would be the last person Alan would tell because she was the only one with whom he was vulnerable. She would immediately recognize his terror, his dreadful lack of confidence. Telling her would be admitting his weakness to himself. The longer she was left in the dark, the longer he could postpone putting his fears into words.

The ringing of the phone startled her. Eleven o'clock. The cocktail party must have been over for at least two hours, but there was no sign of Alan. Nervously, she picked up the receiver. It was George Stanlowski. His voice sounded embarrassed, nervous.

"Elizabeth? George. Hope I didn't awaken you."

"No, I wasn't asleep. What's the matter? Is something wrong?"

He gave a sheepish laugh. "I know this is going to sound kind of silly, but I just wondered if Alan got home all right. He was pretty high when he left the party and since I, uh, saw you go on ahead of him, I just wanted to make sure he was okay."

She tried to sound unconcerned. "That's dear of you, George, but you know Alan. He's perfectly fine."

"Well, good." He laughed again. "I feel like a damned fool calling at this hour, but he was awfully loaded and he kept saying something about going to one of those crummy bars down on Fourteenth Street. Glad he didn't. He might have gotten beaten up and rolled for his dough. Some guys have the damnedest ways of celebrating. I feel like an idiot," he said again, "but I just couldn't get him off my mind. He's a helluva fella, Elizabeth. But I don't have to tell you that, do I?"

"No," she said softly, "you don't. Thanks for your concern, George. Alan's lucky to have such a good friend."

When she replaced the receiver, her palms were wet. She tried not to panic. It was certainly not the first time that Alan had been missing without explanation. She did not really fear for his safety. She simply waited, with dread, for his appearance. He must have been terribly drunk when he left the party if George was concerned enough to call. By now he would be irrational, abusive. She would not be able to talk with him about what she'd learned from George. It would be wiser for her to go to bed now before he came in. But something held her in her chair. An instinct stronger than logic told her to stay where she was, that this would be, at long last, the final confrontation. She almost welcomed the idea.

At two o'clock in the morning she heard his key in the door. Drunker than she'd ever seen him, he staggered into

the living room. He was not alone. With him was a cheaply
dressed, blowsy woman who clung to his arm. A flicker of
surprise crossed his face at the sight of Elizabeth. Then he
gave a coarse laugh.

"Hey, look who stayed up to join the celebration! It's my
devoted, long-suffering little wife! Little wife, like you to
meet little Kitty. Fine girl, Kitty. 'Lizbeth's fine, too, but
she's never been a girl, have you, 'Lizbeth? 'Lizbeth's a lady,
right? No fun celebratin' with a lady. Everybody knows
that. Why don't you go to bed, lady? Kitty and I want to
celebrate!"

Kitty giggled. "Alan, you're a scream! You didn't tell me
you were bringing me to your own house. Jesus, you sure
got nerve!"

"Get out of my house," Elizabeth said quietly. "Whoever
you are, get out of my house."

Alan's voice became rougher. "Hold on. Don't you move,
Kitty. It's my house and you're my guest. You're staying
right here."

Elizabeth ignored him. She got to her feet and took the
woman by the arm. The smell of cheap perfume disgusted
her. "I told you to go. Now go." She gave her a shove. Kitty
looked questioningly at Alan, who was pouring a drink.

"Oh, the hell with it," he said. "You might as well go,
kid. Party's screwed up now anyhow."

"What about my money?"

He reached in his pocket. "Here's twenty. You owe me
one, okay?"

"Sure. Any time."

When the door closed, Elizabeth swallowed hard. For a
moment she was sure she was going to be violently ill. Then
the surge of nausea passed. She was past outrage and disbelief. All she felt was a terrible emptiness. When she could
speak, all she said was, "Why?"

Like an actor slipping into another role, Alan had suddenly changed from a vulgar, raucous drunk into a sullen,
defiant stranger. He seemed to have sobered up in a moment.

"Which 'why' would you like me to answer first? Why did
I bring that whore home? Well, I'll grant you that was ill
advised. I thought you'd be asleep. Stupid of me. Her room
isn't very pretty but it is much more private." He looked at
Elizabeth carefully, measuring the impact of his words. Aside
from her slight trembling, she betrayed nothing. Obviously
she was waiting for him to continue.

"But, shocked as you are, you're even more interested in
why I've suddenly reverted to my old wicked ways, aren't

you? I must be like a bug under a microscope to you,
Elizabeth. It must be fascinating and repulsive to watch me
crawl around, skittering off in all directions at once. Alan
the bewildered beetle. Alan the amorous insect. That's what
I'm like, isn't it?"

She continued to stare at him, saying nothing. Her silence
finally inflamed him.

"For Christ's sake, what are you made of—ice? I've ignored you, ridiculed you, insulted you by bringing a tart
right into your house and you just stand there like some
goddamn marble statue! All you can say is 'Why?' Why
what, Elizabeth? Why was I born? Why did I marry you?
Why am I a lost cause? We've been all over that before.
I'm through with the second-rate confessions and the phony
promises to mend my ways. I'm sick to death of your endless
saintly patience with me. I know what I am and you know
what I am—an unreliable, second-rate dud. I believe it and
you might as well believe it, too. Every time I feel threatened
I go off the deep end. Period. Paragraph. Full stop."

She felt as though she'd been physically whipped. She was
too tired for anger, too weary to do anything but say quietly,
"This is all because of the new job, isn't it?"

Satirically, he applauded, clapping his hands slowly and
loudly. "Bravo! You finally heard about it. That's it. I've got
the big promotion. Fooled 'em again, by God! Mr. Big,
that's me. Lord of all the skies I survey."

"How long have you known?"

"Unofficially? For months. Since before you went to Boston. Of course, I couldn't start officially celebrating until
tonight."

"But it was certain enough to let you start celebrating
while I was away, wasn't it?" Her voice was bitter. "How
clever you were. I didn't suspect. I was so pleased that you
were here every night when I called. How did you manage—
Oh, my God, Alan, you weren't bringing women home while
I was away!"

He seemed unmoved. "I'm amazed that the faithful Mary
didn't report."

An actual physical pain shot through Elizabeth. So that's
what Mary had meant when she'd said the return was wonderful "in many ways." A sudden terrifying thought struck.
The words came slowly.

"The children. *They* didn't see anything, did they?"

Alan looked indignant. "What kind of a monster do you
think I am?"

The absurdity of his question reached Elizabeth. Already

on the brink of hysteria, she began to laugh wildly. "What is there that you could *not* be suspected of? If you're such an insensitive animal that you can bring your women into my bed, why should I doubt that you'd keep the fact from my children? Why should I think you're anything but insane? God knows you must be capable of any kind of sick, degenerate act!" She was weeping and laughing now, half out of her mind. Without warning, she picked up a crystal paperweight and threw it wildly in his direction. It hit him squarely in the center of the forehead. A tiny river of blood began to trickle down his nose. He paid no attention to it. Instead, he walked over to Elizabeth and slapped her hard across the face. "Goddamn you," he said, "why didn't you leave me when I begged you to? Before it was too late."

"You know why," she said between her sobs. "Because I loved you. I thought I could help you. I thought you needed me."

"And now you believe that none of those things is true, don't you?"

"Yes. And now I will leave you, Alan. Just as quickly as I can make arrangements for the children and myself, I'll leave this house."

"I'm sorry, Elizabeth, it's too late." His voice was almost tender. "I've come too far. *We've* come too far. I know you no longer love me. That part is true. But now you *can* help me. Now I *do* need you."

She turned her back on him. "Don't be ridiculous."

"On the contrary, I am being cold-bloodedly practical. This new job makes me a very important man in Washington. There will be a great deal of publicity now, a great deal of high-level entertaining. I need a wife who can handle these things. More importantly, I don't need to look like a fool whose wife has walked out on him. I'm sorry. You had your chance. It may not be pleasant for either of us, but here you are and here you stay."

Elizabeth was aghast. "You really are insane! You can't believe I'm going to stay after this! Even if I could bear the sight of you, I'd die before I'd let my children live in the same house with a madman!"

"Don't worry. There'll be no repetition of tonight. Or of the times when you were in Boston. I promise you that."

"The way you've promised me so many other things," Elizabeth said. "No, Alan, there'll be no more promises, no more chances. If my leaving you now is inconvenient, if it causes you public embarrassment, it's a little late to think of that, isn't it? You've not only disgraced yourself, you've dirtied me. And I'll never let you do that to me again. God knows I won't let you do it to your children!"

"I won't let you go," he said.

"You can't stop me. You don't own me."

He was almost desperate. "Don't you understand? I can't survive without you. Isn't that enough of a victory for you?"

"I don't want a victory," Elizabeth said. "This is not a war. I don't know whether or not you can survive without me. I'm not sure any longer that I even care. But I do know that I cannot survive with you. I've tried. I've put ten years of my life into this hell. I'm still only thirty years old. There must be a chance for me without you. Because there is no chance for you, Alan. Not ever. You'll die of your own diseased mind. I only pray that there's very little of you in your children."

He was blindly angry now. "Who appointed you God? What makes you think you understand me or my mind? Do you know what it's like to live with somebody who's so almighty superior? Maybe I hope that my children don't inherit *your* special brand of Puritan virtue. Maybe I hope they'll grow up not trying to be so stinking perfect, the way their mother tries to be! If you take yourself and those kids out of here, Elizabeth, you'll leave without a penny. I won't give you a dime. Then we'll see how far your stiff-necked New England pride takes you. In the eyes of the law, you're deserting me. Let's find out how *that* sits in court. Or perhaps you'd like to tell the world the details of your happy marriage . . . how your husband drinks and lies and screws everything in sight? I'm sure the judge would be very sympathetic."

He was nearly incoherent now, but Elizabeth felt no pity. She looked at him coldly. "You *are* crazy," she repeated. "I don't want anything from you, Alan. I don't want to know you're alive. I wish I could feel sorry for you, but I can't even manage that. I can't feel anything except the overwhelming urge to get as far away from you as I can. All I want now is to escape."

"Then go ahead and escape," he shouted. "To hell with you. And to hell with all this Washington crap! They can take their job and shove it up their bureaucratic asses! Go on. Get out. And see how well you can manage without me!"

She ran up the stairs and into their room, locking the door behind her. For the rest of the night she heard him stumbling around, crashing into things. Thank God that Mary and the children slept on the third floor, where they could hear nothing.

She could no longer think clearly. Alan, who had tried in every way he could to drive her away; Alan, who had suggested divorce and abortion in the past, now admitted his need of her, selfish though it might be. Or was the excuse of needing her presence at his side in this new period of official prominence just a feeble face-saving device? Perhaps, in spite of everything, he did need her as a wife, as a woman. Perhaps he even loved her in his own confused, psychotic way. He had tried from time to time over the years to be what she wanted, but the efforts were futile and short-lived. So much, she knew, was her fault. There were things she should have done differently, weaknesses in them both that she might have understood and accepted. Alan had been cruel, faithless, and hateful. But there were moments she could remember when he'd been tender and defenseless. Could she try once more? Was there any point in going on with this marriage of two people so ill suited to one another?

In the end, she knew that she could not go on with it. She felt pity for him, but she had no more strength. Whatever was left would have to go into providing for her children and herself. She wanted nothing from Alan. God help us both, she thought. We're so wretchedly imperfect.

At dawn she went downstairs to straighten up the cyclone-struck drawing room before Mary saw it. At some point during the night, Alan had left. She'd heard the front door slam and his car start. By the time the others appeared, she had the room in reasonable order.

"Mr. Whitman went to the office early," she lied to Mary.

The housekeeper nodded. She'd heard it all when she'd gotten up to give Charlene her two-o'clock bottle. It did not surprise Mary that the end had come. Only that it had not come long before.

part III

BETHESDA, MARYLAND 1935-1937

Chapter 5

It was such a funny little house. Not a house, really. Just a rather tumbledown guest cottage on the Parrish-Parker estate in Bethesda, Maryland, just over the district line on the outskirts of Washington. The inspiration to ask for it had come to Elizabeth on that first morning after the final scene with Alan. She had told him she wanted nothing from him, and she meant it. But underneath that proud declaration of independence was near-panic. All she had in the world was eight thousand dollars, the pitifully small sum received from the sale of her father's house. It would not last long when she had to feed, clothe, and house herself and three children. In spite of that, she was determined to get out of Georgetown that very day. It was then that she thought of Marion Parrish-Parker.

Elizabeth had come to know the very social, very rich widow quite well. Marion's huge property was a local showplace. Except for a staff of servants, she lived alone in the main house with its fourteen bedrooms, its much-photographed conservatory, and its fully occupied five-car garage. Dotted around the surrounding forty acres of valuable real estate were five or six guesthouses, all of them in practically abandoned condition. Marion had no use for them. When she had weekend guests there was plenty of room in the big house.

It was contrary to Elizabeth's nature to ask for favors, but on that morning, in her eagerness to escape, she would have done anything. As soon as the hour was decent, she called Marion, explained briefly that she was leaving Alan and asked if she might possibly have the use of one of the cottages.

"I don't know how much rent I can pay," she confessed. "Practically none at the moment. But I'll get a job and make it up to you as quickly as I can."

Like many wealthy women, Marion Parrish-Parker was as kind as she was secure. People who didn't know her were in awe of her impeccable social position, her lavish way of life, her much-publicized Medici Emerald, forty-carat stone which she wore, almost carelessly, on a chain of diamonds. It was said that there was a curse on the glittering green jewel, which had belonged to various ill-fated members of Italian aristocracy. Marion found the superstition amusing. "The only curse is the high insurance rate," she was fond of saying. "Sometimes I think I'd be better off if somebody stole it." Those who knew her found her anything but intimidating. She was amusing, warmhearted and, as now, a totally direct, no-nonsense kind of woman.

"Don't be absurd," she said to Elizabeth. "Of course you may have a cottage. Rent-free, for God's sake. What are you trying to do, sully my reputation by turning me into a slum landlord? I wouldn't dream of charging you, you idiot. Wouldn't know what to ask if I did! You do realize, Elizabeth, that those cottages would never make the pages of *House Beautiful*. The biggest one—which of course you'll need—does have two bedrooms. But the furniture! Well, my dear, it's just a notch above orange crates. Practically Salvation Army rejects. I hope you're planning to bring your own things. Otherwise, my love, you'll be living in absolute squalor."

For the first time, Elizabeth was able to laugh. "I promise you, it will look like Buckingham Palace to me. No, I'm not bringing much furniture. Just a few things that were mine before I was married. And the odds and ends my father left me. It's not important. I'm so grateful that we'll have a place to go. Really, I don't know how to begin to thank you. I'll never be able to tell you what this means to—"

Marion interrupted briskly. "Rubbish. Delighted to have someone making use of one of those dreary little hovels. Just hope it's not too absolutely sordid. My dear, I *am* sorry about you and Alan, but please don't tell me any details. I don't even want to struggle with the temptation to gossip. Seriously, I know you. It must be pretty bad to make you throw in the sponge. So. Come right along. I'll at least have the place cleaned up by the time you get here."

When she hung up, Elizabeth called in Mary and told her that she was leaving Mr. Whitman and taking the children with her.

"I must move today, before he returns," she said. "Will you help me pack our clothes so we can be ready to go when Ann and Quigly get home from school? And Mary, do you by any chance know an inexpensive trucker who can move a few pieces of furniture and small things like china and glass? Mrs. Parrish-Parker is lending me a cottage in Bethesda. That's where we'll be going."

Mary nodded calmly. "I know a private trucker downtown who will probably come this afternoon if I ask him special. He's a friend. Won't charge much. Shall I call him?"

"Yes, please. I'd appreciate it." Elizabeth hesitated. "Whatever will I do without you, Mary? I can't afford to pay you, and there's no room for you to live in. Maybe after I find a job and a better place I could ask you to come back to us. Would you consider it?"

"If it's all right with you, Mrs. Whitman, I'd rather not leave at all. You're going to need help. Somebody has to see to the children while you go out to look for that job. Maybe I could just come in days. Like from eight to seven. Don't worry about the salary. I've got enough put away to see me through for a while, and I can live with my sister for nothin'."

Elizabeth was touched. "It would be a godsend, but it's asking too much."

"I'd like to do it."

"Don't feel you have to," Elizabeth persisted half-heartedly. "You could get a good position anywhere. Half my friends would love to have you. Or you could stay here, I'm sure, and keep house for Mr. Whitman."

The black woman just looked at her expressionlessly. She knows everything, Elizabeth realized. And she blushed.

By the time Alan got home, his family had gone. It didn't really surprise him to walk into the hushed, impersonal house. Maybe it's all to the good, he thought. Eventually he'd get around to finding them. He might even get Ann back. He'd think about it later when he hadn't had so much booze.

Meanwhile, he made another stiff drink and called Kitty. What the hell. She owed him one.

When Ann and Quigly came home from school, their clothes and toys were packed, and Elizabeth, Mary, and the trucker were stowing the last pieces of furniture into a rickety moving van. Ann was the only one of the children old enough to be aware that something was wrong.

"Where are we going, Mama? Why have you put all my things in boxes? Where's Daddy?"

Elizabeth put her arms around her daughter. "We're going to a new house, darling," she said. "You and Quigly and Charlene and Mary and I. Your Daddy can't come with us, but he knows all about it."

Ann looked disbelieving. "Why isn't he here to say goodbye? He wouldn't let us go away without kissing me." She began to cry. "I don't want to go to a new house," she sobbed. "I'm going to stay here and wait for Daddy to come home! You can't make me go!"

Elizabeth was frantic, but she tried to stay outwardly calm. "I'm sorry if you're upset, Ann, but you must do as I say. I'm your mother."

"I don't want you to be my mother!" Ann screamed. "You're a mean, awful old woman!"

Elizabeth had a terrible impulse to slap her. Instead she said coldly, "It's not up to you to want me for a mother, Ann. It's up to you to make me want you for a daughter. And right now, I don't very much want a little girl who's willful and selfish and disobedient. You'll find that you have to earn all the love you get. I don't imagine you can understand that now, but I hope you'll think about it. Whether you love me or hate me is not my primary concern at this moment. Your well-being is. If that makes me a mean, awful old woman in your eyes, I can't really help it. And I really don't have time to worry about it."

This steady stream of adult talk stopped Ann cold. She did not understand much of what her mother was saying, but the tone was as unyielding and authoritative as it was dispassionate. Wide-eyed and subdued, the child fell silent. Within minutes, she found herself wedged into a taxi between her mother and Mary. Charlene was in Mary's arms. Quigly was put in front beside the driver. As they drove away, Ann was the only one who looked back.

Marion Parrish-Parker had not greatly exaggerated in describing the cottage's lack of charm. About the best that could be said of it was that it was solidly built and that it reposed in one of the most beautiful settings in the area. Autumn gold lay richly everywhere—on the huge old elm and maple trees that almost hid the little house, and on the great bursting clumps of yellow chrysanthemums. There was an air of privacy and serenity about it to which Elizabeth's anguished soul responded gratefully. She was not even dismayed by the tiny rooms, the sparse, shabby furniture. In her mind's eye she could see the house as it would be when she carefully arranged her own precious possessions. It would be far from sumptuous, but it would have warmth and a kind of natural beauty. Suddenly she was filled with optimism. She regretted her harshness to Ann and tried immediately to make amends.

"Isn't it nice, darling?" she asked the little girl. "Like a doll's house, don't you think? Wait till we get it all fixed up. We'll have Grandmama's pretty things all around, and lots of candles and flowers. And look at that wonderful fireplace, Ann! We'll be able to make popcorn and toast marshmallows if you want to."

Ann would not be won over. "I hate it," she said stubbornly. "It's ugly here. I want to go back to my own house."

Elizabeth was determined to keep her temper. She realized it must be hard for the child, to be suddenly swept up and transported to this strange new world. And there would be the problem of no Alan. Of them all, Ann was the only one who would miss him.

"What if you make a little playhouse of your own?" Elizabeth coaxed. "You and Quigly could build a secret one right over there under that beautiful fir tree. I'm sure Mary will help you if you ask her nicely."

"Will Mary stay with us?"

"Of course, dear. She won't sleep here because there are only two bedrooms. You and Quigly will share one and I'll take Charlene in with me. But Mary will be here every day, just as she always has been. Of course, you and I will have to help keep house. I'll teach you how to cook. Would you like that?"

"I don't want to cook. When we lived with Daddy you never had to cook."

Elizabeth sighed. "Ann, dear, you must realize that Daddy is staying in Georgetown. He's very, very busy with his important new job."

"Then I'll go and live with him. Who's going to take care of him if we're not there?"

"He'll be just fine," Elizabeth reassured her. "He understands why we're here and he's depending on you to be a big girl. My goodness, you're practically grown up! I'll be depending on you, too. Particularly in helping to take care of Quigly. There's a nice school that both of you can go to. Just two blocks away. You'll take him there and bring him home, won't you? That will be an enormous responsibility. I wouldn't trust it to anyone but a big girl like you."

Ann pouted. "Why can't Mary take him?"

"Because Mary will have to stay here to look after Charlene. You see, Ann, I plan to go out and get a job. That's why you'll have to watch out for Quigly."

The child's face turned scarlet. "I don't want to go to a new school. And I won't take care of Quigly. He's horrible. I hate Quigly!"

"Of course you don't hate your brother, Ann! What a naughty thing to say!"

"I do. I do hate him and I hate this house and I hate you for making us come here! My father wouldn't let us live in a place like this. It smells bad, like old dead animals!" She began to cry. "Why can't I go home, Mama? Please let me go home!"

Elizabeth sighed. Because of Alan, Ann was going to be a problem. She felt sorry for the child. But she was young enough to forget much about her father. In time he would recede further and further from her elder daughter's mind. Meanwhile, Elizabeth would have to be strong and patient. Hopefully she could overcome the sense of displacement that Ann felt. She'd often heard divorced or widowed women worry aloud about the responsibility of being both mother and father to their children. Now she understood what a traumatic thing this could be for both parent and child. She was very gentle with Ann.

"Darling, this is our home now," she said. "I know it's not as pretty as Georgetown was, but just wait and see what a lovely place we'll make it! Come on," she said, putting her arm around Ann, "let's start by unpacking Grandmama Quigly's china. It's always been your favorite. Then you could pick some of those lovely chrysanthemums for the blue and white tureen. We'll make a very special centerpiece for our first dinner in our new house."

Her pretense of lightheartedness did not ring true even to her own ears. Ann was inconsolable. Wordlessly, she wandered off, kicking listlessly at the few tufts of grass that remained on the path in front of the cottage. Worriedly, Elizabeth watched her go. She'd have to keep a close eye on

Ann. She might even try to run away, to get back to the father who had given her such a false sense of security.

Elizabeth went back into the house. Charlene was cooing contentedly in her crib and Mary was making up the three beds with the plain-white, serviceable sheets Marion Parrish-Parker had thoughtfully provided. Quigly was nowhere to be seen. Elizabeth realized suddenly that he had disappeared soon after they arrived. Uneasiness gripped her. He might have wandered off and gotten lost on these enormous grounds. It was beginning to get dark. Anything could happen to a little boy in these dense woods.

"Mary, have you seen Quigly?"

"No, Mrs. Whitman, I thought he was with you."

Elizabeth's heart began to pound. But almost at that moment, Quigly appeared at the door. There was a deep scratch on his cheek, but he was smiling. In his arms he carried one of Marion's prized Siamese cats. The animal was limp, lifeless.

"Quigly! Where have you been? And what are you doing with that cat?"

"It's dead, Mama. Can we give it a funeral?"

"Dead? Where did you find it? And where did you get that scratch on your face?"

"Mean old cat scratched me."

"But when did it—I mean, how did it die?"

"It got drowned. In the fish pool. I had to punish him."

Elizabeth felt ill. "Quigly, what a wicked thing to do! Why did you drown Mrs. Parrish-Parker's cat? What on earth made you do such a terrible thing?"

He looked at her in surprise. "I had to, Mama," he repeated. "He hurt me. See?" He pointed to the claw marks on his face.

She took the wet little body from her child's arms. Horrified, she stood silently in the middle of the living room, holding the animal like a fearful trophy. My God, she thought bleakly, is this the way his mind works? Will he destroy everything and anybody who threatens him? Mary came quickly and took the cat from her, carrying it outside. Elizabeth drew Quigly to her.

"Son," she said, trying to keep her voice calm, "you must never, never kill anything again. We don't harm things or people who hurt us. Not even when we think they should be punished. The Bible teaches us to forgive our enemies, Quigly. That's the way good, Christian people behave. Only uncivilized people do cruel, horrid things to others."

"What's unciverlized mean?"

"It means people who don't live by the rules of the world. Uncivilized people make up their own rules because they don't understand anything of consideration and gentleness. They think only of themselves, of their own protection."

The handsome little face lit up with understanding. "But that's why I did it, Mama. To protect myself. Papa told me to."

She started. "What do you mean? Is Papa here? Did he tell you to drown the cat?"

Quigly shook his head. "No. It was a long time ago. Papa told me to always fight back. He said I'd be a sissy if I ran away. Like a dumb old girl. When the nasty cat scratched me, I only remembered what Papa said." The child was very serious, almost defensive. It was almost as though he was defying her to refute what his father had taught him.

Elizabeth chose her words carefully. The one thing she was determined not to do was to turn her children against Alan. They must never know what kind of man he really was. Yet there was just this kind of misinterpreted advice to be overcome. "Quigly, dear," she said, "you didn't understand what your papa was trying to tell you. He wants you to be a brave man, to stand up for your rights and never to be afraid. But he didn't mean that you should harm people or animals. It is not your right to physically punish others. That's a sin. That's not what Papa meant when he told you not to run away." Her voice trailed off. He was too young to understand. His mind could not yet differentiate between senseless brutality and honorable defense. She tried once more. "Look, dear. Papa meant that if some big bully picked on you, you should stand up to him. Like in the playground. Even if it meant that you came home with a black eye. Papa did *not* mean that you should kill a poor little kitten who scratched you because it didn't know any better. Or maybe because you were teasing it. Do you see the difference?"

He did not answer, but it was obvious that her reasoning was not getting through. Elizabeth tried to console herself that what Quigly had done was just a childish act of cruelty without significance. She would not allow herself to think that her little boy had inherited his father's sadistic streak.

"I hope you do understand," she said finally. "Anyway, tomorrow you and I will go to see Mrs. Parrish-Parker and tell her what you've done. And you will apologize. We will also promise to replace her cat. You see, I'm sure she loved it very much and she'll be sad that you've taken away something she loved. Just as you'd be sad if someone took something precious from you. And one more thing. I want your promise never to hurt another living thing."

There was no response.

"Quigly?"

"It was a bad cat," he said, "and I'm glad I killed it."

In two weeks, the guest cottage underwent an almost miraculous transformation. Not that it approached anything grand or elegant. The tired old living-room furniture refused to be totally disguised, but it took on a more attractive air when Elizabeth arranged it in inviting groups around the fireplace and placed her own few pieces of good furniture in conspicuous spots throughout the house. She hid the worst tears in the sofa with needlepoint pillows, added as many books and pictures as she had managed to bring, and even draped an unsightly table with the embroidered Spanish shawl which had served as her wrap at many a gala evening party. Her one gesture of extravagance was to light the house almost entirely with candles. There were lamps, for safety, in the children's room. Otherwise, except for a reading lamp by her chair, the house glowed softly in warm candlelight. She availed herself of the fall flowers that grew profusely nearby, heaping asters and mums in lavish bouquets in every room. The house was gracious and welcoming, as though it responded to the first gesture of affection anyone had ever given it.

"It's nicer than I dared hope," Elizabeth confessed.

Mary agreed. "That's because there's hope here, Mrs. Whitman. You feel it?"

Elizabeth nodded. She could indeed feel the resurgence of hope, just as she could feel the peaceful process of healing beginning within her. There was, at last, a respite from unhappiness and fear, and she rejoiced in it. She had a wonderful sensation of freedom. She did feel a sense of failure, a self-accusatory regret that she had not been able to make her marriage work. Perhaps, she thought, my standards are unrealistic, my emotional demands too high for any man to meet. If this was so, this was the way she was. She was not foolish enough to think she would change.

Meanwhile, there was this heavenly release from tension. The children seemed to be adjusting to their new life. By no stretch of the imagination could they be said to be bubbling over with happiness, but Ann docilely took her brother to and from school and made no further reference to her father. When she was home, she was withdrawn and uncommunicative, spending her time alone with her books and her drawing pad. She made Annlike pictures. Very stiff and meticulous. Most of them, Elizabeth decided, looked like Ann herself: pages filled with golden-haired girls who appeared to be princesses in heavily guarded castles. Undoubtedly the way Ann thought of her own cloistered life.

Quigly, after making a mumbled apology to Marion Parrish-Parker, seemed to forget all about the incident of the cat. He went about his little-boy business of climbing trees and scaring Elizabeth half to death with his dangerous feats. She supposed he was still proving to an absent father that he was not afraid of anything.

Elizabeth's greatest relief was that there had been no sign of Alan. She had been almost sure that he would find them somehow, although she had told none of their old friends where she and the children were living. It would not have been difficult to track them down if he'd tried, she supposed, but seemingly he had no interest in discovering the whereabouts of his family. Her fears that he would appear raging drunk to create some terrible scene grew less with each passing day. She saw his name in the paper now and then. The official announcement of his promotion had been made and there had been a photograph of him being congratulated by the president. She examined the picture curiously. There was, as far as she could tell, no visible change in him, though she didn't know quite what she expected. He had always been, in public, what he still seemed to be: well groomed, suave, assured, and smiling.

She thought only fleetingly about divorcing Alan. Perhaps she was not yet emotionally ready for this step. Even more concretely, she couldn't afford it. Until she got a job, the few thousand dollars in her bank account were all that stood between her and disaster. She had no reason to want legal freedom. The money could be better spent on other things. She had ruefully parted with seventy-five dollars to buy Marion a new Siamese cat almost as good as the one Quigly had destroyed. Even though that kindhearted lady had protested that there was no need for her to replace it, Elizabeth had been insistent. It was not only a matter of principle, it had become almost a superstition with her, as though the reparation would erase the memory of that awful first day and of Quigly's distorted rationale for his deed.

The first order of business had been to provide some kind of solid surroundings for her children. She had managed a warm, attractive house for them and some sense of continuity through the generous continued presence of Mary. Now she had to quickly set about finding a way to support them all. That would be more difficult. She had no business skills, no training or experience other than volunteer charity work. And it was unlikely that another miracle like Marion Parrish-Parker or Mary Jackson was going to come to her rescue. Fate was not likely to hand her a decent job as it had handed her a house and a housekeeper.

She mentally reviewed her skills: cooking, sewing, needle-point, decorating. She could not visualize herself as a cook or seamstress and she certainly could not earn enough money turning out needlepoint pillows for sale. That left only dec-orating, and even there she was not a professional. Perhaps, she thought, she could get a job selling in some antique shop or furniture store. Yes, that was probably best. The hours would be long, the work tiring, and the salary, she surmised, minimal. But it should bring in enough to keep them alive. Hopefully enough to start paying Mary a little something. She might even be able to take Ann and Quigly to an occasional concert or ballet. In her mind, these things were as important to their mental health as milk and cereal were to their physical well-being. It was an attitude that was to stay with her all her life. The butcher and the grocer might go unpaid for months while she handed over precious dollars for the children to see *Swan Lake* or to hear Grieg's Concerto in A Minor performed by the National Symphony Orchestra. To most of her friends it would seem like an ir-responsible, almost immoral way of looking at things. To Elizabeth, it was as much her duty to feed their minds as it was to fill their stomachs. "What good are their bodies," she said, "if I let their souls die?"

But that was later. Right now she had to find money for both body and soul. Hers as well as theirs.

In 1935, jobs were still hard to come by and men were given preference whenever possible, not because of sex dis-crimination but, quite sensibly, because it was assumed that men usually were the family breadwinners. It was considered almost unpatriotic for a woman to apply for a job that could be done by a man. There were, in fact, very few ads for "saleswomen" in the Washington papers. In all the help-wanted columns of the *Sunday Star, Post,* and *Times-Herald,* there were only three selling positions that Elizabeth thought she might be able to fill. Two were in cheap department stores downtown; the other was in a small fine-furniture shop on Connecticut Avenue where she occasionally had been a customer. She decided to try that one first. It seemed more her kind of thing, and it had the added advantage of being nearer home, though it still required taking two buses each way.

An hour before the shop opened on Monday morning she stationed herself on the sidewalk in front of the door. To her surprise, she was the third applicant to arrive, and within minutes eight other women had silently joined the group. She eyed her competition apprehensively. They seemed remarkably composed, almost stoic, as though they were dutifully pursuing a necessary but futile course. Elizabeth's confidence wavered. Timidly, she spoke to the woman standing next to her.

"I beg your pardon. I suppose you're here about the job?"

The shabbily dressed woman looked at her with bitter amusement. "Oh, no, not me, honey. I'm out here freezing my ass off because I can't wait to buy that French chamberpot in the window."

Elizabeth flushed angrily. "Sorry," she said.

Her companion relented a little. "Sure I'm here for the job. You too? You don't look like you're on your uppers. Where did you work before?"

Elizabeth was embarrassed. She needed this job just as much as the others did. With one probable exception. She had a choice. She could be taken care of if she swallowed her pride and returned to Alan. She doubted that any of the others had even this dubious security to fall back on, and the knowledge made her feel ridiculously guilty. The woman beside her was watching her curiously, waiting for her answer.

"I've never worked," Elizabeth said almost inaudibly. "That is, I've done a lot of volunteer work, but I haven't really held a full-time job." She wondered why she felt so apologetic. Annoyance at herself strengthened her voice. "But I think I'd be very good at selling antiques. I've bought a lot of things here. It's a lovely shop. The clientele is the best in town."

Her companion raised her eyebrows. "Now isn't that wonderful," she said sarcastically. "I do hope you get the job, Countess. It'll be such an amusing experience, slumming on the other side of the counter."

Before Elizabeth could answer, the shop door was opened by a blue-haired, well-coiffed woman whom Elizabeth remembered as the owner.

"Come in please," she said. "I assume you've all come about the position?"

Twelve heads nodded as one.

"All right. I'll interview each of you, so don't trouble about who was first to arrive."

"Swell," the woman beside Elizabeth muttered. "What the hell good does it do anybody to get here early?"

"At least we know we'll all have a chance at it," Elizabeth said. Her naïve comment caused other heads to turn.

"We have a newcomer among us," somebody said.

"You haven't been at this long, have you, dearie?" another voice inquired. "You'll find out. By the time that old bag gets to number six she'll be so fed up that she'll hire one of the first five."

It was all very strange and confusing. They filed in and posted themselves silently around the shop while Mrs. Markham, the proprietor, went to her desk in the rear. From there, she motioned to each in turn to come and sit beside her. Elizabeth was the fourth to be summoned.

"You there," Mrs. Markham called. "You in the black coat. I'll see you now."

Elizabeth went forward, smiling, she hoped, with confidence. Her interview was even shorter than the others. As soon as she disclosed her lack of experience it was all over.

"I'm sorry, Mrs. Whitman. You're the kind of woman I'd enjoy having here. In fact, I remember you, don't I? Haven't you bought from me in the last year or so?"

Elizabeth acknowledged this. "But now I need to work," she said.

Mrs. Markham looked troubled. "I'm sure, my dear. But so do these others. And unfortunately, the three I've already spoken with have done a great deal of selling. I really haven't the time to train you in a thousand and one details. Even then, who knows whether you have an aptitude for this kind of work?"

"I'm sure I have," Elizabeth said eagerly. "And I know I could pick it up quickly."

The shop owner shook her head. Desperately, Elizabeth tried her trump card.

"Also, many of my friends would come in if they knew I was working here."

For a moment, Mrs. Markham wavered. The prospect of a "following" was always tempting, but Elizabeth's was much too tenuous. Again she gave a negative sign. "I'm sorry. That is a point in your favor—knowing so many important women in Washington. But the shop is well established. Your friends already know it. If you had selling experience, I might be inclined to take a chance, but without it, the idea simply isn't practical."

Elizabeth got to her feet. "I understand. Thank you for your time."

"You're very welcome." As she started for the door, Mrs. Markham called after her. "Oh, Mrs. Whitman."

Elizabeth turned back hopefully. "Yes?"

"I do hope you'll remind your friends to come in anyway."

Elizabeth stared at her incredulously. Then she laughed.

The other two leads she followed up were even worse. In the downtown department stores she waited in prisonlike, not very clean personnel offices, filled out elaborate application forms and then waited again in line to be interviewed. The reactions of the bored interviewers were even less considerate than Mrs. Markham's.

"Never worked before? Come back when you have experience."

They did not say how she was to get this precious asset called experience. It was the old, old story. One needs experience to get a job and one can't get a job without experience. Elizabeth felt like Alice in confrontation with the Red Queen. And as the days and weeks passed, the pattern repeated itself over and over again. There were a hundred better-equipped people for each job she went after. Bewilderment gave way to discouragement and discouragement to outright fear. On Thanksgiving evening, when she had fed the children an old-fashioned turkey dinner which she could not afford, she decided that Alan was right: she could not manage without him. Her hand was on the phone to call him when she drew back. "Damned if I will," she said aloud.

Staring into the fireplace which greedily consumed Marion Parrish-Parker's endless (thank God!) supply of wood, Elizabeth reviewed her nonproductive efforts of the past weeks. Obviously, she was going about the business of job-hunting in the wrong way. Nobody was going to hire an amateur when there was so much professional competition in this world of slim employment. It was just stupid to keep answering ads in the papers, registering with employment agencies, doing all the conventional things people did when they looked for work. Suddenly it was so clear to her that she wondered how she could not have realized it: The only way she would ever get a job would be to have an "in" with somebody who knew her as a person, not as an anonymous, inexperienced applicant. She and Alan knew hundreds of people in Washington. She had been in touch with none of them since she left Georgetown, not wanting their pity or their curiosity. Now she was prepared to accept both if need be.

The instinct for survival was stronger than her pride. Let them talk. Who cared as long as one of them had some kind of job she could do? With a sense of anticipation, she methodically began to go through her social address book. By the time she got to "O," her spirits began to sink. Of the dozens of names, all were associated either with the aircraft business or with some governmental branch related to it. Nothing that even began to approach an area in which she could work. It was still another unrealistic, pointless shot in the dark. Then she turned the page and a name jumped out. "Preston, Stuart." A bell rang. Stuart Preston was an important publisher specializing in small, highly profitable newspapers distributed in suburban areas. He also owned a women's magazine, a feature syndicate, and a chain of radio stations in Texas. Stu Preston, an intelligent, attractive, stimulating man in his fifties, and his wife had dined often at the Whitmans'. Elizabeth knew that he liked her. More importantly, she remembered that he'd been almost embarrassingly flattering about the house, the way she had furnished it, and the well-planned little dinners she gave there.

"I'm not sure whether you really do serve the best food in Washington," he'd once said, "but I don't think anyone would notice even if it was bad! You have a genius for creating a very special ambiance, Elizabeth. Everything you do is in such good taste. The whole place is perfection. You missed your calling, my girl. You should have taken up decorating as a profession instead of wasting your time on that sky jockey your married."

They'd laughed about it at the time. She hadn't thought of those words or of Stu Preston in months. Maybe he'd forgotten, too. But tomorrow she'd remind him. Surely in the vast Preston empire there must be some minor job she could do.

She was right that Preston had forgotten that one conversation, but he had not forgotten Elizabeth Whitman. He knew that she and her husband were separated. He even knew why. It was his business to know such things. Not that they were difficult to find out. For all its cosmopolitan reputation, Washington was essentially a small town. The people who "mattered" were relatively few and in constant touch with each other. There had been much head-shaking and speculation over the split between the Whitmans. Most people had been surprised. Stu had not. His newspaper contacts kept him informed of Alan's behavior, and he recognized, soon after the man's arrival in Washington, that he was going to be one of those who couldn't handle privilege and power. He knew about Alan's drinking and his affairs. He even knew of Alan's penchant for picking up dirty little tramps on Fourteenth Street.

He had nothing but disgust for such stupidity. But he felt sorry for Whitman's pretty wife stuck with three children and a husband who was certain to get his comeuppance sooner or later. When he learned that Elizabeth had walked out, he thought of getting in touch with her, maybe offering his help if she needed it. He did not do so. For one thing, he correctly assumed that she would have put a good face on the whole thing and courteously declined his aid. For another, he sensed that he was much too personally taken with her. It would be easy for him to get involved, and Stuart Preston was too smart for that. After twenty years his wife bored him a little. He was not averse to a quick, transient fling when he was on a business trip to Chicago or Los Angeles. But get tangled up with a woman so closely tied in to his own world? No thanks. Such affairs were invariably more trouble than they were worth. As, he thought ruefully, Alan Whitman must have found out.

In spite of his cautiousness, though, Stu felt a little thrill of pleasure when his secretary informed him that "a Mrs. Whitman" was calling. He took up the receiver eagerly.

"Elizabeth? It's good to hear you! How are you?"

"I'm just fine," she said. "Footloose, but fine."

He didn't quite know what that meant. Was she being coy? It didn't fit his impression of her.

"I'd like to see you, Stu, if you have any time."

He hedged. "Of course. Always time for you. What would you like? Lunch? A drink?"

Elizabeth's warm laugh came over the wire. She realized how her opening remarks had sounded. Poor Stu, she thought. I must sound like a discontented, manless female who's looking for company. I probably scared him half to death.

"That's nice of you," she said easily, "but I really want a serious business appointment in your office. If it wouldn't be too great an imposition, I'd like to have your advice. Of course you know that Alan and I have separated."

His relief was almost funny. "For you, I have plenty of valuable time and undoubtedly a plethora of worthless advice. When would you like to come in?"

"Whenever it's convenient."

"Tomorrow? About ten?"

"Thank you. I'll be there."

After they hung up, Preston sat back in his big leather chair and wondered what kind of advice she wanted from him. Could be she wanted him to suggest a divorce lawyer or help her find a house. He knew she was living in one of Marion Parrish-Parker's cottages but he assumed that was only a temporary, expedient move. It never occurred to him that she needed a job.

Being ushered graciously into Preston's private office was like balm to Elizabeth's battered ego after the rude, unfeeling treatment she'd met on her job interviews. Of course, she mused, Stu didn't know this was a job interview. He was simply making time for a friend. He came forward eagerly to greet her, giving her the meaningless little kiss on the cheek that served as a polite salutation in their circle. Settled in a big wing chair beside his desk, she looked around her with pleasure. Preston had a luxurious suite of offices in one of the big buildings on Dupont Circle. From here he kept in touch with all his enterprises. The actual work of producing publications did not take place here, but every decision of importance to a Preston property was made at this vast mahogany desk. "GHQ," his staff called it, and Stu was a quick and decisive commander in chief.

He was smiling at her now. "It really *is* good to see you, Elizabeth. By God, I haven't had a decent dinner in months, now that I think about it."

They laughed. Then Stu's face sobered. "Poor joke, I'm afraid. I really am sorry about you and Alan. And not only for the sake of the marriage and the kids. I think he could fall on his face without you. From what I hear, he's behaving badly. There are even some rumors of his losing out at the BAC. I suppose you know?"

"No. We've had no contact since I left."

"A bad business, that. Seen it happen to a lot of good men in Washington. 'Drunk with power,' as they say. Big jobs go to their heads. They can't handle the fame and flattery. Pretty soon they're hitting the booze and neglecting their work and even being careless about—" He stopped. "Sorry. Afraid I'm out of line. Worse than a gossipy old woman. Tactless of me."

"There's no need to apologize," Elizabeth said. "Why do you think I finally left him?"

Preston frowned. "Goddamn fools. Think they can get away with anything, don't they?" Abruptly, his mood changed.

"So much for that," he said. "Now what about you? You said you needed advice. How can I be of service?"

She came right to the point. "I need more than advice, Stu. I need a job."

He looked faintly surprised. "A job? But surely Alan provides for you."

Pride prompted the instinctive lie. "He would, of course, but I won't let him. Leaving was my choice. I don't think he should have to pay for that."

Preston's look said that she was a damn fool, but he refrained from the obvious reply. He listened carefully as she told him about her job-hunting experiences.

"And so," she concluded, "as you can see, I am unemployable in the accepted sense of the word. No training, no experience, and no way to get either, as far as I can see. I came because I thought that perhaps there might be a place somewhere in your business for a well-meaning matron with no talent at all."

"You're wrong," Preston said.

The short answer startled Elizabeth. She took a few seconds to compose herself. Then she spoke calmly. "I see. You mean there's nothing here. I understand. It was nervy of me to ask. You're a businessman first and a friend second, which is as it should be. There's no question that I hoped to take advantage of your friendship. That will give you a rough idea of how desperate I am. But I'm ashamed that I put you in the position of refusing a charity case." She rose, smiling, from the chair. "Forgive me, Stu. It was a rotten thing to do to a friend."

"Sit down, Elizabeth," he said almost roughly. "And stop behaving like Uriah Heep."

She sank back into the chair. "No wonder you can't get a job," Preston said, "if this is the way you've been approaching it. What's with all this meek, apologetic hand-wringing? You have enough pride when it comes to protecting that blackhearted husband of yours. Why do you go around poor-mouthing yourself? 'A well-meaning matron with no talent at all!' I never heard such a bunch of bull! You're looking for work, not a handout. Well, who the hell do you think is going to hire you if you keep presenting yourself as a 'charity case'?"

A little of the old fight came back into Elizabeth. "That's not fair, Stu! I was talking to you as an old friend. Surely you don't think that's the way I am in front of strangers?"

"You bet I do," he said. "Whether you know it or not, the old confidence has gone out of you. Maybe it's been kicked out. I don't know. Anyway, you're not the lady I knew in Georgetown." His voice softened. "Okay, now you've had your spanking and I doubt that it hurt me worse than it hurt you. But I had to shake you up, Elizabeth, before I *really* tell you why you're wrong." He smiled the attractive smile she remembered. "You're wrong when you call yourself inexperienced and untalented. I've seen your talents firsthand, in your own home. You're exceptionally experienced about entertaining and creating the kind of atmosphere that most women would give their souls to be able to provide. Women are hungry for that kind of information, Elizabeth, and you've got it to burn."

She continued to look puzzled. Stuart kept right on talking in his rapid-fire way. "And the thing you're most wrong about is that there's no place for you in Preston Publications."

She couldn't believe what she was hearing. Preston waited. "Have you lost your hearing along with your confidence?" he asked kindly. "I said I have a job for you, Elizabeth. Aren't you even going to ask what it is? And for God's sake don't go all humble on me again. If you say 'beggars can't be choosers,' I swear I'll hit you."

For a moment she put her hands over her face. When she looked up, her eyes were swimming with tears of gratitude, but her expression was eager, almost merry. A vestige of irrepressible humor was in her voice.

"I know. You're going to make me editor in chief of all the Preston Publications, coast to coast."

He laughed. "That's more like it. No, that's not quite the job I had in mind. You'll have to start a little lower. Only for the moment, of course." His tone became serious. "Have you ever heard of a weekly newspaper called *Wife and Mother?* Probably not. It's what we call in the trade a 'throwaway.' It's given out free, in supermarkets mostly. It's never going to win a Pulitzer Prize for journalism, but five million middle-class women read it every week because it comes home in their grocery bags. It's highly successful because it speaks directly to the kind of woman who receives it. It's aimed at an audience with a life-style much simpler than any you've known. It's a mass publication with just enough class to give the readers something to look up to. They love the ideas that *W and M* gives them about clothes and cooking and decorating and entertaining. And, of course, they like it all the better because it doesn't cost them anything."

"But how do you make money on it if you don't charge for it?" Elizabeth asked.

"That's one thing most people don't understand about publishing. Papers and magazines don't make money on subscriptions. In fact, it costs so much to get circulation that it usually is a losing proposition. Still you must have circulation because that's what the advertising rates are based on. Follow me so far?"

"I think so."

"Good. Then you probably already have figured out that since *Wife and Mother* can prove a circulation of five million hand-picked customers every week, we can—and do—charge whopping rates for our advertising. We're a natural for the big food companies, the soap-flakes boys, the toothpaste makers—all those outfits with enormous ad budgets. They're heavy advertisers, not only because of the size of the weekly audience but because it is one without 'waste circulation.' In other words, unlike a general newspaper where half the readers are men or people not interested in homemaking, *all* our readers are potential buyers of products sold in the stores where they get the paper. It's one of my most successful and profitable ventures. And it's the one where you'll fit in best.

"You finally got lucky, Elizabeth. The decorating editor of the paper left last week and Grace Edwards—she's the editor—has been frantically looking for a replacement. I think she'll snap you up like a gift from the gods."

"Decorating editor!" Elizabeth looked terrified. "Good Lord, Stu, I have no training for that! There must be dozens of writers in Washington who'd be right for that job."

He sighed. "Don't start that again, will you, please? Just take my word for it, there aren't. This isn't New York, where there are plenty of women with experience on magazines and newspapers. This town's business is government. It attracts secretaries and clerks from Iowa. It is not teeming with ladies who have taste and need jobs. Those who qualify are already employed on the big metropolitan dailies. I tell you, Grace hasn't even seen a possible candidate. I'm about to deliver one to her. She'll slobber with gratitude."

Frightened as she was Elizabeth had to laugh at his comic air of resignation. "It sounds wonderful, of course, but please be serious, Stu. What do I really have to do?"

"You have to come up once a week with an idea for a decorating page. Story and pictures. You have to keep in mind that the readers are modest-income families, so there's no point in recommending that they go out and buy Louis

XIV commodes for nonexistent guest rooms. What they want is ideas about arranging furniture, making draperies, grouping pictures. Anything to make their little cottages look better than the woman's next door. Think you can adapt your taste to a slim pocketbook?"

Visualizing her own run-down, borrowed cottage, Elizabeth smiled. "Yes, I can adapt. But what about the writing? I've never written anything more than a term paper or a letter. And the photographs! I haven't a clue how you go about taking newspaper pictures."

"My dear," Preston said, "I told you that this is not great journalism. You are educated and—except for today—articulate. Pretend you're giving advice in a letter to a friend, if you like. You'll get the hang of writing women's features very fast. Besides, we have editors who'll go over your copy and guide you in the beginning. Incidentally, Grace and her girls are very nice young women.

"As for the photographs," he went on, "your only responsibility will be to set up a sample room in a studio or find some real house that's a shining example of great taste on very little money. Then a nice man with a camera will come in and do the picture-taking for you."

"You make it sound wonderfully simple and terribly exciting. I feel like I'm dreaming. You're really sure I can do it?"

"Not really. But about ninety-five per cent."

Elizabeth was overcome by this unexpected stroke of luck. She had dared to hope for something like a receptionist's job. Now this incredible, dynamic man had come up not only with a livelihood but with what sounded like an entree to a whole new world.

"When may I start?"

"Almost immediately, I'd think," Preston said. "Of course, I do have to discuss it with Grace, just as a matter of courtesy. But that's nothing to worry about."

"You're sure she won't mind my coming in like this? Through you, I mean? I don't want her to think I have an in with the big boss."

He looked amused. "Haven't you?" Then, seeing her distress, he added quickly, "Of course she won't mind. There's nothing insecure or petty about our Mrs. Edwards. And she knows I wouldn't hire my own daughter if I didn't think she was right for the job. By the way, Elizabeth, you haven't asked about salary. Newspapers don't pay much. Just between us, the publishers are getting away with murder. Not that it will probably go on much longer. The Newspaper

Guild is getting stronger and stronger. Eventually they'll organize and we'll pay through the nose. Meantime, your spot calls for sixty dollars a week. Can you manage on that? I'd like to do better, but I have to stay in line with the salaries the others are getting."

Right now it sounded like a fortune. "It's fine," she said. "I'll manage beautifully."

"I'm sure you will," Preston said. He didn't tell her that the job really paid fifty. He'd supply the extra ten out of his own pocket and explain the circumstances to Grace. Goddamn that no-good bastard Alan Whitman, he thought. I hope he gets his, the way everybody's saying he will.

Chapter 6

Stuart Preston was right. Alan's world was coming apart in all directions. He knew it and made no attempt to stop it. For a while, after the news of Elizabeth's departure got out, he was a sought-after "extra man," inundated with even more cocktail and dinner party invitations than had deluged the Whitmans in their merry-go-round married life. He accepted them indiscriminately and then behaved so badly that he fell rapidly off the list of one hostess after another. Badly as they needed unattached men, the entertaining ladies of Washington were unwilling to put up with Alan's drunken boorishness, his vulgar comments and obscene jokes. In a town where it was well known that a good haircut and a presentable dinner jacket could get you into the best homes, Alan Whitman was suddenly alone with his paid women and his endless supply of liquor.

The man who had never missed a day's work in his life began to call in sick to the office. At first it was once every couple of weeks. Then weekly. Toward the end, he barely appeared at his desk at all. One morning he came in still drunk and disheveled after a night on the town. George

Stanlowski hustled him home before too many people saw the condition he was in.

Alan's co-worker was appalled by the condition of the Georgetown house. It appeared to have been untouched since Mary Jackson left. The place was filthy. A few dirty dishes stood in the sink and glasses were everywhere, leaving careless rings on the tops of dusty tables. It smelled of whiskey, stale air, and unchanged bed linen. It was no better than a one-man flophouse, George thought. He was embarrassed for Alan, but Alan was beyond caring.

"How 'bout a drink, old buddy?"

"None for me, pal. And none for you, either. Best thing you can do is hit the sack, Alan. You're in bad shape."

Alan poured half a tumbler of whiskey into a used glass. "Never felt better in my life," he said. "I'm a free man. No prissy wife. No kids to worry about. Nothin' to do but enjoy."

George tried to get his attention. "Listen, friend, you've got to pull yourself together. Cut out the boozing. Get back to work. We're all worried about you. There's been a lot of unpleasant talk at the bureau. It's serious. You could lose your job."

"Big deal. Big goddamn deal. Screw the bureau. And screw you, too."

"For Christ sake, Alan, don't you care? You've got it made. Are you going to chuck it all for the sake of another drink?"

Alan stared at him coldly. "They're not going to fire me," he said.

"They are. I swear to God, they are."

"No," Alan said, "they're not." His face looked suddenly old and haggard. It was hard to believe that he was only forty-three. "Tell you a secret. They won't get the chance. I'm going to quit. Decided last night. Tired of Washington. Tired of bein' a big wheel. Tired of you, too. Why don't you get the hell out of here, George?"

"What about Elizabeth?"

"What about her?"

"If you run out on everything you'll never have a chance of getting her back."

Alan stretched out full length on the sofa, the hand holding the glass hanging limply over the edge. He closed his eyes. In the classic manner of the schizoid, his mood had abruptly changed.

"Elizabeth wouldn't come back to me if I were Clark Gable, Charles Lindbergh, and her father rolled into one." He laughed. "I guess that's what she really wanted me to be, now that I think of it. Whatever she wanted, I couldn't deliver. Not really. Not on any kind of permanent basis. To her or any other woman. You see, George, I'm really a lousy husband. A helluva lover, but a lousy husband. Almost as lousy a husband as I am an administrator. I'm not cut out for success." He paused, opening one eye almost comically. "You don't understand one goddamn thing I'm trying to say, do you, George?"

His friend shook his head. "All I know is that you're crazy to talk about resigning. They don't really want to get rid of you down at the bureau. You're forcing them to. Good God, Alan, you're in on the ground floor of the fastest-moving industry in history! Damned few men in the world have your expertise in aviation and the big boys know it. All you have to do is stop this crap and get back to work. Everybody knows what you can do when you want to!"

Alan turned his head away. "That's just the point," he said. "I don't want to."

On the same day that Alan unofficially told his friend that he was abandoning his career, Elizabeth rushed home to Bethesda to announce that she was starting hers. When she dashed into the cottage, her face was as excited as a girl's. She grabbed Mary Jackson and gave her an excited hug.

"It finally happened!" she caroled. "I have a job, Mary. A wonderful one. Remember Mr. Preston? The man who owns all the newspapers? He's going to let me work on one of his papers. Oh, Mary, I can't tell you how happy I am! Where are the children? I want to tell Ann and Quigly the good news."

"Thank the Lord," Mary said. "It's a joy to see you looking like yourself again, Mrs. Whitman."

"I don't feel like myself," Elizabeth said. "I feel like a whole brand-new person. Everything's going to be different. I can take care of us now. I can even pay you. Not as much as you got before, I'm afraid. But something. And more as time goes on." She laughed at herself. "Listen to me! I'm planning on a raise even before I have the final, official okay to go to work." She explained about her interview with Grace Edwards, which was scheduled for the next morning. For a moment, her exuberance subsided. "What if she doesn't like me, Mary? I just haven't let myself think about that."

"Don't you worry. She'll like you. Now you run tell your children. They're right outside playing."

Elizabeth found her two older children a short distance from the house, romping hip-deep in the piles of red and gold leaves which had drifted down from the winter-ready trees. That is, Quigly was romping. Ann, as usual, was simply standing in dignified silence watching his childish antics with an almost superior disdain. Caught unaware, her face was a study in discontent. She still had not adjusted to the loss of her father, the drastic change in her life-style. She was too old to accept without question and too young to be told the sordid events that precipitated the sudden move. After the first few days, she did not mention Alan again. But she could read, and more than once Elizabeth had caught her puzzling over some newspaper story in which her father's name appeared, or looking solemnly at a photograph of him in the business section.

For a moment, Elizabeth watched the children from a little distance. Then she made her voice deliberately gay. "Hey, you two! I have good news!"

Quigly glanced at her with indifference and went back to kicking leaves. For a moment, a ray of hope crossed Ann's face. Then she resumed her solemn expression as she walked slowly toward her mother. "Come on, Quigly," she said over her shoulder. Reluctantly the little boy joined them. Elizabeth told them about her new job, trying to make them feel her excitement.

"How about your mother?" she said. "Remember Mr. Preston who used to come to see us? He's given me a job. I'm going to be a real newspaperwoman. Maybe even have my name on top of my stories. Won't that be something?"

"Will you write about the Washington Senators?" Quigly asked. Baseball was his passion.

"No," Elizabeth said. "I'm going to write about decorating houses and things like that."

"That's dumb."

"Well, maybe some of the ballplayers' wives will have pretty houses that I could write about. That could be exciting, wouldn't it?"

Quigly wandered off without replying. It was silly to expect understanding from a seven-year-old. Yet Elizabeth felt childishly disappointed as she turned to Ann.

"I guess boys don't care much about furniture and things. That's for women, like us. What do you think of my news, Annie?"

"It's very nice," Ann said formally.

"Darling, it's more than nice. It's terribly important. Don't you see? Now I can buy you and Quigly some things to wear. You've just about outgrown everything you have. And I can start paying Mary, who's been so wonderful to us. And we

can do more things together, all of us. We'll be a real family
again."

Ann looked at her with hundred-year-old eyes. "Will we,
Mama?"

"Of course. You just wait and see."

"Can we go back to our nice house in Georgetown? Can
I go back to my old school?"

"Well, no, Ann. Not those things. We're not going to be
rich, dear. Just a great deal more comfortable." The child's
cool manner unnerved her. "I don't understand you, Ann,"
she said. "You used to be such a happy, laughing little girl. I
know you miss your daddy. Someday, when you're older, I'll
try to make you realize why he's no longer with us, even
though he still loves you very much."

"When Daddy was with us we had a nice house and I went
to a nice school. Now we live in this terrible old place and
you're going to go to work. Like Mary. Like a nigger woman."

Instinctively, Elizabeth raised her hand to slap her. She
stopped just in time. She had never physically punished her
children. Reason, she believed, had a greater impact than
force, but Ann was rapidly, perhaps deliberately, pushing her
to the edge of her endurance. She tried to keep her voice
low and calm.

"Don't you ever use an ugly word like 'nigger' again. And
don't you dare refer to Mary in that tone of voice. You're
a spoiled, selfish, heartless human being." With effort she
kept herself from adding "like your father." "I'm sorry,
Elizabeth said cuttingly, "that I cannot treat you like a
princess. I know that's what you've been taught to expect.
Unfortunately, Ann, you are no longer in that pleasant situation. I think it's about time you faced the fact that there can
be very few luxuries for any of us. Not for now, at any
rate."

Ann smiled. A secret smile. "Is Mr. Preston rich?" she
asked innocently.

Elizabeth was taken off guard. "Why, yes, I suppose so.
Why?"

"Maybe he'd get us a nice house if you asked him."

The offices of *Wife and Mother* occupied one floor of a
large building on K Street in downtown Washington. The
rest of the space was given over to the *Chevy Chase Courier*,
the *Alexandria Sentinel* and the *Bowie Bugle*, all suburban
dailies which were part of Preston's newspaper empire.

Entering the front door at nine o'clock the next morning,
Elizabeth was almost bowled over by two young men, one

with a camera, who came barreling out. The cameraless one grinned as he rushed by. "Sorry," he called. "There's a fire that won't keep."

Elizabeth smiled as she took the elevator to the fourth floor. She could feel the air of urgency that pervaded the building and it delighted her. Her experience with the press was limited to a few staid interviews with society reporters and feature writers. Things like fires were something that just happened and mysteriously got into the paper. Maybe now she'd find out how.

She was not prepared for Grace Edwards. Her mental picture of the editor was nothing like the young, pretty, vital woman who greeted her and smiled when she saw the astonishment on Elizabeth's face.

"Well, your reaction's typical," she said. "Everybody expects the editor of *Wife and Mother* to look like a cross between Alice Longworth and Betty Crocker. Hope you're not disappointed by the façade. Don't let it make you feel insecure. I know my business. Started as a copy girl on the *Star* when I was fifteen. That's ten years. Enough time to turn me into a newspaper woman, and a damned good one, if I do say so myself."

Elizabeth liked her instantly. Grace exuded competence, humor, and a nonbitchy femaleness that put her new decorating editor instantly at ease. She was a nonstop talker who looked one squarely in the eye and seemed to be making an instant evaluation even while she rushed on with her energetic, comprehensive rundown of the paper, its audience, its ambitions and its staff.

"We direct ourself to the woman at home," Grace said. "You've heard of her, she's that middle-class dame who serves Jell-O for dessert. Five million of them read *W and M* now. Should be fifty million if Stu Preston would get some of his distribution boys off their fat opinionated behinds. Newspapermen in general don't have much use for women in the business. They think 'hard news' is all that counts and our kind of stuff is fluff. Some fluff! Show me one of those all-male dailies that has our advertising! Anyway, you'll like it around here. Not too many men involved with *Wife and Mother*. Just a couple of photographers, and they're not too happy about it. Of course, there are hundreds of guys but they're on the other floors. I don't mean to make this sound like a convent, but some women don't like to work where there aren't eligible men. Does that bother you?"

"Not in the least," Elizabeth said.

"Good. I mean, you won't find this the Junior League, but

the fourth floor is definitely considered no-man's land. All the same, we're businesslike as hell. We operate as though we're putting out a news daily instead of a pie-crust-and-petticoat weekly. It's still newspapering, and once it gets in your blood there's nothing like it, Elizabeth. You don't mind if I call you Elizabeth? You call me Grace. Everybody does. Anyway, the damned job doesn't pay enough to feed a canary and why we don't all quit and take up nice, lucrative work like prostitution, I'll never know. But we hang on, poverty-stricken and happy. Glad to have you with us. Stu says you're good material. I trust that crusty old s.o.b., but let's get one thing clear: If he's wrong and you don't work out, I'll have to let you go. Okay?"

Elizabeth opened her mouth to agree, but Grace already was racing on. "I know you don't know anything about this business, but you'll pick it up fast. Nobody has time to stop and give you a course in journalism, but everybody will help, I promise you. Now when can you start? Immediately, I hope. The decorating page for next week is bare as a baby's rear end. Well? What do you say?"

Elizabeth hesitated. Grace made it all sound easy, but Elizabeth was terrified at the thought of plunging in and trying to put together a decorating page for next week. She hadn't the faintest idea how to begin. It had never occurred to her that she wouldn't be allowed some small period of apprenticeship. She wanted to bolt, but she couldn't afford to. A chance like this might never come again.

"Where do I hang my hat?" she asked.

Grace smiled approvingly. "Good girl. I'll confess now that I was a little nervous that you might turn out to be one of those la-de-da ladies who'd sit around all day with little white gloves on. You see," she added kindly, "Stu told me a little of your history. I'm sorry about what's happened to you, and I admire your guts." She did not mention the extra ten dollars that Preston was contributing. That was his business, and she was sure that he was telling the truth when he said that Elizabeth knew nothing about it.

As though she didn't want to be thanked for either the job or the sympathy, Grace rushed Elizabeth into a larger room adjoining her office. Three pleasant-looking women were producing an unsynchronized din on their battered typewriters. They paused and glanced up as Grace and her companion entered.

"This is Elizabeth Whitman, everybody," Grace said. "She's our new decorating editor, praise the Lord. Elizabeth, that monument to dress manufacturing over there is our fashion editor, Laurel Lane. Honest to God, it's her real name, no matter how made-up it sounds. She handles the beauty junk as well as fashion. Gets more loot than any of us, by the way, so if you run out of lipstick, she's a great source of supply."

Laurel was a tall, attractive, dark-haired girl about Grace's age. She smiled warmly, acknowledging the breezy introduction.

"Next to Laurel is Maureen Duffy, our food editor. The one who wages the hopeless battle to get our readers off their Jell-O fixation."

Maureen, an ample, brown-haired woman of forty-five or so made a face. "Thankless task," she said humorously. "They just love all those dah-lin' colors the stuff comes in. We'll have to work together, Elizabeth. Some of those silly women write in to ask how to plan a whole table setting around cherry, lemon and lime. Thank God that part is *your* problem."

Grace and the others laughed. "And, finally, our secretary slavey-angel there is Nancy St. John. She's our baby." A pretty youngster, no more than seventeen, smiled brightly at Elizabeth. "Nancy will show you where we keep the copy paper and carbon and stuff," Grace said. "And when you're on assignment, she'll handle your phone. By the way, that elegant corner over there is yours, Elizabeth." She pointed to a disreputable wooden desk piled high with papers. In back of it was a rickety wooden swivel chair and an ancient typewriter. "What the hell is all that stuff on top of the desk, Nancy?" Grace asked.

"Press releases from furniture companies, mostly. Some reader letters asking for advice. And a couple of invitations to press parties."

"Don't let it scare you, Elizabeth," Laurel Lane said. "It's not nearly as frightening as it looks." Elizabeth gave her a grateful smile. Obviously, Grace had told them how completely inexperienced she was. She felt warmed by the easy acceptance of her co-workers.

"Well, let's get to work," Grace said. "Nancy, get Elizabeth a supply of copy paper and pencils, will you? Maureen, maybe you'd let her watch you put your food page together. As for you, Laurel, can you spare a few minutes to give her a conducted tour? I'd like her to see the composing room, the press room, and the photo shop. I'll go over some back issues with you, Elizabeth, when you return, and explain about our deadlines. We all type our own copy, of course, and write the heads and captions. You do type, don't you?"

Elizabeth felt as though she was lost in a welter of new words and unfamiliar procedures. She didn't understand half of what Grace was saying, but she realized that the editor was waiting for an answer.

"Type? Well, yes. Badly, though. With two fingers."

"Perfect," Grace pronounced. "That's the way all good newspapermen type. Didn't you ever see *Front Page?* Laurel, while you're at it, show her the city room. She'll see every damned joker up there pecking away with two fingers."

Laurel rose gracefully. "Put your hat and coat into our armoire," she said, pointing to an out-of-shape Victorian clothes tree in the corner, "and come with me. We'll start with the most interesting and important place of all. Grace didn't mention it because she's endowed with the holding power of royalty, but mere mortals like us occasionally have to know where the ladies' room is."

Grace laughed good-naturedly. "You're right. That should be your first stop. If anything will set the flavor of Elizabeth's new surroundings, our 'powder room' will do it."

Mystified, Elizabeth accompanied Laurel down the hall to a door marked WOMEN. Inside, she couldn't believe her eyes. The room was equipped with the usual cubicles and washbasins. But, in addition, lined up against the wall was a trio of urinals, each holding a potted fern. Laurel burst into laughter at her expression.

"What on earth—"

"Welcome to a man's world," Laurel said. "It's okay. Weird, all right, but okay. Before *Wife and Mother* moved into this building, it was completely a daily paper setup. Nothing but fellas on the premises. Of course, we needed separate accommodations so they just put wo in front of MEN and made it our john."

"But those ferns!" Elizabeth said. "Why the ferns?"

"That was Nancy's idea. I'm sure she thinks the equipment really is meant for planting. Anyway, none of us has the heart to disillusion her. In fact, we've learned to like it. At least it's good for a laugh when things get rough."

Suddenly Elizabeth felt more comfortable. It was a long way from the flower-filled rooms of her Georgetown house to the fern-planted urinals of a shabby newspaper office on K Street, but for the first time this morning she felt she could bridge the gap.

The next hour was a kaleidoscope of hasty impressions. The city room, where the reporters and rewrite men worked, was a madhouse of shirt-sleeved, deafening activity. Clouds of smoke hung in the air, telephones jangled endlessly and constant calls for "Copy!" brought young boys on the run to pick up the long sheets of yellow paper which spewed from a battery of typewriters, all operated, as Grace had promised, in the classic two-fingered hunt-and-peck system, but stepped up to lightning tempo.

The composing room on the floor above was a sea of metal where the pages of the various publications were put into metal, page-sized areas called forms, ready to be sent to the press room at the basement level. Elizabeth was completely confused by the process of "making up a page." At the head and foot of each form, an editor and composing room man faced each other, carefully laying in blocks of type, headlines, and metal engravings, miraculously making the columns fit precisely into the dimension of the page. It was fascinating and mysterious, like a skilled juggling act.

"How can the editors figure out what they're doing?" Elizabeth asked naïvely. "They're looking at everything upside down."

"That's the way it's done," Laurel said. "Not all that difficult, once you get the hang of it. Grace probably will make up your pages at first, but you'll eventually be expected to do it on your own. It's quite fun, once you learn how to stand on your head. Figuratively speaking, of course."

Elizabeth was staggered by the mysteries that unfolded, one after another. She gaped at the huge presses which swallowed up those same metal forms and regurgitated them in the form of thousands of printed newspapers. She was curious about the well-equipped photo lab, but put off by the barely civil reception she received from the two disheveled, aging photographers.

"They don't seem very happy," she volunteered timidly to Laurel. "Everybody else seems to have so much vitality. They act like they're mad at the world."

"I guess they are, poor devils. You see, they're the only men assigned exclusively to us. And they hate it. They'd give their souls to be out covering riots and murders. Instead, they're assigned to fashion shows and cooking classes. Preston has a good retirement policy. They're just marking time until they're eligible. But they're good Joes. You'll find them cooperative and efficient, if not exactly ecstatic about photographing your room settings and flower arrangements."

"Laurel, I'm scared to death." Elizabeth spoke as though the younger girl were her dearest friend. Interestingly, that was the way she felt: that she had made her first close woman friend.

Laurel seemed to feel it, too. "Hey, don't be," she said.

"You're going to be great. Newspaper people are the nicest people in the world. They love to go around acting hard-boiled, but you'll never find a more clannish, sympathetic bunch." She paused. "I think you're nice people, too, Elizabeth. You're going to do just fine."

Elizabeth smiled at her. There was no reason on earth to believe that she'd be all right, but the way this girl said it, Elizabeth did believe it. She had to.

The human spirit, like the human body, has a remarkable ability to adjust quickly to what is asked of it, but even so, Elizabeth was amazed at the ease with which she fell into her new life, her new job. Early on, it became evident to her and to Grace Edwards that fortune and the perceptive eye of Stu Preston had thrown her into a world in which she flourished. She never ceased to marvel at the easy camaraderie, the lack of preoccupation with "status," the generous nature of the women with whom she worked. They were a different breed than the self-involved, sweet-mannered, and ruthlessly ambitious wives of men in government. Laurel was right. Newspaper people acted tough on the outside. But with "their own" they gave generously of their knowledge and support. And they quickly adopted Elizabeth as one of their own.

Peculiarly enough, despite this professional intimacy, Elizabeth knew very little of the personal lives of her co-workers. It was understandable. At the paper, it was "all business." Their kind of work kept them out of the office a great deal, so there was little opportunity for the daily "girl lunches" that women in routine office jobs engage in. In a way, it was just as well. Elizabeth could not have afforded even a moderate restaurant meal every day. Unless she was invited to a press lunch, she usually brought a sandwich from home. Once in a while she and Laurel went to the employees' cafeteria in the building for a quick, cheap bite. They both enjoyed these infrequent excursions, and it was through them that Elizabeth gleaned sparse information about the others in the department.

Grace, Laurel told her, was the only one of the group who was married. Her husband was a lawyer in a big firm. "A nice guy," Laurel said, "but still struggling. Grace's salary is important to them. Someday he'll probably make it big and she won't need to work. Even so, I doubt that she'll quit. She's a natural Nellie Bly. Newspapering is a big part of her life. I don't think she could ever give it up."

"Could you?" Elizabeth asked.

Laurel casually inspected her well-groomed nails painted Raven Red and miraculously unchipped in spite of the furious typing she did. "Me? I don't know. Sure, I guess I could. But I don't think I could ever sit around and do nothing. I can't imagine anything more deadly than just staying home."

"What about children? Wouldn't you like them one day?"

"Can't have any," Laurel said matter-of-factly. "Or so the doctors say."

"I'm sorry."

"Don't be. I'm a terrific honorary aunt to other people's kids. Probably better than I'd be as a mother. How are yours, by the way? I'd like to meet them sometime."

"I'd like you to," Elizabeth said. "Maybe you'd come for dinner one night? I'd especially like Ann to meet you. She's crazy about clothes and all the glamorous stuff. I'm sure you'd be good for her. She probably will have to go to work one day. It would be nice for her to meet an honest-to-God successful career woman. With luck, she'd start to pattern herself after you."

Laurel raised an eyebrow. "Why me? Why not you?"

Elizabeth shook her head. "No chance. I'm beneath her notice. Not her fault, but I'm afraid she's a bit of a snob at ten. Her father told her she was a princess, so she treats the rest of us like peasants."

"She sounds like she could use a good paddling, if you ask me."

Elizabeth didn't answer. "Tell me about Maureen," she said, deliberately changing the subject.

"Well, let's see." Laurel went along with this new tack. "She's a widow. No kids. Went back to live with her mother after her husband was killed in a car crash. Maureen's a masochist, I think. The old lady's a terror. God knows how Maureen stands her. She's a selfish old hypochondriacal bitch. Loaded with dough and perfectly able to live alone, but she won't. Funny how people stay tied to terrible situations even when they don't have to. Somewhere Maureen must be loaded with guilt. I must say, though, she never gripes about Mama. The only reason I know about her is because Maureen once gave her a birthday party and I went, out of some misguided sense of loyalty. Never again, I'll tell you! I'm sorry for Maureen, but wild horses couldn't drag me within twenty miles of the old lady. I may not be Brenda Frazier, but I don't have to spend my evenings that way!" Laurel looked thoughtful. "Would you go out some night with my friends and me, Elizabeth? We have a lot of laughs. And I think you could use some."

Elizabeth smiled appreciatively. "I could indeed," she said, "but I'm afraid you'll have to count me out. My housekeeper doesn't live in. Somebody has to be there at night with the children."

"What about a baby-sitter?"

"Afraid that's out, too. A small matter of finance. Besides, Laurel, you forget that I'm still technically married."

"Listen, it's none of my business, but what are you going to do about that?"

"I don't know. Get a divorce eventually, I suppose. When I can afford it."

"Maybe your husband will meet someone he wants to marry. Then he'll spring for the divorce. It often happens that way. Or are you secretely hoping for a reconciliation?"

"No," Elizabeth said, "I'd never go back to him. And I doubt that he'll want to remarry. Alan isn't cut out for the marriage role. Responsibility is the last thing he wants."

A week after this conversation, Elizabeth read the announcement of Alan's resignation. In spite of everything she knew about him, she was surprised. And in spite of the fact that it did not alter anything about her situation, she was curious enough to call George Stanlowski at his office. He seemed glad to hear from her. Yes, he said, it was true. Alan had handed in his resignation and it had been accepted.

"I tried like hell to talk him out of it, Elizabeth, but it was no use. He just kept saying that he didn't want any part of the whole Washington scene. He's been hitting the booze pretty hard. I hear some pretty scary stories about him."

"I suppose he'll give up the house," Elizabeth said irrelevantly. "We only signed a three-year lease."

"I think he's already moved out. Nobody knows where to reach him. I'm really sorry, Elizabeth. For both of you. And for those kids. Alan is crazy about them, you know that. It's a goddamn shame," George said angrily. "What a stupid waste of talent! That dumb bastard could have owned the world."

"I used to think he would."

George's tone softened. "What about you? Are you all right, you and the children? Everybody asks about you and wonders why you haven't been in touch. We heard you're living on the Parrish-Parker place and that you have a job on *Wife and Mother*. We get the paper at home, but I haven't see your name in it."

"I'm fine, and so are the children. Yes, I'm working on the paper and I love it. But I've only been there a few weeks. I suppose they're waiting to be sure that I'm going to make it before they give me a by-line."

"Well, that's just great," George said heartily. "Listen, stay in touch, will you? Maybe you'd come over for dinner one night. I'll have Lucille call you."

She did not go into explanations as she had with Laurel. "That would be lovely, George. Give Lucille my love. And" —she hesitated—"if you hear anything more about Alan, would you mind calling me at the office?"

"Sure thing. Take care now."

"Thank you. You too."

Although she knew from the day she left Georgetown that Alan was forever out of her life, this latest move of his made the knowledge certain and irrevocable. She would have liked very much to start proceedings for divorce instantly. The scandal he had feared could not hurt him now. Of course, there was no real need to be legally free of him. Lord knows she had not met a man, had not had one social contact in all these months. It didn't matter, really, whether she was married or not, insofar as her activities were concerned. It was just that Elizabeth hated loose ends. She had a sense of orderliness that applied to her life as much as it did to her person or her home. She was uncomfortable with "unfinished business," as she thought of it. She would have felt tidier with her marriage formally dissolved, but she could not squander the hundreds of dollars that step would cost. She had no money for lawyers or trips to Reno even if she had had the time. Divorce simply for the sake of peace of mind was a luxury she could not afford. She accepted that fact with regret.

There was, however, one symbolic step she could take. Grace had told her that beginning next week she would have a by-line, and Elizabeth decided that professionally she would use her maiden name.

When she saw the page proof with the words "by Elizabeth Quigly" at the top of her column, she felt a charge of excitement. It was more than the understandable thrill a writer gets when he first sees public acknowledgment of his efforts. It was her "private divorce." Maybe the only one I'll ever have, she thought, but with it I've regained something of me. Her father came into her mind so strongly that she almost felt he was standing beside her at the splintery old desk where she worked.

"Proud of me, Professor?" she asked silently.

She could imagine his smile. "I've never been anything else," he would have said.

The next eighteen months went by surprisingly quickly and the problems they brought were predictable. The worst of them continued to be lack of money. She had had one raise after a year at the paper which brought her salary to seventy dollars a week, still far from enough to cover anything but the bare essentials. No matter how she economized, the bills each month were higher than the paycheck she brought home. Admittedly, she still succumbed to small extravagances, most of them where the children were concerned. Even so, she did not think of them as extravagances, though Laurel, whose worldly veneer disguised a much more practical nature than Elizabeth's, gently chided her for them.

At Christmas, for example, Elizabeth had bought gifts not only for her family and Mary but for the whole staff of *Wife and Mother,* even including the churlish photographers who had a difficult time maintaining their sour expressions in the face of this unheard-of generosity.

"You are a nut!" Laurel said, exasperated. "My God, you must have spent a hundred bucks just on the office!"

"What's the difference?" Elizabeth asked, smiling. "A hundred dollars won't keep me from starvation if it comes to that. Besides, Laurel, everybody was so pleased. And look at the darling toys they gave the children."

Her friend sighed. "I give up. You're hopeless." The two women had become close friends. Elizabeth still would not double-date with Laurel. Baby-sitters were an extravagance, she explained again, and besides, she was still a legally married woman.

"Oh, sure," Laurel said sarcastically, "baby-sitters are extravagant because that's for *your* pleasure. But expensive cigars for those two old ogres with the flashbulbs are okay because you want to make them happy. What are you bucking for, a halo? For God's sake, Elizabeth, don't you go out of your mind sitting in this house night after night?"

"Thanks to you, no." Elizabeth's tone was affectionate. Laurel had taken to spending one or two evenings a week at the Bethesda cottage. She always insisted on bringing something when she came to dinner—a small present for each child, a bottle of cologne for Mary, or a pint of gin for the martinis that she and Elizabeth enjoyed.

Seven months after the Christmas episode, the two women were sitting comfortably in deck chairs on the front lawn, sipping gin and tonics and chatting easily in the fading light of an early July evening. Elizabeth was discussing plans for Charlene's birthday, two days away.

"She'll be two," Elizabeth said. "I can't believe it. Of

course, she's really too young for a birthday party, but it would be fun to combine it with a Fourth of July celebration."

Laurel pretended sarcasm. "Why have a party at all? We could take her down to the Washington Monument and let her watch the fireworks display. If we don't say anything, she'll think all the hootin' and hollerin' is in her honor."

Elizabeth gave an appreciative chuckle. "You are such a tough lady, Miss Lane," she teased. "Don't try to kid me. You'll be the first one around with some far-too-expensive gift wrapped in red, white, and blue. You're a pushover for Charlene."

"All right," Laurel growled. "So I've got a favorite. Sue me."

"I can't blame you," Elizabeth said ruefully. "I'd just hoped it would be Ann."

"Look, Elizabeth, I love Ann. No, that's not really true. I like Ann. She won't let herself be loved."

"She admires you extravagantly."

"She tries to use me, Elizabeth, and you know it. Maybe it's terrible of me to talk this way to you about one of your brood, but Ann thinks she can wangle anything she wants out of an adult by being fawning and phony. It just doesn't work."

"I know. It only worked on her father."

"And Quigly's a good-looking kid but absolutely unfathomable. He scares me. I always wonder what he's thinking."

Elizabeth nodded sadly. The frank analysis did not offend her. "Isn't it strange, Laurel, how different they all are? It's as though I picked them up on three different street corners. Alan used to say that there's nothing wrong with a parent having a favorite child. I still don't agree with that. I do think it's wrong. But I'm afraid it's inescapably human."

Laurel tried to reassure her. "Well you don't have to worry about fostering any neuroses in this family. If you prefer one, you sure don't show it. They all get equal love and equal treatment from you. If you're acting, it's a damned good performance."

Before Elizabeth could reply, an approaching voice called out to them.

"Yoo-hoo! Are you there Elizabeth?" Marion Parrish-Parker was making her way down the road from the main house.

"Right here, Marion," Elizabeth answered. "Come join us for a drink."

"Oh, you have a guest," Marion said as she came near. "I'll come back another time."

"Don't be silly," Elizabeth said. "You know Laurel."

Marion seemed nervous. "Yes, of course. Nice to see you again."

The younger woman nodded.

Marion was still standing, uncertainly. It was clear that there was something on her mind, something she wanted to say privately to Elizabeth. Laurel picked up the cue.

"Would you two excuse me for a minute?" Laurel said. "I just remembered a call I have to make. To my old mother in Hong Kong."

Mrs. Parrish-Parker looked startled. "My dear, she's not going to call Hong Kong on your telephone, is she? Good heavens, that will cost the earth!"

Elizabeth laughed. "She was just making a joke, Marion. I think she got the idea that you have something to say to me."

Marion fidgeted. Finally she perched tentatively on the chair that Laurel had vacated. "As a matter of fact, Elizabeth, something has come up. Something very nice and yet perhaps not very nice. Oh, gracious, I might just as well come right out with it. I'm getting married!"

"But how wonderful!" Elizabeth said. "Who is he?"

"Dick Aimsley. Richard Aimsley. He's a retired broker. I've known him for years but we hadn't seen each other since, oh, I don't know, maybe 1929. Anyway, we ran into each other in Palm Beach this past winter. It's been one of those rediscovery things. We're not youngsters, and it seems like a good idea to spend our declining years watching the sun sink slowly over Worth Avenue."

Elizabeth was genuinely delighted. "I'm so happy for you, Marion! It's no good being alone."

"I know. And he's not marrying me for my money. He's twenty times richer than I, if you can imagine such a disgusting thing. He has a beautiful house in Palm Beach and a big apartment in New York. We'll divide our time between the two when we're not traveling. Isn't it ridiculous? I feel like a blushing virgin."

"It's marvelous, Marion. Really."

"Yes, of course it is. He could have picked some twenty-year-old. Most of those men do when they suddenly become widowers. I'm really a very fortunate woman." Marion suddenly looked troubled. "There's only one thing that might be bad about it. I won't be keeping this place. I'm putting it up for sale."

"I see," Elizabeth said slowly.

"You don't know how I hate to do this to you, dear, but there's just no point in my hanging on to a big establishment that we'll never occupy."

"Of course not. I understand."

"Naturally, I'll do everything I can to convince the new owners—whoever they are—that they should let you stay on. Though I suppose that strangers would want to charge you rent, even if they did. Let you stay on, I mean. Oh, damn it," Marion said, "I feel just terrible!"

Elizabeth hastened to comfort her. "Please don't. You've been wonderful to let me have this house for almost two years. You really saved my life. I don't know what I'd have done if you hadn't been so generous. I'm working now and I'll find another place. It's all right. Honestly."

Marion wanted to reassure herself as much as she did Elizabeth. "I'm sure it will be some time before we find a buyer. Dick and I are being married next month, but Lord knows when we'll get someone to take this rambling old monster off my hands. So you have time, my dear. And maybe the new owners will let you stay. There's always that chance."

Elizabeth nodded. Marion rose. "It's been wonderful having you here. So comforting to know that there's a friend nearby. I'm sorry to put this burden on you, but I know you'll come up with something. You're so marvelously self-sufficient. Well. Happy Independence Day, Elizabeth."

"Same to you, Marion. And all the luck in the world."

A few minutes later, Laurel peeked around the door. "All clear?" she asked.

"As crystal," Elizabeth said. The troubled tone belied the half-hearted quip.

"I smell disaster." Laurel resumed her seat. "Want to talk about it, or isn't it any of my damned business?"

For the first time since Charles had been her audience, Elizabeth felt free to speak openly about her problems. Holding back nothing, she told her whole story from the beginning, everything that had happened since the day she met Alan. It was uncharacteristic of her, this outpouring of the most intimate details of her life. But it felt good. There had never been another woman in whom she felt free to confide, and there is no replacement, she realized, for the sympathetic understanding of a good friend who can truly identify with such troubles. Neither woman was embarrassed by the story. Elizabeth told it simply, almost unemotionally, not asking for pity or praise. Laurel listened in attentive silence, lighting one cigarette after another, occasionally rising to refill her glass and Elizabeth's without interrupting the flow of words. Elizabeth spoke for nearly an hour and finished, at last, with Marion's disquieting announcement.

"Jesus Christ," Laurel said.

"It's a good time to call on him."

Laurel shook her head in amazement. "Jokes she makes," she said to no one in particular. "Practically out on the street with three kids and seventy bucks a week and she makes jokes!" she paused as a thought struck her. "Hey, something doesn't add up. You said you started at sixty and got a ten-dollar raise, right?"

"Right. Why?"

"Why indeed?" Laurel said. "I happen to know that the starting salary for your job is fifty."

"It is?" Elizabeth was surprised.

"You bet it is. So how come they paid a greenhorn like you more than the basic wage?"

Elizabeth had no idea what she was driving at. "I can't imagine why they did," she said. "Stu Preston distinctly told me that he had to keep within range, because of the other salaries in the department." She clapped her hand over her mouth. "Oh, good Lord, Laurel, I hope you're not upset! I didn't know I was being paid more than the other girls. Truly I didn't."

"Don't be a dope. Of course I'm not upset. None of the others would be, either. We don't have your responsibilities, for God's sake. No, that's not why I'm curious about your salary. I'm thinking it might give us a lead about a way out of this mess for you." Ignoring Elizabeth's puzzled expression, Laurel plunged on. "Think about it. Grace couldn't give you more money or it would show up on the books and some smartass cashier would spread the word. So, your extra pay must come from some off-the-record source. Don't you get it, dimwit? Preston must be anteing up out of his own pocket. He probably realized you couldn't live on less, even rent-free. Ergo, as we say in the Lane family, he's personally interested in your well-being."

Elizabeth was horrified. "You must be wrong. Why would he do such a thing? We're no more than friends, you know that. No, I can't believe that I'm taking charity from Stuart Preston. I could never look him in the eye again!"

"Will you stop with that New England conscience?" Laurel snapped. "Preston would miss ten dollars a week like I'd miss ten cents. Maybe less. Anyway, the hell with that.

Don't you see what this means? He's very fond of you. He's your way out of this housing mess."

Elizabeth looked at her as though she'd lost her mind. "What are you talking about? You're not suggesting that Stu Preston is going to give me an enormous raise, are you? Because that would be ridiculous. I don't deserve it and I'd never accept it. I'm terribly upset even about the ten dollars if your theory is right."

Laurel sighed. "For a bright lady, you can be awfully dense. Of course he can't give you a big raise. He couldn't even officially start you at a higher salary, remember? But he's got all the money in the world. He could lend you some of it. Straight business. With interest and all that. Hell's bells, Elizabeth, you're going to need cash to move and set up a new house. And you've already told me that you've just about gone through your inheritance. You have to hang on to the little you have left. Suppose one of the kids gets sick? You must keep some kind of reserve. Stu's the only answer. You can borrow from him. A few thousand dollars to tide you over."

"Now who's being dense?" Elizabeth asked. "How could I get a loan, even from Stu, without an ounce of collateral? And even if I got it, how would I ever repay it?"

Laurel looked deflated. "Maybe he'd keep you?"

Elizabeth laughed. "My dear, he has a marvelous wife and no interest in me that way at all. Besides, it isn't my style, even if the conditions were right. All I have left in the world is my independence. Don't ask me to let go of that, too."

"I wasn't being serious. Not *really* serious. I was just grasping at straws. Okay, forget his lily-white body and yours. I don't suppose you'd consider hitting that bastard Alan Whitman for some dough?"

"Not even if the idea were feasible," Elizabeth said firmly. "And it's not. From what I hear, he's dropped out of sight. The last that any of his friends heard he was driving a taxi in Baltimore and committing slow suicide on cheap wine. If anything, he's probably closer to starvation than I am."

"That's the only good news of the evening," Laurel said. "I hope he does starve. But you really don't, do you?"

"I'm angry with him. Outraged, if you want a stronger word. But I can't hate him, Laurel. He's sick and has been for years and years. In his defense, he tried to warn me away twice before I went, but I was so sure that I was strong enough for both of us. Well, I found out differently, so here I am. But do you know what *really* frightens me? I *think* that I've learned my lesson, but I'm such a born idiot that under a different guise I'd probably repeat the whole pattern all over again. How's that for the original Dumb Dora?"

"Oh, swell," Laurel said. "I'll make you one promise, unsolicited. If I see you starting on that path again, *ever*, I'll break every bone in your head!"

The mood lightened a little. "All right," Laurel went on, "since I haven't come up with a practical idea, what's the next step?"

"The next step this evening is dinner. There's a thought. Maybe I could get a job as a live-in cook. That would probably pay as much as a decorating editor and give us a roof over our heads to boot."

" 'Us' is right. Who's going to hire a cook with three kids?"

"True," Elizabeth admitted. "They hardly make servants' quarters like that any more, do they? I'd need a whole floor just for my tribe. Maybe I should get a job running a boardinghouse."

Laurel jumped to her feet. "My God, how could I be so dumb! Of course! That's it!"

Elizabeth stared at her. "What's it?"

"Not a *boarding*house, a *rooming* house! You buy a rooming house and run it while you still keep your job at *W and M*. It's perfect. Made to order. I even know the one you can buy!"

"You can't be serious."

"I was never more serious in my life." Laurel was bubbling with excitement. "Listen. Mrs. McBain—whom we irreverently call Lady MacBeth because she haunts the halls at night—wants to sell the rooming house I live in! She's had it on the market for three months. I think she's getting pretty desperate. Wants to go back to Ireland to live. Anyway, you probably could get it for a good price and it's a cinch to run. She only takes four so-called respectable roomers with good references. Each of us keeps our room like it's an apartment. I've even brought in a lot of my own furniture. All Mrs. McB. does is see that the halls are clean and supply fresh towels and sheets. She does it all with one maid. You could do the same with Mary on a fulltime basis. There's plenty of room for you and the kids on the first two floors. You don't need to be around during the day because all of us work, too. You'd live rent-free and make enough extra to pay off the house. How's that for a terrific setup?"

Elizabeth tried not to let Laurel's enthusiasm become contagious. Even so, it did sound like a workable solution. "You're utterly mad," she said unconvincingly. "Assuming I could handle such an undertaking, where would I get the money to buy the house?"

Laurel just looked at her.

"A loan." Elizabeth answered herself flatly. "From Stu Preston."

Laurel nodded.

"Do you really think I should take such a big chance?" Elizabeth asked. "And what about Stu? Will he go along with a calculated risk like this?"

"Why not?" Laurel asked blithely. "If you welsh on the deal he can always garnishee your salary for the next hundred years."

part IV

WASHINGTON, D.C.
1937-1944

Chapter 7

All that Kathleen McBain wanted in this life was to spend
the rest of her days in the little village outside of Dublin
where she'd met and married her Michael, God rest his soul.
They'd come a long way, she and Mike, since they'd landed,
poor Irish immigrants that they were, in the strange place
called Ellis Island in the harbor of New York City. Mike had
done well for himself, there was no doubt of that. He'd
started as a day laborer and worked like a dog until the
day he'd died five years ago. In the thirty-five years between,
Michael McBain had scrimped and saved to build a construction business of his own. It wasn't a big thing, mind you, but
it made a handy living. Handy enough to buy this piece of
property right in the middle of Washington, just a stone's
throw from grand places like the Mayflower Hotel. They'd
turned it into a boardinghouse ten years before, and Kathleen, who had always run it, continued to do so when she
became a widow. Now she was getting too old to be alone,
what with her arthritis and all, and she dreamed of returning
to the gentle land where what was left of her family still
lived.

All this she told Elizabeth when Laurel introduced the two

women next day. It was by way of saying why she had to have cash for the house and why she was making such a sacrifice price. "Fifteen thousand dollars is all I'm asking, dear," she said in the brogue she'd never lost. "Sure and it's worth twice the price. I know that. But these are hard times. People don't have much ready money. The good Lord knows that my Michael, may he rest in peace, would turn over in his grave if he knew what I was willing to let it go for! But I'm that anxious to get home, Mrs. Whitman. There's no life here for me without himself."

Inexperienced though she was, Elizabeth recognized that it was a good deal. The location was not the best; even four blocks from Connecticut Avenue one ran into lower-middle-class mixed neighborhoods like this. But it was no slum, and it was convenient for the working people who roomed there. Elizabeth could walk to the office. Even more importantly, she could be home in a matter of minutes if an emergency arose. The three-story house was unimaginative but substantial and roomy. She could have a bedroom for herself and Charlene on the first floor, along with a small sitting room, dining room, kitchen and bath. Ann and Quigly would each have a room on the second floor, where Laurel Lane lived. The three rooms on the third floor would, she hoped, continue to be occupied by the current trio of residents. There was, regrettably, no place for Mary Jackson to live in, but at least with this new source of income she could afford to pay Mary a decent wage, even have her sleep over in Ann's room from time to time. Maybe, Elizabeth thought hopefully, I'll be able to get out once in a while in the evening. She had not had a night away from home in nearly two years and she felt herself getting stale and uninteresting from lack of stimulating adult companionship.

All these thoughts raced through her mind while Kathleen McBain waited for her reaction. Laurel nudged her. "Bargain," she muttered under her breath. Elizabeth took a deep breath. She had never been good at horse trading.

"The house is very nice," she said, "but it's still a little more than I'd planned to pay. I presume the furniture is included in the price?"

Mrs. McBain looked hurt. "Oh, now, Mrs. Whitman, surely you don't expect me lovely furnishings to be included for such a poor sum! Why, this dining-room suite alone is worth a thousand dollars! To say nothing of the parlor! Oh, no, dear. The price is just for the house. Of course, seeing as how you're going to buy the property, I'd be ever so reasonable about what I'd ask for the beautiful things in it."

Elizabeth had to smile as she looked at "the beautiful things." A matched set of sofa and two chairs that looked as if they came from the cheapest store on Seventh Street. A hideous, heavy old oak dining table and six rickety chairs that Mrs. McBain must have picked up at the Salvation Army Thrift Shop. She had not carefully inspected the rest of the rooms, but she was willing to bet that Mrs. McBain couldn't get more than a thousand dollars for everything in the house if she tried to sell it. And yet if Elizabeth had to go out and replace all this, including beds, chairs and dressers, it would cost six times that much, even with careful shopping. At least she could refinish, slipcover, and paint this awful old stuff, ugly as it was.

"I'm sorry," she said. "If you'd consider including all the furniture, I might be able to offer you thirteen. Cash, of course." She was sure Kathleen would refuse. Instead, the old lady breathed a pathetic sigh.

"It's takin' advantage of me you are," she said, "but I'll accept your offer. Your friend drives a hard bargain, Laurel, me girl." Kathleen smiled impishly. "We simple Irishwomen are no match for an American lady with a good business head on her pretty shoulders."

Laurel cocked a sardonic eyebrow. "If I know you 'simple Irish,' Mrs. McB., you've just made a six-thousand-dollar profit after living ten years rent-free."

Her landlady looked pained. "You've never had a civil tongue in your head the four years I've known you. Saints knows why I should think you'd begin now! So there we are, Mrs. Whitman. All that's left is to draw up the bill of sale. The minute it's done I'll start me packin'."

"I'll try to call you later today and tell you when we can meet," Elizabeth said. "I would like to take occupancy as soon as possible, but I'll have to speak to my people about the money."

As they made their way down the front stairs, those familiar white stone steps, very like the ones the women of Baltimore washed every day of their lives, Laurel clutched Elizabeth's arm and giggled. " 'I'll have to speak to my people about the money.' " She mimicked Elizabeth's voice perfectly. "You are out of this world! If I didn't know better, I'd think you were on your way to your lawyer's to ask which of your gilt-edged securities you should cash in. That was the funniest thing I've ever seen."

Elizabeth was nervous and annoyed. "Funny for you, maybe. I'm scared out of my wits! Do you realize that I have just informally agreed to buy a whole damned three-story house and furniture and I haven't the faintest idea whether or not I can even *get* the money? Suppose Stu won't make the loan, Laurel? And if he does, what do I know about running a rooming house? I'm beginning to get cold feet. Maybe I should never have let you talk me into this."

Laurel stopped dead on the sidewalk. "Oh, no, you don't," she said. "You don't start turning the tables on me that way. All of a sudden *I'm* the improvident one in this team! Who the hell's been spending money on ballets instead of groceries? Who walked out of her marriage without a dime, and with three hungry mouths to feed? Who sat in a cottage last night and painted rosy pictures of how wonderful life would be when she got this bloody rooming house? I *suggested* this idea, sure. It just happens to be the first practical move you've made in two years. But I didn't talk you into it. You jumped at the idea. If you want to talk yourself out of it, that's your affair. Just don't use me as a scapegoat so that any time anything goes wrong in the future you can say 'I wish I hadn't let Laurel talk me into this.' That won't wash, Elizabeth. I won't buy it."

Laurel was angry. And everything she said was undeniably true. For a moment, panic at the enormity of the step she had committed herself to had simply overwhelmed Elizabet. Now she was sincerely apologetic. Laurel hadn't put a gun in Elizabeth's back, forcing her to buy a rooming house. Elizabeth had gotten more and more enthusiastic last evening, knowing instinctively that, mad as it was, it was going to work out. Just as she'd known she had to leave Alan, though she had nowhere to turn.

"I'm so lucky to have you around," she said finally. "Laurel, I'm sorry. What a nitwit I am! You're right, of course, about everything you said. Forgive me?"

"Oh, hell," Laurel said. "What's to forgive?"

Tension gone, they walked up to Dupont Circle where Preston had agreed to meet Elizabeth in his office. At the door of the building they parted.

"Wish me luck," Elizabeth said.

"What's thirteen thousand dollars to Preston?" Laurel said blithely. "He spends that on a new Rolls-Royce when his old one gets dirty." She gave Elizabeth a reassuring wink and strode off rapidly, her pleated skirt and sweater making her look, from the rear, like a sixteen-year-old. Elizabeth smiled, feeling suddenly confident and optimistic. Stu might think she was crazy, but he'd go along.

While he waited for his "protégée" to arrive, Preston reviewed the past eighteen months with almost complete satisfaction. His hunch, for it was no more than that, that Elizabeth would make a good decorating editor had paid off. Grace Edwards gave glowing reports of her, both as an employee and as a person. Stu had noted with interest that her by-line appeared as "Elizabeth Quigly." He did not know whether this was merely to keep her old crowd from moving in on her again or whether it meant that she had irrevocably cut the cord that held her to Alan Whitman. In any case, he approved of the move.

Preston had seen very little of Elizabeth in this period. He did not want to give her the feeling that he was looking over her shoulder. At least that was the explanation he tried to sell himself. Deep down, he knew that he had a more than friendly interest in this quiet woman. With the slightest encouragement, he could become personally entangled with her. He did not intend to give himself an opportunity. Instead, he watched her from a safe distance, glad that she had made friends with Laurel Lane, pleased that she had a safe, if not luxurious, place to live.

He was not a vindictive man, but he could not feel regret at the reports of Whitman's rapid descent to oblivion. Even a layman could see that Alan had a death wish. Stu might have felt pity for that if the man had not tried to drag innocent victims like Elizabeth into an early grave with him. From what he heard, Alan was no more than a bum at this point. It was not within the realm of possibility that he could ever make a comeback. Elizabeth should divorce him, Stu thought. Get him out of her system once and for all. He'd be glad to lend her the money, even arrange a leave of absence if she needed to spend six weeks in Reno. Not that he particularly wanted her to be free. That would only add to his temptation. But he felt that it was the right thing for her. It might even be what she wanted to see him about today. She had given no reason when she asked for the appointment.

To Preston, Elizabeth seemed more beautiful than ever as she walked into the office with the erect posture that made her look much taller than her five feet four. In spite of the two-year-old dress, she was distinguished and elegant, and her expression was radiant. With a sinking feeling, Stu thought that only love could make a woman have such an incandescent glow. Perhaps she had met someone and was here to tell him about it. His unhappy reaction annoyed him. Instead of being a dog in the manger, he should be delighted for her if this was the case. She was still young and desirable. What would be more natural than for her to find another man?

They greeted each other with the warmth of dear friends. Then Preston settled back in his chair and looked at her searchingly.

"I've never seen you looking better," he said. "Newspaper life seems to agree with you."

"I love it. It's the most exciting thing I've ever done."

"It seems to love you back, according to what I hear from Grace. She says you're a natural. I consider that a great tribute to my powers of perception, as well as a compliment to you."

Elizabeth smiled. For a moment, silence filled the room. "Stu," she said at last, "I have something very important to talk to you about. I know you're terribly busy, so I'll get right to it." Rapidly she explained about Marion's decision to sell the estate and then about her own desire to buy the rooming house from Mrs. McBain. "It wouldn't interfere with my job. I have a wonderful housekeeper who could look after things during the day. And it would solve a lot of problems beyond my own housing difficulties. The place is fully rented —Laurel Lane lives there, by the way—and the income would pay off the loan and eventually mean extra money for me." At the mention of "extra money," Elizabeth paused and frowned. She had almost forgotten Laurel's theory that Preston was making a personal contribution to her salary. Now she hesitated, wondering whether this was the moment to mention it. She decided it was.

"This is a bit awkward," Elizabeth said, "but speaking of extra money, I just discovered that I'm being paid ten dollars a week over the going rate for my job. It wouldn't be that you were adding that amount to my salary, would it?"

Preston feigned surprise. "Why should I?" he countered.

"Because you're a very nice man who knew I'd have a hard enough time making out even with the extra you provide."

He looked embarrassed. "You weren't supposed to know. Hell, it doesn't amount to a hill of beans, Elizabeth. Couldn't begin to repay you for all those wonderful meals I've had at your house. I hope you're not going to get all uppity about it. There are no strings attached, you know. I always planned that when you worked yourself up to a livable wage, I'd stop it. Thought of it as a small loan, just enough to help tide you over until you were on your feet. I really didn't want you to find out until that time. Knowing you, I knew you'd get some crazy idea that I was treating you like a help-less female. God knows you're anything but that."

He was so sincerely distressed and so obviously in earnest that Elizabeth lost her own embarrassment. "Thank you," she said simply. "It's dear of you. And I will consider it a loan, hopefully to be repaid one day and certainly to be stopped as soon as possible."

His relief was obvious. "Now about this other matter," Preston said. "I'm perfectly willing to lend you the money for the house. Straight business deal. Five per cent interest. But, Elizabeth, this is a big chunk you're biting off. Have you really given it enough thought? You have a job and three children to worry about. Add the burden of running a rooming house and you've got enough responsibilities for three women! Wouldn't it be a good idea to think it over for a few days? Maybe through the papers we can find you a place to live, something you can afford. There's time, I'm sure. Marion's right, you know. Unloading that white elephant won't be easy. You're bound to have a decent grace period before you have to move. And for all we know, the new owners may be perfectly happy to have you stay there for a nominal rent."

He made perfect sense. But there was this ridiculous, irrational feeling of rightness about the bold move that Elizabeth could neither explain nor deny. She smiled.

"Don't confuse me with the facts," she said. "It's probably crazy of me, Stu, but I just know this is the right move. I'm too much a creature of impulse, I suppose, but my whole life has been like this. As though I really don't control it at all. I guess I believe there's a Master Plan, really. Kismet, destiny, fate—whatever you want to call it. Things just seem to come to me when I need them. Like Marion's house. And the job you had waiting. And finding the rooming house through Laurel. Something pushed me toward these things. And something is pushing me now."

Preston, worried for her, spoke unthinkingly. "The same thing that pushed you toward Alan Whitman, I suppose?" His tone was rougher than he meant it to be.

She understood. "That, too," Elizabeth said. "You forget that without Alan I would never have had Ann and Quigly and Charlene."

He spread his hands in a gesture of good-natured defeat. "Okay. You win. But I insist upon one small practical decision before we shake on the deal. I'll send a good architect over to that house this afternoon. At least," he said with elaborate sarcasm, "we can be sure that termites aren't chew-

ing up the foundation and that the roof doesn't leak. Lovable
Mrs. McBain sounds like the kind of biddy who might de-
camp for Dublin and leave you with corroded water pipes
and an eighteen-ninety furnace. You will agree to that, I
assume?"

"Gratefully."

"Okay," Preston said. "If the house checks out, I'll have
the lawyers start drawing up the papers. How long-term a
loan do you want? Ten years? Twenty?"

"Ten should do it, I think. Four rooms will bring me two
hundred dollars a month income. Even figuring upkeep and
taxes, I should be able to pay you back in ten years."

"That's pretty tight," Stu said. "Of course, we'll hope your
salary will increase, but you're figuring too close, Elizabeth.
I'd think a twenty-year loan would be more realistic. Take
my advice. I know a little more about loans and mortgages
than you do." He looked at her keenly. "Wouldn't it be nice
to have a few bucks in your pocket for a change?"

Elizabeth smiled. "Yes. Very. I can't deny that. But you're
doing me a personal favor. I'd like to repay it as soon as I
possibly can."

"What personal favor? It's a straight business arrangement.
I'll be getting interest on my money, just like any other investment. And I'm not worried about your running out on
the deal. I expect you to be around for a long, long time."

Elizabeth's memory returned to 1924. "We have a government contract with a ten-year completion date," Alan
had said. "That's a lifetime!" the nineteen-year-old Elizabeth
had answered. Was that first meeting only thirteen years ago?
There had been a lifetime of joy and sadness, frustration and
fear crammed into those years. And here she was, agreeing
as though two decades were no more than two grains of sand
in the hourglass of her life. Stu expected her to be around
for a long, long time. She expected nothing. Or, perhaps
more correctly, anything.

"You're very generous," she said. "And I'm more grateful
than I can tell you. I wish there were some way I could
repay you. In more than money, I mean."

Coming from almost any other woman, Stu Preston would
have construed this as an open invitation. He knew Elizabeth
better. In spite of her exposure to worlds she had never
dreamed existed, she remained incredibly innocent. There
was no flirtatiousness in her offer. She had a directness and
an honesty that was unmistakable. It had brought her to
grief, this guileless offering of herself to other people. Probably, Stu thought, it always would.

He rose in a polite gesture of dismissal. "You'll cook me a good dinner in the new house, I hope," he said lightly. "That and your happiness are all the compensation I want."

"Except for the monthly loan payments," she teased.

"You'd better believe it," Preston said. "Those too."

Laurel didn't look in the least surprised when Elizabeth told her about the meeting. "I knew Preston would come through," she said airily. "Hell's bells, he takes that kind of money out of petty cash." Then she couldn't sustain her nonchalance. Exuberantly, she hugged her friend. "I'm so thrilled for you! It's going to make all the difference in your life. I don't know how you've stood it, cooped up in that godforsaken cottage! At least now you'll be able to enjoy a little social life in this town."

Elizabeth was amused. "I've enjoyed the social life of this town," she reminded her. "And I didn't find it such a barrel of laughs."

"Oh, that," Laurel scoffed. "Stuffed-shirt bureaucrats and cornball industrialists from Iowa. You call that a social life? Listen, chum, it's okay to have your name in the society columns and be one of two thousand people invited to a White House reception, but that's not where the real fun is."

"No? Where is it?"

"Break down and come out with my playmates and me and we'll show you."

Elizabeth smiled gratefully. "I'll think about it. What am I saying? I'll *dream* about it! But not for a little while, Laurel. I'm going to have my hands full with the house, assuming Stu's architect gives it the official blessing. And I want to stick pretty close to the kids right now. They're going to be uprooted again, the second time in two years. And just when I was hoping they were adjusting to Bethesda. Now it'll be another new place to live, a different school, strange playmates. It can't be easy for them. Ann and Quigly, I mean. Maybe even Charlene, young as she is, is going to feel a sense of displacement. I wouldn't want to leave them in the evenings for a while. Not even with Mary. But a few months from now maybe we'll talk about it. Fair enough?"

"It's progress, I guess. When will you hear from Stu?"

"In the next few days, I hope."

"Good. By the way, you'll like your other tenants. Betty Kaspar is frightfully grand for a lady who lives in a rooming house, but underneath she's real. And *very* funny. Amelia Neal is one of your harried, intense businesswoman types, but I think you'll take to each other. And Frank Bayard is sweet. Keeps very much to himself, but he's nice. All in all, it's a good group. You won't have any trouble with them. No wild parties and cops arriving in the middle of the night. Best of all, they pay their rent on time."

Elizabeth shook her head. "I still can't believe all this. Who'd ever imagine I'd end up running a rooming house? It's too absurd."

"Yeah," Laurel said, "and you without so much as an Irish brogue."

Within a week, satisfied that the house was structurally sound, Stu Preston gave Elizabeth a cashier's check for thirteen thousand dollars and his unqualified blessing. She gave him a personal note for the loan and an impulsive kiss on the cheek.

"You'll get back every penny, with interest," she promised.

A slightly flustered Preston brushed aside her reassurances. "I'm not worried about the money," he said. "It's a sound investment. The way things are beginning to boil in this town, property will boom in the next few years. Your house will be worth twice what you paid for it. That man in the White House isn't going to let this economy stand still. God knows I hate his guts, but he's an operator. You made a good deal, Elizabeth. You're a shrewd businesswoman."

The very idea amused her. "I'm shot with luck," she said. "I've even made a believer out of you. Or have I?"

"You have," he admitted. "I think you're a witch. A week ago I thought the idea of your holding a job, raising a pack of kids, and running a rooming house was the craziest idea since the bank moratorium. Now I have to admit that you and FDR both know what you're doing."

"That's fast company you put me in."

Preston grinned. "Well, the objectives are different but the personalities are equally irresistible."

Elizabeth was riding high. She could hardly wait to get her hands on the house and move her brood into this permanent-feeling nest. Her excitement was almost immediately diminished, though, by resistance from Ann. Her eleven-year-old had never had any affection for the Parrish-Parker cottage, but she had even less regard for this residence in a seedier part of the city. When Elizabeth took the two older children to see the house, Ann was openly disdainful. She was also embarrassed by the fact that her mother was going to become a landlady. Surprisingly status-conscious for her age, she equated the running of a rooming house with the lowliness of a charwoman. And in positive terms she said so. Elizabeth hated Ann's streak of pretension. For the hundredth time she silently blamed Alan. He had spoiled her so thoroughly in the first nine years of her life that this self-image of superiority probably could never be changed. Ann was still resisting her new life, and short of disillusioning her about her father, there was nothing Elizabeth could do about it.

In contrast to his silent disinterest when they moved to Bethesda, Quigly, too, was more outspoken in his criticism. He was two years older, now, of course, and correspondingly more aware of his surroundings. Aping Ann, he viewed the house, and particularly the busy street, with undisguised disgust.

"There's no place to play," he said. "I don't even see any kids around, except those colored ones down the block."

Elizabeth would cheerfully have hit one child with the other. Instead, she tried to remember how difficult it must be for them. They could not help feeling the effect of the change in their lives these past two years. It wasn't their fault, and it was her duty and her desire to make it up to them. How can I make them understand? she wondered. You can't, a realistic voice said. All you can do is live through each day and hope that time and maturity will solve the problem. She tried gently to attack each of their objections.

"Ann, dear, think of the advantages of living right in the city," she said convincingly. "You can go to the movies on Saturday, all by yourself. There's one right in the next block. And you can even look around in the stores at all the pretty clothes. Now you couldn't do that in Bethesda, could you?"

Her forced cheerfulness did seem to make a slight impression. At the mention of her two favorite pastimes, Ann's face brightened a little. Then the pout returned. "What about school?"

"You'll go to grade school very close to here."

Ann looked down the street at the playing children Quigly had mentioned. "Will there be niggers in my class?"

Hating herself, Elizabeth got angry again. "I warned you about that word before, Ann, and I don't intend to warn you again! As a matter of fact, colored children have their own schools, but it might improve your Christian spirit if they didn't!" She felt the blood rushing to her face. "As for you, Quigly Whitman, you'll play in the schoolyard just as all the other children do. Very few boys, I daresay, have had the run of the woods the way you have. You're both very selfish, uncooperative children and at this moment I don't like either of you very well!"

"I know," Ann said coldly. "The only one you like is Charlene."

For the first and only time in her life, Elizabeth smacked her daughter hard across the face. Ann's eyes opened wide, but she did not cry. It was Elizabeth who burst into tears of remorse.

"Oh, Ann, I'm so sorry, darling! Please forgive me." She reached out her arms. Deliberately, Ann walked out of the room. Quigly scuffed his toe into the well-worn carpet, not looking at his mother. In a moment he followed Ann. Elizabeth looked out of the window. They were sitting like rigid little statues on the top step of the stoop. Their backs were turned away from her. She sank into one of Mrs. McBain's hideous "easy chairs" and buried her head in her hands. Suddenly she saw herself and her house as her children saw them: a middle-class boardinghouse keeper in a shabby setting. It seemed ugly and futile and frighteningly lonely.

Laurel found her there an hour later when she came breezily into the living room.

"Hey, what's with the bookends out front? I couldn't even get a hello out of those kids when I came in. And why the tears? That's a great way to celebrate your new acquisition, I must say!"

Elizabeth tried to smile. "Let's just say that Ann and Quigly aren't exactly overjoyed with the house or the neighborhood. In fact, they're terribly upset."

"Well, now," Laurel said sarcastically, "isn't that just too bad. What would they have preferred—Blair House? I'll have to break the news to them that that's reserved for visiting heads of state. I know they're your own flesh and blood, Elizabeth, but they're goddamned inconsiderate. And you know what? It's your fault, kiddo."

The last words came as a jolt. *"My* fault? Now, look, Laurel, I know I've been directly responsible for the upheaval in their lives these last years, but Lord knows I've tried to do everything I can to make them happy and secure. I'm not looking for any bouquets, but the fact that they're spoiled and selfish is something I'm not responsible for. I've been trying to knock it out of them. I've done everything in my power for them. Maybe it hasn't been enough to compensate for what I did to them in the first place, taking them away from their father, I mean. But damn it, I have made them the focus of my life!"

"Exactly," Laurel said. "And your guilts have given them exactly the weapon they needed to punish you. You've been so busy trying to make everything up to them that you've only encouraged their feeling that they've been badly used. You're so bloody patient and understanding that you let yourself be used as a doormat by those little fiends. Listen, they're damned lucky to have a mother like you. Are you going to spend the rest of your life apologizing to them for picking up the pieces that their rotten father was responsible for in the first place? How about thinking kindly of yourself for a change? This mea culpa crap isn't going to cut any ice with those kids. I know you'll never tell them the truth about Alan, and you're right. But for God's sake will you stop this self-flagellation? I might remind you that there's only one St. Elizabeth in Washington—and it's a mental institution!"

In spite of her bewilderment, Elizabeth had to smile. Then she sobered. "Do you really think that's the way it is?" she asked. "Have I encouraged their willfulness by the guilt feelings I have?"

"I'm no psychiatrist, but that's sure the way it looks to an outsider." Laurel's tone softened. "I didn't mean to be so hard on you, but when I saw those self-righteous faces outside and your devastated one in here, I couldn't hold back any longer. I hope I haven't upset you. It's just that, Jesus, you've got a right to your life, too! When they grow up they'll have theirs. Maybe in twenty years or so they'll understand all you tried to do for them, but what they need right now is a good whipping!"

"Would you settle for a good slap in the face?" Elizabeth asked wryly. "Because that's what I just delivered to Ann."

"Hallelujah! So that accounts for my icy reception! Maybe there's hope for you yet."

"I feel rotten about it."

"No doubt. You would. But I'll give odds that it was not unprovoked. In fact, it must have been a lulu to make you lose control."

"But I've never hit any of them before. I don't believe in that kind of punishment. It's crude and ugly. Maybe I *am* beginning to behave like a landlady."

"Would that be a direct quote from your darling daughter?"

"No. Not direct. By implication, maybe. Laurel, she really is dreadfully unhappy. I don't know what to do about it."

Her friend sighed. "Here we go again," she said. "Be realistic. What's so terrible about having a mother who's able to buy a house big enough to take in roomers? Call them 'paying guests' if that's easier on your sensibilities. You've been damned clever to manage it. And if that fact can't be grasped by an adolescent despot, then it's just tough you-know-what. Holy cow, you're the only woman in the world who doesn't seem to know that the first law is self-preservation. When are you going to get wise?"

Elizabeth was calmer now. Laurel was good for her. The wisecracking, tough attitude was all a cover-up. Underneath there was sympathy and common sense. Elizabeth clung to the reassurance with thankfulness. For one who had never encountered problems like her own, Laurel accurately identified with the self-recrimination and anxiety that plagued Elizabeth. There was always tenderness in her blunt statements, understanding in her intelligent analysis. Mentally, Elizabeth added the friendship of Laurel to her rather limited list of blessings.

Buying the rooming house turned out to be more than an easing of her financial problems. In a slightly removed but pleasant way, it also brought Elizabeth back into much-needed daily contact with people. Her job, of course, had this virtue as well. But it was fun to come home to a house that seemed alive, even when all the occupants were not visible.

The roomers were much as Laurel had briefly described them. Betty Kaspar, a divorcee in her fifties, was, indeed, quite "grand" on the surface, but it was only an act that went with her job as directrice of the Della Dimitri Salon on Connecticut Avenue. The salon, which Elizabeth knew from the old days, was a plush beauty emporium which provided every body-pampering service from exercise to eyebrow-plucking, all at vast cost. As its manager, Betty represented the great Della herself, and in this role she had to, in Laurel's words, "out-snoot the snooty." She dressed always in black from head to toe, as did Mme. Dimitri. And, in the manner of the owner who resided in New York, Miss Kaspar maintained an attitude of superiority which bordered on condescension. The clients ate it up.

Often in the evening Laurel and Betty would join Elizabeth in her tiny sitting room on the first floor, and Betty would have tears of laughter rolling down the faces of the other two as she recited some of the outrageous goings-on in the imposing salon.

"The only way to handle these vain old battle-axes is to

intimidate the hell out of them," Betty confided. "Like today. We have twenty fat ladies enrolled in a reducing course right now, and every morning I line them up for 'inspection' before they start being pummeled and pounded to death. They're supposed to be on a strict diet when they're off the reservation, but of course they cheat like crazy. Well, this morning I just took a wild chance and pounced on Mrs. Clarence Kidlington, who looked very guilty to me. I stared that fat old cow in the eye and said, 'Mrs. Kidlington, I have a strange feeling that you had a *cocktail before dinner last night!*' It was just a guess, but my God, she came apart at the seams. Stammered and blubbered about how it was her husband's birthday and apologized like a schoolgirl. I just kept glaring at her with my famous accusatory look. It really shook up the whole class."

"Aren't women the damnedest creatures?" Laurel said. "They pay five hundred bucks for the privilege of having you give them holy hell."

"Well, we do more than that," Betty said defensively. "We really do get results. They always lose weight."

"Sure," Laurel laughed. "Who wouldn't? They spend the first week of the course on a diet of milk of magnesia. Elizabeth, I must take you to one of Betty's graduations. You won't believe it. The women who finish the make-over course get all dressed up—in new bathing suits. With shoulder corsages, yet! Then they actually participate in a graduation ceremony. It's *hysterical*. There's an audience of family and friends, all applauding like crazy because Big Bertha shed twenty pounds. And the funniest part is to see the fat incoming class in their sweatbands and baggy bloomers, sitting on the floor along the wall, looking pathetic and envious. Some day I'm going to write that performance the way it *really* is, not the glamorous way we report it in *Wife and Mother.*"

"You do and I'll kill you," Betty said. "What's worse, I'll take our advertising out of your silly paper."

It was good to laugh again. Good to forget unpaid bills and ungovernable children and even her own untouched body. It had been more than two years since Elizabeth had made love. She could, she supposed, go along this way forever. Nuns did. But her healthy body enjoyed sex, missed it. Until the very end, she and Alan had had a satisfying physical union. It was the only one she'd ever known, but whatever else he was, she was sure that her husband was a skillful lover.

No replacement for him, in this or any other area, had

even approached her life since the day she left Georgetown. She sensed that she could have some sort of an affair with Preston if she made the slightest effort. This she did not intend to do. The fact that they were both married was not the prime deterrent. In spite of the "saintly" accusations leveled at her by Laurel, Elizabeth was a realist. She was sure that Stu had his little extramarital expeditions and that they posed no threat to Martha Preston. Her rejection of the idea was influenced more by the fact that he was both her employer and her benefactor. She might easily have taken up with some other married man in this period of insecurity, but Stu was out of the question. He was already too much involved in her life.

The only other man even remotely close to her was her only male roomer, Frank Bayard, who wrote a Washington column for a Cincinnati newspaper. He was an attractive man, a few years younger than Elizabeth, and he had made no attempt to conceal his admiration when they first met. "Things are looking up," he said when Laurel introduced them. "Ireland isn't the only place that has gained by Mrs. McBain's departure. Nobody in Ohio will believe that I rent a room from a lady who looks like a movie star. Okay if I extend my stay another forty or fifty years?"

Elizabeth enjoyed the banter. "Sorry, Mr. Bayard, we'll have to take it one year at a time. I'm expecting a call from Hollywood any day now. Renting rooms is simply my avocation between engagements."

He pretended sadness. "The story of my life," he said. "Every beautiful woman I meet is far beyond the reach of a poor newspaper stringer. Oh, well. Back to the girls in the typing pool."

She did not see much of Frank. He checked into her quarters once a month to pay his rent, usually staying long enough to have a sociable drink. But beyond that, Bayard was not really interested in Elizabeth. Nor, for that matter, did she give any serious thought to this pleasant, busy young man. She was happy to have him as a roomer. He was there only to sleep. He came and went quickly to his room on the third floor. Even Betty Kaspar and Amelia Neal, who lived on either side of him, seldom saw Frank or heard him through the solid walls of the house.

Occasionally, Amelia joined Betty, Laurel, and Elizabeth for a pleasant evening of conversation. Like Betty, Amelia Neal had a demanding job. She was the assistant buyer of better dresses at Garfinckel's, Washington's biggest and smartest specialty store. Amelia had worked as a buyer before her marriage to Milton Neal, and after his sudden and untimely death she returned to her career, both for the money and the activity which she thoroughly enjoyed. Amelia was only in her early forties, but she was adamant about the fact that she'd never marry again.

"Not that I didn't enjoy being Milton's wife," she said one night. "He was what my mother calls a 'good provider.' So much so that he made me give up my job when I didn't want to. But I wouldn't do it for any other guy. I *love* working. Isn't that weird? I get a kick out of seeing things sell, especially the few things I'm allowed to buy for the store. I can't wait for my boss to retire so I can really be a big wheel on Seventh Avenue! Assistants don't get much notice. You have to be the buyer with the big pencil. That's when those hoity-toity New York designers really shape up. They know they're at your mercy."

"You're power-mad," Betty Kaspar said.

"Listen who's talking," Amelia answered. "Everybody knows that Joe Kaspar planned to name the Della Dimitri Salon as the corespondent in his petition for divorce."

The words were sharp but the attitude was completely friendly. What an odd lot we are, Elizabeth thought. An unmarried twenty-five-year-old newspaper writer frantic for fun and excitement; a fortyish retailer who dreams of being president of Lord & Taylor; a salon directrice in her fifties who's part slave driver and part prima donna. And then there's me, Elizabeth Whitman *née* Quigly, a lady with two last names and three quite separate and distinct lives, none of which feels entirely comfortable.

As it so often did, a vision of Charles Quigly came into her mind. What if he could see her now? She had no doubt what his troubled reaction would have been. "Come home to the people who love you," Charles would have said. She wondered curiously what her answer would have been.

As though the good Lord knew she needed a respite from upheaval, the next three years of Elizabeth's life were soothingly unremarkable. She found, to her relief, that she could handle the various facets of her life without serious neglect to any. Her job on the paper got easier as she became more confident in it. There were annual raises of ten dollars. Now she earned a hundred dollars a week, a quite respectable salary in 1941. Preston had not yet begun to subtract his donation. She mentioned it to him once but he dismissed the idea.

"I'll let you know when I consider you've reached a living

wage," he said. "Besides, I pick up more than that playing gin rummy with a bunch of patsys at the club every week."

A little ashamed of herself, she did not press him. Her income had increased but so had her expenses. Ann was fifteen years old and in high school. She needed more money for clothes and modest entertainment. Quigly, too, was entitled to a little pocket money, and his wardrobe was a constant drain, for he was growing rapidly and it seemed to Elizabeth that no sooner had she bought him a new pair of pants or shoes than he no longer fit into them. Even Charlene, a cheerful cricket of a child, had to be properly dressed and equipped for first grade.

Elizabeth kept her own expenditures at a minimum. Still, she could not do her job without appearing reasonably well dressed. She was making a name for herself in the decorating field, and even if she had not enjoyed them she would still have had to attend the various cocktail parties and luncheons given by local interior decorators and visiting celebrities from New York, Chicago, and the West Coast.

On top of all this, she felt duty-bound to increase the wages of the eternally faithful Mary Jackson. And she still insisted, despite the resistance of the two older children, on taking her brood to the few plays and concerts that Washington offered.

She also, during this period, began to go out occasionally with Laurel and her "playmates," Harry Thornton and Barney Nash, respectively the drama critic and the nightclub editor of the *Courier*. The "terrible trio," as they called themselves, covered activities in the local nightclubs and hotels, and attended Washington's one legitimate theater, the National. Their excursions were really assignments for either Harry or Barney, but they conveniently expanded to provide free evenings for the four of them. They became, in Harry's words, the "quixotic quartet," dining and dancing at places like the Russian Troika, the faux Spanish Madrillon, and the romantic Shoreham Hotel terrace.

With it all, there was no romance involved. They were simply four good friends. Or, more accurately, four "newspapermen" getting material for their theater or nightclub columns.

Elizabeth did not join them on every excursion. Even though Mary was willing to baby-sit whenever asked, Elizabeth still felt the need to spend as much time as possible with her children. Besides, it was expensive for her to pay Mary for this extra time and she was reluctant to do it too often. But when she did go, she had a marvelous time. She got to see all the new plays that had their tryouts in Washington, ate in restaurants where Alan had never taken her, and, most of all, felt more relaxed and carefree than she had in a long while.

"See?" Laurel said when they got home late one night, giggling like schoolgirls over the antics of the evening. "I told you it would do you a world of good to get out once in a while. At your age and with your looks, it's about time you stopped acting like Whistler's mother."

Elizabeth couldn't deny it. The evenings were fun, mostly because Harry and Barney delighted in being outrageous. That particular night they had dined in a new Hungarian restaurant on Dupont Circle where the service was terrible. After waiting twenty minutes for someone to take their drink order, Barney went out into the lobby and called the restaurant on the pay phone. When it answered, he said, "My friends and I are seated at a table for four near the bandstand and we'd appreciate it very much if you'd send over a waiter." The manager had nearly had a stroke, especially when he realized that he'd incurred the displeasure of the working press.

The camaraderie of the quartet was a delight to Elizabeth. It was all so easy, so undemanding. It did not even trouble her that "legally" she was not free to go out with other men. She no longer felt married. Not that it would have mattered in this group. Whatever romantic adventures Harry and Barney had were conducted with women other than Laurel and herself. "The girls" were more likely to see a drunken Barney Nash to his front door than to worry about his making amorous advances to either of them. It was the same with Harry. Sometimes in the middle of the evening the drama critic would simply disappear without explanation, leaving his three companions to continue their rounds without him. They all did a bit of drinking, Elizabeth slightly less than others, but still consuming her share and joining in the bright banter and nonsense that went on around her.

Sometimes when she was alone she thought of Alan and wondered about his life. It must be a strange one. Even stranger than her own. At least she had some friends, some security. Best of all, she had her children. Alan, she feared, had nothing but a make-believe world.

It was strange. One evening Alan occupied her thoughts so intensely that he seemed to be almost in the room with her. Next morning at the office she found on her desk a letter with his name and return address, a post-office box in Memphis, Tennessee. The effect was like a physical shock.

Her knees began to tremble and her hands shook so violently that she had to wait a moment before she could slit open the envelope. When she did, she pulled out a letter that seemed to quiver of its own will. She spread it flat on the desk. It was Alan's familiar script, but more like an old man's version of it. The words, though loosely strung together, were decipherable, and though the tone was erratic, it was coherent, in a weird way. It was quite a long letter.

Elizabeth, I am sending this to you at the newspaper since I imagine there could be only one Elizabeth Quigly and I do not know where you live. I hope it reaches you, as it is of utmost importance to me.

Since you so selfishly abandoned your marriage and your responsibilities as a wife, I have had no interest in finding you. I could have, if I had wanted to. But I did not wish to and I never shall confront you. I have the right but not the desire to make you face your own terrible, heedless actions. I know God will punish you. That is not for me to do. You deprived me of my rightful role as a father, just as you destroyed me through your relentless domination and demands. You will suffer for this, as I have suffered.

I have been very ill and very despondent. Those who conspired with you to deprive me of my livelihood have seen to it that I could not find work suitable to my ability. I am sure you do not care about any of this. You cared only about trapping me, from the day we met. It has taken me sixteen long, terrible years to get partially free from that trap. Now I wish to be entirely free of it and you.

Providence somehow directed me to this peaceful city where I have been blessed to meet a woman who cares more for me than she does for money, or power or even for herself. She has sheltered me, nursed me through my illness and now I wish to repay her by giving her my name as well as my devotion.

Since I have been a resident here for two years, I am qualified to apply for a divorce on the grounds of your desertion. This I plan to do immediately. My lawyer is sending you the papers to sign. You will be notified when the divorce is final.

Alan.

Incredulous, Elizabeth had read the letter twice again. It had a strange overtone of madness with its piety and its distorted accusations, as though the writer believed himself to be the innocent injured party. There was only one recognizable quality in these strange words—Alan's complete absorption with himself. He had never once asked about the children's health and well-being. His only reference to them, slight as it was, was the charge that she had deprived him of his rightful role as a father. But thank God there was no request to see them or—unthinkable idea—to demand that they spend time with him and his intended bride. Poor Ann, Elizabeth thought suddenly. She would be destroyed if she knew that her still-idolized father never so much as mentioned her name in this first communiqué in five years.

Elizabeth turned to a bulky envelope which had arrived in the same mail. It contained a formal letter from a Memphis attorney, stating that he had been retained by Mr. Whitman to institute divorce proceedings, citing her desertion as grounds for the suit. There were documents enclosed for her signature.

For a few moments Elizabeth hesitated, allowing a flood of mixed emotions to wash over her. She wanted a divorce and this easy method was a stroke of good fortune. It solved everything. It probably would cost her nothing in time or money. The only disagreeable part was allowing herself to be painted as the guilty party. Yet technically even that was true. No matter how compelling the reasons, she *had* deserted Alan. The causes for her desertion were not, in this case, significant. The grounds would not even be a lie, and, for that matter, who would ever know which one of them had finally brought suit? There was absolutely no reason for her not to sign immediately. Still, she could not bring herself to write "Elizabeth Quigly Whitman" on the line the lawyer had indicated with a penciled "x." There was something sad and final about it all. Though it had been a long time since even the pretense of a marriage existed, this man had been her husband, her one and only lover. There was something indecent about the fact that it could be wiped out with three quickly written names on a dotted line.

In the end, of course, she signed. She considered writing to Alan, at least telling him about the children and wishing him well in his second marriage. Then she dismissed the idea. No good could come of any further contact. She was sure she was not dealing with a rational man. Resolutely, she sealed and stamped the envelope addressed to the lawyer. Until she received the final papers, she decided, she would not mention any of this to anyone. Still, she was curious. What was Alan doing in Memphis? And who was this woman whom he described in almost reverent terms? Elizabeth admitted to herself that she would love to know the answers to both those questions.

Idly, she wandered into Grace Edwards' office. "Ask you something?" Elizabeth said.

Grace looked up from her typewriter. "Shoot."

Elizabeth didn't know how to begin. Finally, overriding her intentions of a moment earlier, she told her boss about the letter from Alan and the papers sent for her to sign. "I was wondering whether I should be represented by a lawyer, even though I don't contest the divorce. Would it be an awful nuisance for you to ask Harvey about it tonight before I mail the papers? Maybe if I do need legal counsel he could recommend someone."

"No trouble at all. I imagine you probably should see someone here, even if you don't actually need anybody appearing for you in Memphis. It's probably just a matter of Harvey writing a letter. I'm sure he'd be glad to do it for you himself. I'll let you know tomorrow."

"Thanks very much, Grace. By the way, I'd rather not have this mentioned until it's all signed, sealed, and delivered. In the office, I mean."

"Don't blame you. You're glad about it, though, aren't you?"

"Yes," Elizabeth said, "I'm glad. But it's a funny thing, I feel a little teary at the same time. I guess there's a kind of wrench about a divorce, no matter how much you want it. It's a kind of hollow feeling. Ridiculous, but it's there all the same. And there's something else that I find even more surprising. I'd give a lot to know if Alan is okay."

"That's only human," Grace said. "I'll bet you'd also like to know whom he's going to marry, wouldn't you?"

Elizabeth actually blushed. "I'm ashamed to tell you that I would. Isn't that awful?"

"No," Grace said, "that's female."

The next day, Grace reported that Harvey would call Elizabeth, get a few details, and write a letter to the lawyer in Memphis. "Nothing to it. You don't even need personal representation. I took it on myself to ask my darling husband to do something else, too. He's going to try to find out the answers to those two questions that bother you."

"You shouldn't have troubled him, Grace. I can live without knowing."

"Maybe *you* can, but I can't. Don't worry, good old Harve will check through the firm's office in Memphis or Nashville or wherever the hell they have an outpost in that area. He'll get us the dope."

Within a week, Harvey Edwards had compiled a modest but amazing dossier. Alan Whitman was working as a bartender in a "private club" in Memphis which insiders knew to be a well-run brothel. His "intended," a red-haired lady of sixty, owned the place and managed it as well. To put it bluntly, she was the most famous madam in Memphis. She was also a fire-breathing, off-hours evangelist.

Chapter 8

When the divorce papers were mailed to Elizabeth a few weeks later, a thick envelope addressed in a strong, flamboyant hand was included. In it was a letter from Alan's new wife.

Dear Mrs. Whitman, It seems funny to be writing to somebody with that name when I'm not even used to being called that myself yet. Alan would be mad at me for writing to you at all. I guess you know he's got a pretty quick temper sometimes, but I decided to do it anyhow because the way I look at it, whatever else we are, we're two women who have something in common. Or I guess I should say *someone*.

Anyway, in these past months since Alan and I knew we wanted to get married, I've been trying to think how I'd feel if I was in your shoes. With three kids and all, you must have loved each other once (ha ha) and I thought the decent thing would be to let you know about him. I know *I'd* want to know, even if I didn't love him any more.

There's no use making any bones about it because you'd probably find out sooner or later. I met Alan about a year and a half ago when he came into my club looking for a drink and a woman. I run Sue-Ann's Place in Memphis which provides entertainment for gentlemen. Maybe that will shock you like it shocks a lot of people around here, but I'll tell you what I believe. It seems to me that the Lord didn't mean men to be without female companionship. If they haven't got that at home, then it's better that they get it in clean, decent surroundings than go out and find some tramp who'll give them a disease or something. You'd be surprised how many people agree with me. Even politicians.

I know you come from a high-class family and your father was a professor, but maybe you can understand how somebody like Alan would end up with somebody like me. You see, he feels like he's better than I am. And he is. Not that he'd ever *say* so, but I know he *thinks* it, and that's okay. It's good for a man to feel superior, especially somebody like Alan who doesn't have too much faith in himself. I figured that out almost the minute I met him at the House.

As soon as he came in, I knew he had class. The average person sure wouldn't have guessed it by looking at him. He looked like a bum. He needed a shave and his clothes were all beat up and you could see that he was sick from all the drinking. But the way he talked and acted made me know right away that he'd been somebody once. When you're in my business you can tell the real gents from the tinhorns, no matter how they look. So I struck up a conversation and I was right. I guess he was the loneliest man I ever met.

The rest just happened. I'd been a widow for years—I'm older than Alan, by the way—and I sure never planned on getting married again. But that's the way he wanted it and it's fine with me, though I'd stick to him one way or the other. Who'd ever have thought that little Sue-Ann Temple from the wrong side of Memphis would get a man who'd known the President of the United States? I'm not kidding myself that he's in love with me. Not the way he was with you, I guess. But I think I'm better for him than you were, no offense intended. I think in his way he does feel some love for me. Maybe it's just that he's grateful. He was real sick for a long time. Something with his liver, the doctor said. But he's pretty good now, and he likes his job tending bar. Of course he's not supposed to drink but he does. I guess nobody can cure him of that. Still, it's like he's drinking at home, so at least I can keep an eye on him most of the time without giving him the feeling that he's being watched. He hates that.

There's just one thing more. He showed me the letter he sent you and I thought that if I'd gotten a letter like that I'd wonder why he hadn't asked about his children, particularly Ann who I guess you know is his favorite. He really does want to know about them, but he's too proud to ask. I don't expect you to let Ann come here to visit, but could you send pictures of her and the others? Alan will be furious with me for asking, but I don't care. I know it's the one thing that he'd like to have.

I've just read over what I wrote, Mrs. Whitman, and I don't take back any of it, but I guess there's no use kidding you the way I kind of tried to do. Alan is still sick. The doctor doesn't think he can last too much longer, specially since he won't stop drinking. Maybe that had something to do with us getting married, the idea that he might die soon, I mean. You see, I'm kind of a nut on religion which probably seems funny to you because of the business I'm in. But I've talked to Alan a lot about the mercy of God and the need to make amends for any wrongdoing. I think he wanted to make it all right with God for me before he goes. He doesn't realize that the way I look at it, I'm not a sinner in the eyes of the Lord. Just between us, I don't imagine you are either, but Alan hasn't got to the point where he can forgive you. I don't make any judgment, of course, because I've only heard his side, but I do know men. Some of them are pretty hard for a lady like you to understand.

Excuse me for going on so long. You can tell I'm a preacher in my spare time can't you (ha ha)? I hope you'll accept this letter in the spirit I send it in and most of all that you'll send the pictures to Alan. (I won't show him this, of course.)

Very truly yours,
Sue-Ann Temple Whitman

P.S. Funny that Ann should be part of my name, too, isn't it?

Elizabeth felt a sense of sympathy mixed with relief as she put down the multipaged letter. Sympathy at the knowledge that Alan was going to die; relief that he was in the hands of this remarkably secure and understanding woman. How odd that Alan's endless pursuit of prostitutes had led him finally to one who was such a curious combination of piety, realism, and extraordinary sensitivity. Elizabeth felt no shock or jealousy. Certainly not grief in the way she had experienced it when she knew Charles Quigly was going to die. Alan had hurt her too much for any vestige of love or possessiveness to remain. She regretted the thought of his death as she did that of any human being, but she could not pretend real sadness. It had been coming for so long, slowly, inexorably.

Rising from her desk, she went to the photo lab. Chuck Simmons was on duty.

"Hi," Elizabeth said, "could you use a few extra bucks?"

"Could Stu Preston use a Pulitzer Prize? Sure, how do I get 'em?"

"By coming to my house tomorrow night and taking some pictures of my kids. I'd like one group shot of the three and singles of each of them."

"Why not? How many sets of prints do you need?"

"Just two," Elizabeth said slowly. She'd keep one set for herself. Peculiar. She'd never thought of doing it before.

On the morning of December 7, when the Japanese changed the lives of every American man, woman and child, Elizabeth was almost shamefully untouched. She had no husband or father or brother to be physically threatened by what FDR called "a day that will live in infamy." She thanked God privately that her son was only thirteen, though his tall, muscular build made him look at least three years older. She listened with remote sadness as Barney Nash made hollow, flippant remarks about the inevitability of being drafted. Harry Thornton would not be called, in all probability. The drama critic would be classified 4-F because of poor vision. He made a weak, almost apologetic joke about it.

"I wasn't born half blind," Harry kidded. "I got beat up by an actress who didn't like the blistering review I gave her. Lord love that Amazonian ham! If she ever makes a comeback I'll give her a rave!" Harry fooled no one with his nonsense. His peers at the paper began to vanish methodically and, much as he didn't want to go to war, he felt embarrassed to be left behind.

Within two months, with many of the men gone, Grace Edwards was pressed into service on the news desk of the *Courier* and Laurel was made editor of *Wife and Mother*. Pleased for her, Elizabeth gave a little dinner party, inviting the roomers and the other two members of the Quixotic Quartet. With her release from Alan, Elizabeth now felt really free to join them more often in their after-dark Washington revels. With a completely free mind, she could wholeheartedly enjoy every minute of their nonsense, their unconcealed admiration of each other and of her. It was fun to be with these quick-witted, amusing people who were never at a loss for laughter. Sadly, the war would soon change all that. Washington would be crowded to the limits of its small-town facilities. Nightclubs, restaurants, and hotels would boom. But there would never again be the feeling of easy familiarity, as though the pleasure-seekers of the city belonged to one small, exclusive fraternity. Now their favorite haunts would hold more new faces than familiar ones, and somehow that would take much of the joy out of it all, even, Elizabeth thought, if one still had the heart for such frivolous pursuits.

Frank Bayard chose the middle of Elizabeth's dinner party to make his important announcement. "Fellow inmates and friends," he said, rising to his feet, "may I have your attention, please? I should like to propose a toast. To Elizabeth Quigly, the Elsa Maxwell of paying guest society!" His compliment was enthusiastically applauded. "And," Frank continued, "to the sincere hope that she will find room for me when I return from the wars!"

There was a stunned silence. Finally, Laurel spoke.

"You've been drafted," she said flatly.

Frank shook his head. "Not I, my lovely roofmate. You're talking to Frank Bayard, big-time war correspondent. That's right. The moguls in the head office have decided that any two-bit stringer can cover Washington. What the *Inquirer* needs is Their Man in Action. You are looking at Cincinnati's answer to Ernie Pyle. Ain't that a kick in the head? I went out today and bought an authentic trenchcoat. I may file lousy stories from the front, but I'll sure as hell look authentic doing it!"

Elizabeth looked at him with affection. "That's wonderful, Frank. It's a great opportunity and we're so proud and happy for you."

Frank smiled cynically. "Well, bombs don't understand that they're not supposed to knock off newspapermen," he said, "but the survival rate has got to be better than an infantryman's. And the image is hot stuff. What female can resist a swaggering, tough-talking war correspondent?"

"I don't know," Barney said. "Tokyo Rose, maybe?"

Bayard aped a Humphrey Bogart sneer. "You'll be sorry for that crack, Nash, when my high-powered press jeep splashes mud all over your weary platoon of marching G.I.'s! Better be nice to me, pal, if you want me to write a tearjerking story about the heroism of a former nightclub editor under fire."

They were all being deliberately gay, but a forlorn atmosphere had settled over the little group. This was the way it was happening every day now. The office force was being drained of all but the old, the unfit, or the married men with many dependents. And, of course, it was only the beginning.

"When do you leave?" Elizabeth asked.

"In a couple of weeks. Sorry not to give you more notice, darling landlady, but my Company calls!"

"I'm not worried about that part of it," Elizabeth said. "We're just going to miss you so. Do you realize what you're doing to us, Frank? This house is going to be a nunnery!"

"Yeah, I gotta talk to old Quig about that. At his age, he

should be man enough to handle this henhouse while I'm gone."

When the party broke up, Laurel lingered. "I know you're not worried about renting Frank's room," she said. "There's such a housing shortage already that it's critical. But it would be nice to get somebody attractive, wouldn't it? Another man, anyway."

Elizabeth looked at her suspiciously. "You wouldn't by chance have a candidate in mind, would you?"

"Funny you should ask," Laurel said innocently. "As a matter of fact, a friend of mine told me just yesterday about some Air Force colonel who's been transferred here from California. He's not regular Army. In fact, he was in real estate on the Coast before he applied for a commission. I hear he's absolutely *divine*. About forty. And all craggy, with those sexy, man-of-experience wrinkles around his eyes. Married, of course. But she's staying in their house in Beverly Hills. Wants to hold onto the servants and play golf every day. She's got all the money, by the way. Oh yes, his name's Adam Barnsworth. I'm supposed to have lunch with him tomorrow, specifically for the purpose of recommending a place for him to live. How about if I size him up? If he looks okay I could suggest Frank's old digs."

"I don't mind, but it doesn't sound very likely," Elizabeth said. "From your description, a man like that would surely want a nice apartment. He sounds as though money isn't the problem, even if it isn't his own. Why would he want to live in a rooming house?"

Laurel shrugged. "Maybe he won't. But my friend tells me he doesn't want the fuss of running an apartment. He'll be commuting to California whenever possible. And of course he has no idea how long he'll be assigned here. Could be he'd grab at the idea of having a nice room and no problems. In spite of everybody in town renting everything from maids' rooms to broom closets, there aren't many like this, you know. You've done a sensational job of fixing up this house, Elizabeth. I swear to God I don't know how you've done it."

Elizabeth was pleased. She had worked hard, painting and refinishing furniture, filling the house with plants and pictures, trying to make it a gracious home rather than a sterile, ugly rooming house. She hadn't stopped in her own quarters, either. With her tenants' delighted permission, she had refurbished their rooms as well. It had been hard work but surprisingly inexpensive. She'd used cheap but effective fabrics and lots of warm color, trying to make each room suit the occupant. Frank's, for instance, was distinctly masculine, done in brown and black, the chairs covered in tweedy fabric and the couch bed in strong black, brown, and white stripe. It was a handsome room, far better looking than any furnished studio apartment renting for four times the price.

"Well, I guess there's nothing to lose by mentioning it to your Colonel Barnsworth," she said finally. "Of course he can't have it till Frank leaves. I wouldn't want Frank to think he was being pushed out, not for a million dollars! As we say in New England, 'We wouldn't jump into his grave that fast.'" She stopped. It was, at best, an unfortunate reference.

"Okay, I'll talk to the colonel tomorrow," Laurel said. "If it works it will save everybody a lot of trouble. Both you *and* him. Of course he might turn out to be a horror. In which case I'll advise him to keep on stowing his duffel bag at Wardman Park, where he's living right now."

"Thanks. I don't know why you're always so good to me."

In the doorway, Laurel looked over her shoulder and gave her a broad wink. "Probably because you demand it," she said.

When Laurel explained the room to him over lunch, Adam Barnsworth was delighted with the idea.

"It sounds perfect," he said. "My plans are so unsettled that I can only take something on a month-to-month basis, which rules out any good apartment, even if I wanted one. I'd much prefer this kind of thing for many reasons. I'm not one of those guys who cook—unless you like charred steaks over an outdoor barbecue—so I don't need a kitchen. There's only one thing. It does have its own bath, doesn't it?"

"Blissfully, yes. There are two on the floor. You have one and the other is shared by the two women who also live on the top deck."

"Great. When can I see it?"

"I'll check with Elizabeth. Probably during the day tomorrow when Frank's at work. I'll call you at the hotel and let you know."

"I really appreciate your kindness," Adam said. "It was lucky for me that Sam Griffin put me in touch with you. You've saved me a hell of a lot of aggravation. Are you always so organized?"

"It's one of my worst faults," Laurel said. "All my life I've wanted to be one of those helpless, bubble-headed, beautiful doll-women who have to be constantly pointed in the right direction by some big, strong, protective man. Those are the women men really like. In fact, they're the ones that men marry. Not sturdy, presumably competent, self-sufficient creatures like me."

"You're wrong. I speak only for myself, but if there's anything I can't stand it's a clinging vine. You may think you envy them, but they bore me to death. Give me an independent, intelligent female any time. She has to be good-looking, of course, and feminine enough to bolster my ego. My ideal is serene, too. Warm and understanding. And of course sexy. That goes without saying."

The conversation had suddenly taken a very personal tone for people who were strangers. On the strength of it, Laurel asked an impudent question. "Does your wife fill all those requirements?"

Adam looked startled. Then he smiled. "I guess you could say she fills most of them. Probably *I* lack a lot of things Monica would opt for if she could. Anyway, I'm undoubtedly describing a paragon who doesn't exist. A gem like that would have to have at least a tiny flaw."

Laurel didn't answer. I have a surprise for you, Colonel, she thought. Wait until you meet Elizabeth.

Adam Barnsworth was not remarkably handsome, but he was good-looking enough to make women give him a second, appraising glance, attracted by the strong face with its perennial tan, the deep-set gray eyes, the close-cropped dark hair beginning to go prematurely gray at the edges. A well-built man, he was obviously uncomfortable in the stiff formality of his Air Force uniform. Adam was used to the casual dress of Southern California. The constraining silhouette of his new clothes did not suit him, any more than the role of warrior did. Like most of his fellow officers, he was a civilian in uniform, and the eagles on his shoulders represented no more than a convenient identification of his temporary and unwanted status.

Not that he did not wish to serve his country. He was among the first to volunteer. The easygoing, peace-loving Adam had a broad streak of patriotism, stronger even than the cynical attitude of his wife, who thought that all this business of joining the Air Force was juvenile nonsense. She had said so when he told her his intention.

"Inside every man there's a little boy who likes to play soldier," Monica had said, "but I didn't dream that you marched to that beat. For God's sake, Adam, what do you know about the Air Force? You're a real estate expert. What do you think you can do for the war—re-zone Berlin?"

"I'll do whatever they want," he'd answered. "I'm nearly

forty years old, too old to be a flyboy but not too old to do some of the desk work wherever it's needed."

"You're mad. They'll probably never get around to calling men of your age, but you have to go and volunteer."

Her words irritated him. "What would you have me do, be a Beverly Hills fire warden? It would be very convenient, of course. In case of a blaze I could pump water right out of our swimming pool."

She shrugged. "Do whatever you want. You always have."

Not so, Adam thought. I never really wanted to marry you. He reflected on his seventeen years of life with Monica Collier Barnsworth. They had begun dating while Adam was still at U.C.L.A. and Monica had returned to the family mansion in Bel Air after two undistinguished years at Smith. They appeared to be a well-matched couple, both native Californians with that breed's exaggerated love for athletics, automobiles, and al fresco living. They were both good-looking youngsters. Monica had the lean, graceful body of the well-bred, well-nourished, and well-exercised young California girl. The only obvious disparity in their suitability was a difference in backgrounds. The Colliers were, by any standards, rich, while the Barnsworths were merely upper-middle-class comfortable. It did not seem too great a problem to either family. It seemed no problem at all to the young couple who drifted almost naturally into a relationship which led to marriage when he was twenty-three and she was twenty-one.

They had tried premarital sex and found it mutually satisfying. Adam was much more naïve and romantic about this than his partner. Having slept with Monica, it never crossed his mind not to marry her. She was not his first adventure, but her predecessors were reasonably few, and none of them girls whom he "respected." An "honorable" progression of events, eventually culminating in a wedding ceremony, seemed, to him, called for. It was not a distasteful idea by any means, though even at the time he was not sure that she was the ideal he described to Laurel many years later.

For her part, Monica was sufficiently in love with Adam to encourage his decidedly old-fashioned attitude. She had had other affairs, if one could call them that. They were quick couplings with boys in the East, college kids whose faces and bodies she could barely remember. None had touched her with the gentle, reverent hands of Adam. She was not by nature a giving person, but as much devotion as she was capable of giving she offered to Adam.

Neither of them had any real quarrel with their life together. Adam regretted their childlessness, but Monica did not want children, a fact which she felt honor-bound to reveal to her husband-to-be before their marriage. She did not reveal that she was not a virgin. The latter consideration helped overcome any doubts that the former might have created in Adam's mind. Monica had never before had an opportunity to become pregnant, therefore she might well change her feelings about children. Many other women had. And then, too, there was Adam's belief that he had taken away her virginity. That, to him, was the strongest argument for their marriage.

They had not, of course, had children. Now, in a way, Adam was just as glad. If they'd had a son he would be dangerously close to draft age, and as Adam watched the bright-eyed eighteen-year-old Air Force cadets he was thankful that none of them belonged to him. He was not cowardly for himself, but he doubted that he could have borne the idea of a young Adam Barnsworth's life being ended by a frenzied Japanese or German pilot no older than himself.

He went off willingly for his military indoctrination, proud of his commission, eager to contribute whatever he could to the quick termination of this terrible war. Monica showed no inclination to follow him, even when he was assigned to Washington.

"I hate the East," she said, "and besides, what would I do with myself in a strange, overcrowded city while you were locked up all day in the Pentagon? I'd much rather stay here, if you don't mind. I'll do my bit at the blood bank and the Stage Door Canteen. Besides, since they've locked up Saiko, who'd look after this place if we were both away?"

Adam did not attempt to dissuade her. She was right on all scores, he told himself. Washington in wartime was bound to be jam-packed and uncomfortable and they'd probably have a difficult time finding a place to live. Monica was better off in the big, rambling Beverly Hills house her parents had given them for a wedding present. Not that he really expected her to become a serious gardener. She was easily bored by the kind of tedious chores their now-interned Japanese yard man had performed, and undoubtedly she would find someone to replace him. But Adam knew that without her golf and tennis and swimming, her sleek little convertible and her endless sunbathing, Monica would be miserable and would make him miserable too. What he did not admit, even to himself, was that after seventeen years he looked forward to a vacation from his wife. He supposed that she loved him very much as he loved her—from habit. He was sure that she had been faithful, as he had. Still, after so many years he had a feeling that a separation would be good for both of them. They took each other too much for granted. They seldom argued, but just as rarely did they share any great moments. Their sex life was, he supposed, typical of long-married pairs: infrequent, reasonably satisfying, and totally lacking in surprise.

Despite the fact that she was a hundred times richer than he, Adam had always made it a point to support the household. Monica was free to use her money for luxuries, but his real estate business provided an adequate living and it was a point of honor with him to pay the monthly bills. This fact, too, influenced his lack of pressure on her to go to Washington. He could afford to maintain the California house but he could not support two expensive households. Alone, he could take any kind of modest lodgings, live simply on his Air Force pay, and, through the continuing income from his business, continue to support Monica's life-style in Beverly Hills.

This was his situation when he walked into Elizabeth's house and into her life. Without realizing it, he was ready for her. As she was for him.

Chapter 9

Elizabeth was literally shaken by her initial involuntary reaction to Adam Barnsworth. Though she smiled cordially and offered him a cool, firm hand, her thoughts were as wanton as those of some twenty-year old bar girl waiting for a pick-up. "I'm going to go to bed with this man" was the idea that totally engrossed her. As simple as that. Her own calm, determined attitude shocked her. It was a completely calculated decision, totally uncharacteristic of her, yet as matter-of-fact as if she'd been thinking, "I'm going to invite this man to dinner."

Had she allowed herself the luxury of rationalization, she might have found a valid excuse in the fact that it had been years since any man had made love to her. She was not an old woman nor a cold one, but she had, until now, given abnormally little thought to this repression of her sexual urge. She kept herself too busy to dwell on her unsatisfied needs. More than that, she was too fastidious to simply hop into bed with any man who asked her. There had been a few offers, not all of them unattractive. But something had always made her gracefully step aside. She was too honest with herself for casual physical contact. She envied women who could

173

satisfy themselves the way men did, without sentiment or love, but simply for the sheer, healthy release of it. She was sure she could not be dispassionate in her passion. Therefore, in all the years since Alan, she had never dared risk it.

Small wonder, then, that this irresistible compulsion surprised and, in a way, disgusted her. Until a moment ago, she had never seen the man. Perhaps he was gross or boorish, unclean or even perverted. She did not know, and at this moment she did not care. Any more than she cared about the only fact she knew to be true—that he had a wife in California.

In the way that women have of recognizing such things, she was aware that Adam was drawn to her, too. She doubted that any emotion as quick and strong as her own had crossed his mind, but it was obvious that he looked at her with admiration and more than a faint flash of interest. She wasn't imagining it. Even Laurel, who introduced them, seemed to pick up the vibrations.

"Okay, Colonel," Laurel said, "still think you're looking for a non-existent species?"

Adam actually reddened at her playful words. "Don't go putting ideas in my head, young woman."

Elizabeth stood by quietly, puzzled by the conversation but sensing that she should not press for an explanation.

"The room is just fine," Adam said to her. "I'd like very much to take it on a month-to-month basis if that's all right, Mrs.—uh, by the way, what do I call you? I know your name is Whitman but you write under the name of Quigly. Which do you prefer?"

"Quigly. But I really prefer Elizabeth."

His look seemed so comprehending that her breath came quickly. She went on hurriedly to answer his question. "A month-to-month basis will be fine," she said. "The room will be available in two weeks. Maybe sooner. Will that be convenient, Colonel?"

He nodded. "The sooner the better. And by the way, if you're interested in *my* preference, it's Adam."

After he paid a deposit and left, thanking both of them, Laurel raised a quizzical eyebrow. "Something tells me we like the colonel," she said.

"Yes. Very much."

"He went for you, too. Funny how I knew he would." She recounted their luncheon conversation. Elizabeth tried to look only mildly interested.

"Listen, it's none of my business," Laurel said, "but try

not to go nuts over him, will you? I have a hunch he's not the divorcing kind."

"Don't be ridiculous. I've just met the man."

"Maybe so. But I've never seen you look this way. Now don't sit there and tell me you believe in love at first sight."

Elizabeth considered her answer carefully. "I'm not sure I know what love is," she said. "But I believe in instant chemistry between grown-ups, if that's what you mean."

"Oh, my God," Laurel groaned, "we've been invaded."

Aside from sounding pleased when she called him to say that Frank Bayard would be out of the room in a week, Adam did not evidence any interest in Elizabeth in the days that followed. Out of his sight, her feeling of excitement waned a little. She told herself that it was a momentary aberration and that even Laurel's assessment of the mutual attraction was all out of proportion. Still, she went about making Adam's room as inviting as possible. She put up new curtains, made a new cover for the studio couch, and, feeling guilty about Frank's joking protestations that *he* never had it so good, even invested in a roomy leather chair that she really couldn't afford.

The most significant thing she did, though, was to move Charlene out of her own bedroom into Ann's. The six-year-old was delighted with this idea. She adored her big sister even in the face of Ann's almost complete indifference to her.

"I'm not a baby any more, am I, Mommy?" Charlene crowed. "I'm a grown-up with my own room!"

"Well, half a room, darling," Elizabeth said. "And you must be very neat and tidy in your part of it. You don't want Ann to be angry with you. Remember, it was hers first."

Charlene nodded solemnly, her elfin little face serious with responsibility. "I'll be very, very good," she promised.

Elizabeth hugged her. "Of course you will, angel." She was delighted that Charlene was so happy. She'd been afraid that the little girl would feel rejected. Since the first few months of her life, she'd never slept away from her mother.

Ann was almost hysterically opposed to the idea. "I won't have that little brat in my room! Why should I? She's a baby. She'll have everything a mess. And I'll never have a moment's privacy! It's not fair, Mother!"

Elizabeth tried to calm her. "Ann, dear, she won't be in your way at all. She's so excited about sharing a room with her sister. She worships you. Please don't spoil it for her."

"Spoil it for her! That's all you ever think about, whether

or not Charlene is happy. What about me? Every girl in my class will die laughing when they hear I have to share my room with a six-year-old child! You're just being mean! Charlene's always slept in your room. Why can't she keep on sleeping there?"

Because I want to take a lover there, Elizabeth said silently. Because I'm tired of sleeping alone and aching for the feel and the scent of a man beside me. Because your time for those things is still to come, but mine is slipping away from me. Faster and faster, day by day. Instead, she answered Ann quietly. "I want her with you because it's time for her to be less dependent upon me. It isn't uncommon for sisters to share a room, Ann. I should have started it a year ago. I'm sorry if you're upset, but I forbid you to be horrid to Charlene. I don't think we need discuss it any further. I'm moving her things in today."

Ann looked so miserable that Elizabeth almost regretted her selfishness. But there had to be a place for Adam. She couldn't go creeping up to his room on the third floor, fearful that someone would see or that Charlene would wake in the night and call out to her. No, Elizabeth's quarters afforded the only privacy in the house. And that is where, if he would let her, she would make love to Adam Barnsworth.

The pursuit of Adam was no pursuit at all. If Elizabeth had fears that the attraction was one-sided, those fears vanished the very day he moved in.

"May I cook dinner for you tonight?" she asked when he appeared early in the morning dragging two large suitcases. "If you don't have anything else to do," she added lamely, "I thought you might enjoy a home-cooked meal."

"Lady, there's nothing I'd rather have. After all these weeks, I feel as though I'd been born in a mess hall or a restaurant."

She ducked out of the office early to shop for a thick steak, salad, baked potatoes to be fixed, California style, with heavy globs of butter and sour cream. It wrecked her ration stamps for the week and she couldn't have cared less. She fed the children at six and packed them off to their rooms, assuring Charlene she'd come in later to say good night, reminding the others to be sure to get their homework done. Then she bathed and dressed carefully in a soft, loose housecoat, recklessly using the last of her French perfume on strategic spots, at the base of her throat, the inside of her elbows and in the hollow between her breasts. Deliberately, she kept the lamps low and inviting in her little sitting room, arranging the tiny dining area to glow only in the light of candles.

The elaborately seductive planning made her a little hesitant. Perhaps she was being too obvious. Adam could not fail to get the message. But that's what you want, isn't it? Elizabeth asked herself. Yes, the answer came back, that's exactly what I want.

As she finished the last of her preparations, there was a light tap on the living-room door. Heart beating fast, she opened it. Laurel stood there smiling.

"Hi," Laurel said, "listen, there's a good movie at Keith's. What do you say we— Oops, this is obviously not the night for the Girls Friendly!" She took in the setting and Elizabeth's costume in one comprehensive glance. "Expecting Cary Grant? No, don't tell me. I just remembered. It's D-Day. The invasion has started. What time is he due?"

"Any minute," Elizabeth said pointedly.

"Right. Let it never be said that I can't take a hint. So long, Mata Hari. Don't forget to turn in the military secrets to GHQ."

"Idiot," Elizabeth laughed. "All I've done is invite the man to dinner."

"Sure. Well, if that V-necked number doesn't get him, the smell of Joy will. You *do* know what you're doing, don't you? The guy's married, remember?"

Elizabeth's eyes danced. "Maybe I'll try to forget."

"I'd say you'd already begun," Laurel cracked. "You really sure you can handle this, Elizabeth? I admit he's damned attractive, but the whole setup doesn't exactly seem your style."

Because it was so true, the remark annoyed Elizabeth. "What is my style, Laurel? Keeping house, raising kids, living like a nun? Don't you give me credit for any desire to be just a woman? Or does being thirty-seven years old disqualify me from any further interest in the opposite sex?"

Laurel put her arms in front of her face, burlesquing fear of physical attack. "Okay, okay," she said. "Sorry! I didn't mean to hit a raw nerve. I just don't want you to get hurt. I'm not trying to run your life, for Christ's sake!"

Elizabeth softened. "I know. I'm sorry I blew. Guess I'm a little edgy. You're right, of course. This isn't my style, but it feels so right that it scares me."

Laurel smiled. "Fair enough. All I want to know is that those big blue eyes of yours are wide open going in. Good luck. I really mean it." And with that she was gone.

A few minutes later, the gentle knock that Elizabeth had been waiting for finally came.

They fell easily in an intense, deliriously happy relationship that began that night with the most extraordinary lovemaking either of them had ever known. Strangely enough, for their age they were remarkably untouched people. Adam had known only one woman for seventeen years. Elizabeth had been with only one man in her whole life. Yet of the two, she seemed by far the most experienced, the least inhibited. Her excited response to Adam stirred unexpected things in him. He felt as though he was enjoying the first real sexual satisfaction he'd ever known. There seemed to be no limit to his powers, nor to Elizabeth's free offering of herself in new and provocative ways. Her reaction was the same. Alan's lovemaking had been expert and, she had thought, fulfilling. Now she knew that he had never touched the deep unashamed sexuality that lay within her. There was nothing she would not have done with, for, or to this man. And there was not the least sense of embarrassment about what she gave or took. Only an overwhelming sense of losing herself in this new experience, and a sense of joy in seeing his amazed and delighted face as they made love over and over again.

And, as it never had for either of them, after sex came companionable talk and laughter, far into the night. They lay smoking cigarettes, telling each other about themselves and their lives, occasionally interrupting to kiss and gently fondle one another. Finally, raising himself on one elbow, Adam looked down at her in undisguised wonderment.

"You're miraculous."

She laughed lightheartedly. "On the contrary, my darling, it's you who performed the miracles. Oh, Adam, if I could only tell you."

"You don't have to. I know."

"There's never been anything like this for me before."

"Nor for me. You believe that, don't you?"

She nodded quietly. "Yes, I believe that."

"I don't know where it's all going to go, Elizabeth. I'm not sure it's fair to you. There's the war and . . . other things."

She silenced him with her mouth. "If there was never anything more than this," she said finally, "it would be enough forever."

"You know that's not true. For either of us."

"Yes," Elizabeth said, "it's true."

Try as they did to be discreet about their affair, it was impossible to hide it from the other adults in the house.

Betty and Amelia accepted it as none of their business, discussed it only among themselves, and admitted more envy than condemnation. Laurel made no further reference to the dangerous road that Elizabeth had chosen to travel, but she feared what would happen to her friend if Adam were transferred from Washington or if his wife decided to join him after all. Mary Jackson, who, day after day, made up a rumpled bed that had always before looked unslept in, surmised that Mrs. Whitman had found someone to make her happy. She deserved it, poor lady, Mary thought, after all the years with that terrible man, and all the years without any man at all.

The children were the only ones in the house unaware of what was going on, though Ann, now a very grown-up sixteen, sensed that there was something between her mother and this good-looking officer who had dinner with them almost every night. She knew that Colonel Barnsworth took Elizabeth out once or twice a week, too. It looked suspiciously like a romance, an idea that angered and disgusted Ann. Still loyal to her father, Ann continued to resent Elizabeth for taking them away from him. She stubbornly refused to give her mother the satisfaction of asking her father's whereabouts, and Elizabeth, reluctant to disillusion Ann about Alan's present life, volunteered nothing. Now, Ann suspected, she was further betraying her family by this flirtation with Adam Barnsworth. It was positively sordid at their age. Two old fools making idiots of themselves!

Charlene was too young, of course, to know of such things. She took immediately to Adam and he to her. Their happiness together reminded Elizabeth of Alan's relationship with Ann in the early days, though this one had none of the neurotic possessiveness or destructive permissiveness of that other worrisome situation. Charlene called him Uncle Adam, waited for his arrival every evening and unconsciously substituted him for the father she'd never known. He called her Charley and seemed to fall happily and naturally into the role in which she'd cast him. Charlene was an outgoing, loving child, and Adam was just one more person to love. She gave him the same puppy-dog devotion she gave her sister and brother, "Aunt Laurel," and Mary Jackson. For Elizabeth she reserved a special kind of adoration and, as she had from the first moment, Elizabeth returned it.

In contrast to Ann's thinly veiled hostility and Charlene's all-out embrace, Quigly's attitude toward Adam was, as usual, one of indifference. This was Elizabeth's biggest disappointment. She had hoped that Quigly would find the man-to-man relationship he so badly needed. Instead he brushed off Adam's overtures of friendship. Of all the children, her son was the most difficult to understand, the hardest to love. He seemed to care for no one. He lived in a private world of a few contemporaries, schoolmates whom Elizabeth had never met. Her suggestions that he invite some of the boys to the house were brushed aside.

"You wouldn't like them," he said rudely.

"What makes you so sure? Are they such awful boys?"

"You'd probably think so."

Elizabeth became impatient. "If they're so bad, then perhaps I should forbid you to see them."

Quigly looked at her without expression. "Try it," he said, "and I'll leave home."

"Leave home! I never heard such nonsense! You're only fourteen years old. Where do you think you could go?"

He was defiantly silent.

"Answer me, Quigly!"

"I could lie about my age and join the Army."

Elizabeth sighed. "Don't be ridiculous. They'd never believe you."

"The Merchant Marine, then. They're not so sticky."

She gave up. After that she said nothing more about his friends. She consoled herself with the thought that they probably were very ordinary boys. Quigly would like to make them sound like thugs just to frighten her, to punish her with the sadism that even she could not ignore. His rebellious attitude was, she knew, fostered by Ann. The two of them were quite close. His sister was the only person Quigly talked to, and it stood to reason that his resentment of Elizabeth was in part a direct reflection of Ann's own feelings. This was why she'd hoped that Adam might get through to her son as she never could. Not that she was trying to saddle Adam with the responsibilities of her children. He had simply become so much a part of her life that he seemed as much husband as lover to her. Most of the time she felt young again, and more married than she ever had in all the years with Alan.

Unfortunately, the grim facts of life occasionally reminded her that she was not married to Adam Barnsworth. There was one long terrible weekend when Adam flew to Beverly Hills to be with Monica for their eighteenth wedding anniversary. And another week, even more unbearable, when Monica decided to visit Washington. His wife knew where he lived, of course, but Adam took a hotel suite for the time she was in town, explaining to her that she'd be more comfortable than she would sharing his room.

After his last reunion with Monica, Elizabeth, hating herself, could not keep from questioning him.

"Did you sleep with her?"

Her answer was reproachful silence.

"Well? Did you?" She knew she sounded like a shrew. It was a stupid way to behave. She'd drive him away with such a possessive attitude. Still she had to know.

Adam's voice was dangerously low. "She's my wife, Elizabeth."

"So you did make love to her."

"Yes. Now, are you satisfied?"

The hurt came through in her quick bitter reply. "The question is, are *you?*"

She could have bitten off her tongue. Instantly she was in his arms, crying, apologizing, running her fingers over his hair and face. "Oh, darling, I'm so sorry," she said. "I have no right. I know that. I'm so grateful for what we have. It's unforgivable that I should behave so badly."

"Hush, love," he said. "I know. I know. Let's not discuss it any more, all right?"

Mutely, she agreed. And that night was the most wonderful of all. She vowed never to make such a scene again, but she had finally faced the sickening realization that her passion for Adam was not something she could handle as she'd once thought she could. The future began to frighten her. The thought of life without him was unbearable. One night as he lay in her arms, he sighed deeply.

"I wish I could stay here forever," Adam said.

"Can't you?"

She felt him tense. He pulled away from her. "Nothing is forever, my darling. At any moment I could be ordered somewhere else. You know that, dearest. We must never forget it."

"But you'll come back to me," Elizabeth said. "God won't let you be killed. One day the war will end."

His lack of response was louder than any words he could have spoken. In a panic, she waited for his reassurance.

"You *will* come back, Adam? After the war?"

"How can I? I'm married, Elizabeth. My home and my work are in California."

She felt deathly cold. Slowly, flatly, she pronounced the words. They came out like a death sentence.

"You'll go back to Monica."

"Not by choice. I have no alternative."

Slowly she sat up, switched on the bedside lamp and lit a cigarette. "No alternative?" she repeated idiotically.

"I'm in love with you," he said quietly. "More in love than I've ever been before or ever will be again. I owe you more than I can ever repay. But I can't abandon a woman to whom I've been married for eighteen years. She's done nothing to deserve that. She's been faithful, patient, a good wife in her own way. I'm all she has, Elizabeth. She needs me. I can't disregard that."

She looked at him in astonishment. "And what about me? Don't I need you, too?"

"You and I need each other," Adam said, "but not in the same way. We're strong, Elizabeth. We'll survive, unhappy as we may be about it. I can lose myself in my work. And you have your job, your children, a full life of your own. Monica has nothing but me. How could I cold-bloodedly walk out on her and not feel guilty every day for the rest of my life? What would that eventually do to you and me? I can't be that selfish or that unfair to either of you."

She could not accept what she was hearing. In spite of everything she had told herself, she did not believe that Adam would not get a divorce and marry her. Not till after the war, perhaps, but certainly then. She could not comprehend how a man who loved so deeply could forsake that love for what he thought of as the "honorable" thing to do. Such selflessness was superhuman, unreal. He did not even have the excuse of children to tie him to this loveless marriage. A terrible suspicion that it was not his principles but his weakness that bound him to Monica suddenly crossed her mind. She tried to stay calm.

"How fair are you being to either of us if you live with a woman you don't love and walk away from one you do? It's a curious rationale, Adam. Do you think you'll make either of us happy that way? If she had a choice, do you think Monica would want a husband who stayed with her only out of duty?"

"She'll never know that," he said. "I think she'd kill herself if she knew."

All at once she was angry. "Oh, for God's sake, Adam, don't make excuses for your own spinelessness! Nobody kills himself for love. Especially anyone like Monica, from what you've told me. If she was so dependent upon you, she'd have come to Washington with you. You just don't have the guts to tell her you want out, do you? Or maybe you really do think she can't live without you. If so, you're a fool. She's rich, attractive, and surrounded by friends. She'll make a new life for herself. But what about you? What about your life? Are you going to sacrifice the rest of it

for some stupid Victorian idea of loyalty? It's the only life
you have, Adam. Are you so willing to waste it?"

He was standing now, putting on his clothes, not looking
at her. This is some terrible nightmare, Elizabeth thought.
It can't be true. She ran to him.

"Oh, darling, darling, don't throw it all away." She was
pleading now, the tears running down her cheeks, her naked
body pressed close to him. He took her in his arms.

"My God," he said, "don't you think this is agony for me?
Don't you think I realize what I have to give up? We should
never have started this. I never meant to hurt you so. You
seemed so strong, so sure of what you wanted. I didn't know
if I could handle it, Elizabeth, but I thought you could. Now
look at us. Is all this pain worth the happiness we've had?"

She rushed, sobbing, from his embrace. He finished dressing quietly and came to the bed where she lay huddled in
her misery. Gently he lifted her face and kissed her.

"What now, my love?" he asked. "Shall I go out of your
life tomorrow? It's up to you to decide."

Frantically she threw herself at him. "No, no, no!" She
held him with all her strength. "Not a minute before you
must! Stay with me as long as you can, Adam. There'll be
enough loneliness later."

"Thank you, Elizabeth," he said. "Thank you, my darling."

The glaring truths that had passed between them increased,
rather than diminished, their passion for each other in the
days ahead. Like a woman with a terminal illness, Elizabeth
refused to admit the possibility of the inevitable. She unreasonably clung to the hope that Adam would find himself
unable to live without her. She had to clutch at this one
straw of self-delusion. She had abandoned pride and discipline. All that was left was wishful thinking.

For his part, Adam felt sick with remorse, but he remained committed to the things he told Elizabeth, the things
he really believed. He could not be so callous as to abandon
Monica, the innocent victim. He found himself wishing that
she would write and tell him she'd met someone else, that
she wanted to divorce him. He would have been happy married to Elizabeth, but only if some unlikely stroke of good
fortune would remove the guilt that stood in the way.

Meanwhile, they kept up the pretense that nothing had
changed. Their lovemaking was more obsessive, more violent,
but there were awkward pauses in their conversation, moments of introspection on both sides that had never existed
before. In spite of their best efforts, there was strain between

them, yet they came together at night like desperate, threatened people fighting off a menacing shadow.

In the late fall of 1942, the Air Force took their fate out of their own hands. One night after dinner, Adam pulled Elizabeth down on the couch beside him.

"I have something to tell you," he said. "I got new orders today. I've been reassigned."

She had often tried to imagine this moment. Would she get hysterical, cry, scream, fall apart with misery? She had pictured herself doing any of those things. All of them, maybe. Instead, when it happened she felt only deadly calm, so crushed that she was paralyzed with pain. She managed only one word.

"When?"

"Ten days," he said slowly. "It's overseas. I can't tell you where, exactly, but it's Europe rather than the Pacific."

She struggled for composure. "Ten days," she repeated. "Well, my darling, we'll make every one count. Maybe we could go away somewhere. I'll get time off from the paper. We'll find one of those wonderful old inns down in Virginia and—"

He broke into her frantic planning. "Dearest, we can't."

"Why not? Surely you'll have leave before you ship out."

Adam sighed. "Yes, I'll have leave. Beginning now." His lips tightened. "But I'll have to call Monica tonight and tell her. I'm sure she'll expect me to come home."

"I see. When will you go?" Her voice was flat.

"Day after tomorrow, I suppose. Or whenever they can bump some poor devil of a civilian and give me his seat on a plane." The matter-of-fact tone did not disguise his distress. "Oh, sweetheart, what can I say to you?" he burst out. "I know what you're thinking. I can't be as strong a man as you'd like me to be. You know how I feel. But I'd never forgive myself if I didn't go home."

Elizabeth sounded as though she were sleepwalking. "It's all right, darling. I understand. We still have a little time before you go to California."

"And I'll come back a couple of days early. I promise."

"That will be wonderful," she said woodenly. "Just wonderful."

Chapter 10

Adam did keep his promise to see her once more before he left for Europe. They spent a turbulent, unsatisfactory twenty-four hours together after his return from California. Loving him as she did, Elizabeth tried to put aside the unreasonable resentment she felt, the jealousy brought on by her vivid imagination of the eight days he'd spent with his wife. She did not question him about his trip home and he volunteered nothing beyond the fact that he had seen many of his old friends and that the weather was predictably beautiful.

They talked little, made love violently but with a feeling of urgency far removed from the contented enjoyment of the preceding months. It was as though they were both preparing themselves for a separation that was as final as it was imminent. Elizabeth was torn between never wanting him to go and an almost anxious desire for his departure. Every moment was a strange kind of exquisite pain. She had known from the beginning the transient nature of the affair, yet she had allowed herself to hope against all odds that Adam would find himself unable to live without her. It was not to be, and the bitter realization of that fact made her more scornful of herself than of him. She dreaded his leaving but she could not live for long with the torturous anticipation and helplessness that engulfed her. Better a quick amputation than this slow, agonizing cutting off of a relationship that was beyond any happiness she'd ever known.

He left her bed before dawn on that last morning. Silently she watched him dress, memorizing the way he tied his tie, the quick, impatient way he brushed the short-cropped hair that she used to caress in moments of tenderness. She lay dry-eyed and cold as stone as he came toward her for that final goodbye. He gathered her still figure in his arms, resting his cheek against hers.

"I love you," was all he said. Then he was gone. She had not even been able to reply.

In the awful weeks that followed, Laurel was her only confidante, her sole source of comfort. With her friend, Elizabeth relived the anguish and the ecstasy of this one nearly perfect year of her life. She reviewed it endlessly, examining her own behavior, wondering aloud how she could have handled it better, what she could have done to overcome Adam's inability to accept the future with her that she'd offered him.

Laurel was gentle and patient with her, fully aware that Elizabeth had to talk out her grief and draw whatever comfort she could from going over and over a situation for which she unreasonably blamed only herself. Sorry for her, Laurel had the good grace not to remind Elizabeth that she had known from the start what she was getting into. Elizabeth had forgotten all that. All she could see now was that she had somehow mishandled the affair. That if she'd been smarter, cleverer, Adam would have made plans to divorce Monica and return to the woman who loved him and who, without question, was loved in return.

Sitting in front of the little fire in her sitting room one evening, Elizabeth expressed this thought for the hundredth time.

"Other women get men to leave their wives," she said. "Why couldn't I do it, Laurel? God knows I'd have had no compunction about being a 'homewrecker'! It's not as though there were children to consider, or even a poor, helpless woman whom Adam would have had to support. Monica is rich and strong and independent, from everything I've heard. Yet I couldn't move him. I couldn't get through that blind, stupid sense of obligation. Not even when it meant destroying his life and mine."

Laurel weighed her words carefully. It was time for some plain talk. She had allowed Elizabeth to wallow in her own self-recrimination long enough, half out of her mind with questions to which there were no answers. Wondering whether she was doing the right thing, Laurel changed from the patient, sympathetic listener to the factual voice of reality.

"Look, my dear," she said, "isn't it about time you stopped fantasizing and faced this thing for what it really is? Sure, there are unscrupulous females who might have thought of ways to get Adam for keeps. You could have done any number of things. Gotten pregnant. Called his wife. Threatened suicide. Who knows? But you're not that kind of lady. You wanted him to come to you of his own will. You wanted him to be bigger than his own fears. Well, he wasn't. He isn't. He's a terrific guy, but in this kind of situation he's only running true to form."

Elizabeth was surprised into silence.

"What do you think the odds are on a man breaking up a long-standing marriage for the sake of another woman?" Laurel asked. "Pretty damned slim. For every one you hear about, I'll bet there are ten thousand who do just what Adam did: call it a day. Not that they wouldn't *like* to start over with somebody new. I don't doubt that Adam loves you. More than his wife, I'm sure. But men are different from women. More fearful, more creatures of habit than we are. You know, I really believe that old saying that women always think things will be better but men think maybe they'll be worse. Men don't like change, Elizabeth, but women thrive on it. You seldom see a man rearrange the furniture, much less uproot his life. It's all too troublesome to contemplate. Hell, I've seen guys hang on to secretaries who are so old they fall asleep at their desks, all because it's too difficult to break in a new girl Friday. They flirt with the idea of divorce. And a lot of them, like Adam, would really like it, provided they didn't have to instigate the mess, go through all the trouble, and start out at the age of forty-plus adjusting to a new house, new friends, and a new closet for their golf clubs. When they get that far, they settle for the old, safe rut."

Elizabeth was angry now. "You're being unfair," she said. "Adam wasn't afraid of any of those things. I just couldn't convince him that he wouldn't be hurting a woman who'd done nothing to deserve that hurt. It was his honor, his guilt if you like, that stood in his way. Not fear or lethargy as you'd like me to believe. Don't sit there and tell me that Adam is going back to his marriage just because it's more

comfortable than facing an unpleasant scene. I'll never believe that!"

"Okay," Laurel said easily. "Then let me ask you a question. If the shoe had been on the other foot, what would
you have done? Suppose you were childless, married to a
rich man who'd never done anything really terrible to you.
You meet a guy who's unattached and you fall hard for each
other. Would you have felt compelled to stick by your husband? Or would you assume that even without you he'd pick
up the pieces of his life, go on with his golf games, continue
to live in his beautiful house, and eventually meet someone
and marry her?"

Elizabeth said nothing.

"I'll answer that question for you," Laurel went on. "You
would have had the guts to tell him the truth. Nothing could
have kept you from it. Not only because you'd want to marry
the man, but because you'd have felt dishonest and guilty
staying with your husband when you knew you loved somebody else. That, my pet, is the difference between the mental
processes of the sexes. And in this case, I do not say,
'Vive la différence!' "

Laurel thought she had never seen such sadness on anyone's face. For a moment, she regretted her outburst. Perhaps it would have been better to let Elizabeth go on thinking of Adam as a noble, self-sacrificing man rather than the
quite ordinary male he was. But she couldn't bear to watch
her friend spend every waking hour yearning for a man who
didn't deserve her. Not that Elizabeth would magically recover. But perhaps now, armed with this new thought, she
would stop berating herself for what she thought of as her
own inadequacies. Elizabeth had not had a word from Adam
in the weeks since he'd been gone. He had promised to send
his APO address, but Laurel knew that he had not. She did
not know that Elizabeth wrote to him every night, carefully
saving the growing pile of letters to mail the moment she
knew where to send them. They were stream-of-conscious-
ness letters, full of cheerful bits of gossip, lavishly sprinkled
with reiterations of her devotion and passion, carefully devoid of any self-pitying phrases. They were the only comfort
she had, the last, lingering contact with Adam Barnsworth.

When Laurel went off to her room that night, Elizabeth
unlocked the bureau drawer and read the letters through.
They made a fat stack. Forty-two of them, one for each
day of the six weeks he'd been gone.

They made a pile of fat, curling ashes as she reluctantly
consigned them to the dwindling fire.

After her talk with Laurel, Elizabeth made a determined effort to occupy herself as she had before Adam came into her life. She did not believe the things Laurel had said, but she saw herself through her friend's eyes, a mooning, self-absorbed, quite boring companion. She tried to convince herself that she would never again hear from Adam. Sadly she accepted the fact that she would never even know if he was killed or wounded. They had kept to themselves in their brief happy year. There were no mutual Air Force friends to give her news of her love, no one to tell her whether he was dead or alive. She found herself praying for him every night, but she barely mentioned his name. There was scant occasion to. Laurel and the other women in the house tactfully did not ask questions. Ann and Quigly behaved as though Colonel Barnsworth had never existed. Only Charlene innocently asked when Uncle Adam was coming back.

"One day, perhaps," Elizabeth said gently. "He's off fighting the big war, darling. It may take a long time to win."

"I wish he was here," Charlene said. "Uncle Adam was nice. You liked him, too, didn't you, Mommy?"

"Yes. I liked him very much indeed."

She rented his room to a young man who worked for the Office of Price Administration, consciously selecting a twenty-three-year-old with a solid 4-F rating. There would be no more attractive, mature men in her house. Not, God knows, that she wasn't a burned child. She simply wanted no one who even remotely reminded her of the reaction she'd had at the first sight of Adam.

She threw herself into her work at *Wife and Mother*, helping to train the new fashion editor as Laurel had once helped to train her. She tried to spend more time with her children, no easy task with the older two. At seventeen, Ann had become a young beauty in her third year of high school. Quigly, at fifteen, showed increasingly active signs of rebellion. Twice Elizabeth had to pay damages to an irate store owner whose window had been smashed by Quigly and his friends playing baseball in the street. Once, more seriously, she went to the police station, where her son and two other boys were held, charged with "borrowing" a car for a joyride. As a first offender, Quigly was paroled in her custody. She punished him by confining him to the house every evening for a month, and forbidding him to see any of his unruly companions. She had no way of knowing how he spent the hours between the end of the school day and her return from work in the evening. With neither child could she establish any kind of communication. One evening she tried to discuss the subject of college with Ann.

"Have you given any thought to it?" Elizabeth asked pleasantly. "It's only a year away. We should be making applications. Where are your friends planning to go?"

Ann looked at her coolly. "I don't have friends, Mother. You haven't seen any girls around here, have you?"

"No," Elizabeth admitted, "I haven't. And it worries me, Ann. It's not normal. These are the years when you should be developing a social life."

"With whom? Those terrible girls at school? I wouldn't waste my time. And I know what you're going to ask next, Mother. No, there are no boys I care to go out with either. Not that plenty of them don't ask me. They're trash. I wouldn't wipe my feet on them."

Elizabeth sighed. Ann was still the princess banished to the tower. "Well, anyway, about college. Where would you like to go?"

"Where can you afford to send me?" It was a challenge.

"I'm afraid it will have to be within reason," Elizabeth admitted. "How about George Washington University?"

"And be a *day student?* No thanks."

"I'd love to send you to Smith or Vassar, Ann, but I don't think we can swing it. Maybe one of the Midwestern colleges, if you'd like to go away to school. Why don't we investigate? You could write to a few and then perhaps we could make a trip to look them over. We should be able to manage something fairly nearby."

"Please don't bother, Mother. I'd rather go to work. If I can't go to the right school, I have no interest in second-best. Save your money for Charlene. Maybe by the time she's ready she'll be able to get a *decent* education."

"That's surprisingly generous of you," Elizabeth said wryly. "I didn't know you were so concerned about your little sister."

Ann did not answer.

"Tell me," Elizabeth went on. "What about Quigly? Aren't you interested in his future? You two have always been so close."

The expression on Ann's face was unmistakably cynical. "Who are you trying to fool—yourself or me? Quigly will never amount to anything. He isn't worth educating. He'll probably end up in jail. Or in the electric chair."

"Ann!"

"Well, it's true. He doesn't care about anything. Do you remember when he killed that cat? He loved doing it. He likes doing anything that's destructive and terrible. Which side of the family does he get that from, Mother? Not *yours*, heaven forbid! Must be from our father. After all, any man who'd marry a prostitute must be mentally unbalanced. Do you suppose Quigly has Daddy's genes? We all do, I suppose, but maybe they're stronger in his son."

Elizabeth was horrified. She had been so careful to be evasive on the one or two occasions when Ann had mentioned her father. She had wanted to spare her the truth. Somehow Ann had found out about Alan. From a worshipful child, she had turned into a disgusted, scornful young woman.

"How did you find out? I never wanted you to know."

"I snooped," Ann said without apology. "I found the letters from him and that woman in your dresser drawer. What a dope I was! Always thinking my darling daddy was so perfect. All he is is a no-good drunk. A sick, scared man. No wonder he couldn't stand up to somebody as strong as you. Anybody with so little self-respect must be scared of his own shadow."

"Please don't feel that way," Elizabeth said softly. "Your father had his faults, but he loved you so much. He wanted everything wonderful for you, Ann. So much so that it created this terrible breach between you and me. He didn't mean for that to happen, I'm sure, but it did. Maybe now that it's out in the open, you and I can find a better understanding. Don't hate him, dear. He couldn't help being the way he was. Any more than you and I can help being the way we are. Remember the good things about him, Ann. You were the only thing in his life that really mattered."

"Sure. So much so that he's never sent me so much as a letter in all these years."

"How could he, darling? You'd have wanted to see him and he'd rather have died than let you know what he'd become. He kept quiet for the same reason I did—to keep your memories of him happy ones. I always wondered what I'd tell you if you ever asked about your father. But you never did. I thought it was better not to say anything—not even about the divorce. In light of what's happened, that was a mistake. Finding those letters was a cruel way to learn the truth. I was stupid to think you wouldn't have to know it all one day. I guess I thought it would hurt less when you were more grown up and could have more compassion and tolerance." Elizabeth looked thoughtful. "Why *haven't* you asked about him all these years? It's always puzzled me."

Ann shrugged. "I always expected you to tell me. I wasn't going to come crawling to you, begging for explanations."

She softened a little. "And I guess I always believed that one day he'd send for me. I thought you were deliberately keeping us apart out of spite, because you knew I was his favorite." The words came reluctantly. "I guess I owe you some kind of apology. It must have been pretty rough for you."

Elizabeth had waited years for those words. She knew with what effort a proud girl like Ann managed to say them. "You don't owe me anything," she said gently. "How could you have understood? I'll never know whether I did the right thing, taking you children away from your father. It's easy enough to look back and speculate on what one might have done. All I know is that at the time it seemed the only course to follow, the lesser of the evils. The only thing I want now is for you not to hate your father, Ann. His life was beyond his own control."

All the anger and resentment seemed to have left this strange, remote girl. "Is he still alive?" Ann asked. "Have you heard any more since you sent our pictures? I realize now that that's why you had Chuck take them."

"No. I've heard no more."

"She'd let us know if anything happened to him, wouldn't she?"

"Yes," Elizabeth said, "I'm quite sure she would."

On a Monday afternoon in the fall of 1943, a few months after her talk with Ann, Elizabeth received the telegram she had long expected. "Alan died peacefully this morning," it said. "Services in Memphis on Wednesday. If you wish to come you are welcome. Sue-Ann Temple Whitman."

Elizabeth's first impulse was to wire her condolences and close the book on that chapter of her life which had begun so happily in 1925 and ended so degradingly ten years later. It was farcical to think of attending the funeral of a man she had stopped caring for so long ago, a man whose abused body now belonged to a woman she'd never seen. The very idea bordered on the macabre, and until she told Ann of her father's death, she had totally dismissed any idea of paying her last respects to Alan. Her daughter's unexpected reaction changed her mind.

Ann read the telegram carefully. When she looked at her mother, her eyes were filled with tears. "I'm glad he's gone," she said. "I never really hated him, Mother, in spite of what I said. I guess he was just confused and unhappy. And he couldn't help that, could he?"

"No, darling, he couldn't. And no one else could help him, either."

Ann hesitated. "Are you going to Memphis?"

"I think not. He had made another life for himself, Ann. The appearance of a first wife could only be awkward and uncomfortable for everybody."

"Would you let me go, then?"

Elizabeth was startled. "Let *you* go? Oh, no, dear, I couldn't do that. It would be a terrible experience for you! We have no idea what those people are like. You'd feel unhappy and out of place. I wouldn't dream of sending a seventeen-year-old girl into such a situation. Besides, Ann, what good would it do? Your father isn't there, his soul is gone. He's at peace at last. It would be meaningless torture for you, even if it was feasible for you to make the trip alone. Remember him as you last knew him: in Georgetown when he was a devoted father who adored his firstborn. I promise you that's a better memory than any you might bring back from that unknown world."

Ann seemed to be searching for the right words. "When Grandpa Quigly died, you were there, weren't you, Mother? I mean, you just couldn't have stayed away like it was some stranger, could you?"

Elizabeth looked troubled. "Darling, that wasn't the same thing at all. You know that."

"I know what you mean," Ann admitted, "but one thing was the same: you were his daughter and you loved each other."

The impact of those simple words hit Elizabeth hard. When all the extenuating circumstances were brushed aside, the truth of what Ann said was undeniable. Alan had loved his daughter and she had worshiped him. Still did, probably, in spite of everything she knew, anything she'd said in a fit of outrage and rejection. And there was something else, something Elizabeth recognized from her own experience: barbaric as she considered funerals to be, with their weeping and mourning, their widow's weeds and floral arrangements, they served a purpose which was beyond ritualistic masochism. For some people, the very act of seeing the dead lent a strange, comforting finality to the awful fact. It was, Elizabeth supposed, like women who lost men in the war. Perhaps they never accepted the deaths because there was no visible proof of the terrible happening. As they so often did, her thoughts turned to Adam. Even if she heard tomorrow that he'd been killed, she would never be able to accept the fact that the living, loving man was no more. She realized now why—whenever possible—the bodies of servicemen were shipped home in their flag-draped coffins. It didn't matter to the dead soldiers where they found their final resting place. It only served to make the fact true and bearable for those left behind.

This must be the way Ann felt about Alan. She would be reconciled that her father was lost to her forever only if she physically saw Alan Whitman laid to rest. Elizabeth was appalled by the idea of going to Memphis, of meeting Sue-Ann, of being the focus of curious stares and whispered speculation. But she knew she could do no less for a daughter who, for the first time ever, had come within reaching distance.

"You're sure you really want to go?" she asked one last time.

Ann nodded.

"All right, dear, we'll go tonight. Together."

When she told Laurel her plan and asked her to "baby-sit" with Quigly and Charlene, that outspoken lady looked at her incredulously.

"You must be kidding! You're going to drag yourself and that girl down to Memphis for a funeral where the leading lady is a whorehouse madam who's a free-lance evangelist to boot! Have you lost your mind?"

"Possibly. But I think it's something I have to do for Ann." She recounted the conversation and ended with her own assessment. "This whole thing has been a bad jolt for her. Not just Alan's death, but the awful disillusionment about her father. It was bad that she learned about the divorce and remarriage as she did. I made a mistake in not finding some sensible way to tell her long ago. Thank God she's such a bright child. If anything, in spite of my blundering, I think this has brought us closer. I don't want to let her down now, Laurel. What she'll see in Memphis can't be any worse than what she already imagines."

"I hope you're right," Laurel said. "But don't count on it. At least you're not planning to drag the other two along."

"No. Charlene has no memory of her father and I doubt that Quigly remembers much. In any case, it would mean nothing to him. I'll simply tell them about Alan's death and say that Ann and I are going to the funeral."

"You do have some idea of what you're getting into, don't you? Wait. Don't answer that. I have an eerie feeling that I've said those words before. And if you'll forgive my mentioning it, it didn't work out very well that time either." Elizabeth's stricken face made her feel like an insensitive fool. "Oh, hell, I'm sorry," Laurel apologized. "That was dumb and uncalled for. Me and my big mouth."

"Don't be sorry. It *didn't* work out as I hoped. But I know now that I wouldn't have stopped if I'd known that at the beginning. Adam gave me the best days of my life."

Laurel sighed. "You're the most hopelessly romantic woman I've ever known. As we used to say in Sunday school, 'Behold the dreamer.' "

"Listen to you! Quoting the Bible! I never knew you were so familiar with it."

"Big deal," Laurel said. "I never got past the first book. That's from Genesis."

With Stu Preston's influence, Elizabeth managed to get an upper and lower berth on the night train to Memphis, making return reservations for Wednesday evening. She wired Sue-Ann at her "place of business" and hurriedly packed for herself and Ann. It was the widow's place to wear full mourning. Elizabeth would show respect in her dark costume, but she was careful to avoid any conspicuously funereal garb. Her black dress had white collar and cuffs and the small hat had an upturned brim that fully revealed her face. From Ann's simple wardrobe she chose a navy-blue jumper and white sweater. She hoped they would be virtually unnoticed. In any case, they would be in Memphis hardly long enough to cause a stir. The train would get them there on Wednesday morning and they would leave again that night. There was no need, really, for a hotel room, but Elizabeth telegraphed for one in any case. They would need some place to freshen up after the long train trip and Elizabeth recoiled at the idea that Sue-Ann might offer them the hospitality of her "home." She felt a quite normal anxiety about meeting this unlikely woman who had been Alan's second wife. Though her letter had been diamond-rough it had been touching and yet she was, as Laurel had so blatantly put it, "a whorehouse madam and free-lance evangelist." Elizabeth did not know what to expect. And even more troublesome than her own mixed emotions was her fear of Ann's reaction to this undeniably crude creature who had been part of her father's last years.

Sue-Ann was equally uneasy about meeting Elizabeth and Ann. When she had sent the wire, she'd been sure that the reply would be no more than an acknowledgment of Alan's death and, perhaps, some expression of sympathy. A peculiar sense of the "ladylike thing to do" had made her add the last phrase, saying that Elizabeth would be welcome. It had never occurred to her that the invitation would be accepted.

She grieved "sensibly" for her husband. The grim realities of life and death were all too familiar to her. Alan's death was not unexpected nor, she surmised, really unwelcome to him. He had surrendered to it almost willingly. She was glad that she had been able to make his last few years reasonably comfortable and thoroughly protected. But she knew, with the wisdom of her breed, that she had never really had all of Alan. Despite his bitterness, the real Alan belonged to that cool woman from Boston and to the children she'd given him. Particularly the one who was accompanying her to his last rites.

The "girls" who worked for Sue-Ann were far less contained than their employer. They were hysterical at the news of his death, devastated during the two days that his body lay stiffly and formally dressed in the parlor of the house. The establishment was, of course, closed for business, and the idle young women spent most of their time in their empty rooms, crying theatrically for the man who had been kind and courteous to them, one of the few who had treated them like "ladies."

Sue-Ann's "congregation," fully aware of their spiritual leader's fleshly trade, held regular prayer vigils around the casket, sometimes working themselves into an emotional frenzy, importuning God to receive Alan Whitman's immortal soul. Frequently, Sister Sue-Ann joined in, lending her strong voice in these pleas to the Almighty. None of them saw anything incongruous in this display of religious fervor in a carnal setting. They were earthy, realistic people. Faith was faith. It had nothing to do with the way the Lord saw fit for a good woman to make a living, provided that, like Sue-Ann, it was the only trade she knew.

It was into one of these miniature revival meetings that Elizabeth and Ann walked on Wednesday morning, having stopped briefly at the hotel to leave their bags and wash up after the long, dirty train ride. They stopped abruptly in the bead-curtained doorway of the parlor, their eyes traveling first to the elaborate open coffin which occupied the center of the room. From this distance they could not see its contents, only the blanket of blood-red roses which covered the lower half of the expensive bronze casket. Like a small child, Ann reached for Elizabeth's hand. Together they stood unnoticed for a minute or two, taking in the incredible spectacle.

A heavy-set woman completely enveloped in black crepe stood at the head of the coffin. Only her henna-red hair relieved the monotony of black clothes and dead-white face. Her arms were raised, her eyes closed, and her head thrown back as if in supplication. Her voice rang out above the murmured responses of the ten or twelve men and women who knelt nearby, each holding a lighted candle.

"Take him, Jesus!" the woman's voice commanded. "Sweet, sweet Jesus, receive your servant! Protect him from the hellfire! Give him to your angels, Lord! Raise him up! Now, Jesus! *Now!*"

Elizabeth did not know whether the trembling she felt was her own or Ann's, so strong was the quivering which ran up and down her body. She held Ann's hand tighter, feeling the moisture in its palm run into her own. She forced herself to look away from the woman at the room in front of her. She had never been in a house of prostitution before, but from all she'd heard, this was the prototype, its walls done in red velvet, its long bar, now reverently cleared, surmounted by a cheap painting of a voluptuous nude. Alan's coffin had been placed directly under an ornate crystal chandelier, dimmed now in deference to the dozens of candles which had been placed around the room. The air was stifling and reeked of the sweat of the mourners and the remnants of the prostitutes' perfume.

Her impulse was to take Ann and run. What madness had brought her to this nightmare scene? Instead she stood as though hypnotized, unable even to turn and leave, as though her feet had been nailed forever to the sill of this doorway to hell. At that moment, Sue-Ann opened her eyes and looked directly at Elizabeth. With a little sign, she hushed the mourners, who remained kneeling, heads bowed like some band of unlikely adoring angels. Slowly, with great dignity, she crossed the room.

"I'm glad you came, you and the little girl," she said. The voice was no more the evangelistic trumpeting sound of a moment before. She spoke quietly, with a strong southern accent. Elizabeth tried to answer, but no sound came out of her frightened, constricted throat. Sue-Ann did not seem to notice. "So you're Ann," she said to the white-faced girl. "Your daddy talked about you all the time. He was right. You're a beautiful young lady. You look like him, you know."

Elizabeth was beginning to recover herself. "I'm sorry we didn't telephone," she said. "We seem to have interrupted some kind of special service. The clerk at the hotel told us where to find you, so we just came right over. I didn't expect—"

The red-haired woman smiled knowingly. "You didn't ex-

pect a hellfire and brimstone meeting, is that what you mean?
Well now, I guess that's natural. I expect we do things different here. We never stop praying for the deceased, from
the moment the Lord takes him till we give him back to the
dust he came from. Your way's different, I reckon."

In spite of herself, Elizabeth shuddered. It was all so pa-
gan, so over-blown and distasteful. Even the words Sue-Ann
used were repugnant. Like referring to Alan as "the deceased." With an effort of will, she tried not to show her
revulsion. "It might be best if we come back later," she said.
"What time is the service? The final one, I mean."

"Two o'clock is when we consign his mortal remains to the
ground."

"And the church? Where is that?"

"This is the church, Mrs. Whitman," Sue-Ann said. "My
sect doesn't go in for pews and clergymen in white collars.
For us, God is everywhere." Deliberately, almost cruelly,
she added the final words. "Even in a whorehouse."

I will not give her the satisfaction of seeing how shocked
I am, Elizabeth thought. But I can't subject Ann to any
more of this. If what we've seen is only the continuing
mourning, what in God's name will the final performance
be? She glanced at her daughter. Ann's face was expressionless. She did not even appear to hear Sue-Ann, had not uttered a syllable in response to the woman's earlier words to
her. Ann's gaze was riveted on the coffin, as though she was
trying to absorb the fact that it really was her father who
lay enshrined in this unimaginable setting. For a moment,
both women watched her carefully. Then Sue-Ann spoke
gently.

"Wouldn't you like to look at your daddy, honey? Come.
I'll take you to him."

"No!" Elizabeth's voice was almost a scream. She felt herself losing control. "No," she repeated. "I think we've seen
enough. I don't want Ann to remember her father this way."
She held tightly to Ann's hand. "We'll go now, darling. And
I think the wisest thing is for us not to return. We've seen
what we came to see, dear. There's no need to stay longer.
Your daddy is resting. We'll say a prayer for him in our own
way."

Obediently, Ann turned toward the front door. She had
not uttered a word. Only the stiffness of her body, more pronounced now, and the wetness of her palms betrayed the
horror she felt. She was like a tin soldier. Even her motions
were mechanical. Not once, since the first moments, had she
looked at Sue-Ann or at her mother. She seemed to be in

shock, incapable of thought or speech. What have I done to her? Elizabeth thought. Dear God, what trauma have I created by giving in, once more, to the impetuous, immature wishes of this child?

With a ridiculous attempt at civility, Elizabeth spoke to Sue-Ann. "Thank you for what you did for him," she said. Her voice sounded like that of a well mannered little girl. "Please give our apologies to your pastor for not attending the funeral."

Sue-Ann responded to her first sentence. "He did more for me than I did for him. And now I see why. With me he could be himself and he knew it. Living with you must have been like spending your life in a boarding school—all good manners and everything emotional locked up tight inside you all the time. I pity you, lady. It would do you a lot of good to holler and scream sometime. Maybe that's something you ought to teach your daughter."

Angrily, Elizabeth turned away. At the front door, she heard Sue-Ann's last defiant words.

"Oh, by the way," the madam called after her. "There'll be no need to pass your apologies on to the pastor. I'm the pastor. People like you wear veils and sit off in a little side room during funerals where no one can see you. Me, I'm going to be right out there, telling Jesus and the world what a good man this was. It's a shame you never knew him."

Close to tears, Elizabeth fled down the steps of the bordello, almost dragging the dazed figure of Ann behind her. She picked up their few possessions at the hotel and spent the next eight hours in the anonymity of the railroad station. When the train came she tucked Ann into a lower berth and gave her a sleeping pill. Wearily, Elizabeth climbed into the upper and lay wide awake for hours, not daring to sleep lest Ann call out to her.

As the train made its laborious way north, she thought of Alan, remembering her early hopes for him, reviewing their years together, recalling his fleeting, spectacular success and the promises that were never fulfilled. The man who had been praised by the President of the United States now lay dead in a brothel, his eulogy to be delivered by an unorthodox evangelist who was, incredibly, his wife.

She dared not think what the effect of this experience might have on Ann. At her impressionable age, Elizabeth worried that the strange things she had seen might haunt Ann forever. It had been a terrible, terrible mistake, and Elizabeth prayed that it would have no permanent effect on her daughter. There was no telling how she would react when she came out of her self-imposed silence. She had not spoken a word since they entered that awful house. Would she feel loathing for what her father had become? Would she hate Elizabeth for leaving him? Would she, perhaps, turn against men and marriage, trusting no one, believing in nothing?

Elizabeth tried to find shreds of comfort in the only thing she knew to be true. Ann was a strong personality, a basically, perhaps healthily, selfish one as well. She would never forget what she had seen but perhaps her strong ego would keep her from identifying her parents' failures with her own future.

For the first time, Elizabeth blessed Alan for making Ann so completely sure of her own superiority. Perhaps it was the thing that would save her.

Chapter 11

To all outward appearances, Elizabeth's prayers, delivered so fervently in the jolting upper berth, were answered. Ann did not speak again of her father or of the strange few hours she had spent in Memphis. Instead, she went about her life as she always had, living within herself, not morbidly but with an even more highly accentuated remoteness.

In June she graduated from high school and made good her determination to get a job. She found one, in a bookstore on F Street. Elizabeth still would have preferred her to go to a nearby college. It was true that they could not afford the finest school, but between Elizabeth's salary at the paper and the steady income from the rooming house, she could have managed without too great hardship. In spite of her still modest salary, which, by government decree, had been frozen at the start of the war, she had steadily repaid Stu Preston's loan with interest. In seven years, the house had become an important equity, the only real asset she owned. The few dollars left over each month, after all the bills were paid, went for the "culture" that fed Elizabeth's soul. She continued to take the children to theater and concerts, to buy books and art magazines, to fill the house with plants and blossoms, even though she supposed she should have used every spare penny to build a college fund for Quigly and Charlene.

In 1944, she was thirty-nine years old and at the peak of her attractiveness. Still she sought no man and, strangely, none sought her. The memory of Adam stayed with her, though many months had passed since he left, and she had not had a single word from him. She might have become interested in someone else, time having a way of softening even the most ardent memories, but there was little opportunity to start a new romance. Washington was full of men, but in the words of the wartime song, "they were either too young or too old." Or else they were married, and Elizabeth was determined never to fall into that trap again.

Stu Preston offered the only temptation and she avoided it even more assiduously than he did. They lunched together occasionally, but the atmosphere, as though by mutual consent, remained patently platonic. She did not tell him the full details of her Memphis trip, and Stu did not press her. They did talk of Elizabeth's family. She gratefully used this intelligent man as a sounding board for things that troubled her. In July, she told Preston about Ann's job, expressing regret that the girl did not seem interested in college unless it was a "snobby" school.

Preston did not make much of that fact. "I doubt that's the whole reason," he said. "Ann's a beautiful girl. She'll probably marry early. And *well*. Maybe that's more in the back of her mind than the social status of any female college."

"I can't imagine what would give you that idea. If anything, it's just the opposite. Aside from a few parties that she's gone to with extraordinary reluctance, she doesn't seem to see any young men at all. I don't understand it. At her age, I had more beaux than I could count, and I wasn't half the beauty she is."

"That was a different world," Stu said. "Maybe it's not quite as easy for Ann to meet attractive young men in this impersonal city as it was for you with Cambridge spread out at your feet."

"If it's only that, I won't worry so much."

"What else could it be except lack of opportunity? Don't forget, most of the eligible young men are off to war, God help them."

His words comforted Elizabeth. "I hope you're right, but I can't help feeling anxious. Because of Alan and me. I couldn't stand it if our experience had soured her on marriage."

"Don't be ridiculous. My Lord, Elizabeth, she's not quite eighteen and you're acting like she's an old maid! I wouldn't fret about Ann, if I were you. Believe me, that one will land on her feet. What about your other two?"

Another shadow of unhappiness crossed her face. With Stu, Elizabeth had been quite open about her troubles with Quigly. They had not diminished. He had just turned sixteen but looked three or four years older, with a mature, well-developed physique. Already there were girls and obviously not the right kind of girls. She had found condoms in his dresser when she put his laundry away. She had not discussed her discovery with him, ashamed to have him know what she'd found, even a little fearful of the rebuff she would receive.

"Quigly's just the same," she said finally. "Completely beyond me. He's my own son and I know him less than I know you."

Preston frowned. "What about college for *him* in a couple of years?"

"Your guess is as good as mine. He won't even discuss it."

"Well," Stu said, "at least we can end this conversation on a happy note. Or has Charlene run off with a sword swallower in the circus?"

Elizabeth smiled. "No, I think she'll make it to the age of ten still unmarried, uncomplicated, and utterly irresistible. Would you believe that child has turned into a remarkably good cook? Right now she makes a better chocolate cake than I do—and with ersatz ingredients at that!"

Across the luncheon table they regarded each other with affection. Suddenly Elizabeth reached out and put her hand on Preston's. "What a good friend you are," she said warmly. "You and Laurel. How could I have survived these last years without you?"

He patted the hand that lay on top of his. "You give back every bit as much as you take, Elizabeth. And don't you ever forget it."

She returned to the office considerably heartened by Preston's vote of confidence and relieved by the chance to voice some of the things that troubled her. Her step was almost jaunty as she entered the office of *Wife and Mother.* On her desk, scrawled on a yellow pad, was a brief note. "Check with me when you get back. Important. L." She went immediately to the small office that Laurel had occupied since Grace Edwards left it. Her friend was staring vacantly out of the window.

"Hi. I'm back," Elizabeth said. "What's wrong? Trouble with this week's issue?"

Laurel swiveled around in her chair. Her expression was serious, but her voice had the usual lighthearted ring. "No, everything's tickety-boo, as Winnie the Church is prone to say. The issue is fine. It's the editor who's mixed up. Sit down, friend, and help me make a decision."

Elizabeth took the wooden armchair next to Laurel's desk.

"I got a call from New York about an hour ago," Laurel said. "From *Enchantress* magazine. I used to write some free-lance fashion stuff for them. They want me to come up and talk about a job. In fact, not *a* job, *the* job. They know me and it seems they're dumb enough to think I could be the editor in chief, provided, I suppose, that I pass my Wassermann test."

Elizabeth caught her breath. "But that's wonderful! *Enchantress* is the chic-est fashion magazine in the world! Laurel, what a compliment! Not that you don't deserve it."

"Oh, I deserve it all right," Laurel said mockingly. "The question is, do I want it?"

"But why on earth wouldn't you?"

"That's what I've been sitting here trying to figure out. I can't think of one damned reason why I shouldn't leap on the next plane and accept before they come to their senses. And yet, I don't know. Something's holding me back. Maybe I'm scared that it's too big for me. Maybe I'm just a pretty good weekly newspaper editor but not slick enough for all those highly polished big-city broads who'll probably be out to cut my throat every hour on the hour. Hell, maybe I just don't want to leave Washington. I was born here, you know. Rare native species. Some day they may enshrine me in Smithsonian as a third-generation D.C. bird."

Elizabeth listened carefully to the list of invalid excuses. Laurel could do the job and she knew it. It was a great coup that the fancy magazine had been aware of the talents of a relatively obscure journalist and had sought her out for the key position. All that talk about not wanting to leave Washington was pure nonsense. Laurel was having an unadulterated case of stage fright. It would pass as soon as she walked into the offices of *Enchantress*.

"Laurel, dear, you'd be making the biggest mistake of your life if you passed this up. And there's nothing to hold you here. No family. No important romance. Washington doesn't have enough to offer somebody like you. New York does, and you'll love every minute of it. Lord knows that selfishly I'll hate to see you go, but I'd be a rotten friend if I didn't push you onto that plane."

"Preston will kill me. You know, that son of a bitch has really been good to me."

Elizabeth laughed. "Well, let's say he'll be a little put out. It won't be easy to find your replacement. But he'll survive. In fact, if I know our boss he'll be as happy for you as I am."

"Maybe he'll make you editor."

"I doubt it. Maureen Duffy has seniority and she'd be much better anyway. But let's don't worry about that. You get right on that phone and tell them you're on the way."

Laurel tried to look gloomy but she was already becoming enthusiastic. With her hand on the telephone, she looked impishly at Elizabeth.

"Hey," she said, "I just had a funny thought."

"What?"

"The average woman starts out as an enchantress and ends up a wife and mother. I'm doing it the other way around. Think that's a good omen?"

"Sure-fire," Elizabeth said. "But don't let it go to your head."

In August, Laurel went off to her important new job as editor in chief of *Enchantress* and Maureen slipped into her seat at the paper. As a veteran of almost nine years at *Wife and Mother*, Elizabeth regretted the changes that had taken place in the staff. The replacements for Laurel and now for Maureen were both mere babies, energetic young women who seemed scarcely older than Ann. Little Nancy St. John had married her ensign two years before and still another unfamiliar face dispensed copy paper and telephone messages to the staff. I must be getting old, Elizabeth thought. I hate the impersonal feeling of this office. And most of all I miss Laurel, here and at the house. An undefinable sense of uneasiness overtook her. On the surface, things were quiet. But underneath she felt changes brewing. In her way, she was something of a fatalist. Experience had taught her that things happen when they are supposed to happen. She forced herself to simply wait for the next move in that odd but unalterable master plan that seemed to shape her life.

She did not have long to wait.

Arriving home from the office one evening in early September, she found a solemn, worried-looking Charlene waiting for her at the front door. Wordlessly, the child thrust a piece of paper at her. It was a terse note in Quigly's boyish scrawl.

Mother—
I've been accepted by the Merchant Marine. Was sworn in this morning. They think I'm 18 and there's no use your telling them I'm not. They'd kick me out if you said so but you know I'd just find some other way to get into the war so why bother. I'll write to you when I can. Tell Ann I'm doing her a big favor. Now you can put Charlene into my old room.

Quigly.

Charlene watched her anxiously as she read the defiant message. "Quigly told me to give you that as soon as you came home, Mommy," she said. "He said to tell you he meant it about leaving. Has Quigly gone away forever, Mommy? Won't we ever see him again?" Charlene was on the verge of tears. For some unfathomable reason she adored her brother, worshiped him, as she did Ann, across the gulf of the few but meaningful years that separated them.

Trying to control her own shock, Elizabeth took Charlene in her arms, speaking calmly and soothingly to the distressed child. "Hush, darling," she said. "It's all right. Quigly will be back soon. He loves you very much, baby. See how he trusted you to deliver this important letter? He knows you're a big, responsible girl. There's nothing to worry about, sweetheart. Now how about doing Mommy a favor and setting the table for dinner? I have a telephone call to make. Okay?"

Charlene nodded unhappily. "Will Quigly be here for dinner?"

"No, love. Not tonight. Just set three places, for you, Ann, and me."

When Charlene left the room, Elizabeth called Stu Preston. She hated to bother him, but she did not know where else to turn. Quickly and as unemotionally as possible, she read the letter to him. "I don't know what's right," Elizabeth said. "He is under age and I could get him back, but what then?"

Stu did not give her a direct answer. "Goddamn kids," he said. "Goddamn war."

Elizabeth waited. "Do you think I should get in touch with Merchant Marine recruiting?" she asked finally.

"I can't make that decision for you, Elizabeth. That's something you'll have to figure out for yourself. I will say, though, that he sounds as though he means it. It isn't the first time he's threatened to run away, is it?"

"No," she said slowly, "I think he's wanted to leave almost since the day I took him to Bethesda. Quigly's been a strange, restless boy all his life. I guess I always knew it was just a question of time before I'd lose him." Her voice was sad. "Maybe he always knew he was the left-out one. Ann was Alan's favorite and I'm afraid Charlene is mine. Poor Quigly. He never seemed to fit in at all."

"I think," Preston said quietly, "that you've made your decision."

"I suppose so. How can I fight the inevitable?"

"Now that you've said it, Elizabeth, I'll tell you that I think it's the only one you can make. And for whatever it's worth, you can take comfort in the fact that it could be worse. The Merchant Marine is a helluva sight safer than the infantry, all things being relevant. Maybe you should be glad that Quigly didn't wait to be drafted. Not that this war can last much longer. A few months, maybe, at most. Christ, I don't think any of this is desirable, but it could be worse. May even make a better man of him."

"He's sixteen, Stu. He's not a man. He's just a boy. You know what tough characters sign up for the Merchant Marine. God knows what kind of men he'll be associating with."

In spite of the seriousness of the conversation, Preston had to laugh. "I won't argue that point with you, honey. But I will remind you that a wartime army is not exactly composed of the West Point Glee Club, either."

Even Elizabeth recognized her protective maternalism, ludicrous in this situation, ridiculous, where Quigly was concerned, at any time. She would simply have to accept this as she had learned to live with other uncontrollable events. She prepared to hang up. "Thanks, Stu. I'm sorry to burden you with my problems. I just had to talk to someone."

"Don't ever apologize for calling me. It's a compliment. And Elizabeth, I know it sounds silly, but try not to worry too much. In the morning I'll see what I can find out for you about Quigly's whereabouts. He may even be in touch with you first."

"I doubt it," she said flatly. "Good night," Stu."

As she put down the receiver, Elizabeth thought about the men in her life. I must be some kind of jinx, she mused. Every man I love, I lose. My father, my husband, my lover, and now my son. Two dead. Two missing.

She was right. There was no word from Quigly, but Preston, with his far-flung connections, was able to tell her that her son had shipped out as an ordinary seaman and even give her the name of the merchant ship, which was making the dangerous North Atlantic run. She wrote several letters to Quigly, sending them to the address that Stu provided, but there was no answer. Not even an acknowledgment of her "blessing" nor a response which might have included the one word he left out of his farewell note—the word "love."

Ann seemed reasonably happy in her work at the bookshop. Since the horrible trip to Memphis, she and Elizabeth had tacitly come to a better understanding. Or perhaps it was merely that Ann was acquiring insight with maturity. Her manner, though still withdrawn, was less imperious, less resentful. She even offered to pay room and board, a suggestion that Elizabeth declined with appreciation.

"Use your money for yourself, dear," she said. "It's a great help to me that you're able to buy your own clothes and have pocket money. Your room is here anyway, and heaven knows you don't eat enough to keep a bird alive!"

There were frequent telephone calls and long, sprightly letters from Laurel. She loved her job and was ecstatic about New York. She had found a three-and-a-half-room apartment in mid-Manhattan for the ridiculously low sum of $110 a month.

My rich and social staff thinks I'm quaint to live so modestly. In their minds, I should have, at the very least, a nine-room penthouse. That, of course, is because all the young ladies who work for *Enchantress* seem to come from families with tons of money. A good thing, too. The wages we pay make Stu Preston look like Joe Generous! Fortunately, none of my girls cares. They're working for the sheer glamour of saying they're associated with the magazine. Those who don't live at home (home being a big spread on Park Avenue!) have their own fancy layouts paid for by doting parents. Their salaries are pocket money for buying nylons when those rare gems can be found! It's a wacky world up here. The other day when I told the publisher that one of the secretaries had asked for a raise, he looked at me like I was crazy. "Why on earth would she want a raise?" said he "Has her family cut off her allowance?" Of course, I knew a raise was impossible—legally speaking—because of the wage freeze. But there are ways to slip an employee extra money if you really want to. That's what they had to do to hire me, as you well know. BURN THIS INCRIMINATING ADMISSION!

Love,
Laurel

Elizabeth missed her cheerful friend even more than she'd anticipated. With Laurel's departure, the fun evenings had almost entirely ceased. Life now was boringly routine. The only thing that saved her was her job. It, at least, provided some mental stimulation. Famous names in the home-furnishings and decorating fields continued to come to Washington and were dutifully interviewed by Elizabeth. In return, they provided her with amusing lunches and sophisticated chatter about a New York world which seemed to be populated entirely by people who had cocktails at the Stork Club and dinner at "21."

The most frequent of these visitors was a famous decorator named Robert Gale who arrived every three or four weeks to check on the small shop he maintained in Washington. It was one of many out-of-town branches Gale had established before the war, and it continued, like the others, to flourish among the upper strata of homeowners. Elizabeth had done a piece about him early in her career and an easy friendship had sprung up between them. He called her almost every time he came to town, and she looked forward to her lunches with this witty, urbane fifty-year-old man.

At first, in her naïveté, Elizabeth did not realize that Gale was a discreet but dedicated homosexual. He was extraordinarily attractive, with prematurely snow-white hair and beautiful, London-tailored suits which, since the war, had been replaced by equally elegant custom models from an exclusive New York source. Robert Gale knew how to win over women. It was his business to sell his cultivated charm along with his overpriced furniture. As they came to know each other better, Gale began to put out broad hints about his personal life, so broad that even a remarkably innocent Elizabeth could not mistake the implication. Perhaps he was worried that she would interpret his friendship as something more than what it was. Or perhaps, for one of the few times in his life, Robert had found a woman he could trust. Whichever, she accepted this knowledge without dismay or disapproval. She did not entirely understand such "deviation from the norm," but she did not presume to judge or even question such a highly personal decision. His disclosure did not in the least diminish her affection for him, a fact she made quite plain and one that Gale accepted with almost pathetic relief. Encouraged by her attitude, he talked quite eagerly about the young man who was the center of his life.

"You must meet Tony," he told her one day. "Anthony Alexander, my friend. You'll like each other. Of course, he's much younger than we are, Elizabeth. Only twenty-seven. My God, what I'd give to be twenty-seven again!"

She was amused at the fact that Gale lumped her in his

own age bracket. She was, in fact, right in the middle: eleven years younger than Gale and twelve years older than the young man he obviously adored. It was understandable, she supposed. To Gale she must seem a hundred, with her working daughter and her son in the Merchant Marine. Compared to the women of thirty-nine whom he knew, she must *look* a hundred as well. She had no time or money for the endless facials, body massages, health spas, and hair tinting with which his clients pampered themselves. She did not, in fact, look older than she actually was. But the once dark hair was now generously, though not unbecomingly, salted with white. And the faint, delicate lines around the bright blue eyes reflected the stress of almost twenty hard years.

"I'd like very much to meet Tony," Elizabeth said. As a matter of fact, she was not sure she wanted to meet him at all. What could he be like, this young man who'd involved himself with a patron nearly twice his age? Robert had told her that Tony worked with him in his business; that they had, in fact, met when Gale was invited to speak at the decorating school in which Tony had enrolled after his discharge from the army.

"He was in the army?" Elizabeth's tone betrayed her surprise.

"Sure was. Joined before Pearl Harbor. He was a medic. You couldn't get Tony to carry a gun. Instead, he managed to get himself wounded treating other soldiers in Italy. Even got a medal for bravery under fire." Gale sounded like a proud father. "He's quite a boy. Mystical, somehow. He's deep into all those Far Eastern religions. Oh, I don't mean he's one of those nuts who run around in Indian robes. But he has a kind of, I don't know, I guess you'd call it purity."

Elizabeth was intrigued. She had pictured Tony Alexander as some effeminate, mincing young man with an angelic face and a calculating mind. Instead, a different kind of picture was emerging. It piqued her interest.

"Why don't you bring him with you on your next trip?"

"I have a better idea," Robert said. "Why don't you come up to New York and spend a weekend with us? We'd love to have you. There's a rather pleasant guest suite. And you could see your friend Laurel, who, incidentally, I'd love to meet. The four of us could do the town. See some shows. Take in a couple of good restaurants. What about next weekend? October is nearly gone and you know that's the best time in New York."

To her surprise, Elizabeth heard herself agreeing. In spite of its obvious sincerity, it was a kind of creepy invitation, only because Gale offered it in the exact tone a woman friend would use if she were inviting a guest to visit her and her husband. She supposed his unself-conscious attitude was a tribute to her "broad-mindedness." She was being silly to give it a second thought. Besides, Laurel had been begging her to come for a visit but she had not wanted to impose on her friend's limited quarters. She was ready for a break in her routine and certainly this would be the de luxe way to get it.

"You're sure you really want me to come?"

"My dear, I haven't done anything I didn't want to do since I took my last revolting forkful of spinach at the age of five. If I thought for one moment that you'd be anything less than a perfect guest I wouldn't dream of mentioning it. In fact, I think you should stay over a day or two into the following week. I'm certain that Laurel would like to show you the shops, and they are utterly unbearable on a Saturday!"

When Elizabeth called to tell her the plan, Laurel was delighted. "I'd much rather have you stay with me," she said, "so we could gossip all night. But I must say I'm impressed. Robert Gale's townhouse is supposed to be fabulous! I'm dying to get a look at it. The magazine has photographed there in the past, but that was before my time."

"Do you know the chap who lives with him—Tony Alexander?"

"Never heard of him. Why?"

"No special reason, except he'll be the fourth member of our group, if you have no objection."

"If he wears pants and is ambulatory, I'll welcome him with open arms. Not, I gather, that he'd be interested in them."

"I think not," Elizabeth said. "He's Robert's boy friend. They share the house.

"It figures. Well, who cares? We'll have a marvelous time. And you *will* stay over at least until Wednesday, won't you? We have so much catching up to do. Any word from Quigly?"

"Not directly. Stu says his ship is okay."

"That's a blessing anyhow. The girls all right?"

"Fine. Ann is willing to baby-sit with Charlene the nights I'm away, and of course Mary will be around during the day."

"Bless her heart, she's really Old Faithful, isn't she? When are you arriving?"

"I'll take the Congressional up Friday evening. Don't bother to meet me. Robert is sending his car. I'll call you when I arrive."

Laurel whistled. "Sending his car? Get *you!* Or rather, get *him,* gas rationing and all! Is he really all that madly rich?"

"Well, he's not poor. Which is what I'll be if I don't hang up. This phone call is costing me a fortune."

"Dope! You mean you called me at the office and didn't reverse the charges? Goodbye. See you Friday."

As she settled into her coach seat on the famous Washington-to-New York train, Elizabeth looked forward eagerly to her brief holiday. Aside from the fateful Memphis trip, she couldn't remember the last time she'd been out of Washington. Was it possible that her last journey had been to her dying father's bedside? If so, until now it seemed that every trip she made was a mission of sorrow. This one would be different, she promised herself. She would not allow herself an unhappy thought. She would not even think of Quigly, as she had every night for the past two months.

Gale's smartly uniformed chauffeur was waiting on the platform, his eyes glued to the passengers detraining from the reserved-seat, Pullman-chair section. Elizabeth approached him from behind, carrying her one small suitcase.

"I'm Miss Quigly," she said. "Are you looking for me?"

Hastily the man removed his cap and reached for her bag. "Yes, ma'am. I'm sorry I missed you, Miss Quigly. The train was so full I guess I just didn't see you get off."

"No," Elizabeth said, smiling. "You were just facing the wrong way."

Feeling deliciously luxurious in the rear seat of Gale's pale-gray Bentley, Elizabeth looked out the window with interest as the car made its smooth way uptown. New York was big, dirty, frightening, and insidiously seductive with its glittering shops, its imposing hotels, its crowds of urgent, driven people who seemed to pay no attention to anything around them. She was glad she had not had to fight for a taxi at Pennsylvania Station. They were in very short supply. She had seen two women in a screaming fight for possession of a cab. Each had entered from a different side and each claimed priority. The driver, with the unique imperturbability of New York hackies, simply leaned back and let them verbally slug it out. A fare was a fare, whichever one triumphed. It was all the same to him.

In a few minutes the car slid to a stop on a quiet, tree-lined street in the East Sixties between Madison and Park

Avenues. Robert Gale's black-and-gray townhouse was like an oasis of quiet in the teaming city, its tall French windows delicately curtained against the intrusion of the outside world. The gleaming ebony door bore a warning sign that this dwelling was under the tight security of a professional protection agency.

No wonder there was a burglar-alarm system, Elizabeth thought as she entered. Even the foyer was a treasure house of beautiful things, all selected with Robert Gale's impeccable taste. Their owner came bounding down the stairs to greet her.

"Welcome!" he said. "Was the trip all right? I see that Arthur found you in that hellhole of a Pennsylvania Station!"

"He wasn't hard to recognize," Elizabeth said gaily. "I daresay you're one of the few remaining gentlemen who still has a chauffeur."

"You'd be surprised. There's more money around than ever. Though I like to think that I'm one of the few *legitimate* war profiteers! Most of the rest seem to be making their fortunes in black-market scotch and illegal sales of rationed cigarettes! Come and see the house and meet Tony. Or do you want to unpack first?"

"My extensive wardrobe can wait," she said. "I'm dying to see the house."

"Good. A woman after my own heart!"

He led her into the drawing room off to the right of the entrance hall. It was a gigantic salon with French doors opening out onto a garden carefully planted with orderly patterns of fall flowers. The room was exquisite. It was as though it had been transplanted from the seventeenth century, with every piece of furniture intact, every *objet* a collector's item. Still, much as she admired it, Elizabeth's immediate thought was that it was not a room to live in. It was a showplace that sacrificed comfort for chic, warmth for overwhelming elegance. No wonder *Enchantress* photographed here. It was a background for the effete, the twentieth-century untouchables like Robert Gale. A perfect fire burned noiselessly, as though it knew a crackle or pop would be frowned on. Soft, shaded lamps gave off a flattering glow, but no one would be foolhardy enough to try to read by their light. The silken sofas and delicate French armchairs were meant to be perched on, not sprawled in. Elizabeth thought it was the most beautiful room she'd ever seen. And the most contrived.

The big dining room was more of the same. Perfect in

every detail. The kind of room that called for well-modulated voices and gourmet food, as much of it imported and out of season as possible.

She was sincere in her compliments and Robert seemed delighted by her praise.

"Tony thinks it's a monument to materialism," he laughed.

But not so much that he won't live here, Elizabeth silently answered.

A frown suddenly crossed Gale's face. "Where in hell is that boy? He should have come down to welcome you. He's very anxious to know you, Elizabeth. I've been telling him what a delight you are. That Tony!" Robert shook his head indulgently. "Probably engrossed in some philosophical treatise and, as usual, has lost all sense of time! Come on. We'll go upstairs. I'm sure you'd like to see your room anyway. We're all on the second floor. Arthur and Howard— he's the cook—live on the top. The cleaning woman comes in by the day. Arthur acts as waiter, valet, and chauffeur. It works out well, even though it's a big house for such a small staff. Wartime, you know. Difficult as hell to get help, but we manage."

Thinking of her own domestic situation, Elizabeth suppressed a smile. She had instinctively known better than to ever invite Robert Gale to the rooming house in Washington. He would have fainted.

Chatting easily, Robert led the way. "By the bye," he said, "I took the liberty of inviting your friend Laurel Lane to dinner here this evening. Thought you might be tired and would enjoy a quiet meal at home. Hope that's all right with you. It will give us a chance to get to know each other. Tomorrow night we'll do the town, if that suits you."

"Perfect. It's so thoughtful of you, Robert."

"Here are your digs," he said, opening the first door on the right. "I think you'll find everything you need."

His words were an understatement. The bedroom was a dream, done in pink toile with accents of cherry velvet. Her suitcase lay on a white lacquered rack. Through the bedroom door she could glimpse a sitting room softly decorated in pale-pink silk with antique fruitwood furniture. She could not see the bath, but she was willing to bet that it would be stocked with everything from new toothbrushes to co-ordinated shower caps. Elizabeth caught her breath.

"Robert, it's fabulous!"

"Glad you like it. I think it's nice for a woman. Not that we're lucky enough to have many lady guests. My ancient mother comes in a couple of times a year from Pennsylvania.

And we do have some dear friends who visit New York now and then. You probably know some of them." He named a famous ballerina and a Hollywood actress known to be the darling of the homosexuals. Again, his face darkened. "Damn that, Tony, where is he? You get settled in, Elizabeth, and I'll go see what's happened to him. See you downstairs in about half an hour? Let's see. It's nine o'clock now. Your friend Laurel should be along any time. A bit late for cocktails, but I knew your train didn't leave Washington till four. Hope you're not starving. We'll have a quick drink and dine about ten."

"Thank you. If it's all right, I'll call Ann to tell her I've arrived safely and see how she and Charlene are making out."

In half an hour, having phoned the girls, hung up her few dresses, and given her face a quick, light touch-up, she wandered down to the drawing room. There was no sign of Robert or Tony, but the efficient Arthur appeared to ask if she wanted a drink. She decided to wait for the others. In a moment, she heard the doorbell chime and Laurel was ushered in. The two women hugged each other and exchanged appraising looks.

"My God, it's good to see you!" Laurel said. "You look great!"

"I can say even more about you," Elizabeth responded. "You really look like the successful New York woman. I love your hair. And that dress! Laurel, it's beautiful!"

"You friend Gale said it would be just an informal evening at home, so I didn't go crazy with my chi-chi new wardrobe. I must confess that I've gone a little wild buying clothes. The temptation is irresistible when you have access to the wholesale market. This is what Mainbocher calls one of his 'understated numbers.' You think it looks all right?"

Elizabeth smiled unenviously. "It's a knockout. You never looked prettier."

It was true. Importance and success agreed with Laurel. Always well dressed, she was now head-turning. Tonight she had on a simple, beautifully cut black wool dress that showed off her figure to advantage. Even the costume jewelry looked real. With her dark hair cut short and curled in the current "poodle coif," she was the average woman's dream of a magazine editor. For a moment, Elizabeth feared that she might have changed inwardly as well. Perhaps the super-smooth exterior covered a brittle, nonchalant new attitude that matched the elegant trappings. But Laurel's next words dispelled that worry.

"Jeepers, what a layout! No wonder all the magazines

fight to use this place as a background for pictures. Does anybody actually *live* here, or is it just a place where Robert Gale drops in now and then to drape his arm over the mantelpiece and look glamorous?"

Elizabeth laughed. "Oh, they live here, all right. At least Robert does. So far I haven't seen the mysterious Anthony Alexander."

As though on cue, the two men appeared in the doorway. Gale was immaculately attired in a dark blue velvet "smoking jacket" with a carefully careless ascot. Behind him was a very tall, sensitive-looking young man in a dark tweed suit. Amid Gale's flurry of apologies for their tardiness, introductions were made all around and the omnipresent Arthur took drink orders.

As Robert talked brightly and easily, Elizabeth watched Tony Alexander. She had never seen a face quite so still. When the conversation was directed to him, he answered pleasantly in a gentle, almost soothing voice. Otherwise, he initiated no small talk. Elizabeth tried to read his expression. It was by no means sullen or unhappy. He did not seem bored or even uninterested. And it was not an empty face. It was more as though he was somewhere in a world of his own, far removed from the superficial polite chatter which flowed around him. Perhaps this was part of what Gale had meant when he said that Tony had a kind of "purity." It was a pure face. Incongruous, Elizabeth thought, when one considered the presumably parasitic nature of Tony's relationship with Robert.

During dinner, Tony seemed to come more alive under Elizabeth's sincere interest. While Laurel and Robert exchanged local gossip and played Do You Know? with the names of New York celebrities, Elizabeth talked quietly with Tony, who sat on her right. She learned that he was a native Californian with a patently domineering mother who, early on, had treated him like an adult female companion, including him, at the age of ten, in her bridge games and her shopping expeditions. He spoke of her matter-of-factly and without rancor, but with an intelligent understanding of the way her fierce possessiveness had influenced his life. His father was an unresisting man who had abdicated all parental responsibility in the face of his wife's overpowering personality.

Elizabeth read a great deal between the lines of Tony's recital of his early years. He spoke of both of his parents with affection. Yes, they still lived in California. He visited them once or twice a year. No, they had never been to

New York, but they had met Robert and liked him. In fact, they were pleased that Tony had found such a "good friend and employer." He volunteered the last piece of information with an almost sardonic smile.

"Robert says you were wounded in the war," Elizabeth said conversationally. "What made you enlist in the medical corps?"

"I just wanted to help," he said simply. "I'm not a fighter, I'm a healer. In the literal sense of the word."

Elizabeth raised her eyebrows.

"Some day I'll tell you what I mean," Tony said. "When we have time for a long, private conversation. Somehow I think you'll understand. Most people don't."

With that, he turned away from her and devoted the rest of the dinner hour to Laurel, who seemed charmed by him.

The weekend was an unqualified success. With the pride of "adopted New Yorkers"—even Robert finally admitted that he was Philadelphia-born—the three of them showed Elizabeth every facet of the city's glittering life. They dined in the Cub Room of the Stork Club, the inner sanctum where the famous could stare at each other and avoid being stared at by the tourists who tried to bribe their way past Sherman Billingsly's restraining velvet rope. They had late supper in the bar of "21" after Robert got four impossible-to-buy tickets to the new Broadway hit, *Bloomer Girl*. They lunched at the Colony, drank martinis laced with Pernod in the bar of the Brussels and had Sunday brunch in the Ritz Carlton on Madison Avenue.

On Monday, Laurel gave Elizabeth a tour of her posh offices at *Enchantress*, trying, unsuccessfully, to pretend that she had already gotten used to her fur-covered couches, her multibuttoned telephone with its mysterious intercom system, and her two expensively dressed, if not overefficient, secretaries. Later, the two women lunched at Le Pavillon, where even the unapproachable M. Soulé knew Laurel by sight and gave her the most prominent table in the room.

"Couldn't we sit somewhere farther back where we wouldn't be so conspicuous?" Elizabeth whispered.

"Hush," Laurel said. "You'll ruin my image. Besides, you're so elegant-looking that I'm sure Henri Soulé put you here to dress up the room."

It was a polite fib. Elizabeth could tell from the way Laurel was received everywhere that she had become one of the people who counted in fashionable New York circles. Elizabeth was proud of her friend. Proud of her success and pleased by the way she had so quickly and happily fitted into this big, scary town. Most of all, it was comforting to see that all the publicity, the fawning, and catering had not changed Laurel except for the better. She seemed truly to have found herself. Professionally, at least.

"You really love it here, don't you?"

"Love New York?" Laurel smiled. "Yes, I guess I'm hooked. Sorry about Smithsonian, but I don't think I could ever go back to Washington. You were right about the opportunities here, you know. For anybody who wants a career, this is the place."

"And you want a career." It was more a statement than a question.

For a moment, Laurel looked almost defiant. "That's a funny question. Of course I want a career. What else would I want?"

Elizabeth took a slow sip of her whiskey sour, stalling for time. "I don't know," she said at last, "maybe you want a career and a husband. One or both. A lot of successful women do."

"If you're gently trying to find out about my personal life, luv, you needn't pussyfoot. We haven't had any secrets from each other since practically the day we met. So I don't mind telling you that I haven't met an available man since I've been in New York. Oh, a few grabbers and gropers, but nobody important. You know," Laurel said, slowly eating the cherry out of her drink, "I don't think I'll ever get married. I still entertain the idea that I'd like to, but I'm not even sure that's true. I don't think I have the patience for marriage. For one thing, I'm getting pretty long in the tooth. Things get tougher as you plow deeper into your thirties. You expect more and are willing to put up with less. What I'd really like is a rip-roaring affair with a fascinating man. Somebody bright and attentive and interesting, as well as sexy. A no-strings-attached kind of thing, but good for the ego and the metabolism."

"I'll drink to that," Elizabeth said lightly. "Me, too."

"Baloney. That kind of love-'em-and-leave-'em approach isn't your cup of tea, Elizabeth. You can't handle it. We found that out, didn't we?"

There was a hint of pain in Elizabeth's eyes as she answered. "Yes," she said, "I guess we did."

Chapter 12

In his three years of intimate association with Robert Gale, Tony Alexander had asked for nothing though he had given and gotten much. Discharged from the army after a bullet had gone through him, missing his heart by millimeters, he returned to the States uncertain of what he wanted to do. His almost miraculous escape from death did not surprise him. It was, he knew, not yet time for him to die. He believed he had a special place in the universal scheme of things. He did not think he was the Saviour returned or a superior being destined for sainthood. But he had a firm conviction that he'd been put on the earth for some specific purpose. And that purpose, mysterious as it was even to him, seemed to be an almost eerie ability to heal.

It was what had impelled him to work with the doctors on the battlefield. He had no trouble being accepted by the service. In Tony's mind, there was no such thing as a prefix to the word "sexual"—not hetero or homo or even bi. Consequently, he had none of the "symptoms" which might have caused him to be rejected by army psychiatrists. Even to the professionals, he appeared to be a quiet, thoughtful, physically sound young man. And by enlisting before a war which he knew quite certainly would happen, he was able to select the branch in which he could best contribute his unusual talents.

He had had a chance to try out some of his gifts during his two years in combat. The results were exactly what he expected. There was a strange healing power in his hands. He could hold them a few inches above a bad burn or an ugly cut and within hours the burn would disappear and the cut close over without infection. He did this over and over without his patients' knowledge. All they felt was a strong sensation of warmth, as though intense heat radiated from Tony's body into their own. The more perceptive of his subjects recognized that something strange was taking place, but when they tried to question him, Tony brushed off their curiosity with a laugh. "You're imagining things," he told them, knowing they would never understand. But they were not imagining. He did possess some kind of power that enabled him to see what he thought of as an "aura of energy" around other people. He became convinced that each person radiated a kind of electrical discharge which he could identify, though others, obviously, could not. He believed that this radiation of energy was stronger in some people than in others. Frequently he saw a faint halo around the whole body of another human being. Occasionally, it was so strong as to be practically blinding. In his own case, he reasoned, it explained his healing powers.

He searched for some key to this puzzle in the teachings of the East and found religious beliefs which reinforced his own. He spoke of his strange gifts to no one, content to let his destiny rest in the hands of whatever force ruled his life. He was almost indifferent to the personal pattern of his day-to-day activities. Tony knew only that he had love to give, spiritual as well as physical. He was capable of giving it to either sex as long as it afforded pleasure. And so when Robert Gale came into his life he responded to Gale's needs with gentleness and an almost childlike innocence. It was, peculiarly, his first experience with a member of his own sex. It neither shocked nor appalled him, any more than the one or two physical encounters with girls in California had surprised or even touched him. This, he told himself, was his mission in life: Giving love where it was needed. If his presence, his body, afforded happiness to another, that was where Tony's own happiness lay. He loved both sexes, unquestioningly, unhesitatingly, and with no thought of conventions, which were, after all, man-made.

All these mystical beliefs notwithstanding, he was no

wild-eyed zealot. To him, his discoveries were almost scientifically interesting. He had no taste for spreading his gospel in some freakish, evangelical manner. If anything, his outward appearance and demeanor were exactly opposite; he was unfailingly the composed, relaxed young man Elizabeth met that first evening in New York.

Nor did he consider the luxuries of life evils to be rejected. He did not ask for the material riches that Robert showered on him, but he did not refuse them. He had taste and style, and he appreciated the elegant house, the beautiful clothes, and the good food and drink that his friend supplied. He enjoyed being part of Robert's successful decorating business, finding pleasure in working with fine old woods and exquisitely hand-crafted fabrics. It was this love of the esthetic that had drawn him toward the decorating field in the first place. When he returned to civilian life, he seemed ill fitted for any kind of job. He could have gone back to California, to a job in his father's auto sales showroom, but the idea lacked appeal. He could not picture himself selling secondhand cars to shirt-sleeved middle-aged men and their querulous wives. Nor did he wish to return to his parents' middle-class house in the San Fernando Valley and the smothering influence of the woman who ruled it.

Instead, purely on impulse he had followed up an ad for the New York School of Interior Design, noting that it qualified under the G.I. bill, which provided education for veterans. At the time, he did not know why the ad caught his attention. He had never thought of being a decorator, did not even know anyone who had chosen the profession. Later he realized that it was all part of the Plan. For it was here that he met Robert Gale, come to give a guest lecture. Tony had stayed on after Gale finished speaking, to ask for advice about getting an apprentice job in the field. Instead, Gale had offered a place in his own firm and, within weeks, a place in his own life. Tony accepted both and had had little cause to regret the decision.

The only unpleasant moments in their otherwise satisfactory arrangement came about because of Robert's possessiveness. He was intensely jealous of any man in whom Tony seemed to have more than a cursory interest. It was an attitude that was hard for Tony to understand. The very idea that one human could "own" another was incomprehensible to him, and Gale's occasional rages over some fancied breach of faithfulness left him bewildered and as near to anger as he could come.

"I don't belong to you, Robert," he'd said the first time

Gale accused him of being interested in a young man nearer Tony's own age. "You have no right to tell me whom I can speak to or where I can go. I reserve the right to choose my own friends. It has nothing to do with you."

"Oh, hasn't it?" Gale shouted. "What kind of a fool do you think it makes me look when you're dispensing that innocent boyish charm in all directions? God damn it, Tony, I own you all right, whether you think so or not. I give you the bed you sleep in, the food you eat, the clothes you wear! Without me, you'd be nothing. Just another good-looking kid fresh out of the army. You'd be lucky to be selling ties in Bloomingdale's!"

"I could always do that, too," Tony said quietly. "It doesn't really matter that much to me. In fact, I might prefer it to your childish tantrums."

In an instant, Gale's belligerence was gone, replaced by a frightened apology and promises never to be so petty again. These scenes, played over and over again with minor variations, disturbed them both for different reasons. Tony spoke the truth when he said he would not be owned. He would have walked out on his luxurious life without a qualm if it were only a matter of giving up expensive trappings. But he knew that Robert needed him. He could not walk away from that.

For his part, Gale was disgusted with himself for being so thoroughly captivated by this gentle young creature who really might leave him if the reins were too tightly drawn. He knew that Tony did not care for him in the way that he loved Tony. Gale was the one who was owned, by someone who wished neither to possess nor to be possessed. He tried to keep his fears to himself and his jealousy hidden. Only now and then did his anxiety erupt into one of these confrontations from which he always emerged the loser.

There was no such outburst after Elizabeth's return to Washington. Tony had obviously been enchanted by this sensitive, unpretentious woman and had spent an unusual amount of time talking to her. But this attention did not arouse restless fears in Gale. It really did not occur to him that Tony could have any interest in the opposite sex. He reserved his fury only for the moments when Tony seemed to concentrate on another man.

On the night after Elizabeth's departure, Robert and Tony dined quietly at home. Instead of eating in the formal dining room, Arthur brought them trays in the huge master bedroom they shared. Comfortable in robes, they ate at the Empire desk-table in front of the window. The recorded

music which was piped to every room in the house played
softly in the background. Gale felt very peaceful and expansive. The visit had gone well. He was genuinely fond of
Elizabeth and she had been the perfect houseguest, undemanding and satisfactorily thrilled by the magic world he'd
been able to show her. Even her friend Laurel was a nice
enough woman, not an impossible bitch like most of those
fashion-magazine types. Tony had seemed to enjoy the whole
thing, even going quite willingly to the nightclubs and
pseudo-chic restaurants which he normally professed to hate.

Contentedly, Gale lit an after-dinner cigarette, regarding
even that small comfort with pleased awareness. It had been
clever of him to make that arrangement with the cigar store
on Madison Avenue. In return for a generous weekly bribe,
the owner always had cartons of Gale's favorite brand ready
for Arthur to pick up. Robert was not about to stand in
line, as people did these days, for the privilege of buying
one pack of rationed cigarettes at a time. Nor would he
smoke the unknown wartime brands which less clever—or
less affluent—smokers had to settle for. Money could do anything, he reflected unoriginally. Thank God he'd gotten his
start in the pre-Depression days when it was possible to
make tons of it. Otherwise, he might still be living in South
Philadelphia and eking out a living at some stupid job in that
dead-ass town. Inhaling deeply, he pushed his coffee cup
aside and regarded Tony with affection.

"I'm glad we're alone," he said, "but it was pleasant to
have Elizabeth here, wasn't it? You two seemed to get on
very well."

A warning bell rang in Tony's mind. Was this leading up
to another argument? Did Robert think he'd paid too much
attention to Elizabeth? When he answered, his voice was
noncommittal.

"She's a nice woman."

"Much more than that," Gale said. "She's bright. You
know, Tony, I've been thinking. We could use her in the
business. Might be a very smart idea. I think she'd go over
well with the husbands of some of these stupid females we
have to deal with. And the wives wouldn't feel threatened
by her, the way they might by a young woman."

Tony smiled. "You make her sound ancient. How old is
Elizabeth, anyway? Thirty-eight? Forty?"

"Oh, at least. Not that that's *old*." Robert was suddenly on
dangerous ground. "What I meant was that she's charming
and cultured and not the type to flirt with the clients' husbands. I can think of two or three jobs right now where I'm

in solid with the wives, but the men who pay the bills give me a fishy eye. If I had Elizabeth with me, it might go better."

"It's a thought. And she does have some knowledge because of all those years on the paper."

"Exactly. In addition to which, she has the most important qualification of all: Instinctive good taste. You could tell that by the way she chose the best things in this house to admire. Even some of my best reproductions didn't fool her."

"Do you think she'd be willing to leave Washington?" Tony asked. "After all, she does own a house there, doesn't she? And aren't there a couple of children to consider?"

"I get the impression she's bored and lonely in Washington. As for the house, it should be easy to sell anything in that overcrowded one-horse village. I don't even think the children would be a problem. Her boy's in the Merchant Marine and the oldest girl works in a bookshop. She could get the same kind of job here, I'm sure. That leaves only Charlene—the little one. We'd have to help Elizabeth find an apartment with some kind of decent school nearby."

Tony shrugged. "Sounds reasonable, I guess. Did you have this in mind all the time? I mean, when you asked her here was it a kind of prolonged job interview?"

"Well, it had crossed my mind. And it did seem the only way to really get to know her. But I didn't want to mention it until I was sure she was our kind of people."

"And now you're satisfied that she is?"

"Yes," Robert said. "Why shouldn't I be?"

By contrast to her gay, exciting visit to New York, Elizabeth's life, when she returned to Washington, seemed duller than ever. She gave a carefully edited account of it to Ann and Charlene, describing the wonderful shops, theaters, and restaurants, going into detail about Robert's beautiful townhouse, but omitting any mention of Tony. She reported glowingly on Laurel's job and her appearance. And she produced gifts for both the girls—a twin-sweater set from Bonwit Teller for Ann and, for Charlene, a plaid jumper dress from the famous children's department at Best & Co. They were delighted with their presents.

"Now," Elizabeth said, "tell me what's been going on here. Did you two manage all right?" She wanted to ask if there'd been word from Quigly, but there seemed to be no point. If they'd heard from their brother, the girls would be quick to tell her.

"It's been quiet, as usual," Ann said.

"I made a cake Saturday," Charlene volunteered. "We saved you a piece."

"Did you, darling? How nice!"

"She made a terrible mess of the kitchen," Ann said. "Really, Charlene, you are an awful slob. I can't tell you what a relief it is to have you out of my room." The expressions on the faces of her mother and sister made her realize the implication of her words. She wasn't really glad to be rid of Quigly. But she hoped he would stay away long enough for her to have an apartment of her own when she returned. She had no idea how she was going to manage it. But she would never get used to the idea of being the landlady's daughter. Never.

Three weeks later, Robert Gale came to Washington for the day. He called Elizabeth in advance and asked her to have lunch with him. She accepted eagerly, feeling a little remiss that she did not invite him to dinner at her house, small enough payment for all his hospitality. It would have been the natural thing to do, but something told her not to let Robert know that she ran a rooming house. It was one of her small, rare deceptions. She could imagine him raising horrified eyebrows at the very idea.

She wanted to buy him a house present, but was at a loss to know what to get. Nothing less than a treasure would do, and that she couldn't afford. She fell back on one of her old skills. She made him a small needlepoint picture, sketching the design herself. It was a very personal and charming gift which represented highlights of her visit—a tiny townhouse, a miniature Bentley, a jockey to represent "21" and a tiny stork for the famous restaurant on Easy Fifty-third Street. She entwined these symbols with flowers and made a wreath of them around the initials "R.G." Every evening she worked feverishly on it, determined to have it done in time to present to him at lunch. She finished the last stitch late the night before he arrived. When he opened the package, he was visibly delighted, almost touched.

"What a fantastic idea!" he said. "It's an absolute jewel. I love it! How on earth did you get it done so quickly?"

Elizabeth was pleased. "It was fun to do. Besides, I have plenty of time in the evening."

"Washington a little boring?"

"Well, I'm too old to be a debutante and too poor to be a patroness. There isn't much in between for a single woman in this town."

"Ever thought of leaving?"

Elizabeth looked at him searchingly. This was no offhand question.

Before she could answer, Robert rushed on. "I've been thinking about you, my dear. There's room in my organization for someone with your charm and talent. You're simply being wasted on that hick-town weekly paper. I'd like you to work for me."

For a moment, Elizabeth thought he was offering her a job in his Washington shop. Then remembering his reference to leaving, her eyes widened.

"You mean come to work with you in New York?"

"I've always thought I articulated rather well. That *is* the general idea."

Her surprise was genuine. "I don't know," she said. "It's something I've never thought about. Leaving Washington, I mean. Since my father died, I feel as though my roots are here. There's no one left in Boston. I used to think of that as home. And my children have been moved around so often. I'm not sure that another upheaval—" She stopped abruptly. It was though she was mouthing a stream of consciousness. Robert must think I'm demented, rambling on like this, she thought. If so, he did not show it. He sat quietly across the table, waiting for her answer. She tried to focus on the matter at hand.

"What would I be doing for you?" she asked.

"A little of everything, probably. Including learning a great deal about the most successful decorating business in America, if you'll forgive that immodest but undeniable claim. You'd be somewhat like Tony. He's my right hand. You'd be my left. You'd work with clients from the pursuit of the assignment to its completion. Follow up on eight million details. Deal with impossible carpenters, overpriced painters, temperamental cabinet makers, and notoriously tardy upholsterers. And do a hundred other things. Oh, yes, and I'm prepared to pay you well, if that's of any interest to you. The firm will also assume the costs of moving you and your household to New York."

Elizabeth was bewildered. The offer had come so quickly and unexpectedly that she wasn't sure how she felt about it. It would be an exciting job in a challenging city. In many ways, it would be the final severance with all the old, agonizing memories of Washington—her unhappiness with Alan, her disappointment with Adam. It would be like starting a new life. Yet, on the other side of the coin, it meant a risk. Who knew whether she could count on this relatively unknown, obviously impatient man? He was no Stu Preston in any way. Gale was certain to be quixotic. Perhaps he would change his mind about her after a few months. And there she'd be in New York, jobless and frightened.

There were the children to think of, too. Ann seemed happy in her job. Perhaps she wouldn't want to leave it. Charlene was less of a worry. She was young enough to adjust quickly to new surroundings and she made friends easily. Quigly was still another story. Was it right to take away the only place he had to come home to? But he didn't care about the house. He had been all too anxious to leave it.

The house. She still owed Preston money. But that was no problem. She was sure she could sell the house for at least as much as she'd paid. Maybe more. The loan would be repaid and there might even be—unthinkable idea!—money left over. She was more concerned about abandoning Preston's weekly publication. He'd been so good to her, giving her a job when she was desperate. Was it fair to run out on him now, so soon after he'd lost Laurel?

The thought of Laurel led her back to the positive side of the idea. What joy it would be to live within visiting distance of her best friend, the only woman friend she'd ever had! Elizabeth missed her terribly. Seeing her again in New York had reminded her how lonely she was without Laurel's bright, cheerful companionship, her sure understanding and sympathy.

All this introspection took only a minute or two, but she felt as though she'd been lost in thought for hours. She was being inexcusably rude to her luncheon companion.

"I'm so sorry, Robert," she said. "My mind was jumping from one thing to another."

"Understandable. It's a little more important than buying a new hat."

"I want very much to do it," Elizabeth said, "but there's something I hate to bring up."

"I know. Money. Strange how we all love it and hate to talk about it, isn't it? I have no idea what Preston pays you, but I'm sure I can improve it greatly. It will cost you more to live in New York, for one thing. And for another, I don't believe in taking a job unless one can improve one's income. You do know, don't you, that the wage freeze business is pure nonsense? I can give you your present salary, as I'm required by some stupid law to do, and make up the difference in your expense account. All you do is turn in a nice, fictitious bill for expenses every week. It's slightly larcenous, I suppose, but highly soothing in that the money is tax-free."

Elizabeth stared silently at her plate.

"What's wrong?" Gale asked. "Don't tell me your scruples forbid your going along with that slightly illicit practice. My word, Elizabeth, everybody does it these days!"

"It isn't that," she said. "I don't think that's a big crime. There's something else I've never told you. I have a little more income than my salary." She explained about the rooming house and the extra money it brought in every month. "So you see," she concluded, "I'd have to have quite a big sum to compensate for that loss and for the fact that I'd no longer be living rent-free. I don't know what figure you had in mind. Maybe not as much as I'd need."

Robert let out a surprisingly hearty laugh. "But that's *too* funny!" he said finally. "Of all the people in the world whom I cannot imagine as a stereotyped landlady, you are it! I wondered why you never invited me to your house. My dear, it's so tacky it's positively chic!"

She didn't know whether to be relieved or offended. "You'd get along well with my daughter Ann," she said. "Except that she doesn't think it's chic. Just tacky."

"Now, now, let's not be defensive. I didn't intend to hurt your feelings, Elizabeth. On the contrary, I admire you. It can't be easy, holding down a job and having the responsibility of roomers all at the same time. I'd think you'd be glad to get rid of it, though. All the more reason for accepting my offer. As for the money, I haven't a clue what your total adds up to, but I imagine you make around a hundred dollars a week on the paper. Right?"

She nodded.

"Good. Then that will have to be your salary at Robert Gale Interiors. But each week you will have to be extraordinarily inventive and create a fictitious expense account for another hundred and fifty. Of course you'll have a *real* expense account as well, but that's something apart from your own two hundred and fifty total. Does that strike you as fair?"

She was stunned. "It's more than generous."

"Then you'll come?"

"Yes. If you're really sure."

"I'm really sure," he said gravely. "In fact, I'm delighted. Tony will be, too."

"Tony?"

"Naturally I discussed it with him. After all, the right hand should know what the left is doing." He gave her a disarming smile. "It's going to be marvelous for you, Elizabeth. For us all. I warn you, I'll work your derrière off, but I think you'll like it. Now, when may we expect you? It's mid-November. Think you could tidy things up here and join us by, say, mid-January? I'd like a couple of weeks with you before I go off to Palm Beach in February."

"I don't know," she said. "I have to give Stu Preston notice and try to arrange for the sale of the house. And in between, there are the Christmas holidays, which slow everything down. Oh, and I'll have to find an apartment in New York. Two months doesn't seem like very much time."

"Well, let's aim for it. We can try to handle the new apartment from our end. Line up a few and have you come up one weekend to look them over. Let's see, you'll need at least two bedrooms, of course, and some sort of adequate dining space. And you must be in a decent neighborhood. I should think you could afford to pay around a hundred and fifty dollars a month, wouldn't you? Dear me, that's a dismally small sum, but we'll do what we can." He reached across the table and shook her hand. "So it's a deal?"

Her head was spinning, but she felt wildly excited. The way Laurel must have felt, she thought, when the offer from *Enchantress* came out of the blue. Frightened but happy.

"Yes," she said nervously, "it's a deal."

She was surprised at the comparative ease with which such a big step was accomplished. Stu Preston was genuinely sorry to see her go but he did not try to change her mind.

"I hate the whole idea," he said. "You've made a real contribution to *Wife and Mother*. It won't be easy to replace you, either on the paper or as one of the nice parts of my life. But I think it's a great opportunity, Elizabeth. You could do with a whole new set of people."

"And problems, too," she said ruefully.

"Probably. But I haven't seen one yet that you couldn't handle."

He agreed to accept two weeks' notice and promised to let her know if there was news of Quigly. She would write to what now seemed a mythical mailing address, giving her son her new location, but she had no way of knowing whether he had ever received any of the many letters she'd sent. If he had, he'd never responded. Sometimes she thought that Quigly must be dead, but Stu assured her that this could not be so.

"You would have been notified," he said. "Besides, I'm

sure he's still on the tanker to which he was originally assigned, and it's in active service."

Selling the house took only three weeks. Mrs. McBain had not been as fortunate as Elizabeth. At the end of 1944, with decent housing at a premium, the property was far more desirable and valuable than it had been in 1937. A syndicate which owned other rooming houses in the area snapped it up for twenty thousand dollars. Even after fees and taxes and the repayment in full of her debt to Preston, she was able to realize a substantial profit. Not since Charles Quigly's death had she had even a small nest egg. She determined to guard it carefully. If things came to the worst with Robert Gale, it would tide her over. Or it might be needed for some emergency. It would be nice, for once in her life, to have more than a few dollars in her checking account. Great sums of money were not important to her, but she had known the fears that being virtually penniless could bring. Looking back, she now realized how incredibly lucky she'd been to survive as well as she had. It was as though things had just come along when she needed them—money, housing, friends, even a romance that, ill fated as it was, was also something her battered ego had cried out for.

The luck seemed to continue as the weeks passed. Robert called to say that he and Tony had found an apartment that they thought would do her nicely. Once again on a Friday evening she took the train to New York. On Saturday, the three of them inspected the apartment and Elizabeth pronounced it perfect. It was a floor-through in a converted brownstone on Gramercy Park. From the windows of the small living room, she looked out on a charming square, enclosed and locked, with keys available only to those who lived on the four sides of the park. There were swings and slides for the neighborhood children, and a school for Charlene close by. Grocery stores and cleaners were just a step away on Seventeenth Street, and, despite the fact that it was a fair distance to Gale's offices on East Fifty-seventh, a bus ran right up Madison Avenue, depositing her just a step from the door.

The apartment, while not spacious, was adequate and charming. It had a small, well-proportioned living room with a minuscule working fireplace, a narrow but complete kitchen and two bedrooms, one fair-sized and the other quite small. Elizabeth would take the tiny one for herself. The girls would share the larger one. It seemed to fill all her needs. Even the price was right.

"I'll take it," she said to the agent who accompanied them. "Is a February first occupancy date satisfactory to you?"

"Well, yes, Mrs. Whitman, I suppose so. We had hoped to give a lease beginning January first, but I guess that's unrealistic for someone who has to move from another city. We do require one month's security, of course."

Robert interrupted. "Elizabeth, we have a couple of other apartments lined up for you to look at. Perhaps you should defer your decisions until you've seen them."

She was reminded of the early house-hunting days in Washington, and of dear old Genevieve Chapman's well-bred amazement when Elizabeth settled quickly and firmly on the Georgetown house. People never seemed to understand that certain places gave off special vibrations. This one did. It was a waste of time to look further.

"I honestly don't think I could do better," she said. "It's almost like living in the country with all the conveniences of the city."

Gale shrugged. Elizabeth turned to Alexander. "What do you think, Tony? Am I being too impetuous?"

"I think it's just been waiting for you," he said with a smile. "Go ahead and fill out the application."

It was done as quickly as that. The apartment would be freshly painted ("Matte white throughout," Elizabeth instructed) and a leaky faucet in the one bathroom repaired before she moved in. The agent accepted her check for two months' rent and promised to mail the lease to her in Washington.

"Of course, we'll have to run a routine check on your references, Mrs. Whitman," he said, "but I'm sure there's no problem."

"There had better not be," Robert said haughtily. "I'm Robert Gale and this lady is in my employ."

The agent looked blank. "Of course, Mr. Gale. Like I said, I'm sure there'll be no trouble." It was clear that the name Robert Gale meant nothing to him. Elizabeth and Tony suppressed their amusement and Robert, flushed with indignation, did not pursue the matter.

"There is one more thing," Elizabeth said slowly. "I'd like the lease made out in my professional name—Elizabeth Quigly." It was a decision she'd been toying with since Alan's death. From now on, except where the children were concerned, she would use her maiden name for everything. Whitman was part of another life, a name that belonged to a widow in Memphis. It was a small but terribly significant step. Another tie with the past irrevocably severed.

There was something else that she did not realize until the three of them were in the car heading to the Colony for a celebration lunch. Then it struck her sickeningly that the apartment she had declared so perfect could not possibly accommodate her son if and when he returned. For the first time, she consciously allowed herself to believe that Quigly was not ever coming home.

It had all gone so effortlessly almost from the moment of Robert's offer that Elizabeth knew there would have to be a snag somewhere. As she might have anticipated, the trouble, slight as it was, came from Ann. At first, both girls accepted the decision to move to New York with apparent equanimity. Charlene thought it was exciting, and even Ann was not sorry to leave Washington in general and the rooming house in particular. But later, after Elizabeth had painted a glowing picture of the exciting life they would have, Ann could not resent a subtle jab.

"Do you realize, Mother, that this is the third time in my life that you've told me how wonderful a place was going to be? First it was Bethesda. I remember those lyrical descriptions of country life where Quigly and I could build a playhouse all our own. Then it was this monstrosity where I would be close to the shops and the movies. Now you're selling me Carnegie Hall and the Metropolitan Museum of Art. What's it going to be next—the Blue Ridge Mountains of Virginia?"

The words were said in Ann's old resentful voice, but Elizabeth refused to be upset and conscience-stricken. Her tone was almost playful when she answered.

"No. Actually I was thinking of the cultural advantages of Japan, once the war is over. I hear there's a marvelous little house with a magnificent view of Fujiyama."

Surprisingly, Ann laughed, and Elizabeth felt a momentary sense of identification with her newly grown up daughter. But when she returned from the second trip to New York and told the children about the apartment in Gramercy Park, Ann's face darkened.

"Only two bedrooms? You mean I'm going to have Charlene in with me again?"

"That's what I thought. You two can have the larger bedroom and I'll take the tiny one."

"In other words, *you* still want privacy. What happened? Did Colonel Barnsworth come back?"

Elizabeth was aghast at Ann's impudence. She looked quickly at Charlene, but the child seemed not to understand this vicious attack.

By sheer force of will, Elizabeth restrained herself from slapping Ann. She had done that only once. She would never do it again. Instead, she tried to understand this passion for privacy which seemed to be an area in which Ann was completely uncontrollable. Somehow, her own room meant a great deal to her. It had a disproportionate place in her thinking.

"Very well," Elizabeth said evenly, "if having your own room means so much to you, we'll change the arrangement. You may have the small bedroom and I'll take the larger one with Charlene. I'm not going to fight you on this, Ann. It isn't worth fighting about. I don't understand it, but if it's so important to you, I'll go along with it."

"Thanks."

"There is one thing, though, that I will *not* go along with." Subtly she indicated Charlene. "No matter what you know or think you know, I never want to hear another remark like the one you just made. It was cruel and vulgar."

Ann did not answer. She simply stared unflinchingly at Elizabeth, as though to say, "You never fooled me. You only fooled yourself."

Elizabeth was the first to turn away.

Early in January, they were ready to move. Elizabeth paid one last visit to *Wife and Mother* to say goodbye to Grace Edwards and Maureen Duffy. The parting from Harry Thornton was more difficult than she'd expected. The hard-boiled drama critic actually had tears in his eyes.

"God damn it," he said, "it's like the last-act curtain. First Laurel exits and now you. Worst of all, old Barney's gone."

Elizabeth nodded. Barney Nash had been killed in France. As had Frank Bayard, who had accurately predicted that bombs didn't know they weren't supposed to hit war correspondents.

"We had a lot of fun, didn't we, Elizabeth? Remember those crazy days when the four of us used to do the town? How about that night that Barney volunteered from the audience to help that corny magician at the Shoreham? Did you ever see anybody do a better job of lousing up an act?" His tears were of laughter now, and he took off the thick glasses to wipe his eyes.

"We had fun, Harry. And we'll have more. After all, you

do get to New York now and then to see the new shows. Laurel and I will slip back into our old roles with pleasure!"

"Yeah," he said. "And who'll play Barney?"

Leaving Mary Jackson behind was hardest of all. The black woman was much more than a housekeeper. She had been friend, confidante, and an uncomplaining; unwavering tower of strength for twelve years. Mary was the only person in Washington from whom Elizabeth really hated to part. She even tried to avoid it by suggesting that Mary might find it interesting to move to New York and work for Elizabeth there. She knew it was a silly, desperate suggestion and the refusal did not surprise her.

"I'm going to miss you as much as you and the children will miss me," Mary said, "but I couldn't do that, Mrs. Whitman. My family—what there is of it—is here. I'd be so lonesome I'd be fit to die in New York. Besides, living conditions in this town may not be what you might call fancy for colored people, but from all I hear they're a lot worse in Harlem. You've been good to me and I'm grateful, but this time there's no way I can follow you."

Elizabeth hugged her. "I can't ever repay you for what you've done for us, but maybe you can use this for something you really want. Buy something wonderful, Mary, and think of us." She pressed an envelope into Mary's hands. Inside was twelve weeks' salary and a letter of recommendation couched in superlatives.

"I thank you," Mary said. "And you know the first thing I'm going to buy, Mrs. Whitman? One of those fancy gold four-way frames for pictures of you and the children!"

Elizabeth smiled. "That's very sweet. But I thought you'd save it for a nice trip sometime after the war. I'd pictured you taking a luxury cruise to the Caribbean, maybe."

Mary pretended indignation. "What, and rub elbows with all that West Indian trash?"

The two of them shared affectionate laughter.

On a bleak January afternoon in the beginning of 1945, Elizabeth apprehensively watched the moving van set off with all she owned in the world. The material accumulation of her nearly forty years did not even begin to fill the inside of the lumbering truck. The only worldly evidence of her accomplishments stood beside her on the curb. One waved happily at the good-natured driver. The other, wrapped in her own unreadable thoughts, apparently viewed the departure with no emotion at all.

part V

NEW YORK 1945–1948

Chapter 13

They settled quickly into the new routine. New York seemed bigger and more indifferent than Elizabeth had found it on her two previous visits, but she did not feel as alien as she'd feared she might. The choice of Gramercy Park had been a good one. As opposed to the anonymity of the "smarter sections," with their huge, multidwelling, modern buildings, this area was like a very personal small village in the midst of a big, disinterested city. Within a week they had found their favorite grocer, an amiable dry cleaner, a friendly butcher. There was even a modestly priced restaurant on the next corner, billed as a neighborhood bar but with pleasant tables where families were welcome. They went often in the first two weeks. Exhausted from unpacking and settling in, Elizabeth was sometimes too tired to cook an evening meal. It was a treat for her, as well as for the children, to be served by the pleasant waitress who took a special interest in them, slipping Charlene extra portions of ice cream for dessert and advising Elizabeth which dishes were the best and freshest that night.

Tony and Laurel were very much in evidence those first weeks, coming after work to help with the tedious and

sometimes backbreaking chores. Robert dropped in occasionally to give "moral support." He was not one for un-
crating books and washing kitchen shelves. His contributions
were encouragement and, invariably, a good bottle of
scotch or a precious carton of cigarettes. Elizabeth feared
that he might be displeased by the number of evenings Tony
was spending away from him, but he seemed amenable to
the whole idea. He was anxious for her to get settled so that
she could begin work. If Tony could speed up the process,
so much the better. The dreary mechanics of setting up this
kind of household bored him to tears, but he knew that
Elizabeth could not keep her mind on her job until her personal life was in order. Mostly he stayed away, sending his
love via Tony, along with constant reminders that he expected to see her in the office soon.

Tony was everybody's darling. When Elizabeth introduced
him as "Mr. Gale's assistant," Charlene fell in love with him
on sight, and even the unapproachable Ann seemed charmed
by Tony's warmth and good looks. Laurel had liked him
from the first. And Elizabeth felt herself drawn more and
more to him, not physically but with increasing curiosity
about his mind. She could not forget the tantalizing words
he'd spoken at that first dinner at the townhouse. Something
about being a "healer." There'd been no chance to pursue
it. They were never alone, but sometime they would be.
When that happened, she meant to find out more about this
enchanting young man whose relaxed exterior must mask
some serious thoughts. He was an enigma. Elizabeth suspected that his exotic life-style belied the real, almost
monastic Anthony Alexander.

Mostly, though, she had little time to dwell on the puzzle. She enrolled Charlene in an excellent public school just
three blocks away, where the child seemed happy and where
she quickly made friends with girls of all races. It was one
of the things that pleased Elizabeth enormously, and she
encouraged Charlene to bring home her little Negro and
Chinese playmates for milk and cookies. Unlike Washington, which insisted upon its southern customs including
segregated education, there was no racial discrimination in
the New York school. Elizabeth applauded this as enthusiastically as Ann deplored it.

"How *can* you let her associate with those children?" Ann
asked accusingly. "Don't you find it *embarrassing?*"

"On the contrary, I find it enormously hopeful," Elizabeth answered. "They're very nice little girls with no self-
consciousness about being 'different.' I'm delighted to see

that Charlene finds nothing odd about a playmate whose skin color and eye shape do not duplicate her own. I find bigotry the ultimate vulgarity, Ann. Even in my own daughter."

Ann's eyes widened. "You're accusing me of bigotry?"

"Well," Elizabeth said simply, "how do you plead?"

"I don't plead, Mother. Not in *that* or any *other* sense of the word! You'll never understand, will you? You think the world is some kind of wonderful, do-unto-others place where everybody should be uncritical and sweet and all-forgiving. How can you be so naïve after all that's happened to you? Aren't you ever going to get it through your head that the world is made up of different kinds of people who just don't mesh? I think you wouldn't care if Charlene grew up and married a Jew or a Jap! If he was what you call a 'nice person,' it probably would be just dandy with you!"

"It probably would. If, as you said, he was a 'nice person.' "

Ann turned away in disgust. "That's very easy to say when the question is hypothetical. Lord knows what you'd do if it became a *real* question. And if you let her go on making friends with all the wrong kinds of people, one of these days you just might have to face a problem like that. It'll be interesting to see how you handle it then!"

Elizabeth was not even angry. "My, my," she said, "how *have* you acquired so much wisdom in only eighteen years? It must be wonderful to see everything so black and white. No gray areas for you, are there, Ann? Everything nicely compartmentalized and neatly defined. How simple that must make life."

"You can make fun of it, if you like," Ann said. "But I'm not going to mess up my life the way you messed up yours."

"Fair enough. Each of us has to be happy in his own way, Annie. I hope you get everything you want in this world. Just because you're my daughter doesn't make me expect that you'll adopt my philosophies. But don't make the mistake of thinking that what you consider some of my 'messes' haven't brought me great happiness as well. Maybe, please God, I'm a little better for my mistakes. A little wiser. A little more tolerant. And a little," she concluded pointedly, "less selfish."

Ann was not only angry, she was cruel in the way that only a woman-child can be. She lashed out at Elizabeth.

"You really think you're just a cut below perfection, don't you? You've been playing the heroine role so long that you're beginning to believe it yourself. I honestly think you feel you can make anybody turn out the way you want

them to. You still think Quigly will come home and love you.
You think I'll be the dutiful daughter you'd like to have. Just
like you thought Adam would leave his rich wife because
that's what you wanted. When are you going to wake up,
Mother, and stop trying to make people fit your image of
them? It's going to happen again. I see signs of it now, the
way you look at Tony. You think you're going to reform
him, don't you? My God, can't even *you* see that he's queer?"

Elizabeth was speechless. Such cynicism from an eighteen-
year-old filled her with a bleak feeling of failure. She was
not surprised that Ann knew about her dreams of a life with
Adam. It would have been easy enough for her to overhear
Elizabeth's conversations with Laurel, or even draw her own
conclusions from her mother's despondent period following
her lover's departure. But this unexpected and unwarranted
assumption about Elizabeth's feelings for Tony was pure in-
vention. What did Ann know about homosexuals? And what
would make her accuse Elizabeth of something that had not
even entered her head?

She did not try to answer the cutting questions. She simply stared at Ann, who stared back unflinchingly. It was a
little like those terrible quarrels with Alan that sprang up
over nothing important and ended in irresponsible, unreasonable charges that had no foundation in fact. She felt lost
and confused, unable to cope with this coldly accusatory child.

"Please get out of my sight, Ann," she said almost inaudibly. "I don't know what you're talking about, but I can't
listen to any more of this."

Ann was tempted to press her advantage but suddenly she
couldn't. She was ashamed. When she accused Elizabeth, she
was really condemning herself, using her own frustrations
about Tony as a weapon against Elizabeth. It was Ann who
loved Tony, Ann who would have liked to "reform" him. She
was filled with self-hatred for her own stupidity, disgusted
with herself for entertaining such futile ideas. It was weak
and she had nothing but scorn for weakness. Loving Tony
was an impossible game at which she could only lose. And
like her father, Ann Whitman had no use for losers.

Miraculously, by mid-January, Elizabeth was ready to start
her new job. The apartment, full of familiar, well-loved
things, had begun to feel like home. She found a cleaning
woman who came in twice a week to do the heavy chores.
Between times, she and the girls managed to keep the place
tidy, working out a rotating system of household duties in
which even Charlene participated. If anything, she was mor

help than her sister. Frequently she surprised Elizabeth by
having dinner nearly ready when her mother came home
from work exhausted but exhilarated.

Ann had quickly found a job she liked even better than
the one she'd had in Washington. It was in another bookstore, on Madison Avenue in the Sixties. It specialized in
rare and expensive books, and Ann found the rich clientele
very much to her taste. No more angry words had passed
between her and Elizabeth, though Ann made it a point to
absent herself from Charlene's "interracial" tea parties which
Elizabeth often allowed on Sunday afternoons. Ann was also
noticeably cool to Tony when he came for one of Elizabeth's
simple but delicious dinners. She would sit politely but silently through the meal and then excuse herself, pleading
the need to study up on some of the unfamiliar books she
was called upon to sell.

Tony, sensitive to all the vibrations around him, did not
miss the silent snub. One evening he mentioned it casually to
Elizabeth.

"Seems like I've lost a friend," he said ruefully. "Ann
doesn't seem very happy when I'm around these days. Have
I done something to offend her?"

"Of course not. She's just a moody child."

"Moody, all right. But not a child. In a way, I think she's
more adult than you, Elizabeth. At least, there's a strong
competitive feeling there. This is going to sound a little
egotistical, but she acts as though she's jealous of our friendship."

His perceptive analysis came disquietingly close to the
mark. Tony sensed Ann's resentment of his affection for
Elizabeth and hers for him, but he did not misinterpret it.
He believed that Ann, being nearer to his own age than
Elizabeth was, had a crush on him and was upset by her
mother's place in his life. Elizabeth did not tell him what she
thought—that this suspicious child was concerned only with
the possibility that her mother might make a fool of herself
by falling in love with Tony. Or, she wondered, had Tony
put his finger on something that had not occurred to Elizabeth? Perhaps his instinct was right. Maybe Ann had developed a passion for Tony. Perhaps that explained the
earlier outburst. She might have been unconsciously trans-
ferring her own troubled feelings, using her accusations
against Elizabeth as a defense against the impossible attraction that she herself felt. No. It was impossible. When she
answered, Elizabeth tried to sound unworried.

"I don't think it's anything to worry about. Ann's been a

bit of a problem always. Being the eldest, she was the one who always understood more of the unhappy things that have surrounded us. We have to make allowances for this, Tony. It hasn't been easy for her. She's felt deprived and angry most of her life. I think she'll work her way out of it. It's nothing personal as far as you're concerned," Elizabeth said. "Believe me."

"I'm afraid I don't," he said. "At first I thought she liked me. Now I have the feeling she's disturbed by the sight of me."

"Don't be ridiculous. Every woman you meet feels happier just knowing you."

"I hope so," he said. "And every man, too."

He isn't joking, Elizabeth realized. He really has love for every living thing. He would give it without a qualm, wherever he thought it was needed, and without a second thought. How people must take advantage of him! Perhaps they were all in love with him—not only Ann in her way and Robert in his, but Elizabeth, too. It was possible that Laurel felt the same pull toward him. Thinking back, Elizabeth saw things she had paid no attention to before: "Laurel's unusually quiet, almost devoted attitude in Tony's presence, her slightly husky voice when she mentioned his name. How curious that she'd not realized how they acted when he was around; as though they were all begging for his attention. And what idiots they were. Tony would never belong to any one person. Not even to Robert Gale, who had the greatest claim on him. He was his own master, strong in the security of his own convictions, whatever they were.

For a moment, this seemed to be the ideal time to seek answers to all the questions she had. But as though he anticipated her move, Tony quickly changed the subject.

"Robert's off to Palm Beach day after tomorrow," he said. "You and I will have to keep the empire intact for a month while our leader supervises the installation of solid-gold swimming pools and white-on-white lanais."

"You never go with him, do you?"

"It's never been possible. Somebody had to stay home and mind the store. Of course, the way you're catching on, it might be different next winter. If there *is* a next winter."

Elizabeth looked puzzled. "Now, what does that mean? That you don't think I'll last a year?"

"Far from it. I think you'll last as long as you want to. You could practically run the business now, after only two weeks. No, I just meant that I never let myself think that far ahead. About anything."

"Why not, Tony? You're so young. There's such a great future for you."

"Maybe yes, maybe no. Time doesn't really concern me, past, present, *or* future. I don't believe in it. Just as I don't believe in thinking about people in terms of how old they are. Or how young. Years are just numbers on a page. One lifetime runs into the next. How do you decide where one ends and the next begins—by the number of candles on a birthday cake?"

"I don't understand. People are young and hopeful, middle-aged and mature, old and experienced. How do you deny that?"

"How do *you* accept it? Have you never met a mature young person or an inexperienced middle-aged one? Haven't you ever come in contact with someone who's simply had to have lived a dozen lifetimes before? Who makes up the rules about behavior at a certain point in one's life—the same guys who make calendars?"

"Do you think you've lived before?"

"Of course. Many times. And so, I think, have you."

"Then you believe in reincarnation."

"If you have to give it a word, that will do as well as any," he said. "But I also don't believe in putting labels on credos or beliefs or whatever they are."

."Or on people, either, I'm sure," Elizabeth said.

"Exactly."

They smiled across the littered dinner table, admiring each other in the slowly dimming light of the wax-dripping candles.

"I think you're a remarkable human being," Elizabeth said quietly.

"And I know I love you very much," Tony answered.

She did not reply. She had no idea how to interpret that simple statement.

Robert came back in from Palm Beach suntanned and triumphant. Twice during the month he had sent for Tony to come down for long weekends, presumably to hear how things were going in New York, actually, as Elizabeth knew, because he was desperately lonely for the young man. Tony went obediently and apparently willingly. He brought back good reports on Robert's activities in the fashionable resort.

"The Mandergrove house is shaping up beautifully," he told Elizabeth. "I didn't know there was that much malachite in the world, but Robert seems to have cornered the market on it. Imagine what he could do if he could travel as he used to! Lady Mandergrove would have more treasures in that villa than her Soverign has in Buckingham Palace! And to think that all that opulence is possible because Lord M. makes lovely war planes to kill off half the world."

"While she has sat out the whole thing in Palm Beach, going 'Tut-tut' when she read that half of London was going up in flames. That's disgusting."

Tony looked at the plans spread out on Elizabeth's desk. "Yes, it's not what you call heroic. What is that you're working on?"

"This? The Grimsby townhouse at Fifty-eighth and Park. Complete redo—servants' quarters to wine cellar. You know that. Why do you ask?"

"I just wondered whether you found *it* disgusting. As I recall, the Grimsbys are among the most notorious of our nouveau wartime rich. Let's see." Tony pretended to be thinking. "Ah, yes, I remember now. Farley Grimsby used to be a coat manufacturer on Seventh Avenue until his daughter married somebody with a lot of stars on his shoulder. Then all of a sudden, Grimsby switched from misses' coats to army parkas, and from there to camouflage jungle uniforms and paratrooper jump suits. But that was just good old red, white, and blue American patriotism, wasn't it? Nothing as degrading as making British fighter planes. Thank God it wasn't necessary for Mrs. Grimsby to flee the country. We might be decorating a hacienda in Cuernavaca for her."

Elizabeth threw a package of Gale's black market cigarettes at him. "Rat! Okay, I get the point. 'Let him who is without sin,' etc., etc. You win. One war profiteer is no better—or no worse—than the other. Including, I guess, *us*. Don't you ever feel just a little guilty, Tony? Getting rich on money made out of misery?"

He gave her a quick, light kiss on the top of her head. "The only thing I ever feel guilty about is what I can control," he said. "I know you think I'm an odd character, Elizabeth. And I am. But things like this don't throw me. I'd give my life if I could stop this war. I mean that. Literally. But I can't. Any more than I can stop the Mandergroves or the Grimsbys from making the ingredients that a war requires, and getting rich in the process. If I thought they'd use their profits to help a lot of poor displaced Jews or set up rehabilitation centers for wounded soldiers, I'd never be party to them spending their money on pink marble bidets! But that's stupid and unrealistic. They're riding high in this wartime economy and they'll throw away hundreds of thousands on foolishness, no matter how much we wish they'd use their ill-gotten gains for good. So. We might as well cater to their self-indulgence as the next guy. At least, we're creating some beautiful things—along with some horrors. And if it's any comfort, from Robert Gale Associates they get value received. End of lecture. Time for the question and answer period. Or would you be willing to skip it in favor of lunch?"

"Lunch," Elizabeth said. "On me. In honor of my phony, wartime expense account."

In August, the war blessedly yet horribly crashed to an end. On the day that the Japanese surrender was announced, the Western world went out of its mind with joy, and New York, the biggest, brassiest city of them all, turned on a million neon lights and forgot, for a little time, that it was the citadel of sophistication.

Robert, Tony, and Laurel came tearing down to Elizabeth's apartment that evening, the smiling Arthur piloting the Bentley as though it were a high-powered float in a peace parade. Tony pounded breathlessly up the stairs ahead of the others. He had never seemed so young or so beautiful.

"Come on," he shouted. "Get the girls. We're going to Times Square!"

It was not until they were all in the car, babbling with excitement, that the incongruity of going to Times Square in a chauffeur-driven Bentley struck Elizabeth.

"I never would have believed it," she said to Robert. "You, of all people, heading for that crush! Even on a night like this, I can't imagine you rubbing elbows with hoi polloi!"

Gale smiled. "There's never been a night like this, my dear."

"Please God there never will be again," Laurel said.

And surely there would not be. They had to leave the car blocks from the teeming Forty-second Street district where the mounted police were vainly trying to keep people from killing themselves in a smothering mass of humanity. Strangers hugged and kissed, laughing and crying, blowing horns and tossing streamers and confetti in the air in a demonstration that put any New Year's Eve celebration to shame. There were hundreds of thousands of them—millions, it seemed to Elizabeth—young and old, rich and poor. Boys in sailor suits and girls in short "austerity-length" dresses, soldiers, marines, businessmen, prostitutes and politicians. That night there were no classes, no castes. Just one surging, screaming body of people giving voice to a relief so enormous that it molded them into one vociferous entity.

Elizabeth and her group held hands to keep from being separated by the heedless, overjoyed mob. She held on tightly to Charlene, fearful that the little girl would be swept away in the crowd. After half an hour, they could stand no more. Single file, with Tony clearing the way, they finally made it back to the car and returned to Elizabeth's. Robert had brought champagne, which he insisted upon pouring for everyone, including Charlene and Arthur.

For a moment, as they raised their glasses, there was silence in the apartment.

"To homecomings," Tony said softly.

Laurel put her arm around Elizabeth. On this unforgettable night she knew there were two names in her friend's mind: Quigly and Adam. Who knew whether they would ever come home? For that matter, who knew whether they could?

While his mother and sisters were celebrating V-J Day in New York, Quigly Whitman had just finished commemorating the occasion by smashing up a bar in San Diego, California. Barely seventeen, he now had the look of a tough, weather-beaten seaman and the arrogance that went with it. With his falsified papers, he was able to prove his right to order a drink on those rare occasions when a suspicious bartender questioned his age. He had become a heavy drinker, a brawler, and a woman chaser. Physically mature and sexually experienced, he was still, emotionally, a boy. It was a dangerous combination which had resulted in one serious episode after another. Until now, he had been able, somehow, to extricate himself from his difficulties. His Merchant Marine pay in the past year had gone to compensate bartenders for the damage done to their establishments in Quigly's numerous drunken rows. Several hundred dollars had been grudgingly given over to girls in ports around the world, in payment for their services. Doctors who had treated him for two cases of venereal disease had also cut into whatever money he made. Now he was broke and jobless and in the most serious trouble of his life.

Three months earlier, at the time of V-E Day, Quigly had decided he'd had enough of the sea. When his ship docked in San Diego, he showed an astonished commanding officer his real birth certificate, tossed his seabag over his shoulder, and took leave of his buddies without so much as a word. Not knowing where else to go, he decided to stick around California for a while. He'd never been there before, and the apparently easygoing life appealed to him.

He picked up odd jobs at the shipyards, making enough to rent a shabby room in a waterfront hotel. Almost immediately he also picked up a twenty-three-year-old waitress in the corner bar, waited till she got off work, and then accompanied her to her apartment where he gave her the screwing of her already experienced life. Billie responded ecstatically by offering him the key to her apartment and daily access to her body. He took both as though they were his due. Unfortunately, Billie was as careless as she was passionate. In two months, she informed Quigly that she was pregnant.

At first, he simply shrugged off this unfortunate announcement.

"Tough luck, kid," he said. "You should have been more careful."

Billie looked frightened. "What are you going to do about it?"

His surprise was genuine. "What the hell do you mean, what am *I* going to do about it? I'm not the one who got knocked up."

"But it's your baby."

"Maybe so. Maybe not. How do I know you weren't already that way when I met you? Anyway, there's nothing I can do. You must know the ropes. You had a reputation as a great lay when I met you. To tell you the truth, I've had better. And Christ knows they were smarter."

For a moment, she said nothing. Then very quietly she said, "I think we should get married."

Quigly looked at her as though she'd gone crazy. "Get married! You really gotta be out of your mind! You think I'm gonna marry *you*? Listen, you dumb little tart, you're not good enough to clean my mother's toilet. Marry you? I ought to *kill* you for being so stupid, not *marry* you for it!"

Great, silent tears began to roll down Billie's painted face. It was true that she was a promiscuous, uneducated young woman, but she was not a whore. She had never accepted money for going to bed with a man. She'd had quite a few, but only because she was lonely, or they were. Or because she fancied herself in love with them. It was no fancy that she was in love with Quigly. He was so handsome, so obviously well-born in spite of his rough ways. And he could be, when he chose, utterly charming. She had been happy for the first time in her life, these past two months. Quigly had moved in with her, paid her compliments, made extraordinary love to her. He had even been faithful. Such an apparently durable and unique relationship had made her almost complacent. She believed that she had found her man. And for the first time in her pathetic existence, she had dared to dream of some kind of permanence. It was this confidence that had made her careless. In a way, she supposed, right from the start she had really wanted to get pregnant so that Quigly would have to marry her. Why else would she have been so heedless about the precautions she normally took?

"I don't know what to do," she said finally.

Quigly was sarcastic. "I'd think that would be easy to figure out, even for you. You get an abortion."

"I don't know where to get one."

"Oh, come on," he said impatiently. "You must know a dozen dames who'd be able to tell you. What about your girl friends? Somebody must be able to give you an address, for Christ's sake!"

She shook her head. "I only know one girl who had an abortion. And she died."

Quigly sucked in his breath impatiently. "All right. I'll find out where you can get it done. And you won't die. I hear it's no worse than having your tonsils out."

Billie was used to taking orders. Sadly, docilely, she accepted the destruction of her dream. She told herself that it probably wouldn't have worked anyway. She was a loser. She knew she could not have kept Quigly, even if by some miracle she had persuaded him to marry her. He would have walked out, leaving her with a child to support. She was afraid to have an abortion, but she couldn't think of an alternative to her situation.

"I think abortions are expensive," she said tentatively. "I don't have any money saved up, Quig."

"Well, I sure as hell don't. Jesus God, you don't expect to put the bite on me for everything, do you? I not only have to find the doctor, I have to pay for the goddamned thing too? No chance. You got yourself into this, now get yourself out."

For a moment she showed a spark of defiance. "I didn't get myself into it by myself!"

"Get off my back, Billie!" Quigly's face was ugly. "I don't owe you a thing. I told you before, I'm not even sure this kid is mine. Now, do you want me to dig up an address or don't you?"

From somewhere, for the only time in her life, Billie summoned dignity. "No," she said, "I don't want you to do anything but leave me alone."

"With pleasure!"

In five minutes he'd packed his gear and slammed out of the apartment. On V-J Day, a month later, he was dead drunk, smashing up a bar, breaking up wooden chairs, and throwing them at the mirror, which reflected endless lines of bottles, some of them now in pieces as well. When the melee started, a customer had run out and called the cops. They arrived in minutes and dragged a raging Quigly into the patrol car.

One of the officers questioned the bartender. "What kicked off World War III in here, for God's sake? Looks like a nut got loose! Who started the fight?"

The still-frightened bartender shook his head. "No fight. God-damnedest thing I've ever seen," he said. "That guy you got out there—Whitman—is a regular. Been coming in every night for the last month, beltin' a few, but no trouble. Then tonight, while everybody's celebratin' the Jap surrender, some friend of his comes in looking all white and nervous and tells him something. And whammo! Whitman goes nuts. Starts yellin' and bawlin' and bustin' up the joint. Jesus! I been tending bar twenty years in this town and I never seen nothin' like that!"

"Did you hear what his friend said?"

"Sure. They were both standing right at the bar. Seemed like they were talking about some guy they both knew. The second joker says, 'They just pulled Billy out of the drink. Suicide. You're supposed to go down to the morgue and identify the body.' Yeah, that's what he said. I remember exactly now, because I thought at the time, 'I wonder who Billy is and why he walked in the ocean till his hat floated.' But I sure as hell didn't expect Whitman to go off his rocker. Christ, it was like he wanted to kill everybody! Who do you suppose Billy was, Officer? His brother, maybe?"

"Maybe. We'll find out later. Right now we'll take him downtown and book him. You'll have to come down, too, and prefer charges. You got a helluva lot of damage."

"Yeah. Poor kid. I wonder why he did it. Me, I'd probably go to pieces if my brother took the big dive, but I sure as hell wouldn't go berserk. You think maybe he's a mental case?"

"I'm a patrolman, not a shrink."

"I don't want him to go to jail. Hell, if he can pay for what he did, I'm satisfied. I mean, it's not like some mean drunk who picks a fight. That guy was out of his mind. With grief or something. God knows." The bartender continued to shake his head in disbelief. "I tell you I never seen nothing like it. The look in his eyes. It was enough to make your blood run cold."

The policeman finished making notes and closed his little black book. "You know what they say: There's more nuts out than in. Anyway, you come down to headquarters in the morning. We'll have to book him on a drunk and disorderly. Maybe it'll go easier if you don't push criminal charges."

It was not the first night Quigly had spent in jail. He'd been thrown in the tank before, in other ports, to sleep it off. He'd had money, then, to pay for the damage he'd done in other bars. But that was minor compared to this. Tonight he had almost completely wrecked the establishment. And his total assets in the world amounted to fourteen dollars and change.

He was incoherent when they brought him in, unable to give his full name or to fill in any details of the story that the arresting officer had gotten from the bartender. He did not appear so much drunk as dazed. "Billie," he kept saying over and over. "Billie, why did you do it?"

They tried to find out who the "Billy" was who lay in the morgue, but he met their questions with glazed eyes and endless repetition of the same phrases. He was carrying no identification. Just a wallet with his money and snapshots of a woman and three small children.

"Let's wrap it up for tonight," the sergeant had said finally. "Lock him up. We'll get the story in the morning. No use breaking our asses to check the morgue until tomorrow. Whoever is waiting for him ain't going anyplace."

He slept fitfully on the hard cot and awoke feeling calmer but unutterably depressed. Dimly he remembered the events of the night before. Billie was dead. Billie had killed herself because she either could not arrange an abortion or couldn't afford to pay for one. In either case, it was his fault, just as he knew that the pregnancy was his fault as well. His rage when he'd heard what she'd done was directed against himself, and he struck out in a blind fury against the destructive pattern of his life. He had killed Billie as surely as he had, long ago, held Marion Parrish-Parker's cat under water. It had been a soggy, lifeless mass. As Billie was now. He began to sob bitterly. For all that he was, he was still only seventeen years old.

When they hauled him out later in the morning for questioning, he was able to answer politely and apparently quite openly. Yes, his name was Quigly Whitman and he had left the Merchant Marine three months ago. No, he had no visible means of support. Yes, he knew the Billie Carter who had left a neat note beside her clothes at the water's edge, telling them to inform Quigly Whitman. Yes, they had lived together. Did he know she was pregnant? Yes, he lied, he had offered to marry her but she'd refused and he hadn't seen her in a month.

His excuse for going wild in the bar? He smiled appealingly, helplessly. Surely the officers must know how a man would feel when he received such news about the woman who was carrying his baby. He felt that Billie must have been unbalanced. Otherwise, why would she have taken her life instead of marrying him and having their child? It was wrong of him to do so much damage. He had no excuse except that he was blinded by grief. He would pay all damages, of course. And how would he do that, since he seemed to have no money and no job? Quigly hesitated. His family back East would send him the money, he said. He needed only permission to make a phone call.

It was all very smooth, very convincing. The bartender was agreeable to his release if he guaranteed to make good the fifteen hundred dollars it was estimated that the repairs would cost. Quigly had no idea where he would get such a sum, but he nodded seriously and said that he was sure it would be telegraphed to him within hours.

The sergeant looked at him searchingly. "How old are you, Whitman?"

"Nineteen, sir."

"Christ, you oughta be in diapers instead of knocking up girls and busting up bars."

"Yes, sir." Smug, self-righteous bastard, Quigly thought. Probably got a wife he can't get it up for and a bunch of kids who hate his guts. "I joined the Merchant Marine because I wanted to serve my country. I guess I met some people who were pretty bad influences." He was beginning to enjoy his diffident act. Apparently it was going over well with these dumb cops.

"Okay, make your call. If the money arrives, you can get out of here, this afternoon."

"Thank you very much, sir. I have some sad arrangements to make. Billie had no family. I'm all there was."

"You can make your call over there," the sergeant said. "And if it's long distance, make sure it's collect."

On the way to the phone, Quigly's confidence began to

falter. There was only one person he could call: Elizabeth. The last letter he'd had from her, she'd said she was moving to New York. Going to work for some rich decorator. What was his name. Hale? No. Gale. Yes, that was it, Robert Gale. He probably could reach her there. If she didn't have fifteen hundred, maybe she'd be able to get it from her fancy boss. But what if she turned him down? He dismissed the idea. After all, he was her son.

He got the number through Information and in a few minutes heard the operator ask Elizabeth if she would accept a collect call from Quigly Whitman in San Diego. He could imagine his mother's face. She had probably gone into shock when the nasal, impersonal voice of the telephone company broke more than a year of silence. Her own voice trembled audibly when she said yes, of course, she would accept the charges.

"Your party is on the line," the operator said. "Go ahead."

"Mother?"

"Quigly! Is it really you, darling? Are you all right? What are you doing in California? Why haven't you written?" The questions came in a rush of anxiety.

"I'm okay. I'll explain everything to you later. I'm just fine. Not a scratch on me. But I'm in a little trouble."

"Thank God you're all right," Elizabeth said, hardly hearing the last sentence.

"Mother, I said I'm in a little trouble. I need some money right away. Quite a bit of money. Fifteen hundred dollars, in fact. Can you wire it to me today?"

"Fifteen hundred dollars! Quigly, I don't have that kind of money to spare. What on earth has happened? Why do you need it? Where are you?"

"I told you I'd explain it to you later. It's just a mixup, but I'm at the police station. I need the money before they'll let me go. Can you wire it to me today, care of Western Union, San Diego?"

Obviously she was not going to get the story out of him over the telephone, but he must be desperate to turn to her after all this time.

"All right," she said more calmly. "I'll send you the money but only on one condition: that you come home. I'll add enough for your train fare to New York. Will you do that, Quigly?"

"Absolutely."

"Do you have a pencil?"

"Yes, right here."

"Write down my address and wire me what train you'll

be on. I'll meet you at Grand Central. I'll send the money off right away."

"Thanks, Mother. I really appreciate it. And I'll pay you back."

"We have a lot to talk about when you get here," Elizabeth said. "You won't fail me, now, will you? Word of honor?"

"Word of honor. I'll see you in a few days. I have to go now."

"Quigly! Wait!"

"Yes?"

"I love you, son. And I trust you. You won't disappoint me, will you?"

He tried to hide his exasperation. "I gave you my promise, Mother. I'll be there, don't worry."

"We'll all be waiting, your sisters and I. It will be wonderful to see you again, dear."

"Sure. Right. See you soon. Bye, now."

"Goodbye, darling."

He hung up, elated. Instead of his faltering step to the phone, his return to the sergeant's desk was with his old swagger. "The money will be here in a few hours," he reported.

"Okay, when it comes you can go."

Quigly was overjoyed at the good fortune that had come out of this tight spot. Not only was Elizabeth going to bail him out, she was actually going to send him extra money. The train fare would keep him going for a few weeks, anyway. Maybe he'd go to Los Angeles. He'd always liked the sound of it. One thing was sure, he had no intention of going to New York. He didn't have to throw away his mother's address. He'd never even bothered to write it down.

As she rushed to the bank to draw two thousand dollars out of her precious savings account, Elizabeth felt thankful and happy. It was providential that she'd sold the Washington house and banked the small profit. Otherwise, she didn't know where she could have found the money Quigly needed, particularly on such notice. It was good that she'd kept writing to him, too. If she hadn't given him her new business address he'd never have been able to find her when he needed her. There had been moments of anger and rejection in the past year when she'd nearly decided to stop sending the unanswered letters. Thank God she hadn't.

She was disturbed by the idea that he was in trouble with

the police, of course. But whatever it was, it couldn't be too serious if it could be solved by something as relatively unimportant as the payment of money. She surmised that he'd gotten into a fight and had to pay for some damage he'd done. The idea did not surprise her. Quigly had grown up with a chip on his shoulder. She did not doubt that his quick temper had gotten him into still another boyish scrape.

She was eager to know the whole story. Where he'd been, what he'd been doing. She presumed he was out of the Merchant Marine. She speculated upon how he would look, what he would say when he came home. She could hardly wait. Anyway, she thought optimistically, I won't have to wait long. There should be a telegram later today, telling me what train he's taking. Then she'd only have to contain herself for four days and three nights while he traveled across the country.

She would not allow herself to entertain the idea that he would not do exactly what he promised. He'd been a difficult child, an elusive one. But his biggest sin had always been secretiveness, not dishonesty. It was unthinkable that he would not keep his word.

But as one day and then another passed without the arrival of a telegram, Elizabeth grew increasingly pessimistic. For a week she clung to the idea that he was going to surprise her. That the doorbell would ring one evening and there he'd be. But after two weeks of silence she knew better. Finally, without much hope, she wired Police Headquarters in San Diego, inquiring as to the whereabouts of Quigly Whitman. The terse answer came back, "Whitman left city August 8. No forwarding address." That was the day after she had spoken with him.

She had told no one that she'd heard from Quigly. Originally, she'd planned it as a surprise. But as the days went on and her hopes dimmed, she kept quiet, not wanting the others to know how uncaring her son was. They would have been angry for her sake, and probably contemptuous of her gullibility as well. She had thrown away two thousand hard-earned dollars on a dream. Perhaps Ann was right. Maybe Elizabeth was eternally trying to make people into what she wanted them to be. If so, she'd failed again with Quigly. But even so, she could not have done anything other than what she did.

She accused herself of sentimentality, illogic, even the kind of ego-pampering that Quigly's return probably would have satisfied. Cold-bloodedly, she condemned herself for once again trying to play God. She was, in her own mind, a naïve fool for believing what she so desperately wanted to hear. In fact, she had only done what most mothers would do—respond to her child's plea for help.

Once again, she had offered forgiveness and love. And once again it was rejected.

Chapter 14

Ann Treadwell Whitman was a strange mixture of inherited and adopted traits. Like her brother, she could be distant, cold, even cruel in her dealings with people. She was selfish and opinionated, not easy to understand. These were qualities she had gotten from Alan. But from him, too, she had inherited a better than average mind, a feminized version of his good looks and, like Quigly, an ability to be completely charming when she chose to be.

From Elizabeth's genes had come her good health, her inborn sense of discipline and her desire to be surrounded by lovely things, though in Ann's case, "lovely things" were more conventional and stereotyped than those in which her mother found beauty. She did not have Elizabeth's outgoingness and tolerance. She did not indulge herself—as Elizabeth had pointed out—in any "gray areas" of indecision or self-doubt.

To the qualities that her parents had bequeathed her, she added her own. She was more materialistic than Elizabeth or Alan and far more ambitious than either of them. But Ann's ambition and materialism did not lie in the direction of a career. She had decided early on that the quickest, easiest and surest way to be comfortable and secure was to marry the right young man who could give her the kind of home and social status she was determined to have.

Not that her sights were set unrealistically high. She did not delude herself that she would marry into "high society" or that she would ever enjoy enormous wealth. Ann was, above all, a realist. She did not come from a prominent family, had not made a debut, would not, in all probability, be acceptable to the world of the Whitneys, the Astors, or the Rockefellers. She would be perfectly content with an attractive Protestant male, already established in a good job. He would possibly—and preferably—come from well-off parents who would ultimately die and leave him a respectable if not staggering inheritance. They would live in the suburbs, where she would be important in local activities such as the Garden Club, the Book Club, and the PTA. They might belong to the Country Club as well. She would have two, possibly three children, a new house decorated by Sloan's and a second car which would, of course, be a station wagon. Their friends would be couples like themselves, young marrieds with whom they would play bridge and come into the city occasionally for dinner and the theater. Her children would play with their children. And all of them would be part of a stable, orderly community in which excessive drunkenness, serious philandering, and menial work and money problems would never threaten their lives.

Ann dreamed of this upper-middle-class life which would be far removed from any she'd known. It seemed to her that she had spent nineteen years on a teeter-totter. There were still vivid recollections of her "princess period" when her father had been important in Washington and the little Georgetown house had glittered with famous and influential names of the Roosevelt era. FDR was gone now and so was everything she identified with that period—her father, the money, the private schools, and the sense of importance that a nine-year-old girl had felt. That was the top of the seesaw. As it began its descent it went through the Bethesda strata, the poor house on the rich estate, the first public schools, the knowledge that sometimes there was barely enough to eat, the fear in Elizabeth's eyes that she thought her young daughter did not see.

But even that period was not as gloomy as when the imaginary board she'd straddled really came down to earth. The rooming house in the mediocre neighborhood, the ill-bred children who were her classmates and whom she consistently ignored, the indignity of having to share a room with her baby sister and the ultimate disgust of knowing that her mother was having an affair with a married man. All these were worse than anything that had gone before. New York was a slight improvement, but still a far cry from the security she craved.

Falling in love with Tony, even if he returned her affection, did not fit in with her plans. Even if he did not belong to Robert, he could not give her the solid things she needed. She was tired of a false world in which even Laurel and Elizabeth represented nothing but affectation.

Only at the bookshop did she seem to find the kind of substantial, unthreatening atmosphere with which she wished to identify.

She liked her job there. The shop had a sense of orderliness and peace, and most of the customers were serious, erudite booklovers. There were some chi-chi matrons interested only in expensive leather bindings which matched the decor of their libraries, and a few grubby bookworms in search of obscure titles at bargain prices. The shop's clientele also occasionally included a literary celebrity, which was exciting. But the usual browser was an upstanding, thoughtful man or woman who appreciated literature and did not belong to the school that read only mystery stories and trashy novels.

Unfortunately, most of them were old enough to be Ann's parents or grandparents. After six months, she reluctantly began to think of changing her job, for the life plan she had made for herself was not likely to be fulfilled by one of these customers. She hated to think of leaving the shop, but her priority was to be where she would meet the right young man. Her young WASP might never find her in this remote, soft-spoken world. She would have to pursue him into his own environment—Wall Street, perhaps, or one of the big Fifth Avenue banks. Or even, as a last resort, seek him out in the slightly less solid atmosphere of a Madison Avenue advertising agency. She could take a quick typing course, maybe even learn shorthand, and get a job where the kind of husband she wanted was already in a junior executive position.

She had just about decided to give notice at the bookshop when Peter Richards walked in. Outwardly, he was the man Ann had imagined. About twenty-five or so, she thought. Good-looking, but not in a movie-star way. The close-cropped hair was freshly trimmed, the Brooks Brothers suit was well but not rigidly pressed, as though he took care of his clothes but was not obsessed by them. He wore no

jewelry, no self-conscious gold crest ring, and, more important, no wedding band. He carried a neat briefcase and a
copy of the *Wall Street Journal* under his arm. As Ann approached him, he was looking vaguely at a shelf of hand-
somely illustrated books on flowers, a half-annoyed frown on
his face.

"May I help you?" she asked.

"Yes, please. What do you have in a book on Japanese
flower arrangements? Something brand-new, preferably. We
seem to have every one ever issued before 1945."

Who was "we," Ann wondered? He and his wife? The
lack of a wedding ring didn't necessarily mean that he was
unmarried. Or maybe the "we" was himself and a roommate. God forbid he was another Tony Alexander!

"We have one that just came in," Ann said. "It's quite
beautifully done. The author spent twenty years in Japan before the war, so it's extremely authentic."

She handed him the slim volume, which he leafed through
absently, finally returning to the inside flap.

"Wow!" he said, grinning. "Twenty-five dollars! At that
price it should be autographed by Hirohito."

Ann smiled back. "I think he's been a little busy lately,
authorizing documents of surrender. Would you like to see
something less expensive?"

"No, no," Peter said. "This will be fine. At least I'll be
sure it's one she doesn't have."

Ann looked slightly curious.

"It's for my mother's birthday," he said. "She's a nut on
Japanese flower arranging. Personally, I don't understand all
that subtle understatement, but she's crazy about it."

"It *can* be lovely," Ann said demurely. "My mother adores
things like that, too. I must confess, though, that I'm like
you. The meaning of it all rather escapes me. I like big,
happy bunches of flowers. Especially ones you can grow
yourself."

"You grow flowers?"

"Not any more. New York apartment life just isn't geared
for that kind of thing. But when I lived outside of Washington, it was an absolute wonderland. I miss it terribly—all
those huge old trees and great masses of plants!" She sighed
romantically. "Sometimes I'd give anything for the feel of
earth under my hands. I guess I'm just a country girl at
heart." She stopped abruptly. "Oh, I'm so sorry to be taking
up your time with such nonsense! Do forgive me. I'm sure
you're in a rush. Shall I have this gift-wrapped for you? And
is it cash or charge?"

Peter was intrigued. "I'm not in a rush at all. I'm on my lunch hour, but there's no deadline. I was just going to have a sandwich and read the paper. Maybe I'm holding *you* up, in fact. What time do you eat?"

Ann glanced at her watch. "In about five minutes," she said matter-of-factly. "Now, did you say cash or charge?"

"Charge. It's in my father's name, but that's the same as mine. Except for the Junior, of course. Is it okay if I charge it to him and send it to the house?"

"Of course." Ann prepared to write up the sales slip. "To whom will it be charged?"

"Mr. Peter Richards, 902 Van Cortland Drive, Scarsdale, New York. And send it to Mrs. Peter Richards, same address."

"Do you want to enclose a card?"

He nodded. "I'll write it while you're finishing up. And then maybe you'd do me another favor?"

"If I can," Ann said pleasantly.

"Would you have lunch with me? You probably know this neighborhood better than I. Besides which, you're terrible pretty, Miss . . ."

"Whitman. Ann Whitman. Like the candy company, but no relation, unfortunately."

Peter laughed. "Okay, will you accept my invitation? I don't mean to be fresh, honestly. I just think you're a nice girl, and you've been a lifesaver in helping me solve my problem. Will you come?"

Ann forced herself to hesitate for a moment. "All right, Mr. Richards, I will. With pleasure."

If he had answered a classified ad headed "Wanted: Husband for Ann Whitman," Peter could not have been a more perfect candidate. He was bright enough to hold down a good job in a famous brokerage house with a branch office on Park Avenue, but he was not smart enough to see through the act that Ann put on for him. During lunch, she was shy without being coy, modest but subtly inviting, interested in him without appearing aggressively overeager. She encouraged him to talk about himself. He was, as she'd guessed, twenty-five. Had done a two-year hitch in the army as a second lieutenant. He had graduated from Harvard. And he'd just returned to civilian life and to his job at Fennerman, Whitehouse, and Stokes where a place had been held for him while he was in the service. He did not live with his parents, but shared a flat with another young man in a big apartment house on East Fifty-seventh Street.

"The folks wanted me to live at home," he told Ann,

"but Scarsdale's no place for a single guy. Too much trouble trying to commute late at night, after a date. I like being in the city for other reasons, too. I can walk to the office, and Joe Albertine is great to share an apartment with—mostly because we almost never see each other. He's the district manager for a big printing company. Travels most of the time, so I really have the place to myself about three weeks out of every month. It works out fine," he laughed, "especially since Joe pays half the rent."

"Do you have brothers and sisters?" Ann asked.

"Nope. Just me. That's why Mom and Dad were dying to have me come home, I guess. They just rattle around in that big old house. I go home for weekends now and then, especially in the summer. *Somebody* has to use the pool and the tennis court." He paused. "Hey, will you listen to me! I've spent the whole time telling you the dull story of my life. What about you, Ann? What's your life like?"

She told him the almost-true facts about herself. "My father's dead," she said. "He was one of the pioneers in the aviation business. My mother is an associate in an interior decorating firm called Robert Gale. I'm the eldest of three. I have a brother, Quigly, who's not living at home, and a little sister Charlene. We live on Gramercy Park. That's about it. Dull, isn't it?"

"Not at all. But why aren't you in college?"

"Mother wanted me to go to Smith or Vassar, but I really didn't want to leave her and Charlene, especially with Quigly away. Besides, I love what I'm doing. Sometimes I think I'm getting a better education than I could have gotten in school. And," she added naïvely, "I do meet the most interesting people."

Peter smiled. She was incredibly beautiful, this girl, and refreshing. He thought of some of the girls he'd been dating. They were great for laughs. They could match him drink for drink, and most of them were not averse to coming up to the apartment for at least part of the night when Joe was away. But he didn't take any of them seriously. He could get very interested in this soft-spoken, self-effacing Ann Whitman. He'd even give odds that she was a virgin. He had a hunch that she was brighter than she would like him to think, but that was all to the good. Dumb girls bored him to death, but he could not imagine himself getting involved with a real brain or one of those overambitious career types with which New York abounded. Marriage to one of them would be a constant competition. Not that he considered marrying Ann Whitman, on the basis of one very pleasant lunch. In fact, he had no intention of marrying anyone for the next four or five years. Being a bachelor in this town was too much fun. Still, it might be interesting to ask her for a date. He couldn't quite figure her out. Maybe she wasn't quite as wholesome as she appeared.

Ann could almost read his mind. He's going to ask me for a date, she thought. I mustn't seem too anxious. She glanced at her watch.

"Good Lord, it's nearly two o'clock!" she said. "If I don't get back to the shop, I'll get fired! Thank you so much for lunch, Peter. I do hope your mother likes the book. If she doesn't, we'll be glad to exchange it."

He signaled for the check. "I'll walk you back," he said. "It's nice of you to offer to exchange the book. I'll tell Mother, though I'm sure she'll be delighted with it."

Ann's heart sank. Maybe he wasn't going to ask her out. Why should he? A young, attractive guy like Peter must have dozens of glamorous girls after him—particularly if they knew he came from a family as well off as the Richardses must be. What did he need with an uneducated shop girl who lived with her mother and sister?

They strolled back to the shop in the soft September sunshine, chatting amiably about inconsequential things. At the doorway, Peter held out his hand.

"It's been one of the nicest lunches I've had in a long time," he said. "Maybe we can do it again sometime?"

"That would be nice." Deliberately, she let a little note of disappointment creep into her voice. It was the cue that Peter had been waiting for.

"Listen," he said, as though he'd just thought of it, "I've got a better idea. Maybe you'd have dinner with me instead. Then we won't be pressured for time. What about Friday evening? Are you free?"

For an instant, she hesitated. Should she pretend to be terribly booked up for the next week or so? Play hard to get? Friday was only two days away. It wouldn't do to appear too available. The hell with it, she thought. Strike while the iron's hot. In a week, he might have changed his mind.

"Friday will be fine," she said.

"Great. Give me your address and I'll pick you up about seven-thirty, okay?"

Ann would have preferred to meet him somewhere. The apartment was presentable enough and Elizabeth could be counted on to exude ladylike charm, but there was always the chance that Robert Gale or Tony or even Laurel would be around, their ultrasophistication giving the lie to the homespun picture Ann had tried to paint. But meeting him out-side her home would be even more out of character. The girl she was projecting would not have gone out with any young man who hadn't been properly introduced to her mother. She scribbled her address and phone number on a piece of paper.

"The phone number is in case you change your mind," she said. "Of course, if you lose it, you can always reach me here at the shop."

Peter gave her a long look. "Don't worry, I won't change my mind. Just be sure you don't change yours."

"Not likely," she said truthfully.

At dinner that evening, Ann started preparing the way for Peter's arrival.

"By the way, Mother, I have a date Friday evening."

Elizabeth looked surprised and pleased. "Oh? How nice, Ann! With whom?"

"His name is Peter Richards. I met him when he came into the shop today to buy a book."

Elizabeth's eyebrows lifted slightly. It troubled her that Ann never seemed to meet anyone, never had gone out socially in the nine months they'd lived in New York. But to pick up a date in the bookshop? It hardly seemed Ann's style. Stupidly, she voiced her surprise.

"I'm delighted that you're going out, but with a perfect stranger? Isn't that a little risky? I mean, planning an evening with someone you don't know anything about?"

Ann looked at her with exasperation. "There's just no pleasing you, is there? First you worry that I don't go out at all, and now you complain because I've made a date."

"It isn't that, Ann. I'm glad that you're going out. I was just surprised that it was with someone who wandered in off the street."

"Where else would I meet somebody—through Robert or Tony or Laurel? I haven't noticed them offering to produce an interesting young man for me. Not that they could. I'd be amazed if they knew anybody who wasn't part of their decadent circle!"

Elizabeth shook her head in warning. Charlene was all ears. This was no conversation for a ten-year-old. Ann ignored the signal.

"Which brings me to something else, Mother. Peter is picking me up here at seven-thirty. I'd appreciate it enor-mously if you'd keep the fashion and decorating crowd away that evening. And I wouldn't be annoyed if Charlene was in bed, too."

"I *never* go to bed at seven-thirty," Charlene said indignantly. "And Friday night I can stay up even later than usual because there's no school next day! Mother, I don't have to go to bed just because Ann's got somebody coming here, do I?"

"Of course not," Elizabeth said soothingly. "You'll be allowed to stay up as you are on any other Friday night. I'm sure your sister's new friend would be very pleased to meet you."

Mollified, Charlene went on with her dinner. "As for your other request, Ann," Elizabeth said, "I think we should discuss that privately." Her tone barely disguised her annoyance.

Ann shrugged. "As you like."

Later, when Charlene had gone to bed, Elizabeth faced her older daughter.

"All right, now, what's this all about? Who is Peter Richards and what do you know about him?"

"He's young and good-looking and works for a brokerage house. *And* he comes from a very nice, normal family in Scarsdale. He was buying his mother a book on Japanese flower arranging and he took me out to lunch afterward and asked me to go out Friday night." Her tone was irritatingly put upon. "Oh, yes, he also went to Harvard and was in the army for two years. He reads the *Wall Street Journal* and his table manners are impeccable. Does that make you feel better?"

"There's no need for such elaborate sarcasm, Ann. I don't think I should be boiled in oil for wanting to know about someone you're going out with. Especially when it's a pick-up."

The minute the last two words were out of her mouth, Elizabeth regretted them. She was being as nasty as Ann was. Damn this child, she thought. She can always manage to reduce me to her level of pettiness!

"I'm sorry," Elizabeth apologized, "that was not a very nice thing to say. You have a good point when you say that you don't have much opportunity to meet young men. I'm glad that your Peter Richards is so attractive. Nothing would make me happier than for you to start going out and having fun, Ann. At your age, I'd already met your father and decided to marry him."

"I think I'm going to marry Peter Richards," Ann said.

Elizabeth did not know whether to laugh or not. She managed not to show her amusement.

"On the basis of one lunch? Aren't you rushing things a little, Ann? You are a most attractive young woman, but how can you be so certain that *he'll* want to marry *you?*"

"He will," she said blithely. "He can be handled. Of course, first I'll find out if we're physically compatible. If we are, then he's everything I want. Attractive, bright enough, and from the kind of background I'd like to be part of—solid and substantial."

It was as though their roles were reversed. Elizabeth was the one who felt young and naïve, while Ann spoke unemotionally, almost clinically, of her plan to catch Peter Richards. She did not mention love or voice any of the dreamy, romantic hopes that Elizabeth had felt when she met Alan Whitman twenty years before. This was to be a competent campaign, including, apparently, the strategy of going to bed with Peter before she finally made up her mind to marry him.

Elizabeth did not know what to say. "You don't mean that, Ann," she finally protested. "About finding out whether you're physically compatible. That is, you don't mean it *literally.*"

"Of course I mean it. Two people who get married without finding out whether they like sex together are just crazy. If it isn't good, it can ruin the whole thing." She seemed surprised by Elizabeth's shocked reaction. "For God's sake, Mother, I thought you were such a liberal, advanced freethinker. Didn't you think I knew about the birds and the bees? Don't worry. I won't get pregnant. I'm sure Peter will see to that, even though I'm not prepared."

Elizabeth was stunned. Of course she knew that Ann knew about sex. But this casual approach still came as a complete surprise. Against her will, she had to ask the next, obvious question.

"Ann are you still . . . That is, have you ever . . . ?"

"Have I ever slept with anybody? No. A couple of times I thought about it in Washingon, but those boys didn't appeal to me enough. Besides, I decided to use my virginity as a nice trading point. I just knew it might come in handy when I met the man I wanted to marry. And you see? It has."

"You're very sure of yourself," Elizabeth sid feebly.

"Yes, I am. Everything is going to go exactly the way I want it. Which is why I'd like you to keep Gale and the others out of the way Friday night. Peter Richards is going to think he's taking out a very sheltered, unworldly girl. Not one whose mother spends her time with gay decorators and tough magazine editors. Let's keep it all candlelight and needlepoint for the time being, okay? He'll find out soon enough what weirdos hang out here. But by that time he'll be hooked."

Elizabeth was finally, vocally angry. "How dare you! Those people have been the best friends we've ever had in this world! They've literally kept us from starving—and that means you and Quigly and Charlene as well as me. Now you'd like me to kick them out of the way so you can impress some upper-middle-class young snob who's probably only taking you out so *he* can get *you* into bed. And don't think it'll be for a lifetime, Ann. It's much more likely to be one night or two. You're not only a terrible, ungrateful girl, but you're a stupid one as well. I should forbid your even going out with Peter Richards after what you've told me. Not that I blame him. You've done everything but take your clothes off already. And you have the audacity to put your level of morality above that of the people you don't want him to meet!"

Ann's lips were compressed in a tight, determined line. "You can't stop me from seeing him, Mother. You know that. And if you feel so strongly about introducing him to our select group of depraved friends, then I'll just have to arrange to meet him outside of the house. It won't look as good, but I'll explain it somehow. I want to create the right impression. Is that so difficult to understand? Peter's been brought up in a very conventional atmosphere. I'm sure of that from the things he said. I'm not going to ruin my chances at the start by letting him think that we're practically *bohemians!* If that's too much to ask, I'm sorry. I've never asked much of you until now. I'm not suggesting that you give up your friends. I'm just making a simple request that for one night this apartment look like a sober, quiet, refined background for me."

All Elizabeth's arguments collapsed. She felt like a traitor to the three loyal people whom Ann did not consider "good enough" for Peter to meet. And she was sickened by the mental image of her untouched young daughter in bed with some faceless young man. But there was nothing she could do about the latter. She couldn't chain Ann up, forbid her to leave the house, or lock her into a chastity belt. As for Ann's attitude about Elizabeth's dearest friends, there was no way to change that, either. Helplessly, she retreated into silence. Ann recognized it as consent.

"Thank you, Mother," she said quietly. "I won't ask you for this favor often, I promise. Peter Richards is going to find himself engaged very quickly. Then I don't care whom he meets—or even what he finds out about us."

"What about the other thing?" Elizabeth asked.

"You mean will I go to bed with him Friday? Oh, no, you don't have to worry about that. Not on the first date. That would be dumb. It will take two or three evenings of reluctance before I allow myself to be seduced. He has to be good and steamed up, and then *terribly* remorseful."

Ann smiled an angelic smile as she left the room. Elizabeth sat up for hours. How could she have borne two such unfeeling children? She still had not recovered from Quigly's deception. Even Stu Preston, whom she had called to ask veiled questions, had no help to offer her. Quigly was out of the Merchant Marine, so his whereabouts were no longer traceable. It might be years before she heard from her son again. And now Ann, always secretive and resentful, had revealed another side of herself—a scheming, devious nature. Worst of all, Elizabeth felt that Ann's strategy was going to work. Women like that always got what they wanted.

Much as she didn't want to, Elizabeth had to admire Ann's choice when Peter Richards arrived on Friday night. He was charming, well-spoken, courteous, and already interested enough, Elizabeth could see, to fall into Ann's clutches. Peter was a "catch" who was ready.

The apartment was as requested. Elizabeth was alone except for Charlene, who looked angelic in her pink quilted robe and slippers. It was a cool enough evening to have a fire going and there were candles and fresh flowers, the amenities that Elizabeth insisted upon even when they were not "setting the stage," as they were this evening.

The few minutes before the young couple left were pleasant and relaxed. Ann was playing a role. Tony would have called it "the compleat ingénue." She showed enormous affection for her mother and sister, sat quietly while Peter and Elizabeth exchanged small talk, finally departed with a blown kiss to a nauseated Elizabeth and a baffled Charlene.

Though she had not told her the details, Elizabeth had confided to Laurel that Ann was going out with a new beau. She dialed Laurel's number as soon as the young pair had left and Charlene had gone off to the bedroom to play with her large family of paper dolls.

"How did it go?" Laurel asked.

"I feel like a cross between the Madonna and Emily Post. It went fine, I guess. He's very attractive and polite and treated me like I was a hundred and two."

"What did Ann wear?" It was a typical Laurel question.

"Her new black velvet suit with the white satin edging. It was just right, I thought. She looked grown up and demure all at the same time."

"Good choice. I'm glad she's finally met somebody nice. Hope it takes. That child is overdue for some social life."

"Yes," Elizabeth said, "she is. But I have a feeling she's going to make up for lost time."

Elizabeth made it a point not to wait up for Ann, but she was still sleepless at 2 A.M. when she heard the key in the door. She would have loved to have gotten up and gone into Ann's room to hear how the evening went, but she hesitated to intrude. Maybe, she thought, I'm a little afraid to find out.

Having volunteered what was, for her, an extraordinary amount of information, Ann said almost nothing more about her romance with Peter. It was apparent, though, that it was going swimmingly and according to plan.

Peter took Ann out again on Sunday, after that first Friday date, and they saw each other three times again in the following week. Ann no longer asked her mother to keep her "weird friends" away from the apartment. She had taken to meeting Peter directly after work, returning home long after Elizabeth had retired. After the fifth date, Elizabeth awoke, as she always did when she heard the front door softly open and close. It was still dark, but the hands on the radium-dial clock by her bed said five-thirty. She knew then that Ann's strategy was in full operation. She turned over quietly so as not to disturb Charlene sleeping peacefully in the other bed and lay staring toward the ceiling. She supposed she should feel outraged or apprehensive, certain that Ann had "traded her virginity" in a gamble for marriage. Instead, she felt only old and tired. I only hope she gets what she wants, Elizabeth thought. And then, almost irrelevantly, Poor Peter.

The next morning was Saturday, Ann's day off as well as Elizabeth's. It was well after noon when Elizabeth went in to wake her. For a few seconds she stood looking down at the perfect, peaceful face, the silky blond hair curling over one white shoulder as though Ann had arranged it that way before she slept. No more little girl. Even now she looked seductive, satisfied and womanly. Elizabeth shook her gently.

"Ann. Ann, wake up. Peter's on the phone."

"What time is it?"

"Going on one o'clock. Peter's on the telephone," she repeated.

"All right. I'll be right there."

Elizabeth told herself that she was trying not to eavesdrop on the conversation but of course that was a lie. She couldn't hear the low-spoken words on Ann's end of the line, but the tone of voice was unmistakably intimate and punctuated with soft laughter. Finally Ann hung up and wandered out into the kitchen. Elizabeth's unspoken questions hung in the air as she poured her daughter a cup of coffee.

Ann took her time drinking her coffee. Then she yawned hugely, leaned back in her chair and said, "Well, I guess I'm engaged."

Elizabeth could not hide her astonishment. "So soon? Ann, you've only known him a week!"

"Ten days, to be exact."

"Darling, are you sure this is what you really want? How can you know a man in such a short time? You're talking about someone you hope to spend your life with!"

Ann looked at her coolly. "How long did it take you to decide about Adam?"

"That was quite different. We were both mature."

"Only in age, Mother. I think you were more of a romantic at thirty-nine than I am at nineteen. Anyway, I told you even before I went out with him that this was the one I wanted, provided everything was satisfactory."

Elizabeth's answer seemed to come from somewhere near the pit of her stomach. "And everything was, I assume, 'satisfactory'?"

"Yes. Quite. Of course, he was in a state when he found out that this was my first experience. But once he got over the shock, it didn't seem to be much of a problem."

I simply do not believe this conversation, Elizabeth thought. It's unreal. Ann apparently found nothing unusual about it. She was more than composed. She was positively smug.

"Anyway, when it was over, I cried a little, though I actually felt marvelous. That's when Peter asked me to marry him."

"And you accepted."

"Not exactly. I told him he didn't have to marry me just because he was my first lover. I was very convincing. I told him that I'd wanted it just as much as he, and that it was my responsibility as much as his and that he needn't feel that there were any strings attached. So you see he really had an easy out if he'd wanted to take it."

"But you gambled that he wouldn't."

"It wasn't much of a gamble. He's in love with me. Anyway, I said I wouldn't accept his proposal until he made it again in the cold light of the morning after. That way I'd be sure that it was what he wanted, not just something he felt he had to do. He proposed again on the telephone just now. And this time I accepted. We're going to go looking for a ring this afternoon."

"Ann, do you love him? Or are you like Quigly, just looking for a way to escape?"

"Quigly's a clod," she said coldly. "If I'd wanted to escape in some dumb way I could have gotten myself a room at the Barbizon Hotel for Women. Don't compare me with Quigly."

"All right, but you haven't answered my question. Do you love him?"

"Of course I love him," Ann said impatiently. "And I love the life he's going to give me."

"That most of all," Elizabeth said.

"Yes, Mother. That most of all."

The quick romance was followed by a short engagement. Peter took Ann to meet his mother and father in Scarsdale and she returned triumphant with her future in-laws' blessings.

"They want to meet you, Mother. And they'd like to have the wedding out there, if you wouldn't be offended. I told them you'd love the idea. There's a nice little church in the town and their house is big enough for a reception. In fact, I think it's a godsend. We'd have had to go to terrible expense, renting a hotel suite here in town."

"I'm sure Robert would have been happy to have offered you his house for the reception," Elizabeth said.

"You're kidding! Mr. Richards would faint if he saw that faggoty house! I wish I didn't even have to invite the group to the wedding, but I suppose you'll insist."

"Yes, I will insist. In fact, I'm not so sure that I still wouldn't prefer to give you the wedding reception in a hotel. It's the duty of the bride's parents, after all."

"Oh, Mother, for once in your life be practical! Anyway, if I got married in New York, whom would we invite? At least out there the Richards have scads of friends who might not come into town for the wedding. Did I tell you we're planning it just before Christmas? December twenty-third, we decided."

"No. You've told me very little. I feel more like a spectator than the mother of the bride."

"I'm sorry." Ann seemed honestly contrite. "I know it all seems very rush-rush, but if we get married then, Peter can get time off over the holidays. We thought we'd like to go to Bermuda for our wedding trip."

"Very original," Elizabeth said drily.

The slight sarcasm went right over Ann's head. "Now about our plans. It'll be a small wedding and not too big a reception. Let's face it. We don't have many people to ask and I'd hate to look silly with Peter's guest list two hundred and mine maybe a dozen. Anyway, I do want to wear white. Unless," she said impishly, "you think it should be off white."

Elizabeth's troubled face was more expressive than words. Even Ann realized how calculating she must sound.

"You think I'm terrible, don't you? Please try to see it my way, Mother. I'm not blind to what you've tried to do for us. You may not believe it, but I really admire you. I think you have more guts than any human being I've ever known. I suppose in a way I'm jealous of you. Maybe that's why I'm always trying to hurt your feelings, to shock you. Probably I'm envious of the way everybody adores you because you're so damned good and trusting. I'm sure that a psychiatrist would say I'm trying to compete on a different level. I'll never be the woman you are, so I have to beat you in a different way—by showing you that I can order my life, the way you never could control yours. I don't think I've ever said it to you in my whole life, Mother, but I really love you."

Under this unexpected confession, Elizabeth melted. She was close to tears as she listened to the things that it must have been difficult for the proud, remote young woman to say. She experienced an uncontrollable surge of love for her daughter. How analytical she was for her age! And how comforting to know that at least she recognized her motives. Ann's self-appraisal was a revelation to Elizabeth, and she sought the right words to tell her child how much this long-awaited communication meant. It explained so much that had been, until now, inexplicable.

"Darling," she said finally, "thank you. Thank you so much. What a tender person you are under all that defensive armor. And how amazing that you recognize things that most people twice your age could never figure out by themselves. I'm so proud of you, Ann. And I love you so much. But darling, don't get married just to prove something to me. Please. Now that it's out in the open, can't you see how unnecessary that is? You don't have to create a model life just to show me that you can do something I failed at. It's not worth it. Give it a little time, dear. Don't rush into this just to show me you can do it. Maybe in a year or so you'll still want to marry Peter. And you'll have my blessing. But you could also meet someone else in that time, someone you'd really love more than you love Peter. That person could give you the same sense of protection and security, and a lot more beside."

When she answered, it was the old, unemotional Ann speaking. "Look. I wanted to tell you the naked truth just once. But it doesn't alter anything. It doesn't really change the way I feel or the things I have to prove. Not just to you. To myself. I don't want to have to worry about money and fatherless children and all those terrible things. I won't, that's all. I just plain won't."

"But, sweetheart, the Richardses aren't millionaires, are they? And Peter has a good job, but he doesn't make a fortune, I'm sure. Why do you think this is all such great insurance?"

"Because I don't expect to be terribly rich or grand or powerful. What I want is what I guess you'd call a dull suburban life. A house and kids and all the nice middle-class trappings. Peter will be able to provide those. He'll commute to wherever we live and I'll meet him at the station every night at six-nineteen. I'll drink coffee with the other wives in the neighborhood and exchange recipes and get pregnant and shop at the supermarket. And I'll love every safe, unthreatened minute of it. I know that doesn't fit your picture, Mother, but it's the picture I want. I want roots. Good, permanent, dull roots. I've never felt that I had any."

Elizabeth made one last protest. "But it's such a dreary, undemanding picture, Ann. Won't you be bored with it?"

"No. It's the only real power there is for a woman. You thrive on challenge, Mother, but I don't. I want to be the unthreatened queen of my nice little limited world. I want to live in a restricted neighborhood where my children go to school with kids just like themselves. I want them to grow up in one house, with one set of parents who are so normal that they could come right out of the pages of *Good Housekeeping*. I've had enough chaos, enough divided loyalties, and enough fright. I don't want any more of it. I told you. I'm not like you. And I'm not going to be like my father."

"And Peter? Is he ready for this cookie-cutter mold of a life?"

Ann smiled. "He may not know it, but he's ready. It's the kind of life he comes from. He's basically a conventional, responsible, rather innocent young man. If he weren't, he wouldn't have been so easily grabbed off by the first tearful virgin he seduced, now would he?"

Elizabeth only sighed in response.

"Don't worry," Ann said. "I'll make him a good wife. He'll be happy. He doesn't have the kind of emotional problems my father had. Thank God for that. He won't make my life hell or pass his neurotic moods on to *his* kids."

There was no arguing with her. There never was with Ann. Elizabeth could only be grateful that for at least a few precious moments her daughter had let down her guard long enough to admit her weakness and, best of all, articulate the love that Elizabeth had never been certain she felt. The life that Ann quite clearly wanted would have driven Elizabeth out of her mind. But what is one person's idea of happiness is not necessarily another's. I can't set her standards by my own, Elizabeth thought. Any more than she can set mine by hers.

"It's your life, my darling," she said finally. "I may not understand it, but I'll never criticize it." Her voice became businesslike. "Well, then, I think we'd better make some plans. First of all, I'd like to invite the Richardses, en famille, to dinner here. I'll get a girl in to cook and serve. All right?"

Ann nodded.

"And then we must shop for a dress for you, a trousseau really. And we'll need to make a list of people you'd like to have at the wedding. It would be nice to invite a few old Washington friends, if you agree. Like the Prestons. And Betty Kaspar and Amelia Neal. They were always so fond of you. Maybe a few others. As you say, we have to have *some* people sitting on the bride's side of the church!"

"Do you think Stuart Preston would give me away?"

Elizabeth looked surprised. She hadn't given that subject a thought. Actually, it made sense. Ann would never, of course, consider Robert or Tony, the only two men they knew well. And the nationally famous publisher would fit in with Ann's mental image of a "respectable girl's" escort down the aisle.

"I'm sure he would," Elizabeth said. "Unless, of course, he's planning to be away somewhere. Incidentally, what about attendants?"

"Joe Albertine, Peter's roommate, will be his best man."

"And your maid of honor?"

"I don't know. I guess it will have to be Stacey Farmer." Ann named the other young woman who worked at the bookshop. "Isn't it ridiculous? I don't really have a close friend."

Elizabeth felt a pang of sympathy. She had never had a close woman friend either until she met Laurel. Poor Ann. It's as though she's been living in a vacuum all these years, with no one to talk to.

"Sounds fine," Elizabeth said cheerfully. "Would it be a nice touch to have Charlene as a junior bridesmaid?"

"No," Ann said. "It would be sickening."

Chapter 15

She hoped she didn't show it, but Elizabeth cringed inwardly all the way through the "family dinner" with Peter and his parents. Not that it didn't seem to go well. Elizabeth had forgotten none of the niceties that had once made her a much-envied Washington hostess, and even with limited facilities and the help of one less-than-perfect waitress, the meal was delicious and attractively served.

Before the Richardses arrived, Ann was as nervous as a cat, fussing over the look of the table, toying with the already arranged flowers, even hanging over her mother's shoulder as Elizabeth prepared the food.

Elizabeth tried to be understanding. Of course the child would be anxious to have everything turn out perfectly, but Ann's hen-on-a-hot-griddle hovering finally exasperated her to the point where she ordered her out of the kitchen.

"For heaven's sake, Ann, will you please leave me alone? You're doing nothing but getting in the way. I'll never finish in time if I keep stepping on you ever time I turn around!"

"But it's got to be right, Mother. Everything at the Richardses' is so beautifully done."

"Then we should have let *them* give the dinner," Elizabeth snapped. Then she laughed. She was as edgy as Ann. "I'm sorry, darling," she said, "I know this is an important evening. I don't blame you for wanting everything right, and it will be. This is one area I do know a little something about. You wouldn't remember, but in Georgetown we entertained cabinet officers and diplomats. I used to be known as a pretty good hostess."

"I remember," Ann said. "I remember everything."

"Then have faith," Elizabeth said gaily. "Go take a nice long tub and make yourself even more beautiful. And do me one favor, please. Double-check to see that Charlene washes behind her ears."

Ann made a face. "Isn't that child old enough to keep herself clean?"

Elizabeth refused to allow herself to be goaded into another silly spat. "Suit yourself," she said lightly. "But if you want everything around here to be flawless tonight, you might just as well include your sister's bathing habits."

The three Richardses arrived promptly, and the atmosphere, somewhat stiff at first, gradually relaxed over the second cocktail. Joanne Richards was a recognizable suburban matron type, tall, simply dressed, well-spoken, very much like the Cambridge ladies Elizabeth remembered from the days when she was Ann's age. She was easy to know, pleasant to be with, and Elizabeth liked her very much. The two women were unalike but not incompatible. Elizabeth could never endure the kind of garden-club, passively proper life that Joanne personified, but she had no quarrel with it, for those whom it suited. She watched Ann's obvious admiration for her future mother-in-law. She would pattern herself as closely as possible after the senior Mrs. Richards, who represented all that Ann thought of as serene and soothingly conventional. The idea did not disturb Elizabeth. She did feel a little pang of jealousy, realizing that this was the kind of mother Ann would have chosen if she could. But she could handle the hurt better now, knowing that Ann loved and admired her too, even though she wanted to be nothing like her. Best of all, Joanne seemed devoted to Ann. And that was what really counted.

Peter Richards, Sr., was another story. He looked like an older version of his son, and though he was amiable and seemingly satisfied with his prospective daughter-in-law, it was not ten minutes before Elizabeth recognized him for what he was: a smug, narrow-minded, highly opinionated semityrant with deep prejudices and a kind of heavy-handed humor that went over big in the locker room of the golf club. At dinner, his conversation reinforced Elizabeth's quick appraisal.

"Well, now, Elizabeth," he said, "Pete tells me that you and your husband were in Washington when the late unlamented President Rosenfeld had us by our throats."

Out of the corner of her eye, Elizabeth saw Ann dart her a pleading look. Elizabeth smiled calmly.

"Yes. My husband served in the government under President Roosevelt. It was a very interesting time to be there, although he was active only at the very beginning of the administration, from 1933 to 1935."

"Had a bellyful by that time, eh?"

"No. My husband became ill." She did not elaborate.

"Shouldn't wonder," Richards said. "That man would have made anybody sick. And that wife! I swear, I've never struck a woman in my life, but I believe I'd have taken a stick to her."

"Dad," Peter said, "nobody wants to talk politics, particularly tonight." Almost imperceptibly he indicated a silver-framed picture on a side table. It was a signed photograph of Eleanor Roosevelt. His father frowned.

"Oh. Sorry, Elizabeth. I didn't know she was a friend of yours."

"We aren't close friends," Elizabeth said, "but I admire Mrs. Roosevelt enormously."

"So do I," Joanne said. "I think she got into a lot of areas where a woman doesn't really belong, but I'm sure she did it only to help her husband. They say that with him so terribly handicapped, she really had to be his eyes and ears as well as his legs."

"Really?" Richards said. "Then how come she doesn't go back to being a mother and a grandmother now? Seems to me those kids of hers could use a lot of handling. She might do more good there than she will getting mixed up in the United Nations thing. Or do you think the Little Haberdasher needs legs, too?"

There was an awkward pause. "Ann tells me you're with Robert Gale Associates," Joanne said chattily. "It must be fascinating. I've seen pictures of so many houses he's done. Absolutely beautiful. He must have great taste. He's too expensive for us, but how I'd love to have him do our house!"

Her husband snorted. "If he did, you'd live in it with another husband, old girl. No matter how much money I had, I wouldn't let one of those fairies within ten miles of any place of mine."

Elizabeth pointedly ignored him. "I think Robert Gale is incapable of an error in taste. In any direction. But his real genius is in decorating to suit the personality of the client. Do you know that we send out elaborate questionnaires before we accept an assignment? They're like psychology tests, full of seemingly unrelated questions about preferences in books, sports, even radio programs. The answers are analyzed, and from them Robert selects color schemes, period furniture, and accessories which are compatible with the client's way of life."

"What a marvelous idea!" Joanne said.

"What a great promotional stunt," Richards snorted. "I'll bet you fifty dollars that he doesn't pay any attention to those answers. Probably just reaches for plan B or C and goes right ahead making every house look like a queer's paradise."

Elizabeth held her tongue. Had it not been for Ann, she would have cut this stupid boor down to size, and she was perfectly capable of doing it. But it was her house and he was her guest as well as her daughter's soon-to-be father-in-law, God help her. Ann was fidgeting nervously with her napkin. Young Peter looked embarrassed. Charlene sat wide-eyed and quiet, uncomprehending but sensitive to the tension in the air.

"You know the children are planning to look for a house somewhere in our area, don't you?" Joanne asked pleasantly.

"Yes, Ann told me. They were fortunate to get the little furnished sublet in Greenwhich Village for a few months," Elizabeth said. "It will give them a chance to look for a house and take their time about choosing furniture."

"Handy to have somebody in the family with contacts in the wholesale furniture market, too," Richards said jovially.

His attempt at humor fell flat. Joanne graciously attempted another recovery.

"There really are some charming houses quite near us. I hope you'll come for a weekend soon, Elizabeth. Do you know the area? No? Well, I'd love to show you around."

"Better make it quick," Richards said. "Even Scarsdale is beginning to attract the wrong element. They built a synagogue in the next town to us. Next thing you know, we'll have the colored."

Elizabeth gave Ann a searching look that seemed to say, "Is this the 'nice, normal family' you're so anxious to marry into? The mother seems like a reasonably nice woman, but Peter Richards, Sr., is the worst kind of intolerant, well-to-do, middle-class snob."

Somehow they got through the evening. In her nervousness, Ann chattered interminably, probably afraid that Elizabeth was going to openly show her distaste for Mr. Richards or that Charlene would decide to mention some of her unacceptable playmates. Only once more, however, did they come near the brink of a disastrous confrontation. That was when the subject of the wedding party came up. Elizabeth had telephoned Stu Preston and received his delighted agreement to give Ann away. Both the Prestons would come, of course, and the senior Richardses seemed impressed.

"I've read a lot about Stuart Preston," Peter Richards said grudgingly. "Very important man. Sounds like an intelligent one, for a Democrat. Is he an old friend of the family?"

"Yes," Elizabeth said. "He knew both my husband and me. Later he gave me a job on one of his papers. And lent me the money to buy my rooming house in Washington."

There was a horrified silence. Joanne Richards looked startled. Even young Peter looked surprised. And his father's face darkened. Ann jumped into the breach.

"Mother loves to tease about it," she said with a laugh. "It's her own private joke. Mr. Preston did arrange for the financing of the townhouse we bought when we left Bethesda. Mother called it a 'rooming house' because it was always teeming with overnight guests. My grandfather was a Harvard professor, you know, and so many of his old friends came to stay when they were in the city. And of course there were always people like Mrs. Parrish-Parker, who's one of Mother's dearest friends. She married Richard Aimsley of New York and Palm Beach. I'm sure you've heard of him, Mr. Richards. He was well known in Wall Street before he retired."

Elizabeth was torn between anger and pity as Ann chattered nervously and all too obviously, frantically trying to turn the casual reference to the rooming house into some kind of snobbish joke. She was angry that Ann was ashamed of the truth. At the same time she felt sorry for the girl's insecurity. It was so terribly important to Ann that these people believe she came from what they considered a proper background. Her values were so shallow, so wrong. She was so unsure of herself that she was willing to be a pretentious, absurd little liar. Elizabeth would not expose the lie, but neither would she openly condone it.

"Well, all that was a long time ago," she said when Ann finally stopped.

"Really?" Joanne Richards asked. "I thought you'd been in New York less than a year."

"That's correct," Elizabeth answered. "But we hadn't seen the people Ann mentioned for quite some time before we left." It was a stupid answer and she was angry that she'd been forced to add one deception on top of another. How dare Ann make us look so foolish? Surely these people know she's trying to cover up something. All that going on about her grandfather's friends and Marion Parrish-Parker! It was too elaborate to be believable.

Before they got into deeper water, young Peter rose, looking at his watch. "It's getting pretty late, Dad," he said, "and you and Mom have quite a drive." Playfully he picked up Charlene and swung her into the air. "As for you, mouse," he said, "you've been so quiet all evening we almost forgot you were here! I know. You did it on purpose so you wouldn't get sent to bed, right?"

Charlene laughed, her arms tight around Peter's neck. "I don't go to bed early any more," she said. "I'm ten and a half years old."

"My, my! As old as that! Pretty soon we'll be marrying *you* off, baby sister."

Elizabeth was grateful to him. His light touch had saved what threatened to become a sticky moment. She found the Richardses' coats while Joanne and her son kissed Ann good night and Peter, Sr., gave her a little pat on the cheek.

"Thank you for a lovely evening and a delicious dinner," Joanne said. "Now don't forget, you're coming to us for a weekend before the wedding. All of you."

"We'd love to if we can," Elizabeth smiled. "But you know how much there is to do to get the bride ready. By the way, it's charming of you to have the reception. I'm really grateful. As you can see, we're hardly equipped for big parties, and hotels are so impersonal."

"I'm grateful to *you* for letting us do it," Joanne said. "I'm really being selfish. You see, I'll never have a daughter to marry off. At least you have a second chance with Charlene."

"Nice evening," Mr. Richards said. "Many thanks. Come on, Joanne."

"You were great, Mrs. W." Peter whispered, kissing her on the cheek. "Don't pay too much attention to Pop. His bark is worse than his bite, but thanks for being so patient."

The minute they left, Charlene was packed off to bed. "Skedaddle," Elizabeth said. "You were a perfect little lady tonight, baby. But bedtime is long overdue."

Charlene kissed her. "Peter's so nice, isn't he, Mommy? When I grow up I'm going to marry somebody just like him."

"Yes, he's very nice," Elizabeth agreed. He'd be even nicer, she thought, if he were an orphan.

Ann, emptying ashtrays and taking glasses into the kitchen, seemed anxious to avoid any discussion of the evening. Elizabeth was not going to let her off so easily.

"That's quite a family you're marrying into," Elizabeth said. "Peter's a darling and his mother is really very nice. But that father! Ann, doesn't it frighten you that some of that bigotry might rub off?"

Ann was defensive. "What's so terrible about him? That he didn't like FDR? Millions of people didn't, you know. And that because he's a real man he doesn't go for swishy decorators like Robert Gale? Or is it news to you that an awful lot of nice people in this country don't have your ultraliberal views about Negroes and Jews? Okay, he's not your type, Mother, but I assure you that he represents the great majority of solid Americans, whether you want to believe so or not!"

"You don't have to be so violent about it, Ann. I agree that everyone is entitled to his own opinions, even when they're as small-minded as Mr. Richards'. What I hate most is the way you seem to have accepted them. That ridiculous, overdone act you put on about the rooming house! Couldn't you see what a fool you were making of yourself?"

"I wouldn't have had to make a fool of myself, if that's what you call it, if you hadn't deliberately brought it up. You just had to make a point of the fact that we took in roomers, didn't you? You knew damned well how something like that would sit with those people!"

"I won't deny that I was up to *here* with Mr. Richards," Elizabeth admitted, "but I didn't do it to deliberately embarrass you. It was just a natural part of my explanation about Stu Preston. I had no idea it would bring on such hysteria. I'm sorry to say, dear, that it made me ashamed of you."

"It made *you* ashamed of *me!*" Ann was enraged. "How do you think I felt all those years, having a landlady for a mother!"

"Perhaps you'd rather have starved."

"Oh, don't talk nonsense, Mother. You could have managed some other way if Laurel hadn't talked you into it. She's always been the world's worst influence. You can even blame her for bringing Adam Barnsworth into your life."

Elizabeth was impassive. "Or, more correctly, thank her," she said. "Anyway, we're not talking about Laurel. We're talking about this tight, hidebound little world you're going to be part of. Don't go into it with any secrets, Ann. You'll never be able to keep them. Besides, you have nothing to be ashamed of."

"Haven't I?" The tone was heavy with sarcasm.

"No. Certainly nothing of your own making. Besides, I might remind you that when you asked me to keep Robert and Tony away the first night Peter called for you here, you said quite clearly that you didn't care what he found out later, once you 'had him hooked' as you so elegantly put it. I gather that's no longer true."

"No, it isn't true. But I know there's nothing I can do about it. Sooner or later the Richardses will meet your friends and co-workers. But now I wish to God we hadn't invited Betty Kaspar and Amelia Neal to the wedding! There's not much hope that they won't blab their heads off about living in your rooming house."

Elizabeth shook her head. "I can't understand this fixation of yours, Ann. Good Lord, it's not as though I ran a bawdy house!"

"Speaking of which," Ann said bitterly, "I'm grateful that you didn't manage to work in some reference to Sue-Ann and the good old days in Memphis."

"Listening to you," Elizabeth said, "I almost wish I had."

Ann stared at her mother with disbelief. "I really think you want to ruin my life," she said slowly. "I think you're more competitive with me than I've ever been with you. I think you'd like to prevent this marriage if you could. Maybe you envy what I'm going to have."

It was hopeless. Ann would never grasp the fact that all Elizabeth wanted was for her not to turn into a self-righteous little prig. It was clear that this was the direction in which she was headed. Maybe this was the kind of wife Peter wanted. For both their sakes, Elizabeth hoped so.

"Darling," she said quietly, "we've been under a strain this evening. Let's not go on with this emotional conversation. We're both saying things we don't mean. Come on, kitten, its time to turn in. I've said my last word about the Richardses. It's your life, Ann. You're marrying Peter, not his family. And he's quite a boy. I know you're going to be very happy. And that will make me happy."

The quiet tone seemed to appease Ann. But at the doorway of her room, she turned. "There's just one thing more, Mother. The Richardses know I have a brother, but they don't know much about him. I've said he's living in Europe, studying to become a wine importer. That's the first thing that came into my mind when Mrs. Richards asked whether Quigly could come home for the wedding. Imagine," she said, shuddering. "All I'd need is for him to turn up at the wrong moment."

"Good night, Ann," Elizabeth said quietly. "Sleep well."

The girl did not notice the irony in her mother's voice.

"I will," she said cheerfully. "I always do."

The wedding came off as scheduled, without a hitch. Ann condescended to be driven to Scarsdale in Robert's Bentley, the chic of the car and chauffeur overcoming her distaste for its owner. The ceremony was simple and brief, and Ann looked radiant in the simply cut ivory satin wedding gown which showed off her beautiful figure and her pale, flawless complexion. Her dark-haired attendant, Stacey Farmer, complemented the bride in red velvet, exactly the color of the Christmas poinsettias with which the little church was decorated.

As he led Ann down the aisle, Stu Preston was handsome and impressive in his cutaway. He gave Elizabeth a wink as they passed the first pew where she sat with Charlene, Martha Preston, Laurel, Robert, Tony, Betty, and Amelia. Mr. and Mrs. Richard Aimsley, who had been invited, but declined, sent the bride an ornate silver coffee service, a gift that amused Elizabeth. Ann had never polished a piece of silver in her life. Now, thanks to Marion and quite a few other impractical well-wishers, she'd learn what a burden the material trappings of life could be. Thank God, Elizabeth thought, she knows a little about basic cooking. It might be a while before the house and the full-time maid Ann envisaged would replace the tiny sublet that she and Peter would occupy when they came back from Bermuda.

There were no awkward moments at the reception, either. Tony completely charmed all the Scarsdale matrons and Robert Gale was set upon as a celebrity. He even graciously accepted an invitation to address the Women's Club at one of their "Famous People Luncheons" the following April. The Prestons were perfect in their roles, delighting Ann with their references to her as a beautiful pampered child in Georgetown. It was all like a well-rehearsed scene out of a polite, drawing-room drama. Even Laurel created a pleasant sensation when the ladies discovered that she was actually the editor in chief of *Enchantress*. Ann's worries about the bride's invitation list had proved more than groundless. Her guests were far more interesting and glamorous than the collection of stockbrokers, bank officials, and real estate developers who seemed to encompass the bulk of the Richardses' friends.

As she and Peter prepared to leave for the airport, Ann, under the pretense of hugging her mother, whispered in Elizabeth's ear. "I take it back," she said. "Your crazy friends have been the hit of the show. Thanks, Mother. For everything."

Elizabeth kissed her. "Be happy," she said. For a moment, she was sorry she had not given Ann the diamond-and-sapphire pendant that had belonged to her grandmother, the one Elizabeth had worn on her own wedding day. She had thought about it and decided that although Ann would admire it as a piece of good jewelry, she would not really be touched by its history or cherish it as Elizabeth always had. It lay in the safe-deposit box at the bank, waiting for its time to go around the throat of a more sentimental bride, one who was now only ten and a half years old. It was a right decision, Elizabeth concluded after that one moment of regret. The pendant properly should have gone to the elder daughter, but Ann was far more thrilled with the platinum ruby and diamond "cocktail ring" that had been a gift from her new in-laws.

Elizabeth and "her group" left the reception soon after the young couple departed. Stu Preston offered to take them all to the St. Regis for a nightcap. He and Martha were staying there overnight. Betty and Amelia would sleep at the apartment. Elizabeth declined with thanks.

"Charlene's out on her feet," she said, "and I'm feeling a bit of a let-down myself. Of course, you're all welcome to come back to the apartment. We can kick off our shoes and relax."

The others decided against it. It had been a long, tiring day, with the Washington arrivals making the trip up early in the morning and planning to return first thing the next day. Before they climbed into their cars, though, Stuart drew Elizabeth aside.

"Is everything going all right with you?" he asked. "The job okay? And what about Quigly? Any news?"

"I'm fine," she said. "Robert's wonderful to work for. Almost as nice as you. As for Quigly—nothing. I have no idea where he is or what he's doing. I try not to think about it too often."

His voice was full of sympathy. "I know. But he'll turn up. I'm sure of it."

Elizabeth nodded silent agreement. "Stu, I can't thank you enough for coming all the way up here to give Ann away. You were every girl's dream of the father of the bride."

He smiled. "I was honored. I have only one regret. I wish I really were the father of that particular bride."

Elizabeth tried to sidestep the implication. "You don't know what a handful she is," she said ruefully, "or you might not make that wish."

She wasn't fooling him with her pretense of misunderstanding. What a goddamn fool I was to let this woman get away from me, Preston thought. When she was vulnerable, I was too cautious. Now it's too late for anything but friendship. Well, he'd settle for that. He gave her an innocuous kiss on the forehead. "You'll call me if you need anything?"

"I always have," Elizabeth said simply, "and I guess I always will."

With Ann married and gone, the little apartment on Gramercy Square seemed strangely empty. The wedding, taking place only two days before Christmas, had left Elizabeth little time to prepare for the holidays. On Christmas Eve, she and Charlene scurried out and bought a tree, which they decorated with all the old, familiar ornaments. During the day, Elizabeth quickly picked up food and gifts for Charlene, Laurel, Tony, and Robert, inviting her New York group of "waifs and strays" to come for dinner on Christmas Day—a bidding they accepted with alacrity. In spite of its impromptu air, it was one of the happiest celebrations Elizabeth remembered in years. The tension which Ann always unwittingly created was missing. The room seemed to be alive with love as they opened their gifts and drank toasts in Robert-donated champagne to the newlyweds and their happy future.

At ten o'clock, when Charlene was excused, she kissed them all, saving the last good night for Elizabeth.

"Could I see you alone for a minute, Mommy?"

"Of course, darling."

They went into Ann's old room, which Elizabeth had immediately turned over to Charlene for her private domain.

"This is my best Christmas present of all," the child said, indicating the bedroom. She looked very serious. "Do you know it's the very first time I've ever had a room all to myself? Not that I didn't like sleeping with you, Mommy, or with Ann in the other house, but it makes me feel very grown up to have my own room."

"I'm glad, darling. You *are* very grown up, Charlene."

"And you'll see. I'll be a big help to you."

Elizabeth squeezed her hard. "I know that, love. You're a very sufficient ten-year-old."

"Ten and a *half*," Charlene reminded her. "I can do a lot more things for you now, Mommy. I can even shop for food and get dinner ready when you come home from work." She looked wistful. "I know you're going to miss Ann a lot. Like you miss Quigly. But I'll try to make up for it."

Elizabeth was touched. This was the child she'd always wanted—gentle, giving, wise beyond her years. Charlene was her hope, her final fulfillment, the person her mother had felt she'd be since the day she was born. Still, Charlene's vulnerability almost frightened her. There was something ethereal about her extraordinary sensitivity and her understanding of responsibilities that would not even occur to the average child. She was a delicate little girl, yet she had the strength and endurance which Elizabeth gratefully recognized as purely Quigly traits.

"We're going to do just fine," Elizabeth assured her. "I'll depend on you a great deal, baby. And I know you're up to it."

As Elizabeth prepared to turn out the light, Charlene smiled at her mischievously. "I just thought of something funny, Mommy."

"What's that?"

"Ann always hated sharing a room with anybody. Now she'll have to share one for the rest of her life, won't she?"

Elizabeth couldn't restrain a laugh. "Minx! You would think of that, wouldn't you? Now get to sleep! Good night, ex-roommate!"

There was no answer. Charlene was already half asleep with a contented smile on her face.

When she returned to the living room, the others were deep in a discussion of plans for New Year's Eve. Robert had decided to have a big party at his house.

"We'll make it a double celebration," he said. "Not only the birth of 1946, but we'll cheat by a couple of weeks and make it the anniversary of Elizabeth Quigly's first year as a member of Robert Gale Associates."

"That's sweet, Robert," Elizabeth said, "but I really hate New Year's Eve parties. All that forced gaiety just because the calendar has flipped another page."

Robert looked at her sternly. "If you think, dear girl,

that a Robert Gale party bears any resemblance to the usual dreary fetes where the guests get drunk and put lampshades on their heads, you are sadly mistaken. We do not go for noisemakers, streamers, or the appearance of old men with scythes and naked children dressed only in banners saying 'Happy 1946.' Any party I give, Elizabeth, will be a study in unequivocal elegance. Frankly, I'm deeply wounded that you would compare it with some strange mental image you must have of a middle-class orgy at the Scarsdale Country Club."

Elizabeth made a deep, mocking bow. "Forgive me, master. Humble apologies from these unworthy lips. Provided I can get a baby-sitter, I accept with deepest pleasure."

"Well, that's more like it," Robert said. "What's more, you will act as my official hostess. And we'll see if we can round up thirty or forty other amiable souls to decorate the rooms. Now, let's see. We know plenty of attractive men, but not enough good-looking girls. What about some of those snappy young things who work with you, Laurel?"

"Those little snobs? Most of them will be off breaking their legs on the slopes of St.-Moritz, I imagine. And those who aren't probably already have plans for the Big Night. Besides, Robert, what do you want with my bunch of industrial debutantes?"

Robert shook his head. "You just don't understand business, Laurel, dear. Those debutantes invariably grow up to be rich young society matrons with triplexes which have to be decorated by Robert Gale. What's more, their names on my guest list add a certain cachet which goes over well in the society columns."

Laurel continued to look uncertain. "I don't know. I'm sure the ones who are in town will already have plans. Besides, I've never made a point of mingling with them socially. Won't they think it's a little odd if I suddenly invite them to a gala?"

"Not," Robert said loftily, "if the gala is *chez moi*. Tell them to bring their dates. Those are the rich young bucks they'll eventually marry anyhow. Take my word for it, they'll come with bells on. Curiosity about Gale's private way of life will be stronger than any reticence about mixing with the boss. Of course, realistically, we won't depend on the *Enchantress* chorus line for the bulk of the guest list. Whatever you may think, I do know some snappy ladies in this town. All I want is a good cross section of the best rich people in New York."

Through all this, Tony had not uttered a word. Elizabeth could see that he found it unappealing. Like herself, Tony probably would have preferred a quiet evening with a very few people he loved. Not this flamboyant scene that Robert obviously was determined to arrange. She suspected that Tony viewed New Year's Eve much as she did—as a time for quiet introspection, a thinking back to the sad and happy times of the past year and a mild curiosity about what might lie ahead. He would hate being surrounded by strangers, curiosity-seekers, hangers-on, this night above all. But there was nothing he could do about it. He was committed to Robert in matters like this. Only in such small ways was he able to "repay his debt." In the year they had worked together, Elizabeth felt she knew Tony both well and not at all. She had seldom been alone with him except at the office or at an occasional quick lunch. In the evening, Laurel was always around, or Robert. Both of them, Elizabeth sensed, felt intensively possessive about Tony. She understood Robert's proprietary air, of course, but lately Laurel's attitude confused her. It was almost as though she, too, felt that she had some special claim on Tony Alexander. How wonderful it must be to so thoroughly captivate everyone you meet. And, at the same time, what a dreadful responsibility for someone as gentle as Tony. She admitted that she, too, was ensnared by the inner and outer beauty of this young man. Had been from the beginning. He seemed to have some irresistible attraction for every one of them, all the more strange because he did nothing overt to seek their devotion. He simply commanded it by being alive, by being in their orbit. Even Charlene followed him like an adoring puppy. Only Ann had seemed immune. Once again, the old doubt struck Elizabeth. Perhaps Ann had been the most captivated of all and, realizing it, had gone out of her way to pretend an active dislike for Tony. It would be like her to recognize a hopeless candidate and deliberately turn her back on him. He was poor, by Ann's standards, and he was of questionable virility. Neither quality would have suited the eminently practical Ann. Even if she had entertained some foolish hope of attracting Tony, she would have made herself dismiss it as an unrealistic, emotional indulgence. She would, in fact, have swung completely in the other direction, expressing nothing but disinterest, even dislike.

Perhaps none of this reasoning was true, Elizabeth told herself. Yet watching the adoration that the others, including herself, had for Tony, she wondered whether she had accidentally discovered a chink in Ann's armor. It would not be out of character for her daughter to put reality ahead of emotion. It would even explain why Ann had so quickly and

calculatingly settled on Peter Richards who represented
safety and protection from foolish temptation.

What utter nonsense, Elizabeth told herself. Ann was in
love with Peter. He was the perfect husband for her.
Chances were that an attachment to Tony had never entered her head. And if it had, the danger had passed. The
new Mrs. Richards was married and married to stay. Elizabeth would bet her life on that.

In the next two weeks, prosaic but happy-sounding postcards came from Bermuda. The weather was lovely. They'd
been bicycling all over the island and Peter was teaching
his bride to play golf, "in preparation," Ann wrote, "for my
future as a Westchester wife."

The New Year's Eve party was big, grand, and, at least to
Elizabeth, intensely boring. Robert had been right. At least a
dozen of Laurel's editors came with their rich young escorts. They pretended to be terribly blasé but they were
visibly impressed by the grandeur of the Gale townhouse. To
Elizabeth's relief, there seemed to be very few of "the boys"
in evidence. She did not know whether Robert had carefully
screened the guest list to eliminate notoriously fey young
men or whether it was his custom to keep his worlds carefully separated. In any case, only a few famous and well-
accepted homosexuals were in evidence—a much-admired ballet dancer, a prominent photographer, and a sought-after
costume designer seemed to be the only representatives of
Robert's "other life." The rest of those present were mostly
young, chic businesswomen, Laurel's editors, a sprinkling of
high-level retail executives from the most exclusive fashion
stores, a handful of society reporters and gossip columnists,
and a smattering of post-debutantes, all accompanied by
suitable escorts wearing impeccable dinner jackets and polite, vacant smiles.

Elizabeth was bored because she knew almost no one and
because she had to act out the role Robert had chosen for
her: the welcoming, gracious hostess of the evening. Robert
had overlooked nothing. There was dancing and champagne
and, at eleven o'clcok, a perfect sit-down dinner for fifty at
five tables for ten set up in the cleared dining room and done
in pale-yellow linen cloths exactly matching the yellow
roses and tiny orchids which formed the centerpieces. True
to his word, Robert's party was devoid of silly paper hats,
raucous tin horns, holiday bunting. Promptly at midnight, the
host struck a resounding note on a sixth-century Chinese
temple gong. The startling, dramatic peal brought instant

quiet throughout the rooms. Raising his champagne glass, Robert smiled graciously, almost benevolently.

"Ladies and gentlemen," he said, "may I never behold anything less beautiful than those within my vision in this first minute of 1946. You do me honor by being here at the beginning of the first year of peace. To health, wealth, and serenity for each of you." He drained the thin crystal glass and sent it smashing into the fireplace. In seconds, forty-nine others followed it.

While the guests were drinking, breaking their glasses, and exchanging kisses in various degrees of fervor, Robert leaned close to Laurel. "Happy New Year, pet," he said. "And how did you like that little piece of showmanship?"

Laurel looked at five hundred dollars' worth of broken crystal spilling out of the fireplace.

"How come you used the second best set of champagne glasses?" she asked wryly. "What are you saving the good ones for—English royalty?"

Robert dropped his usual suave mask. He looked at her with undisguised hatred.

"No, my dear, I'm saving the best crystal for the day you marry or die or get out of town. To be exact, for the moment that you leave Tony the hell alone."

He knows, Laurel thought. He knows about Tony and me. She tried to bluff her way out of it.

"Are you drunk, Robert? What on earth are you talking about?"

"Don't play cute with me, Laurel. I've lived through this before. Just don't delude yourself. Because Tony's been to bed with you doesn't mean a thing. You wouldn't understand that, but I assure you it's true."

Angered, she lashed out at him. "Oh, doesn't it? Then why are you so upset? You're insanely jealous!"

Robert smiled. "Believe me, I am neither. I find Tony's selflessness a little boring at times, that's all. When he gets into one of his godlike moods, it all becomes quite inconvenient, even though I've learned that it's only temporary. Somehow you've made him feel that you need him. It is a situation that he finds impossible to resist, no matter how distasteful to him it may be. But you don't understand what I'm telling you, do you? I knew you wouldn't. Just remember I warned you."

He turned his back on her. Across the room she saw Tony smiling his heart-melting smile at a pretty girl in a pink chiffon dress. It was the same way he smiled at Laurel. Suddenly she couldn't bear it. She ran to the guest bedroom and got her coat. Without a word to anyone, she left the house. Uncaring that it was after midnight and bitterly cold, she walked the more than twenty blocks to her apartment. A few passersby turned to look at the beautiful, elegant woman in the long black velvet coat striding heedlessly alone down Park Avenue. Once or twice, oblivious to the red traffic signal against her, she was almost hit by a car. She didn't seem to notice the cars or the drivers who swore at her.

"Whatsamatter lady? You drunk or blind or sumpin'?" the motorists shouted.

She did not even acknowledge their fright. All she could hear were Robert's terrible, venomous words, his malicious, threatening voice, his almost detached recital of a situation he cynically recognized, probably, she thought, from previous experience.

And somehow she knew that he did not lie. It had no real meaning for Tony.

Chapter 16

Elizabeth had not been a witness to the bitter exchange between Laurel and Robert on New Year's Eve, but the repercussions touched her life and made her uneasy. If she asked Laurel to the apartment, her friend immediately inquired whether Robert and Tony were coming. If the answer was yes, Laurel made some transparent excuse. There did not seem to be the same reticence on the part of the two men, yet Elizabeth felt that they were relieved never to find Laurel present when they came to visit. None of the three openly discussed the breach. And in spite of her closeness to Laurel, Elizabeth did not feel free to ask questions. Laurel felt deeply about something involving herself, Tony, and Robert. Too deeply, apparently, to discuss it even with Elizabeth, who knew only that the trouble had begun at Robert's party.

That night when Laurel abruptly left alone, without explanation, Elizabeth had questioned Robert. He pretended surprised innocence. Even Tony seemed amazed that Laurel had departed without a word. Troubled, Elizabeth had kept phoning Laurel's apartment until she answered.

"Laurel, dear, what's wrong? Why did you leave? Are you ill?"

The voice sounded fuzzy, as though its owner had been crying, but she admitted nothing. "I'm okay," she said. "I just suddenly had enough of that whole phony scene."

"But you should have let someone take you home! I know that Tony would have been glad to."

Laurel's sarcasm was apparent. "Yes, I'm sure he would have. Tony's a very obliging fella."

Elizabeth let it drop. "Well, if you're sure you're all right," she said reluctantly, "I'll call you tomorrow."

"Fine. Enjoy the rest of the party."

From that moment on, the estrangment had begun. It was like a silent, hostile conspiracy which bewildered Elizabeth, yet she could not bring herself to ask any of them what had happened. Instead, she continued her friendship with all three, but there were no more happy foursomes. She saw them separately, or Robert and Tony together. It was concern, more than curiosity, that made her hope that Laurel would volunteer the truth. But this she did not choose to do. Nor did either of the others apparently wish to enlighten her. As though by tacit, mutual consent, they picked their way through a once close relationship as though they were tiptoeing around a time bomb. Whatever had happened was too painful for Laurel to discuss. Whether Robert and Tony's silence was pain or anger, Elizabeth did not know.

On a Saturday afternoon in mid-January, the newlyweds came home suntanned and exuberant. The wedding trip, Ann reported, had been a dream.

Peter was grinning from ear to ear. We were damned lucky with the weather," he reported. "I was worried about that. Bermuda can be awful in winter. The island's like a ship at sea. Completely unpredictable. But we struck a perfect couple of weeks."

Elizabeth found their presence like a breath of fresh air. Ann had never looked prettier or more content. Even her usually offhand manner had softened, under Peter's enamored, indulgent care. She had what she wanted now, and it became her.

"How's everybody?" Ann asked. "I'll bet Charlene loves having that room all to herself."

"She does," Elizabeth answered. "In fact, she feels a little sorry for you, Ann." She recounted Charlene's comment about her sister never being able to sleep alone again.

Ann looked smug. "She'll find out it's not too bad."

Peter pretended to be serious. "I don't know. She has a point. It's a little disillusioning to share a room with a woman who puts her hair up in curlers and wears cold cream to bed. Besides, Mrs. W., my bride snores a lot."

Ann was indignant. "Peter Richards, I do not do any of those things!"

"Well, maybe not. But you do insist on wearing a nightgown to bed. Any enlightened doctor will tell you that it's much healthier to sleep in the buff. Lets the body loose from the constriction of clothes."

As her mother and husband laughed, Ann actually blushed. Then she joined the slightly bawdy teasing.

"And everybody, including doctors, knows that a little mystery keeps romance going," she said. "Isn't a woman at her most alluring in a nightgown?"

"Absolutely," Peter agreed. "Particularly for about thirty seconds."

Their uninhibited happiness was contagious. It was good to see Ann so lighthearted and frivolous. Elizabeth wanted to keep them around for a while. Perhaps it was all the more because their carefree manner was in such marked contrast to the feeling of secrecy and barely veiled anger which her friends exuded these days.

"You'll stay for dinner, won't you?" Elizabeth asked. "I'm dying to hear more about your trip."

"Oh, Mother, we'd love to," Ann said, "but we promised Peter's folks we'd come out there after we saw you. In fact, we're going to stay with them for a few days."

Elizabeth was disappointed. "I know they're anxious to see you, but how come you're staying? The apartment is ready for you, isn't it? I thought you'd be in town for a while."

"We will be," Ann assured her. "But while we were gone Mrs. Richards lined up two or three houses near them for us to look at. I don't want to camp out in that furnished dump in the Village any longer than necessary. If we find a house quickly, I can start buying furniture. Don't worry. We'll be around a lot for a while. You'll have plenty of opportunity to feed us! And when you see the way my husband eats, you'll probably take back the offer!"

Ann obviously couldn't wait to start her life in the suburbs.

"Well, consider this a second home," Elizabeth said. "Charlene and I really miss you. And unless Ann's cooking has improved dramatically, Peter, you might be glad to patronize this Gramercy Park boardinghouse."

Ann laughed. "That reminds me, Mother. Mrs. Richards says there's an excellent cooking school in Scarsdale. I think she has about as much faith in me as you do!"

"Give them both my love," Elizabeth said. "By the way, Laurel, Tony, and Robert sent theirs to you."

"Give them ours," Peter answered. "Hope we see them soon."

Ann said nothing. That part of her life was over, and she was glad.

Although the young Richardses did move into town within a few days, Elizabeth saw little of them. For one thing, they had found a house in Scarsdale and Ann was frantically shopping for furniture. Moreover, they had their own crowd of young friends, all of them originally Peter's. Except for an occasional courtesy call, they were very little in evidence at Gramercy Park. When they did come, it seemed almost deliberate that they chose evenings when they knew that only Elizabeth and Charlene would be at home. Ann's dislike for her mother's friends had not abated. If anything, it seemed to have increased. She barely asked for Laurel and Robert, and when Tony's name was mentioned, she deftly changed the subject.

It probably was a blessing that Elizabeth had little time to wonder about it. As they had a year ago, she and Tony were working feverishly, getting Robert ready for his annual winter pilgrimage to Palm Beach. There were several new commissions which threw them into a frenzy of preparation. More than once, Elizabeth reluctantly had to call Charlene at six o'clock and ask if she could get her own dinner because Elizabeth would be tied up at the office until at least eight.

"I can manage just fine, Mommy," Charlene said. "I'll keep your dinner hot until you come home."

Elizabeth worried. "Now remember, you're not to open the door for anyone. That's an order!"

"I won't," the self-reliant voice answered. "Is it all right if I listen to the radio a while?"

"Of course. But don't forget the homework, baby."

When Elizabeth finally would get home after eleven hours of grueling work, Charlene always had a plate of food ready for her and a happy, welcoming smile to go with it. Over and over again, Elizabeth reminded herself how blessed she was to have this cheerful, uncomplaining child, such a far cry from the difficult Ann and the uncaring, still unheard-from Quigly. Still, she almost wished that Charlene could be more childish. It was unnatural to see a little girl not yet eleven years old so willing to take on adult responsibilities, and so capable of handling them. Charlene knew how to cook and sew, to clean, to shop, and to do all of them with an expertise that

Ann probably would never master or even try to. Elizabeth was grateful for the help that Charlene gave her. At the same time, she felt guiltily that she was robbing her of her childhood. The chores Charlene so willingly assumed—often unasked—deprived her of normal playtime, and Elizabeth worried that she did not get enough sunshine and fresh air. She was too thin, a little too pale. And yet the yearly medical examination showed nothing except a slight tendency toward underweight, which the doctor dismissed as a phase she'd grow out of.

On weekends, Elizabeth spent every minute with Charlene, enjoying her company as though she were another adult. They explored the Metropolitan Museum, the Museum of Natural History, and the Museum of Modern Art. They gazed openmouthed at the rococo splendor of the Frick Collection with its rooms full of ornate Fragonards and delicate French furniture. They ate lunch at the Fulton Fish Market and fed the seals in Central Park, went to the top of the Empire State Building, and ventured into the dark, scary underground recesses of New York's maze of subways. After Robert left for Florida, Tony began to accompany them on these expeditions, and then Charlene's joy—as well as Elizabeth's—was complete. He loved New York as they did and was more content eating a hot dog in the zoo than a Chateaubriand at "21."

One Saturday evening as they returned exhausted from a trip to the Statue of Liberty, Tony spoke quietly to Elizabeth.

"May I stay for dinner?"

She looked at him quizzically. "Well, of course, Tony. But what an odd question! You usually have dinner with Charlene and me after our outings. Why the special request?"

He looked almost sheepish. "I just wanted to make sure you expected me and didn't have anybody else coming. I need to talk to you alone."

The implication was obvious. He knew that in a year she had made no close friends in New York. Robert was in Palm Beach. The only other person who might have been coming would have been Laurel. She forced herself to sound as though nothing were unusual.

"You'll have me all to yourself, as soon as the president of your fan club goes to bed."

They settled down over brandies when Charlene was tucked in. It had begun to snow lightly, giving New York that rare momentary illusion of cleanliness and quiet that would disappear with the first rush of morning traffic. In spite of the tranquil atmosphere, Tony seemed visibly agitated. For a while, neither of them spoke. Then, twirling his brandy glass lightly, Tony abruptly plunged into what was troubling him.

"I guess you know what's wrong between Laurel and Robert and me, don't you?"

"No. Not only what's wrong between you three but between all of us. What is it, Tony? What's happened?"

"Laurel thinks she's in love with me."

Elizabeth gave a little laugh. "Well, that hardly makes her unique, does it? You seem to have a capacity for inspiring devotion. Or is this more serious than the crush each of us has on you?"

"It's more serious. And it's my own stupid fault. You see, Elizabeth, I've been to bed with Laurel. Twice. And she interpreted that as love. At least she did until Robert disillusioned her on New Year's Eve."

Elizabeth was thoroughly mystified. "I'm afraid I don't understand. I didn't know you cared for Laurel that way. I thought that you and Robert—"

"Were lovers? We are. But I don't buy the idea of love in the way most people do. If my body makes Robert happy then I gladly give it to him. And if it fulfills a need for Laurel then she, too, is welcome. People don't have sexes to me, they have souls. If they enjoy any kind of spiritual or emotional or physical contact with me, I see nothing immoral in that. I enjoy it, too. Unfortunately, I don't seem to be able to communicate this to the people I become involved with. They become possessive, demanding, jealous. The way Robert has always been. And the way Laurel is now. They tear me apart with their desire to own. And I won't be owned. Robert knows that. He lives with it, even though emotionally he's incapable of accepting it. That's why in his jealousy and anger he attacked Laurel. And now Laurel hates us both. My God, why can't those two understand that there's enough love in me for both of them—and for anyone else who needs it?"

Elizabeth tried desperately to digest what he was saying. It was, of course, totally unrealistic of Tony to think that ordinary people could accept his kind of "love" and make no claims on him. Was he really no naïve? Did he really not know that human emotions weren't as lofty as he wanted them to be? He must realize it. Otherwise he would not be so troubled. Nor would he have said, as he had at the beginning, that Laurel's love for him was his "own stupid fault."

Poor Laurel. God knows what Robert had said to her. Slowly, Elizabeth tried to sort out the facts.

"How did Robert find out about you and Laurel?"

"I told him. I've told him every time I've been with someone else. Man or woman. He must learn to accept this as part of me. He knows that. He knows I'll leave him in a moment unless he understands that I belong to no one and everyone."

"But that's childish, Tony! People can't accept that."

"I can. Why can't they? Robert knows I'd do anything in the world for him. Care for him if he was sick. Go with him anywhere he needed me. Why can't he see that any relationship with other people doesn't in the least diminish what I feel for him?"

Elizabeth sighed. "Because his passions are more worldly than yours. Just as Laurel's are. Most people believe that the physical act of love, done with tenderness and consideration, is a commitment, a vow of fidelity."

"Remember your Bible, Elizabeth? 'God so loved the world that he gave his only begotten son.' "

For an instant, Elizabeth lost her patience. "But you're not God, Tony! Nor, I daresay, his son!"

He smiled. "No. Of course I'm not. But I do love the world. Every man, woman, and child in it. This is my only contribution. I want to give. To love. To help. And never to hurt."

"Then why have you deliberately hurt two people who love you? In the name of honesty? In the attempt to convert them to your particular view of intimate relationships? How could you, Tony? How dare you set yourself up to judge what other people must accept? It's you who's selfish and egotistical, not them!"

Her words did not anger him. "I only know one thing," he said. "If they want me, they must accept me on my terms, because that's how I see love. Is that so bad, Elizabeth? If you needed the comfort of my arms, the warmth of my body right now, would you expect me to become exclusively, eternally your possession? Is it so unthinkable that joy can be an undemanding thing, accepted when the time is right, relinquished with grace when the need is answered? Why do people have to flaunt their conquests, prove to the world that someone is entirely their own? What kind of vanity requires them to make a continuous public display of a private moment of happiness?"

Thinking of her own hopes of marriage to Adam Barnsworth, Elizabeth shook her head. "You ask too much, Tony.

I don't know how men like Robert feel, but my heart aches for Laurel. A woman wants the world to know that she is exclusively, selfishly loved. She wants to speak of it, proudly and freely. It's part of her emotional security. Oh, I grant you it's sometimes stupidly sentimental. As sorry as I am for Laurel, I'm amazed she could think that being in bed with a man twice makes him her own. I suppose her only excuse is that you are such a different kind of man. I'm sure that, considering what she knows, she must have believed that you had found, at last, the one woman who could take you away from Robert and his kind of life. She must have felt that she alone could 'reform you,' if you will. You see, my dear, I never dreamed that *any* woman could interest you physically. Probably Laurel felt the same. I suppose when you made love to her, she read too much into it. She saw it as the beginning of a new kind of life for both of you. Many women dream of making that happen. Unfortunately, it rarely does. And it must hurt." Elizabeth paused. "I'm glad you told me about it, Tony, but I don't know exactly why you did."

"Because you're her best friend, and you've got to make her understand."

"Isn't that *your* job?"

"I've tried. She won't listen. She insists that I couldn't have shown such passion unless I felt deeply about her. She blames most of it on Robert. She seems to think he has some diabolical hold on me that is keeping me from her. I swear to you, Elizabeth, I told her exactly what I've told you, but she wouldn't believe me."

"How could she, Tony? She's in love with you. You made her feel that she had some special quality, and now you want her to accept the fact that you were only doing her a favor!"

For the first time, he winced. "You know that isn't true. I love Laurel. The way I love Charlene and Ann and Robert. She must understand the way I feel about people."

"How very easy that is for you to say since you've never really been in love with anyone. My God, how did this whole terrible mess ever happen?"

"The way it always does," he said. "The first time was the night you had the Richardses here for dinner. Laurel was alone and depressed. I went over to see her and she told me how low she was. We talked a long while. And finally she asked me to make love to her."

"So of course you did. Compassion on demand." Elizabeth's voice was scornful.

"All right. If that's the way you want to put it, yes. She seemed happy, gay afterward, and I thought she understood it for what it was—two dear friends, two adults sharing a moment of forgetfulness. I went home feeling good. Not only physically. I thought I'd helped Laurel through a bad time, given her the reassurance she needed. Then two nights later she called me. I went over, and after a lot of talk, somehow we ended up in bed again. I tried to tell her then that she was precious to me, but that I wasn't in love with her. She threatened to tell Robert. I said that wouldn't be necessary. That I'd tell him myself. I know she didn't believe that I would. But of course I did. I had to. She found out on New Year's Eve that Robert knew all about it. As you know, she's refused to see him or me ever since. She's turned her back on me even more obviously than Ann did."

The last words triggered the troublesome thought that had, for so many months, nagged Elizabeth and which now came back to haunt her.

"Tony, I must ask you one difficult question. And you must answer me truthfully, no matter how reluctant you might be." She paused. "Did you ever go to bed with Ann?"

There was a fraction of a second's pause before he answered. "On my word of honor, Elizabeth, I never did."

"But she tried to get you to, didn't she?"

He looked pained. "My dear, where is all this leading us? It has nothing to do with the Laurel problem."

"Then why did you mention Ann? Perhaps it was subconscious, but it might well have to do with my daughter's behavior. You don't have to answer. I know now that she was in love with you. I think I've always known it. Nothing else would explain her irrational dislike of you and Robert. I've always thought she married too quickly. And I suppose I always really knew why."

"I swear to you, Elizabeth, that I never gave Ann the slightest encouragement."

"I believe that. I really do. Ann was a confused eighteen-year-old girl and Laurel is a thirty-three-year-old experienced woman. Yet neither of them could resist you as a challenge. I only pray to God that Laurel will regain her perspective about you as Ann seems to have. Ann will make a life with Peter. I'm sure of that now. She'll have babies and dogs and all the things that most girls want. But Laurel? What's going to happen to Laurel, Tony?"

He was not pretending. He was deeply troubled. "I don't know. I hoped you could help."

"How? By telling her that I know what a fool she made of herself? I wouldn't humiliate her by letting her know that I knew, and now I understand why she hasn't been willing to talk to me about it. What would you have me say to her? That you're so lofty you fancy yourself above ordinary human emotions? That she must share you with anyone who you decide has need of you? Or should I remind her that for all your sweetness and charm you still are only a twenty-eight-year-old with godlike delusions? It's no good, Tony. If she decides to discuss it with me, I'll do what I can for both of you. But if she doesn't come to me and won't listen to you, how can either of us help her?"

"You sound as though I disgust you."

"No," Elizabeth said wearily, "you make me afraid for you and for the people you unintentionally hurt. I've never met anyone like you, Tony. You're not a bad person. In your own way you try to be a good one. Funny. In a way you remind me of myself twenty years ago. I was so sure that I could help the world, that I had the magic formula for making other people happy. Oh, I never had your 'mystical' attitude toward it. My approach was more personal, maybe in a way even more egotistical, particularly where my husband was concerned. I had the ridiculous idea that I was the influence he needed, the guiding spirit that could steer him right. And he ended up hating me for it. It's too bad that Laurel has turned her hatred toward you and Robert, but it's easy to understand. In all this talk of 'giving love,' only Robert has won a victory, Tony. What have you gained? What has Laurel?"

Without warning, he began to cry. Openly, unashamedly, like a wretched child. For a moment or two, Elizabeth watched him helplessly. He was such a little boy, such a confused, well-meaning idealist. He was not the composed, unselfish dispenser of favors he wanted to be. As though the conversation about Laurel had never happened, Elizabeth went to him and held him in her arms, making soothing, reassuring sounds, cradling his head against her breast. He calmed down, finally, and looked up at her with despair.

"Help me," he said. "I don't know what I am or where I'm going. I haven't been truthful with you, Elizabeth. I can't even be truthful with myself. I hate Robert. It makes me sick when he touches me. Yet I accept his favors and pretend that I'm making the sacrifice for him. All I'm doing is trying to justify the fact that I'm no better than a male whore he could pick up anywhere. A little more presentable, maybe. A little more useful in his business. But a liar to him and to myself."

She said nothing. There was, she knew, more to come. Tomorrow Tony might regret the first honest self-appraisal he'd ever made. But tonight it was important to him to tell the truth. He continued to cling to her almost desperately, the way even her own children had never clung to her.

"I play at being homosexual with Robert," he said, "but a woman can arouse me just as well. I didn't go to bed with Laurel because I felt she needed me. I did it because for that moment I wanted a woman and she was willing. I didn't have to take her the second time. I wanted that, too. She had reason to think I was in love with her. I told her so over and over those nights. Just as I've told it to Robert." He paused. "Just as, dear God, I almost once told it to Ann. But that I couldn't do. You do believe that, Elizabeth? I never laid a hand on Ann."

"Yes, I believe that." It was Ann who was the fake, Elizabeth thought. Ann who so offhandedly talked of using her virginity as a trading position for marriage. She had done it, all right. But would she have if Tony had been willing to be her lover? Or did Ann imagine that she could have bargained with Tony as she later had with Peter?

"What's wrong with me, Elizabeth?" His voice was pathetic. "Am I psychotic? Am I some sort of degenerate? Are all the things I've believed about 'giving of myself' just a cover-up for indiscriminate lust? When I was in the army, I found out that I had some special kind of power, some strange effect that made people happy, sometimes even seemed to make them well. I know that's true, even now. But why am I misusing this gift? Why can't I be as truly selfless as I want to be? Why must I be tortured by these terrible selfish feelings that I want to reject? I'm so mixed up, Elizabeth. I'm so terribly guilt-ridden and torn apart. I'm ashamed of the unhappiness I cause. And yet, in spite of my shame, I really can't belong to anyone. All I can do is feel scorn for them because they want to own me. What kind of curse is it that makes me torture everyone who loves me?"

He was making only half sense to Elizabeth. She knew nothing of Tony's almost mystical powers to heal, his "religious" experiences. She could only guess at his sincerity even now. Maybe he himself did not know which was the "real Tony"—the one whose love of people transcended man-made conventions or the all too human young man who could not resist normal self-gratification? Perhaps he was a little mad. An eavesdropper on this strange conversation certainly would have thought so. She thought—as she had with Alan—of suggesting professional help, but she feared that even the suggestion would destroy this delicate thread of communication between them. She was sure that Tony had never talked this way to anyone. She had been given an insight into a be-wildered mind. At this point, at least, she could not jeopardize Tony's one slim hold on reality. He was looking to her for answers, and she had none to give. Instead, as was her way, she turned to practical considerations, trite as they seemed.

"Tony, dear," she said gently, "I think the thing you need most now is rest. Go on home and get some sleep. We can talk more tomorrow, if you like."

He shook his head. "I can't. I can't be alone. I don't dare be. Please let me stay here tonight."

With a sinking heart she understood what he meant. In this mood of self-hatred he might do anything, even destroy himself. For a moment, she thought he was going to ask to go to bed with her. Even worse, in that split second she knew she might acquiesce. Not because she wanted him. After all he'd told her, the thought of sex with Tony seemed indecent. But her pity for him was so overpowering, her distress so acute, that she might have taken him to her as she would have comforted any wounded friend.

As though he read her mind, Tony smiled wistfully. "No, Elizabeth," he said gently, "even I would not suggest that."

Startled at his perception, she reddened.

"But I'd be grateful if you'd let me stay in the apartment," he said. "I can sleep on the couch. I need to be near someone. No, that's not precisely true, either. I need to be near you. Not in your bed. I just need to know that you're there. Even with a door closed between us, I'll know you're there." He gave a little laugh. "It can even be a locked door if you like. I wouldn't blame you. But please let me stay."

"Of course you may stay. I'll make up the couch for you. And I won't lock my door. I know I don't have to."

In the morning, a surprised and delighted Charlene discovered her adored Tony asleep on the living-room couch. She peeked into her mother's room, where Elizabeth lay fast asleep. Quietly, the capable child began preparing Sunday breakfast. She wondered why Tony had not gone home. Probably because of the big snowstorm. She wished she could wake up every morning and find Tony there. She loved him very much. He was the kind of man she was going to marry, she decided. She liked him even better than she did her new brother-in-law.

Chapter 17

While Robert was in Palm Beach, Elizabeth continued to see Tony and Laurel, always separately. Now it was also Tony who inquired whether Elizabeth would be "alone" before he came to the apartment. They did not refer again to that strange conversation on the snowy February night. But an even greater affection and understanding had been born. Elizabeth had gained some small insight into Tony's troubled thoughts. And he seemed more relaxed, as though his confession—or confessions—had shifted some of the burden from his shoulders to Elizabeth's.

Laurel still had made no reference to the affair with Tony or to Robert's knowledge of it. Sometimes Elizabeth suspected that Laurel knew Tony had talked to her about it, but for the first time in their friendship there was a taboo subject: Anthony Alexander. Elizabeth tried to handle it naturally, casually mentioning Tony or speaking of Robert's success in Palm Beach, bigger than ever in this postwar period. Laurel seemed distant and uninterested when the conversation took that turn. There was an air of bitterness about her these days, a self-condemnation implicit in her manner. Tony had lied to her, used her, and she had opted for silence about it, even in the presence of her closest friend. It was no good that Tony was contrite. Laurel thought she hated him for making a fool of her, and hated herself even more for believing him in those two brief, passionate interludes.

But in honest moments of introspection, she knew she did not hate Tony. She loved him. She hungered for him. And everything inside her wished that when he said he loved her it had been true. The realistic Laurel knew it was not. And the sensible Laurel knew that the only way to prevent a repetition of disaster was to stay away from him.

Early in March, Robert summoned Tony to join him.

"No worry about leaving you in charge *this* year," Tony said. "This time I'm absolutely positive that you can run the business better than either of us. Which reminds me. Do you realize that you haven't had a vacation since you joined us? When Robert and I get back, why don't you think about taking some time off? Vacations are very important. You could use a change of scene."

"What about you and Robert?" Elizabeth parried. "I haven't noticed either of you going on holiday since I've been here."

"True. But don't let Robert kid you. In spite of his stories about how hard we work in Palm Beach, it's still more sunshine than slavery. The only sweat we work up is at the pool at the Breakers! Besides, he has mentioned going to Europe in the spring. It's the first year he's been able to go since the war, and it's important for him to get over there and buy up half the antiques on the Continent. The trip masquerades as business for the benefit of Internal Revenue, but my hunch is that it's a great tax-deductible vacation."

"Will you go with him?"

"I suppose so. It'll be strange to see London without buzz bombs. And I never have seen Paris. They shipped me home before we got that far. Anyway, Robert plans to stay at least six weeks. And you know better than anybody else that he wouldn't trust me out of his sight that long."

It was the first even offhand reference Tony had made to their conversation. "By the way," he said slowly, "how's Laurel?"

"All right, I guess. I don't think she looks well, but she seems to be very busy. She's making a great success of the magazine. They've extended her contract and given her a big raise." Elizabeth paused. "She mentioned the other night that she might be going to Europe this summer. A few of the Paris couture showings will be starting up again and she'll probably go over in July for the fashion openings."

"That'll be nice for her." He hesitated. "Has she ever mentioned the thing with me?"

"Never."

"I'm sorry she hasn't," Tony said frankly. "I was hoping she'd get the same comfort from you that I got."

Elizabeth looked surprised. "That's nice of you, Tony, but I honestly don't remember giving you much comfort."

"You did," he said. "Someday I'll tell you how."

Elizabeth did not take the vacation that Tony had suggested. With Quigly gone and Ann married, she could have afforded to take Charlene somewhere, particularly since Robert had given her two quite handsome salary increases in the year and a half she'd worked for him. But there seemed no place to go. None, that is, within reason. She would have loved to go somewhere exciting and exotic, like the Orient, but that was out of the question. It was still too soon to visit Japan, even if she could have afforded it. Then Laurel, in a burst of the old warmth, suggested that Elizabeth might accompany her to Europe in July. In April, when Robert and Tony had already set sail for their six weeks' buying trip, they discussed the idea.

"We could have a marvelous time," Laurel said over lunch. "The magazine will send me first class all the way and you could share my stateroom and hotel room in Paris. Come on, Elizabeth, plan on it. It won't cost much, and I can just imagine how you'd love it. It would almost be worth paying you to go with me, just for the fun of watching you go crazy at the sight of the Champs Elysées!"

It was a tempting idea. Laurel seemed to be coming out of her depression. She was almost the old, gay Laurel of the Washington days, a little sleeker and more sophisticated, perhaps, but still the wonderful friend and companion who had seen Elizabeth through those black days years before. On the surface at least, she seemed to have recovered from the emotional hurt she'd suffered. She still expressed no interest in Tony or Robert and was careful to avoid any contact with them. But Elizabeth was relieved to see that common sense had finally overcome the self-pity and resentment which her confusing encounter with Tony had engendered. Like Ann, Elizabeth thought, only with a more concrete reason to feel rejected.

"I don't know," Elizabeth said. "I'd give anything to do it. All my life I've dreamed of seeing the world, and do you know I've never gotten farther than a few cities on the East Coast? What a limited horizon for a middle-aged lady!

Now that I think of it, I can't even remember when I last had a vacation. My lord, it must be more than twenty years! Between babies and disasters, I guess the last real pleasure trip I took was to Saratoga on my honeymoon!"

"All the more reason," Laurel said. "Will you go?"

"What about Charlene?"

"Can't she stay with Ann and Peter? Now that they have that stultifyingly middle-class house in the suburbs, they surely could keep her for three weeks this summer when she's out of school. Or would Ann be afraid she'd scuff up the wall-to-wall carpeting in that *Ladies' Home Journal* living room?"

Elizabeth laughed. Secretly she shared Laurel's horror at the prim, stiff house that Ann had created. There was nothing really bad in it, there simply was nothing warm or personal. Everything matched too perfectly, like all the upholstered furniture and what Ann irritatingly insisted upon referring to as the "drapes." Lamps and vases were firmly in pairs; ashtrays were too small to be usable, since Ann didn't smoke and had insisted that Peter quit. It was like some self-conscious model house in a new-development tract, with everything perfectly equipped and blandly anonymous. There were no books in sight and there was only one photograph— Ann in her wedding dress. Even the "den," where the young couple spent their evenings, had none of the charming disorder that goes with a happy, relaxed home. Elizabeth did concede that Ann had surprised her by becoming an excellent housekeeper. In the pattern of the other young wives in the community, she had gone to cooking school and had become a good, plain cook, though given to cake mixes and horrid little salads of canned pears and creamed cheese. On the whole, though, Ann had turned into a reasonably efficient, if not imaginative, homemaker. She had only a part-time cleaning woman instead of the full-time maid she'd planned on, but she had the two cars, the house, the country club membership and the smug, self-righteous attitude of the wife of a rising executive. She had gone as far away from Elizabeth's idea of a life-style as she could.

Mrs. Richards, Sr., could now, indeed, have been Ann's mother. A stranger comparing Elizabeth and Joanne would most certainly have pointed to the latter as the woman who had given birth to this insular, self-satisfied young matron. Elizabeth was glad that Ann was so happy with her narrow little life, and equally glad that she lived it some distance away. The truth was that she bored Elizabeth to tears. On the rare occasions when she visited her daughter in Scarsdale or when Ann and Peter came in town to visit her, Elizabeth could hardly wait for the evenings to be over. She had no interest in Ann's local gossip, her civic activities, or her new recipes, just as Ann did not relate to Elizabeth's work, or to the areas of art or music or politics which her mother futilely tried to introduce as topics of conversation. Even Peter seemed to grow daily more like his father. He was becoming a serious, self-opinionated young man, already verging on the pompous. To each his own, Elizabeth told herself. Thank God in a way for Ann's highly developed sense of self-preservation. For one thing, it had warned her to get out of the reach of Anthony Alexander.

Now Elizabeth addressed herself to Laurel's provocative question about Europe. It would be a dirty trick to play on Charlene, banishing her to that sterile world even for three weeks, but she knew that the child would not be affected as Elizabeth was by the stifling atmosphere of Ann's existence. She might even consider it fun to spend a vacation "in the country," as the locals called it.

"Okay," Elizabeth said, "you're on! I'll call Ann tonight and ask her whether she'll look after Charlene while I'm gone. Oh, Laurel, I can't believe it! I'm really going to Europe! I don't know how I'll live through the next three months!"

That evening at dinner, she broached the subject to Charlene. As she'd expected, the child was almost as excited about her mother's trip as Elizabeth was. Her only instinctive doubt was about staying with Ann.

"Are you sure she won't mind, Mommy? Ann's awfully particular about her house. Maybe she'll think I'll mess it up."

"Darling, what nonsense! Of course she won't think anything of the kind! She knows what a marvelously neat little girl you are. Far neater than *she* ever was at your age! And I do think it will be fun for you, baby. You don't have enough opportunity to play outdoors. Ann and Peter have joined the country club, you know. I'm sure you'll be able to go swimming every day and you'll probably meet a lot of nice children your own age."

Charlene warmed to the prospect. As rude as Ann had been to her, she worshiped her big sister and idolized Peter. Still, with her uncanny sensitivity, she had reservations about her welcome in Ann's house.

"Maybe it would be better if I could stay with Tony and Mr. Gale."

"No, dear. I'd really like you to be in the country for a few weeks. Get some roses in those cheeks. And don't worry that it will be inconvenient for Ann. She'll adore having you."

On her way to the telephone, Elizabeth wished she were as positive of that as she had sounded. She dialed Ann. Peter answered.

"Hi, Mrs. W.," he said. "What a coincidence! Ann and I were just getting ready to call you."

"Really? What about?"

"I'll let Ann tell you herself. Wait a second. Here she is."

"Mother? I'm so glad you phoned. I just finished talking to Mother Richards and I was about to call you. Guess what? I'm going to have a baby! In October. Isn't that terrific? How do you think you'll like being a grandmother?"

Elizabeth's reactions came swiftly. First was happiness for Ann. Then an unreasonable little twinge of jealousy that she had called Joanne Richards first. And finally, the disappointing realization that a six months pregnant Ann could not be asked to take care of Charlene. She would be much too involved in herself and her own well-being to take on even this minor added responsibility. It would not do to mention it. She forced herself to sound wholeheartedly delighted.

"Darling, I'm thrilled for you both! How are you feeling?"

"Superhuman. A little morning sickness, but nothing insurmountable. It's Peter I'm really worried about. I don't think he'll survive impending fatherhood. He's already bringing me breakfast in bed, not that it stays with me very long."

"But you're sure you're okay?" Elizabeth's own pregnancies had been remarkably easy, but the thought of her own mother never ceased to haunt her.

"Absolutely peachy," Ann reassured her. "Everything is on schedule, including this baby. We plan three, you know. Two years apart."

"I see," Elizabeth said drily. "And of course the first will be a boy?"

"Naturally. It's much more convenient for girls to have an older brother who can introduce them to his friends. I always thought it was a bore that I came before Quigly. He was no help when it came to getting dates for me."

Ann was chattering frivolously, but Elizabeth knew that beneath the nonsense, the girl was completely serious, confident that she could will the sex of her children as methodically as she arranged everything else about her neatly boxed-in existence.

"Oh, by the way," Ann added. "Peter insists on our getting a full-time housekeeper now. Isn't he too much? I have to run now, Mother, but I'll be in touch."

"Take good care of yourself. And congratulate Peter for Charlene and me."

"I will." Then, almost as an afterthought, "How is Charlene?"

"She's fine," Elizabeth said. "I was thinking maybe I'd send her to day camp this summer. Anything to get her out of this hot, steamy city." For a wild moment, Elizabeth hoped that Ann would offer to have Charlene spend a little time with the Richardses. Unsurprisingly, she did not. Maybe Charlene's intuition was better than mine all along, Elizabeth thought. Maybe Ann wouldn't have taken her for a few weeks even if she hadn't been pregnant.

When she told Charlene that Ann was going to have a baby, the child's face lit up. Then, almost immediately, it fell. "She won't want me this summer, then, will she?"

"It's not that she doesn't want you, darling, but I think it might be too much for her to have any guest in the house. Don't worry, though. I had another idea. How would you like to go to day camp? There are some nice ones. They pick you up every morning in a bus with a lot of other children and you spend the day in the country and come home to sleep at night. Doesn't that sound like fun?"

Charlene seemed reluctant. "I guess so. But why couldn't I just stay home, Mommy? I can play in the park." Suddenly she realized what this turn of events did to Elizabeth's plans. "What about the trip you were going to take with Aunt Laurel! Won't you be able to go?" Charlene was on the verge of tears.

"Hush," Elizabeth said. "It's not all that important, sweetheart. There'll be other years for me to go to Europe. Maybe by the time I go you'll be able to go with me. Wouldn't that be something? Think about London! 'They're changing the guard at Buckingham Palace. Christopher Robin went down with Alice.' Remember that poem, Charlene? It was always one of our favorites."

The child made one last try. "Maybe I *could* stay with Tony?"

"No, dear. Tony and Mr. Gale will have their own plans this summer, I'm sure. They're invited away lots of weekends, you know, and we wouldn't want to interfere with their summer. Anyway, cheer up. Remember, Fourth of July is coming! We'll plan something extra special this year for your birthday."

When Elizabeth broke the news to Laurel, the editor of *Enchantress* unreasonably exploded. "Goddamn that Ann! Wouldn't you know she'd pull something like this just in time to spoil the first real bit of fun you'd have had in years?"

Elizabeth couldn't help laughing. "For heaven's sake, Laurel, you make it sound as though she got pregnant just to spite me."

"I wouldn't put it past her," Laurel grumbled.

"You're being silly."

"I know I am. But damn it, it does seem almost spooky. It couldn't be worse timing if she *had* figured it out."

"Well, she didn't," Elizabeth said. "So that's that for Europe as far as I'm concerned. This year, at least."

"Oh, sure. And next year Ann won't be able to take Charlene because she'll have a new baby. And the year after that she'll be pregnant again according to her timetable."

"Laurel, dear, I'm more disappointed than you, but there's really no use batting our heads against the wall. The trip's off for me. I'll just have to enjoy it vicariously through your postcards."

"What about Charlene? You were so anxious for her to breathe some good clean air for a change."

"I thought maybe a day camp this summer. At least she'd get out of the city while I'm at the office."

"Wait a minute," Laurel said. "Why don't we send her to camp for the whole summer? That would solve everything. If it's money you're worried about, I can help you out."

Elizabeth regarded her affectionately. "Dear Laurel, you really are so generous. But it isn't just money. I don't want to ship her off with strangers. I know that a lot of children younger than Charlene go away to camp, but I don't think she's ready for that kind of prolonged separation from me. If she could have been with Ann, I'd have felt all right about it. But abandoning her for my own pleasure is something I just can't do. I know. You think I'm being ridiculous. You're going to tell me that she's the most mature child for her age that you've ever seen. And in many ways she is. But emotionally, she's far from secure. She'd pretend that it was fine for her, but I think she'd feel tossed around again. She's lost so much, Laurel. Her father and her brother, even in a way her sister. She's been plopped down in strange houses since the day she was born. Outwardly, she has responded better than the other two, but she's much more sensitive, no matter how adult she seems. No, I just can't go off to another country and leave her with strangers. Not at this stage."

"Well, what the hell. Let's take her with us."

Elizabeth shook her head. "You know that wouldn't work."

"No, I suppose not. But damn it, Elizabeth, it seems so unfair!"

"I'm sure those were the very words that Helen Hayes's producer used when she told him about her 'act-of-God baby.' "

Laurel sighed. "Do you always have to be so bloody philosophical about your kids?"

"Don't be deceived," Elizabeth said. "Beneath this calm exterior beats the heart of a Margaret Sanger."

"It should have started palpitating twenty-one years ago. If it had, you'd be free, white, and forty-one."

"Touché," Elizabeth said. "But I'd have missed an awful lot of interesting things in the meantime."

In July, Elizabeth and Charlene saw Laurel off to Europe on the *Queen Mary*, refurbished now from a troop ship into the greatest luxury liner on the transatlantic run. Elizabeth could have wept with disappointment as she joined the little midmorning party in Laurel's flower-filled stateroom. The very smell of the ship, the bustle of stewards rushing in with champagne goblets and late-arriving bouquets, even the feeble little trays of limp cheese and anchovy canapes which were standard fare at sailing parties all seemed part of a glamorous, remote world which Elizabeth might have shared. There was such an air of urgency and excitement in the corridors, such a feeling of expectancy among the passengers, among the first to go on postwar business or pleasure to Europe, that Elizabeth had an urge to thrust the bright-eyed Charlene into the arms of a very pregnant Ann and simply announce that she was staying aboard this floating palace.

Of course she would not. Instead, she radiated enthusiasm as she circulated among Laurel's friends, most of them from the staff of *Enchantress*. It was curious, really, that Laurel had made no more friends in New York than Elizabeth had. There were a few faces that Elizabeth knew, men and women whom Laurel obviously counted among her closer acquaintances. But for the most part the party consisted of business associates, both on the magazine and in the fashion industry. More strangers than friends, really, with the exception of Elizabeth and Charlene. Ann and Peter had come with the senior Richardses. More, one suspected, out of curiosity than affection. Tony and Robert were conspicuously absent, uninvited of course. But Elizabeth was surprised to see one beautiful, deep red rose lying in a slim florist's box. She glanced at the card tossed onto the waxed paper. It said simply, "Tony." Laurel had not even had the flower put into a vase. Perhaps it gave her pleasure to see it lying there, slowly dying. It was an unexpected but not unlikely gesture, as ambivalent as the sender, as stubborn as the receiver.

They watched the *Queen* sail majestically away from its dock, and waved at the small figure of Laurel at the rail of the promenade deck. Finally, anticlimactically, they turned away. Ann and Mrs. Richards climbed into the car for the drive back to Scarsdale, the two Richards men headed south toward their offices, and Elizabeth and Charlene hailed a cab for the return to Gramercy Park.

Elizabeth couldn't remember when she'd felt so low. It was a blistering hot Friday noon and already the streets of New York were beginning to empty as the frenetically sun-worshiping Manhattanites headed for weekends in the Hamptons, Fire Island, or the Jersey Shore. Even Charlene had been asked away for the weekend. One of her schoolmates' family had a house in Westhampton and the little girl's mother had called to ask Elizabeth's permission for Charlene to spend a few days with them.

"My husband drives out about three o'clock on Friday," Mrs. Spencer had said on the phone. "He'll be glad to pick up Charlene and bring her back early Monday morning. We'd love to have her, Mrs. Whitman. She and Joyce are very good friends and I think she'd enjoy it."

Charlene wanted to go and Elizabeth gladly agreed. She had met the Spencers at one or two parents' nights at the school and found them charming, agreeable people who lived just down the street. She packed a new bathing suit, some playclothes and underwear in a small suitcase when they got home and had Charlene ready when Mr. Spencer arrived shortly before three.

"Be a good girl," Elizabeth said as she kissed her. "And do exactly what Mrs. Spencer tells you."

"I will," Charlene promised solemnly. "Will you be all right without me?"

Elizabeth smiled. "Well, it won't be nearly as much fun for me, but I'll manage, as long as it's only for a few days." She and Mr. Spencer exchanged amused glances.

"We'll take good care of her, Mrs. Whitman," he said. "I'll have her back about ten o'clock Monday morning if that's okay."

"That will be fine. I've already told them at my office that I'll be a little late on Monday. I'll be here when you return. Thanks so much, Mr. Spencer. And please thank your wife for me. It's a great treat for Charlene."

When they left, it was strange to be so physically alone. Ann was a million light-years away in Scarsdale, Laurel was on the high seas, Charlene was making her first "grown-up" visit to another woman's house. And Quigly? God alone knew where Quigly was. It had been almost a year since she'd heard from him. Even Tony and Robert had been invited to Fire Island for the weekend. Tony had mentioned it yesterday when she told him about Charlene's invitation. He'd seemed disturbed.

"I hate to think of you being all alone the whole weekend," he said.

Elizabeth had laughed it off. "It's not exactly a national disaster. As a matter of fact, I'm rather looking forward to it. I can't remember when I've had forty-eight hours all to myself. I have a hundred things to do around the house and I probably won't do a damned one of them. I just might be a lazy slob and read and sleep the whole weekend. Live on peanut-butter sandwiches and not even cook a meal for the first time in a hundred years! I love all of you, but there are times when a girl *needs* to be alone."

She had really believed it when she said it. It had been years since there were neither family nor friends to make demands on her time, her interest, and her energies. It had seemed like bliss to think of being left utterly, peacefully alone. She would read and listen to music and go to a movie if she felt like getting out of the house. She'd be able to "recharge her batteries," as she thought of it, let her mind go limp, and be thoroughly refreshed for the return to the responsibilities of motherhood, housekeeping, and career.

Now, in reality, it appeared to be a gloomy prospect. The apartment seemed terribly still and lonely. Listlessly, she stripped off her clothes and got into a loose housecoat, made herself a glass of iced tea, turned on the electric fan in the living room, and picked up one of the three books which she thought she'd been dying to read. But she could not lose herself in the pages of the latest best seller. Her mind kept going to the people she loved. She thought of Adam, wondering whether he came home safely from the war, whether he had picked up his life in California, and whether he ever wondered about her as she did about him. She could close her eyes and remember every detail of their lovemaking. How long ago it was! Almost four years since she'd felt desired and responded to that desire. She'd kept herself very busy. God knows it hadn't been difficult, with all that had happened, to keep from thinking of her own needs. Yet, once in a while as she lay in bed, she was conscious of her own body, feeling the loneliness of a still passionate woman who went untouched year after year. But mostly, she had been too tired, or too preoccupied with Ann's or Quigly's problems, or Laurel's or Tony's, to linger on the restlessness that was always within her.

At that instant, the phone rang. She looked at her watch. Four o'clock. It must be Tony, she thought, checking on her before he and Robert left for the Island. But when she picked it up, it was not Tony. It was an unmistakable, unforgettable voice.

"Elizabeth? It's Adam."

She began to shake, quite literally. It was a fantasy, her mind said. It was not possible. She stood helplessly holding the receiver, unable to utter a syllable.

"Elizabeth? Are you there?"

She tried to control her trembling. "Where are you?" she managed finally.

"In New York. How are you, darling?"

"Fine," she stammered. "Just fine. How are you?"

"I'm all right," he said. "I was in Washington this week on business and I tried to find you. Betty Kaspar gave me your address and phone number. Elizabeth, I'd like to see you. May I?"

No, she thought. Don't ask to see me. Don't come back in my life like some ghost who'll stay a minute and drift away again, having rekindled all the suppressed desires. You're alive and well. At least I know that. But I can't handle seeing you again.

Instead, she said simply, "Of course."

There was no mistaking the relief in his voice. "May I come right now? I'm staying at the Plaza. I could be there in fifteen minutes."

"That will be fine," she said woodenly.

"I love you, darling," he said. "I have so much to tell you."

In a daze, she showered quickly and wasted three precious minutes wondering what to put on. She remembered the first night she had dressed seductively and set the stage for lovemaking. But that was a different Elizabeth, emotionally uninvolved at that point, almost calculatingly intent on starting an affair which she did not know would turn into the focus of her life. Or was that Elizabeth really any different from this one, whose body once again quivered at the thought of being touched by those gentle, familiar hands? She forced herself to stop daydreaming. He had said, "I love you," but what did that mean? He'd loved her before, or said he did. Yet he'd put her out of his life with excuses of "duty" and "honor." Why had he come back? In a little irrational flurry of hope, she allowed herself to wonder whether things had changed for him. Perhaps Monica had met someone else, as he'd always said he hoped. Perhaps he was free.

With an effort of will, she put such unlikely notions out of her mind. If such had been the case, he would have found her sooner, would have written to her or called from California. No, she knew what the story would be. Business had brought him East, had provided an easy opportunity for him to see her. Maybe he did still love her in his own way. But she knew in her heart that nothing had changed in his life. Nor would it. She was a fool to even see him again, to even chance becoming the pawn she'd been the first time. This time she'd be strong.

She deliberately put on a simple, almost prim little linen dress. Nothing provocative or misleading. She brushed her hair and quickly applied makeup. Thank God it was broad summer daylight. She could not be tempted to light candles or start a romantic blaze in the fireplace. She would see him and they would talk like old friends. Perhaps the old dreams would go away when the memory reappeared as a living thing. Childishly, she hoped he would be fat or bald or boring, and that she would feel nothing for him.

She put out ice cubes and glasses. Then she sat quietly and waited for Adam.

He was there in twelve minutes. They'd both timed it.

Chapter 18

Of course she had been kidding herself. It was as though he'd been gone a few days, rather than years. There was an initial moment of awkwardness as Elizabeth opened the door. They stood looking at each other, a tentative smile on her face, a look close to anxiety on his. Then he stepped into the apartment and took her in his arms, holding her close.

"Oh, God, Elizabeth," he said. "Oh, my God."

She felt curiously detached at that instant. Now it was Adam who was incoherent and trembling. Gently, she patted the familiar close-cropped hair, touched the strong, slightly rough cheek. Then, carefully, she withdrew from his arms, stepping back to look at him. How could he be so little changed? Aside from the unfamiliar civilian clothes, he could have been the man who went off to war in 1942, handsome, straight in his bearing and as physically attractive as he'd been that first time he came to the house in Washington. In a typically feminine reaction, she wondered how he saw her. Was she, too, the same? Or did Adam find her a little older, a little less compelling than before?

As though he read her thoughts, he looked deeply into her eyes. "I didn't think I'd forgotten a single thing about you," he said, "but I was wrong. I'd forgotten how beautiful you are. Or perhaps you've become even more beautiful." He looked around. "You are everywhere in every home you make, aren't you? So many things I remember, and all of them uniquely, wonderfully you."

Through these first minutes, Elizabeth had said nothing. Now she drew him to a chair and when he was seated, she suddenly felt ill at ease. She still stood, feeling disturbed and unsure of herself. Finally, she said, "Would you like a drink?" Then she laughed superficially. "What inane words to say to an ex-lover whom you haven't seen in nearly four years! When you leave, Adam, I'll be furious with myself for not having come up with some frightfully clever opening line! Something straight out of Noel Coward would be much more apt than 'Would you like a drink?' Dear me, I must be losing my touch. New York doesn't seem to have made me a whit more sophisticated, does it?"

"Don't, darling," he said. "Please don't."

"Don't what? Don't make you a drink?"

"Don't pretend with me. I don't recognize the brittle Elizabeth. And I don't think I want to."

"What *do* you want, Adam?"

"Make me that drink, and I'll try to tell you."

"Gin and tonic? Or have your tastes changed?"

"Gin and tonic. And no, they haven't changed at all."

She made their drinks and took the chair opposite his.

"Now," he said, "bring me up to date."

"I'd rather you told me about you."

"No, please, you first. We have so many more frames of reference in your life than in mine."

She fought back the obvious, snappish retort. "All right, I'll try to make it short." Quickly she told him about Quigly's leaving and the last word she'd had from him. About Ann's marriage and her pregnancy. About Laurel's job and, of course, about "Charley," as he'd always called the little girl. She told him how she got her present job and briefly mentioned Robert and Tony only in context with her work.

Adam listened attentively. He presumed there was much she was leaving out.

"Do you hear anything from Alan Whitman?" he asked.

"He died," Elizabeth said, and let it go at that.

"Maybe I have no right to ask," Adam said slowly, "but I have to know. Is there someone in your life now, Elizabeth?"

She hesitated. A voice inside of her said, Lie to him. Tell him you're in love. End it now before it starts all over again.

That's the easy, facesaving way. Don't let him know you've been unable to even look at another man since you met him. Don't let him think he can walk in and out of your life anytime he chooses. Have you no pride? She heard the warning and ignored it.

"No, Adam," she said. "There's no one in my life now." She paused. "And what about you?"

He began to walk restlessly up and down the room. "I'm back with Monica. But I suppose you've already surmised that. I was discharged after V-E Day and went straight to California. Picked up my business and what I laughingly call my married life. I've done well. Real estate is booming in that area. I've made a dozen trips East since I saw you, but I never had the courage to call you. I thought you might hang up in my face. No reason why you shouldn't, God knows, after the way I behaved."

She was very quiet. It hurt to know that he'd been near before without her knowing. It was cruel of him not to at least have let her know that he was alive. She waited for him to go on.

"I know you're wondering why you never heard a word from me. Christ, the things you must have thought of me! And you were right. For all my wartime heroics, I'm a pretty spineless guy. I couldn't bring myself to face a nasty breakup with Monica, but I couldn't be rotten enough to keep cluttering up your life. I convinced myself that the kindest thing I could do for you was to stay the hell out of your sight forever. I told myself that anything else was unfair to you. You had a right to happiness, and I suppose it sounds insanely egotistical but I thought that you'd never marry again until you put me completely out of your mind. I've been tempted a thousand times to write to you or call you. You see, it's not true that I just found out where you were. Betty Kaspar didn't tell me. I learned that from Stu Preston the minute I got back to Washington. But I cared too much to cause you more pain. That's my only excuse. It seemed the best thing I could do for the only woman I've ever loved."

"Do you think it was your right to make that decision alone, Adam? Since I was involved, wasn't I entitled to share in it?"

He looked at her intently. "If I had come home from the war, told you I still couldn't divorce Monica and asked you to be my lover on a very part-time basis, would you have bought it?"

Her answer came without hesitation. "Yes, I would have bought it."

He shook his head. "But how long, Elizabeth? How long before you would have despised me? How long before you'd have resented me for turning up for a day or two every couple of months and then leaving you? Where would I be all the times you needed me? And don't say you'd have moved to California to be near me. That would have been worse. You're not cut out for sneaking around dark corners, spending secret evenings whenever I could get out of the house. It's not your style. I don't even think it's mine." He paused. "There is something I want you to know, though. While I was overseas I did decide to ask Monica for a divorce. When I came home I told her I was in love with someone. She laughed it off. Said it was no more than she expected—a wartime romance. The wife of every serviceman went through it, she said, even the wives of the top brass. She said it had nothing to do with her and me. She still liked her life and she'd never divorce me. I never brought it up again."

"But you could have divorced her."

"On what grounds, my darling? Even if I'd found the legal ones, the moral hangups and stupid sense of obligation wouldn't go away. I damned near lost my life a couple of times but I couldn't lose my ridiculous conscience. It's a lousy marriage, but I guess it's till death do us part."

She looked at him questioningly.

"I know what you're thinking," Adam said. " 'So what is he doing here now?' " He shook his head. "I'm not sure, except that this trip I *had* to see you. I couldn't resist any longer. Sitting in that hotel room an hour ago I felt as though you were calling out to me. It was as if I were reading your thoughts. I've needed you so much. I've wanted you until I ached with it. And I was ashamed to face you. But this afternoon I just dialed and prayed. And you answered. Now I know I was right. Damn the consequences. I've only been half alive without you."

"And I without you," Elizabeth said.

He came to her and gently lifted her to her feet. "Does that mean what I hope it does? *Can* you live with the only kind of situation I can offer you—being together for a day or two every month or six weeks? Can you stand that without eventually hating me? It's no life for any woman, darling, and especially not for a woman like you. You should never have to take second place."

She put her face close to his. "Am I second place with you, Adam?"

"Of course not. I've just told you that."

"Then I'm not really second place at all, am I?"

His kiss was at first gentle, then eager and finally demanding. She felt the old, wonderful weakness come over her, the marvelous helplessness return. There were no more words just then. Simply hours of indescribable, insatiable acts of love.

Much later they dressed and went to the outdoor garden of the Ritz for dinner. Over the meal in the nearly empty restaurant they held hands and kissed, unself-consciously, like young lovers. There was time for talk, now. Some of it bright and gay, like Elizabeth's description of Ann's prudish little house and her self-satisfied life; some of it tragic and terrible, like the nightmare of the funeral in Memphis; some of it sad, like the endless worry over Quigly.

"I'll start doing some checking when I get back to California," Adam promised. "He can't have just dropped off the face of the earth, darling. We'll find him."

A shadow crossed Elizabeth's face. "I'm almost afraid of what we'll find if we do. But I have to know. No matter how bad it is, I have to know, Adam. Just as I couldn't rest until I knew about you."

He pressed his lips to the palm of her hand. "I hope I did right, coming back. God knows it's selfish of me."

Elizabeth smiled wickedly. "Let's go home," she said, "so you can be selfish some more."

They spent most of their weekend making love, going out only for dinner and returning quickly to lie in each other's arms. Adam told her of his war experiences, and she held him tighter, terrified even now at the thought that he might have been killed or wounded. They did not speak of Monica or of his life in California. And as if by tacit agreement, they did not again mention his scheduled departure on Sunday night, once he had told her exactly when he had to leave.

"I'll say it just once, and then we'll never have to go over it again," Adam said. "I promise to be with you in New York or somewhere at least once a month, and more often if I can manage it. I'll phone you whenever I can. And you are to call me at my office if anything comes up that I should know about. My secretary is Miss Varick. She'll know that you're an important name and will find me wherever I am if you need to speak to me. You will always know where I am, and you must always let me know where you are. And you must promise to say to yourself ten times a day, 'Adam loves me.' Okay?"

With her mouth on his, Elizabeth said ten times, "Adam loves me. Will that do for today?"

"No, my love. That's only for when I'm not here to say it

myself. When I'm around, you are supposed to say, 'I love you, Adam.' "

"Oh, I do, my darling. I do. I do!"

He held her so tightly that it hurt. A delicious pain. "You're so much more than I deserve. And I'm so much less than you should have. You've given me a second chance, sweetheart. I promise you that I'll never let you go again, unless you want to go."

This time, their parting was different. Elizabeth insisted on riding to Idlewild with him in the taxi, and much as she hated to see him go, there was no sense of desperation in her. She had the future to look forward to. Meager as it might be in terms of hours, it was rich in the promise of love and tenderness. Now there was anticipation in her life once again, something she had not felt in a long, long time. Bolstered by it, she could stand the separation, even endure the anonymous role she had to play in Adam Barnsworth's life. On the way out they kissed and touched each other, unmindful of the driver's interested observation through the rear-view mirror.

Elizabeth giggled. "We're necking like teen-agers. He must think we're a couple of middle-aged nuts."

"Let him," Adam said. "He probably has a fat, ugly, slovenly wife who lets him come near her for twenty minutes every other Saturday night. Poor, jealous bastard. I feel sorry for him."

At the terminal, Adam spoke to the driver. "Want to make the return fare and a good bonus?"

"Sure. Why not?"

"Okay. Then wait here a few minutes and drive my wife back home. She'll triple the meter."

The cabbie regarded him suspiciously. "Look, mister, how do I know your wife ain't getting on the airplane with you and I'll never even see the fare *out* here?"

Adam reverted suddenly to a colonel. His voice was that of a man used to giving commands.

"Because I'm telling you. That's how you know. Don't give me any flak, buster. If you want the deal, okay. If you don't, I'll pay you off now and you can get your ass out of here."

"Okay, okay! I'll wait right over there, lady. How long will you be?"

"She'll be back in ten minutes," Adam said.

Walking toward the gate, Elizabeth was strangely silent. Adam squeezed her hand.

"Please don't be sad," he said. "I'll be back very soon."

A tear rolled slowly down her face. "It isn't that."

"Then why are you crying, sweetheart?"

She managed a smile. "Because I'm a silly woman. You told the cab driver I was your wife. And those were the most beautiful words I ever heard."

He stopped walking. He set his briefcase down and took her by both shoulders, looking intently into her happy face.

"I know what I said. And it was no accident."

Around them, the other passengers jostled and pushed their way toward the waiting airplane, but they stood quite alone, caught in their private stillness, silently exchanging vows. Nothing reached them in that moment. Not the babble of the crowd nor the nasal voice of the P.A. system slurring its endless unintelligible announcements. Unaware of anything but themselves, they kissed deeply yet calmly. Then Elizabeth turned and walked slowly out of the airport. Neither of them looked back.

Charlene came home the next morning, chattering excitedly about her weekend. She'd been on a picnic and Mr. Spencer was teaching her how to swim! They wanted her to come for another weekend before the summer was over, if Elizabeth would let her.

"May I go again, Mommy? Maybe next month?"

"Of course, baby, as long as the Spencers are nice enough to invite you." Guiltily, she hoped the next invitation would coincide with Adam's return so that they could have the apartment all to themselves. What a beast I am! Elizabeth thought. Wanting to get my own child out of the way so I can be free! Not that they wouldn't eventually have to make different arrangements anyway. She supposed that Adam could always quietly come into her bed, even when Charlene was home. But it wouldn't be the same. He'd not be able to stay the whole night, nor could they make love in the somehow even more exciting daylight hours. Elizabeth could not visualize herself sneaking into Adam's hotel room in the middle of the afternoon. Yet she would. Their moments were too precious to waste on prudish reluctance.

"Did you miss me?" Charlene asked. "Were you lonesome?"

"I missed you very much, but I knew you were having a good time, so that made it all right. Besides, I had a very pleasant surprise. Guess who turned up in New York? Your uncle Adam! Remember? The nice man who roomed with us in Washington?"

"Uncle Adam? The one who went off to war and made you so unhappy?"

Elizabeth was startled. She knew that Ann had been aware of her depression when Adam left, but Ann was nine years older than Charlene. How could a seven-year-old have been so conscious of her misery? Unless, of course, her older sister had told her.

"I was unhappy when any of our friends went to war," Elizabeth said reasonably. "Remember how I felt when Barney Nash left? And Frank Bayard, who had the room before Uncle Adam? War is a sad thing, Charlene. All grown-ups grieve when they see men going off to risk their lives for their country."

Charlene was not put off. "But Uncle Adam was special, wasn't he?"

Elizabeth had never deliberately lied to her children. She had been protective, even evasive, when she felt the cause was justified. But she had never lied and she would not start now.

"You're a very wise little lady," she said. "Yes, Uncle Adam was special. He was very precious to me. And he still is."

"Then I'm glad he's back," Charlene said emphatically. "Will we see him a lot, like we used to?"

"No. Not like that. He lives in California now. But he'll visit us whenever he comes to New York. Maybe as soon as next month."

"I hope I'm not away when he comes next time."

Elizabeth would not lie, but she did not answer. "My gosh, look at the time!" she said instead. "I'd better get to the office before Mr. Gale fires me!"

Charlene looked serious. "He wouldn't do that, would he, Mommy? Tony wouldn't let him."

Elizabeth laughed. "Of course not, you goose. But I do have to go, sweetie. Can you unpack your things? There's something for your lunch in the refrigerator. I thought we'd go down to the corner for dinner tonight to celebrate your return. Maybe Tony and Mr. Gale will come with us. We'll have a homecoming party for you. How does that sound?"

"Nice. But you don't have to give me a party. I've only been gone since Friday afternoon!"

"I know," Elizabeth said, "but it was a very important weekend."

She arrived at the office looking refreshed and glowing in spite of the fact that she'd had very little sleep in the past forty-eight hours. Those beauty editors don't know what they're talking about when they say that sleep is the best beauty treatment, Elizabeth thought with amusement. Sex can replace it and then some!

"Well, *you're* looking very chipper this morning," Robert said. "Have a good weekend?"

"Marvelous. What about yours?"

"Positively ghastly. Tony was the invisible companion. When he wasn't asleep he was lying out on the dunes trying to soak up enough solar energy to heat an eight-room house! I swear to you, Elizabeth, he's going to get skin cancer from all that burning stuff. But he won't listen. I even caught him once lying with his fingers spread apart so that the goddamn sun would tan him evenly on the inside of his hands!"

Tony listened with amusement. "Never try to come between a native Californian and his worship of the great outdoors," he said easily. "You effete Easterners prefer to go around looking all wan and washed out, like you spend your lives in dark saloons, which of course you do."

"And a damned good thing for you that we do," Robert snapped. "Some of our most profitable assignments come out of the entertaining I do in those 'dark saloons.' "

Robert was obviously in a vile mood. Tony must have virtually ignored him all weekend. Elizabeth pretended not to notice the tense atmosphere.

"Well, your friend Charlene enjoyed *her* country visit," she said. "The first weekend away from Mama was a huge success. In fact, I told her I'd take her out for a modest dinner to celebrate her return. How about you two joining us?"

"No, thanks," Robert said. "The last thing I need tonight is a wholesome description of bucolic life. I can't wait to get home to my nice, dark, decadent townhouse."

"Tony?"

"Love to. I could do with a little enthusiasm for the simple things. Besides," he said, "I want to hear about your weekend. I'm glad you weren't bored to death with nobody in town."

"As a matter of fact, it worked out very well. An old friend of mine happened to be in New York. Colonel Barnsworth. He used to rent a room from me in Washington."

She didn't know why she'd mentioned Adam's name. It was as though she wanted somebody to hear it from her own lips. I must be discreet, she cautioned herself. But damn it, I don't want to be.

Tony did not seem to notice. He merely said, "I'll go

straight home with you from work. We can have an early meal."

"Then kindly do me the courtesy," Robert said frostily, "of calling Arthur and telling him you won't be home for dinner."

"Aye, aye, sir," Tony mocked. "I'll report in."

"All right, madam," Tony said to Charlene when they'd settled in at the little neighborhood restaurant, "you have the microphone. Now tell us everything that happened from Friday afternoon till Monday morning."

Charlene eagerly recounted every detail of her weekend with the Spencers. She was most enthusiastic about the swimming. "I wish I could do it every day. Really learn to be a good swimmer, I mean. The day camp is nice, but that's one thing they don't teach us. Mommy, do you think that maybe next year I could go away to camp? Where they have a lake? I'll be twelve."

"I don't see why not," Elizabeth said. She was surprised that Charlene seemed to adjust so well to being away from her. Maybe I've been foolishly overprotective, she thought. Or maybe I'm thinking of an empty apartment and Adam.

"Tell you what, Charlene," Tony said. "If your mother agrees, I'll help you learn to swim well even *before* next summer. This winter we could go to an indoor pool on weekends. I love it, but I never have anybody to go with."

Charlene was ecstatic. "*Do* you agree, Mommy? May I do that with Tony?"

"If he's kind enough to offer, I think it would be wonderful. Now finish your dinner, love, and let's get home. You must be tired. You had to get up awfully early this morning to drive all the way in from the Hamptons."

"I'm so excited I'll never get to sleep! Not for hours and hours!"

"Want to bet?" Elizabeth asked.

Charlene was in bed and sound asleep within half an hour after they got home. In fact, she was almost nodding over the extra portion of ice cream that the waitress brought her. Elizabeth tucked her in and tiptoed out of her room, quietly closing the door. Tony stood at the open window of the living room, staring silently out into the darkness of Gramercy Park.

"Make you a drink?" Elizabeth smiled involuntarily at the memory of having said almost those same words three days before.

"No, thanks. But I would like to talk."

"Of course. Sit down, Tony, dear. What's wrong? Bad weekend?"

"Bad weekend, bad weeks," he said. "Elizabeth, I don't know what I'm going to do."

"About Robert?"

"That's part of it. But it's really what I'm going to do about me. I've got to figure out where I belong. Come out for something. Decide where I stand and where I'm going. How the hell does Anthony Alexander plan to spend the rest of his life? And with whom?"

Since the night he told her about Laurel, Elizabeth had known that this was a deeply troubled young man. She was not surprised that he was still tormenting himself, seeking his real identity, trying to sort out his loyalties and learn to accept and come to terms with himself. But that had been going on for months. Years, probably. What had finally triggered this desperate soul-searching? The incidents with Laurel? Greater demands from Robert? Or had she somehow been the spark that touched off this increased self-examination? She remembered Tony's oblique reference to her having given him "comfort" in that almost embarrassingly frank talk months before. Did his distress now have something to do with that evening? If so, perhaps she had created more chaos than relief. His sexual confusion was very real, made worse by the peculiar semireligious obsession. Tony Alexander was twenty-nine years old. In some ways he was a hundred; in others no older than Charlene. He so clearly wanted to talk, and just as plainly did not know how to begin. She groped for a way to help him. In her own rediscovered happiness, she felt more than ever the desire to help those she loved. And though she was not old enough to be his mother, in a way she felt toward him as she would have felt toward an unhappy son.

"Start anywhere," she said finally. "Just talk, Tony. Get rid of it, whatever it is that's eating you. Maybe by simply saying the words you'll understand yourself."

"All right, Elizabeth. I'm in love with you."

It was literally the last thing in the world she expected him to say. For a moment, she thought he was trying to make a joke before he began to talk about what was really on his mind. But this was no joke. He was in earnest. Or at least, Elizabeth told herself, he believed that he was. She could not hurt him by making light of it. Yet to take it seriously was madness. How was she to answer this unexpected declaration of love? Tony might have reason to think she was in love with him, too. There had been such closeness, such af-

fection between them. Perhaps this was what he meant when
he spoke of the comfort she had given him. Perhaps, had it
not been for the reappearance of Adam, she might even have
been tempted to accept his love. He was much younger than
she, but, as she had told herself a few minutes before, in
many ways he was old and wise. Their minds worked well
together and probably so would their bodies. But that, for
Elizabeth, was yesterday. Now that she knew that Adam was
alive and still wanted her, there could be no one else for her.

"Well?" Tony said. "Aren't you even going to answer?"

She tried to smile. She hoped her voice was steady. "I'm
trying to digest what I think I heard," she said lightly.

"I said I'm in love with you. Not that I love you. Don't
overlook the distinction, Elizabeth. It was you who made me
realize it in the first place. I've loved lots of people. But I've
never been in love with anyone before. That's what's eating
me. That's what's driving me out of my mind."

She felt helpless. Had the situation not been so tragic, it
would have been comical. For years she had wanted to be
loved, and nothing had happened. Now, within the space of
three days, two men had declared their love for her. One
had hurt her badly. And the other she might well hurt ir-
reparably. She had grave doubts that Tony knew his own
mind. He was grasping at straws, perhaps seeing in her the
solidity he so desperately wanted. But she could not gamble
with his emotions. He was so completely distraught and defenseless.

"Tony, dear, are you certain of what you feel? Or is this
perhaps just an understandable attempt to do what you said
earlier—figure out where you stand in this crazy, mixed-up
world?"

"I'm certain," he said. "I know you're the answer for me.
I've thought about it for weeks. With you I can be honest. I
can become something. I want to spend the rest of my life
with you. I know I can't answer the endless needs of other
people. I don't care whether our love outrages Robert or
wounds Laurel. All I want now is to put a stop to this terrible sense of being nothing, belonging to no one. I think I
began to realize it that night we talked about Laurel. The
night you let me sleep here. I didn't trust my impulses then.
I wanted you, but I wasn't sure whether it was really you I
wanted or just another woman. The way I wanted Laurel.
I've thought about it ever since, Elizabeth. I know now that I
want you. I'll never want anyone else. I want to marry you.
To take care of you and Charlene. We'll go to California,
away from Robert and his hold on us both. Away from

Laurel's unspoken accusations. I love you completely. Say you're in love with me. Please say it."

She shook her head slowly. "I can't, Tony. And I can't give you what I once accused you of giving: compassion on demand. You don't want me, my dear. You want an anchor, a concrete way to stop your drifting. I do love you, Tony. But I'm not in love with you. Funny," she said sadly, "a week ago I think I might have said 'Let's try it.' We were just two lonely, compatible souls then. We might have given each other a kind of unorthodox but satisfactory life. Neither of us had much to lose. And perhaps we could have found some kind of serenity together. But it's different for me now. I think you're trying to convince yourself that you're in love with me because you think it's your best option. Once I might have been glad to settle for that. To buy some happiness for you and for myself. But now I can't even pretend to be in love with you, darling, because I'm still so very much in love with someone else."

His shocked face tore at her heart. "I don't believe you," he said. "I know you're in love with me."

"No," Elizabeth said. "Tony, dear, I knew that someday I'd tell you about my real love, even though I thought it would be telling you about the past. But what happened this weekend and what you've said tonight makes you entitled to know everything."

She told him about Adam. From the Washington days until the weekend that had just passed. He sat staring at her, angry at first, not willing to believe, then finally accepting that what she said was true. His happiness was important to her, and taking away his dream of it made her remorseful. Without thinking of what she was doing, she came close and put her arms around him. Her touch seemed to shatter his last vestige of control. He began to kiss her frantically, ripping her dress, running his hands over her breasts. She did not resist as he tried to make her respond, but there was no response in her. Her only fear was that Tony would try to force himself on her. Please God, don't let him, she thought, because he'll never forgive himself.

As suddenly as the attack began, it ended. Abruptly he released her and stood looking at her half-exposed body. She made no effort to cover herself up. She was not being provocative. She was simply saying without words, "I'm not frightened or angry or repelled. If you want me on these terms, take me. This is what it means to 'give love' simply to make someone else happy."

He looked away. "It's stupid to say I'm sorry. I wish you wanted me the way I want you."

She spoke gently. "I wish so, too. I truly do. But I think we've both learned something, Tony."

"What? That I'm damned near capable of rape?"

"No. That you really are a man who wants more than sex. Otherwise you would have taken me. You want love in its real sense. You can be healthily selfish. That's a beginning. That's a step toward reality."

He didn't believe her. "All I can see is that it's probably the end of you and me."

"Never. We may never make love to each other, but we're more intimate than most lovers. I think tonight you've become dearer than ever to me. I do love you, Tony. And I'll never stop being grateful that you wanted me so much. Don't let this make a difference between us."

"Don't talk rot, Elizabeth. Of course it will make a difference. My God, I offer you love and marriage and you can't accept them."

"That doesn't mean that someone else can't or won't. You know now what *you* can feel. Things can change for you. You proved that to yourself and to me. Maybe your life won't go the way you thought it might when you came here this evening, but it can go differently now."

"Sure it can," he said crudely. "By the law of averages, I can outlive Robert, who'll leave me a lot of money. Then I can buy myself a Tony."

She was outraged. "Stop feeling so damned sorry for yourself! What are you trying to do, make me think I'm the only woman you could ever care for? You have everything in the world to offer, Tony. But for God's sake stop acting like a sacrificial lamb! Go find yourself a woman who'll return what you have to give. Or if you decide it's not a woman you want, then choose a man you can care for. It's no disgrace. The only disgrace will be your refusal to fight for the reality of love, whatever it is for you!"

Her outburst surprised her, but she was not sorry for it. Tony had to make his choice and stop feeling guilty about it. Somewhere he had to find the truth about himself and live with it. For a moment she'd thought she'd glimpsed the real humanly selfish Tony. Now she was uncertain once again.

At the door he stopped. "May I say one more thing?"

"Of course. Anything."

"Then I say, God damn Adam Barnsworth. I wish the Nazis had blown him straight to hell."

In less violent terms, Laurel's reaction was almost the same when she returned from Europe and Elizabeth told her about the reappearance of Adam. Her response, though less cruel, was equally dismayed.

"Oh, no! That bastard hasn't come back into your life! My God, what ego! I suppose he just walked right in and said, 'Hi, honey, I'm home. Let's pick up where we left off four years ago.'"

Elizabeth was not angry. She knew that Laurel was only concerned that Adam would hurt her again. This was a possibility that Elizabeth would not concede. She realized how it must look. Adam had abandoned her. Not that his leave-taking was voluntary, but his long silence was. Laurel resented it for Elizabeth. Just as she resented his return, still unable to offer Elizabeth anything but a secret, part-time liaison.

"I know how it must seem, Laurel," she said, "but I love him and he loves me. He can't do anything about his wife. And he thought by staying away that he was doing the kindest thing for me."

"Well, he was right there," Laurel snapped. "So why the hell didn't he keep on observing his Boy Scout oath?"

"It *wasn't* the kindest thing for me. I didn't know how miserable I'd been until I felt how happy I was to be with him again. Look. I know it isn't rational or practical, but it's the only thing in the world I want. I'd rather have two days with Adam once a month than twenty-four hours a day with some nice, predictable man I didn't love. Call me crazy. Maybe you're right. By the world's standards, I'm the champion patsy of all time, but that's how it is. Or, rather, that's how *I am*."

"Yeah. Dumb. A glutton for punishment. You're the eternal innocent, Elizabeth. Nobody can be mad at you for your unrealistic dreams, but Adam knows better. He wants you and he also wants to stay married. Somebody ought to invent a slogan to go with that. Something like 'Have your cake and eat it, too.'"

"I hoped that you, of all people, would understand."

"Oh, I understand, all right. I just hope that this time *you* do! For God's sake, be realistic, Elizabeth. Adam Barnsworth has been honest with you. I'll give him that. But what's to prevent his having another attack of 'conscience' about what he's doing to you? How are you going to handle it next time he decides to disappear into the woodwork?"

"How can I answer that? How does anyone know how he or she will behave under any given set of circumstances? Right now, I don't think it will happen again. But I know I can't be sure of that, any more than I can be sure of anything in this world. All I know, is that I'd be a fool to turn my back on this happiness for however long it lasts. If I lose Adam again, I suppose I'll live through it, as I did before. But I can't think about that now. All I can do is live for the moment."

Laurel softened. "I know. I just don't want you to be so terribly hurt again. And I'd be so happy if there was some security in your life for once. Some guy who'd take care of you."

"I know," Elizabeth said, "and you make perfect, unemotional sense. I'd probably give the same kind of advice to you if I thought you were heading for trouble. But try to see it from my point of view. More than half my life is over. I've been married and I've produced three children and I'm on my way to being a grandmother. Am I supposed to wait around for a suitable, aging gentleman who'll do me the honor of proposing companionship in our declining years? Or am I not entitled to grab at the kind of love that makes me feel twenty years old and irresistible in spite of my rapidly graying hairs? What would you have me do, Laurel? Spend the rest of my life slowly atrophying because the only man I want wants me in a selfish way? As far as Adam is concerned, he's not trying to fool me. And this time I'm not trying to fool myself."

Laurel sighed. "Women! What idiots we are! Our favorite indoor sport seems to be kidding ourselves about men. Or about our own ability to handle whatever they choose to dish out. I have one hell of a nerve lecturing you about a hopeless situation, I guess. I went into a funk over one myself not too long ago. I imagine you had a pretty good idea of what was going on then, but you didn't get all high and mighty and lecture me about falling in love with a no-future guy, did you?"

Elizabeth didn't want to talk about it. She didn't want to hear Laurel admit that she'd made a fool of herself over Tony, or, more correctly, that Tony had made a fool of her.

"Come on," Laurel said lightly, "you know I had a little fling with Tony. You're never dumb about other people. I'm sure he told you his version of it. If he told Robert, he surely told you. To tell you the truth, I'd be rather curious to know how he saw the whole thing. What did he tell you—that I'd seduced him?"

"No. He said that he'd found you very desirable. That he'd wanted to make love to you and that he did." She paused. "But you read too much into it. You understandably thought he was in love with you and you were angry and bitter when you found out he wasn't."

"Well, that's more or less accurate reporting," Laurel said. "A little shaded in his favor, maybe, but not exactly untrue. I've always been attracted to him. You know that. But I never gave it any real, serious thought because I figured he belonged to Robert. And then out of the blue came those protestations of love, accompanied by some pretty impressive physical manifestations of same. I had enough ego to say to myself, Well, well! Laurel, old girl, you're the woman who can do it! You can turn the genes around or change the psyche or whatever it takes to transform a queen into a king. Boy, did I have the wrong number! Robert made sure that I knew this wasn't the first time Tony had experimented. That was the big New Year's Eve scene. Yes, sir. 'Happy New Year, Laurel, you dope.' For a minute our Tony strayed from the fold, but his heart belongs to Daddy. Imagine me being dumb enough to think that Tony could really love a woman. Christ, that faker! Anything for kicks, I guess. He must have had a pretty good laugh over it with Robert."

"You mustn't believe that. Tony wouldn't intentionally hurt you. Maybe he did get carried away, but at the moment he meant it. I'm sure of that. Have you discussed it with him since, Laurel?"

"Of course not. Robert's message came through loud and clear."

"But didn't you feel the need for a frank talk with Tony?"

Laurel's laugh was bitter. "Did he feel the need for one with me? He never came near me after the second time. And I hardly think it's the kind of thing you can handle gracefully by asking your lover to tea and inquiring politely whether he's an irretrievable homosexual. His silence was convincing enough. Tony may have brief moments of doubts about which sex he prefers, but when the chips are down, honey, he puts his money on the stronger one. I don't have to have that spelled out for me. Anthony Alexander is incapable of a permanent attachment to any woman. Rita Hayworth couldn't hold him, much less Laurel Lane!"

Until now, Elizabeth had not realized the depths of Laurel's misery. Self-confident creature that she was, her unexpected vulnerability must have come as a shock, and its betrayal as a pill almost too bitter to swallow. Her only consolation was her firm belief that Tony could never love any woman. If she found out otherwise, the knowledge would destroy her. And if that other woman happened to be her best friend, she'd be alienated beyond any hope of reconciliation.

But Laurel would never find out from her. And it was unthinkable that Tony would tell Robert anything that had passed between him and Elizabeth, as he had told Robert about his experience with Laurel. The difference in intensity between the two episodes was too deep for that.

There was no justice, Elizabeth thought. How simple and wonderful it would have been if Tony had felt for Laurel what he professed to feel for her. Maybe now that he knew Elizabeth loved someone else, he'd pick up the affair with Laurel, and this time he might really mean it. But even as she wished it, Elizabeth knew it was not going to happen that way. He had tried, through her, to escape a life he believed he didn't really want. When that failed, he would, in his own fatalistic way, interpret it as a sign that he was meant to stay with Robert. And stay he surely would. Tony, like the rest of them, was not incapable of feeling rejection. He would run from it to the dubious safety of a world that he knew wanted him.

"Hey," Laurel said, "come back. You're a million miles away. Look. It's over and done with. I know you hate to see me hurt, but I've pretty well recovered from my girlish dream. Maybe I can even be friends with Tony again sometime. Don't look like you've just heard my last will and testament! I was a dope, but it hasn't turned me off men forever. Only next time, you can be sure that before I fall I'll make sure it's Bluebeard and not Little Boy Blue."

"Seems like a rotten choice," Elizabeth smiled.

"What the hell," Laurel said typically. "It's a rotten world."

Chapter 19

Between Adam's visits, the demands of her job, and the concern for Ann's condition and Charlene's well-being, Elizabeth did not, in the fall of 1946, have time to brood over the unfortunate situation which involved Tony, Laurel, and herself. Laurel was busy at the magazine. This was the peak season in the fashion business. And Tony spent all his time with Robert and Robert's friends. He did not see Elizabeth outside of business hours, but he did take Charlene swimming every weekend. The child learned to swim well, and though she did not gain weight, she had endless vigor and energy. Unlike Ann who had been blasé at eleven, Charlene had boundless enthusiasm for everything, from her outings with Tony to her delighted reunions with "Uncle Adam."

The latter had more than kept his word. He telephoned several times a week to say how much he loved Elizabeth and missed her. Driven by the need to share her happiness, Elizabeth reported his calls to Laurel, who responded with a slightly cynical thrust.

"At least he's got the time difference working for him," she said. "It's three hours earlier in California, so the great man can call you at home while he's still in his office."

Elizabeth refused to allow Laurel's jaundiced view to spoil any part of her pleasure. The calls were her life's blood, and so were the letters which came between. They were the first she'd ever had from Adam. And though they were brief and almost boyishly awkward, they held back nothing. She cherished them above anything she owned, reading and re-reading the extravagant praise of her beauty, her desirability, and her necessity to him.

Most wonderful of all were Adam's visits. He came into New York for two or three days every month. Unfortunately, since the pretense was business, he was usually there in mid-week. So between the appointments he actually kept and Elizabeth's job, there was little chance to meet during the day. But during each trip, they would steal an afternoon and spend it in Adam's suite at the Plaza. He would order lunch sent up from room service and they would eat quickly, calling down to have the table removed as soon as possible. Then Adam would hang the "Do not disturb" sign on both the living-room and bedroom doors.

They teased each other affectionately about their limitless passion. Lying in bed smoking cigarettes, they were almost amused by their unquenchable desire.

"You are a wanton woman," Adam said in mock severity.

"And you're an oversexed man," Elizabeth accused.

"The least you could do, Elizabeth, would be to get up and look out the window. That view of Central Park is costing me fifty dollars a day. Have you no civic pride? Don't you want to see how glorious your city looks with all the trees turning color?"

She rolled over on her side. "*You* get up and look," she said. "You're the visiting fireman. I can see Central Park any day. Frankly, I'd rather just look at you."

They were together every evening and most of the night in Elizabeth's bed. Usually, they dined at home with Charlene. She adored Adam and he returned the affection in full measure.

"You're wonderful with her," Elizabeth said.

"It's easy. I'm almost as crazy about her as I am about her mother." His voice turned serious. "I wish she were mine. I always wanted a little girl. And if I could have had one, Charley would have been my idea of the perfect daughter. You've done a helluva job on her, Elizabeth."

"She's done it on herself."

"Wrong. A child is the product of her surroundings and her early influences. I believe that."

"Then tell me, Dr. Freud, how do you account for the

other two? They struggled up under the same set of circumstances, and Ann has turned out to be somebody I can't relate to and Quigly has disowned me completely."

"Good point, I admit. I can't answer that. Unless maybe the difference in their ages and Charlene's has something to do with it. The other two did have more conscious exposure to your late husband. Maybe they absorbed too much of the early horror. And speaking of Quigly, I'm sorry to say that I'm nowhere. He seems to have vanished after San Diego. I've put out all kinds of feelers up and down the whole West Coast and I've come up with zero. I can only assume that he's left that part of the world or is living in it under a different name."

"But how can an eighteen-year-old boy manage to exist so thoroughly on his own?"

"My dear, he was doing that long before he was eighteen. Don't give up hope, darling. I haven't. We'll find him yet."

Elizabeth nodded. "I believe that. I will till the day I die. Anyway, thank God the other two are all right. I wish you could see Ann's baby, Adam. He really is adorable."

In October, Ann had given birth to a seven-pound boy who, to no one's surprise, was promptly christened Peter Richards III. Propped up in the hospital bed ("Absolutely awash in lace and ruffles," Elizabeth laughingly reported to Laurel) Ann looked like a magazine photograph of a new mother, her blond hair caught with a pink ribbon and her expression triumphant when Elizabeth exclaimed over her son.

"Told you it would be a boy," Ann said.

"You surely did," Elizabeth said. "And he's beautiful. *You* look beautiful, too, Ann. Not too bad a time?"

Ann managed to register a look of remembered suffering for the benefit of her husband, who hovered nearby. "Only we know what it's like, don't we, Mother?" She sighed theatrically. "But it was all worth it to give Peter a son."

I just might gag, Elizabeth thought. But she's smart, I can't deny that. Peter will be waiting on her hand and foot for weeks, probably wondering what he can do next to make up to her for the pain she allows him to think he's caused.

As though on cue, the enraptured Peter approached the bed. He held a small blue-velvet box in his hand.

"This seems as good a time as any," he said. "A little reward for a very brave girl."

Ann opened the box. Inside was a gold bracelet from which hung a gold and diamond charm in the shape of the numeral one.

"Turn it over," Peter said eagerly.

Ann read the inscription aloud. "For my first lady and our first child. With all my love, Peter."

"How thoughtful, Peter!" Elizabeth said.

Ann smiled at him tenderly. "Yes, darling, it's lovely. And how smart of you to leave space for additions."

Peter grinned. "It's been ready for weeks. When shall I get the next one going?"

"Men!" Ann said to her mother. "Aren't they the biggest babies of all?"

Elizabeth did not give either Laurel or Adam the full account of that syrupy hospital scene. It was too embarrassing. Still, she supposed she should not quarrel with Ann's adroit handling of Peter. He seemed to like it. And Ann seemed to get everything she wanted. A nurse would come home with her for the first month while she "regained her strength." After that, Elizabeth was quite sure who would get up for the three A.M. feeding, and who, probably ever after, would answer calls in the night for glasses of water or trips to the toilet. Maybe I really envy her, Elizabeth mused. Ann had developed selfishness to a fine subtle art. For everything she gave, there would always be return in full measure. She won't get hurt often, and never by a selfish partner. But neither will she know what it's like to be stupidly, heedlessly in love. A damned good thing that virtue like Ann's is its own reward, Elizabeth thought frivolously. It sure bores the hell out of everybody else.

Life settled down into a pattern that, while not perfect, was at least satisfying. Adam continued his visits and his attentions. One weekend in the spring of 1947 they were even able to sneak away to the Greenbriar in White Sulphur Springs, West Virginia. Laurel volunteered to keep Charlene, and since Monica was visiting relatives in San Francisco, Adam did not have to hurry home as he normally did. They had a delicious time. The countryside was in full bloom and Elizabeth thought she had never seen anything as voluptuous as the magnolias and dogwoods. They delighted her senses, reminding her of how beautiful Washington was in the spring. But the wonders of nature were nothing compared to the ecstasy of being alone with Adam for long, lazy days and softly scented nights. It was ironic, yet miraculous, that this was exactly the kind of trip she'd visualized their taking before Adam went off to war. Perhaps he remembered how she'd wanted to go away with him then and was making it up to her now, just as he was trying to compensate through his devotion for so much of the past.

She felt as though it was the first honeymoon she'd ever had. That young girl who had believed herself so in love in Saratoga had had no idea of the meaning of gentleness, laughter, and passion. Heedlessly, Adam had registered them as "Mr. and Mrs. Adam Barnsworth." Even Elizabeth questioned the wisdom of that.

"Should you have given the right name?" she asked almost shyly when they were alone in their room. "Not that *I* have any reason to mind. I just wouldn't want it to cause difficulties for you."

"Darling, you don't seriously think I'd register us as 'Mr. and Mrs. John Smith,' do you? Give me credit for a little more respect for you." He smiled reassuringly. 'Besides who's ever likely to check a register in a hotel in West Virginia? I know what you're worried about, and I tell you to stop worrying. The only person who could have any possible interest in that guest book would be Monica, and, unfortunately, that's highly unlikely."

"Unfortunately?"

"Yes. Because if it came to checking hotels, it would mean she was looking for grounds for divorce. And nothing would please me more."

"As long as she initiated it," Elizabeth said.

"I'm afraid so. I'm still your spineless wonder, remember?"

"You're still my lover, my idol, my hero, and my friend, *that's* what you are. Now be quiet and kiss me."

"My pleasure," he said.

It was almost as though she'd had a premonition about the registration. On the second morning she went downstairs ahead of Adam to ask about the car they'd ordered for the day. At the main desk, she inquired whether Mr. Barnsworth's request for a convertible had been arranged. The clerk checked.

"Yes indeed, Mrs. Barnsworth. It's all ready for you."

She was not conscious of the man who stood behind her, waiting his turn to speak to the desk clerk. "Thank you," she said, and turned to look straight into the surprised eyes of Stuart Preston.

"Stuart! I don't believe it! What on earth are you doing at the Greenbriar? Is Martha with you?"

His manner showed clearly that he had overheard her conversation about the car. "No," he said rather stiffly. "I'm here with a group of executives from my office. We come once a year for our physical examinations. They have full facilities for that here, did you know?"

"No. How extraordinary! I thought it was just a resort."

"It is primarily, but they do have this program of complete and very top-notch medicals for businessmen. It's a good idea. We get checked over each morning and have the afternoon for golf. Gives us a little relaxation while we're getting the once-a-year okay for the benefit of our insurance agents." He paused. "I won't be coy and ask what you're doing here. I heard the clerk call you by name. So Adam found you, did he? I wondered whether he'd follow up the information I rather reluctantly gave him."

Elizabeth was not embarrassed. "Yes, he found me. But not until last year. Bless you for telling him where I was, Stu."

Of the two, only Preston seemed uncomfortable. "Listen, I hope running into me doesn't upset you. I mean, you know I'll not mention it to anyone. Hell, I won't even speak to you in the dining room."

Elizabeth was so happy she couldn't resist teasing him. "Why, Stuart, what makes you jump to immoral conclusions? How do you know that Adam and I aren't married?"

He looked startled. "Are you?"

"No, darling, of course not. You know you would have heard. We're just two grown-up people spending a little time together and making sure that nobody gets hurt."

"You love him very much, don't you?"

"More than I could ever tell you."

Preston grinned wistfully. "God bless you," he said. "That's the kind of thing I'm always happy to hear about people I'm fond of. Take whatever happiness you can find, Elizabeth. You deserve it. Wish I'd been smart enough to offer first."

"What are you looking so Cheshire cat about?" Adam asked when he joined her at the front door a few minutes later.

"You'll never guess whom I just bumped into." She told him about the meeting with Stuart. "See?" she teased. "I warned you not to register us under your name."

"Darling, he'd have recognized you anyway."

"Yes, but he wouldn't have heard me called Mrs. Barnsworth. Anyway, it doesn't really matter. He was happy for us, and he's the last person in the world to gossip. This place is so big we probably won't even run into him again, so we can just forget it. I know *he* will."

Adam looked thoughtful. "What a crazy thing. Imagine running into Stu Preston here."

"You're not worried about it, are you? I know he won't tell anybody."

"I'm not worried about that or anything else," Adam said. "I'm much too damned happy to worry. I just think it's curious. Stu Preston, of all people. You know, he's always been in love with you, Elizabeth."

"Oh, darling, what nonsense! He's been one of the best friends I've ever had. But in love with me? Don't be silly!"

"Don't kid your lover," Adam said. "You know it's true."

"I know no such thing. So help me, if I hadn't stupidly let you become so sure of me, I'd swear you were jealous."

Adam kissed her. "I *am* jealous, you sexy creature. And you should be glad."

She considered that for a moment. Then her eyes lit up. "You know something? You're right. I *am* glad."

They didn't see Stu again that weekend, nor did they meet any other familiar faces when they returned to the Greenbriar in August while Charlene was away at camp. There was no gossip about them from Stu or any other quarter. In New York, they were discreet about appearing in public. It was no sacrifice. They much preferred to be alone together at home than to suffer through the polite restraint of a restaurant dinner where they might easily run into one of Adam's business associates. Aside from Charlene, who saw him at the apartment, and Laurel, whom Elizabeth always told of his visits, no one in Elizabeth's New York orbit was aware of Adam's return. Except, of course, Tony. But neither of them had ever again referred to Adam Barnsworth or any other part of that painful evening.

In the late autumn, of 1947, Charlene began to catch a series of colds. She recovered from them quickly, and at first Elizabeth, used to minor illnesses in children, paid only routine attention. She kept Charlene home from school for a couple of days each time and plied her with fruit juice and aspirin. But when the colds came one on top of each other and left a lingering, hacking cough, Elizabeth began to worry. Watching Charlene closely, she didn't like what she saw. The child seemed listless and tired, though she managed to summon up some reserve of liveliness when it seemed called for, and was disappointed when Elizabeth told her she thought they'd better cancel the swimming excursions with Tony for a while.

"In fact, love, I think we'd better let Dr. Martin have a look at you. It's been a year since you had a complete physical. Probably you need vitamins or something. We might as well build you up so you don't keep getting these pesky colds."

Elizabeth made the appointment for the first week in December and told Tony she'd need to take a morning off to go with Charlene to the pediatrician.

"What's wrong? Can I do anything to help?"

"Thanks, but I'm sure it's nothing serious. She just keeps getting one cold after another and lately she's been running a low-grade fever with them. I think she's run-down and I don't want to take chances in the bad weather. It's time she had a checkup anyway. Don't worry. I'm sure she's okay. And I'll be back in the office in the afternoon."

Dr. Martin listened to Charlene's chest and frowned. Then he called the nurse and told her to take the little girl to the lab on the lower floor of the medical building and have them do a chest X ray. Standing by, Elizabeth felt unreasonably frightened, but after that first frown, the doctor's manner was relaxed and reassuring.

"Tell the boys to give me the X rays right away," he told the nurse. "Mrs. Whitman's a busy lady who has to get back to her job. As for the little glamour girl," he said, indicating Charlene, "she's probably anxious to get back to school. What grade are you in, honey?"

"Seventh," Charlene said proudly. "I skipped a year."

"Think of that! Then you're old enough to go down by yourself and let them get a snapshot of your back, aren't you? Miss Laval will take you. You don't need Mother along, do you?"

"Will it hurt?"

"Nope. All you have to do is hold your breath for a couple of seconds."

When Charlene and the nurse left, Dr. Martin took Elizabeth into his office.

"I hate to alarm you before I'm absolutely certain," he said, "but I don't like what I see and hear. The symptoms you describe and what I can detect even without X rays and smears and cultures look an awful lot like tuberculosis."

Elizabeth turned deathly pale. "Oh, no! It can't be!"

"Now, let's don't panic until we're sure. I might be just picking up a bad bronchial infection, nothing worse. Hopefully the X rays will confirm that. We'll go ahead with other tests when Charlene comes back upstairs, but I think it would be a good idea if you stayed around until we get the prints developed. If it turns out to be what I suspect, we'll have to make some immediate plans. I know you're not the hysterical type, and that's why I'm prematurely suggesting this possibility. As I say, I can be dead wrong. Believe me, it won't be the first time."

Elizabeth tried to hang on to the thin thread of hope he offered, but she already knew—as she was certain Dr. Martin did—that Charlene was seriously ill. He was not an alarmist. He would not even have mentioned TB if he was not already positive that his diagnosis was correct.

Willing herself to be calm, she tried to return his reassuring smile.

"God knows how I hope you're wrong!" she said. "But if you're not, what then? What's the treatment, Doctor?"

He shook his head. "Unfortunately, we don't have drugs for this. Plenty of research going on in this area, but no real breakthrough yet. Meanwhile, all we can do is treat it with complete bed rest in an environment of good clean air. If she has a light case, we can expect complete recovery within months."

"And if it's not a light case?"

"I really don't think we have to worry about that."

"Please. I want to know."

"All right, in really severe cases it is sometimes necessary to collapse a lung or even remove one. But," he added hurriedly, "I'm sure we're not up against anything that bad. I told you before, we might not even be dealing with the disease at all. She hasn't coughed up blood, has she?"

"No. Of course not. I'd have had her here in five minutes! It's been constant colds, a persistent cough, and a somewhat lethargic attitude. Doctor, when will we know?"

"Very shortly. That's why I told them to rush the X rays." He looked at her sympathetically. "I have to see some other patients in the meanwhile, but why don't you just stay here and take it easy? Charlene will be having blood, urine, and sputum tests, and by the time they're through we should have the pictures."

"Shouldn't I stay with her while she has the other tests? She's so little to go through all that alone."

His expression was firm but kind. "She'll be all right. The nurses are marvelous with kids. Besides," he said gently, "if the report is bad, Charlene will have to be without you for weeks at a time, you know."

"What are you talking about?"

"What I said before. She'll have to be hospitalized out of New York. I'm assuming that you'd have to keep your job here while she's undergoing treatment in some place like Denver."

She looked at him in amazement. "You think I'd stay here

and let her go off alone to some strange hospital? What kind of a mother do you think I am?"

"Now sit down and cool off," he said sharply. "I know what kind of a mother you are. A good one. With a good, level head. That's why I assumed that you'd be practical about this. Even if you followed Charlene to wherever she was hospitalized, you couldn't see her very often, and how would you live? It just wouldn't be sensible for you to give up an excellent job here. Doesn't it make better sense for you to keep on making good money so that you can ensure her care? Anyway, my dear, we're both getting ahead of ourselves. We can have this discussion after we get the reports. Hopefully then we won't need it."

Elizabeth knew that he was only taking the conscientious physician's cautious attitude until he had proof in hand. She was not misled by the possibility of a reprieve. Charlene was sick. She would have to go away. And it was unthinkable that Elizabeth would not go with her. She could earn some kind of living anywhere. She'd managed before. Hadn't she left Alan when she had three small children and only a few dollars to her name? She had provided for them then. And she would provide for Charlene now.

It seemed hours, though it was less than one, before Stan Martin came back with the reports and the X rays in his hand. He didn't have to speak. His distressed face told her the story.

"You were right," Elizabeth said flatly.

"Yes. Thank God it doesn't seem to be terribly advanced, but she does have tuberculosis. Now I think we have to discuss the future."

Elizabeth nodded. She was numb with pain.

"If you agree, I'll place a call to an old friend of mine, Dan Abrams. He's one of the doctors working at the National Jewish Hospital in Denver. They specialize in this disease and they're tops when it comes to the care of children. It's a fine institution, Elizabeth. Charlene will get the world's best medical care there. And there's something else that should relieve you of a great burden: her care will cost you nothing."

She looked at him in amazement. "Cost me nothing? I don't understand. I'm not putting Charlene into some charity hospital. I can work and earn enough to pay for her care!"

"National Jewish is not what you think of as a 'charity hospital.' It is supported by contributions from generous private sources, principally Jewish, though the hospital is nonsectarian. It's a philanthropic endeavor financed by thousands of concerned people. I've been all through it with Dr. Abrams. It's a wonderful place. You'll know that the minute you see it. There's a sign firmly planted on the front lawn which says, 'None may enter who can pay. None can pay who enter.' "

Elizabeth looked bewildered.

"I recommend we get Charlene there as quickly as possible," Dr. Martin went on. "As I told you, it's the best. And since you are determined to be near her, at least you'll only have to worry about supporting yourself for however long it takes for her to recover."

Elizabeth, remembering Charles Quigly, grabbed greedily at the last words. "Then she will recover? She'll eventually be well?"

"I can see no reason in the world why not. I don't know how long it will take. Hopefully, she'll make speedy progress once she's there. But I can't give you a time limit on that recovery. I don't think even the doctors at N.J. will do that. You'll have to take it day by day. Probably month by month." He hesitated. "Face it, Elizabeth. It could even be year by year. But with proper care Charlene will get well."

She began to breathe again. Terrible as it was, it was not a death sentence.

"Tuberculosis," she said. "My father died of it. Is it hereditary?"

"No. It's a germ. Anybody can catch it. Even a child who lives in good surroundings and eats proper food and is clean and well cared for. But it is contagious in some stages. So until we get Charlene to Denver, there are certain precautions I want you to take." He explained to her about keeping Charlene away from direct contact with other people, particularly other children. He told her that the dishes and glasses Charlene used must be kept separate from any others, and sterilized after use. "Above all, use common sense," he said. "You are dealing with a disease that can easily be transmitted, even to you. *Particularly* to you because you will have the closest contact with her. No matter how much you want to hug and kiss her right now, for God's sake don't. Remember that you can't afford to get sick. You have to look after Charlene."

"I understand. How quickly can we go to Denver?"

"Tomorrow, if you say so." She put things like jobs, leases, material possessions out of her mind. Laurel or Tony would deal with her furniture, and as for the lease, let the landlord sue her, for all she cared. She'd get some kind of job in

Denver and live near the hospital. It didn't matter what kind of job as long as it paid her rent.

"I'll call Dan right away and see when she can be admitted. I'm sure there'll be no great delay once I explain the circumstances."

"Thank you," Elizabeth said. "I'll wait to hear from you."

She found Charlene dressed and waiting for her. Elizabeth took the child's hand and smiled her thanks to the nurse.

"By the way," she said, "is there some prescription I should have filled? Dr. Martin didn't mention any medication."

"No, Mrs. Whitman," the nurse said compassionately. "There is no medication."

In the taxi, Charlene seemed almost like her old, bouncy self. Obviously she was relieved to have the extensive examination over.

"If I don't have to take any medicine, I must be okay," she said happily. "I hate medicine. Ugh!"

"Me, too," Elizabeth said absently. Already she was searching for a way to tell Charlene what lay ahead without frightening the little girl. How could she possibly understand the nature of her disease or endure the long-range recovery that would cut her off from a normal life? Even Elizabeth found it hard to accept the idea that rest alone would cure this illness. It seemed like such an ineffectual weapon with which to fight a potential killer.

When they got to the apartment, Elizabeth knew she had to face telling Charlene immediately. In addition to the other precautions, Dr. Martin had ordered her to keep the child in bed until it was time for them to leave for Denver. There would have to be an explanation of why. Why many things. Why did she have to stay in bed? Why was Elizabeth going to stay home with her? Why, ultimately, was she going to a hospital in a far-away city?

"Baby," Elizabeth said, "we have to have a little talk. But first you're going to get into your nightie and hop into bed. Then I'll tell you what Dr. Martin said. Everything's okay. I promise you that. I just want to explain to you about a bug you picked up somewhere."

Charlene looked puzzled. "Why do I have to go to bed in the middle of the day? I feel fine. I don't even have to take any medicine."

"*That's* what I'm going to explain to you, Miss Nosy, as soon as you climb under the covers. Now get going before I paddle you!"

"Don't you have to go work?"

"Nope. Got the day off. You and I will have lunch on trays in your room."

Elizabeth's nonchalance did not fool Charlene, but she went obediently to her room without further questions and began to prepare for bed. She was sick after all, she supposed. It was funny. She felt all right. A little tired, so that unaccustomed as she was to resting during the day, the cool, clean sheets felt good when she slipped into them. She wondered what her mother was going to tell her. It was all very mysterious.

Elizabeth made two quick, quiet phone calls. The first was to Tony. Briefly but calmly she told him the bad news. "Tell Robert I'll speak to him later. I'm sorry to have to leave you two, but of course I won't be coming back to the office. I can't leave Charlene."

"Naturally," Tony said. "Oh, God, I'm so sorry, Elizabeth. I know you can't talk now, but I'll come down this evening, okay?"

"Yes, of course. I'd appreciate it if you would."

She spoke next to Laurel and again explained Charlene's illness and what she planned to do. Laurel began to cry.

"Please don't do that," Elizabeth said. "If you break down, Laurel, I will, too. And I can't afford that."

"I'm sorry." Laurel managed to get herself under control. "I'm coming right over."

"Thank you, dear, but it would be better if you didn't. You see, I haven't explained it to Charlene yet. I think we'll need this afternoon for a little quiet talking."

"All right, then I'll be there this evening."

Elizabeth didn't answer.

"What's the matter?" Laurel asked. "Don't you want me to come at all?"

"Of course I do. God, I haven't even begun to think of all the things I'll have to ask you to do to help me! It's just that, well, Laurel, you should know that Tony's coming tonight, too."

"So what? Good God, what does that stupid feud mean in the face of this? Tony and I are your best friends, Elizabeth. We'd be pretty poor ones if we let our own problems interfere with anything we can do for you and Charlene! I can't speak for him, but I know damned well that I'd work with Jack the Ripper right now if it could take some of the load off you. And I'm sure Tony feels the same. I'll see you later. Anything you need in the meantime?"

"No. Nothing."

She changed into a comfortable housedress and fixed two

lunch trays, methodically deciding which china, silver, and glassware she'd keep aside from now on for Charlene. The thought made her feel physically sick, but she knew that Dr. Martin was right. She had to stay well.

Calmly she carried Charlene's tray into the bedroom, where the child was propped up, unsmiling, on her pillows. In a minute she returned with her own tray, which she placed on the desk facing the bed. Elizabeth settled herself in the desk chair and picked up her fork.

"Now," she said gently, "let's chat while we eat. We have a lot to discuss, woman to woman."

When Laurel and Tony arrived that evening, they found Elizabeth looking strained but momentarily relieved and decidedly pleased that they came in together. If nothing else, she thought irrelevantly, this tragedy may at least make them friends again.

As though she read her thoughts, Laurel spoke first. "I called Tony after we talked this afternoon. He picked me up. You can relax, dear. All we care about is you and the little one."

Tony nodded. "How is she?"

"Tremendous. We talked for more than an hour this afternoon, and once she understood, it was more as though she was reassuring me. I know she's frightened, but she's not going to let anyone know it. I told her just about everything Stan Martin told me. About the disease and the hospital and the fact that it might take a long time for her to get well again. I didn't lie to her or try to make it sound like nothing more than a bad cold. She knows it's serious, but she also knows, as I do, that she's going to get well. I'm satisfied she believes that, though I doubt that she realizes what a long, hard road she has ahead. I'm not sure I can grasp it myself just yet."

For a long moment, the three of them sat in silence, each involved in his or her own disbelief, sorrow, and pity. Finally, Tony glanced at his watch.

"It's just eight," he said. "She won't be asleep yet, will she? Could I go in and visit with her a little?"

"Of course," Elizabeth said. "But," it almost killed her to say it, "don't get too close, Tony."

"Want to come with me, Laurel?"

"I'll go in when you come out. Might be too much excitement for both of us to descend on her at once."

When he'd gone, Laurel spoke to Elizabeth. "I suppose you've called Adam?"

Elizabeth just stared at her. It wasn't possible but it was true. In these last nightmare hours she had not even thought of Adam. How could such a thing be? Not once in more than five years had a day gone by without her thinking of him. Yet today it was as though her whole world revolved around one small figure in the next room, and around those to whom she had turned for help. This, she supposed, was what he had meant when he wondered whether she could endure their kind of "arrangement." Love her as he did, he was not free to be with her when she needed him most.

"No," Elizabeth said slowly, "I haven't called Adam. Isn't that strange? I suppose I knew he was too far away to help."

"Why don't you slip in and do it now," Laurel suggested gently. "It's only five o'clock in California."

Mechanically, Elizabeth moved toward her bedroom. Though she had never used it before, she had memorized Adam's number at his office. She placed the call and a crisp voice answered.

"Mr. Barnsworth's office."

"May I speak with him please? It's Elizabeth Quigly."

"Yes."

"This is Miss Varick, Mrs. Quigly. Mr. Barnsworth is not in his office, but I think he's nearby. Do you want to hold on while I try to find him?"

"Yes, I'll hold on."

In a minute she heard the familiar, loving voice.

"Elizabeth? Darling, is something wrong?"

She told him about Charlene, and for the first time that day she could not hold back her tears. Almost incoherently, she sobbed out her dreadful news.

"Sweetheart, please try to get hold of yourself," Adam begged. "Are you alone? Is anyone with you?"

"Laurel's here. And Tony Alexander."

"Do you want me to come? It might take a day or two for me to settle things here, but then I can break away for a couple of days. God help us, what you must be going through!"

Of course she wanted him to come. She wanted his strength and his comfort. She wanted him near her as she went through the bewildering acceptance of what had happened to her child and the awful uncertainty of what was to become of her. But she didn't want him for a few hours, flying in on a suddenly arranged "business trip" that had to be explained to his wife. For the first time since they had found each other again, Elizabeth knew that she was still alone. She loved Adam and he loved her. But it was a love meant for happiness, not for stress. It was her choice and she had made it. Even now she had no regrets. When she answered, her voice was firm and without a hint of reproach.

"No, darling, there's nothing you can do now. Later, maybe, when I know my plans. I just wanted you to know about Charlene."

She thought he sounded relieved, but perhaps that was only because every one of her nerve ends seemed acutely sensitive.

"You're sure?" he asked. "You know I'll come."

"Quite sure. There's no reason for you to be here." No reason, she thought, except that I love you and need you.

"I'll call you tomorrow," Adam said. "And if anything happens in the meantime, you call Miss Varick at home. Got a pencil? Here's her number. She can always reach me at my house."

"All right." Elizabeth did not even write down the number. "But nothing's going to happen immediately."

"Nevertheless, you call her if you need anything in a hurry. Money. Anything. Be brave and strong, my darling, as you always are. Remember I'm only a few hours away. I love you, dearest. Kiss Charlene for me."

Elizabeth gave a mirthless little laugh. "I can't even do that," she said. "Adam?"

"Yes, dearest?"

She wanted to say, "Come to me. I'm so frightened." Instead she said, as she had a thousand times before, "I love you."

"And I worship you," he answered. "Try to get some rest, my darling. I'll talk to you tomorrow."

Wearily she returned to the living room.

"Did you get him?" Laurel asked. "Is he coming?"

"I got him, but he's not coming. Oh, he offered," she said defensively, "but I told him I'd need him more later."

Laurel didn't answer. The expression in her eyes said it all.

part VI

DENVER, COLORADO

1948-1949

Chapter 20

In spite of her impatience to get Charlene to Denver, it was a month before all the arrangements could be made. Everyone was the soul of kindness in that seemingly interminable period. Between them, Laurel and Tony made arrangements to have her furniture packed and put into storage. Elizabeth's first impulse was simply to sell everything and use the money to finance her unknown future, but her friends talked her out of it. It made much more sense, they argued, to hold on to her possessions until she knew where she was going to settle. Things could always be sold later, storage was not that expensive, and Robert insisted upon making her a five-thousand-dollar loan to tide her over and be repaid whenever she could.

There seemed to be an unspoken agreement that she was not coming back to New York. They all assumed that once Charlene was well Elizabeth would not bring her back into the uncertain climate and demanding atmosphere of the East. Not that she had any specific plans. She was living one day at a time, now, and those nearest to her understood that her whole mind was absorbed with the urgency to get Charlene started on her program of recovery.

Even Ann came down off her lofty plateau to offer sympathy and encouragement, if nothing else. She did not come into New York, pleading that she dared not risk the danger of exposure for the sake of a flourishing little Peter Richards III. It was far-fetched, but Elizabeth understood. Ann called daily, solicitously, offering to notify anyone that her mother wanted her to. Elizabeth, knowing that Ann felt guilty about her absence, suggested that she take over the job of notifying Stu Preston and their other friends in Washington. She was simply to write and tell them of Charlene's illness and that Elizabeth was taking her to National Jewish Hospital. She could notify them later of Elizabeth's address in Denver. There was one sticky, stupid moment when Ann learned the name of the hospital.

"National *Jewish?*" she asked.

Elizabeth had no time for nonsense. "Yes, the best in the world," she said. "And you can tell your liberal friends in Scarsdale that it's nonsectarian."

"Mother, you know I didn't mean it that way."

"Of course you did," Elizabeth said. "Fortunately, it's not important."

A week after she called him, Adam flew into New York. He had telephoned her every night since she'd given him the bad news, and his concern for her and Charlene was real. She welcomed his arrival with open arms, but without the ecstatic elation she'd always felt. She loved him and knew that the love was returned. But the greatest crisis of her life had done something to her emotions. She was incapable of the passionate response to Adam that had always been instantaneous and overwhelming. It was as though he was a wonderful sidelight of her life, rather than the center of the universe as she'd thought. They made love the night he arrived, but the fierce, complete abandonment was not there. Adam recognized it and was unusually gentle. He knew that Elizabeth had finally come face to face with the one fact that she had never been willing to admit, even to herself. She had had to make herself realize that he was not, in actuality, her husband. That he could not be at her side all through this time of fear, and that her desperate need of him was an obligation he could not fulfill in the unstinting way she deserved. It did not matter that all this had been true from the beginning. Now it had become reality. And while Elizabeth loved him no less strongly, it was only human that she harbored an unreasonable resentment of the role she had chosen.

He tried, tenderly, to tell her that he knew what she was

feeling. She denied it violently. More, he guessed, for herself than for him. She did not want to admit, even to herself, that, deep and true as it was, her relationship with Adam still had its limitations. Her ecstasy was a little feigned, her responses a shade more inhibited. Try as she would to overcome it, there was disappointment within her. She tried to brush away the evidence of her lessened passion with explanations and apologies.

"I'm sorry," she said when he failed to rouse her as he always had. "It has nothing to do with us, my darling. I'm exhausted by this last week. Drained of everything, I suppose. I can't seem to lose myself in anything right now. Not even in your wonderful lovemaking."

He kissed her limp body. "How else could you feel after what you've been through?" he said softly. "Don't you think I understand, my love? Don't you think I'm just as aware as you are of how inadequate I've been? I should have come instantly and stayed until things were settled. I should have said to hell with anything else. I wanted to, and I couldn't."

"Hush," she said. "We made an agreement long ago. You haven't failed me, Adam. You tried to prepare me for something exactly like this. You're the most honest man I know."

He held her close. "I was an insensitive clod," he said. "This was not the time for lovemaking and I knew it. I just couldn't stay away from you. I never have been able to."

She took his head between her hands. "Don't ever say that. There will never be a time when I don't want you to make love to me. I just never want to cheat you."

For a long time they lay together, not speaking. Elizabeth closed her eyes and tried to think of nothing but the body that fitted every contour of her own. But it was no good. The sleeping child in the next room might just as well have been in bed with them, so strongly did she dominate Elizabeth's thoughts. Finally, she kissed Adam and slipped out of bed. For the first time in years, she put on a robe before she lit a cigarette. Usually she walked about naked and proud, reveling in his undisguised admiration of her. Adam was aware of the unconscious gesture of withdrawal. Pulling the covers over him, he sat up and lit a cigarette, watching her as she paced restlessly around the room.

"When will you leave for Denver?" he asked quietly.

"The minute Dr. Martin gives us the word. Damn this holiday season," she said. "It slows up everything. Stan Martin says we probably won't be able to go until right after the first of the year."

"Any idea where you'll be?"

"I'm not sure. I've talked to the assistant administrator of the hospital. Sounds like a very nice man. His name is Lance Milford. He suggested I probably could get an apartment in someplace called Yates Court. It's just a ten-minute walk from the hospital. But of course I'll let you know the minute I'm settled."

"I probably won't be able to get back here before you leave," he said. His voice was miserable but resigned. "As you said, these goddamn Christmas holidays louse up everything."

Elizabeth was not surprised. "I know," she said. "I understand."

"But I'll call you every day. That goes without saying. Are you sure you don't need money?"

"No. I'm fine, Adam. Truly. I'll yell if I do."

He banged his fist on the night table. "Jesus Christ! How can I let you go through this alone? What shall I do, Elizabeth? I can't live with myself this way! Do you want me to tell Monica everything and beg her to give me a divorce? I'll do it. I swear I will. God knows I owe you that!"

She came back to the bed and cradled him in her arms. "Dear love, please don't hate yourself. We're all right. All of us. Nothing has changed between you and me, Adam. Stop punishing yourself. I accepted the terms long ago, and nothing has happened to alter them. Not even this. I've always wanted to marry you. You know that. But not because you owe it to me, sweetheart. You owe me nothing. Not now or ever. You've given me life, on the only terms you could. Don't read the wrong things into the way I'm reacting at this particular point in time. This is not the moment for decisions based on guilt or pity or desperation. Just stay as near me as you can. Talk to me often. Come to Denver when I'm calmer and you can manage it. That's all I want right now. That's all I'm capable of accepting."

Suddenly overwhelming desire engulfed them. This time it was a violent, almost brutal coming together that left them wringing wet and exhausted. It was almost as though they sensed that it would be a long time before they knew each other's body again.

And now here she was in a compartment with Charlene on the Union Pacific City of Denver train headed toward a world completely strange to her. She had slept little on the trip. Her mind was full of a thousand memories and as many questions. She remembered Tony, Laurel, and Robert on the platform at the station, looking worried as they tried to make feeble jokes about how lucky she and Charlene were to be getting out of the New York rat race. Giving Laurel one last hug, she reminded her again of her promise.

"If you hear anything from Quigly, you'll let me know instantly? He may contact you or Stu Preston if he doesn't reach me. I'll be at Yates Court. I've told Stuart, too, just in case."

"Yes, darling, of course. You know I'll call you instantly. And you promise to let *us* know about everything just as soon as you can. We'll be frantic until we hear from you. Elizabeth, are you positive you don't want me to come with you? I could get a berth on the train even now, I'm sure. And one of the kids at the office could send me some clothes."

Elizabeth shook her head. "We'll be all right. Please don't worry." She turned to Robert and kissed him warmly on the cheek. "Thank you so much for everything. I'll repay you as soon as I get a job."

"Don't be an ass," Robert said gruffly. "Stop stewing about that piddling little loan. And remember there's more where that came from. I can overdecorate one Central Park duplex and send you enough money to keep you in style for a year in that godforsaken town!"

She smiled at him gratefully. In spite of his pretended sophistication, Robert was touched by her trouble. She knew he meant every word of his offer of help, no matter how flippantly he chose to phrase it.

Her last goodbye was to Tony, who held her gently and lovingly for a long moment. There was so much, and so little, between them. It was such a strange case of what might have been.

"Goodbye for now, Tony, dear. Try to be happy."

"Take care of yourself," he said. "And remember, we love you."

Elizabeth awakened in the upper berth of the compartment. Her watch said seven o'clock. They were due in Union Station at eight-thirty that morning. It had been a tiring trip, with the change of trains in Chicago and the confinement of the compartment. A nice, cheerful porter had brought all their meals in. Charlene, of course, had spent the entire time in bed, sleeping a great deal, occasionally rousing to look at the bleak unfamiliar landscape as they sped across the country.

Elizabeth slipped out of bed and looked at it now. To her Eastern eyes it was like another planet. As the morning light took over, she could see a clear blue, cloudless sky and beyond the flat landscape, a glimpse of high plains. The countryside itself was barren and forbidding, dry and sandy, dotted with dead sage and yucca. The only vegetation was a few sparse trees along the creek beds. She recognized willows but the cottonwoods were unfamiliar to her. An occasional lonely-looking ranch house broke the monotony of the silent scene, with dismal windbreaks planted on the north and west sides. In the feed lots near the railroad tracks, Elizabeth could see cattle, their breath steaming in the high dry cold air. There seemed nothing welcoming about this approach through northeastern Colorado. She hoped that Denver would make her feel less like a stranger in a foreign land.

She dressed Charlene and then rang for the porter, ordering breakfast when he poked his beaming black face in the door.

"Yes, ma'am," he said. "Breakfast comin' up! By the way, Miz Whitman, if you and the little lady look out there you'll begin to see some mountains now. Most folks find it mighty impressive, first time they see 'em."

The mountains, now faintly visible from their side of the train were, indeed, impressive. Fascinated by their majesty, Elizabeth could not tear her eyes away from the snow-topped peaks. Even as she and Charlene ate their breakfast, she continued to look at the strangely hypnotic land, observing its undulations and upward pitch to the foothills. Like many a traveler before her, she wondered how the pioneers had ever managed to cross this harsh, treeless, shrubless country. How had they reached the golden West, thwarted by this bleak countryside and challenged by the mountains that lay beyond it?

The mountains were more sharply in focus now, breathtaking in their unassailability. The train rushed over crossings, sped through towns so small that they flashed past almost unnoticed. Soon, whistling in triumph, the train slowed, edging its way haughtily through the outer industrial section of Denver, pulling up at last into the dimness of the station.

The sense of unfamiliarity was secondary, now, to the urgency of getting Charlene to National Jewish. A porter on the platform took their bags, led them through a circuitous route of tunnels and ramps to a taxi outside. Their first breath of Colorado's dry, cold air almost seemed to burn their lungs with its sharpness, and the mile-high altitude of Denver made them gasp for breath. Despite the snow on the ground, though, it did not seem bitterly cold. They were to learn later that the dryness of the air was quite different from the wet, heavy hand of winter in New York. They would discover, too, that although Denver could be pounded by blizzards that dumped inches of snow on the city, all but mere traces of the white, powdery stuff usually were gone by noon of the following day.

The cab sped them to the hospital by way of East Colfax Avenue. Trying to control her nervousness, Elizabeth made idle talk with Charlene.

"Look, darling," she said, "we're going through a thriving community. It looks quite different from what we saw from the train, doesn't it?"

It did, indeed. In 1948, Colfax Avenue was crowded with liquor and grocery stores, filling stations, an occasional movie house, and two or three grubby-looking nightclubs, and dry cleaners who advertised "uniforms done overnight."

"All happened during the war," the cab driver volunteered over his shoulder. "Lowry Field's just over there a way. It was a big U. S. Army Air Force base, you know. The area just kind of grew up to take care of the soldiers and their families."

Within minutes, they drew up in front of the hospital. The first thing Elizabeth saw was the sign that Stan Martin had told her about. Somehow it was comforting, a recognizable landmark that seemed to give reality to this otherwise unreal situation. Even more reassuring was the fact that when she approached the front desk and gave her name, the receptionist responded immediately with a welcome smile.

"Mrs. Whitman? Of course. Mr. Milford asked that he be notified as soon as you arrived. Just sit down right over there and I'll call him."

In seconds, Lance Milford appeared. He was young, about thirty-one or -two, Elizabeth judged, and he projected kindness and empathy.

"I'm glad you're here," he said simply. "Dr. Abrams is anxious to meet you, too. You both got some pretty good advance press notices from Dr. Martin." He crouched down so that his face was on the level with Charlene's. "So this is our new friend," he said. "Hi, Charlene."

"This is Mr. Milford, honey," Elizabeth said. "He works here."

"Are you a doctor?" Charlene asked.

"No, I just help those important fellas. You know, Charlene, I came here just like you. Fighting the same bug. That was ten years ago. I lived in New York, too, just like you do."

"Ten years ago!" Charlene looked frightened.

He hastened to reassure her. "Oh, they got me well in no time. The thing is, I liked it here so much that I applied for a job working in the hospital. It's a terrific place, Charlene. You're going to meet some wonderful people. We have lots of little boys and girls here, just about your age. What do you say we all go meet some of them?"

Elizabeth suspected they were getting special attention and was grateful for it.

"We came straight from the train," she said. "May I leave my bags here for a while? Once Charlene is settled, I'll go to see about an apartment I've arranged for. One you suggested—in Yates Court."

"Perfect. Okay, Charlene, let's go. We're going to put you in a building with a funny name. It's called Pisko."

The area in which Charlene would live was on the second floor. There was a circular arrangement with six beds divided into two-bed cubbyholes with curtains between. It was spotless, bright, and, for what it was, reasonably cheerful. A trim young nurse came forward to greet them and Lance introduced her to Elizabeth and Charlene.

"This is one of our guardian angels," he said. "Her name is Miss Riddle."

The nurse's eyes twinkled. "And I *don't* have the answers," she said teasingly. "So don't let my name fool you, Charlene."

For the first time, Charlene smiled. "Riddles aren't any good unless they have answers," she said.

"Hah!" the nurse said admiringly. "I've got a smart one here! You'd be surprised how many people miss the point of that joke. It's become my own little private test for a sense of humor. You passed with flying colors!"

Elizabeth could have kissed her with gratitude. The ease with which Lance Milford and Miss Riddle handled these first terrifying moments filled her with assurance. It was not going to be easy, any of it. But thank God for the help of these relaxed, compassionate people.

"Now," Miss Riddle said briskly, "how would you like to meet your roommate? She's twelve. How old are you?"

"I'll be twelve on the Fourth of July."

"No fooling!" Miss Riddle looked impressed. "So *you're* the reason they have parades and shoot off fireworks! I always wondered what all the fuss was about."

The nurse ushered Charlene and Elizabeth to one of the two-bed cubicles. The occupant of the second bed was a broadly beaming little girl whose hair was caught with blue ribbons and whose skin was the color of polished ebony.

For a second, Elizabeth caught her breath. Somehow she had not expected Charlene's companion to be a Negro child. Not that it disturbed her. And she knew it would not seem unusual to Charlene. How lucky we lived in New York, Elizabeth thought, remembering that some of Charlene's best friends at school were as black as this poor little bedridden thing. The children acknowledged the introductions shyly. Then Clara Jenkins looked at Elizabeth, two hundred years of cautiousness in her eyes.

Elizabeth took the child's hand. "I'm so glad that Charlene has a new friend, Clara," she said. "And such a pretty one."

"Charlene's pretty, too," she said softly.

"Okay," Miss Riddle announced. "Mutual admiration society is adjourned. We're going to get you into bed, Miss Fourth of July."

"Right," Lance Milford said. "I'm sure Dr. Abrams will be in his office now, Mrs. Whitman. He'll want to have a few words with you, and then we'll inundate you with a thousand yards of hospital red tape."

Charlene was busily getting into a hospital gown. "You won't have to wear this unstylish thing very long," Miss Riddle promised her. "It's just the accepted uniform while we run a few routine check-out procedures. Then you can wear those pretty pajamas and robes your mother has tucked into your suitcase."

"How do you know I have any?" Charlene asked. "We haven't unpacked yet."

"Want to bet a quarter that I'm wrong?"

Charlene looked at her appraisingly. Then she grinned. "Nope. You're right. I've got a whole lot of nice new things. Mommy bought some, but most of them were presents from our friends."

Elizabeth had a lump in her throat. Charlene was being so brave, making it easy for all of them. I am *not* prejudiced, Elizabeth told herself. She *is* an extraordinarily perceptive child.

"I'll be back in a little while, darling. After I've met Dr. Abrams. He must be great if he's such a good friend of our Dr. Martin." She hoped she sounded as untroubled as she wanted to.

"I'll vouch for that," Miss Riddle said. "Every nurse in the hospital is secretly in love with him."

Milford led her back to Daniel Abrams' office. The doctor greeted her pleasantly and Elizabeth could see why all the nurses were devoted to him. He was in his early fifties with a shock of coal-black hair and deep brown eyes that looked as though they could identify with emotional as well as physical suffering.

He asked politely for Stan Martin and then got right down to business. "I'm sure you understand the nature of this disease, Mrs. Whitman. Dr. Martin tells me he's explained pretty much to you what we can do for Charlene. I've studied the X rays from New York and she seems to have a light case and it's been caught in time. We can be thankful for that. Of course, we'll do many more X rays and tests here, but I doubt that our findings will be any different from the ones she's already had. The only treatment we have now is rest. Complete bed rest at first. As she improves, we'll let her get up for short periods. That's the semiambulatory stage. When she becomes even better, she'll be ambulatory and eventually she'll be able to go with you for outside visits."

"Perhaps it's a foolish question, Doctor, but have you any idea how long it will be before she's well?"

"No, Mrs. Whitman, I can't give you an answer to that. It depends upon how she responds. Sometimes the germs even change composition, which alters the course of treatment. It's a helluva disease, but we're on the verge of licking it. One day there will be drugs available that will make this prolonged treatment of bed rest unnecessary. Unfortunately, we don't have them yet. So we have to depend largely on the healing power of nature—which is a pretty frustrating thing for a so-called man of science to have to admit. However, we know it works. And in Charlene's case, I don't think you have to fear thoracic surgery or anything of a drastic nature. It will just take time and lots of patience. Keeping Charlene's morale high will be an important part of the treatment. We can do a lot, but you can do most of all."

"When will we know how she's progressing?" Elizabeth asked.

"As I told you, we'll be checking her constantly. But we can't declare her cured until six direct smears and six direct cultures have been analyzed and pronounced negative. I must warn you, Mrs. Whitman, that you can't expect overnight miracles. But I think you're one of the lucky parents. At least you can feel sure that no matter how long it takes, barring unforeseen developments, your child will eventually be able to lead a full, healthy, normal life."

She was grateful for his forthrightness. He was considerate but he didn't try to raise false hopes about the rapidity of Charlene's recovery. Nor did he alarm her, as so many doctors might have, about the threat of sudden serious developments.

"Thank you, Dr. Abrams. I know that Charlene is in wonderful hands. And she's a strong child, mentally and emotionally. I know I have a lot to be thankful for. All of you here are so kind."

"We're doing what we want to do, Mrs. Whitman. All we're waiting for is the day we can do more."

Lance Milford was waiting for her outside of Abrams' office.

"Terrific guy, isn't he?"

"Extraordinary," Elizabeth said. "You all are."

"Buy you a cup of coffee before you go back to Charlene?"

"If you can spare the time, I'd like that."

In the cafeteria, Lance began to talk easily. "What I told Charlene was true, you know. I had a pretty good job in New York by the time I was twenty-one. Just out of college and lucky enough to land a promising spot in an advertising agency. Then I got TB. The really bad version. They had to remove a lung. Funny how fate works," he said. "All through college I'd kind of flirted with the idea of becoming a doctor, but my family didn't have any money and it's a long expensive grind, so I gave up the idea. Then, when I got here and these people saved my life, I realized two things. One was that for the sake of my health I should always live in this climate. And the second was that if I couldn't be a doctor, I could help doctors. So, as I told Charlene, I asked for an office job and got it. I've done well and I love every minute of it. Even got married three years ago. You must meet Janie and our two-year-old, Nancy. They're something extra that fate handed me. Jane's a Denver girl. I would never have met her if I hadn't decided to stay." He paused. "I'll bet you're wondering why I'm telling you the story of my life when you've got so much on your mind."

"No," Elizabeth said, "I'm sure I know why. Your story is inspirational. It gives one hope that there really is a master plan."

"I don't know if it's as dramatic as all that," Lance said, "but I can imagine what you're feeling right now. I thought maybe it would help to hear a horror story with a happy ending."

"You were right. It does. I know that what Charlene has to overcome is nothing as bad as what you faced. It must have been terrible for you. Twenty-one. Just at the beginning of an adult life and a career, and suddenly you're presented with the very real possibility of death. Thank God Charlene doesn't have that to fear."

"She's a lucky kid," he said. "And she has something I didn't have: Somebody like you standing by."

"Didn't you have parents?"

"Just a widowed mother. Constantly hysterical. She was in such a state that she made me much worse, poor thing. She didn't mean to, of course. But I spent so much time worrying about her that Dr. Abrams finally suggested she go back to New York. From then on, I got better. My recovery was being hindered by her lack of control. In Charlene's case, her improvement will go all the faster because of your attitude."

"Thank you," Elizabeth said, "but how can you be so sure? Right now I'm a bundle of helpless, quivering fright."

"Probably so. But she'll never know that. I've gotten pretty good at judging people these last few years, Mrs. Whitman. I saw how you behaved over in Pisko. Slow and easy. And, God bless you, you didn't bat an eye when you saw Charlene's roommate."

"I don't have the energy to waste on prejudice, Mr. Milford. There are too many real problems in this world."

He nodded approvingly. "Now, let me tell you the most important thing. At the moment, while Charlene is in the complete bed-rest stage, you'll be able to visit her twice a week, on Tuesday and Friday after 5 P.M. and from three to five o'clock on Sunday. It doesn't sound like much, I know. But them's orders."

Elizabeth was disappointed but she accepted this piece of bad news without protest.

"If those are the rules, those are the rules. Anything else?"

"Just a million forms you'll have to fill out. Lots of background information and that kind of thing. There are no charges here, you know, but what we give up in fees we take back in terms of your time. We need to know everything about Charlene and you and her whole family history. It's like writing the story of your life. Want to get started?"

"Yes. And I can see Charlene again, before I leave, can't I, Mr. Milford?"

"Of course. By the way, I wish you'd call me Lance."

"Thanks. I'm Elizabeth."

"Good enough. Here we go, Elizabeth. Get ready for writer's cramp!"

Milford had not exaggerated. There did, indeed, seem to be an endless amount of information required. Elizabeth had no trouble answering the questions about her side of the family, even the painful admission that her father had died of tuberculosis. But when it came to Alan's history, she was at a loss. It occurred to her that she knew surprisingly little about his family, and nothing at all of the medical history of his parents. Grimly she noted the cause of Alan's death as "acute alcoholism" and added "possible paranoid complications."

It took her almost an hour to complete the lengthy forms, supplying financial information and giving her address as Yates Court, though she wasn't completely sure that she would take the apartment there. For Charlene's next of kin, after herself, she wrote in "Mrs. Peter Richards, Jr., Scarsdale, N.Y." It was technically true, though Laurel Lane, Tony Alexander, and Adam Barnsworth were much more "family" to Charlene than her sister.

She finished at last and went back to the Pisko building. Elizabeth's heart contracted at the sight of the tiny figure in the impersonal hospital bed, but Charlene seemed calm and relaxed.

"Everything all right, darling?" Elizabeth asked.

"Sure, Mommy, I'm fine. Everybody's very nice here. Clara and I are going to be friends. Do you know she's been here three months and they're already letting her get up every day?"

Clara beamed. "It's okay here, Mrs. Whitman. The food is real good. Don't you worry. I'll look after Charley."

Elizabeth started at Clara's use of Adam's nickname for Charlene.

"I told Clara that that's what Uncle Adam calls me," the child explained. "She likes it better than Charlene. Miss Riddle calls me all kind of things like 'George M. Cohan.' What does that mean, anyway?"

Elizabeth smiled. "He was a famous actor who sang a song about being born on the Fourth of July. Miss Riddle is quite a lady, isn't she?"

"She's fun. Dr. Abrams is nice, too. He came to see me while you were gone." Charlene looked troubled. "He said I might be here quite a while."

"We knew that, darling," Elizabeth said soothingly. "It will be hard for you, I know, but the important thing is that you'll be getting well. Hospitals are very boring, sweetheart. I guess that's why the person in one has to be called a patient."

Clara grinned from the next bed. "My mama says that that's why they say doctors 'practice'—'cause that's all they really do."

The three of them laughed. Then Charlene turned serious again.

"I wasn't thinking about me," she said. "I'm worrying about you, Mommy. Where are you going to live? Will you get a job here? You won't have any friends and I'm afraid you're going to be terribly lonesome without Tony and Aunt Laurel and Uncle Adam and me. I feel bad causing you all this trouble."

Remembering Lance Milford's worries about his own mother, Elizabeth hastened to dispel Charlene's fears.

"Hey," she said, "who's in charge of this family all of a sudden, you or me? Are you insinuating that I can't take care of myself in a strange town? Me, who conquered New York single-handed? Why, Denver is going to be a snap! In a few minutes, darling, I'll have to leave you and go look at that apartment I heard about. Then I'll see about something to keep me busy between visits to you." There was no point in worrying Charlene about money. The necessity to work was much better passed off as something to occupy Elizabeth's time. "As for our friends," she went on, "you know we're going to be smothered with attention. I bet they'll be calling me every day for a report on you. I wouldn't be surprised if we had some visits from them, too. Now, Miss Worry Wart, will you relax in that bed and try not to fuss? It's Friday—visiting day—so I'll be back after five o'clock to stay as long as they'll let me."

Reassured, Charlene smiled and waved goodbye. "Try to find an apartment with a nice view," she said. "Like Gramercy Park."

Yates Court did not have the charm of their New York apartment, but it had enough advantages to make Elizabeth decide to take one of the less expensive units on the garden level. The building appeared to be about forty years old, a U-shaped structure with a court entrance and two-story wings faced with balconies supported by vast, out-of-proportion Greek columns made of wood. It reminded Elizabeth of a solid, no-nonsense matron, arms akimbo, complacently gazing at the beautiful City Park just across the way.

The apartment itself was dark and tight-feeling, rather drably furnished, but reasonably priced. And when Elizabeth explained her circumstances, an understanding superintendent said he was sure that occupancy could be arranged on a month-to-month basis. Approaching the building, Elizabeth had correctly guessed that this had once been an elegant neighborhood, now slightly down at the heels but still reputable and even pretty, with great elm trees lining the street.

But in addition to its low rent and its proximity to the hospital, what really clinched her decision to live there was City Park. It was huge, beautifully landscaped, and tended with the affection of those who have had to plant every tree, shrub, and blade of grass, for nothing grew naturally in this area. On the east edge of the park stood the Museum of Natural History, in which Elizabeth was to while away many lonesome hours. Not too far into the park was a band shell where she could drink in the music that had always been her joy. There was a great view of the mountains as well, and she knew she would never tire of looking at their ancient grandeur which seemed to give everything a sense of continuity. She looked forward to the day when she could show City Park to Charlene. There was a lake and a duck pond which undoubtedly would be inhabited by the time she could bring her child to see it.

She moved immediately into an available furnished apartment, waiving a new paint job in favor of the flexible arrangement on the lease. Even before she unpacked her bags, she called Laurel collect from a public telephone booth, apologizing for the expense and promising to make up for it when she got a phone of her own.

"Who cares about the dumb collect call?" Laurel said. "How is everything? How is Charlene? And how are you?"

Elizabeth told her all that had happened since her arrival. Was it only this morning? Already it seemed as if days had passed, so much had been accomplished. She gave Laurel her new address and the address of the hospital and asked her to relay all the information to Tony and Ann.

"I'll call you as soon as I get my own phone," she said. "Should be in a day or two. I understand the phone company gives priority when they know the hospital might have to reach you."

"Sure there's nothing you need?"

"No. Just keep your fingers crossed."

Miss Varick accepted the collect call to Adam and he came on the line immediately. She repeated the information she'd given Laurel, trying even harder to make a joke of the dreary little apartment, praying that he would tell her when he was coming to see it.

"Thank God it's gone so well this far," he said instead. "Darling, are you sure you don't need money?"

Money seemed to be uppermost in his mind. She tried hard not to feel that he was more concerned with the material problems of her life than with the emotional ones. She supposed that to him they went hand in hand. A practical man like Adam was only showing his concern for her, trying to make sure that she was not in need. It was his way of expressing his love for her. But what she needed, of course, was what he could not give her: himself.

"So far I'm in good shape," she assured him once again. "Monday I'll see about some kind of a job, but if things get tough I won't hesitate to ask. Honestly, darling."

"You make sure you *don't* hesitate," he said. "I know you and your bloody New England pride. Call me collect every day, sweetheart, until you get your phone. Then I can call you. And give my love to Charley."

"I will, Adam."

"And remember what you're supposed to say ten times a day when I'm not there."

"I never fail," Elizabeth said softly.

She hung up feeling depressed. His voice had been warm and tender, his concern for her apparent and his reminder to say "Adam loves me" was his way of reassuring and supporting her. But there was no mention of coming to Denver. Not even a vague promise.

By the time she returned to the hospital at five, she had managed to shake off the sense of uneasiness. She regaled Charlene with news of the apartment and the exciting park across the street, told her of the conversation with Laurel, and said that everyone, including Uncle Adam, had sent his dearest love. At the mention of his name, Charlene's eyes lit up.

"When is he coming to see us, Mommy?"

"I don't know, darling. He's a very busy man. But it will be soon, I'm sure."

Charlene smiled contentedly. This was like hearing that her father would come to visit. She was confident that he would hurry to Denver.

Elizabeth wished she shared that confidence.

Chapter 21

Elizabeth's life in Denver evolved into an unspectacular routine. She went to work. She went to the hospital. She went home. There was the constant, nagging worry about Charlene, though Dr. Abrams assured her that the progress was good and the prognosis excellent. Still, in those winter months when she could visit the bedridden child only three times a week it was a wrench to see her so helplessly confined.

In a way, it was worse for Elizabeth than it was for Charlene. The latter seemed to take her illness almost philosophically, never complaining about the enforced rest and never greeting her mother with anything but cheerfulness.

Elizabeth knew they were pretending. With their extraordinary closeness, each sought to protect the other. Their visits were determinedly gay. Charlene chattered about her new-found friends, the wry Miss Riddle and the companionable Clara Jenkins. Clara, in particular, was a source of endless interest to Charlene, and the Jenkins family came to be almost as much her visitors as Clara's.

Elizabeth saw them every time she went to the hospital.

They were solid, pleasant people, long-time Denverites. Mrs. Jenkins worked as a maid for one of the "old families" while Mr. Jenkins was employed as a garage mechanic. There were two other children: five-year-old Lucy, who was too young to visit her sister, and sixteen-year-old James, a handsome, polite boy who exuded gentle assurance without a trace of servility. Jim, ambitious and intelligent, was quick to confide to Elizabeth that he hoped to become an aeronautical engineer.

"What a coincidence," she said. "That was my husband's work."

"No kidding! When was that?"

"Light-years ago," Elizabeth said. "He was with Moreford Aircraft when we were married in nineteen twenty-five and he'd been in the industry some time before that. You'd think of him as a pioneer."

"Yes, ma'am. Those early men paved the way."

"Where do you plan to go to school?" she asked.

"I haven't decided yet. Cal Tech, maybe."

Overhearing, his mother beamed. "There's a special piggy bank for Jim's education, Mrs. Whitman. By the time he's ready for college, we'll be ready to send him to the best there is. You know," she said, looking lovingly at Clara, "there's nothing like the health and happiness of your children. I feel sorry for people who're so wrapped up in themselves that they don't have time for their kids. Lord knows it's no sacrifice. It's the greatest reward there is. Of course, *you* know that. Look how you just dropped everything and came out here to Denver. I don't know what we'd have done if we hadn't been lucky enough to live here."

Elizabeth smiled. "There's no mystery about that, Mrs. Jenkins. You'd have done exactly what I did. Without a second thought."

"Of course we would have. All it means is finding a way to make a living in a different town. Still, it can't be easy to pull up roots and leave your home and your friends."

"Home can be anywhere. And real friends are never lost."

Addie Jenkins nodded. "Charlene says you found yourself a nice job in an antique shop near the Brown Palace Hotel. You like it?"

"Very much. Mr. Lederer is a most considerate employer. He's so kind about letting me leave early on Tuesday and Friday so I can be here at five o'clock."

"He'd be the first one to understand. He came here thirty years ago with TB. Got cured and never left."

Elizabeth was surprised. "Really? He's the second one I've

heard of. Mr. Milford, in the office, told me he did the same thing."

"Oh, Denver's full of them," Mrs. Jenkins said. "Fact is, that's how the city got built up. A lot of very rich men in this town came here first with the sickness. Then they stayed on and started all kinds of businesses. Some of our best families began that way a long time ago."

She spoke simply but proudly. Though formally uneducated, Addie Jenkins was anything but the stereotype of the subservient cleaning woman. She had a soft, pleasant speaking voice and a dignified, erect carriage. Elizabeth judged her to be in her late thirties, a handsome woman, devoted to a kind, hard-working husband, her three children, and to the city in which she did not feel herself an outcast.

"I wish we could visit sometime, Mrs. Jenkins," Elizabeth said impulsively. "Perhaps you and your family would come for dinner one evening. I don't have much of an apartment, but I'm still a pretty fair cook."

Addie looked at her with new respect. She had gathered enough from Clara to know that the Whitmans had once been "somebody." In her eyes, Elizabeth was a real lady. At this moment in time, there was no difference between the white woman whose father had been a professor and the black one who'd been sired by a porter at Union Station.

"We'd be glad to do that, Mrs. Whitman," she said. "And mighty pleased to have you come and see us, too."

Charlene and Clara were delighted. They had become "best friends." It was only natural to them that their families should strike up a warm friendship, too.

As the winter passed, Elizabeth had no reason to doubt her statement that real friends are never lost. Laurel and Tony called at least twice a week. They were seeing more of each other now. The momentary affair seemingly had been transformed into something close to the old comradeship. At least once a week one or the other sent Charlene a gift—a game, a book, or some silly, frivolous thing like a pair of bedroom slippers with a poodle's face on the instep. Charlene improved daily. In two months she became semiambulatory, allowed to get out of bed for short periods each day, but not permitted to leave the hospital. By late March, Elizabeth finally allowed herself to believe that what Dr. Abrams had told her really would come true.

Ann wrote from time to time, her letters always full of her daily activities and the remarkable achievements of Peter Richards III. At the beginning of April, she wrote that she was pregnant again, with another baby expected in October.

"We're delighted, of course," her letter said, "even though we're not terribly surprised. You remember, Mother, that we planned three children, two years apart, so we're keeping to the timetable. This time I want a girl. Wouldn't it be crazy if she was born on Ditto's birthday?"

Elizabeth cringed at the nickname Ann and Peter had given their son. It was too cute for words. What was worse, it probably would follow the poor child through his life, the way football players were called "Snooky" or "Sonny." Elizabeth had gently protested the appellation when she'd first heard it in New York, warning Ann that the name would probably stick with him. Ann was annoyed.

"We think it's amusing," she'd said. "His grandfather is Senior, his father Junior, and this one is ditto."

"I *understand* it, Ann," Elizabeth had answered. "But it seems so damned coy."

"You never thought it was coy when Adam Barnsworth used to call Charlene 'Charley.' That seemed pretty sticky to *me*."

Elizabeth gave up. "Ditto" went with the other incomprehensible trappings of Ann's new life. Like the hand-painted roses on the kitchen cabinets and the Civil War musket which had been transformed into a standing lamp in the den.

Elizabeth answered the letter announcing the second pregnancy with warmth and congratulations. "I hope by the time your 'daughter' arrives, we'll know more about our plans. Charlene is making marvelous progress and life here is really quite pleasant, but I doubt that we'll settle permanently in Denver. I've been giving some thought to going to Arizona or maybe California. The climate is better and the pace, I hear, is much less hectic than in the East. Charlene will have a long recuperative period once she's released. At least I plan on that, though the doctors say she'll be fully recovered when they let her go. I don't want to bring her back into the demanding life of New York and you know that your crazy mother would *really* go stark, raving mad in the suburbs." She hesitated over that last. It was a little dig, but she couldn't resist it. Ann was so irritatingly positive that Scarsdale and all that went with it was the closest thing to heaven on earth. Elizabeth was even mischievous enough to close with a line that she knew would drive Ann up the wall. "By the way," she wrote, "did I tell you that Charlene and I have made some wonderful

new friends? They're a family called Jankins. Their daughter
shares the cubicle with Charlene and they have two other
darling children. The mother is a cleaning woman and the
father works at a garage. They've been to my apartment for
dinner once or twice and I've been to their house. It's
such a joy to have a little company, and they're so kind and
intelligent. I never even think about the fact that they're
Negroes."

Ann's next letter completely ignored the reference to the
Jenkinses. Probably, Elizabeth thought, she was too horrified by the idea to dignify it with a reply.

The greatest source of uneasiness in this period was
Adam. He did not call every day, but he did telephone two
or three times a week, always with protestations of love and
apologies for his inability to get to Denver. Still, instinct
told her that something was wrong.

"Sweetheart, you know how I feel," he said. "My God,
this separation is killing me! Isn't it ludicrous? Geographical-
ly you're closer than ever and yet I see you less than when
you were in New York. You do understand, don't you?
I could always find a legitimate business excuse for going
to New York, but how can I explain a sudden trip to
Colorado?"

The hurt Elizabeth felt came out as iciness in her voice.
"Must you explain it?" she asked coldly. "Surely there's more
real estate to be investigated in Colorado than in Manhattan,
if it's an excuse you need."

"Darling, that's not like you. You know I have to leave
word where I can be reached whenever I go away. My
business associates know damn well that we have nothing
going in Denver."

She had an urge to strike back. "Your business associates?" she echoed. "I thought it was your wife you worried about."

There was a long moment of silence.

"Maybe I'd better call you in a day or two when you're
feeling better," Adam said quietly. "Give my love to
Charley."

Suddenly Elizabeth was frantic. "Oh, Adam, I'm sorry!
Please forgive me! I miss you so much. Charlene does too.
She keeps asking when you're coming to see her. I know I'm
behaving badly. It's just because I love you and I'm lonely for
you. Sometimes I feel as though I'm never going to see you
again. I get scared and angry. Please find a way to come,
Adam. Please."

"All right," he said, "I'll find a way. Within the next two weeks."

"Promise?"

"Since when did you have to ask for promises? I'll be there. I'll let you know exactly when."

That was in early April. He did not, in fact, manage to come until May. Rationally, Elizabeth understood the difficulties, but emotionally she was distraught. In the black moments of the night she tried not to think that the affair had at last become too difficult for Adam, that his passion had succumbed to overwhelming, endless obstacles. She clung to the anticipation of his visit, making herself believe that she was wrong, but when at last he called and told her that he would come for two days she was as apprehensive as she was ecstatic.

She counted the moments until his arrival, which was planned for a Monday afternoon. She was happy that that spring Denver was enjoying soft weather. He would see it in all its beauty—its clear sunlight-speckled mountains, its bravely budding trees. But on Sunday a heavy, wet snow began to fall in great globs, causing the leafed-out branches to bend and even break under the weight. For hours the city was buried under the heavy downfall. Elizabeth fretted that the airport would be closed, but on Monday morning when she took the electric bus to work, the streets were passable but slushy, and the air bright and clear.

The understanding Mr. Lederer had given her two days off when she explained that a dear friend was coming to see Charlene. When she left the shop at noon, she thanked him.

"Don't thank me," he said. "I know what it's like to see someone from home. It will do you and Charlene a world of good. You and that child are entitled to a little happiness."

But Adam's long-awaited visit did not bring happiness to Elizabeth. It was a bewildering forty-eight hours of mystery and passion, culminating in agony. From the moment he walked into the Denver airport, she sensed that something was wrong. There was an artificial jauntiness about him, like a man who had something to hide. His kiss seemed rehearsed. And in contrast to their postwar reunion in New York, the atmosphere between them seemed strained and unnatural.

At first, Elizabeth told herself she was imagining things. He was there, wasn't he? If he no longer loved her, he need not have come at all. Yet he seemed to have a withdrawn, troubled quality. She wondered whether it was she who had changed. Perhaps the strain of these past months had taken away some of the spontaneous delight she'd always felt when she saw him. But she knew this was not true. The sight of him stirred her as it always had. This time it was Adam who was holding back.

Whatever it was, he did not tell her about it on Monday night.

"I've checked into the Brown Palace Hotel," he told her, "but if you have no objection, I don't intend to sleep there."

She raised her eyebrows. "No objection? Remember me?"

Adam smiled. "I must take you down to see my suite, all the same. You won't believe it. They must have designed it for a lecherous cattle baron. The sitting room is aggressively Western, all masculine knotty pine and burlap curtains with cow brands all over them. But the bedroom is an invitation to seduction! Blue satin sheets on a king-size French bed, among other things. It's the damnedest place you've ever seen. I suppose some rich rancher in town for a couple of days could do his business with the boys in that cowhand living room and then take his lady love into a whole different atmosphere. Either that, or it was decorated by a schizophrenic interior designer."

"Quite a contrast to my seedy flat."

He kissed her, more easily this time. "You are incapable of living in a seedy flat," he said. "I've told you before, my darling, that you have a magic touch with a home. I admit I miss your own things, the ones you had in Washington and New York, but the Elizabethan touch is here somehow. Even in unlovely Yates Court."

They dined at home, toasting each other over the wine and talking far into the night. Never before had they waited so long to make love. Finally, Adam rose.

"Isn't it about time we got out of this living room?"

"I thought you'd never ask," Elizabeth said, trying to keep her voice light.

There was, again, the remembered rapture, and for a little while Elizabeth chided herself for her fears. He was full of desire for her, thrilling her with his touch and his whispered words of love. They slept late next morning and awoke in each other's arms, ready to come together in the union that each found endlessly remarkable.

Adam took her to the hotel and they laughed at the ridiculous suite with the saloon-type bar in the living room and the mirrored ceiling in the bedroom. On impulse they made love in the oversized bed, giggling like youngsters at the ostentatious surroundings.

Even when he excused himself to call his office and check for messages, Elizabeth did not feel shut out of his life. She had by now convinced herself that she had imagined his initial hesitation when he arrived. And when they went to visit Charlene, she was sure that any change in Adam was a figment of her imagination. If anything, he was more tender and loving with the child than he'd ever been. Charlene was enchanted to see him, introducing him proudly to Clara and her family, begging Miss Riddle to come and meet her uncle Adam. In turn, he was more than ever like her father. For a moment, Elizabeth saw tears in his eyes, tears he was careful to hide from the little girl. Elizabeth had never seen him so touched. And she had never loved him more.

When they returned to her apartment, Adam made himself a stiff drink. He seemed terribly unhappy. She tried to comfort him.

"Darling, I know that seeing Charlene has affected you tremendously," Elizabeth said, "but she's going to be all right. Having you come was the best medicine in the world for both of us. She loves you, too. Like mother, like daughter."

He turned away as though she'd struck him.

"Adam, what is it?"

He blurted it out. "Monica's going to have a baby."

She stared at him stupidly. "I don't believe it," she said at last. "Monica is pregnant? You two are going to have a child?"

He nodded grimly. "Why do you think I haven't been able to face you all these months? Christ, Elizabeth, I know you've always realized that I had to perform my occasional husbandly obligations, but how could I tell you this?"

She said the first trite thing that came to her mind. "But Monica never wanted children. And to have one now at—how old is she, forty-five? Why, Adam?"

"God knows it wasn't planned. It's a change-of-life baby." The expression on his face was unfathomable. "She thought she was long past that danger, so she was careless. The doctor says it happens quite often. She didn't even know she was pregnant until she was four months gone."

Elizabeth hung on to the edge of her chair. The room was swimming. Adam's childlessness had always been one of the things for which she was grateful. It made her seem less of a thief. Less, perhaps, like some of the women who had not cared that Alan Whitman had not only a wife but children as well. Now Adam was going to be a father. An unwilling one, but a father all the same. Or, she wondered, was the idea that distasteful to him after all?

"How do you feel about the baby?" she asked quietly.

He answered her honestly. "I don't know. I never expected to have children of my own. Charley was my little girl, you know that. At the time Monica and I should have been having them, she wanted no part of it. Hell, she still wants no part of it. But as for me, well, it's strange. The *real* part of me, the part that loves you, wants no child unless it's yours. But the ego in me feels stimulated. I can't lie to you about that, Elizabeth. I can't deny that there's a certain thrill in knowing you're buying a little share of immortality, no matter how accidentally you got it. I feel a crazy obligation to this unborn child. I don't love its mother. But she's carrying part of me."

"Therefore you feel a greater obligation toward Monica." It was not a question, it was a statement.

"I don't know," Adam repeated. "As God is my judge, Elizabeth, I don't know what I feel. I know I love you. But now there's an even stronger claim on me than just the fact of my marriage. I can't sort out my emotions. I keep telling myself that this doesn't make any difference between us. It certainly doesn't make me care for Monica again. It doesn't make me feel that I'm robbing her by wanting to be with you, any more than it ever did. And yet there's this terrible guilt. This awful, unreasonable conflict between wanting to belong to you and feeling that for the first time it's wrong because we could hurt someone innocent, someone who isn't even born yet. I know it doesn't make sense, but the whole insane accident has done something to me."

"Yes," Elizabeth said slowly, "I know it has. I knew from the first minute you came in that something had changed." She felt dead. "I think we'd better not see each other any more, Adam."

"No," he protested, "don't make that judgment now, darling. I can't lose you again, Elizabeth. Please give me time. I've been thrown by this, but I've never had a moment's doubt of what I feel for you. Nothing can change that. Once the baby's born, I know I'll get back on the track. I'm not seeing the whole thing clearly now, but I will."

She shook her head. "You've always felt guilty about Monica. You'll be even more remorseful when there's a child involved. It won't work, Adam. You can't be torn apart like this. And neither can I."

He refused to accept it. "I've never felt guilty about Monica. Obligated, yes. So much so that I couldn't leave her. But not guilty. She's never given me what you have."

"But now she can give you more," Elizabeth said. "Now she's going to give you a child. How will you feel, Adam, sneaking off to see me when there's a child? How will *I* feel, knowing I'm taking part of you that belongs to someone else?"

"That's nonsense!"

"Is it? The way you're behaving already, even before the baby's born, must be some sign of how you'll feel when it really exists and needs you."

"I won't give you up."

"You must," Elizabeth said. Suddenly she was bitterly disappointed in him. Not at the full realization that Adam and Monica slept together. She was not so naïve as to think they did not. It was that once again Adam had found an excuse to turn away from her. And, like the first time, though he believed it, it *was* an excuse. He'd said before, long ago, that he wasn't being fair to her, that the "best thing he could do for her" was not to reappear after the war. She'd bought that excuse, made herself believe it because he believed it. She had clung to the idea that his concern for her was greater than his own desire. Now he was questioning whether his impending fatherhood had greater claim on him than her love, her need, her faithfulness. Her reaction was, at last, healthily self-protective. When there was a problem, it was she who was dispensable. Not Monica. Not the marriage. Not the unborn baby. They would stay. It was Elizabeth who was expected to wait on his pleasure, to understand and never complain. She was angry with him, but she was much more angry with herself. He spoke the truth. In time, Adam would come around again. But this time, Elizabeth must not be waiting. She had been at his command long enough. Adam was a good man. But he was also essentially a selfish one, even if he did not realize it.

"I think you should go to the hotel tonight," she said wearily.

He was genuinely surprised. His expression finally drove her to articulate rage.

"Does that come as such a shock to you?" she demanded. "Did you really expect one more night of lovemaking before you go home to your pregnant wife? Wasn't last night enough of a farce? My God, Adam, do you think *I'm* without feelings, too? Doesn't it ever occur to you that I have emotions? I love you. God help me, I love you. But I can't go on forever trying to understand your priorities. You've been honest. You've admitted that you don't know how you feel about this arrangement. Well, neither do I. But I know that right now it's no good between us. Maybe it never will be again. This time if you said that the kindest thing would be to leave me alone, I'd have to agree with you. It's like tearing my heart out, but I want you to go away and not come back. Let me live, Adam. Help me to stop making such a fool out of myself. I'm no superbeing. I'm an ordinary woman. You expect too much of me. I can't give that much any more."

He didn't fight her. He felt trapped by his conscience, fenced in by his own responsibilities. Adam was torn in many directions. Beyond the strange, almost incomprehensible happiness of knowing he would be a father, he also knew that Elizabeth was the only woman he wanted, and the two facts were irreconcilable. God knows life with Monica offered no joy. Not that she was a shrew. On the contrary, until the past few months she had been an amiable, complacent wife, like all the other wives in their orbit who had settled into a marriage and, after more than twenty years of it, did not consider the possibility that the way of life could change. Their married friends were carbon copies of themselves. The men succeeded in business, played golf, occasionally took up with another woman, but never moved to make the outside relationship permanent. The women kept beautiful houses and entertained graciously, played golf, and sometimes suspected their husbands of lapses of fidelity, a fact they did not regard as a serious threat to their own security. That had been Monica's attitude when Adam returned from the war. It was, he supposed, her attitude today. She might have wondered what he did on his frequent trips to New York, but outwardly she gave no sign that they were anything but a well-suited, faithful, long-married couple.

The pregnancy had come as a shock to both of them. Sex between them had long since become rare and routine, as much a part of the normal pattern of married life as their dinner parties. At first, Monica had thought she was going into menopause. When the doctor pronounced a quite different verdict, she was stunned. She had never wanted children and had avoided them through all the "dangerous" years. To be "caught," as she thought of it, at this late stage was as unfair as it was unseemly. Her friends had grandchildren. And here she was, at her age, about to give birth. Without even telling Adam, she discussed with the doctor the idea of terminating the pregnancy.

"I couldn't do that, Mrs. Barnsworth," he told her. "You are in excellent physical and mental health. No medical board of review would approve a therapeutic abortion. There's no reason. And don't go getting crazy ideas about an illegal job. Your pregnancy is too far advanced for that kind of amateurish blundering. You could die in the hands of some kitchen-table butcher! Besides, I'd think you and your husband would be happy, after all these years, to have a child. It should be a great joy to you both."

"Doctor," Monica had said coldly, "you are an ass. I'm nearly forty-five years old. It's too late for me to start with diapers and 4 A.M. feedings. Adam and I never wanted children when we were young. My God, what will we do with one now? Do you realize that by the time this child is in high school we'll both be in our sixties? What kind of ridiculous relationship will that be? The Barnsworths with a baby! We'll be the laughingstock of Beverly Hills!"

"Be that as it may," he'd said. "You are going to have your child in about five months. I hope you'll see it differently by that time."

Monica had recited the conversation word for word to Adam in February. He had tried to calm her, to even sound pleased, but all the while he wished it were not true. It had not been a lie when he told Elizabeth that he had mixed emotions about fatherhood. It made him feel strangely young and virile. And at the same time it represented unseverable bondage to Monica and the marriage. He had always hoped one day to be painlessly free, to marry Elizabeth. He did not know how or when this would come about. But this made the romantic dream impossible. Unless, he'd thought, something happens to Monica or she miscarries. He had been revolted by his own involuntary reaction. He was wishing one or the other dead! The idea that he could think that way had been so abhorrent to him that he pushed it into the back of his mind. He thought, instead, of Elizabeth, alone in Denver with the sick child whom he loved like his own. He could not face her. Could not tell her that while she'd been saving every ounce of herself for him, he had impregnated a woman in an unemotional ritual that now left him feeling guilty about his wife, his unborn child, and his one real love.

All this came to him again as he heard Elizabeth sending him away. She was right, of course. He could not desert Monica now. And to pretend that her pregnancy did not affect his relationship with Elizabeth was unrealistic, almost obscene. He could not see her and make love to her while Monica grew heavier and more unhappy with each passing day. She was having a hard time with this first, late pregnancy. She was ill-tempered, resentful, and unwell most of the time. Yet she clung to him as she never had. Even this two-day separation had caused the first scene of its kind in all their married life. She had not wanted him to go away. And he had been torn between guilt at leaving her and desire to see Elizabeth. And in the end, he had done neither woman a favor.

"All right, Elizabeth," he said finally, "I'll leave you now. But I can't promise it will be forever. You're the most of me, my love. The best of me. No matter what kind of upheaval is going on inside me now, it doesn't change the part of me that belongs to you and always will. I can't argue with the way you feel. God knows you have every right to want me to go away and leave you in peace. I'll try, darling. But I don't know when I'll come crawling back, asking just to be near you. I know how selfish that is. But I know what I feel. I tried once before to put you out of my life and I couldn't. I can't guarantee that this time I'll succeed. Can *you* be so sure that we can live without each other?"

Her anger was gone. She was dry-eyed and lifeless. "I can't be sure of anything any more, Adam," she said. "Except that I love you. But that's not enough. Not this time. I'm going to try to forget. I want you to do the same. There's nothing for us now except a new barrier to any hopes we might once have had. We've been happy, but we've been hoping against hope for a miracle. It's not going to happen. Let's face that like two grown-up people. We're not Romeo and Juliet. We're adults with responsibilities. I have Charlene. You have Monica and your child. Maybe it's time we stopped thinking only about ourselves."

His agony matched her own. He wanted to wash away the bitter taste of truth. The thought of never seeing or hearing from her again was unendurable and inescapable.

"I can't just walk away like this," he said. "I have to know where you are, how you and Charlene are. What will you do when she's well? Where will you live? You must promise to let me know, Elizabeth. Please. I beg you."

She recognized his suffering as her own, but she dared not weaken. "I'll get word to you," she said finally. "But don't call me then. Don't torment me or yourself."

He took a step toward her. "Kiss me, darling, just once more. Let me leave remembering the feel of your mouth on mine."

She turned away. "No. I can't. If there's anything to remember, let it be yesterday."

She told no one, not even Laurel, of the outcome of Adam's visit, and he respected her wishes to be left alone. With the exception of a little note on his office pad, he did not try to reach her. The familiar scrawl, dated July 12, 1948, simply said, "Catherine Barnsworth born this morning. I love you. Adam." She did not acknowledge it, but in spite of her pain, she was glad that Adam had a daughter. Remembering his devotion to Charlene, she could imagine how he would make his Catherine happy. Alan and Adam, she thought. The two men in her life. So very different and yet with one thing in common—their gentleness with little girls. She wondered about the baby. Did she look like Adam? Was she, as Alan had said of Ann, "born for good luck"? In Ann's case, at least, the prediction seemed to have come true. She had found luck, though not until early maturity. Catherine would be more fortunate. She had a father who would never leave her.

In October, with irritating efficiency, Ann delivered the girl she wanted. Peter called to give Elizabeth the good news.

"Everything's fine," he said. "Six pounds, four ounces, and Ann was in labor only four hours. By the way, Mrs. W., we've named her Elizabeth Joanne. Hope that's okay with you."

"I'm complimented and delighted! I wish I could see her. Give Ann a kiss for me, Peter. And the same for my new granddaughter."

"How's Charlene?"

"Doing fabulously, thank the Lord. In fact, the doctors think that by the end of the year she'll be fully recovered. They won't put a firm date on it, of course. But Dr. Abrams cautiously encourages me to think that perhaps we can move on by next January."

"Move on? You're coming home, aren't you?"

"I'm not sure, Peter. As I wrote Ann a while back, I might look for a better climate than New York."

Since Dr. Abrams had given her reason to think that Charlene might be well in a few months, Elizabeth had been pondering her future. She felt strongly that for Charlene's sake New York was not the best place to live. There was nothing for them any more in Washington or Boston. And Denver, pleasant as it was, was not her idea of a permanent home. Aside from the Jenkinses and Lance Milford, she had made no real friends, felt no ties to this pleasant but impersonal city. Most of all, she wanted to get away from the reminder of Charlene's illness and from the apartment in which she had said her final goodbye to Adam.

She bought a book on Arizona and toyed with the idea of moving to Phoenix or Tucson, but the photographs of the desert, for all its majesty, did not have allure for a New Englander who had grown up with a love for lush foliage and a sense of identity with the nearness of a great body of water. She knew where she wanted to go, of course. To California. She dreamed of the Pacific, imagined it as even more awesome than the East Coast ocean she knew. She loved the idea of sunshine and year-round flowers, of tropical, voluptuous blossoms and greenery. But California meant proximity to Adam. Not that Southern California wasn't big enough to lose oneself in. She might never run into Adam, particularly if she settled in some part of it far from Beverly Hills. But she was afraid, unsure of her own strength to resist the ease of making a local call to his office, uncertain that in some lonely moment she would not tell him that she was nearby, knowing with certainty that within minutes he would be at her side.

In December, somewhat to her own chagrin, she allowed herself to believe that fate had made the decision for her. Tony called to say that he was on his way to the Coast and would stop over in Denver for a day to see her and Charlene. Elizabeth was overjoyed to see him. It had been almost a year, and though he was unchanged in appearance, Elizabeth felt that he was even warmer and dearer. Time had eased the embarrassment of that one strange evening when Tony had declared his love for her. Now they embraced warmly and happily, delighted to be reunited.

"Why are you going to California?" Elizabeth asked. "To see your family?"

"That's secondary. Robert's opening a shop in Beverly Hills. I'm going out to supervise the remodeling of the store he's leased on Rodeo Drive. Need I tell you that it's in perfect condition but naturally Mr. Gale wants it gutted and everything done from scratch?"

They laughed. It was so typical. No matter how beautiful the place might be, Robert would consider it unfit for his occupancy unless he designed every inch of it.

"How will you handle it, staffwise? Will you and Robert become commuters?"

"Undoubtedly," Tony said. "You know that the Great Man will make all the contacts for decorating those Bel Air socialites' houses and doing the movie stars' little places in Palm Springs. But good old Tony will constantly keep running out to pick up the pieces. Of course, we'll need some-body permanently on the scene. In fact, Elizabeth, that's partly why I stopped off to see you. It was a great excuse to visit you and Charlene, but it's also official business. Ann told Laurel that you were quite definite about not coming back to New York. When Robert heard that, he decided that you should move to California and run the Los Angeles branch of Robert Gale Associates. How does the idea strike you?"

She hesitated. Tony misunderstood her hesitation.

"Before you say anything," he went on, "let me give you the full story. This wouldn't be just a little job running a West Coast show room. Robert wants you to be part of the business. He'd like to make you a limited partner, as he has me. Of course, you won't own quite a large share of the business, but you'll have holdings in the company and participate in the profits, over and above your salary. I think it's a great opportunity for the future, as well as solving a lot of im-mediate problems."

"A great opportunity! It's like a dream! To work with both of you again would be enough. To really own even a little piece of Robert Gale Associates is something I never even thought of. I'm overcome, Tony, but I don't quite un-derstand why Robert is offering me this."

Tony looked sober. "Robert will tell you that it's because he knows he'll get twice as much work out of you if you share in the profits. That's pure baloney. You wouldn't work a bit less hard if you were on straight salary, and we know it. The fact is, Elizabeth, that Robert is setting his house in order. There are very few people he cares about, but you are one of them. Next to me, I guess he loves you more than anybody else. He wants to make sure that if something hap-pens to him you'll be protected. It's his legacy to you, as well as his insurance that the business he loves so much will go on."

"I don't understand," she said. "Are you telling me that Robert's dying?"

"No. That is, there's no time limit. But he did have a minor heart attack a few months ago. Nothing too serious, but the doctor has told him it's a warning. He's only fifty-five, but he drives himself like he's twenty. The doctor has ordered him to slow down. If he has another attack it could be serious. He's frightened, Elizabeth, though you'd never know it. He doesn't want anybody—not even you—to know that he has a bad heart. But he knows he could go, just like that, any minute. He calls the doctor a quack to his face and says he should be drummed out of the A.M.A., but he knows that he might live twenty years or twenty minutes. That's why, in that sentimental way that he'd never let anybody see, he wants you to come back and be around if he's not."

Elizabeth was terribly distressed. "Is he taking it easier? Are you able to talk some sense into him about taking care of himself?"

Tony shook his head. "You know better than that. No chance. Look at this new move—opening an office three thousand miles from New York! Does that sound like a man who has any intention of changing his ways?"

"No," Elizabeth admitted, "it doesn't. I suppose, if anything, news like this would only make him drive harder. Robert would choose to die with a glass of champagne in one hand and a spoonful of caviar in the other. I don't know that I blame him. I wouldn't really want him to change."

"Nor I. Though he has changed without realizing it. Not in the ways we've been talking about. He's softer in private, more grateful for every minute I spend with him. He never mentions it, but I think he's spent a lot of time reevaluating his life. That's why he wants to do something special for you and me." Tony laughed indulgently. "He doesn't even raise hell about my seeing other people. So of course I don't. Perverse creature that I am, once I know I'm not expected to belong, I'm willing to belong. It's the way I feel about you, Elizabeth. You'd never try to own me, which is why I've always wanted to be owned. Whether you know it or not, you're stuck with me, even if you refused the offer. It probably was very smart of you."

Thinking of Adam, Elizabeth smiled wryly. The whole course of her life would have been changed if he'd not reappeared just before Tony's declaration of love. But the whole course of Robert's life would have changed, too. He'd have lost Tony, this gentle man who was now the only person other than herself who brought him loyalty and devotion. There is a master plan, Elizabeth told herself. It was meant for Tony to stay with Robert. Meant for her to lose Adam. Meant for this new life to begin.

"Who knows what's smart?" she said now. "It seemed the only wise thing to do at the time. For all of us. Now we know it was also the kind thing, don't we?"

The room was very quiet. Outside, winter pushed at the windows as it had in the little apartment on Gramercy Park the night they'd talked. Elizabeth recalled Tony's bitter words. Something like, "Robert will die and leave me a lot of money." She hoped he didn't remember that statement.

There was every chance now that it would come true. And if it did, would Tony "buy himself a Tony" as he'd cynically promised that night? She thought not.

"Well, what about it?" he asked. "I think you'd like California. You could have a house and a garden and a solid future, being a partner in the business. It would make Robert and me happy, Elizabeth. And give us a chance to see a lot of each other."

"Does Laurel know about this?"

"She doesn't know about Robert's health. Nobody does except you and the doctor. But I did tell her about the offer. She thinks it would be terrific for you. She said that maybe you'd even be able to find out something about Quigly, provided he's still in California. No word, I suppose?"

"No. None at all. He just seems to have vanished. I can only believe that that's the way he wants it, Tony. If so, I have to accept that. If he's alive and wants to see me, he knows he can always find me." She thought for a few more moments. The idea of being so near Adam was the only thing standing in the way of her acceptance of this generous offer. It was stupid to turn down a made-to-order future for fear of a chance meeting or an impulsive telephone call.

"I accept the proposition with pleasure and gratitude," she said. "I'll write to Robert tomorrow, and as soon as Charlene is discharged we'll head straight for California. Things *do* happen to me just when I need them. Even when you and Robert seem to be the ones who always make them happen!" Suddenly she was excited. She was going where she wanted to go. Sight unseen she knew she'd love California. And to go with a wonderful, secure future was more than she could have hoped for. God was good. She'd find a little house where Charlene could grow up like a normal, happy young girl. Ann was safe and serene. If only her lost child would reappear, her world would be complete. Except for Adam. There was no hope of that happiness. She would not keep her last promise to him, either: the promise to always let him know where she was. He must not know she was in California. He must not know, ever again, where to find her.

part VII

CALIFORNIA 1949-1972

Chapter 22

Perhaps because she was so strangely drawn to it, California seemed to Elizabeth everything she had hoped for and more. She did not see the gaudy houses painted in fluorescent "Spanish" colors, nor the shabby shops with their displays of ceramics and carved coconuts, nor the masses of outlandishly dressed people of all ages who had flocked to this promised land in which they hoped to spend their sunshine days or their sunset years. She saw neat little houses with carefully tended gardens, the elegant shopping area of Wilshire Boulevard with stores that rivaled the splendor of Fifth Avenue. She saw tanned, smiling people who looked unhurried and unharassed.

Leaving Denver had been an unexpected wrench. The Jenkinses gave a farewell party for Charlene, to which they also invited Lance Milford and his family. It was a happy, touching occasion, with exchanged promises to keep in touch. Miss Riddle and Dr. Abrams were on hand the day Elizabeth took her child from the hospital. The former hugged Charlene tightly and declared she'd never had a more lovable patient. And the latter pronounced himself more than satisfied with Charlene's recovery.

"She can live a perfectly normal life," he assured Elizabeth. Then he frowned. "Just don't let her pick up that big smoking habit you have. Wouldn't be a bad idea if you gave it up yourself, Mrs. Whitman."

She blushed guiltily. "I'll try," she promised, knowing that she wouldn't.

Tony had made reservations for them in an apartment hotel just off the Sunset Strip, a base from which Elizabeth would look for a small house. He made a special trip to escort them to Los Angeles, and as a surprise Laurel came along. The two women shed happy tears at their reunion. It had been almost exactly a year since they'd met, and though neither mentioned it, each found the other not a little changed in appearance. Always fashion-conscious, Laurel was now the height of elegance with her Balenciaga dresses and her John Fredericks hats. Her lips and nails were more fashionably deep red than ever, and she was one of the few women outside of New York who wore obvious eye makeup. By contrast, Elizabeth felt old and shabby. She had spent almost nothing on clothes in the past year, even less than she had in New York, which was little enough. The dark hair, which had begun to go gray a few years earlier, was now almost snow-white. She really had been unaware of her appearance until she was side by side with Laurel. Then she felt that in contrast with her thirty-seven-year-old friend she looked a hundred years older than her forty-four.

It was not true, of course. The white hair only added to the beauty of her still young, surprisingly unlined face. And though the clothes she wore were not highly styled, they could not disguise the figure that remained youthful and appealingly curved. She was truly handsome now, not in a matronly way, but in the manner of a woman to whom the years has brought added wisdom, intelligence, and an almost earthy kind of sexiness. There was a ripeness about her that the pencil-thin, ultrachic Laurel could not match, for all her expensive trappings.

But the changes in the two were only external. They still admired the very qualities that made them so different and brought them so close. Elizabeth did not have Laurel's quick wit, the slightly ribald humor, or the veneer of sophistication, all of which delighted her friend. And Laurel could never achieve the gentleness and simple acceptance of life that sustained Elizabeth. The disparities in their natures only enhanced their mutual affection, each wistfully trying to emulate, to some degree, the attributes of the other.

"My God!" Laurel said, looking around the Yates Court

apartment. "You didn't tell me you'd been living in a mole hole!"

"Come on," Elizabeth chided. "It's not all that bad. A little dark, maybe, but that's my best lighting lately."

"Like hell it is," Tony said. "You never looked better. As for Charlene, she's a different person. She told me she'd put on ten pounds. She's going to be a knockout in a couple of years, Elizabeth. You'll have your hands full with those Hollywood wolves!"

The idea of Charlene, whom she still thought of us as a baby, being pursued by young men with "evil intentions" made Elizabeth laugh. But it could be true. She'd be fourteen this summer. Her "little girl" was almost a young woman. Now that Tony had mentioned it, Elizabeth wondered why she had been so unaware. Charlene's delicate little figure already was beginning to fill out, with a soft swelling of the breasts and a hint of womanly roundness to the hips. She had seen her only as a small, sick child. A less involved observer already saw the makings of a beautiful adult, not only physically but spiritually.

The four of them spent an exhausting week house-hunting in the Los Angeles area. Used to the compactness of big cities, Elizabeth was fascinated and dismayed by the distances people routinely drove every day to work. She had assumed that she'd have to live in Beverly Hills, near the shop. Now she saw that she could choose from a staggering variety of locations if she was willing to drive fifteen or twenty miles, as hundreds of thousands of others did, from home to office and back again. She didn't relish the idea of that. She never had enjoyed driving, but in this part of the world it was a way of life, and even if she chose to live close to Rodeo Drive, she'd still need a car to travel to and from appointments. Might as well get used to it. It was strange that no one seemed to walk. She asked Tony about it.

"Out here, we consider it not only immoral but practically illegal," he said. "Don't decide to go for a nice walk in Beverly Hills after dinner. Before you know what happened the cops will appear and pick you up as a suspicious character. Literally."

She disliked the thought of navigating through the heavy traffic twice a day, but in a way she was relieved that she didn't have to live as well as work in the same area where Adam and Monica had a house. She knew that his office was in downtown Los Angeles, "a million miles away," so there'd be little chance of running into him during the day. After-hours and weekends were better spent in some section where there was no chance of an accidental encounter with the Barnsworths.

It was stupid to let her fears about running into Adam influence her choice of a house, but to some degree at least, it did. She was also swayed by the choice of the best neighborhood for Charlene, one where there were good schools and some feeling of stability. She was reaching back for the safety of her own childhood, she supposed. Remembering the small-town atmosphere of Cambridge, where she had grown up in an environment of "normality," she wanted Charlene to have a group of friends whom she saw regularly, to have a house where they were welcome, to participate in the safe, mundane activities of a quiet community.

With all these considerations in mind, she rejected the idea of a house "at the beach." Had she been alone, she would have chosen to live in Redondo or one of the other Pacific shore towns that dotted the coastline. But the atmosphere was too relaxed, too bohemian for an impressionable young girl. There were solid-looking houses, to be sure, but there were also beach cottages and local bars where the young surfers and sun-worshipers gathered. The ocean still beckoned to Elizabeth, but the resortlike, permissive ambiance of these freethinking settlements would not do.

Neither would the suburban (shades of the Richardses!) atmosphere of Westwood, nor the anonymous aura of the houses on the side streets farther downtown off Wilshire Boulevard. The Hollywood area and the hills behind it seemed too artificial. Bel Air was for millionaires and Beverly Hills was, as noted, clearly out of the question. After a week, Laurel and even Tony began to lose patience with her.

"For Pete's sake," Laurel said, "we've seen half a dozen places you could afford to buy. And all of them terrific, except that you always manage to find something wrong with each location! What's left?"

Tony agreed. "She's right, Elizabeth. What are you visualizing, a nice little house in Pasadena?"

"Why not?" Elizabeth asked. "We haven't looked there."

Laurel shrugged. "Why not indeed? Somewhere in this Tinker Toy town there must be a house she won't find fault with. I don't know any more about Pasadena than I do about the rest of this part of the world, except that I hear part of it's very social and the rest is for little old ladies in tennis shoes."

"It's pretty far from the office," Tony said hesitantly. "And you know how you hate to drive. That's some traffic to buck twice a day."

"I'm going to hate driving whether it's twenty blocks or twenty miles," Elizabeth said. "The main thing is that I find the right house at the right price in the right location."

"Dear God," Laurel sighed. "The woman is demented. I doubt she'll know it when she sees it, if she ever does."

"I'll know it," Elizabeth smiled. "I'll smell it."

It was, as Tony had promised, a long drive, and a frightening one even in those days when there were far fewer maniacal commuters on the Freeway. Halfway to Pasadena, Elizabeth began to lose courage. I'd never be able to do this morning and evening, she thought. I'd have a nervous breakdown. But when they approached Pasadena, she forgot all that. This was what she'd been looking for—tree-lined streets, fabulous old Victorian mansions benevolently over-looking small, well-cared-for houses with lovingly tended gardens. Children rode bicycles, women pushed shopping carts. They passed a high school which was just disgorging its students, and Elizabeth looked with pleasure at the casually dressed, seemingly healthy and vigorous youngsters who were piling into jalopies or strolling casually away from the handsome building. They drove around for a few minutes, inspecting the shopping centers, the small downtown section with its few shops and respectable-looking restaurants. Elizabeth de-lightedly spotted the Pasadena Playhouse and the Museum of Art. And she knew she was home.

Within two hours she had decided on a tiny house set well back from the street and surrounded by trees and shrubbery. There was a small, pachysandra-covered front lawn and a back garden which she would transform from neglected nothingness to an informal riot of fragrance and color. The house was small but adequate, with two bedrooms and a medium-sized living room which contained the one thing Elizabeth could not live without—a working fireplace. The house was about forty years old, unprepossessing but undeniably inviting. It needed paint and repairs. The old couple who had owned it had not made improvements in years, she guessed, but she brushed aside the agent's unnecessary reassurances that it needed only a little fixing up to make it beautiful. It would take time, work, and money, but she had enough of all three. She'd be happy here. And so would Charlene. There were neighbors near enough to be called in an emergency, or so she hoped. Her only worry was leaving Charlene all day and she crossed her fingers that whoever lived nearby would be friendly enough to be counted on if, God forbid, something happened while she was at work. She was glad that the nearest houses could be glimpsed through the trees on her property. She wanted privacy but not isolation for her daughter's sake.

"I'll take it," she told a surprised agent. Remembering her house-hunting in Washington, she smiled. "And you don't need to show me any others. I buy houses like I buy dresses. I know what's right when I see it, without even trying it on."

"Mrs. Whitman has an extraordinary sense of smell," Laurel explained gravely to the bewildered real estate man. "I suppose you've noticed it too?"

He clearly thought they were all crazy. "Noticed what?"

"The smell," Tony said. "It's unmistakable."

The agent sniffed. "Well, it's a little musty, maybe, but that'll go away in a couple of days as soon as the house is opened up."

Laurel laughed. "We're not very nice to tease you this way. Forgive us. It's an inside joke."

When he left them, Elizabeth looked fondly at her friends. "There *is* a smell, you know, at least in my head. It's like turning over new soil and putting down fresh roots."

Within forty-eight hours, with Tony's help, she had negotiated a bank loan, bought a sturdy, sedate Ford ("No smart little convertibles for me," she'd said over Laurel's protests. "The way I drive I'd feel safer in an armored tank!"), and made arrangements to have the house painted so that she and Charlene could move in within two weeks. When Laurel and Tony left, she went into an orgy of shopping for the necessities of life, from beds to patio furniture. With the exception of her mother's antiques, her books and pictures and a few staple things such as blankets and kitchen equipment, she told Laurel to get everything else out of storage and sell it. "Furniture that looks right in New York just doesn't work out here," she said. "This house is going to be bright and airy and mostly contemporary. I don't want to be shut in with heavy curtains and tons of fabric. I want to breathe fresh air and wallow in sunshine."

She felt heady with success and excitement. To her profound amazement, she even passed her California driving test on the first try, a good omen, since she hadn't driven a car since her Georgetown days. Charlene was enrolled in the very high school they'd passed and liked on sight, and it was only three blocks from the house. The neighbors on either side were cordial but not overpowering. Each of the pleasant young women who lived beside Elizabeth dropped in the first weekend she was in residence, offered to help if she needed them, and then mercifully disappeared. Neither of them worked and both had small children, another discovery that added to Elizabeth's peace of mind.

She never really got used to getting behind the wheel of "Fred the Fiend" as Charlene laughingly named the car. She was a terrible driver, but she nervously navigated the long trip to and from the Beverly Hills shop, suffering nothing worse than the curses of more confident drivers who dashed past her as she proceeded slowly and cautiously in the right-hand slow lane.

Getting the shop ready for opening took all her concentration and energy. In a strange city, it was difficult to know where to find the best workmen, how to go about hiring the two assistants she needed, even where to go for a snack at lunchtime. But somehow she managed. And by the time Robert arrived in March, people were beginning to talk about the chic new decorating service and its already famous owner.

It was the first time Elizabeth had seen him in well over a year. She searched his face for signs of illness and found none. Nor did he seem changed in any other way. He brushed aside her attempts to thank him for her partnership.

"Don't be a crashing bore about all that," Robert said. "It's purely selfish, my dear. If you have an interest in the business, you'll work even harder. Even that lazy Tony has perked up since he's become one of the principals. He's driving me mad. Always underfoot lately!"

Elizabeth loved him for the act he was putting on. She knew that Tony was now making him happy and she knew why. Robert was in many ways like a woman pretending that a lover simply couldn't leave her alone and delighted to let the world know it was so.

They worked like slaves getting ready for the cocktail party that would officially open Robert Gale Associates in Beverly Hills. Tony came out a week ahead to help with the final details while Robert pursued his endless stream of contacts among potential clients and the all-important press. Glancing over the list of guests to whom invitations would be sent, it gave Elizabeth a shock to see "Mr. and Mrs. Adam Barnsworth." She shouldn't have been surprised. Every rich homeowner in the area had been asked to the party from a list supplied by Robert's local press agent. But the idea that Adam might appear filled her with panic. Probably he would not. It didn't seem the kind of thing he would have any interest in. But Monica surely would come,

even without him. For a moment she hesitated, torn between curiosity to see Adam's wife and the certainty that the
prospect would make her so apprehensive that she'd be
absolutely useless before and during the party. Besides, there
was always the outside possibility that Monica would insist on
Adam's accompanying her. For the first time in her business
life Elizabeth did something dishonest. She quietly put a
pencil line through the two names and noted beside them,
"Out of town. Regretted." Robert didn't know them. There'd
be no questions asked. And if Monica wondered why she,
among all her friends, had been excluded, she would probably not mention this loss of face to Adam or anyone else.
If Elizabeth gauged her correctly, she would tell her cronies
that the Barnsworths "simply couldn't make it that evening."

It worried Elizabeth that all the upcoming publicity would
alert Adam to the fact that Robert Gale was opening a
shop in the area. But he'd have no reason to tie her into it.
For all he knew, she was still in Denver. She realized that the
fear of seeing him again was an obsession with her. She
thought of it sometimes as she drove to work. What if
Adam's car should pull up at the stop light next to her?
What if she bumped into him in a drugstore? What if, recognizing the name of the firm, he simply wandered into the
shop one day out of idle curiosity?

Well, what if he did? she asked herself defiantly. Did that
mean that he would expect—or even want—to see her
again? And did she have no strength of character at all?
Couldn't she send him away as she had before, back to his
wife and to the child who was now real? She didn't know
those answers. She only prayed that she'd never be faced
with the questions.

The opening went well. The shop was crowded, mostly
with expensively dressed women and a few unwilling and
bored husbands and lovers. Robert and Tony were charming, and Elizabeth, feeling confident in the new cocktail
dress that Robert had insisted upon treating her to at I.
Magnin, was caught up in the excitement of the party, the
glitter of chandeliers and diamonds, the smell of flower arrangements and French perfume. Her only bad moments
were spent fending off reporters and photographers. Robert
kept expansively mentioning his two partners, and Elizabeth gave her full attention to avoiding cameras and assuring interviewers that the only name they should mention was
Robert Gale's. She was relieved next day to see that apparently she had succeeded. Robert's picture and quotes

were the only ones used in the newspaper stories. Apparently the reporters accepted the fact that only one name in the company made news. Thank God there were enough socialites present for the press to concentrate on without having to fall back on Gale's associates for names to pad out their stories.

For a few seconds during the party, Elizabeth took Tony aside. "Is Robert all right, do you think? This is really strenuous. He's being pulled at from all directions."

"He's okay. I made him rest for a couple of hours this afternoon. Besides, you know this is really what he loves most."

Robert did seem to be enjoying it. He fancied himself a cross between Noel Coward and Clifton Webb, full of urbane charm and rapier wit. The ladies adored him, more so, it seemed, when he was insulting them than when he was paying them a rare compliment. Or perhaps they did not recognize the difference between the two. Hovering nearby as Robert talked to three prominent women—a film star, a famous director's wife, and the mistress of an oil magnate— Elizabeth shook her head in amazement as she overheard the conversation.

"Darlings," Robert was saying, "apparently I arrived just in the nick of time! Like the second coming of you know who! I'm here to rescue you from the sins of abysmal taste! I've seen your houses and they're pure disasters, my dears, pure disasters! Well, we'll soon take care of that, won't we? Beautiful, glamorous creatures like you should have backgrounds *worthy* of you. Poor angels, there's never been anyone around to help you before, has there? Never fear. Robert Gale and his associates will turn your vulgar dwellings into palaces fit for the queens that you are!"

As the evening wore on, Robert's happiness increased. He was in his element surrounded by famous names and uncountable wealth. Already he'd made six definite appointments for the next day. Elizabeth worried. He was pushing himself too hard. She told him so, cautiously, later that night when the last guest departed and the three of them had gone to the Beverly Hills Hotel for a late dinner.

"What are you trying to do?" she scolded him lightly. "Do you think you can redecorate all of Southern California in the next three days? For heaven's sake, leave some unexplored territory for me when you go back to New York."

"This is only the beginning," Robert said. "This branch is going to be terrific. Maybe better than New York or Palm Beach. They're all so marvelously nouveau riche and eager.

Like Texans. Maybe the next branch should be in Dallas, Tony. What do you think? They're absolutely sloshing around in oil wells down there, though God knows where one would stay if one had to spend time in Dallas. I'm sure there's no equivalent of the Beverly Hills Hotel." He looked around with satisfaction. "You're the lucky one, Elizabeth, living in all this magnificence while we struggle along in the squalor of New York."

She smiled. "You haven't been to Pasadena yet. It's not exactly the same. But I love California. I really do. I love it more every day."

"Good. Maybe you should move to Beverly Hills, though. Tony says it's to hell and gone where you live. The way this thing is starting out, you may be on call day and night. Be better if you lived nearer the clients, don't you think?"

"Sorry. No. And we'd better get one thing straight, Robert, dear. I just can't be on call twenty-four hours a day the way you are. I have Charlene, remember? Besides, I honestly couldn't stand those simpering women twenty-four hours a day, seven days a week. I'm delighted when I can retreat to my funny little house in dull old Pasadena. Speaking of which, are you ever coming to see it? You'll hate it, you great snob, but I would like you to come."

"Maybe next trip. By the way, where is Charlene this evening?"

"Sleeping over at a school chum's house. I figured it would be a late night and I wouldn't trust myself to drive home. So I took a room here, at your expense, of course."

Robert's eyes twinkled. "My God, the way you two take advantage of me!" Abruptly he sobered. "And you can, you know. Both of you. I enjoy it. You're the only two people in the world I really love. I'm grateful for your devotion, even if I don't often show it."

Neither Tony nor Elizabeth knew what to say. This unexpected public show of emotion and tenderness was so out of character for Robert that it took them off guard. It was he who rescued the situation. In a second, he was the old Robert.

"Well, if you two want to go have a good blubber, for God's sake go to your respective johns and do it! As for me, I'm starving. I'm going to have some of that indecently expensive Alaska king crab, a Caesar salad and the best bottle of bubbly in this crummy, provincial hotel."

The upbeat mood restored, they dined and talked late into the night. At 2 A.M., Tony walked Elizabeth to her room while Robert weaved cheerfully off to the enormous cottage on the hotel grounds that he shared with Tony.

"See you right after breakfast," he called as he made his way up the dimly lighted path. "I don't show my ugly face until after coffee, but you'd better be up and at 'em by nine, Elizabeth. Remember, there could always be another stock market crash. We have to get the girls while they still have more money than brains. God knows there are plenty of them out here with those soothing qualifications!"

On their way through the corridor, Elizabeth and Tony found themselves smiling indulgently.

"He's quite a guy," Tony said. "For all that brittle façade, he's as sentimental as a valentine. He really does love us, you know. And he knows we care for him."

"It was a marvelous night for him. For us all. Bless you, Tony, for being so good to me and to Robert." She kissed him lightly. "You're being wonderful to him."

"I'm not playing games, you know. It's not even pity any more. It's real affection. I'll be with him as long as he needs me."

"I know," Elizabeth said. "See you in the morning. Like the boss said, 'Up and at 'em by nine.' "

But she was not to start her day with Robert as they had planned. At eight o'clock the phone rang while she was having breakfast in her room. It was Tony calling to say that he had just gone into Robert's bedroom to waken him, but there was no Robert to awaken. After his triumphant evening, Robert Gale had gone to bed happy. And sometime during the night, without a sound, he had died peacefully in his sleep.

Chapter 23

In Los Angeles the day after Robert Gale's successful opening, the morning papers carried candid pictures of the smiling decorator greeting world-famous film stars. The evening papers carried a studio portrait of Robert Gale and the staggering news of his death from a heart attack in a cottage at the Beverly Hills Hotel.

Two men read the news with no small degree of personal interest, though neither had ever met Robert Gale. One was Adam Barnsworth. The other was Quigly Whitman.

They had, peculiarly, a number of things in common. Both lived with beautiful women in Beverly Hills. Both were surrounded by luxury. Both of them loved Elizabeth Quigly and neither had any idea, until they read the evening paper, that she was within thousands of miles of them. There was one other bond they shared: the question of whether to get in touch with her.

Heedless of the inevitable exposure she dreaded, Elizabeth had taken over the handling of the press when the announcement of Robert's death was made. She had no choice. Tony was prostrate with grief in the beginning, then involved in making arrangements for the return of Robert's body to Philadelphia to be buried in his family's cemetery plot. It was left to Elizabeth to answer the reporters' questions and to issue necessary statements concerning the fact that the business would continue under the direction of Anthony Alexander and herself, the surviving partners.

Throughout the nightmare of that day, as she tried to talk calmly to the newspapers, it did occur to her briefly that now Adam would know where she was. In the face of this shattering tragedy it seemed irrelevant. Struggling for composure, stunned by Robert's death and concerned for Tony's devastated reaction, she knew only that Robert would want his business to go on, and that it was crucial to assure the world that it would. She had no idea whether the statements she gave out were true. Tony, who held the controlling interest, might well wish to sell out or liquidate the whole thing. Perhaps without Robert he would feel unable to continue the business, or, even more likely, would have no wish to. But until there was time to think clearly the enterprise had to be protected, and Elizabeth was the spokesman for its future. Her personal life at this moment was secondary. One way or the other it would be drastically affected by the death of her friend. Hiding from Adam became a childish consideration, unworthy of her attention.

She had immediately telephoned Laurel, gratefully refusing her offer to fly out and help. She'd also called Ann, who responded without emotion about Robert's death but with some interest in how it would affect Elizabeth's future, a question to which Elizabeth could not provide an answer. Charlene was deeply affected by the event, and her concern for her mother and Tony was genuine and touching. Beyond these people, Elizabeth did not know whom to notify. To her knowledge, Robert had no family, but if there was anyone, Tony would see to that part of it, just as he would see to the burial. She had been rather surprised that Robert would lie in the family plot in Philadelphia. He seemed, in life, to have no interest in his hometown, and Elizabeth would have guessed that he would have wanted to spend eternity somewhere near the New York he loved. But Tony had had instructions from Robert about this eventuality.

"He told me several times that if anything happened, he wanted to be buried near his mother," Tony said. "It was part of that sentimental streak we saw last night, I suppose. Anyway, that's where I'll take him."

"Do you want me to go with you? I think I should. You'll need someone. It's too difficult to go through things like this alone."

Tony shook his head. "No, dear. There's no need. You know my feelings about death. Robert's still alive for me. Still a spark of energy that can't be destroyed. I'll miss him. But the funeral is nothing but rote. I've had my moment of shock and grief. From here on, I'll simply be carrying out the wishes of a friend, as quickly and quietly as possible."

He left on the train that night with Robert's body. There had been no talk of the future. It was not the moment for that.

It was not the moment either, Adam Barnsworth decided, to get in touch with Elizabeth. He had been startled to learn that she was living in Los Angeles, puzzled that she had not let him know, as she'd promised, where she was. He admitted to himself that his ego was hurt. He could not understand how she could be so near and not even call him. Logically, he understood it. Emotionally he found it difficult to accept. In a way, he supposed, it was his own fault. After all, had he not once told her that they couldn't live in the same city? That neither of them was cut out for quick, stolen, secret evenings? He regretted those cavalier statements. He longed to see her. But he would wait. She would be upset now. He realized that it was not the propitious time to seek a reconcilation.

It was a different story with Quigly Whitman. He, too, wanted to see Elizabeth, but he was nervous about facing her. There was the underhanded way he had handled the situation in San Diego. More than that, he knew how Elizabeth would feel if she found out how he'd been living for the past year. She probably would not love him less. But she would be disappointed and troubled that Quigly was being kept by a woman more than twice his age. It was not the kind of arrangement Elizabeth would understand.

It was strange how he had drifted into his present situation. He'd hightailed it out of San Diego, trying to put behind him the memory of Billie, justifying his own part in the episode by rationalizing that only an unstable girl would kill herself over anything as minor as a broken romance and an easily terminated pregnancy. For months he'd simply wandered up the coast of California, directionless and uncaring.

He'd lived by doing odd jobs. He'd been a filling-station attendant, a member of a construction crew and, finally, a carhop at a drive-in restaurant on Sunset Boulevard. That was where he'd met Theresa Isherwood. She'd driven in one day in her white Rolls-Royce and Quigly had taken her order for a cottage cheese salad and black coffee. They had boldly and quite openly taken stock of each other. Quigly saw a good-looking woman in expensive sports clothes. About thirty-five, he'd guessed, and definitely on the make. Terry had seen a handsome, sexy-looking kid whose hand did not accidentally touch hers as he handed over the salad and the steaming mug of coffee. Ready for anything, she thought. Probably out here trying to make it in films, like a hundred thousand others. She judged his age at about twenty-two. They were both wrong. Quigly was not yet twenty. And Theresa Isherwood's forty-second birthday was just around the corner.

She watched him moving easily to the other cars and knew that though he didn't look her way he was aware that her eyes were on the slightly too tight trousers and the carelessly half unbuttoned shirt. When he came back to collect the tray, she said simply, "What time do you get off work?"

As though he expected it, Quigly said, "Five o'clock."

She started the motor. "I'll pick you up."

Promptly at five she appeared and drove him to her house in Bel Air Estates. During the twenty-minute trip, neither spoke. When he saw the big house with its swimming pool and tennis court he didn't even comment. Inside, Terry finally broke the silence.

"Like a drink?"

"Sure. Scotch. Double."

"Good choice." Her voice was matter-of-fact. "Let's have it in my bedroom."

Theresa Isherwood had been prepared for a one-night stand. She'd had plenty of them, and when she saw a man who interested her she did not waste time with girlish amenities. A well-known Hollywood agent, she was twice divorced, highly successful. She lived alone, except for a discreet housekeeper, in a beautiful twelve-room house on some of the most expensive real estate in Southern California. She was also a nymphomaniac. Her two husbands had found that out a little too late. The first one quietly retreated from a hopelessly unfaithful wife. The second had caught her with the gardener in the very bed she now occupied with Quigly. He'd gotten rid of her, and soon thereafter she got rid of the gardener. She'd thought maybe it would be different with a Japanese. It wasn't.

Since then, she picked up whatever caught her eye. She supposed that it might be dangerous, bringing these stalwart strangers home. One of them might rob her or even kill her. But she didn't really expect that, and she didn't really care.

So far she'd been lucky. She was businesslike about it. It gave her a perverse pleasure to pay them, and most had been satisfactory studs who had gone away obediently, grateful for fifty unexpected dollars in their pockets. Only one or two had tried to prolong the relationship. With them she used the excuse that she was married and that her husband, though impotent, was insanely jealous. The mythical husband was always away on an overnight business trip, but the implication was that he would return the next day, revolver in hand.

None of this troubled her conscience, nor did it interfere with her work. She was one of the most highly sought after actor's agents, and her client list read like a history of the Academy Awards. Her personal life, though well known and gossiped about in Hollywood, was her own. As long as it did not diminish her productivity, it was nobody's goddamn business. She'd never marry again. She did not even want any kind of continuing arrangement. There were plenty of presentable men to take her to public events like previews and industry dinners. She did not sleep with them. She never mixed business with pleasure.

She was pleased that Quigly seemed to know exactly what he was there for and didn't try to make small talk or ask boring questions. For some reason, she did not mention his "fee." Drinks in hand, they undressed quickly and began to make love, still with no more than a dozen words exchanged. She was startled to find herself unusually excited. Quigly's lovemaking was surprisingly expert and just rough enough to suit her. It was apparently also passionately dispassionate. "Workmanlike" was the word that came into her head as the night proceeded. He seemed tireless. Between explosive bursts of sex, he went out and refilled their glasses, bringing them silently back into the bedroom. To her pleasure, he showed no lack of virility despite the vast amount of scotch he consumed.

They did not sleep at all that night, and at about eight o'clock Quigly got up, used her shower without permission, and began to get into his clothes. Terry watched him.

"Where the hell do you think you're going?"

"To work, lady. I'm due at the drive-in at ten. Any objections?"

She looked at him curiously. "You don't even know my name."

"That makes us even. You don't know mine either. So

what? We both got what we wanted, didn't we?" He smiled unpleasantly. "Or weren't you pleased with the performance?"

For the first time, Terry didn't want it to end. "You're cool," she said "Aren't you the slightest bit curious about me?"

"Should I be? You wanted to get laid. So did I. It wasn't half bad. Next time you get the urge, drop around for a hamburger. Maybe I'll still be there."

He had her now, and he knew it. She tried to keep up the pretense of indifference, but the act wasn't going very well.

"Look, Hercules," she said, "I think maybe we've got something here. What's your name?"

"Jack the Ripper."

"Very funny."

"Okay. Little Lord Fauntleroy, then. What's yours—Rebecca of Sunnybrook Farm?"

"It's Theresa Isherwood." She waited.

"Is that supposed to mean something to me?"

"If you're looking for a break in movies, it might. I'm an agent, and a damned good one."

"I'm impressed," Quigly said, "but not interested. I'm not looking for a break in the movies. Cary Grant's already got all the parts I'd be good in."

"Who are you?" Terry demanded. "And if you're not a would-be actor, what the hell are you?"

"I'm a poet, a dreamer, a nomad, and currently a carhop who's not adverse to bouncing around attractive older ladies."

"You're also a son of a bitch."

"Yeah, that too. Well, see you over the french fries."

He was a new experience to her. Somebody who wanted nothing from her. Not a chance to stay in her house or in her life. Not a job. Not, presumably, even money in return for his services. She couldn't believe it. Even that nasty crack about "older ladies" didn't anger her as it normally would have. She had never seen a young man so uncaring and, so indifferent, she guessed, to what happened to him.

"I like you," she said. "Probably because you have even less heart than I. I'd like you to stay around awhile. Believe me, I never say that to anybody. Will you stay? Can you? Or do you have a faithful little wife waiting at home?"

"I don't have a wife," Quigly said. "No family at all. And no plans. But what's 'awhile' in your language? A day? A week? A month? And what's in it for me besides three squares and access to your lily-white body?"

"Don't knock those last two advantages," she said. "As

for the duration, who knows? You can stay until I get tired of you. Or you of me. Or until we get bored with each other. One thing's sure. It beats hell out of hustling hash browns."

For the first time, he laughed. "You put it on the line pretty good, don't you? If I stay, what are my duties? Besides the ones I performed last night, I mean."

"Just be quiet and tough. Both seem to come easily to you. Oh, yes, and you might supply a name. It could get tiresome referring to you as 'Hey you.' "

Quigly thought for a moment. What did he have to lose? He was just about to tell them to take the carhop job and shove it. Theresa was old enough to be his mother, probably, but she was good in the hay. And there was this super house with a pool. She'd probably buy him clothes. Maybe even a car. She'd give him money, too. For some reason, he'd gotten to her. Who cared how long it lasted? It was better than being on the bum, working your ass off for a few dollars and sleeping in smelly boardinghouses. He turned on his charm, but not too much. She liked to be treated like a tart. He mustn't forget that. That, with his physical prowess, was probably what had done it.

"Well, Christ, why not?" he said finally. "If it gets too creepy, I'll blow out of here. My name's Alan. Alan Whitman."

It was a nice touch using his father's name. He'd inherited the old man's genes and his rottenness. Might as well appropriate his name as well. It was somehow fitting that he'd end up with a whore. God knows his father had had enough of them. Ann had told him about that.

Theresa smiled, a satisfied, catlike smile. "All right, lover. Enough yammering. You've made yourself a deal. Now come back to bed. I don't have an appointment until lunchtime."

That had been a year ago. To the surprise of both of them, Quigly was still established in the Bel Air mansion. He was well kept and only moderately bored. Terry was never seen with him in public. They did not go out in the evening, and if she had a "duty appearance" to make she went alone or told him to keep out of sight when her escort came to pick her up. His days were pretty much his own. He occupied some of them shopping for clothes from the generous allowance Terry gave him. Now and then he drove around aimlessly in the new convertible she'd brought home as a surprise after they'd been together for six months.

"Happy anniversary," she'd said sardonically. "We've

made it through six months. Hell, that's a record. Neither of my marriages lasted that long."

If she went to bed with other men, Quigly didn't know it. He rather doubted that she did. Their lovemaking should have been enough even for Terry. God knows it was more sex than he'd had in his whole life! She was insatiable. No wonder those husbands took off so fast. Strong and virile as he was, her demands left him so drained that most days he simply lay around the pool, gathering his strength for the night. There wasn't enough energy left to go looking for a young girl who might be free during the day. He probably wouldn't have done her much good if he'd found her.

From his vantage point of not quite twenty-one. Terry seemed ancient to him. By snooping through her personal possessions including her passport, he'd discovered that she was twice as old as him. Damned near Mother's age, he thought, and still going strong. He had never thought of women over forty as still being so interested in sex. For the first time, he came close to understanding Elizabeth's attachment for that Colonel Barnsworth back in Washington. It seemed laughable to think of them thrashing around in bed together, but when that was going on Elizabeth was almost Terry's age. At least, he thought, she had enough decency to pick somebody her own age, a bright guy, even if the bastard was married. Terry got her kicks from young bodies. It didn't matter whether they had minds. She wasn't interested in conversation. So far, though, Quigly didn't seem to bore her. That was surprising. He'd figured the set-up good for maybe a couple of months until she spotted his replacement. So far she hadn't, and meanwhile Quigly was amassing a sharp wardrobe and a fair amount of cash to take care of him for a while after he left Terry, however or whenever that might be.

Waiting for his benefactress to come home that spring evening, he'd picked up the paper and read about Robert Gale. His mother was quoted throughout the story and billed as one of the partners in the decorating business. I'll be goddamned. Quigly thought. All this time she's been working not more than five miles from where he lived. He wondered what had happened to Ann and Charlene, whether Elizabeth had remarried. It was impossible to tell. She was still using her business name of Quigly.

Like Adam, he debated whether to get in touch with her. He could imagine her look of disapproval when she found out about Terry. But why did she have to find out? He could pretend to have a good job. Maybe he could say he

was Miss Isherwood's secretary. No, Elizabeth would never believe that. How would an uneducated clown like Quigly
get to be anybody's secretary? Her chauffeur, then. That
was better. That would account for the expensive convertible, his free periods during the day, and his on-call obligations at night.

Suddenly he was excited about seeing Elizabeth and the
girls again. He'd make up some story to explain the San
Diego thing. He could always say that he'd gotten mixed up
with a bad bunch of guys and been picked up on an assault
and battery charge. He'd been innocent, of course, but too
ashamed of his behavior to face her. She'd buy that. He'd
remind her of how she'd cautioned him, way back in
Bethesda, against hurting innocent things. Even cats.

It probably was too late to call her at the shop tonight.
He'd do that tomorrow after Terry went to work.

At eleven-thirty the next morning, one of the girls in the
shop told Elizabeth that she was wanted on the phone.

"Not another reporter," Elizabeth pleaded. "I can't stand
it."

"No, Miss Quigly, he says he's your son."

Her heart began to race as she heard Quigly's voice. It
had been so long. She'd almost given up hope.

"Mother? How are you? I've been reading all the publicity. Too bad about Mr. Gale."

"Quigly! Where are you?"

"About a block away in a phone booth. I was afraid to
come in until I'd called to see whether you were still speaking to me."

"Speaking to you! Darling, I've done everything I could
think of to find you!"

"I'm glad. I mean I'm sorry I've caused you so much trouble. How are the girls?"

"They're fine now. Charlene's been very sick, but she's
all right again. Ann's living back East and— Quigly, why are
we going into all this on the phone? I want to see you and
hear all about what's happened. Can you come to the shop
right now?"

"I sure can. How about lunch, Mother?"

"Of course. I'll be waiting."

She couldn't believe that the grown-up, beautifully dressed
young man who appeared five minutes later was the rebellious boy who'd run away to join the Merchant Marine. He
was very like Alan. For a moment, the resemblance jolted
her. There was the same winning smile, the same good

looks, the same outward, easy assurance that made her own behavior seem gauche and clumsy. He greeted her with a quick little kiss, as though he had seen her yesterday.

"You look terrific," he said. "I like your hair. Funny, it makes you look younger."

She had a hundred questions, but she'd save them till they left the shop. All she said was, "I'm so happy to see you, Quigly."

She suggested a small coffee shop nearby where she frequently lunched, but he would not hear of it.

"None of that," he said. "I made a reservation at Perrino's. This is a celebration. Nothing but the best for our reunion."

"Quigly, that's one of the most expensive restaurants in town! Darling, we don't have to go there. It'll cost a fortune!"

"Now don't start bossing me around," he teased. "In a couple of months I'll be a full-grown man. Besides, it's a good place. I go there a lot."

It was a lie. He'd never been there in his life, but he'd heard Terry mention it often, knew it was a smart spot to lunch. He also knew that Terry was not lunching there that day.

He helped her courteously into the expensive car. She looked surprised.

"Like it?" he asked. "Unfortunately it isn't mine. Belongs to my boss. I'm working for a big-shot lady agent. I'm her chauffeur, but she likes to drive herself in the Rolls during the day. This car is for going to the market." He laughed. "Weird, right? Any other dame would use this one and save the Rolls for night, which is mostly when I drive her. But not Miss Isherwood. She thinks it's 'chic'—to use her favorite word—to trundle around the big horsepower herself during the day. Makes people remember her, she says."

Elizabeth did not understand but she was not unduly suspicious. Hollywood people were notoriously eccentric. She supposed that this Miss Isherwood needed to be even more outlandish than her clients.

"How long have you worked for her?"

"About a year. I have quarters over the garage in her place in Bel Air. She's kind of a nutty old dame, but she pays well. It's not a bad job."

"But you don't plan to be a chauffeur forever, do you?"

"Of course not."

"What *are* your plans, Quigly?"

He concentrated on maneuvering through the heavy traffic. "I'm not sure," he said. "Maybe I'll work part time and go back to school." He pulled up in front of the restaurant, where a parking attendant took the car. Elizabeth had been in Perrino's once or twice with Robert Gale. She knew the way through the ornate foyer to the dining room and she realized immediately that Quigly did not. He hadn't told the truth about coming here often. She was touched. He wanted so much to have her think that he was doing well, that he dined often in the most expensive places. Probably he was spending a week's pay on this lunch. He was trying very hard to play the man about town, and she'd do nothing to spoil the illusion. She stood back diffidently as Quigly spoke to the headwaiter.

"Reservation for Whitman," he said. "My usual table will be fine."

The captain looked puzzled, but experience and the five-dollar bill Quigly pressed into his hand produced a smooth, instantaneous reactions.

"Of course, Mr. Whitman. Nice to see you again. Right this way, please."

They ordered cocktails. A martini for Elizabeth and a double scotch for this suddenly grown-up son.

"Okay," Quigly said, "now bring me up to date."

She wanted to hear about him, where he'd been, what he'd been doing, why he hadn't sent a word to her. But perhaps he needed time to relax, to down his drink and have another before he tried to explain. Obediently, she told him about Ann's marriage and her two children, about Charlene's long struggle in Denver, about Laurel's great success as a career woman and her dearness as a friend. She filled him in on how she'd gotten to New York through Robert Gale and briefly mentioned Tony.

"So here I am," she said finally. "The house in Pasadena is really enchanting. I can't wait for you to see it. And of course Charlene will go out of her mind when she hears you're back! When can you come out? Tonight? We could have dinner."

Terry was planning to be home that night. "I'm sorry, Mother. Not tonight. I have to drive Miss Isherwood. But one evening soon, for sure. I never know when I'll be off duty."

There was a pause while they ordered luncheon. Again, Elizabeth was aware that Quigly was not used to fancy menus. She considerately chose Poulet Florentine from the bewildering list of French dishes. "I don't know why they have to be so fancy about chicken," she laughed. "Probably to justify the prices."

Quigly smiled with relief. "I'll have the same," he told the waiter.

"All right now, darling," Elizabeth said, "tell me about you."

"Not much to tell. The Merchant Marine was okay, but I was glad to get out. Sorry about that mess in San Diego, Mother." He told her the lie about getting mixed up with a bad bunch. "I was too ashamed to face you," he said. "I guess I've been ashamed ever since I ran away. I got your letters, some of them anyway, but I was all mixed up about everything. I didn't think I wanted any more family problems, after Dad and all that. I know it was lousy of me, but I had a kid's idea that I could start all over, away from everybody and everything. I always felt like the unwanted one in the family. Dad never could see anybody but Ann, and I even thought Charlene was the only one you cared about. That's nuts, of course, but that's how I felt. And to tell you the God's truth, Ann didn't help. She always acted like we were allies or something. But at the same time she was always telling me what a rotten deal Dad had gotten from you, and how we needn't have been so shoved around if you'd had a little more patience. She even got me all riled up about that Barnsworth guy. Said you cared a hell of a lot more about him than you did about either of us."

He continued to eat as he talked. His table manners were rough, additional evidence that the worldly act was nothing more than that. But Elizabeth scarcely noticed. She was much too caught up in what he was saying. It was affirmation of what she had long ago concluded—Quigly's rebellion, his feeling of being less loved, and, of course, his deep, frustrated yearning for her approval. Listening carefully, she felt that she had failed him miserably. But she supposed she had always known that. His analysis was disgracefully accurate. Probably it was the real reason why she had not stopped him from leaving home. She was more guilty about Quigly than he was about her.

"I'm not trying to pass the buck," he was saying now. "I mean, hell, I guess Ann really believed what she was saying. I didn't have to listen to her or believe her. But it seemed like everything that happened proved she was right. Like your taking her and not Charlene and me to Dad's funeral. And the way you moved Charlene in with Ann when Barnsworth came. I don't know. It was just a combination of everything, I guess. I was too young to get in the Army but I wanted to get away, so I lied my way into the Merchant Marine. You know, Mother, I always thought you'd stop me. I kept expecting them to hear from you and send me home."

There was sorrow in Elizabeth's eyes. "Do you wish I had, Quigly?"

He toyed with his chicken. "I don't know. Sometimes I wished you had. But it probably was good that you didn't. At least I grew up fast. I'd probably have been in a helluva lot more trouble hanging around you and the girls."

"I'm sorry, darling, that I let you down. I didn't know what to do—what was best for you. I've always loved you. I never meant to neglect you."

"That goes double," he said.

She blinked back the tears. "Well, it's over now, thank God. Oh, Quigly, I'm so glad you came back! Maybe we can be some kind of a family again."

"You asked me about my plans," he said. "What about yours? Now that Gale's dead, will you and this Tony Alexander run the business? Will you stay in California?"

"There's been no chance to discuss the business." She told him about Tony's return to the East with Robert's body. "When things are settled, I'll know where I stand. I suppose there's a will. And I imagine that Robert left everything to Tony."

"It was that way between 'em, huh?"

"They loved each other," Elizabeth said simply. "It wasn't sordid or ugly. Robert Gale was a marvelous person. He was kinder to me than you can imagine. And Tony is very special. You'll see when you meet him."

Quigly cocked an eyebrow. "Maybe. But I've met a lot of fruits in the last few years. Some of them went for me, but that's not my kind of thing."

For a moment, Elizabeth was angry. "Don't classify Tony with any peculiar creatures you may have met in your travels, Quigly! He's one of my dearest friends."

"I'm sorry. That was a rotten thing to say. If you like him, I'm sure he's a great guy."

She relented. "I know how it must sound, but Tony's out of the ordinary. It's too long a story for now. But you'll like him. Charlene adores him."

Quigly didn't answer. Charlene adored everybody, even the brother and sister who hadn't made the least effort to return her love. Charlene had adored Adam Barnsworth too.

"By the way," Quigly said, "whatever happened to the colonel? He make it through the war okay? Do you ever hear from him?"

"He made it. In fact, the last I heard he was living in

Beverly Hills, but we don't stay in touch any more. He's still married. In fact," the words came with difficulty, "he and his wife recently had a little girl. Their first."

"At *their* age?"

"Darling, women in their forties can still be attractive. That may sound incredible to you now, but someday you'll realize it."

"Yeah," Quigly said. "Maybe so. But most of them don't start having babies then."

"No, they don't. But that doesn't mean they can't."

Her words gave him a chill. Holy Jesus, what if he knocked up Terry one of these nights! He laughed at himself. Terry was too smart for that. And if some stupid accident did happen, she'd take care of it pronto. She wasn't a dumb kid like Billie.

He paid the check and drove Elizabeth back to the shop. She gave him her address and telephone number and asked for his.

"I don't mind giving it to you, Mother, but I'm pretty hard to find. In and out all the time, all hours of the day and night. I'm never sure when Miss Isherwood will need my services, and she doesn't like it much when I get personal calls. There's no phone where I sleep. I have to go over to the main house and sometimes it gets her kind of mad."

His explanation didn't quite ring true. "But I must know where you are," Elizabeth protested. "I promise I won't bother you if it will jeopardize your job, but I can't stand the idea of having you go off again without leaving me a clue as to where you are."

He couldn't figure out how to get out of that one. He scribbled the address and phone number on a slip of paper. "Okay, but don't call me there, please. I told you, the old girl gets annoyed. Look, I'll call you in a couple of days and come out to dinner. I want to see the house and Charlene. Probably won't recognize that pipsqueak. How old is she now, twelve?"

"Believe it or not, your little sister will celebrate her fourteenth birthday on the Fourth of July. She's in high school and terribly grown up."

"Son of a gun," Quigly said. *"This* I have to see."

"You'd better. And be quick about it. Thank you, sweetheart, for a lovely lunch. And thank you more for coming home."

She jumped out of the car and disappeared into the shop. He watched her speculatively, wondering whether he'd been convincing. Most of all, he hoped that he'd gotten across the idea that she was not to phone him "at work." Jesus, she'd probably ask for Quigly Whitman and announce that his mother was calling! That would take some explaining since Terry thought he was an orphan named Alan. It amused him to think that the picture he'd painted of Terry made her sound like a doddering old screwball. One thing was sure: those two must never meet. It was important to him that they both thought him honest and, in one way or another, admirable. He had no idea how much his mind was working like his father's.

Chapter 24

Three nights later, Theresa having announced that she would be out for the evening, Quigly arranged to have dinner with Elizabeth and Charlene in Pasadena. The three of them had a wonderful time. Quigly was loud in his praise of the little house and full of appreciation for what he declared to be the first decent meal he'd had since the Washington days. As for his admiration of Charlene, it was enough to set the child's head spinning.

"You've really turned out to be a raving beauty!" he said. "What happened to that funny little kid I remember? Next thing you know, I'll be sizing up some guy who wants to marry you! Believe me, he'd better be perfect or as the man of the family I won't give my okay!"

Charlene blushed with delight. Her adoration of this handsome big brother was overwhelming. Elizabeth felt almost the same. This was a different Quigly. More mature than his years and much more out-going than the boy who had left her. The publicity she'd feared had turned out to be all to the good. There had been no word from Adam as a result of her name appearing in the papers. Instead there was this bonus of Quigly's easy, laughing presence in their

415

lives, a plus that seemed to give the move to California extra dimension and meaning.

When he left, promising to call in a day or two, Elizabeth and Charlene hugged each other.

"Isn't he wonderful?" Charlene caroled. "I hope he comes over some weekday so I can show him off to the girls at school. They'll go crazy about him!"

Elizabeth smiled. "Yes, darling, he's wonderful. But he's nearly twenty-one. I don't think he'll appreciate other teen-agers the way he does his sister."

"I don't want him to. I just want *them* to know what a handsome brother I have." For a moment she looked troubled. "The only thing I can't figure out, Mommy, is why he stayed away so long. It was wrong of him to worry you the way he did."

"He had his reasons, dear. He was a confused, unhappy boy. He didn't mean to worry me. Anyway, that's ancient history, isn't it? Quigly's come home now. That's all that matters, isn't it?"

Charlene nodded. "I wish he *really* would come home. To live, I mean. Couldn't he stay with us instead of sleeping over a garage? We could make room for him. You and I could share a room like we did a long time ago."

"I don't think that's possible right now. He needs to be nearby when Miss Isherwood wants him to drive her some-where. Pasadena's too far away. Maybe something will work out later. He doesn't plan to keep this job forever. Meantime, it's lovely to know we can be together now and then."

"Wouldn't it be simply perfect if Ann and Peter moved to California with Ditto and Elizabeth?" Charlene's face glowed at the idea. "Then we'd *really* be a family."

"I wouldn't count on that," Elizabeth said. "But maybe they'll come to visit one day. Or we'll go back sometime and see them."

"We *are* going to stay in California, aren't we? I love it here."

"Yes, we're going to stay. I love it, too."

Elizabeth had already made up her mind about that. No matter what happened to Robert Gale Associates, she would stay in California. It was as though she'd finally found the place she belonged.

Tony telephoned from New York two days later to say that Robert had been buried in Philadelphia and that under the terms of the will the bulk of his estate had been left to Tony. "There was one thing I didn't know about," he told Elizabeth, "and I have mixed feelings about it. That is, I'm glad for you, but not so sure I'm happy for me. The will stipulates that Robert Gale Associates may not be sold for twenty years and that ownership is fifty-fifty between you and me. How do you like that? We're equal partners in a business we can't sell!"

The news took Elizabeth's breath away. Humanly, she was overcome by her good fortune. She knew that the business as it stood showed a clear profit of one hundred thousand dollars a year. It was possible that without Robert it might not do as well. On the other hand, with careful management, it might even grow. The idea of having an income of fifty thousand dollars made her giddy. But, as she'd feared, Tony didn't sound too happy about the prospect of carrying on. He hated all the socializing and contact-making that was a big part of the success of this kind of business. She was sure that he'd have preferred to sell the name and give her the equivalent of her share of the partnership, a share they'd all thought was only ten per cent, the original agreement when she came to California. She felt sorry for Tony, still held by a hand that directed his life even from the grave.

"Is that legal?" she asked. "Can one put such a restriction on what's done with a business? If you and I wanted to sell the company, couldn't that part of the will be overturned?"

"I don't know," Tony said, "but unless you want to sell, I don't even plan to see whether the request is binding. I look at it as an obligation to Robert. If he wanted Gale Associates to stay alive for twenty years more, then my vote is to try and make it happen. The clause was added right after you took the California job, by the way. Robert knew damned well that I couldn't manage alone. He was counting on you to keep the whole thing healthy. That's why he made you an equal partner—to assure his immortality for a while, at least." Tony laughed affectionately. "Smart bastard," he said. "He knew I wouldn't give a damn for any of this. I'd probably have sold the business for peanuts and accidentally gyped you as well as myself."

"We can make it go, Tony. Robert knew that. We'll have a long talk about it when you get here. Or do you want me to come to New York?"

"It would be wonderful if you could come here for a week or so. I have so damned much to do. I'm going to sell the house, of course. I'd really like to move to California, but I guess that won't be possible. You'll have to oversee that operation while I take care of New York, Washington, and Palm Beach." He sounded almost frightened. "My God,

Elizabeth, how am I going to handle it? You know I never was any good with the clients! Maybe we should reverse it. You come back and run the East and I'll take over out there."

"Tony, dear, we can't settle this on long distance. Now stop worrying. I'll be there in about ten days. The girls we hired here can hold down the fort while I'm away."

"What about Charlene?"

"I'll bring her. She can stay with Ann and meet her new niece. The timing is good. School's closed for Easter vacation and Charlene was just saying how much she'd like to see Ann and her family."

Relief allowed a trace of amusement to creep back into Tony's voice. "Great. But how much will Ann like to see her?"

"I'm tired of worrying about what suits Ann. This time she'll take her sister as a houseguest and no excuses accepted!"

"It won't be too convenient for you to stay in Scarsdale."

"No," Elizabeth said, "it won't. Will you make a hotel reservation for me?"

"Why don't you stay here? There's plenty of room and the house seems awfully empty these days."

Elizabeth hesitated. Then she decided she was being foolish. "That's perfect," she said. "I'll call you as soon as we have train reservations."

"You could fly."

"I know. But somehow I'd like to make *one* train trip that wasn't connected with disaster."

He understood. He remembered watching the train pull out as she and Charlene left for Denver. He didn't even know about the horror of the hasty trip to Memphis with Ann.

"Call me when you know the schedule. I'm glad you're coming, Elizabeth. I need you."

The next forty-eight hours were frantic. She called Ann and received a lukewarm acceptance of Charlene's impending visit. She wondered how to let Quigly know they were leaving for a couple of weeks. He'd been so specific about her not telephoning. Perhaps a note would be better. Hastily she wrote one, care of Theresa Isherwood at the address in Bel Air, but before she could mail it, her son called. He had been very good about checking in by phone nearly every day since his reappearance. Elizabeth hated herself for the suspicion that it might be more to prevent her calling him than any act of filial devotion. There was something wrong about that part of his story. His repeated overinsistence seemed unnecessary. It was hard to believe that even the most intolerant employer would be angered by an occasional call from her chauffeur's mother. For the moment she put that question aside. She'd discuss it with Quigly when she returned. For now, she was preoccupied with briefing her two employees, trying to anticipate any problems that might arise in her absence. They had two big jobs in the works, both agreements finalized after Robert's death, though it was he who had made the initial contacts. Things should proceed smoothly at this point. She had spoken to the clients, gotten approval on the general direction of the decor. The girls in the shop could carry on with the preliminary gathering of swatches and colors while she was away.

In the midst of one of these frantic days, the call she'd been half expecting finally came. It was not the shock it had been in New York. She was relieved to find herself reasonably calm as she picked up the receiver and heard Adam's voice.

"You didn't keep your promise," he said. "I had to read in the paper that you were here."

"I know. I'm sorry, Adam. It seemed better that way."

"How's Charley?"

"She's fine. Perfect, thank God. How's Catherine?" What an inane conversation, she thought. Like strangers asking after the health of each other's children. Adam sensed it, too.

"She's doing better than her parents," he said in reply to Elizabeth's polite question. "Fortunately, we found a good, young nanny. Monica and I must seem more like inept grandparents than parents." He paused. "I didn't call to make small talk about children. I want to know when I'm going to see you."

"I don't know. I think maybe never, Adam. I meant what I said in Denver. It won't work for us. I can't handle it. What's the point in starting again?"

"Things are different," he insisted. "I wasn't myself in Denver. I wasn't thinking straight. Now that Cathy's here, I love her but I realize that she hasn't changed anything for Monica and me. She never will, really. She came too late. Elizabeth, I want to be with you whenever and however I can. I don't believe that you don't want to be with me, too. We'll work it out somehow, darling. My God, let's not sacrifice whatever time we have left!"

In spite of everything, Elizabeth felt herself drawn to him, hypnotized by the urgency in his voice, excited by the prospect of seeing him. He could still do that to her. She supposed she still loved him. And she knew she was lonely for love. It would have been easy to say yes. It was impossible to say no. Yet some inner source of strength kept her from saying either. Instead, she hedged.

"I'm going to New York tomorrow for a couple of weeks," she said. "Let me think about it, Adam. I'll call you when I get back."

At least she had left the door open. He consoled himself with the fact that she hadn't totally rejected the possibility of seeing him. If she was wavering, there was always hope.

"Do you really mean it this time? Do you promise to call when you return? If you don't, I'll come looking for you."

"I'll call," she said.

"I'll be waiting. Have a good trip. And think right thoughts, darling."

She hung up without answering. Afterward, she realized that she had not told him about finding Quigly. She owed him that. He had done so much in the beginning to try to help her. No matter. She'd tell him about Quigly when she called to give him her decision about them. She wondered whether she had subconsciously forgotten to tell him about Quigly because it was an acceptable reason to call him again. Perhaps she needed justification for a move that she knew was wrong and foolish.

Tony was waiting for them at Grand Central early on Saturday morning and Laurel was with him. Standing in the middle of the crowded terminal they all hugged and kissed, ignoring the annoyed travelers who had to detour around them, almost being run down by Redcaps with trucks piled high with luggage. Ann had not come but she was expecting them for lunch. They'd drop Elizabeth's bags at Robert's townhouse—Tony's now—and drive directly to Scarsdale. The faithful Arthur was still behind the wheel of the Bentley. He was flustered but pleased when Elizabeth hugged him, too.

The drive to Scarsdale was beautiful. Elizabeth felt the excitement of the changing seasons. It was the one thing she missed about the East. California's sunshine, interspersed by only an occasional rainy spell, could grow monotonous. Even though one could drive a comparatively short distance from Pasadena to ski country, it was not the same as seeing the environment take on four quite different guises during the year. This one was the best—spring, with its soft air, its delicately emerging greenery, its stubtle flowers that contrasted strongly with the passionate explosion of hibiscus and poinsettias that grew even along the main traffic arteries of Los Angeles. In this part of the world things were more neatly contained. Manhattan kept its landscaping tightly controlled within the limits of Central Park. Its midtown streets were all sterile efficiency. Sensibly, New York left it to the suburbs to go wild with a profusion of spring scent and color edging the winding roads that led upstate.

Ann had gone to some effort to make the luncheon festive. Peter and his parents were also present when the New York group arrived. Ann came out to meet them, carrying a solemn six-month-old Elizabeth Joanne. Ditto, now two and a half, toddled forward to kiss his grandmother and lisp a carefully rehearsed greeting that came out sounding something like "Wekkom, Ganmomma." Elizabeth was delighted with them. The children were beautiful, and though the taste level of the Richardses' house still was beyond her comprehension, she did her best to sound approving when Ann asked for her opinion. She obviously was proud of her home, and content in it. She seemed genuinely delighted to see Charlene, promising that they'd have a very good time together in the next week. Even Tony and Laurel were cordially received. There had been a big change in Ann since her marriage. In some ways, her stuffiness had increased. Where was the girl who had coldly schemed to marry the first man she went to bed with? She had become self-righteous, almost priggish. Yet she had softened, too. Security had given her a feeling of superiority that enabled her to be pleasant even to Laurel and Tony, whom she had once professed to despise.

All in all, it went well. Mrs. Richards, Sr., made a great fuss over Charlene, and her husband seemed almost jolly, barely mentioning the fact that he "didn't mind sacrificing his Saturday golf game for such a happy reunion." To Elizabeth's relief, there was no talk of minority groups or racial prejudices. Had there been, she was afraid that Charlene might launch into an enthusiastic description of her friends the Jenkinses. It was a sure thing that Ann had never mentioned them to her in-laws. There was a good chance that she'd never even told Peter about the black family who'd been so kind to Elizabeth and Charlene.

After lunch—chicken salad heavy with mayonnaise and a chocolate cake which Ann had made, a combination that made the calorie-conscious Laurel go green with horror—Elizabeth drew her daughter aside for a private chat. She filled her in on what she knew of the business situation and then, her voice full of unconcealed delight, she said, "But

I've saved the best surprise for last. Quigly's back!" She told Ann all about Quigly's reappearance, how grown up and wonderful he looked, how he seemed to have mellowed. She made no reference to his comments about Ann's influence, simply passing over his early behavior, as she had with Charlene, with the offhand comment that he'd been a confused and unhappy boy.

"But that seems to be over now," Elizabeth said. "It's like a sad story with a happy ending. I don't know what his plans are, but right now he has a good job as a chauffeur for an important actor's agent. He seems to like it. At least it pays well and he has a great sense of responsibility about his work. I think that's the most important part of all. He's behaving like a man."

Ann looked shocked. "A chauffeur! Why, he's nothing more than a servant! He's like Arthur, being sent into the village to have his lunch!" She tapped her foot impatiently. "Of course, I don't know why I'm so surprised. I always knew Quigly would never amount to anything. I was the only one who wasn't the least surprised when he ran off and joined the Merchant Marine."

"No," Elizabeth said quietly, "I'm sure you weren't. But I do think you're overreacting about his job. There's nothing terrible about driving someone for a living. It's honest work and Quigly takes pride in it. Remember, Ann, he's had very little education. I hope he'll go back to school and eventually get into a career with a better future. But for now, I'm very proud of him. And if he shouldn't ever progress beyond this kind of work I'd still be proud of him. He didn't have it easy when he was growing up. I realize that now, more than ever. I'm grateful that he's turned out to be as poised and charming and conscientious as he has."

"Baloney! Quigly didn't have it any worse than the rest of us! He was always a mean, surly child. He never gave anything to anybody. All he ever knew how to do was get into trouble. He never had an ounce of ambition. He didn't give a thought to planning his life."

"The way you did," Elizabeth said.

"Yes, Mother, the way I did. After you left Daddy, I don't remember anybody covering *me* with love and affection. I had to plot my own course and I did. I know you tried, in your own way, to be a good mother to all of us. I realize that with working and running that terrible rooming house and all the rest you didn't have time to worry about whether any of us had it easy. But that didn't make me end up a cocktail waitress or a maid!"

Elizabeth was silent. It was all technically true, she supposed. All except the statement that she didn't worry about them all. She had always been concerned for their happiness. It was just that she had never been able to reach any of them, except Charlene.

Ann's anger had turned to distress now. Her voice was almost pleading. "Listen, Mother, promise you won't say a word about this to Peter or his family. And tell Charlene she mustn't mention it, either. I think they'd die if they knew the truth about Quigly. They still think he's living in Europe."

"Is it so important to you, Ann?"

She looked defiant. "Yes, it is. I know you think that's snobbish and horrible, but I can't help it if you do. The Richardses are very impressed right now that you're a full partner in Robert Gale Associates. That makes me important, too. But having a brother who's a domestic is not my idea of anything to brag about. Besides, they'd know I lied about why Quigly didn't come to my wedding."

"All right," Elizabeth said wearily, "I won't mention it, but I can't vouch for Charlene. The one thing I will not do is make her ashamed of her brother. She's very bright, Ann. There's no way I can think of to ask her not to talk about Quigly without telling her the reason behind it."

"Then I'll handle it myself."

That was the most appalling idea of all. "No, I don't want you to do that. All right, I'll find some way to speak to her about it before I leave. And don't you *dare* say to her any of the things you've said to me! I won't have that child subjected to a false set of values, not by you or anybody else. Do I have your word, Ann?"

"I suppose so. Yes. As long as *you* promise she won't mention Quigly. I want to be sure of that before you leave today, Mother."

Before she left with Laurel and Tony, Elizabeth invited Charlene to go for a walk around the garden.

"You're going to be all right here, love? I'll get back sometime during the week, but I'm not sure just when. Tony and I have an awful lot of things to do before you and I go back to California."

"I'll be fine," Charlene said. "It's fun to see Ann and Peter again, and I'll have such a good time playing with the babies. They're adorable. It makes me feel very grown up to be an aunt."

Elizabeth took the opening. "There's something else. Something I think you're grown up enough to understand.

You see, darling, lots of people have ideas that you and I don't agree with. But everyone has his reasons for his beliefs and we must accept the right of others to think as they do, even if we don't go along with that thinking. Ann, for instance, sees some things much differently than you and I. That's because she lives in a world where rules are more rigid and differences between people are much more important to them than they might be to us. When you're a grown-up, you recognize that people often take different views about the same subject. And while you might find their views distasteful, you learn to be tolerant of their right to hold them."

The puzzled look on Charlene's face told Elizabeth that she was taking a very convoluted way to get to the point. "What I'm saying, in my roundabout way, is that your sister thinks that Quigly should be in some profession other than the one he's in. She feels that while there's nothing wrong with being a chauffeur, she's afraid that people around here might not understand how a boy from a good family could take what some of them think of as a very insignificant job. I don't agree, of course. But I understand Ann's thinking and, most importantly, the segment of society she lives in that makes her think that way. So, she's asked us not to mention Quigly right now. She'd rather talk about him when he's back in school or doing some other kind of work. Do you understand, sweetheart? It's one of those silly ideas that go with living in a small, close-minded community. But if it makes Ann happy for neither of us to talk about Quigly, I guess we can do her that favor, can't we?"

Charlene wasn't quite sure of Elizabeth's full meaning, but she grasped the general idea. Ann was ashamed of having a chauffeur for a brother. It wasn't very nice, Charlene thought. She should love him whatever he did. But she supposed that's what her mother had meant about being grown up and tolerant. Maybe Ann had reasons that she didn't understand, but she had asked this favor and Charlene would grant it.

"All right," she said slowly. "If Ann doesn't want me to talk about Quigly I won't. I think she's wrong, though, Mommy."

"Between us, I do, too, darling. But it is her right to feel as she does. It's not our right to demand that she agree with us, and we don't love her any the less for it." Elizabeth took a deep breath. Might as well go the whole way. "It's the same thing about the Jenkinses, honey. Ann has never known black people as friends. She doesn't understand how wonderful they can be."

Charlene was quick. "So I shouldn't talk about the Jenkinses while I'm here either. Is that what you mean?"

"Yes, sweetheart. No use stirring up unhappiness. One of these days your sister will understand more about the world than she does now. But for the moment, let's just stay off both those subjects. It's not that Ann is unkind, dear. She simply has to go along with the way the people around her think. They're nice people, Charlene. They wouldn't harm anyone. But they put special value on things like the kind of work a man does, or the color of his skin. They wouldn't understand about Quigly or the Jenkinses. And we wouldn't want Ann upset, would we?"

"No. I love her. I think Ann's beautiful."

Elizabeth gave her a tender kiss. "And so are you, baby."

As she climbed into the Bentley, Elizabeth spoke to Ann in a low warning voice. "It's fixed," she said. "I talked to Charlene. She loves you. I think you'd better leave it that way."

The three friends dined quietly at home that evening. Elizabeth told them about Quigly, and their reactions matched her own. Laurel declared it a miracle and Tony expressed his eagerness to meet her son.

"Who knows? Maybe he can come into our business," Tony said.

Elizabeth shook her head. "I doubt that. Quigly doesn't seem cut out for the decorating world. He's much too male and lusty." She stopped, dismayed by her thoughtless put-down of men in their profession. Damn! What a stupid thing to say in front of Tony.

He seemed unruffled. In fact, his amused smile seemed to say only, "You know better than that." Laurel, uncomfortable, jumped into the breach.

"Speaking of business," she said, "what *are* your plans? Tony's told me the terms of Robert's will. Are you two going to carry on?"

Elizabeth and Tony looked at each other. "We haven't had much of a chance to talk about it," he said, "but I think we both respect Robert's wishes. I'm not sure how it's going to turn out. The name is well established, but it was Robert who really made it work. Elizabeth's talent will carry a big part of the load, and I've learned to be a pretty good detail man. I don't know what my partner thinks, but what worries me most is the contact area. I'm lousy at that. And

Elizabeth, for all her charm, has other obligations. Knowing the right people and spending most of your life with them is the name of the game. All the talent and efficiency in the world isn't going to save us if we don't attract new clients."

Elizabeth agreed. "The missing link now is the person who knows a lot of rich people. Somebody who's terribly chic. Hopefully somebody who can create publicity for the company. A person who's super-sophisticated, creative, and already known and accepted by the chi-chi world that never heard of Tony and me. It's going to be a killing problem to find someone with all those qualities."

"Is it?" Tony asked. "Maybe we're looking at her right now."

The almost offhand remark was electrifying. Elizabeth's expression was one of amazed delight.

"My God! Of course! Tony you're so right! I've just described Laurel! It's a brilliant idea! Oh, Laurel, please say you'll do it! Come into the business with us and handle the contacts. You know everybody and everybody knows you. It would be the coup of the century for Robert Gale Associates! We'd be such a wonderful working team, and there's a great future for all of us." She looked at Tony. "I'd be willing to give you a share in the business if Tony agrees. The way Robert originally included me."

Tony nodded. "We might even be able to do a little better. In any case, Laurel, you'd be part of something you had a real stake in. And Elizabeth's right. She did describe you without realizing it. There's something else, too. Something she left out. The person we'd want is also someone we admire and trust. You fit those requirements as well."

The unflappable Laurel was speechless. "Now hold on a minute, you two," she said when she finally recovered. "This is all going a little too fast. Fashion's my business, remember? Not decorating. And if I do say so immodestly, I'm pretty well set at *Enchantress*. Much as I love the idea of being a part owner of a business, I have to think about taking such a calculated risk. Suppose I can't deliver the clients? What if the three of us can't keep Robert Gale Associates on top? I hate to seem so mercenary and selfish, but I have to think about my own security. I'm thirty-seven years old, chums. In a couple of years it'll be too late for me to start over if this doesn't work out. I envy the kind of blind faith you two have always had, but I haven't got it. I keep seeing myself as a lonely little old lady begging for pennies on the street corner. Let's just say I'm chicken. Big risks always scare me. You know that, Elizabeth. Remember how terrified I was when *Enchantress* offered me the job? If you hadn't propped me up, I'd probably still be the fashion editor of *Wife and Mother*."

"But don't you see that that's exactly the kind of practicality that Tony and I need? In his funny way, Robert had the same qualities. He pushed himself out of fear of failure, I think, because he cared terribly, as you do, about financial security. Tony and I don't have that same kind of admirably sensible drive. And that's the ingredient that's needed."

"She's right," Tony said. "Robert was a talented interior designer, but he wasn't as good at it as Elizabeth is. His forte was charming people, shocking them, intriguing them with his outrageousness. He had a marvelously imperious quality that inspired confidence in clients. You have it too, Laurel. There's no need to worry about the details. Elizabeth and I will see that the job is done, once you get the jobs for us to do."

"I don't know," Laurel said. "It's all too sudden. Let me think about it for a day or two. And you two had better do some serious reconsidering as well. It's just as important for you not to make a mistake as it is for me. You're both swept away with what you think is a stroke of genius, but we'd better talk about it again in the cold light of day. Sometimes dear friends make rotten business associates, you know."

Elizabeth walked her to the door when she was ready to leave.

"I think maybe I know what's really on your mind," Elizabeth said. "You're afraid to be around Tony day after day, aren't you? You're still in love with him, aren't you?"

"I'm not sure. Maybe. We've struck a nice, impersonal balance in the last year and a half since you and Charlene left. We've seen each other outside the office from time to time, but there's been no repetition of that situation that threw me into a tailspin. I'm scared of falling back into the same trap. But the other things I said weren't lies. It is a risk that I'm not sure I'm prepared to take. I have a very comfortable life, Elizabeth. I don't do things by instinct, the way you do. I wish I could. But I'm not made that way. Anyway, we'll see. You and Tony talk it over seriously. And I'll think, too. We'll reach a decision in a couple of days."

Elizabeth went back into the living room, where Tony was slouched in a chair. He looked up at her.

"Well?"

"I think she'll do it, but she needs time to think. There's more involved than she said, you know."

"I guessed as much. It's me, isn't it?"

"Yes. She still isn't sure of her feelings for you, Tony. She's terrified of making a fool of herself again."

"I was afraid of that." He stood up. "Make you a night-cap?"

She nodded. While he poured the brandy, Elizabeth sat lost in thought. She could identify so easily with Laurel's fears. They were like her own about Adam, so drawn to him and so terribly aware that giving in again to her desires could only bring her more frustration and pain. Adam. She'd have to decide what to do about him, too. The relationship could be resumed in an instant, but to what purpose? In the scary way he had of reading her thoughts, Tony took the chair opposite hers and said, "Not to change the subject, but whatever happened to Adam Barnsworth?" She started.

"What on earth made you bring that up right now?"

"Seeing you sitting there looking so beautiful. Remembering that you told me there was only one man in the world you loved. Realizing for the thousandth time that there is only one woman I can ever love."

She ignored his disturbing statements. Instead, she told him about Adam and their last meeting in Denver. "He called me just before I left for this trip. He wants to see me again when I return."

Tony's face was expressionless. "And will you go back to him?"

In that split second, Elizabeth made up her mind. "No," she said slowly, "I won't."

There was a long pause. "What are you going to do with your life, Elizabeth?"

She tried to smile. "Keep it very busy," she said. "Work like hell to make us successful. Try to help Quigly find himself. Search for some kind of understanding with Ann. Enjoy my grandchildren. Watch Charlene grow up and hope she finds the kind of happy future she deserves."

"And for yourself?"

"Those things *are* for myself. But if you mean really, *really* for me, I have one secret ambition. I went to see one of our clients up on the Monterey peninsula just before I left. I fell in love with that part of the world. I'd like one day to buy some land and build the kind of house I've always wanted—overlooking the sea, spacious and beautiful and serene. When my children are safe and settled and we've fulfilled our promise to Robert, I'll retire there and read every book I've ever wanted to read, do all the gardening

I've longed to do. I'll be sixty-five years old in nineteen sixty-nine, Tony. Just the right age to disappear gracefully."

"Twenty years is a long time off, my dear."

"I know. I mean to buy some property and start building soon. I'll go there weekends and holidays when there's a house. Hopefully, if all goes well, that will be in the near future. But the day I long for is when I can go and stay forever. I can't do that now for many reasons. Money. Responsibilities. For that matter, I don't even have the need for it now. But I will one day." She stopped. "And what about you? What is your life plan?"

"Not as neatly mapped out as yours, I'm afraid. I've thought about it a lot in the last couple of years, but now I don't know. I'd thought that if something happened to Robert I'd just chuck everything. I really don't give a damn for possessions, you know. I thought about maybe going to India, to see whether I could get some insight into the knowledge that seems to be just beyond my grasp. I even thought of going back to California and trying to find peace in one of the monasteries there. This strange sense of having been given a gift has always persisted, and I've never known what to do with it. But things are different now. I'm bound to try to make Robert's business work for him. It's a debt I have to pay off. I don't want any more of the kind of life I lived with him. I've made it clear to all his friends that that episode is over." He paused. "I guess I've really faced the fact that all the things I said about loving everyone in the world were as unrealistic as you once told me they were. Only one thing hasn't changed for me, Elizabeth. And you must hear it again, even if you choose to ignore it. I love you. If I could choose the course of my life, I'd spend it with you."

The lump in her throat made words impossible.

"Don't say anything now," he pleaded. "We need time. Too much has happened too fast. Just know that for me you are the ultimate fulfillment. Go to bed, darling. Your old room is waiting for you. Sleep well."

She went silently to her room, unpacked, and climbed wearily into bed. But she slept fitfully, her rest disturbed by dreams so vivid that they kept awakening her. In one of them, she seemed to be in an enormous forest where she was marrying someone. The wedding guests wore strange costumes. There was a heavily veiled woman, like a nun, whom she recognized as Laurel. There was a nurse who seemed to be Charlene, and a man dressed in a devil's suit who kept screaming wildly that the ceremony must be stopped. She couldn't make out his face, but it was a voice she knew. The sound of it woke her. She lay in a cold sweat, trembling. It was a long time before she fell back into a troubled, uneasy sleep.

Chapter 25

By the time Elizabeth and Charlene boarded the Twentieth Century Limited a week later, many things had been resolved. For one, Laurel had agreed to join them for an excellent salary and a fifteen per cent share of the profits. She would make her headquarters in New York, and she and Tony would alternate trips to California, interspersed with Elizabeth's occasional visits to New York. Once she'd decided to make the big step, Laurel threw herself enthusiastically into the project. Even before Elizabeth left town, announcements of the new partner in Robert Gale Associates appeared in the daily papers and she'd been invited to appear on several daytime interview radio shows. Tony and Elizabeth were pleased by the rapid progress. The people Laurel had come to know through *Enchantress* were already beginning to call with discreet inquiries about the services her new firm offered. Laurel would become as famous as Robert Gale in the circle that changed its decor almost as regularly as it replaced its wardrobe.

Tony had put the townhouse on the market and found a small, bright flat on Beekman Place for himself. They decided to keep the Bentley and Arthur. Laurel would need them both to enhance the image of elegance that Robert had initiated, and both car and chauffeur were, in any case, part of the company's expenses. Robert's personal possessions, all bequeathed to Tony, were put into the resources of the business. As they were sold to clients, the money would be returned to him. He wanted nothing for himself except his books and records and one small Fabergé box which Robert had loved most among all the things he owned. He offered Elizabeth anything she wanted from the house before its contents were turned over to the business. She chose, oddly, an antique gold ring that had belonged to Robert. It was neither a man's ring nor a woman's, but could be worn by either. It was a simple ornament, unjeweled but delicately formed in the shape of two clasped hands. She had never seen Robert wear it, nor had Tony. It simply lay among the clutter of sapphire cuff links and diamond and platinum studs in Robert's jewelry case. She didn't know exactly why she wanted it. It was of no great value and she didn't even plan to wear it. She disliked jewelry of any kind. But the very simplicity of it seemed to demand attention. It caught her eye among all the dazzle of precious stones, and she kept coming back to it as she made her choice.

"Take something more important," Tony urged. "Robert would have wanted you to have a couple of his paintings or some of the furniture."

She refused with thanks. "Those things are part of another kind of life," she said. "You know they don't go with Pasadena."

Tony smiled at the idea of Robert's elegant metropolitan accessories in her simple little house. "Then take some things and save them for the house you're going to build."

"No, that house won't suit them either. I see it as open and spacious, with lots of rough-hewn beams and white-washed walls and acres of glass walls. All these beautiful old things would hate me for putting them in such a contemporary setting. I think Robert would rather see them in a Park Avenue triplex where they belong."

He acquiesced. "All right, but I've chosen something for Charlene." He handed Elizabeth a delicate miniature painting on ivory. It was a sunny landscape washed in tones of gold and soft green. "It's always reminded me of her," he said. "Gentle and warm and above any awareness of unpleasant things."

On the train, watching Charlene admire her gift for the dozenth time, Elizabeth thought lovingly of Tony. She was not in love with him. She had refused to give him an answer to his offer of marriage. They had discussed it only once again during that week, and Tony had not pressed. "I'll wait," he'd said. "However long it takes for you to make up your mind. At least you haven't said 'Never.' That's enough for now."

She thought, too, of Laurel. They had talked frankly, alone, just before Laurel had decided to come into business with them. The younger woman's reasoning had been almost brutally honest.

"I'm saying yes for several reasons, Elizabeth, and you might as well know them all. The one thing I'd never do is lie to you. You and Tony are offering me a damned good proposition and a chance to make more money than I ever could at *Enchantress*. I think I can do what you need done. I can play the phony game, kiss asses the way Robert did. It doesn't bother me. In fact, I'll enjoy the socializing and the publicity. But the main thing is that I've decided I really want Tony. I'm past all that wounded pride stuff of a few years ago. He's the only man I want to marry, and proximity isn't going to hurt my chances. He's through with the limp-wristed set, now that Robert's dead. I think he only played that game out of loyalty and some stupid sense of 'divine obligation.' He's free now. Handsome, white, and over twenty-one. Sure, he's five years younger than I am, but so what? I'm the right woman for him, Elizabeth. And by God before he knows what happened he's going to realize that, even if I have to seduce him in every hotel room between here and Palm Beach."

She took Elizabeth's worried silence for disapproval. "Do you think that's so awful? Do you hate me for being such a predatory, conniving bitch? I love him. And I can make him happy."

"Of course I don't hate you," Elizabeth said. "Why shouldn't you go after what you want, especially when it's something you believe is best for both of you? But don't set your heart on something that may not happen. I don't want to see you hurt again, and Tony is very much his own person, you know. His ideas about everything have always been quite definite. He's not easily swayed. For all that soft, sensitive exterior, he's used to having his own way."

"So am I," Laurel said.

The conversation disturbed Elizabeth. She would not be unhappy if Laurel succeeded in making Tony fall in love with her. I'm not a dog in the manger, she thought. Just because I can't marry him doesn't mean I wouldn't like to see him married and happy. Particularly to my best friend. But she knew Tony better than Laurel did. She knew he would never fall in love with Laurel and she suspected, after that earlier episode, that he would not even go to bed with her. As for Tony's feelings about herself, Elizabeth was almost embarrassed to realize that she did believe they would not change. What unutterable ego, she scolded herself! Laurel was only five years older than Tony but she was twelve years his senior! Even if she had been in love with him, the age difference would frighten her. Still, it did not frighten Tony. He'd said he'd wait for her to make up her mind to marry him. And he meant it. God help us all if Laurel ever found out whom he really loved, Elizabeth thought. But a considerate Tony would never tell her. And neither, of course, would Elizabeth.

She and Charlene changed to the Super-Chief in Chicago, and as the endless, boring countryside slid by, Elizabeth thought with regret of Adam. She couldn't explain the sudden decision that had made her tell Tony she would not go back to Adam. It had nothing to do with Tony. But sitting in that chair, the first night in New York, she suddenly knew that she could not return to the old, hidden life with Adam. The brief moments of forgetfulness were not worth the days of guilt nor the nights of loneliness. Perhaps she had finally matured to the point where love was not more enticing because it was forbidden. She wanted love and sex. She was still only forty-four years old. But she needed more. She needed unswerving devotion. Let the past sit for its portrait, she thought. She had to paint new pictures now. Bright, open ones—as sun-filled as the little ivory that Charlene cherished. Not dark, romantic studies like the ones in Robert's collection. She knew now why she had not taken any of the old, brooding things that Tony had generously offered. It was not that they did not fit into her house. They did not fit into her life.

A few days later she called Adam at his office and told him that she could not see him again. "We can't pick up where we left off," she said. "Just leave it alone, Adam. It was a wonderful part of our lives, but it's over."

She expected heated protestations but he was surprisingly docile. "My darling, if that's your decision I can do nothing but accept it. I only want one favor. I want to hear that from your own lips. I want to see your face when you say goodbye."

"No. It's pointless. I'm not going to change my mind."

"It's not pointless for me. It will help me erase the memory of the last time you sent me away. As long as I live I'll never forget the way you looked in Denver. At least let me see you once more, even if this really is the last time."

She didn't believe him. Worse, she didn't trust herself to be alone with him, not anywhere that he might touch her. But if her resolve was real, it could stand the test of seeing him. She couldn't hide from him forever. At any time he chose he could walk into the shop.

"All right," she said. "I'll have lunch with you tomorrow."

He picked her up at the shop and began to drive north through Beverly Hills. They had exchanged only a few words of greeting, not even a kiss on the cheek.

"Where are we going?" Elizabeth asked.

"What about the Bel Air Hotel? Ever been there?"

Elizabeth shook her head.

"It's pretty," Adam said. "And very quiet. I don't know why they keep the restaurant open for lunch. Nobody ever seems to be there. At least we can be undisturbed."

"And unrecognized," Elizabeth said.

He was right, it was pretty. And quiet. They crossed a charming little bridge over a man-made lake in which white swans swam in dignified pairs, and made their way up a winding, flower-lined walk to the restaurant. It was empty except for one mutually enchanted couple in a far corner of the big room.

"Honeymooners, no doubt," Adam said indicating the pair. "That's about all this hotel attracts. Except for rich recluses and, I suppose, occasional assignations. It's too far out of town for most people. And at night *nothing* happens here. Nothing in public, that is."

He ordered their drinks, not asking what she wanted. "Now," he said, "tell me what's been happening."

It was like her lunch with Quigly. Except that that was a beginning and this was a finale. Remembering Quigly gave her her clue.

"I suppose the most important thing, except for Charlene's recovery, is that Quigly has come back." Once again she recounted the story. At the beginning, Adam looked pleased, then amused to think that the same newspaper story had alerted them both to her presence in Los Angeles. But when she told him about Quigly's job as Theresa Isherwood's "chauffeur," Adam's face darkened.

"What's wrong?" Elizabeth asked. "Do you share Ann's view that being a chauffeur is so demeaning?"

"No. Of course not. But I do know Theresa Isherwood. At least I know about her. She needs a chauffeur like I need

real estate in Death Valley. What's Quigly *really* doing
there?"

"I don't know what you're getting at. I told you. Quigly's
been driving her for more than a year."

"I'll bet he has. Elizabeth, don't you know about Terry
Isherwood? She's the biggest nympho in town. Specializes
in young boys. Keeps them very well for a while and then
replaces them with some new body. She's also very big
on booze, and there's even talk of drugs, though I doubt
that. The two don't usually go together from what I hear.
I'll bet Quigly lives there, doesn't he? And five'll get you
ten that he's very seldom available at night."

Elizabeth felt sick.

"I don't believe any of it," she said.

"Sweetheart, you'd better. And you'd better get Quigly
out of there as fast as you can."

The sight of her stricken face made Adam curse himself.
Not for telling her. It was better that she find out and try
to do something about it before it was too late. But what
really made him want to kick himself was his timing. He
should have waited until the end of lunch to tell her about
Isherwood. Now her mind was only on Quigly. He had
damned little chance of refocusing her attention on their
problem. Unless, he thought, I can use this to convince her
of how much she needs a man to help her. He took her hand
gently.

"Don't look so frightened, love," he said gently. "I'm
sorry that I had to be the one to tell you, but it's better
that you know. My God, Elizabeth, you are such an innocent!" He felt her hand trembling as it lay loosely in his.
"Let me help you. I'll talk to Quigly. He never liked me
very much, I know, but maybe he'll listen to another man."

She looked up at him, her eyes wide and haunted.

"Darling, you need me," he said. "And I'm here. I'll always be here, Elizabeth."

For a moment she wanted to throw herself into his arms.
She had almost forgotten why they had come here. She
wanted to cling to him as she had in the past, to delude
herself with the belief in his love and faithfulness. And then
she remembered the thin surface of reality on which their
relationship had been built. She'd always been alone, she
thought. Always faced her problems by herself. Maybe not
handled them as well as she should, but gotten through
them somehow. She would not use Quigly's ugly situation as
an excuse to go back to Adam. Shoulders temporarily lent

were all she'd ever had to lean on. She wanted no more of them.

"I'm sorry, Adam. What I said on the phone still goes. It was wonderful, but it's over. You wanted to watch me say it. Now I have. I care for you. I always will. But I won't live through it all again. I don't want to exist on sentimental memories of the past and stolen scraps of happiness in the future. It's not good enough. Maybe, somehow, I haven't thought I really deserved any more than a piece of somebody's love. But I don't think that way any more. I'm willing to give, but I know that I have to be on the receiving end too. You said it once. I'm not cut out for 'Back Street' living."

He did not understand this "new" Elizabeth who had always been so eager to give, so undemanding and unselfish. Suddenly she was sounding like most of the women she knew, including Monica. He didn't realize that, with every ounce of strength, she was fighting for her life.

"There's someone else, isn't there?"

Adam would have to think that way. It would be the only explanation his ego could accept.

"Yes," she lied, "there's someone else. I'm going to marry him."

She waited for his reaction. Would he plead with her to change her mind? Would he offer to divorce Monica and marry her? He did neither. He didn't even ask her who the man was. Nor did he make a pretense of wishing her happiness. All he said was, "Would you like to order lunch?"

"I'm not really hungry, are you?"

"No. I'll drive you back."

They were silent all the way back to Rodeo Drive. At the curb he leaned across and opened the door for her. The feel of his body as it brushed her produced a quiver of excitement. She jumped quickly out of the car, closing the door behind her.

"Goodbye, Adam," she said through the open window.

He didn't answer. The car roared into gear and he was gone.

Though she felt she should, Elizabeth hesitated to confront her son with what she'd heard about the way he was living and the woman he was living with. For one thing, she was uncertain of what his reaction would be. He might be violently angry at her "snooping." She realized that even now she was a little afraid of him. His relaxed, nonhostile attitude might be just a cover-up for the still inwardly raging

Quigly of his boyhood. Since he was so secretive about his life, there was no question that he was ashamed of it. Even if he was not angry, he would be deeply disturbed by her knowledge.

Elizabeth was not shocked by the unorthodox arrangement, but she was terribly troubled. Much as she was repelled by any man—especially her own son—being kept by a woman, she was more worried about Adam's warnings of excessive drinking and perhaps even drugs. She had not seen Quigly take more than two or three drinks and he had handled them well. But so, in the beginning, had Alan. She waited for the right moment to talk to him, and it came in June, the evening after his twenty-first birthday. He was free that night and came to Pasadena to have dinner with her and Charlene. They made a little party of it, with a cake and twenty-one candles. Charlene had bought him a sport shirt which he seemed to love. Elizabeth's gift was a modest wristwatch, silver, with clean, modern lines. He seemed disconcerted as he opened her gift and it was then, for the first time, that she noticed a flash of gold under his shirt sleeve. Unthinkingly, she reached over and pulled up his cuff. On his left wrist was an obviously expensive, unmistakably new watch. At first, the significance of it didn't reach her.

"Oh, Quigly, what a bore!" she said. "I didn't realize you *had* a wristwatch! I don't remember ever seeing it before."

"As a matter of fact, I just got it. It was a birthday present from my boss. Nice of her, wasn't it? But it's too fancy for my taste. I like this one much better. Thanks so much. It's really great-looking."

The moment passed. It was not until Charlene had reluctantly gone to bed that Elizabeth brought up the subject again.

"That's a pretty expensive gift your boss gave you," she said casually. "She must think highly of you."

"Yeah, I guess so. I try to please."

"So I've heard. You and quite a few others before you." His eyes narrowed. "What does that mean?"

"Why have you lied to me, Quigly? You're not Miss Isherwood's chauffeur. She's keeping you, the way she's kept a lot of other boys."

He retreated behind the sullen expression she remembered.

"Darling, I know you didn't want me to find out, and I didn't suspect. The information came gratuitously. But that's not important. What matters is that it's no kind of life for you,

living with a woman like that. I hate what I hear about her.
And I'm afraid of what she's going to do to you. I'm not
being righteous about it, Quigly, but I am frightened. Where
can all this lead? You're only twenty-one. Surely you don't
expect to spend the rest of your life being taken care of by
Theresa Isherwood or women like her."

"Have you got a better idea?"

"Of course I have. Finish high school and go to college.
You can live here with Charlene and me, or we'll find a
bigger place. I'll gladly make a home for you."

"You did once before and I couldn't wait to get the hell
away from it."

"But you were a child then. A rebellious boy. You're a
man now. You must give some thought to your future.
There's no future in what you're doing!"

His voice was harsh. "Forget it, Mother. I'm sorry you
found out, but that's not going to make me move to Pasadena and start trying to get a high school diploma like some
old fathead or immigrant! No chance. You're right, I don't
know what the future is. Do you know what *yours* is? Does
anybody know what his is? Maybe Terry will throw me out
tomorrow. Maybe I'll get sore and walk out. How the hell do
I know? But I'm not equipped to do anything. So maybe
I'm goddamn lucky that these old nymphos find me so red-hot.
At least I can stash away a few bucks between hungry broads.
Maybe I can make a career of being passed from one to
another, the same way they trade butlers!"

His voice kept rising as he talked. It all made no sense.
Even if he could stomach this life, he must know that in a
few years he'd be replaced by a younger, less used lover.
Elizabeth tried once more.

"You're not thinking straight. You're only twenty-one.
That's not too old to go back to school, to begin planning
some kind of career. Quigly, you must get your life in some
kind of focus. There are so many years ahead of you.
Don't you want to marry one day? To support a wife and
children? Don't you care anything about making something
of yourself?"

"I'm doing all right," he said flatly. "I'm not going to start
breaking my butt for a lousy sheepskin. As for the wife and
kids and career stuff, I don't give a damn for any of that. Let
Ann have the vine-covered cottage and the runny-nosed
babies and the whole respectable scene. And let that husband of hers worry about life insurance and mortgages. Not
for me. There's no security anywhere. You know that. Look
at the man *you* married. Big job. Hot stuff. Snappy house in

Georgetown. And where did it get you *or* him? Where did it get any of us?"

It was like arguing with a drunk, except that Quigly was perfectly sober. Elizabeth fell quiet. She was wasting her breath. "I'm sorry for you," she said finally.

"Well, don't be. You've worked like a dog for the last fifteen years and I'll bet I've got more cash in the bank than you have."

"You know I wasn't talking about money, Quigly."

"What else counts, Mother? Haven't you found that out by now?"

It was pointless to go on with this conversation.

"Please think about what I've said," Elizabeth begged. "We can talk about it more next time you come."

"You mean I'm still welcome? In spite of my 'shameful existence'?"

"You're my son and I love you. There'd never be a house in which you weren't welcome."

His answer came with a wry smile. "Someday you may regret those words. Anyway, I'm glad you mean them now."

Chapter 26

The success of Robert Gale Associates was as rewarding as it was hard-won. In the beginning it was not easy to covince women that the much-publicized, flamboyant decorator was replaceable. He had become an institution, but without his presence some of his old East Coast customers felt uneasy, and the new branch in Beverly Hills was bad-mouthed by the established Los Angeles interior designers. It was fortunate for the business that Robert had already locked in a few assignments in the weeks preceding his death. Elizabeth and her small staff did a superb job of execution on these, and word quickly spread that despite the demise of the founder, Robert Gale Associates was still *the* name to drop if you had a house to be done or redone.

Elizabeth drove herself hard to get and keep clients. She sat through boring lunches with self-indulgent women, spent hours listening to their uninformed views of decorating, and was pleasantly surprised to find that they respected and even liked her. She retained the publicity agent whose job it was to get photographs of Gale-designed houses in the Sunday supplements and to drop names of the clients into the local newspaper gossip columns. Within a few months, the results began to show up in more work than they could handle. Fortunately, the status-conscious community was willing to wait. It became almost a mark of snobbism to be "on the list," waiting your turn to be decorated by Gale Associates.

Things were going equally well in the East, and by the beginning of 1950, Elizabeth, Tony, and Laurel knew that they had a business that would provide a more than comfortable life for them. The three partners exchanged visits frequently, but they were seldom together. Tony and Laurel came separately to the Coast, but Elizabeth made only one quick trip, in the fall, to New York. She had no desire to return to the East, not even to see Ann. And in any case the travel schedules of the other two were much more flexible. Elizabeth still had a young daughter to think about. At fifteen, Charlene could not be left alone in the house for long periods of time, and Quigly, of course, offered no help in this direction.

He did continue to visit regularly. His liaison with Theresa Isherwood showed no signs of change, though Quigly did. He had put on weight. The once sinewy body was already showing signs of bloat from too much drinking and too little outdoor activity. He and Elizabeth did not discuss his situation after that first evening. She tried once more to bring up the serious subject of his future, but he made it plain that if she wanted to keep seeing him, that topic was off limits, just as any contact with him at the Bel Air mansion was.

There had been no further word from Adam. She made herself believe that she was glad. She thought of him often, but with decreasing pain. It was as though he were part of some other sequence, dimly and wistfully half remembered.

In February of 1950, Ann had her third planned child, a boy whom she named Alan. Elizabeth wondered a little at the choice of name. Apparently Ann had succeeded in blocking out the last little piece of her past life and the unhappiness that went with it. Perhaps her only memories of her father were of the laughing, handsome man who had spoiled her so shamelessly. If so, it was just as well. Ann would try to paint a flattering picture of the grandfather they'd never seen for her own children. Just as Elizabeth had tried to hide the truth about Alan from Ann, Quigly, and Charlene. Only Laurel knew everything. Even Tony knew only some of the sordid story of Elizabeth's married life. It was ancient history. Even the woman who had lived it had managed to forget much of the horror.

From their separate visits, it was easy to see that the relationship between Tony and Laurel had not progressed the way the latter had planned it. It was an amiable working arrangement and a highly profitable one, but no more than that. On her latest trip to California, Laurel had seemed unusually depressed.

"Damn that Tony," she said, "I'm getting nowhere with him. I swear, he's the next thing to a priest! I think he's taken some private vow of celibacy. He's working hard, of course. But when he isn't, he's fooling around with some nutty Eastern religious junk. I don't know what he does at night. He says he reads and listens to music. I think he's contemplating his navel or praying to Buddha! It wouldn't surprise me if he showed up one day wearing a habit and a cowl. It's a far cry from his old life with Robert, in more ways than one."

"Don't press him," Elizabeth said. "Let it work itself out. It will anyway, you know."

"Terrific! While you're being fatalistic about my future I'm spending half my life at the beauty shop getting my gray roots touched up. On you, white hair looks sexy. On me it doesn't look like platinum blond!"

On Tony's next visit, without divulging her conversation with Laurel, Elizabeth casually brought up the subject of his "studies."

"I remember what you told me about wishing you could go to India or somewhere," she said. "Does the mystical life still intrigue you? I confess it does me. I've been doing a little reading on the subject, just out of curiosity. I don't understand much, but enough to see why anyone could be interested."

"You mean you don't think I'm an absolute nut?" Tony smiled. "Laurel does, you know. She gives me a fishy eye every time I tell her I'd rather dig into one of my musty old books than take her out to dinner."

"Well, you must admit that's not very flattering."

"I suppose not, but you know I don't feel anything but friendship for Laurel. I don't mean to hurt her. I just don't want to get involved with her outside of business. As for the religious stuff, it gives me great serenity. I know now that I don't have a real 'calling,' but there's so much I'd like to know. The little I have learned is a great antidote for the feeling of futility."

"What about the healing? Any more experience with that?"

"I haven't tried it for years. I believe that the power is somehow still there, but maybe age has made me cautious. The idea used to excite me. Now it scares me. Hopefully, that's a sign of some kind of maturity at long last. I've given up those godlike delusions. I'll be content just to come to terms with life. That's very important to me, because, you see, I don't think my life is going to be a very long one by normal standards. I'd like to know who I am before I become the spark of energy that will go through eternity as the real me. I'm thirty-three. I don't think I have more than, say, another seven years."

Elizabeth made an impatient gesture. "That's the most ridiculous nonsense I've ever heard. What would give you such a silly idea?"

"Nothing physical. I'm in good health. I've just always believed that I'd never live past forty. It doesn't bother me. But I'd like to know what this life is all about before I tackle the next one."

"Tony, you're talking absolute rubbish. My God, you can't predict the future! I thought you said something about 'signs of maturity.' You're talking like a melodramatic teenager!"

He teased her. "There you go again. Wrong reaction. You're supposed to be overcome with pity, not chastising me like a schoolboy. Why don't you ever do what I expect? When I tell you that I don't think I'll live more than another seven years, you should rush out and marry me right now, so we can have those few precious remaining days together."

She didn't know whether he was serious about any of it, but for the first time the reaffirmation of his devotion did not distress her. She left warmed by his persistent love. The talk of dying around the age of forty was nonsense, of course. The idea of living with Tony was not within the realm of possibility either, but it was good to know that he cared.

"We'll talk about it again when you're forty-five and out of danger," she said lightly.

"No, we'll talk about it sooner than that. Not today or tomorrow. But soon." Abruptly he changed the subject. "Now that the business is going so well, have you given any more thought to buying some property up the coast?"

"I *think* about it often, but I haven't *done* anything about it. You know me. I hate driving so much that I haven't even had the courage to do much looking."

"Why don't we go Sunday? Charlene can come along. We can easily do a hundred miles or so. It would be fun."

That was how she came to find the land she'd always wanted. It was about forty miles north of Los Angeles. Three acres of oceanfront property that looked as though no one had ever stepped foot on it before. On high ground, the view was breathtaking, the property thick with heavy, ancient trees and beyond them black rocks and the Pacific pounding at the strip of beach over which the land rose precipitously. There were only two or three houses within miles. "Her property," as she instantly thought of it, had nothing but nature for company. Yet for all its splendid isolation, it was only an hour's drive from Los Angeles. Charlene gave a sigh of admiration when she saw it.

"Oh, Mommy, it's beautiful!"

Elizabeth couldn't speak. It was just as she'd dreamed it. She looked at Tony, who nodded.

"Let's go find the agent," he said.

Before Tony went back to New York, the property was hers. It would be a while before she could begin to build on it. Just buying the land was, she supposed, a foolish extravagance at this point, but she didn't care. Someday she'd have her house here, just the way she visualized that too. Meanwhile, she could come and sit under a tree and lose herself in the welcoming embrace of the land. She could dream and plan. And now the fantasies had a real foundation.

The time flew. She was busy and reasonably content. She should have made a trip to New York, not only for business, but to see her third grandchild. She kept postponing it. She was ashamed of the fact that she really had no desire to spend time with Ann. She'd have liked to see the children, especially the new one, but the thought of all the Richardses and their stupid prejudices filled her with impatience and distaste. She had never really forgiven Ann for her lies about Quigly. Her daughter, she thought, finally facing the facts objectively, was selfish and petty. Not the kind of person she'd waste an instant on if there'd been no blood ties. By the world's standards, that was shocking. One was supposed to love one's parents and children blindly, even if they were unlovable. The truth was that she simply couldn't love Ann because she couldn't like her. None of this logic, however, kept her from feeling guilty about it. Instead, she invented excuses for not going to New York. The latest was a supper-dance she was planning for Charlene's sixteenth birthday on July 4, 1951.

It was Charlene's first "grown-up party" and it was a toss-up whether she or her mother was more excited about it. Elizabeth arranged to have the event at the only big hotel in Pasadena. There were twenty boys and girls invited, all of them Charlene's schoolmates. It was a "long dress evening" and Charlene had her first floor-length gown, a pale-blue mousseline de soie with short puffed sleeves and a skirt with dozens of yards of filmy fabric. It was far too expensive, but she had looked like a dream in it when she tried it on at the store. The hell with the price, Elizabeth thought. Three years ago I wasn't sure she'd ever live to be sixteen. Now she's well and beautiful and too good to be true. Why should I worry about a dress or party that would cost a couple of hundred dollars? The kids would have a marvelous time, having dinner in the hotel and dancing. Even Tony was coming out for the birthday. He would escort Elizabeth, though they'd simply greet the guests and leave before dinner. This was Charlene's night. Elizabeth had explained that to Quigly.

"I know that Charlene would love to have you at the party," she'd said, "but it's not for adults. Tony and I are not even staying. So I hope you don't mind, darling, that you're not invited. You will come over during the day, though, won't you? Charlene will want to see you. Maybe Tony will be here when you come. I can't believe that you two have never met."

At first he said that he understood about the party and promised that he'd try to come over during the day. Then he hedged. He couldn't be sure, of course. It was a holiday and he might be required to be with Terry.

"Can't you tell her it's your sister's sixteenth birthday?"

In an instant he became angry. He wasn't invited to the party, but that "swish" Tony Alexander was flying out for the evening and would be Elizabeth's escort. That should have been my job, Quigly thought. I should have been the one to escort my mother to the party. Not some fancy queer.

"Terry doesn't even know that I have a sister. Or a mother. She doesn't even know my right name. She thinks it's Alan."

The pain in Elizabeth's eyes pleased him. Serves her right, he thought, for not asking me to take her. The fact that she could never count on him didn't cross his mind. But he did realize that he was resentful of the mysterious Tony Alexander. Quigly would come to Pasadena on July 4 somehow, no matter how much Terry wanted to stay in bed all day. He had to get a look at this guy who was so important to Elizabeth. Goddamn phony, he thought. Making up to a woman almost old enough to be his mother. Quigly hoped that Elizabeth wasn't going to get involved with a jerk like that. She never did have any sense about men.

July 4 promised to be a scorcher. Elizabeth woke early, as she did even on holidays, and went into her little garden.

The neighborhood, like Charlene, was still sleeping. She brought out a cup of coffee and sat contentedly in her favorite wicker chair, anticipating the day and the evening. Tony had arrived at the Beverly Hills Hotel the night before and promised to be over by lunchtime. Quigly, too, had phoned yesterday and said he'd come by late in the afternoon. His tone had been completely different from the one he'd used when they'd last talked. It was all sweetness and light. He was looking forward to meeting Tony, and he'd come as late as possible because he wanted to see Charlene in her party dress. Meteoric, Elizabeth thought. Quigly was, in the phrase she remembered from her childhood, "as changeable as the weather." She hoped he would be cordial to Tony, not only because she wanted them to like each other, but also because on this day, of all days, nothing must be allowed to spoil Charlene's happiness.

The young girl joined her now, her expression full of excitement and her whole attitude vibrantly, joyously alive. Charlene was always wide awake from the moment she opened her eyes, as though every day were a brand-new adventure. She accepted Elizabeth's birthday wishes with a kiss and Elizabeth's birthday gift, a small string of cultured pearls, with appreciation worthy of a strand of priceless rubies. She put the pearls on immediately and turned around and around in the sunlight, watching the light reflecting on the luminous beads.

"They're fabulous, Mommy! You shouldn't have! You're doing so much—the party, the new dress, everything! But I love them!"

"I'm glad, baby. And they'll look even better with your evening gown than they do with those funny pajamas."

Charlene laughed, but before she could answer, the phone rang. "I'll get it," Charlene said. "Maybe it's Tony or Quigly."

Through the open window, Elizabeth could hear her voice, at first startled and then rising an octave in delight. She couldn't make out the words, but whoever was on the other end of the wire was obviously a surprise, and a pleasant one.

Charlene came back to the garden. "You'll never guess who that was!" She looked as though she'd just gotten another birthday present. "Jim Jenkins! Would you believe it? He's living in California and going to school at Cal Tech. He called to wish me a happy birthday and I invited him to the party tonight, Mommy. Was that all right? We can always squeeze one more in at the table, can't we? I'm so excited about seeing him! He says Clara is fine and the whole family sends love."

"Whoa," Elizabeth said. "Take it easy. You're going to make yourself sick with all this excitement!" She was stalling for time. She'd be delighted to see Jim. Even though the families had not kept in touch since she and Charlene had left Denver, Elizabeth had fond memories of them and their kindness. She'd particularly liked Jim, but how would Charlene's new friends react to him? Elizabeth had made a deliberate effort not to involve herself in the community, but she suspected that in its own way it was another Scarsdale, conservative, insular, and anything but liberal. What would the reaction be when Charlene introduced her black friend to her "normal" schoolmates? For that matter, what about the hotel? Elizabeth had never seen a black person in the dining room, except for those who quietly and unobtrusively served the meals. It was not herself or Charlene she worried about, it was Jim. If anyone was rude to him at the party or if, God forbid, the hotel refused to serve him, the evening would be an agony of embarrassment for him.

"I take it that Jim had no reservations about accepting your invitation," Elizabeth said.

"Of course not! Why would he? I don't think he knows anyone here, and I'm sure he was pleased to be asked to a party."

"Did you mention where the party was being held?"

"No. I thought it would be better if he came here and went over with us." Charlene began to look worried. "What's wrong? Didn't you want me to ask him? I thought you liked the Jenkinses."

"I do like them, darling. Very much. But, Charlene, how will your friends feel about Jim? Are there other Negroes in your group? I know it's hateful, but I hope we haven't created a situation that could make him uncomfortable. I'm not even sure about the policy of the hotel. They may not serve colored people."

Charlene was aghast. Such problems had never entered her head. To her, Jim was a beloved friend, and having him at her birthday party made the evening absolutely perfect. It was like that awful business with Ann when she went to visit. She couldn't believe that people in Pasadena felt as Ann's friends did. For a moment she wondered whether Elizabeth felt that way too. Tears came into her eyes, but involuntarily her spine stiffened. At that moment, she was very like her mother.

"If my friends don't like Jim, then they don't have to like

me," she said firmly. "As for the hotel, Mommy, if you think he can't go there, then I don't want to go either. I'd rather call off the party."

Elizabeth felt very proud. "That's the way I feel, too. But let's hope it won't come to that. Why don't I call the hotel and see what I can find out?"

What she found was a politely evasive assistant manager whose implication was unmistakable. When she explained that she wanted to increase the table to twenty-one, there was no problem. But when she deliberately added that the new guest was a young colored man, the assistant manager's voice suddenly took on a new, hesitant quality.

"Could you hold on just a moment, please, Mrs. Whitman? I'd better check our reservations for this evening. It's a holiday night, you know, and we're heavily booked." He paused for a few seconds, presumably to verify. When he came back on the line, he was full of apologies. "I don't know what to say to you," he lied, "but it turns out to be just what I feared. We can't accommodate one additional person at that table. There wouldn't be enough space for the waiters to get around. We're lucky that we could make room for as large a party as twenty. There's just no way we could stretch it to twenty-one. I'm terribly sorry. Perhaps if we'd known sooner . . ."

Elizabeth knew this was how it was going to be. "I see. Well, in that case, I'm going to make your life easier. Just cancel the whole reservation, please. Now you'll have room for twenty nice, white guests."

The assistant manager spluttered. "Now don't get the wrong idea, Mrs. Whitman. I wouldn't want you to think—"

She interrupted. "I don't have to think. I know." Without another word she put the receiver in place. Charlene stood quietly by, listening. Elizabeth did not have to explain. They were both bitterly disappointed, but Charlene was the first to recover. She nodded approvingly at her mother.

"I'll call everybody and tell them the party's off."

"Wait a minute," Elizabeth said. "Why should it be off? We'll just transfer the location and have it here."

"But there's no time! It's a holiday, Mommy. The stores are all closed. We couldn't even shop for food!"

Elizabeth smiled. "How would you like to have your party catered by the Beverly Hills Hotel? Look, sweetie, I'll call Tony and explain what happened. I'm sure that the manager at the hotel will whip up some kind of supper that Tony can bring over. Robert Gale Associates is a good customer. I'll bet you anything that we can produce the best party of the year right in this house—long dresses and all. You may have to settle for phonograph records instead of a real band, but otherwise we have all day to pull together the kind of birthday celebration that you deserve!"

"Do you really think so, Mother? That's even better than the hotel! I'll call everybody and tell them to come here." She paused. "What should I tell them about why we've changed?"

"How about the truth?" Elizabeth said. "That way they'll also know about Jim."

Charlene obediently went off to telephone her friends. Elizabeth wondered how many of them would come when they heard about the unexpected guest. Charlene might have some very sad surprises in store, but she was mature enough to handle them. It suddenly occurred to her that Charlene was very grown up indeed, the way she had stood up for Jim, the way she was willing to sacrifice her party for what she instinctively knew was right. Elizabeth recognized still another evidence of outgrown childishness: It was the first time Charlene had ever called her "Mother."

By the time Charlene returned from making her calls, Elizabeth had already gotten out all her china and silver and was setting up a long table under the living room windows as a buffet. The expression on her child's face told her the story.

"Well, I guess I know who my real friends are," she said. "Only eight people are coming." She seemed more sad than upset. "The other twelve said okay until I told them about Jim. Then they all had dumb excuses about why they couldn't make it." Charlene managed to smile. "Boy, there sure must be an epidemic of sudden colds in Pasadena!"

Elizabeth's heart ached for her. "Did any of them come right out and say they didn't want to mix with Negroes?"

"Nope. I think I'd have respected them more if they had." Her face clouded. "How can people *think* like that, Mother? They don't even know Jim! All they know is that he's not white!"

Elizabeth put her arms around her child. They hugged each other wordlessly. Thank you, Lord, for this one, Elizabeth said silently. She's going to have her head knocked off regularly, but damn it, she's going to be quite a woman.

"Okay, kitten, no time for moping. We have work to do. Let's see, now. Eight guests, plus you and Jim. And I suppose Tony and I'd better hang around since the party's at home. Makes it all look properly chaperoned, you know. That's twelve. And if Quigly stays, we'll be thirteen. Good thing we're not superstitious! Out of my way, young lady, I've got to get to that telephone. Tony doesn't know he's about to be a messenger boy transporting thirteen dinners to Pasadena. It's time I told him the good news."

There was no way of knowing that that hastily rearranged birthday party would set off a chain of events that would touch and alter the lives of many of the people there. On the surface, the gathering was an unqualified success. But beneath the laughter and merriment, unformed thoughts became eventual realities; predetermined opinions gelled into solid convictions; unthinkable possibilities ultimately turned into acceptable events. Some of these things happened the very night of the party. Others were years in the making. But all of them were touched off by passions that lit up the July night as dramatically as the skyrockets that were ignited after supper on the lawn of the little house in Pasadena.

The predetermined opinions were Quigly's. He was prepared to hate Tony on sight and he did. In his distorted view, the handsome thirty-four-year-old man whose devotion to Elizabeth was so quietly apparent was an unwelcome intruder. He loathed Tony's easy charm, his obvious familiarity with the layout of the house (Tony knew exactly where to look for extra glasses and where to go to fetch a light shawl when Elizabeth felt chilly later in the evening) and, most of all, Quigly was jealous of Charlene's adoration and Elizabeth's affectionate dependence on this stranger. Knowing Terry would raise hell because he was so late getting home, Quigly nonetheless stayed for most of the party. He had not intended to. He'd come about five-thirty, an hour before the guests were due, to see Charlene in her new dress. But Tony had already arrived, and the compulsion to watch the behavior of Elizabeth in his presence caused Quigly to change his plans and stay on. He didn't even call Terry to make up some story about his delay. He simply hung around, saying little, unnerving Elizabeth with his sullen presence.

"Quigly, dear," Elizabeth said at one point, "I'm so glad you decided to stay for the party, but you don't seem to be having much fun. What's wrong? I know these young people seem like babies to you, but you've hardly said a word all evening."

"I'm an interested spectator. So that's your wonderful Tony Alexander, is it? He's a phony. What do you see in him?"

Elizabeth gave a slightly exasperated sigh. This was not the time for a heart-to-heart talk about Tony. Besides, what was there to say? Quigly knew how good Tony had been to her and Charlene. If he was irritable about Tony's place in her life, innocent as it was, there still was no way—indeed, no need—to explain her affection for her business partner. She was sorry that Quigly had not taken to Tony, but she hadn't expected him to. She wished Quigly would go away. His sulky concentration on the man was spoiling the party for Elizabeth. Fortunately no one else seemed aware of it except Tony, who made one or two attempts to talk to Quigly and was rudely rebuffed. After these efforts, Tony simply raised his eyebrows at Elizabeth and did not go near her son again.

James Jenkins, who unknowingly had been the cause of the frantic last-minute change of plans, was the hit of the evening. At nineteen, he had the poise of twenty-nine. He was warm and charming, free of self-consciousness about his beautiful, light-chocolate skin, and amusing about the reactions of his classmates at Cal Tech. "I think it's come as kind of a shock to them to find themselves in the same classroom with a Negro," he said laughingly to the group of young people who clustered around him. "They keep waiting for me to pick up my banjo and go into a Little Black Sambo shuffle. I'm sure they expect me to bring a slice of watermelon to school for lunch." He was making a joke of it, but Elizabeth felt sorry for him. It couldn't be easy. Even if many people—like the youngsters who had come tonight—felt no prejudice, there must be many more in Jim's school who resented the presence of this "ignorant nigger" who had the presumption to think that he could become an aeronautical engineer. Thank the Lord, Elizabeth thought, for the minority who saw the inner person, not the outer skin. The kids who were here tonight were among those who rejected discrimination, either through their own thought processes or with the guidance of intelligent parents. In either case, they took to Jim wholeheartedly. The girls thought he was handsome and interesting. The boys accepted him as a "good guy." And Charlene, always happy, was positively radiant.

"That's a terrific youngster," Tony said quietly. "He's a beautiful person."

"Extraordinary," Elizabeth agreed. "So are his parents. I must write Addie Jenkins tomorrow and tell her how happy we are that Jim is in California and how wonderfully well he's doing."

Quigly left at ten, saying good night to no one except

Elizabeth and Charlene. The latter thanked him again for the well-chosen white handbag he'd brought her.

"I'm glad you like it," he said. "I picked it out myself. Do you approve, Mother?"

"Of course. It's in perfect taste, Quigly. And entirely suitable for Charlene. It's a lovely present, dear."

He smiled triumphantly. "Sometimes I surprise you, don't I?"

Elizabeth pretended not to read anything into the remark. She simply returned his smile and kissed him good night.

When Tony and the others left about midnight, Charlene dragged her mother into the kitchen. "Let's have a glass of milk and talk about the party?" she said excitedly. "Wasn't it absolutely the best ever? That food Tony brought was out of this world! And everybody seemed to be having such fun, didn't you think? Isn't it funny how it worked out? This morning I was so upset that we couldn't go to the hotel, and now I'm so glad we didn't!"

Elizabeth agreed. "Not," she said ruefully, "that I wouldn't welcome an army of waiters to clean up this mess."

"Oh, pooh! We can do that in half an hour!"

"Sure we can. I was just trying to be funny." She looked searchingly at Charlene. "The only thing I regret, honey, is that some of your friends didn't come because of Jim."

"I know. I'm sorry. But maybe it's just as well we found out how they feel. I mean, now that Jim's here I hope he'll be around a lot. At least we'll know who'll be glad to see him. The kids were crazy about him, Mother. I think he's the nicest boy I ever met. He said he was going to ask you if he could take me to a drive-in movie next weekend. You will let me go, won't you?"

Elizabeth was startled. She was not yet used to the idea that Charlene was old enough to have dates. But of course Charlene was. Particularly with someone as responsible as Jim Jenkins. And yet, much as she disliked herself for the thought, she knew that her child would be stared at, whispered about, if Elizabeth allowed her to go out with a Negro boy. A party was one thing. A twosome was another. Nonsense, she told herself sternly. Let people talk. Jim Jenkins was their friend. This wasn't Scarsdale and Elizabeth wasn't Ann.

"If Jim wants to take you to a movie, it's fine with me," Elizabeth said. "He's a very dependable, lovable boy."

And that, though she didn't know it, was the beginning of one of the unformed thoughts that became eventual realities.

Chapter 27

For the next two years, she watched helplessly as the romance between Charlene and Jim Jenkins slowly blossomed. In June of 1952 Charlene finished high school and Jim got his engineering degree from Cal Tech. He graduated in the top ten of his class and immediately got an offer of a job in the Santa Monica plant of Douglas Aircraft. On Charlene's eighteenth birthday, they came to her and said they wanted to be married.

Elizabeth panicked. She had known it would happen, but she kept thrusting the idea away from her. She'd been glad, almost hopeful, when for one six-month period Jim didn't come around and Charlene went out with other young men. But even a fool could see that she had no interest in anyone but Jim. Elizabeth sometimes imagined that Charlene only accepted these other invitations at Jim's insistence. In point of fact, this was precisely true. He knew that he loved Charlene and that she loved him, but he was painfully aware of the racial problem and as troubled by it as Charlene was undismayed.

"You must see other people," he had said to her a year after they'd started going together. "Charlene, we know how we feel about each other, but you don't understand how impossible it is. A white girl married to a colored man. You'd be hurt a hundred times a day! What would your family think? My God, they'd go out of their minds!"

"You're wrong," Charlene said firmly. "Mother loves you. And the most important thing to her is that I be happy." She didn't mention Ann's reaction. It would be predictable and volcanic, but that couldn't be helped. As for Quigly, they saw less and less of him lately. He still "worked" for Theresa Isherwood. Elizabeth had finally told Charlene the whole story, deciding that it would be better for her to hear it from her mother than from some chance outsider. Charlene had been upset at first, then understanding and even sorry for Quigly. She shared Elizabeth's worries for his future, but she also reluctantly accepted the fact that there was nothing they could do about it. He was twenty-four years old and looked thirty-five. He no longer bothered to disguise his alcoholism. When he came to see them, he brought his own bottle and consumed most of it during the visit. The look on Elizabeth's face as she watched her son grow steadily more incoherent saddened Charlene. She did not know that Elizabeth also saw a repetition of Alan and was only waiting for some ultimate, terrible disaster.

But Charlene said none of this to Jim as they discussed their future. She was well aware, as Jim was, that a marriage between them would distress Elizabeth. She could not fully foresee all the problems, but she knew there would be many. They didn't matter to her in comparison with her love for him. Finally, to soothe him, she'd reluctantly agreed to a pact. They would not see each other for six months. She would go out with other young men and he would take out other girls.

"But if at the end of that time we still feel the same," Charlene warned, "I'm not listening to any more arguments. We'll get married."

It was the best he could hope for. He could have gone away, but he wasn't sure that would solve anything. They loved each other and he knew in his heart that six months was not going to change the way Charlene felt, any more than it would give him time to get over her. He'd been in love with her since the first day he'd seen her, a pixielike little adolescent in the hospital bed next to his sister's. He hadn't known it then, of course. But he'd never forgotten her from that moment until the night of her sixteenth birthday. And in two years he had reluctantly faced the fact that she was the wife he wanted.

He knew that Elizabeth was aware and frightened by what was happening. She had a right to be. The world was not ready for mixed marriages. It set out to destroy the people who dared to make them. Angry at being thwarted, society struck back in endless ways, ostracizing the offenders and penalizing the offspring of the "guilty" pair. Even his own parents, he knew, would be devastated. They had their own kind of pride. And they loved him as much as Elizabeth loved Charlene.

The "trial separation" had been pointless. If anything, it only served to convince Charlene that in comparison to Jim other young men were crude and shallow. Jim didn't see anyone during that period. He spent long hours pacing the floor of his rented room, one moment grimly facing the impossibility of it all and the next allowing himself to hope that in spite of everything such a marriage could work. In the end, when Charlene called and said she'd kept her part of the bargain and it was a stupid idea, he'd raced to her.

Now, as the two of them sat facing Elizabeth, Jim identified once again with the fears that Charlene's mother felt. He could hardly bring himself to look at her. Charlene held his hand tightly, her little face sympathetic but determined.

"We know there'll be problems, Mother," she was saying, "but we're prepared for them. We're not trying to pretend that this is an ordinary marriage. *We* think it is, but we know the world won't agree. We just love each other, that's all."

That's all, Elizabeth echoed silently. Would that it were as simple as that. She was sure that Charlene could not conceive of the slights and insults that lay ahead. Even Jim, who had intimate knowledge of it, could only imagine, as Elizabeth could, the kind of pain that people would inflict. None of them would know the depths of human cruelty until they lived through it.

"I sympathize with you both so much," Elizabeth said. She groped for words. "I want your happiness more than anything on earth. But what you're suggesting would test the love of *any* two people. I don't know a finer young man than you, Jim. I'm so proud of you, of the things you've accomplished. I know you have a good job and can take care of Charlene. And I know how much you care for each other. But there are so many things to think about. Not just the two of you. What about children? Are you prepared for the way they'll be treated? Won't your heart break every time a child of yours comes home asking questions or crying from some ugly slur? What will you say to your children? What can I say to you?"

"Nothing I haven't said to myself—and to Charlene—a hundred times, Mrs. Whitman. I've thought about going away. She's very young. I suppose in time she'd get over this. I know that's what I *should* do, but God help me I can't make myself do it."

A scene like a flashback came into Elizabeth's mind. "I thought that if I didn't stay away you'd never marry anyone else," Adam had said. But his staying away hadn't mattered. She had only hungered for him more in his absence, as Charlene would hunger for Jim. In all probability the girl would recover. But she'd never love anyone the way she loved this boy. Elizabeth was certain of that. Does the world and its man-made conventions have the right to deprive her of such happiness? Elizabeth wondered. For that matter, do I? I can't protect her from the bad times. I can only stand by her while she endures them. She held out her hands to them. It was the hardest decision of her life, but she made it. "If this is what you both want, then, my dears, what can I say but God bless you?"

Charlene came running to her. "Oh, Mother, thank you! I'm so happy! I knew you wouldn't fail us! And we'll be fine. You'll see."

Jim stood back, saying nothing. He knew what it had cost Elizabeth to give that blessing. He realized the value she put on love. It was an obligation he took very seriously. He and his mother-in-law-to-be looked at each other with solemn understanding. I'll do everything I can to shield her, his eyes said. Hers answered him calmly, with a trace of sadness, I know you will.

In the weeks that followed, not only did Elizabeth agonize over the reluctant approval she'd given to Charlene and Jim's marriage, but her doubts were reinforced by nearly everyone close to her.

It was no surprise that Ann was horrified beyond description. Her disgust did not disturb Elizabeth nearly as much as the disapproval of some other people whom she had not expected to react with such violent distaste. Laurel, for one, was as upset as Ann, though for quite different reasons. Laurel was concerned for Charlene, while Ann thought only of "what people would say" if, God forbid, they found out that her sister was married to a Negro. On the phone, Laurel sounded nearly hysterical.

"Are you crazy? You can't let Charlene do this! Elizabeth, for God's sake, use your head! I'm sure he's a perfectly nice, bright boy and maybe they are in love, but even *you* can't believe that this kind of a marriage can work! She's going to be terribly, terribly hurt. Not only during the marriage but even more so when it breaks up. She might even have a baby before it does! It's inconceivable that you're letting this happen, the way you love Charlene! She's a baby. She doesn't know what she's doing!"

"She knows she's in love," Elizabeth said weakly. "They've had two years to be sure of that."

"Oh, swell! Two years between the ages of sixteen and eighteen and Charlene thinks its a lifetime commitment. Elizabeth, I don't understand you."

"Nor I you. Of everyone I know, Laurel, I thought you would be the most tolerant. You have lots of friends who aren't white. It never seemed to matter to you."

"The operative word is 'friends,' not 'husband,'" Laurel snapped. "I'm crazy about Duke Ellington but I haven't tried to marry him. *Nor* am I eighteen years old!"

When Elizabeth broke the news to Quigly, he acted as though it didn't penetrate. For a minute, Elizabeth thought his mind was so sodden with liquor that he couldn't absorb what she was saying. She repeated it.

"Quigly, dear, did you hear me? I said that Charlene is going to marry Jim Jenkins."

They were alone in Elizabeth's living room. Quigly looked at her over the rim of his glass.

"I heard you, Mother."

"Well?"

His expression didn't change. "I'm going to kill that black son of a bitch."

Her whole body went cold. "Quigly, don't even say such a monstrous thing! That's not funny."

"It's not supposed to be. Somebody has to do something. Since it doesn't look like you're going to stop Charlene from marrying this nigger, I guess it's up to me. And I suppose the only way to do that is to kill the bastard. Maybe they'll catch me and put me in the electric chair. I don't care. My sister is not going to marry some black buck. I'll burn before I'll let that happen."

He did not even raise his voice as he spoke. It was as though he were going to step on a cockroach. It seemed no more important than that. No more emotional.

Her stomach churning, Elizabeth tried to speak calmly. "Darling, if you love your sister you'll try to understand and be happy for her. We all know it's a dangerous, maybe foolhardy, thing she's doing. You're not the first to criticize me for allowing it. But I have to allow her to live her life,

Quigly. Just as I must let you live yours and Ann hers. I understand how you feel, all of you. God knows I wish she hadn't fallen in love with Jim. But she has. Nothing will change that. Not even killing Jim. All that would accomplish would be to break Charlene's heart and mine. I think that's the last thing you want to do, isn't it?"

Somehow her words reached him. For the first time, he allowed his anguish to show.

"You've got to stop her," he said. "You're the only one who can." His voice was louder now. "For Christ's sake, Mother, promise me you'll stop her!"

"All right, dear," Elizabeth said soothingly, "I promise I'll try again. I'll tell her how worried you are and how concerned. But no more wild talk of violence, Quigly. That will solve nothing. *You've* got to promise *me* that. If you did something terrible to Jim, I'd lose all of you. Keep reminding yourself of that, son. If you care for me, spare me that agony. It would be unendurable."

It was the only way to reach him. Hopefully, the desire for her love was stronger than his protective instinct for his sister. It was a long chance, and not one to be counted on, but it was the only one she had. For the moment, at least, it seemed to be working.

"You promise you'll stop her?" His voice was suspicious.

"I promise I'll try. And what about your promise to me?"

His eyes focused vaguely on her troubled face. "I didn't think what killing the bastard would do to you. I don't care about him or myself. And Charlene would get over it. But you'd care if they killed *me* for doing it, wouldn't you? You'd really care."

"Yes, darling, I'd really care. I couldn't live if that happened to you."

His whole mood changed. It was as though he'd forgotten why he'd threatened murder. He seemed suddenly happy.

"You do love me, don't you?"

"With all my heart."

He nodded and smiled, apparently satisfied. "I think I'd better lie down for a while before I drive home," he said. "Maybe had a drink or two too many."

He stretched out in Elizabeth's room and she covered him with a light quilt. In seconds he was sound asleep. She stood for a long while looking down at him, asking God for help. She was convinced that her son was verging on madness. He had his father's urge for self-destruction and his father's need for approval. She didn't believe he'd really kill Jim Jenkins. It was much more possible—and equally horrible—to believe that Quigly would eventually kill himself.

The news of Charlene's engagement was not happily received by Addie and Fred Jenkins, either. A few days after Jim called them in Denver, Elizabeth received a letter from Addie. Like the one she had gotten so long ago from Sue-Ann Temple, this one was full of errors in grammar, spelling, and punctuation, but its content was touchingly sincere. Elizabeth read it with sadness.

Dear Elizabeth,
James called to tell us that he wants to marry your Charlene and you have agreed that he can. Fred and I are verry upset. Not because we dont love her she is a wonderful child but we know that this is bad for both of them Elizabeth. We are verry proud of our son and want him to be successfull and happy which is what we know you want for Charlene. They dont relize that the world wont let them be that way if they get marryed. People will brake their hearts Elizabeth and ours too. We love you and Charlene almost as much as we love James. That is why we are beging you to stop it if you can. Clara is the only one who is happy because she is young and cant beleve how the world really is but we know dont we? Please do this for Fred and I. But mostly do it for our children. I know you feel just like we do.

Sincerely your friend
Addie Jenkins

She managed to get Jim alone and show him the letter from his mother.

"I know," he said sadly. "They're terribly upset, and they're right. I'm doing a terrible thing to Charlene, Mrs. Whitman. I realize it more every day. It's like I live every minute on guard. What restaurants can I take her to where we won't be turned away? What will happen when we run into someone either of us knows? Why do you think we always go to drive-in movies instead of regular theaters? Good Lord, I feel like a leper! And if it's this bad now, what will it be like later? Where will we live? Who will our friends be? How many times a day will she be snubbed and sneered at? I've asked myself a thousand times if I can put her through this. I'm used to it. But it will be new and horrifying to Charlene. She doesn't realize it yet. I've been careful about avoiding dangerous situations, but once we're married I won't be able to stand between her and embarrassment twenty-four hours a day. I don't know what to do, Mrs. Whitman. I don't know whether I have the guts to watch her suffer. I don't know whether I have the right to drag her into this kind of a life. And yet, so help me, I don't know how I can leave her."

Charlene, who'd been in her room dressing, spoke from the doorway.

"I've had just about enough of everybody worrying about my life." Elizabeth looked up, surprised. She'd never heard her daughter sound so hostile.

"I heard most of what you said, Jim, and I'm serving notice on all of you right now that I am not made out of spun sugar. Everybody's hysterical that I'm going to be destroyed by other people. It seems like the whole world thinks I should be hermetically sealed, as though I have no strength and no ability to give as good as I get. Well, you're all wrong. I'm willing to fight for the right to be happy. I don't give a damn whether it's the world's idea of a suitable marriage, it's mine. And I swear that the next person who goes around wringing his hands and worrying that poor little Charlene will be wounded is going to get a good punch right in the mouth!"

It was such an un-Charlenelike speech that her mother and her fiancé were stunned into silence. Their faces made the girl break into a grin.

"You two look as though I'd suddenly turned into Frankenstein's monster! Does it come as such a terrible surprise that I do have a little backbone? Come on, Mother. I'm one of your three headstrong children. Ann and Quigly have done what *they* wanted with their lives. What makes *me* so different?"

"Your brother and sister haven't defied the world the way you're about to do," Jim said. "From what I hear of Ann, her only sin is being a little insular. As for Quigly, the little I know about him, I'd guess that the worst accusation you could make is that he's not particularly ambitious. You can't really compare this step with their paths, can you?"

Elizabeth interrupted. "What you say is more or less true, Jim. But Charlene's right, too. Her way is going to be overtly harder, but I believe that the gains will be greater. She's not fooling herself about what she'll suffer. The difference is that she's sensibly but cheerfully willing to sacrifice. I wish I could say the same for most people. Including myself."

Charlene smiled at her gratefully. "Nothing worth having comes easily, right?"

"I'm not sure about that," Elizabeth teased. "You didn't give me much trouble eighteen years ago."

The conversation did not magically dispel their apprehensions, but it did, somehow, make them all feel better. It was all out in the open, and as far as could be anticipated they were prepared to expect the worst from friends, family, and strangers. They were strengthened by the knowledge they stood together, with Charlene the strongest of them all. Let the mischief-makers and the spokesmen for "morality" do their worst, Elizabeth thought. These kids are going to make it. In a crazy way, they would start off better prepared than most young couples. They were braced for trouble, not lost in unrealistic, storybook expectations of married life.

She wrote what she hoped was a reassuring letter to Addie and Fred Jenkins, trying to explain the awareness of the children and herself, along with their unshakable determination. There was no direct reply, but Jim told her later that the letter had made his parents feel a little more reconciled though they continued to disapprove. Almost daily, Elizabeth got a letter from Ann, letters that worked themselves up to an increasingly feverish pitch and finally culminated in one which Ann declared that not only would none of the Richardses come to the wedding but that she never wished to see her sister again. "I have not told Peter or his parents any of this," Ann wrote. "When this insane marriage has taken place, I will simply let them know that Charlene has married an aeronautical engineer. Period. God knows how I'll keep them from eventually finding out the truth, but you can be quite sure that I'll try!"

Elizabeth tore up the letter, more in sadness than in rage. Ann's whole life was built on lies. Lies about her background, her mother and father, her brother, and now her sister. She even lied to herself, Elizabeth thought, about the kind of person she was. Except by now Ann undoubtedly believed in the fictitious creature who was Mrs. Peter Richards, Jr.

After her first outburst, Laurel subsided into defeated acceptance of the matter. She wrote a warm note of good wishes to Charlene and sent her a lacy negligee as an engagement present. Elizabeth and Charlene giggled over the gift. It was even more impractical than some of the ornate silver Ann had received.

"Can't you just see me in this at six-thirty in the morning, trailing around the kitchen of our apartment, fixing Jim his breakfast?" Charlene asked.

"Maybe you can wear it on your wedding trip, at least," Elizabeth said. The pair had decided to drive down to Mexico for a few days after the ceremony, which was now planned for mid-November. When they returned, they would live in a little apartment in Manhattan Beach, one of the oceanfront communities Elizabeth had looked at before settling on Pasadena. The apartment was not too far from Jim's work. Best of all, it was a live-and-let-live settlement where a great many of the inhabitants were young and freethinking.

Quigly had lapsed into an almost indifferent attitude. There were no more ugly threats. When Elizabeth told him that Charlene wanted him to give her away at the wedding, he agreed with sullen nonchalance. "If that's what she wants, okay."

Elizabeth was pleasantly amazed. Charlene and Jim knew nothing of Quigly's violent reaction when he first heard the news, but Elizabeth had been almost certain that restraint was the most she could hope for from him. Whether this dispassionate acquiescence was the result of her pleading or simply additional evidence of his increasing withdrawal from reality, Elizabeth could not be sure. Practically, she was concerned only that he behave well at the ceremony and that, above all, he be sober. Charlene knew that Quigly was drinking heavily, but she had no idea of the extent of his deterioration nor of the danger he presented. She was delighted but not surprised when she learned that he would act as father of the bride. Jim had asked Tony to be best man. And Clara Jenkins would serve as Charlene's maid of honor.

It was to be the simplest of ceremonies. They'd be married at the Los Angeles courthouse and return to Pasadena for champagne and wedding cake. They were taking no chances on some minister refusing to marry them. In any case, neither was a formally religious person. Elizabeth hadn't gone to church in years, nor had her children. Only the Jenkinses regularly attended Baptist services in Denver, but even they were wise enough to know that the quieter and more impersonal this wedding, the better. They would come, of course. As would Laurel. Aside from "family" there would be no guests. Jim and Charlene had a few friends, mostly the handful who had been at the sixteenth birthday party, but they decided against inviting even those sympathetic outsiders. Somehow, Elizabeth found this the saddest part of all. It was as though they knew they would have to exist only for each other and were preparing themselves for it even on the first day of their married life.

Through it all, Tony was a tower of strength. His joy for

Charlene was beautiful to watch, and the admiration he'd expressed for Jim the first day they met seemed to increase as the two sensitive men grew to know each other better.

As the wedding day drew closer, Tony's calming influence was the only thing that kept Elizabeth from shaking to pieces with nervousness. Her main concern was Quigly. Was it possible that he really was going to behave? Or would the sight of Charlene giving her hand to this Negro boy set off that ungovernable anger again? And how would he react when he actually met Addie, Fred, and Clara Jenkins? For that matter, even the presence of Tony could be enough to transform him from the robotlike figure of the past few weeks into an unreasonable monster. She thought seriously of how she could change the plans, keep Quigly away from the wedding. But there was no way. The commitment had been made and Charlene had her heart set on it. Nor was Quigly likely to quietly agree to withdraw, even if she had the temerity to ask him. No, all she could do was cross her fingers and believe what Tony told her: Quigly's devotion to Charlene and to her would motivate him to behave like the head of the family.

"He'll play his part," Tony assured her. "I'm confident of it. You were smart to plan an early ceremony. Ten in the morning should be just about right. Enough time to get over a hangover and not enough to get loaded again. We'll watch him at the reception. I'll tell Laurel to hang on to his coattails, if necessary. She can keep anybody distracted! Stop worrying, dear. It's going to go all right."

To her eternal relief, he turned out to be an accurate prophet. Quigly came to pick up Charlene and Elizabeth promptly at nine o'clock in the morning and drove them silently but expertly to City Hall. He was red-eyed and puffy, but neatly dressed and almost theatrically polite. The others were waiting for them when they arrived—Jim with the look of adoration in his eyes, Tony smiling calmly, Clara a bundle of excited happiness. Laurel and the Jenkins family were solemn, and ten-year-old Lucy, whom most of them had never met, stood quietly near her mother, interested by the sight of these strange people who would soon be part of her family.

Charlene, in a short white silk dress with her grandmother's necklace at the simple V neckline, looked like the heroine of a children's story. Elizabeth knew that she, Laurel, and Tony were contrasting this demure bride and this brief ceremony with Ann's opulent wedding. This was no show put on for the benefit of strangers and members of the suburban press. This was a simple, lifetime promise between two people who made the dreary surroundings and even the undeniable tensions of the witnesses fade into nothingness. It was all brief and touching, serious yet joyful. Even Quigly, Elizabeth realized wonderingly, was almost tender as he brought his sister to the young man he had threatened to kill. She realized, almost with awe, that it all emanated from Charlene—her serenity, her happiness and her sublime confidence that she was surrounded by love. No one could have been inhuman enough to destroy her moment by a single misplaced word or deed.

And no one did. Back at the house, the atmosphere of rightness persisted as though they were all caught up in the spell of Charlene's most wonderful day. Tony was especially attentive to the Jenkinses. And Laurel, apparently having been given her orders by Tony, stuck close to Quigly, somehow even leading him into occasional laughter. Still, it was as though everyone knew it was not wise to push their luck. By half past twelve, the newlyweds were in their car on the way to Mexico, the Jenkinses said their polite goodbyes, graciously refusing Elizabeth's invitation to stay for lunch. A few minutes after their departure, Quigly prepared to leave too. Elizabeth walked with him to his car and kissed him warmly.

"You were wonderful, darling," she said. "Everything was wonderful. Thank you for being so dear with Charlene and everyone."

"Surprised you again, huh? You probably thought I was going to get drunk and make a scene, didn't you?"

"No, of course not. I knew you wouldn't do that to your sister."

"You're really a lousy liar, Mother. You've been looking anxious since nine o'clock this morning." He started the engine. "That marriage isn't going to work, you know," he said quietly. "But I won't have to kill him. Charlene will be back home within a year. That's why I figured there was no use making any more of a stink about it. It'll blow up of its own accord. And fast."

He drove off quickly. She was not to see him again for a very long time.

For the first time in her life Elizabeth now lived alone. It reminded her of all those dreary magazine articles about women in their forties and fifties who suddenly woke up and found their children married and gone and themselves depressingly free and unneeded. Not that there were no demands on her. Robert Gale Associates was thriving in a way that even its ambitious founder would have approved. Her days started early and ended late, and there were no weekday hours when she was not fully engrossed and interested in the business, which was providing the kind of living she'd never dreamed of having. But on nights and weekends the little house begged for the sound of Charlene's bright voice. There was a limit to the amount of gardening she could do on Saturday and Sunday and a point at which the solitary reading time she had always longed for became nothing more than a way to kill the evening. She realized that she had too much time to think. She felt boxed in in this little house she'd always loved. Uninterrupted for hours, she indulged in the fruitless pastime of going back over her life, reviewing her mistakes and stupidly wishing she had done many things differently. She blamed herself for her estrangement from Ann and Quigly, refusing herself the solace of the truth, which was that she could not have controlled them in any case. All she could see, in this period of depression, was that somehow she had not given them what they needed and they had turned their backs on her.

She wrote to Ann, a long, loving letter, telling her of Charlene's happiness and begging for her elder daughter's understanding. Ann did not reply. She had not even sent her sister a wedding gift, and Charlene, instinctively aware, had never mentioned Ann, had not even brought up her name when the wedding was being planned and the "family" invited. She knew, without being told, what the reaction must have been when her mother told Ann about Jim. With a pride inherited from Elizabeth, Charlene chose not to speak of her sister. But Elizabeth knew it must hurt, and in this introspective time she blamed herself, more than Ann, for the breach between her two girls.

She blamed herself for Quigly, too. If she had stopped him from running off to the Merchant Marine, if she could have held on to him just a little longer in those formative years, maybe, just maybe, he would not be the self-loathing parasite he'd become. She had heard nothing from him since the day of the wedding weeks before, yet she hesitated to call him in Bel Air. She could not bring herself to telephone that house and ask for "Alan Whitman."

Just before Christmas, she went into a preholiday slump. She spoke to Charlene nearly every day, cheerfully disguising her low spirits, matching her own tone of voice to Charlene's blissfully happy account of her wonderful new life. They arranged to be together on Christmas. Jim would come and fetch her on Christmas Eve and she would sleep over on the convertible couch in the Jenkinses' little apartment. She hesitated at first, but Charlene was so distressed by the idea that they would not be together that she finally relented.

"Why don't you and Jim come here?" Elizabeth asked. "There's a little more room and I can do a big dinner with all the trimmings."

"I'd really rather have *you* come *here,* Mother, if you don't mind. It's my first Christmas as a housewife and I'm dying to show off! Besides, you love the ocean—even at its bleakest—and it's marvelous now. Sort of lonely and grand without all the surfers and the beach umbrellas."

The prospect of being with Charlene and Jim helped to sustain her though a dreary Thanksgiving and a December that seemed to offer very little in the way of cheer. She talked to Tony and Laurel often, but they were busy in New York, with no plans to come West until after the first of the year. She realized that she had made no friends in California. She and her next-door neighbors exchanged cheerful waves across their lawns, but Elizabeth had never had the time nor the inclination for neighborly visits and it was too late to begin now. She couldn't picture herself running over for a chat with the women who lived nearby or inviting them and their husbands for cocktails. It simply wasn't her style.

In this quite out of character period of self-pity, she even came close to calling Adam. She'd had a note from him just after the wedding, a brief, almost formal little communiqué that said simply, "Dear Elizabeth, I read a notice of Charley's marriage in the newspaper. If you think it appropriate, give her my love and my warmest wishes for her happiness. As always, Adam." Between the lines she read that he was willing to see her again if she was still free. For all he knew, he might have married the man she'd invented as an excuse to finally drive Adam away. It would be easy to call him and say that there was no man, to pick up again with Adam and fill at least some of the lonely hours, even if the idea was futureless. She was tempted, but she gritted her teeth and resisted. That was no answer. That, like her failure with Ann and Quigly, was part of an irreparable past. She had to have something in her life that was her own. Something to fill her with pride and a sense of purpose. Something to serve as a goal for the future.

In the middle of the night she awoke, knowing what she wanted: her house. She would begin building her house. Now she could afford to. In her mind she could see it, distilled from

the hundreds of idle sketches she'd made. Tomorrow she'd
find a good architect. She knew just how she wanted it—not
grand and formal but spacious and perfect. There would be
room for Charlene and Jim whenever they wanted to come.
And for Tony and Laurel. Perhaps Quigly might even want
to live there. Maybe in time Ann would relent and bring her
three children to visit. Elizabeth had never even seen little
Alan Richards.

Suddenly she felt happy, purposeful. Even without those
she loved she would be content on that high cliff overlooking the woods and the sea. She would not be lonely there, as
she was in this little house, which used to seem warm and
cozy and now seemed like a container for the ashes of her
memories. Elated by the idea, warmed by it as she might
have been by the presence of a lover, she lay awake for
hours, making plans. To most people it would seem ridiculous, this idea of an inanimate heap of wood and stone promising the joy and comfort it did. Some of those very people
she wanted to build the house for would think she was
crazy. Why did she need a big house in a desolate section?
they'd ask. Ann would never comprehend. She needed the
security of her peer group. Laurel, too, would shudder at the
thought of such isolation. Even Charlene and Jim might
think it wiser and safer for her to stay in "civilization." But
one person would understand. Even before she called the
architect tomorrow, she'd call Tony.

Anticipating his enthusiasm, she fell blissfully back to
sleep.

Chapter 28

Just after Christmas, Laurel and Tony had a serious talk. It was Laurel who initiated the discussion, emboldened, perhaps, by the memory of Charlene's wedding, and using it, in any case, as an opening wedge.

"Maybe I'm having a bad case of the romantics," she said casually over lunch with Tony, "but in spite of my better judgment, I'm coming to the conclusion that the only way civilized people can be content is to form some kind of permanent, relaxed attachment. I fought the idea of Charlene's marriage to Jim. But, my God, the peaceful look on their faces when they took those vows! It was as though they could handle anything as long as they were together. I can't get that ceremony out of my mind."

An unsuspecting Tony agreed. "No matter how sophisticated or intellectual they like to think they are, most people need to belong in order to survive. Those kids know it instinctively. Older people sometimes have to find it out the hard way."

"Exactly." Laurel took a deep breath. "Tony, what year is it?"

He looked at her with amusement. "What do you mean,

'What year is it?' Chinese style, like the Year of the Dragon? Or the year five thousand and something on the Hebrew calendar? Or do you mean what year is it according to how I date my checks? In the latter case, it is December 27, 1953. What kind of a news flash is that? Don't tell me I forgot your birthday!"

"No, *I'm* the one who keeps trying to forget that. I just thought maybe it was leap year."

He looked away from her.

"Don't play dumb," Laurel said. "I'm proposing to you. Tony, let's get married."

Pretending it was a joke, he tried to spare her. "What, and spoil a beautiful friendship? You're kidding, Laurel. What would you want with a husband like me?"

"I've always wanted you," she said steadily. "I only went into partnership with you and Elizabeth to be near you. I love you, Tony. I'm right for you. Why should we both be alone? You just said it a few minutes ago—people need to belong."

"Laurel, I'm devoted to you. You know that. But we're *not* right for each other."

"Am I all that unattractive? You didn't think so once."

The barb stung. "You don't need to be reassured of your charms," he said. "They're still there. Stronger than ever. But what else would hold us together? The business? Other than that, we don't even like the same kind of life. You'd go out of your mind sitting home every night while I lost myself in those old books you've always resented. You wouldn't understand my lack of interest in fashionable people and places. You'd hate living in my spartan little apartment and I'd go crazy in your chic-ed up penthouse. What would we have in common except sex and Robert Gale Associates?"

"That's at least one thing more than we've got now."

In spite of the serious tone of the discussion, he had to smile at the quick little retort. Then he spoke again, earnestly.

"I'm flattered by this, dear. What man wouldn't be? You're a famous, exciting woman, and a wonderful one. But I'm not in love with you, Laurel. I couldn't make you happy."

"You're not telling the truth, are you? There's something else in the way."

"Something else?"

"Yes. Maybe it's age. I'm five years older than you are. That bothers you, doesn't it?"

The irony of it was almost too much. He couldn't marry Laurel because he loved Elizabeth. Elizabeth, who was not five years older than him, but twelve. Elizabeth, who probably would never accept him even as a lover, much less a husband.

"You know better than that," he finally answered. "The age thing couldn't be less important."

"Then what is it, Tony?"

He tried to be patient. "I've just told you, dear. We don't share the same interests and attitudes. We can work together in complete harmony. But trying to live together would be a disaster."

"I can change. If I have you, I won't want all the other things. For God's sake, Tony, must I get down on my knees to you? Don't you see how humiliating this is for me? But it's worth it if I can only make you see how right it is! You haven't given me one valid reason why our marriage would be a disaster. It wouldn't be, you know. It would be good. Solid. We'd be part of something. And we both need that. I don't care whether you're in love with me as long as you're not in love with . . ." Her voice trailed off. Her eyes narrowed. "That's it, isn't it? That's what's standing in the way. You're in love with someone else. Of course. It's Elizabeth. It's always been Elizabeth, hasn't it? Even when you lived with Robert you loved her. Even when you made love to me you loved her. Dear God, how could I have been so blind? Why didn't I see through the act you two have been putting on all these years? What an absolute, utter fool you must both think me!"

He tried to calm her, but the words continued to rush out.

"My best friend," Laurel said. "What a colossal joke! Trying to comfort me when Robert cut me to ribbons years ago. Sympathizing about the way you used me. Even pretending to understand when I told her the main reason I was coming into the business! 'Let things work themselves out,' she said." Laurel laughed bitterly. "She knew how they'd work out, all right. She's had you in the palm of her hand since the first night you met. She knew it. And she let me go on thinking there was a chance."

"Stop it! You're reading it all wrong! Yes, I'm in love with Elizabeth. I've begged her to marry me. But she's not in love with me. You know that better than almost anyone else. You know it's always been Adam Barnsworth for her. Never me. She wasn't pretending when she tried to console you. She adores you, Laurel. You can't doubt that after all these years. If she said nothing about my feeling for her it wasn't out of duplicity. She was trying to help you through a hard time. My God, Elizabeth is the last person in the world who'd mock you! Maybe she even believed there was a chance that

I'd get over her and turn to you. Maybe she hoped for that.
I don't know. I do know that my love has been a burden
for her in many ways, because she's never wanted to hurt
me any more than she would hurt you. Don't blame Elizabeth
for any of this, Laurel. If you must blame someone, blame
me."

She was quieter now, but the resentment had not left her.
"You can try to protect her if you like," Laurel said, "but
you can't whitewash her, Tony. She should have let me know
how you felt about her. She could have spared me years of
hopeless dreams. The least my 'dear friend' could have done
would have been to tell me the truth. But she didn't. She
even let me change my whole way of life when one single
word of discouragement could have stopped it. She knew why
I threw over a good career to risk my future: just to be
near *you*. She let me take a gamble that she knew was
futile because *her* future depended on it. What a charming
little charade we played that night at Robert's house! Elizabeth 'accidentally' describing me. And you 'instinctively' recognizing that I fitted all the qualifications! How wonderful to
find out that your closest friend and the man you love are
conspiring for the sole purpose of feathering their own
nests!"

"I don't think you believe a word of what you're saying."
Tony spoke very softly. Other diners in the restaurant were
beginning to look over at their table as Laurel's voice became increasingly shrill. "I don't think you possibly could accept that cold-blooded evaluation of Elizabeth. You know
her better than that, Laurel. She was as delighted for you as
she was for us when you joined the business. And whether
you believe it or not, so was I."

"Oh, *absolutely!*" Laurel's voice was thick with sarcasm.
"You two were positively philanthropic. What a break for
me! I don't know how to thank you both."

"You're being ridiculous. You're twisting everything to excuse your own childish attachment to me. Nobody offered
you Tony Alexander as part of the deal. You invented that
reason for yourself. Elizabeth and I presented you with a
sound business proposition. The fact that you thought you
could use it to get closer to me was the product of your
own egotistical assumption that your nearness would be irresistible. Who was going to disabuse you? Elizabeth? Me? We
had to hope that you'd come to your senses in your own
good time, as you seemed to have done once before. I never
gave you encouragement, Laurel. If anything, I made every
effort to keep away from you except during business hours.

But you wouldn't face the truth. Now that you have, you're jealous and outraged and blaming everybody except yourself."

In spite of his tough accusations, he felt sorry for her. She was angry and humiliated. Even so, he was not prepared for her next words.

"I want to leave the business," Laurel said suddenly. "You and Elizabeth can afford to buy me out. Don't worry, I've got it in good shape now. You'll both be fine financially. Robert Gale Associates can run on its own momentum for the twenty years. And you and Elizabeth won't have to worry any more about keeping your little secret from me. I never intend to see either of you again."

He pleaded with her. "You're being ridiculous! Elizabeth and I have no 'little secret.' We've never been closer than you and I. For that matter, we've never been physically as close. There's no reason why you should give up a damned profitable livelihood just because of hurt pride and mistaken beliefs! Or throw away the best friendship you have because of some silly idea that Elizabeth and I betrayed you! It doesn't make sense to destroy your future in a fit of personal pique. It's not like you, Laurel. You're much too level-headed for such an emotional off-the-cuff move!"

"I want out," she said coldly. "Discuss it with your lawyers. And above all, don't let Elizabeth call me. I won't speak to her." She rose abruptly from the table. "Goodbye, Tony. It was fun."

Helplessly, hardly able to believe it, he watched her leave the restaurant. He dreaded telling Elizabeth. She was so happy now with the plans for her new house, so enthusiastic about the place where they would all spend warm, companionable hours together. She would be crushed to know how Laurel felt about her, but, of course, she had to be told immediately. He'd have to do it in person. It was important that he be there when he tried to explain Laurel's behavior.

He made a reservation on the next morning's plane to Los Angeles. Then he called Elizabeth and told her he was coming out. She was overjoyed.

She was waiting for him at the airport. When he saw her smiling face, Tony wanted to turn and run. Elizabeth threw her arms around him and kissed him, childishly excited and happy. She'd been on the upgrade ever since she'd made the decision to start building her house. As she'd expected, Tony had shared her delight when she phoned him the morning after she'd made the decision. Now she plunged right into the subject, hardly letting him get a word in. She'd found a marvelous local architect, one they wouldn't dream of using on Robert Gale jobs because his taste ran to the kind of pure lines that their clients wouldn't understand. He was doing plans right now, many of them based on what she called her own noodlings. With any luck, the contractor would start early in the spring and surely by a year from now, if not before, Tony and Laurel and all of them could have Christmas in the new house! Would he drive up with her tomorrow to see again how breathtakingly beautiful the site was?

"Tomorrow is Saturday," Elizabeth bubbled on, "so whatever work you've come out to do can wait till Monday, okay?" She cocked her head inquisitively. "By the way, what *is* it you've come out to do? Now that I think of it, this is a sudden trip. Has something happened or"—she pretended to be flirtatious—"did you just decide that you had to spend New Year's Eve with me?"

Tony, driving "Fred the Fiend," did not take his eyes off the road. "Both," he said. "Made any plans for the arrival of nineteen fifty-four?"

("What year is this?" Laurel had asked yesterday. "I thought maybe it was leap year.")

"Nary a plan," Elizabeth answered. "What would you like to do? Not that we have much choice. We're not the type for nightclubs and funny hats. And I've turned down three invitations from well-heeled clients to celebrate in their Beverly Hills haciendas. Of course, I could still accept one of them, but we'd hate it."

"I vote for Pasadena. I could take you out to dinner and then we could go back to the house and cower as nineteen fifty-four blasts its way into the world."

"I don't feel like cowering. I'm very high on life these days. What I'd really like to do next Tuesday night is cook you a good dinner and break out a bottle of champagne at midnight. Deal?"

"Deal," Tony said. Tuesday is four days away, he thought. I'll have to tell her about Laurel before then. I wonder how much celebrating we'll be in the mood to do.

"Now what about the thing that really brought on this sudden trip? Has something happened back in New York?" She began to sound worried. "Ann and the children are all right, aren't they? You'd have told me if there was anything wrong. Or Laurel would have called."

"As far as I know, they're fine." He pulled up in front of the Beverly Hills Hotel. "Let's have a drink and a sandwich," he said. "I can't eat that garbage they serve on the plane. I'll tell you all about it as soon as I've checked in."

They settled themselves at a back table in the dark recesses of the Polo Lounge. It was midafternoon and the room was almost deserted. As calmly as he could, Tony told her about the scene with Laurel, watching the dismay come over Elizabeth's face. He spared her nothing, and she responded to Laurel's bitter denunciations with genuine sympathy and grief.

"It's not possible," she said over and over. "She can't really believe that we've used her. It just isn't Laurel to think that way!"

"I know. But it's not you she resents, Elizabeth. When she calms down, she'll realize that. Right now, she's seeing you only as the obstacle to her plans for me. I'm the one she hates. Hell hath no fury. This is the second time she's been rejected. It's too much for her."

"Poor baby. Poor Laurel. Underneath all that sophistication she's more naïve than Charlene. So romantic. So vulnerable. Tony, I'm going to call her. I'm sure I can make her understand. She mustn't leave the business. Even if she can't forgive us, we mustn't let her throw away her future. There must be a way I can get through to her. We've always been able to talk."

"I honestly wouldn't advise it. Not right now, anyway."

"But what are we going to do about her?"

"For the moment, nothing," Tony said. "Let's give it a week. Fortunately we're in the middle of the holidays. We couldn't get to the lawyers if we wanted to. I think we should leave Laurel alone for a little while. I'll talk to her as soon as I get back to New York. Maybe by that time I can make her see at least the practical side of the problem. As for recapturing the closeness we all had, I doubt that even time will do that."

Elizabeth wanted to weep. It was all so unnecessary, so foolish. She and Laurel had shared so much, lived through so many changes. It was impossible to think that the only dear woman friend she had in the world hated her, never wanted to see her again. Tony was wrong; Laurel did resent her, probably even more than she resented Tony. A change of heart from him could restore Laurel's love. But nothing Elizabeth could say or do would convince her friend that she had not been secretive and selfish. One by one I lose all the people I care for, Elizabeth thought. Alan. Adam. Ann. Quigly. And now Laurel. Some she had run from. Others had judged her and found her wanting. She blamed herself for their loss. She had expected too much of them, had unwittingly tried to make them perfect because she looked for perfection in the people she loved. When they did not live up to her standards, she thought the fault lay in them. She accused herself in this moment of self-examination. The idealist in her had been her greatest enemy. She talked a glib story about "human failings," but when it came to the humans who "belonged to her" she had remarkably little tolerance for their weaknesses.

A gentle touch brought her back to reality. It reminded her that there were three who still cared. She still had Charlene, Jim, and Tony. She covered the hand that lay on hers, fiercely, possessively as though she'd never let it go.

Tony called her early the next morning. She was sure that he'd had no more sleep than she, but his voice sounded alert and cheerful.

"What time do you want to leave?" he asked.

For a moment she couldn't remember where they were going. She'd forgotten her suggestion that they drive up the coast today. Her impulse was to cancel the expedition. She had no heart for it.

As though he anticipated her thoughts, Tony chided her. "Hey, if you're thinking of calling off our drive, that's a bad idea. What we need today is a look at things that are bigger and more important than we are. I'll pick you up in an hour."

It had been a right decision. As they came closer to the wooded area that belonged to her, Elizabeth felt a sense of peace. She stood on the edge of her cliff, looking at a world that had endured for thousands of years, letting the soft Pacific wind blow away the petty clouds of self-doubt that cluttered her mind. She wished the house was built. She wished she could stay there forever. Tony seemed to share the serenity that this vast expanse of natural beauty offered. He stood quietly at her side, drinking in the grandeur of it.

"What little specks of nothing we really are," he said finally. "When I look at this, things slide back into proportion."

Elizabeth picked up a pebble and tossed it idly down the cliff. She watched as it skipped and jumped and finally came to rest at the bottom of the steep incline.

"That's me," she said. "Starting so high, bouncing off one plateau after another, and finally coming to a halt at the depths. I'm like that little piece of stone. Except that it will endure."

His arm encircled her, a protective, impersonal gesture. "Do you think you're alone, lady? That's everybody's life you're describing."

The simple words were what she needed. He could not have talked her out of her self-hatred with reassurances of her virtues or her accomplishments. He could not have brought her out of despair with compliments or denials of the flaws she recognized within herself. All he could do was remind her that she was human and therefore destined to make mistakes. She envied Tony his inner strength. More than that, she blessed him for the capacity to give of himself, but only to the limits of the recipient's ability to receive.

It was a good day, a good weekend. On Sunday they drove down to see Charlene and Jim, who seemed blissfully happy in their little apartment.

"We had such a wonderful Christmas, didn't we, Mother?" Charlene said. "I wish you could have been with us, Tony. You and Laurel. How is she?"

Tony glanced at Elizabeth. Not yet, she signaled.

"Laurel's fine," he said. "Like the rest of us, she survived the holidays and probably will drown her sorrows on New Year's Eve. By the way, what are you kids doing that night?"

Charlene looked embarrassed. Jim answered for her.

"My bride's afraid you'll think we're crazy if she tells you that we're going to a drive-in movie," he said.

Elizabeth looked puzzled. "A drive-in movie?"

"It's where Jim and I went on our first date, remember, Mother?" Charlene explained. "I'm a silly, sentimental slob, but that's where I want to be on the first night of our first full year together."

"Of course," Elizabeth said. "I think it's a perfect idea." She didn't think so at all. She suspected that they didn't want to go to some public place where they might be stared at or even turned away. She wondered whether they had friends. Charlene spoke of "the neighbors," but Elizabeth had never seen any of them. Perhaps even the easy beach community looked down on this black-and-white marriage. They were young. It would have been natural for them to have been going to a New Year's Eve party or giving one. She might even have understood if they'd simply planned to stay home and make love on that most sentimental of all nights. But to go to a drive-in movie was like admitting that they wanted to be part of a celebrating world and knew they had no entree to it. They can't exist alone forever, Elizabeth worried. In this honeymoon stage it didn't matter, but one day soon they'd need outside interests and stimulation. Suddenly she realized what she was doing. Damn you, Elizabeth, she scolded herself, don't start meddling! What do you want to do, drive these two away too? They're grown-up, married people. Let them solve their own problems. Stop seeing bogeymen around every corner. *They* don't. Why should you? She had to get over this habit of interfering under the guise of affection. No matter that the concern was sincere. The truth was that she couldn't put herself inside other people's heads, couldn't live their lives for them or presume to tell them how they should. The sooner she accepted that, the better for everyone.

On the way home from the beach, Tony said, "You're worried about them, aren't you?"

Elizabeth looked straight ahead. "I'm trying hard not to be. I can't wish things right for them. I know that. I'd give my soul if it would guarantee that they'd never have to suffer, but I know there's nothing I can do except pray that they'll make it."

"You have a right to worry, not that it will help. But they'll make it, Elizabeth. With a lot of bumps and bounces, probably, but eventually they'll come to rest safely. Remember the pebble? Nothing could stop its inevitable progression."

"You *do* believe in fate, don't you?"

"Unswervingly," Tony said. "Fate. Destiny. Kismet. A master plan. Call it anything you like, but what's to be will be. I always thought you felt that way, too."

"I've always given it lip service," she said, "but I've *behaved* as though I had the ability to fix the course of my life and other people's. I was thinking of that as I listened to Charlene and Jim. I found myself wishing I could *make* the world accept them. It's not the first time I've wanted to rewrite that master plan. It's a kind of Don Quixote idea that's been with me all my life. Even my father warned me against it. I just can't sit back and resign myself to the fact that life is prearranged and nothing I can do will really change it. That's always seemed such a defeatist thing. Like taking the easy way out."

"Is that so bad? Haven't you done enough fighting and struggling? There's a big difference between giving up and giving in. How about just rolling with the punches for a change?"

Elizabeth managed a laugh. "What do I do—give up or give in?"

"You'll never give up," he said.

The change in Quigly that was apparent to Elizabeth was even more obvious to Theresa Isherwood. She and Quigly had been together for nearly four years, a uniquely long-lasting arrangement for this woman whose sexual experiences had always been transient and whose marriages had never survived more than a few short months. In those four years she had looked elsewhere only two or three times, found no one as satisfying as her surly young lover, and, with no small degree of surprise, had almost accepted the fact that she had settled down with one man. But in the last few months, she'd begun to have her doubts. Quigly's drinking was finally affecting his sexual prowess as well as his looks. His nastiness increased, though she didn't mind that. A masochist, she almost enjoyed his boorish behavior. But she liked handsome bodies and, most of all, virile ones. Since Quigly was losing both of these attributes, she began to think seriously of losing Quigly.

It might not be too easy. He was thoroughly spoiled by now. He considered the house, the car, and even the housekeeper as much his as hers. No doubt he had forgotten the terms on which he came there. She had had no idea that "a while" would become almost four years, and it was a fair bet that he now felt thoroughly entrenched. Most of all, she was more than a little afraid of what he'd do if she told him to leave. His temper was monumental. Several times he'd hit her, and once had beaten her so badly that she couldn't leave the house for a week. She'd gotten a sick thrill out of that physical violence, something no one had ever dared inflict on her before. But now she was frightened by the image of the ungovernable rage his dismissal might provoke, and for the first time the thought crossed her mind that he might seriously maim or even kill her. But she'd have to take that chance. She was tired of Quigly. He left her cold. And time was slipping by. She was past forty-five now, and there were fewer and fewer years left in which she could attract and excite young men. She wasn't going to waste them on a bloated, lethargic creature who no longer could give her the satisfaction she required. In less blunt words, she told him this on an evening in the spring of 1954, breaking the customary silence at the dinner table with the announcement of her decision.

"Alan," she said without preamble, "I've been thinking about us. I think it's time we called it a day."

He went on eating as though he'd not heard her.

"It's lasted a lot longer than either of us ever thought it would," Terry went on. "Damn near four years. But I'm ready for a change. It's been good, lover, but the bloom is off. You're not making it any more."

Still he said nothing. His silence began to unnerve her. "I know you've put aside some money," she continued, "and I want you to keep your car, of course. But I think you'd better pack tonight and be on your way tomorrow."

He pushed his chair back and came around to her side of the table, seizing her roughly by the shoulders and pulling her to her feet. His flushed face was close to hers and his whiskey breath felt hot on her skin.

"You goddamn slut," he said, "do you think it's going to be as easy as that? You think I'm going to settle for a few lousy bucks and a car? You must be crazy. What the hell do you think I am, some poolboy you can fire without notice?"

Though she was trembling inside, she put on an air of bravado. "What do you have to bitch about?" she asked. "You came here for one night and I've kept you for four years. If it wasn't for me, you'd be slinging hash in some beanery on Ventura Boulevard! You've got money and clothes and you've learned how to behave in a house with servants. Christ knows you're leaving with a thousand times more than you came in with!"

"I'm not leaving at all," Quigly said. "I like it here. I earn my keep. If we're less hot in bed, that's your fault, not mine." His face was ugly and determined. "You should be grateful. Screwing you is like doing it to a withered-up old woman. Better hang on to what you've got, baby. You're about as sexy these days as a mother superior. I'm making it better than *anybody* could with an old bag like you!"

She hit him hard in the face with her clenched fist. "You lousy bastard," she screamed, "don't you dare talk to me that way! You with your drunken impotence! Get the hell out of here *now!* Tonight! You're nothing but a sodden bum. I've always known you were slovenly and vicious, but now I realize how stupid and filthy you are as well. You must *really* come from the slums! Who the hell gave birth to you —a pimp and a whore?"

A fury unlike any he'd known came over him. He saw blackness everywhere except around the figure of this shrill, screaming woman who shouted vile lies about his background. Blindly he began to strike out, his strong fists hitting her again and again, smashing her face and body, even after she fell to the floor of the dining room. After the first scream, she was unconscious, but he continued to beat her, first with his fists, then with strong bone-crushing kicks to her body.

It was all over in a few minutes but it seemed to him like hours, like a lifetime of trying to destroy everything ugly.

When he finally stopped, he could not look at the broken, bleeding woman at his feet. He supposed he had killed her. He wondered why the housekeeper had not come running at Terry's first scream. Then he remembered that it was Thursday, her evening out. I'm a murderer, he thought dully, the police will come looking for me. I've got to get out of here.

The woman on the floor did not appear to be breathing. Stumbling, he hurried to his room and packed his clothes, stopping only long enough to go into Terry's bedroom and remove the money in her purse. For good measure, he also scooped the contents of her jewelry box into his pocket. Maybe he cold get out of the country. It would be hours before the housekeeper returned. Sometimes she even stayed overnight with her daughter. He had time to get a plane for Mexico before Terry's body was discovered. Maybe he'd go on from there to South America or someplace where the cops couldn't get at him.

He thought of calling Elizabeth to say he was leaving town, but decided against it. She'd know soon enough what he'd done when the newspaper headlines screamed that Theresa Isherwood was dead and Alan Whitman had disappeared. It would be better if Elizabeth could honestly say that she had no knowledge of his whereabouts. Maybe he'd send her a postcard later on, from Brazil or someplace. Or maybe, better still, this time he'd really drop out of her life for good.

There were no headlines. When the housekeeper returned late that night, she found Miss Isherwood unconscious on the dining-room floor. Rushed to the hospital for emergency surgery, she miraculously survived, though for forty-eight hours it was touch and go. The housekeeper, knowing well that Miss Isherwood would want it that way, wisely kept quiet about Quigly. She told the doctors and the police that some intruder must have broken in and robbed her employer, probably beating her when she tried to resist. They and the newspapers accepted that story and the press gave it space on page three, describing it as another burglary and brutal assault in the swank Bel Air section. When Theresa regained consciousness, she confirmed the story. And when the police matched Quigly's fingerprints, which were all over the house, to those of a young man with an arrest record in San Diego, she said that Mr. Whitman had visited her often but she hadn't seen him in several days. The masked man who robbed and beat her, she said, was young and black. She didn't think she could identify him.

Elizabeth read the newspaper stories with despair. She instinctively knew the truth, but there was nothing to be done about it. She was glad she did not know where Quigly was and that even if somehow they linked him to her she could honestly say that her son had not contacted her in months. There had not been a word from him since the day of Charlene's wedding. Not even a message at Christmas. Perhaps, she thought hopefully, he really had gone away before this terrible thing happened. Maybe that's why she hadn't heard from him. But she knew that that couldn't be true. His fingerprints were all over Theresa Isherwood's house. She was sure that Quigly had done this terrible thing.

Charlene called, troubled by the newspaper story about Quigly's employer. Elizabeth tried to reassure her and failed miserably.

"I'm sure Quigly had nothing to do with it," Elizabeth lied. "Even Miss Isherwood said it was a stranger."

"But why haven't we heard from him?" Charlene persisted. "It's all so odd, Mother. I thought surely we'd see him at Christmas and we didn't hear a word. Did you try to reach him?"

"No, I didn't, darling. I've finally learned that when your brother wants to see us, he gets in touch. I'm sure he's all right. He probably will be calling when he reads about this awful thing. My guess is that he left his job some time ago and didn't want us to know." She hoped that Charlene would not figure out the time discrepancy between Quigly's disappearance and his still evident fingerprints. That, of course, was hoping for too much.

"But he'd been there recently," Charlene said. "They found his fingerprints. Even Miss Isherwood said she'd seen him a few days before. He must have still been working there."

"Maybe so, dear. I just don't know."

"Did you know that Quigly had been arrested in San Diego?"

"Yes. But it was just a misdemeanor. A fight in a bar."

Charlene sighed. "Do you really think we'll hear from him?"

"Of course we will. We know he had nothing to do with this. If he had, Miss Isherwood would have said so."

Elizabeth didn't believe a word of what she was saying, and she knew that Charlene didn't either. They both sensed that this awful act had been Quigly's doing and that the victim was lying for reasons of her own.

The only other person who saw the story in the Los Angeles papers and connected it to Elizabeth was Adam Barnsworth. He debated whether to call her and rejected the idea. She was through with him. She had not even acknowledged his note sending his love to Charlene. He wondered whether Elizabeth had remarried. Several times he'd been tempted to drop in to the shop, just to see her. But each time his better judgment kept him away. He still missed her. And he still, in his own way, loved her for herself and for the marvelously uplifting effect she'd always had on his ego. He needed that buildup more than ever these days. He was fifty-three years old, a depressing time of life when one is neither young nor old, but unhappily aware that the joys of sex and romance are slowly diminishing. God knows Monica did nothing to make him feel young and attractive. She was much too concerned with fighting the evidence of her own fading charms. Even five-year-old Catherine, dear as she was and much as he adored her, only reminded him that he would have been more properly cast as her grandfather. He spoiled her endlessly and she responded with affection. But all the while he knew that father and child could never really communicate. There were too many years separating them. He felt sorry for this little girl deprived of the understanding of young parents, and he tried to make it up to her. But of course he couldn't. She was a lonely child. And Adam was a lonely man. What was worse, it was his own fault, and too late to rectify. Elizabeth had given him three chances and he'd thrown them all away. He did not have the courage to try again after the last rebuff.

He read about Quigly, shook his head sadly, and tried to put the boy and his mother out of his thoughts. Elizabeth had enough troubles. She didn't need another person making demands on her, drawing on her strength, using up her seemingly endless supply of courage. He hoped she was happily married. She needed someone to lean on, to take from, Adam thought. And in this, for once, he was completely and selflessly right.

Chapter 29

When Tony returned to New York, his first move was to call Laurel's apartment. Her maid answered and said that Miss Lane had left on a trip. No, Miss Lane had ordered her not to give an address to anyone. No, she had no idea how long Miss Lane planned to be away.

"She did say, though, that if you called, Mr. Alexander, you should get in touch with her lawyers. Miss Lane said they'd be handling everything for her."

The lawyers were no more communicative about Laurel's whereabouts, but they were quite prepared to discuss the settlement their client demanded. After two hours of legal double-talk, a review of "past performance" and "future growth," and veiled insinuations that Miss Lane had been "responsible for keeping the firm of Robert Gale Associates from foundering," it netted out to the fact that Laurel would accept a flat sum of three hundred and fifty thousand dollars for her fifteen per cent ownership of the business.

Before calling Elizabeth, Tony turned to his own lawyer for advice.

"Highway robbery," the attorney said. "You'd be a fool to agree. Everything is on your side. Miss Lane is the one who wants to sell her shares and there's no way that fifteen per cent of a business grossing slightly over a million dollars a year is worth that kind of payoff. Sounds more like blackmail than business. If you want to be very generous, offer her fifty thousand dollars. Even then you'll be Santa Claus."

"And if she refuses?"

"Then she can retain her minority ownership and share the profits as you and Miss Quigly do. You've given her an interest in the business, so she's entitled to participate in the profits, probably to the tune of fifteen or twenty thousand dollars a year. You can handle that, but a lump sum, even if they compromised on a quarter of a million, would mean going into hock. You'd have to take out a big loan—assuming you could find someone to take the risk. Funny," the lawyer said, "I didn't figure her for that kind of a woman. Sounds like she's out as much for revenge as for money. Either that or she's in the hands of a bunch of shysters who think they can gouge hell out of you."

"Could she take the case to court?"

"Sure. I don't think she could win it, but she could try. Probably kick up a lot of dust about how she saved the company and base her case on future growth, which she'll claim to have initiated." He paused. "And of course if there's anything personal in this, the publicity could be bad. Which, I'm sure, is what she'd be counting on. Since Gale's death, you're like a new company. How old now —three years? A nasty, mudslinging battle in the tabloids could put you out of business. If," the lawyer said meaningfully, "there's any mud to sling."

Tony didn't answer. Laurel was bitter enough to open up any number of skeleton-filled closets. She'd make hay out of his relationship with Robert. She might even portray herself as the trusting victim of a lustful, lying man and a woman who pretended to be her friend but was an adulteress and a heartless mother whose own children had rejected her. None of these charges would affect the actual outcome of her case, Tony was sure, but they'd make juicy headlines if Laurel chose to level them.

Tony wasn't seriously worried about bad publicity destroying the business. He didn't even care about any exposé of his own life. But he couldn't let it happen to Elizabeth. He couldn't let Laurel paint her friend as the ex-wife of a drunken bum who died in a whorehouse, or as the mistress of a prominent California businessman, or as the mother of a psychotic son with God knows what in his background, and of a daughter married to a black man. None of this would win Laurel's case for her, and in time the public would forget, after they'd had a few lip-smacking weeks of yellow journalism. But Elizabeth would never recover.

"I'll have to talk it over with my partner," Tony said finally, "but I don't think we can let this go to court. Too many people will get hurt if Laurel is as vindictive as I think she is. If we make a counteroffer, what do you *really* think it would have to be?"

The lawyer made a quick assessment. "If the business is grossing around a million dollars annually, her shares now would be worth about a hundred and fifty thousand dollars. Can't start with much less. Probably, if you're lucky, they might settle for two hundred thousand in a flat payment. Can you swing that?"

"I don't know how, but we'll have to."

"I think we could get a much better deal if we fought it."

"I'll let you know in a few days," Tony said.

He explained it on the phone to Elizabeth that night. At that time, the robbery and assault of Theresa Isherwood had not taken place. Even so, Elizabeth knew that the airing of her life was unthinkable. Charlene must be protected and even Ann, unlovable as she was, did not deserve to have her world destroyed by the whisperings of her friends and the taunts of the children who played with hers. There was even Adam to be thought of, and his family as well. It would be a malicious witch-hunt, supported by the bare bones of truth with none of the softening excuses of extenuating circumstances. She found it almost impossible to accept the fact that Laurel really would use her intimate knowledge to wreck so many lives. Yet they dare not take the chance. Like Tony, Elizabeth did not care for her own sake. But she couldn't live with the knowledge that all these things, some of her own making, others pure happenstance, would bring devastation into the lives of innocent people.

"Would Laurel really do this?" she asked. "Can she hate us so much, Tony? If only I could talk to her," Elizabeth said again. "I know I could make her understand."

"She's unreachable, dear. Physically as well as emotionally. If you agree, I think the only thing we can do is try to come to terms with her. Let the lawyers fight it out. It won't be easy to raise a big amount of cash, but we'll get it somehow, though it will considerably reduce our incomes for years while we pay off a big loan. Of course, we could look for outside money. Somebody to invest in the business. Another partner."

"After this, I'd rather manage without, if we can."

"I, too," Tony said, "even though we'll pay through the nose for our independence. I don't know what we'll net for a long, long time. I can manage and I'm sure you can too, but, for one thing, I'm thinking about your house. You may have to put off building for God knows how long, and I know how much you want it."

"It can wait," Elizabeth said. "It's worth waiting for."

It took weeks of haggling between the lawyers to arrive, finally, at a settlement. Laurel remained out of sight and her representatives would disclose only that she was "somewhere in Europe." Meanwhile, "the parties of the first part and the parties of the second part" settled on a lump sum payment of two hundred thousand dollars for Laurel's share, and the attorney for Robert Gale Associates, working with Tony's accountants, managed somehow to negotiate a ten-year loan for the company. It meant repaying twenty thousand dollars a year plus interest—sizable reparation, Tony thought ruefully, for a breach of no-promise. He took all the blame for it. So much so that he offered to handle the debt himself.

"I've been thinking about this," he told Elizabeth later. "The whole damned thing is my fault. Laurel only wants revenge on me. It's wrong that you should be penalized, too. Hell, I can make it easily without your giving up anything. I think this loan should be my responsibility, Elizabeth. I want you to continue to draw your full share of the profits, regardless of this debt."

She shook her head. "Absolutely not. We're partners. Our business obligations are mutual. So, for that matter, are our personal ones. No matter what you think, Tony, in Laurel's eyes we share equal guilt and deserve equal punishment. Maybe we are guilty of a crime against her, if only by default."

"I still think you're getting the short end of the stick."

"No, I'm paying for a lot of blind moments, just as you are. Thank God we can afford the price of Laurel's silence. Particularly now."

The Isherwood story had just broken. If they had risked a court fight with Laurel, Elizabeth thought, what fuel this would have added to the fire!

"I know that if it wasn't for me and my children and some other people, you'd have let her bring the case to court," Elizabeth added. "The very least I can do, Tony, is to pay my part, and with gratitude." Her voice lightened. "Besides, it's not so terrible, is it? We've both lived on a lot less money than we'll bring home even now. I have no children to support, I own a piece of land, and while Pasadena isn't where I want to end my days, it's not exactly skid row. Charlene and Ann are secure. The business is doing well, even without Laurel's contacts. It's a long way from Marion Parrish-Parker's free cottage and sixty dollars a week at *Wife and Mother!* Look, my dearest friend, I'm a big blessing-counter. In spite of everything, the last twenty years haven't been all bad. For one thing, they've brought me you."

They were sitting in the back garden of Elizabeth's house, the last rays of sunlight bathing them in a soft, benevolent wash of gold. In the face of all her troubles, Elizabeth managed to look serene and beautiful. Tony knew she must be frantic about Quigly, disappointed in Ann, troubled about Charlene. He knew, too, that stopping the work on the new house was a bitter disappointment. And yet she showed none of this. With it all, she could find much to be grateful for, including, happily, Tony himself. It was almost impossible not to reassert his love for her. He wanted to offer himself, his devotion, to beg to be with her fully and completely and forever. If she sensed this, she gave no sign. The smile she gave him was openly affectionate but not provocative, warm and tender but without fire. She was not ready to let him take away the worst burden of all, her loneliness. Deep in his thoughts, he realized he had not heard what she'd just said to him.

"I'm sorry," he apologized. "I was a million miles away. What did you say?"

"I asked whether you'd been to visit your parents on this trip. I haven't heard you mention them lately."

Reluctantly, he came back to a part of his life that he managed to think about as little as possible: the early part.

"I drove over to see them yesterday," he said. "Nothing changes. When I walk into that house, it's as though I go back thirty years in time and I'm seven years old instead of thirty-seven. Mother complains and Dad smiles. He talks about retiring in a few years and she says she'll go crazy if he hangs around the house all day. He's tired. He's sixty-three years old and he'd like to putter in his workshop and tend his garden. He'd be happy doing it. But Mother won't let him. She thinks that men who retire just wither up and die. At least that's what she says. What she means is that the less she sees of him the better. Which is what I've always known. He worships her and she's merely suffered him all these years. No wonder she tried to make a little husband out of me. She's still all over me with the kind of affection that Dad would give his soul for. I'm sorry for her, but she suffocates me. I hate going there. I even hate talking about it."

Elizabeth said nothing. A motherless child, it was hard for her to imagine a mother as anything except warm and giving, but never at the expense of the man she married, especially one as obviously patient and devoted as Mr. Alexander seemed to be. She remembered stories that her own father had told of the woman she'd never known—the woman who cared so much for him that she'd died giving him the child he wanted. That was the kind of mother Tony should have had. Even now, she thought realistically, it may be the one he's still searching for.

"I know what you're thinking," he said.

"Do you?"

"Your mind is working like a textbook. You're telling yourself that my pattern is classic—the momma's boy who becomes a homosexual and then gravitates toward the older woman who's really a mother image. A nice, neat package of curbstone psychoanalysis, Elizabeth, but unfortunately it doesn't fit. If anything, I've patterned myself after my father —at least in the sense that I'm willing to be used if that makes someone I love happy. As for looking for 'another mother,' the last thing I want is a possessive relationship. Her kind of smothering domination is what I've run away from all my life. It's probably the real reason I could never respond to Laurel. She'd have put me in chains if I'd let her. I'd have become the child she's never been able to have."

"You contradict yourself," Elizabeth said. "If you're willing to be used to make people you love happy, you might have given Laurel that opportunity."

"You overlook a fine point of distinction. I never loved Laurel. Not that way. And I don't think she ever really loved me. If she had, she wouldn't be punishing us now. By my definition, love never wounds the loved. It regrets, perhaps, but it doesn't respond to disappointment with the deliberate intent to destroy. That's not love, Elizabeth. That's false pride, the distasteful acknowledgment of one's own insecurity."

"The thought's provocative," Elizabeth admitted, "but then how do you explain the jealous 'love-nest murders' that make headlines? How can people do the terrible things they do to each other in the divorce courts if they don't want to wound the ones they loved?"

"Why don't you look close to home for that answer?" Tony was very serious. "Did you seek revenge for all the horrible things Alan Whitman did to you? Did you try to actively punish him for the humiliation and disillusionment you took? What about Adam Barnsworth? Have you done anything to ruffle his life, even after all he put you through? No, Elizabeth. You understand love. It doesn't come with a price tag. The heart can't write an I.O.U. Love is a loan, but those who give or receive it shouldn't demand reparation if, unfortunately, its term expires. The wise ones write it off, having enjoyed its use for a little while or a lifetime."

Elizabeth smiled. "You still expect a great deal of people, don't you Tony?"

"Only of a handful with the real capacity for love. Those are the only ones I expect anything of—the ones who understand the tenuousness of that emotion. They're the Elizabeths of this world. All the others are the Laurels."

"Don't be too hard on her, Tony. With all the surface success, she hasn't had much of a life. She's frightened and lonely. That's what her bitterness says to me. I know the feeling, including the bitterness. It's not easy for a woman to be alone, but it's almost unbearable when she's never been loved even in the past. Without memories of yesterday to sustain us, what's our defense against the emptiness of today and tomorrow?"

"Perhaps the hope of a better future."

"Easy enough to say. Unfortunately, you can't just summon love and companionship anytime you need it."

"*You* can," Tony said. "Elizabeth, let's stop playing this old game. I love you. I want you. There's nothing standing between us any more. Not a friend. Not a child. Not a lover. There's so much that's right between us. Why do we waste more years pretending that friendship is enough? We both need more, and I'm not sure there's that much time. I wasn't being dramatic when I said I expect to die early. I really do. And whatever years are left I want to spend close to you. Marry me, please. I beg you."

"Darling," she said, "it's wrong for you. You're thirty-seven years old, Tony, and I'm forty-nine. When you're a vigorous fifty, I'll be in my sixties. I have grandchildren. I'm a white-haired old lady now, in the eyes of the world. People will laugh at us, Tony."

She didn't fool him. He was confident at last, sensing that the long-desired victory was at hand. So happy that he could afford to drop his urgent, tense, argumentative tone.

"Since when have we cared about people, either of us? Besides, my darling, you forget: I won't live to be fifty."

Her unwillingness to accept that sharpened her voice. "When you talk like that, I *know* you're too young for me!

I've told you before: Stop spouting juvenile nonsense! Nobody can predict his own death. You drive me crazy with
that silly premonition!"

"All right," he said, "I'll never mention it again. I'll even
try to believe that I'll be a virile fifty saddled with an ancient
wife of sixty-two, as long as you have settled for that idea."

In spite of herself, she had to laugh. "Tony, Tony, what
can I do with you?"

"I've already told you. Look, let's even be practical about
it if that will make you feel less guilty. We'll close the New
York office and operate from here. Even if we do less business, we'll reduce our enormous overhead *and* have a combined income. We'll be able to build the house on the sea and
commute to Beverly Hills. My lord, woman, you'll even have
a free chauffeur!"

He looked more than ever like a boy in love, yet he spoke
with a man's sense of practicality.

"It makes sense, Elizabeth, from every angle. But most of
all, it's the kind of rightness you feel under the surface of
your skin. It's taken a long time, but you know you need me
as much as I need you. Are we going to be stopped by trivia
like rules about who's older than whom? Or are you afraid
that Ann will recoil with as much horror as she did when
Charlene married Jim? Maybe you think that Quigly's dislike
of me is a roadblock, even if he's not around to erect it?
Sweetheart, we can't even hurt Laurel any more. I think
that's always been between us, like Robert was."

She could not deny that the thought of her children's reactions had crossed her mind. Only Charlene would rejoice
for her. As for the others, what difference did it really make?
Ann had disowned her for permitting the mixed marriage.
Quigly was gone again, without a word, heedlessly, perhaps
forever. Laurel knew where Tony's love lay. And, most important of all, Elizabeth permitted herself to finally accept
the idea that she loved Tony. Perhaps she always had, even
when she refused to seriously entertain the idea in New York,
even in Denver when she allowed herself to continue her
romantic, passionate, unrealistic longing for Adam.

Because, she saw now, Tony had always been there, waiting. He had quietly moved beside her through the turmoil of
these last years, only once permitting herself the luxury of
showing selfish physical desires. In times of trouble, she
turned to Tony. In moments of joy, he was the one with
whom she shared them. In her agonies of self-doubt, it was
Tony who calmed and reassured her. His gentleness belied
his strength. Of all the people in the world, only Tony saw

through the facade of self-sufficiency to the inner woman who yearned for the comfort of someone stronger than she.

Suddenly she felt the peace of dependence. She savored the idea of abdicating responsibility and decision. In a way, Tony's brisk, businesslike assessment of the practical aspects had been the unexpected key that unlocked the possibility of marriage to him. Not that she would go into the union simply because it was "sensible." But the decisiveness of his plans somehow gave a dimension of worldly reality to the physical and emotional depths of his attractiveness. This was not the helpless, unmaterialistic dreamer that Robert had tried to make him seem. Nor the mystical, remote character Laurel had mooned over. This was a man who planned for his woman, even as he loved her. She was seeing the first person in her life who did not believe she was self-sufficient. Tony would never treat her as though she had no need of help. He knew her well. She was not a woman to be coddled and pampered, like a mindless doll. But she needed to be complimented with respect and cared for in the shelter of a man's supporting arms.

It seemed to her that he must be able to read all these revelations in her eyes. So much so that when she answered she did not say, "I love you, I want you, I need you and I go down on my knees to you in gratitude and understanding."

She simply said, "Yes."

They were married on Thanksgiving Day in 1954 in the nearly completed house high on the cliffs overlooking the Pacific. Their decision once made, Tony had returned to New York to close the office there, get out of his lease on the Beekman Place apartment and arrange to have his precious books and records stored for later shipment to California. Elizabeth had joyfully called the contractor and pressed him for a November completion date on the house, shamelessly playing on his sentiment by telling him of her marriage plans. She and Tony were determined to start their new life in this house. Every second was suddenly precious, and throughout the summer and early fall Elizabeth hovered like an anxious bride, charming the workmen and their boss, producing near-miracles simply through the happiness and anticipation she radiated. Everything seemed to work right, and by the day of her wedding, like a good omen, the house was not only built but sufficiently furnished to live in. It was a house, Elizabeth decided, that never really would be finished. Every room seemed to offer endless possibilities for improvements that she would add through the years. But even in this semicompleted state it was beautiful. All the spacious rooms, with their rough-plaster white walls and carved-oak beams, were planned to have a view of the sea. The house sprawled comfortably, uncluttered but welcoming, watched over by the massive trees that surrounded and sheltered it without disturbing the vista beyond. There were so many fireplaces that Tony teased her about them.

"I think you're an arsonist at heart," he said. "My God, there's a fireplace in every room in this house. We could burn the place down and still have seven chimneys left!"

It was true. There was a huge fireplace in the living room and another in the big kitchen, where they'd have most of their meals. Each of the three bedrooms had a fireplace and so did the little library. Fulfilling a lifelong dream, Elizabeth also managed a corner fireplace in the bathroom adjoining the master bedroom that she and Tony would share. She could think of nothing more luxurious than lying in a warm tub staring into dancing firelight. Long ago she'd decided that if ever she built a house, this would be one of the unexpected delights in it. That and a kitchen big enough to hold rocking chairs and a big round dining table, as well as space for copper cooking pots and tiers of potted plants to bring the greenery of the countryside into the heart of the house.

In spite of its space and touches of extravagance, it was far from a mansion, not imposing by Bel Air or Beverly Hills or Malibu standards. But it had dignity and grace and every inch of it bore the imprint of Elizabeth's infallible taste.

Though she really couldn't afford such an expansive gesture, Elizabeth had, with Tony's blessing, given the little Pasadena house to Charlene and Jim. The mortgage payments were even less than the rent they paid at the beach and, in any case, they would have had to move to more expensive quarters. Charlene was expecting a baby in April, an event that filled her with delight and her mother and her husband with hidden apprehension. Both Elizabeth and Jim had mixed emotions about the pregnancy. Jim even had doubts about the move to Pasadena, which he quietly expressed to Elizabeth.

"Do you think we'll be welcome there? It's just great of you to give us the house, but how will the Jenkins family go over in that super-conventional neighborhood, Mrs. Whitman? I still remember Charlene's sixteenth birthday. We all pretended that nothing was out of the ordinary, but I know darned well that a lot of her friends in Pasadena didn't show up that night. You didn't have to be bright to figure out the reason. Do you think it's wise of us to try to live here, especially now that we'll have a child?"

Elizabeth had the same realistic doubts, but she would not admit them, even to herself. Instead, she took a down-to-earth stance.

"Look, Jim, we know there'll be people in Pasadena who won't welcome you and your family. But that will happen wherever you go. You could move to Watts and Charlene wouldn't be accepted, would she? I think you have to expect some trouble, hopefully little. But there'll be bigots everywhere, all your life. You knew that when you married. We all did. And we all decided that your happiness and Charlene's was much more important than an occasional snub from some ignorant, narrow-minded outsider. You made the choice and you've made some adjustments already. This is just one more. You can't hide, dear. And you can't change the color of your skin, even if you wanted to. All in all, I think you two have been handling it pretty well. I know Charlene is happy. I hope you are."

"I never knew there was such happiness," he said. "I just don't want her hurt."

Same old refrain, Elizabeth thought. Same futile hope. "You can't prevent it," she said gently. "All you can do is help her through it."

In the end they took the house and moved in as soon as Elizabeth moved out. There was no overt protest in the neighborhood. There was simply chilling silence, even from the same two neighbors who had been so friendly toward Elizabeth and Charlene. Elizabeth knew that the side glances and the whispered comments hurt Charlene as she moved about her daily chores at the supermarket and the drugstore. But she never spoke of them. She seemed happy to be back in the security of the house she'd once shared with her mother. And she waited for her child with the same touching complacency that surrounded any contented, pregnant "normal" young woman.

Antoinette Jenkins arrived on April 4, 1955, three months before her mother's twentieth birthday. Though she was a tiny baby, Charlene had a long, agonizing period of labor before she produced this doll-like, café-au-lait child. Jim was out of his mind during the endless wait at the hospital. Even Elizabeth and Tony could not distract or comfort him.

"If anything happens to her," he kept saying again and again, never finishing the sentence. "My God, if anything happens to Charlene!"

"Nothing's going to happen," Elizabeth promised him,

wishing she felt as relaxed as she sounded. "Charlene's going to be perfectly fine, dear."

Addie and Fred Jenkins had flown in from Denver when Jim called to say that Charlene was on her way to the hospital. That was almost twenty-four hours ago and none of them had left the waiting room since. The Jenkinses' patient, almost mournful faces unnerved Elizabeth. They had never really accepted this marriage and Elizabeth thought she knew what was going through their minds now: this was God's punishment to the young people who had broken the rules. She knew they were praying for Charlene. She was not so sure that they were asking the Lord for the survival of a grandchild. Damn it! Why did Charlene have to be the only woman in this family who had such a difficult and precarious time giving birth? Both Elizabeth and Ann had delivered their children with almost disgraceful ease. Neither of them had suffered the way Charlene was suffering now. Maybe the primitive instincts of the senior Jenkinses were right. Perhaps God didn't want this baby born, for its own sake. Maybe it was significant that only its mother anticipated its arrival with joy. Jim had never once mentioned the baby; he was concerned with the survival of his wife. And when, at last, the tired obstetrician appeared, Jim rushed to him with only one question.

"My wife, Doctor, is she all right?"

"She's all right, Mr. Jenkins. You can see her in a little while."

Jim's body went weak with relief. "Thank God," he said. "I thought I was going to lose her."

The doctor patted his shoulder. "Now that it's safely over, I don't mind telling you that I had some pretty bad moments myself." He seemed to hesitate, as though there was something he was reluctant to add.

Jim nodded. "I'm grateful to you for saving Charlene."

What's the matter with him? Elizabeth wondered. Isn't he going to ask about the baby? Doesn't he sense that there's something the doctor isn't telling us? She waited, but Jim was being cradled like a baby himself in his mother's strong arms. Both of them were crying unashamedly as Fred Jenkins gently caressed his son's head. Elizabeth finally couldn't stand it any longer.

"What about the baby, Doctor?"

"A beautiful, perfect little girl," he said. "Such a tiny thing to give so much trouble! Just over five pounds, but every ounce of it in good condition." He looked over at Jim. "There is something else I have to tell you, Mr. Jenkins. You have a lovely daughter, but I'm afraid that's it as far as a family is concerned. Charlene must not have another baby. I'm sorry, but you two will have to make up your minds to that. She couldn't survive another pregnancy." The doctor frowned. "It's a damned shame," he said. "Charlene's a wonderful young woman. I've never seen a braver one. She's the kind who should have half a dozen kids."

For the first time ever, Elizabeth heard hardness in Jim's voice. "Look at us, Doctor. Look at the whole family. You've given us *good* news. One half-black baby is enough. God knows we don't need to multiply our problems by two or four or six!"

The doctor looked embarrassed. "Well, that's a personal matter, isn't it? I can only give you a medical view. Good night, Mr. Jenkins."

Elizabeth was shocked. She knew that Jim would have preferred to be childless, but Charlene would be heartbroken when she learned that she couldn't have more babies. Jim felt her curious stare.

"I must sound like some kind of monster to you," he said, looking squarely at Elizabeth, "but you'll never understand what it's like to be black and to be responsible for bringing outcast children into the world. I'll love my daughter, but every time somebody calls her a nigger or reminds her of her daddy's color I'll wish she'd never been born. How much of that punishment do you think I can take? How much can Charlene? We shouldn't have had one child. It was an accident. I'm just thankful we can't keep on compounding our mistake."

"Didn't Charlene want to have children?"

"Sure. But she couldn't grasp what it meant any more than you can. Oh, you have an intellectual understanding, Elizabeth. You mentioned it before we married. I agreed with you. I never intended for us to have children, ever. Charlene didn't know that. Well, at least we won't have to quarrel over the size of our family. We'll just do the best we can for the one we have, God help her." He sighed. "Let's find out if we can see Charlene and the baby for a minute. Then maybe we can all go home and get some sleep."

They were able to see a drowsy but happy Charlene and a tiny bundle that was like a miniature edition of her with toast-colored skin. Even Jim softened when he saw his child.

"She's so little," he said gently. "So helpless."

As they left the hospital, Jim turned to Tony. "We discussed names before the baby was born. Charlene said that if it was a girl she'd like to call her Antoinette. That okay with you?"

"Thank you, Jim." He looked at Elizabeth. "It's the second best compliment anybody ever paid me."

Chapter 30

Although Elizabeth dutifully wrote to Ann, telling her in long, loving letters of her marriage to Tony, of Charlene's baby, of the contentment which was upon them and the love and longing they still felt for all the Richardses, no letter with a Scarsdale postmark appeared in the mailbox on the road that led to the Alexanders' house. Nor, in the next two years, was there any word of Quigly. He had simply been swallowed up the night he ran from Theresa Isherwood's house. For all Elizabeth knew, he could be dead.

There was surprising, secondhand word of Laurel. Stu Preston, long since retired, still kept in touch with Elizabeth. And it was in one of his letters that they learned that Laurel had returned to Washington.

Our little Laurel has become quite the Washington hostess. She came back to our very much-changed town after a year of living it up in the capitals of Europe and has just about taken over this one. She has a local television show which is doing well, and an apartment on Wisconsin Avenue that is constantly cluttered with Eisenhower big shots. She and Perle Mesta are in silent competition, I think. Each has ammunition. Perle has the money, but Laurel has the looks.

She's also become a femme fatale (or so those younger and better qualified to judge tell me!) and the gossip columns link her with a different man every week. I see her for lunch now and then, but despite the romantic rumors she doesn't give any indication of a serious attachment. Too bad, I think. Laurel needs a husband, if only to round off some of the hard edges which this old codger finds uncomfortably abrasive. She's not the girl we knew, Elizabeth. If I sound nostalgic, it's only because I am.

Two years of life together had also brought changes in Tony and Elizabeth. Their business prospered to the extent that they were able to hire competent people, expand the Beverly Hills headquarters, and gradually turn over more and more of the management to their employees. They still drove into town four days a week, leaving the house early and waiting impatiently for the moment when they could get back to it.

They saw very few people and needed no one. Except for Charlene, Jim, and the adorable Antionette, they selfishly guarded their privacy and their totally fulfilling companionship. As though by silent agreement, they spoke little of the past, partly because there were some things that were painful and pointless to rehash and partly because each felt he had experienced a rebirth through the other.

It was impossible, of course, to block out all reminders of the life that preceded their marriage. Tony still reluctantly and infrequently went to see his parents, angered by the fact that his mother refused to meet Elizabeth, whom she referred to as "that old woman you married." Had it not been for his affection for his father and for Elizabeth's urging, he would not have gone to his parents' house at all. Elizabeth insisted that he do so.

"Darling, we understand your mother," she said. "It's not me she hates. She wouldn't have accepted any woman you married. Besides, I know what it's like to have children you never see. It comes under the heading of cruel and unusual punishment."

So he dutifully appeared every few weeks at his parents' home and came racing back as though he'd escaped from the jaws of hell. On the nights he'd seen his mother, Elizabeth was aware that his lovemaking was exceptionally ardent, as though he could find sanity only in her arms. Not that their marriage lacked physical excitement at all times. Elizabeth was a passionate woman and her desire was more than matched by Tony's ability to arouse her with a word, a touch, a look. It was the kind of love she'd never known even with

Adam. With him she'd thought she'd achieved the ultimate in ecstasy. With Tony it was this and more, for as her body came to his she felt the permanence of it, the security that filled her as completely as his physical prowess that brought the act to mutual completion. Even when she had first admitted her love for him and warily consented to marriage, she had not known the depths of Tony's devotion or visualized the joy he would bring her. She knew at last what it meant to be unselfishly adored.

Sometimes, alone in her firelit bathroom, she examined her body anxiously for signs of aging. She did not fear growing old except that she did not want to see the excitement and wonder disappear from her husband's face. She wanted to be beautiful for him. Not that her physical perfection was all-important to Tony. He worshiped her body, but she knew with a wonderful sense of confidence that he saw the whole Elizabeth, the inner shape of her even more clearly, perhaps, than the outer. Still she was glad that the breasts were still quite firm and upright, the buttocks as yet unwrinkled and sagging. Quite a stroke of luck, she told herself, for a lady who'd lived more than half a century. And who took almost that long to find out what love was really all about.

Although they had agreed never to discuss it, Elizabeth was so secure, so certain of their good fortune, that on Tony's fortieth birthday she brought up his old superstition, chiding him gently about the nonsense of believing he wouldn't live past that age.

"Happy birthday, my darling," she said over cocktails, "and a toast to the *next* forty years! Look at you, love. Can this be the same fellow who knew he'd never make it into the fifth decade? Where's your premonition now, Anthony Alexander? And however are you going to explain being eighty with a ninety-two-year-old wife?"

He caught her up in his arms, laughing. "Witch! You broke the spell! Made a fool of me, didn't you?" He began to kiss her, but she broke away.

"None of that," she said with mock severity. "You're not going to have your way with me at five o'clock in the afternoon!"

"What's wrong with five o'clock in the afternoon? Besides, the afternoon sun does sexy things to your face." He turned her toward a mirror. "See there? Tell me, did you ever see a sexier five-o'clock look?"

"That's a blurred, two-martini look," Elizabeth teased. "Anyway, I want to give you your present. It's one you have to share with me." She handed him a small blue-velvet box and waited for him to open it. All at once she was nervous. The idea which had seemed inspired when she thought of it now made her anxious. What if Tony misinterpreted the gift? What if it brought back painful, unwanted memories instead of symbolizing, as she intended, the permanence and security she felt? She held her breath as he opened the box. Inside was the gold ring that had belonged to Robert, the one she had selected when Tony gave her her choice. And beside it was an exact duplicate.

For a moment he stared at her. His eyes went back to the two bands with their delicately entwined hands. And then he smiled with such pure, happy comprehension that Elizabeth's heart felt as though it were coming through her breast.

"Mrs. Alexander, you're extraordinary," he said. "Do you know I've never worn a ring in my whole life? Never wanted one until this moment." He slipped the original on the third finger of Elizabeth's left hand in front of the plain gold wedding band she wore. "Now you're twice married to me," Tony said. For a moment, he kept the twin in his hand, then he held it out toward her.

She put the matching one on his finger, pressing her lips to it as she did.

"I must have known, somehow, why I chose it," Elizabeth said softly. "I must have known, even then, that one day it could say everything I hoped to feel, much more adequately than any words."

He locked his hand into hers. "Till death do us part," Tony promised. "And may that be a long, long time from now."

While Elizabeth and Tony were reaffirming their vows, Ann Whitman Richards in Scarsdale was tearfully considering breaking hers. It seemed to her that she had done nothing but weep for a week, ever since she discovered that Peter wanted to end their marriage. She had had no suspicion. There had been nights when he'd been late getting home from the office, but that in itself was not cause for alarm. Every husband in their set sometimes put in overtime at his office. Nor did it trouble Ann that Peter had attended three week-long conferences in Washington without suggesting that she go along. It would have been impractical for her to arrange a baby-sitter, and the idea of a week in Washington— a town that held nothing but unpleasant memories for her— had no appeal. Besides, she was much too busy with her house, her children, and her endless community activities. She was president of the Literary Club now and spent a part of every day working on the monthly meetings, arranging speakers for "Book and Author" luncheons which gave recently published authors a chance to plug their newest works and provided members of the club with an afternoon of "culture." She also was chairman of the fund-raising committee for the March of Dimes. And she served on the board of directors of the Country Club, a distinct honor since all the other directors were male.

Until a week ago, she'd considered herself a model wife in every sense. Twelve years married, she had not, for one moment, "let herself go." She was always perfectly groomed, endlessly competent and unfailingly interesting. She was not like some of her less energetic suburban friends who had nothing to tell their husbands in the evening beyond a dull recital of the children's behavior or a boring account of the crisis when the dishwasher broke down. Her house was spotless, her meals well planned and acceptably cooked by the full-time maid. Even her sex life was more than dutiful. If Peter did not thrill her, she was careful not to let him know. She was good at playacting in bed. It was no trick to pretend that she reached a climax with him. She never did, but it pleased him to think so. Not once in a dozen years had she refused him with excuses of being too tired or of having a headache. It had been somewhat of a relief that in the past six months his ardor had somewhat abated, a fact that did not seem unremarkable in a solid, not particularly imaginative man approaching "middle age."

With everything going for her, nothing could have been further from her mind than Peter's suddenly blurted out request for a divorce.

A week ago he had come home as usual, listened quietly to the recital of her well-organized, active day, poured himself a drink and said, without preamble, "Ann, I want a divorce."

For a second, she thought this was one of Peter's painful attempts at humor, but a look at his unhappy face confirmed that it was no joke. She was, for once, speechless.

"I know it's a shock," he said, "but I've met someone else. I'm sorry to hurt you. I know you've tried to be a good wife, but I want more out of life than this."

"Tried to be a good wife!" Her voice shook with fury. "I've run your house, had your children, submitted to your clumsy lovemaking! I've spent twelve years making myself into the kind of woman I thought you wanted, doing things the way your mother does them, even cutting myself off from my own family because I was afraid their unconventional ideas would displease you! I've made myself over for you, Peter, and now you dare to sit there and tell me you want more than this! You expect me to accept that? Do you really think that because you've met some woman you fancy yourself in love with I'm going to allow all our lives to be uprooted and rearranged? You must be out of your mind! Perhaps you forget how you begged me to marry you, how you rushed me into it! And now that you're bored with the arrangement, you have the nerve to tell me that you 'know I've tried to be a good wife'! I *am* a good wife, damn you! And what's more, I'm the one you chose!"

He seemed untouched by her words. "Everything you've said is true, Ann, except for those last words. You're *not* the wife I chose. I chose a soft, gentle, helpless girl. But I find I've married a computer. You're programed to function as efficiently as a machine. You run a perfect house, take your children to the dentist twice a year, involve yourself in all kinds of do-gooder projects. But there's not an ounce of warmth in you, Ann. There's no love anywhere. Just this wild desire for perfection—deadly, stifling, predictable perfection. I can't stand that for the rest of my life. I can't endure any more of your competence. You're choking me with your goddamned well-ordered world."

She couldn't believe it. The ingratitude of it. And from Peter, of all people. Dull, upper-middle-class Peter, who had seemed so thoroughly indoctrinated with suburban conventionality was now behaving like some irresponsible, aging roué. All the hard work she'd done to make herself part of "their world," all the attitudes she'd adopted because she thought that's how Peter Richards' wife should feel and act —all these were now turned against her by the very man she thought she was pleasing. She'd forgotten that she'd wanted this tight little life for herself and that she'd felt safe and unthreatened in it. All she could think of was that Peter had wanted her to become what she was, and having achieved that he now wanted no more of it.

"Who's the woman?"

"You don't know her," he said. "She lives in Washington. I don't want to discuss her, Ann. It's true that I've fallen in love with her, but I'm honest enough to know that if it hadn't been her it would have been someone else. She didn't steal me from you. You pushed me away, bit by bit, year by year. Can't you remember what we were like when we met? I picked you up in the bookshop and I thought you were the most refreshing, charming, unselfish girl I'd ever known. You seemed so undemanding, so filled with easy happiness. When

I found that I was the first man you'd ever had, you wouldn't even let me feel guilty. I couldn't believe that you'd make no demands on me. And when you didn't, I felt that you were the most guileless, innocent creature I'd ever met. I didn't rush you into marriage. I know now that it was part of a plan from the first moment you saw me. I didn't realize it for years. I even began to fall into the heavy, pompous ways of my father, because you took on more of the crisply organized pattern of my mother. But a couple of years ago I saw what was happening to us. Our planned children were here. Our planned social set was functioning. Even our sex life had a plan—Monday, Wednesday, and Saturday, whether we wanted to or not. I'm too young for that kind of rut, Ann. And so are you. We've got to get away from each other."

Her voice was heavy with sarcasm. "So you've decided to chuck it all and run to some woman who'll let you be the boy in the bookstore again."

"No. He's gone. But I'd like to be the man who wakes up every day with some sense of anticipation."

"And where does that leave me? Like my mother? Alone at thirty-one with three children to bring up? Oh, don't tell me you'll provide. Of course you'll provide—*money*. But who'll provide a father for those kids? Who'll provide for my new, husbandless role in this community?"

"You'll marry again, Ann. You're much too clever not to find another husband. You'll figure out a plan. That's what you're best at."

"Wrong," she said coldly. "What I'm best at is being Mrs. Peter Richards, Jr. And *that's* what I'm planning to remain." She started for the stairs. "I'm sure you'll want to sleep in the den tonight. There are blankets in the hall closet."

"And that's how you think you're going to leave it?"

For the first time that evening, she spoke with a touch of humility. "Peter, this is much too serious for sudden decisions. Believe it or not, I love you. I need time to think about what you've said. I'm shocked and hurt and angry, but I believe in my marriage, *our* marriage. Let's be sure of what we're doing before we wreck everything. There's more involved here than just you and me."

The thought crossed his mind that she was scheming again, stalling for time to construct a plan to keep him. Still, she was right. He'd had years to think through all this. Ann had had only a few minutes. It was only fair to let her come to the decision, as he had, that their life together was stale and better ended. He'd lied about the other woman. There was one, but he did not plan to marry again, ever. He'd had enough of the sameness that seemed synonymous with the state of matrimony. He'd reached the limits of boredom.

"All right, Ann. We'll talk more tomorrow."

They had talked every night for a week, sometimes calmly, sometimes screaming at each other. Midway through it, Peter admitted that the other woman wasn't really important. Ann didn't believe him, but she was prepared to forgive his infidelity if only she could hold this marriage together. At the end of seven days they were no closer to understanding each other than they'd been at the beginning, and it was then, wearily, that Peter made his unorthodox suggestion.

"Look," he said, "we can't take much more of this. We're just covering the same ground. I think we should really get away from each other for a week or two. Why don't you go to California and visit your mother? I'll take care of the kids."

The idea was so absurd that Ann began to laugh.

"Visit my mother? What in God's name are you talking about, Peter? You know I haven't even been in touch with her for four years! She'd think I was insane if I suddenly showed up on her doorstep after all this time!"

"That's part of the problem. You've even come to disapprove of your whole family. I think you underrate your mother. I don't think you understand her even as well as I do. I know you get letters from her all the time. I've read most of them. I know she still loves you. And I happen to think she's a very wise woman. The best one you could turn to right now. You need her, Ann. Why can't you admit it?"

She wavered. "I wouldn't know what to say to her. I don't even know whether I want to see her."

Peter's voice was gentle. "You'll know what to say when you see her. Go call her, dear."

When Elizabeth returned from the telephone, she looked as though she'd seen a ghost.

"Tony, that was Ann."

He looked up from his paper, startled. "Ann? Is something wrong?"

"Yes and no. I mean, she wouldn't discuss it on the phone. All she said was that she needed to get away for a week or so and could she come here for a little visit."

"Hard as it is to believe, that sounds like trouble with Peter."

Elizabeth agreed. "That's what I think, too. Anyway, darling, I told her to come ahead. I hope that's all right with you."

"On the contrary, I absolutely forbid it."

She looked at him wide-eyed. Then he laughed.

"You nut," Tony said affectionately. "You didn't think for one second that I meant that, did you? Darling, she's in some kind of trouble and she needs you. I'm just amazed and delighted that she has sense enough to realize it. Is she bringing her kids?"

"Don't ever scare me like that again," Elizabeth said. "For a second I really thought you didn't want her to come."

"I know. Then you thought the honeymoon was over and I was so bored with you that I'd even welcome your not too cordial daughter."

"Be serious. She's behaved so badly, Tony. About Charlene as well as us. It must be something really drastic to make her unbend even to the extent of speaking to me, much less coming to visit. And to answer your question, no, she's not bringing the children. I asked her to, but she said she wanted to come alone. She'll be here day after tomorrow."

"You going to tell Charlene?"

"I don't know. I think not, at least until Ann gets here and I find out what this is all about."

"Good thinking. Lord, this is about the last thing we expected, isn't it?" He pulled her into his lap. "You'd better be extra nice to me tonight and tomorrow," he said. "I have a feeling I'm not going to have you much to myself for a while."

On the long plane trip to the Coast, Ann felt a mixture of relief and anxiety. It was good to be alone, even for a few hours. This last week with Peter had used every ounce of her strength. They had talked and argued through most of the nights. Neither of them had gotten much sleep, and Peter's face when he drove her to the airport looked lined and weary. I'm sure mine does too, Ann thought. Mother will be shocked when she sees me. Damn her. She probably looks young and prettier and happier than ever.

The thought of a reunion with Elizabeth made her almost as uneasy as the fears about her possible divorce. She still disapproved of Elizabeth for permitting Charlene to marry a colored man. And now, to make matters worse, they'd had a baby. Ann also continued to be upset by the marriage between her mother and Tony. She told herself that it was unsuitable, degrading. How could Elizabeth have married a man so much younger than herself, and particularly one whose past was as unpalatable as his? Ann had made her position unmistakably clear through silence. How would Elizabeth receive her now? And what should her own attitude be? She simply couldn't apologize for the way she felt. Her own desperate situation had not magically made the other things right, she reasoned. She couldn't pretend that she'd changed her views. But what then, she asked herself, was her justification for running to this woman who condoned all that Ann rejected?

As the plane got nearer to Los Angeles, she wished she had not let Peter talk her into this insane trip. He had suggested it in desperation. And in a moment of weakness she had grasped at this last remaining straw. She was sorry now that she had.

And yet, when she saw Elizabeth at the gate, she almost ran to her mother's arms. Tony watched quietly as the two women hugged each other, the light tears on their faces intermingling like their voices, which said over and over how happy they were to see each other again.

"Hey, what about me?" Tony finally said.

Ann turned to him almost shyly. "Hello, Tony. Congratulations."

"Hi, Ann," he answered. "Welcome home."

The first twenty-four hours of Ann's visit were uncomfortable for the three of them. After that first spontaneous moment at the airport, Ann seemed to withdraw into the aloof, guarded self that Elizabeth and Tony remembered all too well. She replied politely to their questions about the children. Ditto was eleven, Elizabeth Joanne nine, and Alan seven. They were nice, well-adjusted children, she said almost defiantly, who lived a normal life. Encouraged by Elizabeth's careful questions, Ann spoke of her local activities, of her in-laws, her excellent maid, and the changes she'd made in the Scarsdale house. What she said was less significant than what she did not say. Her husband's name did not cross her lips. Nor did she so much as inquire after Charlene and Quigly. Fully aware of these omissions, neither Elizabeth nor Tony introduced the subjects. It made for an unnatural, stilted first day.

On the second morning, Elizabeth suggested that Tony go to the office without her.

"I think I'll take a few days off, if that's all right with you, darling," she said. "Ann isn't here to make small talk. Pretty soon she's got to get around to whatever is really on her mind. Maybe if the two of us are here alone during the day she'll relax enough to tell me about it. I don't think she'll open up while the three of us are together."

Tony agreed. He even offered to go further. "If you think it will help, I could stay a couple of nights with my folks. It's a God-awful thought, but it won't kill me."

"Not on your life!" Elizabeth said. "I never want to sleep alone again as long as I live. You've spoiled me rotten in two years. I don't think I could close my eyes if you weren't beside me."

"Now that," he said, "is the kind of talk I like to hear."

She waved cheerfully at him as he drove off to Los Angeles. "Drive carefully," she called. "And hurry back!"

He flapped his hand at her outside the car window, as if to say, "Don't worry; I'll be back to rescue you."

There was no sign of Ann when she went back into the house, but within half an hour her daughter wandered into the kitchen, still in her robe and yawning hugely. It reminded Elizabeth of the old days. Particularly of the morning when Ann had announced that Peter had proposed.

"Sleep well?" Elizabeth asked, handing her a cup of coffee.

"Better than I have in a week." Ann looked out the big kitchen window. "It's beautiful here, Mother. So quiet and sheltered. I envy you."

Elizabeth didn't answer. Instead, she busied herself making a second breakfast for Ann. She and Tony had had theirs an hour before.

"Just toast, please," Ann said.

"Oh, have a nice big breakfast, sweetheart. We can take it out on the patio and I'll join you for my fourth cup of coffee. Besides, you look too thin to me. Maybe we can fatten you up a little while you're here."

Ann shook her head. "I'm not hungry. Honestly. But I'm a coffee fiend, like you. It would be nice to sit outside and have gallons of it."

They settled themselves in comfortable chaises on the stone terrace outside the living room. For a long while, neither spoke, each lost in her thoughts. Finally, Elizabeth lit a cigarette and inhaled deeply.

"Want to talk about it, Annie?"

Ann kept her eyes on the view. "All right," she said finally. "Peter wants a divorce."

It was a thunderbolt, but Elizabeth didn't visibly turn a hair.

"And you?"

"I'm so mixed up I don't know how I feel any more.

When he first mentioned it, a week ago, it was out of the blue. I had no idea that he'd ever considered such a thing, any more than I had. I flatly refused. I still don't want it. But now I don't know if there's anything left to keep us going, even if I convinced him to stay."

"Tell me what happened, Ann. Has Peter met someone else?"

"Yes, there's another woman, but that's not really it, Mother. I mean, that was the final push, maybe, but it's not that serious. The real trouble is that Peter's bored with our life, and with me. I think his expression was that he chose a soft, gentle girl and found out he'd married a computer. How about that for irony? I've spent twelve years trying to be the kind of well-organized wife I thought he wanted, only to find out that he really prefers a clinging vine. He says I'm a cold, efficient machine who plans every step of my life and his. He finds our marriage stifling and predictable." Ann's face darkened. "It's so bloody unfair! In the beginning *he* wanted the house in Scarsdale and the three children and the nice, normal life. Now he's changed his mind and *I'm* supposed to accept that without so much as a protest!"

Elizabeth had the sensation of picking her way across thin ice. There was irony here, but not the kind that Ann recognized. What was sadly, painfully ironic was that Ann had really believed she could arrange her life and Peter's just the way Elizabeth had once thought she could control her destiny with Alan. We're very much alike in many ways, Elizabeth thought, and there's a parallel in the years leading up to our final discovery. But Ann has one thing in her favor: Peter will help her to change if she's willing. She can save her marriage if she can swallow her pride.

"Do you love him, Ann?"

The girl bristled. "What do you mean? I married him, didn't I? I had his children and kept his house and tried to give him the kind of background that would help his career. We're very well known in the community, and the contacts I've made haven't hurt Peter's business, you can be sure of that. I've never cheated on him. I've tried to stay attractive and interesting. My God, what else should I be—Marilyn Monroe?"

"You still haven't answered my question."

Ann refused to look at her.

"Then I'll answer it for you," Elizabeth said. "You've never really loved Peter. From the moment you planned to marry him he was an escape from your past, from insecurity and emotional upheaval. Peter didn't realize it for a long time, Ann, but we know that you used him to get away from me and all that I represented. You swung so far in the opposite direction that I think you really did turn yourself into a kind of living organization chart. He doesn't need that. He needs a wife who needs him, flatters him, makes him feel that she can't live without him. Did you tell him those things when he told you he wanted to leave?"

Still there was no answer.

"If I know you, Ann, you didn't. I'm quite sure you spoke of yourself, your sacrifices, and, probably, your concern for your own future as a divorced woman with three children. Can you tell me that isn't true? Can you really tell me that you told Peter how much he meant to you as a husband, a lover, a man?"

Ann jumped to her feet, livid with anger. "I don't know why I came here," she said. "I should have known what to expect from you—sermons and accusations. I was a fool to think you'd understand. You've never made any sense out of your own life. Why in God's name did I think that by running to you I could make any sense out of my own?"

"Sit down, darling," Elizabeth said. "Please. You're so full of pain and, believe me, I'm not trying to add more. I love you, Ann. We may never see things the same way, but you can't stop me from loving you and wanting to help. I'm not foolish enough to think that you can profit by my experience. The only way to learn about life is by living it. But there comes a time when the lessons have to pay off or you'll spend the rest of your days regretting that you ignored them."

Rebelliously, Ann went back to her chair. "So what *are* the lessons I'm supposed to have learned? That it's stupid to be ambitious for your family? That it's dumb to devote your whole life to creating some kind of atmosphere of normalcy and sanity? What's your prescription, Doctor—a closetful of black lace nightgowns and a big bottle of Shalimar?"

Elizabeth couldn't help smiling, but she quickly hid her momentary amusement. She'd like to have said that sexy nightgowns and perfume might be a very good start, but Ann was in no mood for humor. Instead, she said, "Ann, let me ask you something. Do you truly want to look at Peter twenty-five years from now and see his blustering, bigoted father? Do you really want to be another Joanne Richards with nothing more stimulating in her life than Japanese flower arrangements? Is that the answer to life? Peter doesn't think it is. Neither do I. And in your heart I suspect that neither do you."

"What's so wrong with it?" Ann said. "That's the way

most Americans live, if they're lucky. They don't go charging around through life looking for excitement and romance and that one great overwhelming love."

"No, they don't," Elizabeth agreed. "They settle for mediocrity. Year after year of the same, uninterested marriage partner. The same group of friends making the same heavy pronouncements about business and schools and household help and taxes. They live in a gilt-edged ghetto, walled in by their tight little fears of the future. That was the course you chose, Ann. You didn't know quite how limited a route through life it was, and Peter was too blindly in love with you to think further ahead than tomorrow. But that's changed for him now. And if you want to keep him, it had better change for you."

"Why should it? Why should *I* change?"

"Because *he* has, my dear. It's as simple as that."

Ann's teeth were clenched so tightly that the veins in her neck stood out. With all her will she resisted what she'd heard. She told herself that she'd been wronged, that the things she valued and concentrated on were the right things, the only meaningful things. It was easy enough for Elizabeth to tell her to change. But she didn't know how to go about doing it, even if she were to try. Suddenly her whole face and body seemed to crumple. She curled up in a corner of the chaise and let the tears come. In an instant, Elizabeth was beside her, making little soothing sounds.

"I do need him, Mother," Ann sobbed. "I know I've been selfish. I haven't meant to be, but I haven't thought about what Peter was feeling. Not for years. I've been so busy making myself a big woman in my town that I've been no woman at all to him. Oh, God, I never really realized how much I don't want to lose him!"

"No one ever does, darling, until they're faced with the loss."

Ann was off on an orgy of self-recrimination now. "I haven't even been honest with him. I've never told him the truth about Quigly or Charlene. I was too ashamed, too fearful that I might be connected with any kind of imperfection. I remember how he reacted when I told him about you and Tony."

Elizabeth was human enough to be curious. "And how was that?"

"He didn't think it was terrible at all. I was furious with him. He said, 'Ann, I should think you'd be happy for your mother. It's taken her a long time to find someone who can give back as much love as she's given. Some people never find that in a lifetime of searching.' I was too angry with you to pay attention to what he meant. I think I see it now. Two years ago he was asking me to love him more than I loved myself."

"Or more than you loved the picture you had of yourself."

"Is that really it, Mother? Have I spent all these years making up an Ann Whitman? Can I ever be some kind of a whole, real person?"

"Oh, darling, of course you can! It won't happen overnight, but every day you'll find a new, nice piece of the real Ann. Just to make the start, to admit that you need to change, is enough for now, isn't it? You can't unscramble twenty-five years of hostility and self-protection over one cup of coffee, my love."

Ann got to her feet, calmly this time. "I'm going to call Peter. I want to tell him that I'll change. I really will."

"Take a piece of advice?" Elizabeth asked. "Wait a few days. There are a couple of things I'd like you to do first."

"What things?"

"I'd like you to see how happy Tony and I are, and what it means to think first of the other person. And then," Elizabeth said slowly, "I'd like us to go and visit Charlene and Jim."

Ann swallowed hard. "All right. I'll go see Charlene. I think I'd like to. I owe her an apology."

"No, Ann, she doesn't expect or want one. She doesn't need your regrets or even your approval. She needs your love."

"What about Quigly?"

Elizabeth sighed. "I'll tell you all about that. Later."

A week later, a much transformed Ann flew home to her husband. The reunion of the sisters had gone even more easily and warmly than Elizabeth had prayed. After an almost timid introduction, Ann and Jim seemed at ease with each other. Antoinette, of course, would have charmed the leader of the Ku Klux Klan and in minutes she had captivated her newly discovered aunt.

Driving home from Pasadena, Ann had sounded wistful. "There's so much real happiness in that little house," she said. "And they have such terrible problems, poor kids. Not much money. The whole racial thing. My God, they have guts."

"Nope," Tony said over his shoulder. "They have another four-letter word. It's a printable one beginning with L."

"I know," Ann joked. "Lust."

"Right," Tony said, looking at Elizabeth. "Doesn't everybody?"

Chapter 31

Within four days of her return to New York, there was a letter from Ann in the Alexanders' mailbox. It was one that Elizabeth had never even dared hope to receive.

Ann wrote at length of her return to Peter, admitting that she had all but gone down on her knees to him and reporting, joyfully, that he was willing to try again. They were planning to sell the house in Scarsdale and move back to the city. They could afford good private schools for the children and as soon as they found a pleasant apartment they'd leave the "gilded ghetto" behind. Ann had resigned all her "important" presidencies and chairmanships. "From now on," she wrote, "I'm going to be that nice, anonymous Mrs. Richards who forgets to send out the laundry! Maybe I'll be able to get into some charity work, like reading for Recording for the Blind or helping out in one of the hospitals. But no more big-shot jobs that occupy all my thoughts. I know now where the emphasis of my attention must be. 'You let me have it good' —and I hope and pray the message really got through. I'm sure it did."

But it was the last paragraph that pleased Elizabeth most of all. "I don't quite know how to say this, Mother, but I think that what really worked a minor miracle was seeing you and Tony together. It made me so ashamed of the nasty little narrow-minded attitude I'd taken. But best of all, it made me realize what kind of honest harmony can exist between two people. It's as though you two are one. That's what I mean to make happen between Peter and me, if I can. There's no way to say thank you—not just for the California visit but for a lifetime of caring about me. All I can say is that I respect you deeply and love you very much, both of you."

Elizabeth showed the letter to Tony. "I think she means it," she said. "It's taken her a long time to find out that she can let down her defenses and believe in someone besides herself. Peter gave her a good scare. I don't think she'll soon forget how close she came to losing everything that really matters."

He read the letter carefully. "I hope you're right, darling, but people have a way of forgetting pain after a while. Let's just hope that Ann doesn't have a relapse into her old, hostile, self-serving ways. Maybe you should send her the prayer that every young Hindu bride memorizes."

"What's that?"

Tony smiled. "It's one that an independent woman like Ann would have a hard time accepting," he said. "It was said by Sita, the wife of Rama, who was one of the nine forms of the incarnation of Vishnu, the god of love. In the Hindu religion, Rama was unjustly banished by his father, and his loyal wife Sita followed him, saying:

> Car and steed and gilded palace,
> vain are these to woman's life;
> Dearer is her husband's shadow
> to the loved and loving wife."

Elizabeth looked at him pensively. In these last two years, Tony had gone deeper and deeper into his search for ultimate truth. His ever-increasing fascination with all religions had become one of the many things he shared with Elizabeth. He no longer talked of going to the East to find truth, as he had many years before, but his interest in the beliefs of that part of the world continued to intrigue him. Hinduism seemed to hold the most meaning for him, and Elizabeth often questioned him about it with sincere interest. She did some reading on her own, and while she was by no means the scholar that Tony was, she found herself caught up more and more in the subject. It seemed to her convoluted and even contradictory. What did one make of a religion that had one God and 330 million gods? Yet how did one discount a faith built on the belief that human equalities result from man's own doing, not from the action of the gods. This article of faith—reincarnation really—could explain why some of the world seemed to have everything and some of it nothing. If one accepted the fact, simplified to its barest form, that a person is born into his present life as he has lived in a past life, then much of the injustice that troubled any thinking person might be explained away. And if it followed that one was reborn into a future life according to how he'd behaved in this one, then there was reason to adhere to the basic ideals of Hinduism: purity, self-control, detachment, nonviolence, charity, truth, and deep compassion for every man and animal who lives and breathes.

"Tony," Elizabeth said suddenly, "do you still believe in reincarnation? We talked about it once, long ago. You used to say you believed in an eternal spark of energy. Is it the same, really?"

"I can't answer that, darling. I don't know enough. I can't yet accept that a man who's greedy in this life literally comes back in the next as a pig. But I do think a little piece of us goes on somehow forever, and maybe Hinduism comes closest to what I'd like to believe. I'm not sure about all their confusing gods and devils, but I'm inclined to agree with their wise men who believe that this world is temporal and that worldly desires lead to frustration and frustration to human suffering. Maybe the answer lies in God. Or maybe it is as simple as what one philosopher advises us to do— think steadily on life's mysteries until we reach the highest revelation."

Sometimes Elizabeth tried to challenge him. "It seems to me that Hinduism is the simplest of religions and the most complicated to understand. It's kind of permissive, don't you think? Some of its philosophers say that every man has a right to choose the religion that most appeals to him. By trying to stand for everything, doesn't it really stand for nothing?"

"You're not the first critic who's leveled that accusation, and I'm not the first proponent who's been unable to refute it. Hell, darling, I'm not even sure I'm a proponent. I'm more like an inquiring reporter. But I know one thing. Something exists. Maybe it's just man's endless yearning to believe in something—to worship something. Maybe you're my god, my Brahman, as the Hindus call their supreme power. You know, when they speak of Brahman, they say, 'Thou art woman. Thou art man. Thou are the dark-blue bee and the green parrot with red eyes. Thou hast the lightning as thy child. Thou art the seasons and the seas. Thou does abide with all-pervadingness. Wherefrom all things are born.' Now, my love, to me that describes you."

From time to time they picked up conversations as strange as this one, or they talked of "the temporal things" that touched their daily lives: "Our" children, as Tony called them. Or "our" grandchildren. Except for the thought of Quigly, who was never far from her mind, Elizabeth was happy about her family. Charlene and Jim did not seem to have as many problems as one might have feared. Jim was doing well at Douglas now. He'd had two promotions since their marriage and loved his work, his wife, and his daughter. Charlene had been bereft, at first, at the knowledge that she could not have more children, but she seemed to have adjusted to the unhappy idea and spoke instead of how fortunate she was to have the perfect one she had.

The reports from New York continued to be good. The Richardses had gone ahead with their plans, left Scarsdale, and "started over" with a new communication that came through in Ann's frequent and sensible letters. Elizabeth suspected that the adjustment was not quite as easy as Ann wanted it to sound. She had forgiven, but probably would never forget, Peter's unfaithfulness, though that aspect of the problem was never again mentioned. Elizabeth imagined that Peter, too, was making an extraordinary effort. Ann would never entirely change. Surely there were moments when she unwittingly reverted to her old selfishness, but Peter wanted his marriage enough to know that she was trying, not only with outward changes but with an inner determination to be a more giving, more loving, more flexible person. Both her girls would make it, Elizabeth thought. If only she knew what had happened to her son—whatever it was—she believed that her mind would be truly at peace.

Life with Tony was day after day of bliss, the tranquil melding of mutual interests and mutual love. She never stopped being her own person, nor he his. But together they formed a unity that spoke with one voice and one heart.

Robert Gale Associates, no more a dubious enterprise, was now a solid, flourishing business. Tony and Elizabeth were pleased with the people they'd found and delighted with the loyalty of their employees, who obviously were happy working for Mr. Alexander and "Miss Quigly." They'd discovered a charming man who was willing and eager to do the contact work that had once been Laurel's great contribution, and though they would have liked to give him a small share in the business, they dared not. Not at this point, anyway. The profits were good, but there was the house to pay off and the loan, which stretched ahead for years. They had no problem meeting their expenses. Their payroll was higher, but so were their profits. They lived well but modestly. Remembering the old "hand-to-mouth" days when she avoided the butcher and the grocer, Elizabeth gave thanks for her worldly blessings. They had all come from Robert Gale, she thought—the unexpected financial security and the undreamed-of-happiness with Tony. She hoped that somehow Robert knew and approved.

They decided to give a New Year's Eve party to welcome the new decade marked by the year 1960. They'd been married six wonderful years and in all that time they'd never had a big gathering in their beloved house. The party was Elizabeth's idea. She wasn't sure how Tony would take to the thought, particularly to one phase of it.

"Darling," she said one night in early November, "why don't we have a big celebration this New Year's?"

He looked faintly surprised. "Well, sure, if you want to, but I thought you hated organized fun. What do you want to do—go out or invite a few people here?"

"I'd like to invite a lot of people here. The gang from the office. Charlene and Jim. Your parents, if they'd come—"

Tony snorted. "Hah! Stop right there. In the first place we couldn't get them, and in the second place I don't want them. You'd have about as much chance of an acceptance from them as you would from Mamie Eisenhower or her new buddy Laurel Lane!"

"Funny you mentioned Laurel," Elizabeth said slowly. "I thought I'd like to invite her."

He stared at her, dumbfounded. "Sweetheart, you're crazy! What in the name of God makes you think she'd come? And why would you want to ask her?" He gave her a sudden look of understanding. "Oh, I get it," he said. "You know she won't come, but you're still hoping for some kind of reconciliation, aren't you? Don't you ever give up, Elizabeth? I know exactly what's going through your mind. Laurel won't come, but she might answer your letter. And then that would open the door to some kind of dialogue. Honey, forget it. She'll only snub you, if she answers at all."

"Is there anything to lose by trying? I know she was obsessed by the desire for revenge because she honestly believed that we used her. But we had so many good years, Tony. So many in which she was dear and kind to me. I've never stopped feeling that I could make her understand, if only she'd talk to me."

"Sweetheart, I love you for the generous way you think, but please don't start this up again."

She looked at him pleadingly.

"Oh, all right," Tony said reluctantly. "Invite her if you like, but don't be surprised or crushed by her reply. Or more likely her lack of it."

"I won't. I promise." She kissed him. "I have another idea, too. One I'm sure you'll like better."

He raised a dubious eyebrow.

"How about asking Ann and Peter and their children? I think it would be exciting for them and we have plenty of room to put them up for a few days. Besides, I've never even seen Alan and he's nine years old!"

"Fine with me, darling. But are you sure you want to see our grandson or do you want to check up on the progress of the Richardses' marriage?"

"To-ny!" Elizabeth's voice was reproachful.

"Okay, I take it back. Anyway, it's a good idea. You know, we never have had this whole family together, have we? But leave mine out, all right?"

"You mean I mustn't even *ask* them?"

"That's exactly what I mean. If you want a sure-fire guaranteed Grade-A joy-killer, just get my mother over here. I'm dead certain she wouldn't come, but let's not even take the million-to-one gamble."

Elizabeth pretended disappointment. "You won't pamper me, not even on New Year's Eve?"

"No, love, I will not pamper you. Not on New Year's Eve or any other eve. I will love you, admire you, rejoice in you and offer you my life, but pampering is for spoiled babies and foolish women, of which you are neither, thank God."

She laughed. "Deprive me of a mother-in-law, will you? I've never *had* one, you know. I've always just *been* one."

Tony went back to his book. "Some people never know when they're well off," he said. "Sorry, darling. Subject closed."

When Laurel Lane opened her morning mail a week later, she was amazed to find, inside a letter from Stu Preston, a sealed envelope that simply said "Laurel" in a handwriting she instantly recognized. Stu's note explained briefly that Elizabeth, not knowing Laurel's Washington address, had asked him to forward the enclosed. For a moment she was afraid to open it. After all this time, Elizabeth surely would not get in touch with her unless it was something very important, some kind of trouble. Perhaps it had to do with Tony. Maybe, God forbid, something had happened to him. Laurel knew about the marriage. The news had not surprised her. Knowing the depths of Tony's feelings and guessing at the ultimate surrender of Elizabeth, their union was predictable. She no longer felt bitterness. Six years had done much to dispel the outrage. But scorn for her own blindness about Tony persisted. She had behaved like a romantic schoolgirl, not once but twice. It was a role that did not suit Laurel's carefully cultivated image of herself. Almost reluctantly, she opened the envelope.

The invitation to California was the last thing she expected. Couched in Elizabeth's gentle tones, Laurel could almost hear her voice as she read the quite long letter. It was a simple statement of unwavering affection. It spoke freely of their difficulties, without apology and without malice. Mostly, it dwelt at length on the early years when Laurel, Elizabeth said, had given so much to her and her children, when she had been so much a part of their world.

> And so, dearest Laurel, I seem to end as I began—asking for your presence in my life. All that has gone before, both good and bad, is nothing compared to the loss I feel. True friendships are so strong and resilient that by their very nature they have the ability to span the chasm of misunderstanding. You are still my friend, the only woman not born of me whom I truly love. I know that seeing me again, and seeing me with Tony, is not an easy thing to ask. But I like to think that the follies of our early years need not remain as a barrier to devotion in our later ones. Please come to us. There is so much to share.

It was not an ordinary letter, but the writer was not an ordinary woman. Like Tony, Laurel knew that Elizabeth did not really expect her to come, but that she hoped for the reestablishment of contact with one who'd always been important to her. For the first time, Laurel sensed a different Elizabeth, one not quite so strong and capable. The Elizabeth who had written this had the same deep needs and insecurities that beset weaker women. It was not the Elizabeth who had fallen apart over a disastrous love affair with Adam Barnsworth. Nor the one who had despaired when her only son ran off. This was an Elizabeth looking over her shoulder at the specter of age, which ran faster as she moved slower: a woman who had been admired by many but befriended by few. And of those few, the only woman Elizabeth had ever been close to was Laurel Lane.

Impulsively, she went to the typewriter and answered the letter.

> I'm glad you wrote. More than glad—touched and happy and full of admiration. Were our roles reversed, I don't think I could find such generosity of spirit. But then, I never have been the woman you are, Elizabeth. Which, of course, is why Tony always wanted you. He was right, you know, and your happiness proves that he was.
>
> I wish I were big enough, strong enough, and nice enough to say that I would come to see you, but I'm not. Not that I still harbor the old grudges or nourish the old resentments. I'm ashamed of the things I've done and said. Not just the money, which I know was a hardship for you, but the hateful thoughts I've had, the self-pity I've wallowed in, the childish frustrations which I allowed to become banners of martyrdom.
>
> To have—unasked for—both your forgiveness and the confirmation of your continuing love is, I know, more than I deserve. And yet with all this, I feel somehow that it is best if we don't see each other now. One day, perhaps, I'll be grown up enough to share. When that day comes, I will know that I can come to you. And you must know, in return, that if you have real need of me at any time, I shall be at your side . . . spanning those chasms with a friendship that has never died, but has only been in hibernation.

After he'd read Laurel's letter, Tony made no comment about it. He simply looked at Elizabeth with a tender smile.

"Feel better now?"

"Yes," she said. "I feel cleansed and comforted."

The other invitations elicited prompt and delighted response. The Richards clan en masse accepted with pleasure for a long weekend. So did the Jenkins family, who would stay overnight.

"That'll be quite a crew," Tony said. "What are you planning to do, swing hammocks from the ceiling? Thank God the office bunch can make their drunken way back to Los Angeles!"

"No problem. There's plenty of room. It'll be fun. Imagine! All the children will be meeting their cousins for the first time. And even the brothers-in-law have never seen one another. Isn't it ridiculous? You'd think we lived millions of miles from each other instead of just across the country."

Tony was a little more cautious in his enthusiasm. "Let's

just hope that it turns out to be one big happy family," he said. "Geography, my darling, is sometimes much more than a matter of distance, and kids can be very unkind."

"You're thinking of Antoinette, aren't you?"

"Yep. She's the only namesake I'll ever have and I admit to bias, but I'm damned if I'll let those New York smart alecks say one word to hurt her. I hope Ann tells them the facts of life before they meet their little brown-skinned cousin."

"Don't worry, love, she will. I'm sure of it."

"Well, set my mind at ease and remind her of it when you write, will you? Maybe she'd better let Peter explain it. Even with his 'impeccable Scarsdale background,' I think he has a lot more sensitivity than our daughter, in spite of her so-called metamorphosis."

"You still don't believe that Ann has changed, do you?"

"Darling, she's innocent till proved guilty. I know that's not very noble of me, but Ann has always been Academy Award material. Let's just hope this new tolerance and humility isn't just a bid for a matrimonial Oscar."

Elizabeth was unhappy about Tony's reservations. She wanted so much to believe that her daughter had really faced her own flaws and was working hard to erase them. Yet Tony had reason to distrust the "new Ann." He still remembered the old one who had tried and failed, at an early age, to interest the man who was now her mother's husband. It was an ugly thing to remember and she put it out of her mind. Ann was so young then. And she was not the only one who'd been in love with Tony. More ancient history, Elizabeth told herself impatiently. It has nothing to do with today. Look how Ann had behaved when she'd come alone to visit. Despite the closeness of their ages, she'd treated Tony with almost daughterly deference. Unlike Laurel, she'd gotten over her childish fantasies about him. All Ann wanted now was a good marriage to the man she really loved, the father of her children. Elizabeth would, of course, caution her to prepare the small Richardses for a cousin and an uncle who must not, under any circumstances, come as a surprise to them. Probably Ann already had. But it couldn't do any harm to make sure. As for any lingering attachment to Tony, that was as ridiculous as it was distasteful. He was her stepfather.

As Thanksgiving approached, Elizabeth planned a quiet dinner—just Charlene and Jim invited, with Antoinette, of course. That was all the immediate family there was. Besides, it was more than just the traditional holiday. It was their wedding anniversary. They would share it with no one except the two who had stood up for them at the ceremony.

A Yankee at heart, Elizabeth refused to deviate one iota from the enormous Thanksgiving dinner menu of her childhood. Although they would be just five at the table, she prepared a banquet that would feed twice that many. She didn't care. Thanksgiving wasn't real unless the table groaned with turkey, stuffing, and four different vegetables, two kinds of pie, and all the trimmings. It was a time to be surrounded by a feeling of plenty—from food to love. She stayed home from the office the day before to prepare the meal, working happily in her cheerful kitchen, looking forward to the groans of protest and pleasure which would greet her efforts. She was glad that she and Tony had chosen that day on which to be married. It gave special meaning to the word "thanksgiving."

Early in the afternoon, Charlene called. Her voice was strange, as though she was choosing her words carefully for the benefit of an audience. There was a false cheerfulness about it.

"Mother, you'll never guess who just arrived at my house. It's Quigly. He's right here beside me."

Elizabeth caught her breath. "Is he all right, Charlene?"

There was a moment of hesitation. "Yes, of course."

"You can't speak freely, can you?"

"That's right."

"Before you put him on the phone, dear, just answer one or two questions. Is he drunk?"

"No, Mother. Not now."

"But he's been drinking."

"Yes indeed," Charlene tried to sound sprightly.

"I see. Are you all right?"

"Of course, dear, I'll let Quigly speak to you now."

The sound of her son's voice caught at Elizabeth's heart. It was the old, accusatory voice, devoid of amenities even after all these years.

"I came looking for you," he said without preamble. "I didn't know you'd moved."

"Quigly, darling, how wonderful that you've come home! How are you? Where have you been? We've been so worried."

"Don't start with the questions to *me*, Mother. I've got a few of my own. Charlene says you're married to Tony Alexander! For Christ's sake, why?"

"I don't think this is the time to discuss that," Elizabeth

said. "I couldn't very well let you know, since I had no idea where you were. Anyway, there's plenty of time to talk, now that you've come back. I'm very happy, Quigly. Totally happy now that you're here. Where are you living?"

"No place. I just got to Los Angeles. Took the bus out here, thinking my mother would have room for me. I don't know what I'll do now. Maybe leave town again." He laughed. "One thing's for damned sure: I can't go back to Bel Air."

Unthinkingly, Elizabeth said the first thing that came into her mind. "You'll come here until you're settled," she said. "We have plenty of room. I'm sure Charlene can put you up tonight and you can drive out with her and Jim tomorrow. Once you're here, we can make plans. Please don't run off again, Quigly. There's always room for you in my house."

"Yeah? Maybe so. But will your husband feel the same way?"

"Yes," Elizabeth said, "he will."

Quigly's voice was disbelieving. "Well, I'll come tomorrow," he said, "but then we'll see. Here's Charlene. She wants to speak to you again."

"Quigly can stay with us, Mother. We can make room if he doesn't mind the pullout bed in the living room."

"No, darling, I've told him he's to come here. If you can manage tonight, I'll take over from there. He's in bad shape, isn't he?"

"Yes," Charlene answered. "See you tomorrow."

Only when she'd hung up did the realization of what she'd done come over Elizabeth. This wasn't just her house, it was also Tony's. She had no right to invite anyone to stay without discussing it with him. Not even her own son. For that matter, she thought realistically, *least of all* her own son—a moody, angry, unpredictable man who had never liked Tony and obviously could not comprehend or accept the idea of her marriage to him.

As she'd been so many times before, Elizabeth was torn between opposing forces. She was being unfair to Tony. She knew he would go along with whatever made her happy, but he could hardly be expected to welcome this hostile guest. Yet she couldn't let Quigly simply wander off again, leaving her with a hundred unanswered questions to which her vivid imagination provided dreadful answers.

I take advantage of Tony, she thought with remorse. First with Ann. Now with Quigly. Only a man with his compassion and devotion would put up with it. She tried to assuage her guilt with the thought that it would be only for a few days.

Quigly had come back. That meant something. Perhaps, like Ann, he could be made to see what he was doing to himself, as well as to those who loved him. He was a thirty-one-year-old drifter, no more emotionally mature, Elizabeth felt sure, than when he'd run off at sixteen. His life added up to nothing, and from the sound of him he had no more plans for his future than he'd had when she'd tried to convince him to leave Terry Isherwood, go back to school, ultimately get a job and build a solid existence for himself. If he'd rejected that at twenty-one, what hope was there for him now? He'd left Terry, Elizabeth thought ruefully, but under circumstances that no one could have imagined. He was lucky that the agent wanted no ugly publicity. He could have been spending these last years in jail instead of in hiding. God knows where he's been or what he's done. Maybe he wasn't so lucky. Maybe even jail would have been better.

When Tony came home, she told him what had happened. If he was upset, he didn't show it. Instead of recriminations he offered comfort.

"My poor darling," he said, taking Elizabeth into his arms. "You've spent the whole day worrying about how I'd feel, haven't you?"

He felt her head nod against his chest. "I had no right to ask him here without your permission," the muffled voice said. "I knew you'd be wonderful about it, but I can't lie, Tony; I didn't even think of you when I told him to come. Nothing seemed to matter except reaching out to him again. That was terribly wrong of me, terribly stupid and selfish. I don't deserve to be forgiven."

He lifted her tear-stained face. "Sweetheart, there's nothing wrong in what you've done. I'm not in competition with your children. I know my special place in your life. Haven't we always shared the hard things as well as the happy times? This is *our* home, Elizabeth, and anyone either of us invites into it is *our* guest. Besides," he added sensibly, "why are we anticipating the worst? We haven't seen Quigly for years. His visit may be just as surprisingly pleasant as Ann's was—and you know what trepidation we both had about that."

Elizabeth shook her head. "There's nothing I'd rather believe, but I don't hope for a second miracle. You didn't hear his voice on the phone, or Charlene's. No, darling. Quigly won't bring us happiness, much as I'd like to be optimistic about it. I want to see him. I want to find out for myself. But I promise you that it will be a short visit, and I'll try to spare you as much as possible."

"That's not like you," Tony said. "To take such a defeatist

attitude about anything. He's come looking for you again, Elizabeth. He needs you. I'd be the world's most ungrateful man if I didn't do anything I could to repay you for these last years. Don't worry about Quigly and me, and don't talk nonsense about asking my permission for anything you ever decide to do. With one exception. If you ask for a divorce, I'll say no."

She finally managed a smile. "I wish I could tell you how I love you. Without you there'd be no life for me."

He cradled her in his arms. "We'll never be apart," he said. "That much I promise you."

She thought she was prepared for the worst, but the sight of Quigly shocked her when he arrived with the Jenkinses the next day. The bloated look of the heavy drinker was there, more obvious than ever now. He looked, Elizabeth thought to her own shame, like a bum. The cheap, ill-fitting suit was stained and rumpled and he wore no tie under the frayed collar of his soiled shirt. In his hand he carried a small canvas bag, a pitiful container for the few things he owned. Almost recoiling, she went to him and put her arms around him. He stood quietly, arms at his sides, not returning her embrace. His eyes sought Tony's and then shifted away under his stepfather's steady, unreadable scrutiny. Behind Quigly's back, Charlene shook her head at her mother, in a gesture that was either hopelessness or warning.

With determined gaiety, Elizabeth ushered them all into the house, making small, cheerful comments to cover her anxiety. Over and over she told Quigly how happy they were to see him, how incredibly wonderful that the family could be together on this special day.

"It isn't just Thanksgiving, dear," she said, "it's also our wedding anniversary! And now you've made a double celebration a triple one! Oh, Quigly, it's so marvelous to have you home again."

"Is it?" he asked. "Why? Just because it's the return of the prodigal?" He looked down at his clothes. "I certainly don't add anything to the classy tone of the gathering."

"You add something better," Tony said quietly. "Peace of mind for your mother. As for the clothes, how about going into town with us tomorrow and picking up some new things? Californians have a style of their own—casual and comfortable."

"I know," Quigly said. "I lived here once, remember? No thanks. I don't think I'll be around long enough to worry about fitting in with the atmosphere. Not any part of it."

The dinner, which was to be a joyous thing, was tense, with long periods of silence between compliments to Elizabeth on the excellent meal and abortive efforts by Charlene and Elizabeth to keep some kind of normal conversation flowing. Jim had hardly said a word since they arrived. It was obvious that he was troubled by the whole affair. His devotion to Elizabeth and Tony was deep; he didn't like the look, sound, or smell of this interloper who ate with the table manners of a longshoreman and refilled his wineglass constantly without even offering to help anyone else to the contents of the bottle which stood between him and Elizabeth.

Antoinette in her high chair between Tony and Charlene, was the only thing that saved the day. When all else failed, all of them concentrated on the happy, bright-eyed little girl, commenting inanely on how well she handled her food and how pretty she looked in her pumpkin-colored dress. None of them could wait for the meal to be over. All of Elizabeth's preparation and anticipation were spoiled by the presence of the angry stranger who sat at her right, openly scornful of them all.

At nine o'clock, the Jenkinses prepared to leave.

"I think I'll hitch a ride into town with you," Quigly said unexpectedly.

Elizabeth was appalled. "What are you talking about? You're going to stay with us. That's what we arranged yesterday."

"I only make arrangements one day at a time," Quigly said. "Today I feel different. It was a nice dinner. Thanks a lot."

Tony intervened. "Come on, fella," he said easily, "that doesn't make sense. We want you here. We were looking forward to your spending some time with us."

" 'We'?" Quigly's smile was mirthless. "You mean 'she,' don't you? Mother'd probably like to keep me around so she could pump me about where I've been and what I've been doing, but don't tell me *you* want me to stay. I stopped believing in fairytales a long time ago, Alexander."

If there was a subtle implication in his last words, Tony chose to ignore it, just as he elected to remain unruffled by Quigly's boorishness.

"I speak for both of us, Quigly," he said. "Your mother and I want you to stay for a while."

"Don't give me that noble crap. I know you hate my guts."

"No, I have no reason to hate you." Tony's tone was reasonable. "Nor do I have reason to like you. I don't know

you, Quigly, any more than you know me. I don't feel anything for you, but I feel a great deal for your mother. I
doubt that she could produce a child who didn't have some
redeeming features. Maybe I'd like a chance to find out what
they are."

"Oh, Jesus, I think I'm going to puke! What are you, a
fancy preacher? And what the hell do you think your wife is,
some kind of saint? You make me sick!"

"Quigly, that's enough!" Elizabeth's voice was loud and
firm. She was angry, not for herself but for the vicious, unwarranted attack on Tony. "Tony has every right and every
reason to throw you out of this house. He wants you to stay
and so do I, but if you can only answer kindness with crud-
ity, then you don't belong here at all. Go on back to town.
Go wherever you want. Get out of our lives and this time
stay out!"

He was as surprised as if she had physically struck him.
He had expected her to plead with him to stay. The sadistic
streak in him wanted to watch her beg. Confused, he hesitated. In the background, Jim and Charlene stood silently,
Antoinette asleep in her father's arms. The adults looked at
him with expressions that ranged from Jim's outright disgust
to Tony's still unperturbed face.

"Well, what the hell," he said finally. "What's a day or
two more or less? Where do I sack out?"

"Down that hall," Tony said. "First door to the right."

Charlene lingered after Quigly had made his way to his
room and Jim had taken Antoinette out to the car.

"Are you sure he should stay?" she asked them. "He was
so strange last night. I heard him stumbling around in the
living room until all hours, talking to himself. I'm afraid of
him, Mother. I can't forget that awful business with the
Isherwood woman, I don't know what it is, but I think his
mind is affected. Maybe we should just let him go. I know
you don't want to, but I don't think he's responsible. And
with the way he feels about Tony—"

"I'm a big boy, love," Tony said. "I can take care of
myself *and* your mother. You know we can't just turn him
out, Charlene. He has nowhere else to go."

"We'll be all right," Elizabeth echoed. "You go home with
that worn-out child. I'll talk to you in the morning."

When the car drove off, Elizabeth turned a despairing face
to her husband. "She's right, you know. He acts as though
he is unbalanced. I suppose all the drinking has affected his
mind, the way it did his father's. Tony, what are we going to
do?"

"We're going to see what the next few days bring," he said. "Let's wait till Monday. The shop is closed till then and I won't leave you alone in the house with him for a minute."

"He wouldn't hurt me," Elizabeth said. "I'm sure of that. But I don't think I can help him."

"You can talk to him," Tony answered. "When you do, you'll know soon enough."

Chapter 32

The smiling, well-scrubbed Quigly who appeared for breakfast the next morning was almost more of a shock than the surly boor of the previous evening. He sat down at the table with Tony and Elizabeth and gave them a shamefaced, boyish smile.

"I don't know how to apologize for last night," he said. "I guess I had too much wine. Combined with all the emotion, I must have been a pretty ugly character. I hope you'll forgive me. Especially you, Tony."

It was not a very good act, and his audience was undeceived. If anything, this sly change of attitude frightened Elizabeth more than ever. It reminded her of Alan Whitman: one minute the charming, guileless gentleman, the next a raging, threatening brute. Even Tony, without a similar frame of reference, was not so easily taken in by this pretense of an overnight transformation, and Quigly was not stupid enough to think he was fooling either of them. He shrugged his shoulders. "Okay," he said. "Forget it. I was soberer last night than I've been in years. And as for emotion, that's a laugh. Being here doesn't mean any more to me than anywhere else I've been lately. Sorry about that, folks.

If you expected a repentant sinner you're in for a big disappointment."

"I don't know *what* we expected," Elizabeth said. "At least, I don't know what *I* expected. Tony doesn't know you well enough to have any predetermined opinions, good or bad."

Quigly looked impatient. "Come on, Mother, you don't really think I'm going to swallow that one. I know damned well you've told him everything about me from the day I was born. He knew what to expect. The same as you did."

"You're right," Tony said. "I know all about you—including the way your mother loves you. There's only one thing I don't know, Quigly. Why have you come back? Because you had no place else to go?"

"Bingo! Right on the nose! I got tired of running. I figured that Pasadena was as good a berth as any for a guy who was fresh out of dough. Of course, I didn't know how the setup had changed. That kind of loused up my plans." He yawned, pretending indifference. "Well, that's the breaks, right? I'll get moving right after breakfast. Three's a crowd in your little love nest."

Elizabeth was determined to let Tony make this decision. She had asked Quigly here without consulting him. She would not urge him to stay without some sign from her husband, and she would bite off her tongue before she'd ask her son where he'd been all this time.

"Where will you go?" Tony asked quietly.

"Who the hell knows? Maybe back to Mexico." He looked at Elizabeth. "I know you've been dying to ask, Mother. Well, that's where I went after I had the run-in with Terry and took off. It's a nice little country to get lost in, and the living's cheap. What I took from Terry kept me going for quite a while. After that money ran out I picked up odd jobs, showing the tourists around and working on fishing boats out of Baja. It was okay, but it got boring as hell. That's why, when I heard she hadn't died I figured it was safe, so I decided to come back to the dear old U.S. of A." He laughed. "Maybe I even had some crazy sentimental idea of being with my mother in her declining years. I pictured you as a lonely old lady. How about that? Instead, you've got yourself a young husband, a big house, and a fat wallet. Terrific! I should have known you'd come up smelling like roses. You always have."

Elizabeth could not restrain herself. "Why did you do it, Quigly? Why did you assault and rob Terry Isherwood? God

knows it wasn't a very pretty setup, but in her own way she
was good to you."

"Good to me? Sure, she was good to me. She gave me
money and clothes and a car and all the booze I could
drink. Why not? I was the lay she paid for. She was good to
me the way she was good to any servant. And she thought
she could kick me out the same way she'd fire a maid who
didn't suit her any more. I don't take that kind of treatment
from anybody. I leave when *I'm* ready to leave. Not when
some cheap tramp tells me to. She knew what a bitch she
was. Look how she covered my tracks for me. It wasn't
kindness, you can believe that. She was goddamned scared
that if the police caught me I'd tell the world what she is.
She got what she deserved from me, the stinking, lousy
bitch."

Elizabeth thought she was going to be sick. Only the firm
pressure of Tony's hand on hers kept her from giving in to
her physical revulsion. There was not an ounce of remorse in
Quigly. He had freely admitted assault and robbery, yet he
had no more guilt about it than if he had killed a bee that
had stung him. He was psychotic. The right thing to do was
to have him committed to an institution for his own safety
and the protection of others. It would be pointless to call
the police, even if she could bring herself to do it. Terry
would not press charges and Quigly would never admit what
he had told her and Tony. She supposed she could have him
declared mentally incompetent, but the thought of Quigly
locked away in an asylum was as terrible in its way as the
idea of Quigly loose and destined to do other brutal things
without a twinge of conscience.

Like his wife, Tony had listened with disgust to this de-
ranged tale of violence and revenge. Quigly was the per-
sonfication of evil, but he was also a sick man. And above
all, he was Elizabeth's child. When Tony finally spoke, his
voice was calm and reassuring.

"All right, Quigly," he said. "So much for the past. Nothing to be done about it in this life. Let's think about the
future. You say you expected to come home and be with
your mother. In a way, I'm responsible for the foul-up in
your plans. If you'll let me, I'd like to help you figure out
where you go from here. You can't spend your life drifting
without purpose. Maybe together the three of us can help
you find a better way to live."

Quigly rolled his eyes toward heaven. "Jesus Christ, you
really are a preacher, aren't you? Don't be a jerk. I'm not
interested in all that mealymouthed junk about a better life.

Life stinks. It ain't worth a plug nickel. Not yours or mine. Nothing goes right. Nobody's any damned good. The world is full of phonies and grafters and pious do-gooders who'd carve your heart out and tell you it was for your own good. Thanks a lot, but I'm cutting out of here. Good riddance to you know what."

"Quigly, you're a fool." Elizabeth's voice shook. "Tony doesn't care about you. Why should he? But he knows that I care. I gave birth to you, and that's a fact bigger than all my logical reservations. I'm stubborn enough not to step aside and let you destroy yourself if there's the slightest chance that you can be helped. Tony knows that. He's willing to make the effort for me. Can't you do the same?"

Her son looked away from her. "I'm not worth it," he said. "I'll screw up your life. You don't know me. I get these crazy periods when I know I'm off my rocker. When I'm making sense, I know the best thing for everybody would be for me to kill myself. And when I go nuts, there's no telling what I'm liable to do. I talk big. Big man. Tough. But I'm nothing but a scared drunk, like my old man was. Remember when I got in that trouble in San Diego? I smashed up a bar because I was out of my head. Because a dumb little broad with my baby in her killed herself because of me. I went nuts that time. I've done it before. I did it later, with Terry. And God help me, Mother, how do you know I won't do it again?"

This was one of the rare lucid, honest moments of Quigly's life. Everything hangs in the balance at this instant, Elizabeth thought. If we can get to him now, maybe there's a chance.

"I don't know that you won't do it again," Elizabeth said. "None of us knows that. But if Tony and I think it's worth the risk, what do you have to lose? Stay with us for a while, Quigly. Give yourself a chance at a little peace and quiet at least. We won't bother you. I won't nag or question or try to push you. Maybe here, where nature is so overwhelming that we all feel humble, you'll be able to sort out your life. And anytime you want to go, you'll be free to go. You're not a prisoner here. You're a welcome member of the family."

Even as a child Quigly had never cried. But now a trace of moisture came into his eyes. "I'm afraid," he said. "I want to stay. I don't want to start out again with no direction, bumming my way to nowhere. But, damn it, I have to be honest." He turned to Tony. "The only person I've ever cared about is my mother. Charlene's okay, but I never really got to know her. She was always like a little doll. As for Ann, I used to think she was my best friend, but now I know that she's as much of a fake in her way as I am in mine. As for you, Tony, I don't like you. I never have. I don't trust all that self-sacrificing goodness. I think you've used Mother, just as the rest of us have—"

Elizabeth tried to interrupt, to protest Quigly's cutting, slow-measured words, but Tony silenced her.

"Let him go on," Tony said. "It's better that he does."

Quigly smiled. The tears were gone now, the old, hard-bitten expression returned. "See what I mean? That's what I don't trust. Any red-blooded guy who'd let somebody tell him that that person didn't like him or trust him would punch the bastard in the mouth and throw him out of the house. Unless he had some very good reason to keep on playing a phony game. I don't know what yours is, Tony. But if I stay here, you can be damned sure I'll find out."

"You can't find out what doesn't exist," Tony said, "but you're welcome to try. Just as you're still welcome to stay. I don't think it's going to be a very pleasant interval for any of us, but at least you're open about it. I can't say I like what I've heard, but I respect your courage in saying it. And since the one thing we do have in common is love for the same woman, we might at least try to accept each other for her sake."

The two men faced each other, one with open hostility, the other with cool disdain.

"Have I nothing to say about this?" Elizabeth asked. "Or do I simply stand by and wait for you two to decide whether you can live under the same roof?"

"Darling, the decision is yours. You know that," Tony said.

" 'Darling, the decision is yours,' " Quigly mimicked. "You're really smart, aren't you, Tony? When the chips are down, you don't take any responsibility for the wayward son. You can always say that it was her choice. If I set fire to the house or beat up the gardener, you won't even have to say 'I told you so.' She'll know that without being told."

"Quigly, shut up!" Elizabeth's voice was a command. "I must be the one who's crazy, to let you stay here. The risks are all on our side, Tony's and mine, remember? We've been happy with our marriage and our home. Do you think I'm looking forward to the disruption of the most wonderful time of my life? I can be honest, too: I'm more frightened of having you stay here than you are of staying. Not because I think you'll do anything violent, but because if your warped mind even vaguely threatens what Tony and I have between us, I think I might kill you myself!"

Neither of them had ever seen her so angry, so out of control.

"I have no right to make demands on you, Quigly, or you on me," Elizabeth went on. "Yes, I want to help you because there are blood ties between us. But you'll have to make me think you're salvageable. And that, I admit before God, I've never been able to do. I've loved you as a mother. But I find you inadequate as a man and pathetic as a human being. Now you know it all. If you want to stay and behave yourself, Tony and I will try to be your friends. If you can't accept Tony as the head of this house, as my husband and the man I love, then we'd better make some other arrangements. You see, son, I'm not as good as Tony. I'm trying to be. I'm trying to live up to the kind of compassionate person he is. And God knows he's never proved himself more than he has today."

She expected Quigly to slam out of the door, and in her heart she wished he would. It was madness to take this crude, insulting, dangerous young man into their home. She would be playing a far too dangerous game with her way of life and Tony's. Give him up, she told herself. It's like bringing a loaded revolver into the house.

But he didn't leave. In another of those split-second changes of personality he became, if not pleasant, at least docile.

"Okay," he said. "I'll stay a little while if you'll let me. It won't be for long. Just till I can figure out where to go from here. I'm sorry, Tony. I don't take back what I said, but I won't ever say it again. That's a promise." He got up from the table. "I think I'll take a walk, if you don't mind."

When he'd disappeared, Elizabeth put her head in her hands. "My God, what have I done? How can I inflict this on you?"

"Sweetheart, it isn't tragic," Tony said. "It's sad, for you and for him. He thinks he doesn't want help, Elizabeth, but we both know he's crying out for it in the only way he knows how. Look, it won't be easy having Quigly around, but I don't think it will be for long. He needs more help than we can give him. You have to face that. One of these days he'll just cut and run. You must start adjusting to that idea."

"Right now I'm ashamed to tell you that I wish he would."

"I know. And it's nothing to be ashamed of. Quigly won't give an inch. I don't think there's anything we can do about it except to stand by until he decides to take off again."

"But it's all so futile," Elizabeth said. "And I was telling the truth. I am afraid that having him around will do something to us. I'm convinced that he's mentally unsound. I wish I could bring myself to have him put somewhere for treatment, but I can't face it. I can't face anything, it seems. Not the threat of having him here and not the anxiety of seeing him disappear again. Oh, Tony, promise me that whatever happens it won't make any difference between us!"

"Nothing could make any difference between us." He tried to cheer her up. "Not a dozen Quiglys, not an earthquake, not even my mother."

She managed a smile. "Thank you, darling."

"Thank *you*, darling, for agreeing to be stuck with me through a thousand reincarnations."

Quigley's visit stretched into a week, then a month. There were no more scenes like that one of the first morning. There was nothing. They seemed to be playing a watchful waiting game, calm on the surface, abnormally normal. Elizabeth felt like a character in a surrealistic dream. She and Tony resumed their daily normal lives, going into the office four days a week. Quigly never left the house, and each time Elizabeth returned to it she wondered whether she'd find that he'd gone berserk in their absence or whether he'd be there at all. If he was thinking about his future he did not discuss it, and neither Elizabeth nor Tony mentioned it. Quigly seemed to be marking time, as they all were. Only when she was alone with Tony in their room did she feel even remotely like herself. The rest of the time she seemed to be walking on tiptoes, holding her breath, listening for the explosion.

At Christmas, they went to Charlene's for dinner. It was the first time in a month that Elizabeth felt any relaxation of tension, and that was because Antoinette was now old enough to really enjoy the day and her excitement was contagious even to the unreadable and uncommunicative Quigly. Charlene, though she spoke to her mother daily on the telephone and knew the uneasy truce in which she lived, had begun to feel a little easier about her brother. He had been drinking almost nothing during this last month, Elizabeth reported, and had seemed to be using the Alexanders' house as a rest home, sleeping late, eating well, and taking long solitary walks along the beach. Charlene knew that it was a taut-wire atmosphere, but she was glad to see Quigly looking almost like the handsome young man she remembered. He had lost much of his bloat and had even accepted

Elizabeth's offer of some new clothes, mumbling his thanks as she went with him to pick out two new suits and everything that went with them, from the skin out. .

During the course of the Christmas celebration, Charlene got Tony aside for a low-voiced conversation.

"How's it going?" she asked.

Tony smiled. "Almost too uneventfully," he admitted. "I worry about your mother. She's on the alert every minute. Can't say I blame her. From what I know of Quigly, this acquiescent attitude is too exaggerated to be real. It's weird. It really is."

"Does he say anything about what he's going to do?"

"Nothing. But some kind of move will have to be made, Charlene. He can't be with us the rest of our lives—not for his sake or ours."

"Mother says he never leaves the house except to go for walks. I wish he'd start looking for some kind of job and get his own place. What are you and Mother going to do, Tony?"

"I'm not sure, honey, but we'll have to do something right after New Year's. I think maybe Elizabeth is hoping that the sight of you and Ann with your families may jar Quigly into the realization that each of you kids has to find a life of your own. Anyway, we'll get through the holidays and if Quigly doesn't look like he's going to make a move, I'm afraid we'll just have to risk an explosion and tell him it's time to start job-hunting."

Charlene sighed. "You are really the soul of patience, both of you. I can't figure out what Quigly has in mind. Surely he knows he can't live with you and Mother forever."

"I'm surprised he's lasted this long, the way he feels about me. I hate to sound cynical, but I think he was just physically exhausted when he came to us. I believe that's the only reason he has stayed. Maybe I'm hoping that now he's back in shape, he'll begin to make plans."

"Me, too," Charlene said. "Anyway, New Year's will be fun. I can't wait to see Ann and Peter and their children. When do they arrive?"

"December twenty-ninth. They'll be with us till the third of January."

"Poor Tony. You really married a familyful, didn't you?"

He laughed. "Wouldn't have it any other way. Well, *almost* any other way."

Quigly politely declined the invitation to go to the airport to meet the Richardses. "Seven of you in the station wagon with luggage seems enough," he said. "Besides, I'll have the martinis chilled when you get here." Elizabeth's worried look did not escape him. "Don't worry, Mother, I won't sample them. I'll be cold sober when I meet my very proper brother-in-law. Besides, haven't you noticed what a model of temperance I've been this past month? I don't drink as many martinis as you do."

"That fact has crossed my mind," Elizabeth said, "with pleasant awareness. You're looking very well these days, Quigly. I know Ann will be so happy to see you in such good shape."

"Has she changed much?"

"Yes, I think you'll find her quite a different girl. What am I saying? Girl! Good lord, Ann's going to be thirty-four on her next birthday! I just can't believe it. Anyway, she's gained a lot of awareness. I'm very pleased with her. You will be, too."

Quigly's only answer was a sardonic smile.

The Richardses arrived like a breath of crisp, fresh air from the East. They were a strikingly beautiful family. The handsome, successful young father. The well-dressed young mother. And three children whose good manners spoke of a well-ordered home life laced with the kind of social poise that reasonably affluent New York children acquire early in life.

Elizabeth couldn't get over her grandchildren. Peter III, still called Ditto, of course, was a tall, good-looking boy of thirteen. Elizabeth Joanne, at eleven, had her mother's blond beauty and a gentle shyness that was reminiscent of Charlene at the same age. But it was little Alan who really captured his grandmother's heart on sight. Perhaps it was because she had never seen him, this child who was born during the period of Elizabeth's estrangement from Ann. Until this moment, Alan Richards had been only a name and a photograph. Now he became a nine-year-old delightful reality with an impish face, a perpetual grin and an irrepressible curiosity about California.

"Does the sun really shine here all year long, Grandmama?" he asked as they started the long homeward drive.

"Well, no, darling, not exactly," Elizabeth said. "Sometimes we get a good bit of rain. And at this time of year it can even be quite chilly. But we don't have changes of seasons, the way you do."

He thought about that for a moment. "You mean it never

snows. I don't think I'd like that. I couldn't go skating in Central Park."

"You mean *ice*-skating, dopey," Ditto said from the superiority of his teen-age knowledge. "You can *roller*-skate here all year round. And Mom says Grandmama's house is right on the ocean. Boy! I'd like to learn how to surf! I bet that's a heck of a lot more exciting than dumb old skates!" He turned to Tony. "Do you know how to surf, uh . . . Sorry, sir, what do I call you?"

" 'Tony' will do fine. As for surfing, I'm no expert but I manage. I was brought up here, Ditto. All California kids learn to swim about the same time they learn to walk. Surfing comes a little later, but we all take a whack at it."

"I can swim," Alan said proudly. "We all learned how at Grandmama Richards'. Even Jo, and she's only a girl."

"Okay, kids," Ann said, "let's not monopolize the conversation. I'd like to get a word in edgewise, and so would your father."

"Obediently, her brood subsided. Ann's word obviously was law, but there was no rebellion against the order to be quiet. She's doing a good job, Elizabeth thought happily. She's mastered the fine art of discipline without making her children feel put upon or unloved.

For the next half hour, the adults chatted amiably, each family bringing the other up to date on their news while the children quietly looked out the car window and made occasional comments on palm trees, orange groves, and other fascinating discoveries in this strange new land. Finally, Elizabeth turned to the children.

"You have a lot of lovely surprises in store," she said. "I'm sure your mommy and daddy told you that you're going to meet your uncle Quigly for the first time ever. And your uncle Jim, too. Ditto, you and Elizabeth Joanne have met Aunt Charlene, but I doubt that you'll even remember her, it was so long ago. And there's a baby cousin, too. Her name's Antoinette."

A strange silence settled over the car. Elizabeth looked questioningly at Ann. Ann seemed uncomfortable and Peter frowned.

"I've told the children that their uncle Quigly has been traveling for many years," she said.

Elizabeth waited.

"And they understand that Aunt Charlene's husband and baby are a little different than the people we know. But they're well-brought-up children," Ann added hastily, speaking more to them than to Elizabeth, "and they know that nice people don't comment on others who are not as fortunate as themselves. They're very anxious to meet their cousin Antoinette and their uncle Jim."

"Mommy says we have to be nice to them even though they're Negroes," Alan piped up innocently. Ditto punched his little brother hard in the ribs.

"Shut up, dummy! You know we're not supposed to mention that!"

Elizabeth felt sick at heart. She looked at Ann, who blushed and then raised her chin in the old defiant way.

"How would *you* have explained it, Mother?" she asked.

Elizabeth didn't answer. She certainly was not going to have an argument with Ann in front of her children, but she knew how she would have explained it. She would have spoken of the great love between Charlene and Jim, and the beautiful baby whom they adored. Admittedly, it was a subject that took careful exposition, not an easy situation for children or, for that matter, adults to grasp. But one thing she knew she would not have done: she would not have implanted the idea that Charlene's niece and nephew "had to be nice" to their "less fortunate" uncle and cousin. She took what comfort she could from the knowledge that they did, indeed, seem to be well-mannered children, but they were only children nonetheless, and heedless of the hurt they could inflict. Probably Ditto was old enough to watch what he said, and little Jo, as they called her, seemed a quiet, almost spiritual child who seemed to have great sensitivity. If an awkward moment came, it would be through some spontaneous curious comment from the exuberant youngest Richards.

Tony took his hand off the wheel for a moment to gently pat her knee. "Don't worry," he said under his breath. "Jim can handle it. And Antoinette's only four."

It wasn't so much the idea of what might be said, Elizabeth realized, as the recognition that Ann hadn't really changed as much as her mother had hoped. She was still a snob, still a hopelessly bigoted, basically ignorant girl. Those few days in California had not really changed her outlook. They simply represented a period when she was repentant and worried, full of a determination to change which, no doubt, she meant at the moment but which Elizabeth now saw clearly was no more than expedience. Tony had said that time had a way of making people relapse into their old ways after a crisis had passed. In Ann's case, he'd accurately predicted what had happened. She had changed her address and her activities, but it was clear that the old attitudes were no different than they'd ever been.

Elizabeth looked at Peter, who had barely spoken a word since he'd arrived. He seemed to have the insulated air of a man who had settled for less than what he wanted, but who no longer was interested enough to fight. Elizabeth guessed that Peter had become a younger Adam Barnsworth—a man who would stay with his wife through a sense of obligation and duty but who no longer loved her. Like Adam, Peter would cheat. And like Monica, Ann would pretend that none of it was happening. Elizabeth felt sorry for them both. Peter was trapped by his own conscience, as Adam had been. As for Ann, despite her disappointing reversion to type, Elizabeth pitied this young woman who could not rise above her opinionated little view of what life was all about.

An unsmiling but sober Quigly awaited them. He was polite as he was introduced to Peter and the children, but when he turned to his sister and kissed her lightly on the cheek, it was with something close to indifference. Even Ann could not let the chilly reception pass unremarked.

"Well, Quigly, after all this time I'd hardly call that an enthusiastic greeting," she said. "We haven't seen each other in more than fifteen years!"

"I know. You haven't changed."

"Neither, apparently, have you," she said tartly.

"I guess whatever we are, we only become more so as we get older." Quigly's voice was unpleasant. "Nice people become nicer." The unfinished implication made Ann go white with anger.

Uncomprehending, the children stood silent and bewildered until Elizabeth hastily interrupted. "Come along, and we'll show you where everybody beds down. Ann, you and Peter will have the guest room next to Quigly's. The boys will go in there. Quigly says he can make do on the living room couch. Charlene and Jim will take the smallest guest room. They'll only stay overnight, and then Quigly can take that room."

"What about me, Grandmama?" A wistful Elizabeth Joanne looked up at her.

"For you, love, we have a little surprise. I'm going to tuck you and Antoinette into the open-out couch in the library. You're such a big girl that you can look after your little cousin, okay?"

Jo looked almost frightened. "You mean I have to sleep in the same bed with her?"

"Darling, we're guests," Ann said quickly. "Grandmama has a full house. You don't mind sharing a room for one night, do you? She has her own room at home," Ann explained to Elizabeth, "that's all she means."

"Is it?" Elizabeth asked frostily. "I'm glad to hear that." She put her arm around Jo. "Wait till you see Antoinette, sweetheart. She's like a little angel."

Alan hooted. "You're funny, Grandmama! How can Antoinette be an angel? They're white and she's black."

Peter Richards spoke sharply. "That's enough, Alan!" Then his voice softened. "Angels don't have any special color. They're not the way you see them in books, son. Besides, your grandmother wasn't talking about that kind of angel. She meant a dear little girl who is your first cousin, your mother's sister's child whom we'll all love very much. I know."

Alan retreated. "Yes, sir," he said. Then, determined to have the last word, he teased his sister. "I'm sure glad Aunt Charlene didn't have a boy. 'Cause maybe I'd have to share the bed instead of you!"

"You be quiet, Alan Richards!" Jo shouted. "Just wait and see. I'll get back at you, you rotten, nasty little brat!"

The sudden outburst from this demure child startled Elizabeth. It wasn't only Alan who'd been brainwashed about Negroes. They all had. Probably Ditto, too, though he was old enough not to show it.

Peter took charge. "I'm ashamed of both of you," he said. "So is your mother. Now get moving, all of you. You're big enough to unpack your own clothes, so get at it."

"Come on, boys, I'll show you your bunks," Quigly said.

"And I'll escort you to the library, madame," Tony announced gravely to Jo.

"I know where our room is," Ann said. "I'll go settle in."

Elizabeth and Peter were left alone in the living room.

"I'm sorry," he said. "I don't think there'll be any more trouble. You know how kids are, Elizabeth."

She smiled at him affectionately. "Yes, I know how they are. I also know they have to be taught to hate and fear. Just the way it says in that song from *South Pacific*. 'It has to be drummed in their dear little ears. They have to be carefully taught.' "

"Ann tried to prepare them. She really did."

"Don't feel you have to defend her, Peter," Elizabeth said sadly. "I know my own daughter. I also know the limits of her tolerance."

He didn't answer.

"I wish it had turned out to be what you deserve. You're a very nice man."

It was his turn to smile with fondness. "It's not all that

bad, really. In her own way, Ann has tried harder ever since she came back from the visit with you. Life is somewhat improved. In fact, it's quite a remarkable change in many ways. I know marriages that are a helluva lot worse."

"And some that are a helluva lot better."

"Yes," Peter agreed. "Yours, for instance. From what I've seen, you and Tony have the kind of marriage they write about in storybooks."

"We have," Elizabeth said. "But don't forget that for me it took two tries, and at least one major mistake in between."

The next day Tony volunteered to drive the Richardses into Los Angeles for a sight-seeing trip. The children and Peter accepted enthusiastically, but Ann elected not to go.

"I've seen it before," she said. "Peter and the kids never have. I'll stay here. Maybe I can help Mother with some of the preparations for tomorrow night."

"Everything's under control," Elizabeth assured her. "Do go if you like, Ann."

"No, I'd rather stay here with you and Quigly, if you don't mind."

"Of course I don't mind," Elizabeth said.

Ann glanced at Quigly, who was sitting with his feet propped up, reading a news magazine.

"What about you, dear brother? Mind having me around?"

He didn't look up. "Doesn't make any difference to me," he said.

Ann approached his chair. "Mother says you do a lot of walking. How about taking me on a conducted tour of the beach? It's a nice day."

For a moment she thought he was going to refuse, but he put down his magazine and got to his feet.

"Okay, if you want to."

They made their way down the steep incline from the house to the edge of the ocean by way of a series of rough, treacherous stones which served as a precarious stairway to the beach. Twice Ann slipped and would have fallen if Quigly hadn't caught her.

"My God," she said breathlessly, "this was a little more than I bargained for. Isn't there an easier way?"

He shook his head. "This is the only path. I like it. It's dangerous. Do you know, Ann, that if I hadn't grabbed you, you could have fallen all the way to the bottom? You probably would have been killed. Better be sure the kids don't try this unless there's a grown-up holding on to them."

She looked at him suspiciously. "I don't believe that this is the only path, Quigly. Mother wouldn't navigate this, and she'd have warned me about it for the children's sake. You're lying. Of course! I remember now, from my last visit. There's a perfectly good flight of steps going down the other side. I'll bet Mother doesn't even know these are here! Damn you, Quigly, you just wanted to scare me, didn't you? It gives you some kind of sick pleasure to frighten people. You really are a monster!"

He laughed. "Better keep your eyes open and your mouth shut, Ann. We're still a long way from the bottom."

Furious, she took his advice. When they reached the safety of the sand, she faced him, eyes blazing. "What the hell's wrong with you? What have I ever done to you? Hurt your precious ego? Just because I lied about your being a common sailor because I knew the Richardses wouldn't understand? Is that any reason to hate me? You do hate me, Quigley. You've made that very clear."

He looked out at the ocean. "You're not worth hating, Ann. I don't feel any emotion except distrust. When we were very young I loved you because I thought you were the only person in the family who loved me. Later on I realized you never cared, not about me or anybody except yourself. You pretended to be close to me, but it was only to have me on your side, against Mother and Charlene. You did some bad things to me, Ann. Things that are too late to undo. But I don't care about that any more. I don't care about myself, but I do care about Mother. You never stop hurting her, do you? Like yesterday. You must have done a great job on those kids preparing them to meet their new relatives. And I watched you last night. You were trying to flirt with Tony. I don't know who else saw it, but believe me, little sister, I didn't miss it. You've got big eyes for him, haven't you? You're a bitch, Ann. You're the most immoral woman I've ever known."

"How dare you! You of all people! God knows what kind of things you've done in these last fifteen years! And you stand there and accuse *me* of being immoral!!"

"Your morality is only technical. Maybe you've only slept with one guy in your life, but in my book the way you think makes you more of a slut than the worst whore on the waterfront. Oh, you keep your body very pure. But your mind is as dirty as a pimp's. We're a great pair, you and I: the prissy daughter with hot pants for her stepfather and the nasty, crazy son with the lurid past. We're cute, you and I. Just what Mother deserves."

She ignored the upsetting reference to her feelings for Tony. "I find your sudden concern for Mother very touching," Ann said sarcastically. "Where the hell were you all the years she needed you?"

"Where you were: a million miles away."

"And I presume that moving in and sponging on her now is supposed to make up for all the geographical absence?"

"No. When I came home I didn't know she'd married. At first I was wild. I hated Tony Alexander. I told them both I didn't trust him. I thought he was using her. I guess that's because I thought everybody used her, the way you and I always did."

"And now you've changed your mind?"

"Hard as it is to believe, the answer is yes. I'm glad she has Tony. He has more guts than any of us. And he really cares for her, which is more than we've ever done. That's why I didn't like what I saw last night. You stay the hell away from Tony, do you hear me? If that tight-assed husband of yours isn't man enough to keep you in line, I sure as hell am."

Suddenly she was frightened because there was truth to what he was saying. She had tried to be a little flirtatious around Tony last night, but she told herself that it didn't mean anything. After all, she had thought she was in love with him once, but that was all over. She'd wanted to show Peter that she was desirable to other men. That's all it was. Now she knew that Quigly saw what she'd denied even to herself. She had been making a play for Tony. Her brother's mind, distorted by years of resentment against her, had read the true meaning in her actions. He had made her face her own unspeakable desires, and she didn't doubt for a moment that he really would kill her if he thought she was going to pursue them.

"Quigly," she said reasonably, "maybe you have reason to dislike me for what I used to be. But I'm different now. I love my husband and my children. I love Mother. I came all the way out here to ask her for help when I thought my marriage was breaking up. I did think I was in love with Tony once, but I swear to you, on my children's lives, that I haven't had that kind of a thought about him since the day I met Peter. And that's the God's truth!"

"What would you know about the truth? Or God either? Just watch your step, Ann. I'm warning you."

He turned away and walked up the beach, leaving her to find her way back to the house. Just as she remembered, there was a very safe flight of wooden steps leading directly up the cliff.

Chapter 33

On the morning of the last day of the year 1959, Elizabeth awoke reluctantly, her whole body feeling leaden, as though it was too heavy to get out of bed. This sense of exhaustion was strange for her. Usually she came back from sleep alert and eager to explore a new day. Her strong, healthy body was capable of carrying her through hours of strenuous activity, and her agile mind was always curious about what lay ahead.

But this morning she was reluctant to move. The place beside her was empty. Tony had quietly crept out of the room without disturbing her. Dimly, she could hear sounds of activity in the house—the high-pitched voices of Ann's children and the rumbling sounds of the three men who already were moving about. It was past nine o'clock. Almost two hours later than she normally slept. And still she did not get up. She lay on her back, staring at the ceiling, dreading the moment when she would have to become part of this troubled household.

The day before had been ominous. After the walk from which Ann and Quigly returned separately, the two had not exchanged a single word. Even when Tony and Peter and the children came back from their drive, Ann did not immediately come out of the guest room to greet them. Right after a lunch in which her two children did not speak to each other, Ann had retired to her bed, pleading a headache. She stayed there until dinner time.

In midafternoon, Elizabeth tiptoed in to see if she was all right. Ann was lying on her side, her face to the wall.

"Ann, are you awake?" Elizabeth whispered.

"Yes."

"Are you all right? Is there anything I can do for you?"

"No, nothing, thanks. I just want to be left alone."

Elizabeth frowned. "Did something happen between you and Quigly? Did you have an argument?"

"Please, Mother, I don't feel like talking." Ann was trying to be patient. Elizabeth knew she should leave, but she didn't. Instead, she sat on the edge of the bed.

"Darling, if Quigly upset you, I wish you'd tell me about it. He's highly volatile, but he can't help himself. Tony and I have come to realize that this past month. For days and weeks he can seem perfectly normal, and then the slightest little thing can set him off. He's a sick boy."

Ann sat bolt upright. "Are you blind? A sick boy? He's a maniac! Do you know he tried to kill me this morning?" Her voice was shrill, almost a scream.

Elizabeth tried to quiet her. "Hush, Ann. Quigly will hear you."

"Let him! He's crazy, I tell you! That dirty, depraved mind of his! He should be put away!"

"Sweetheart, what's this all about? What makes you think he tried to kill you?"

Ann told her about the dangerous steps. Elizabeth paled. She knew of no such steps. Quigly had either discovered them or else he'd spent all those days alone at the house painstakingly constructing a useless and dangerous trail on the side of the cliff.

"He hates me," Ann insisted. "He hoped I'd fall and kill myself. I almost did, twice. If he hadn't caught me, I'd have gone plunging to the bottom."

Elizabeth looked at her. "But he did catch you, didn't he? So he couldn't have meant for you to fall. It doesn't make sense, Ann. I don't know what those steps are all about, but if Quigly wanted you to be killed, it sounds as though it would have been easy enough for him to have let it happen."

For a moment, the logic of this stopped Ann, but then the fear and dislike of her brother returned.

"Don't you see? It was like a warning. He wanted me to

know how easily he could get at me. It was a warning about Tony."

"What about Tony?" Elizabeth asked. "What does all this have to do with him?"

"I keep telling you. Your son is crazy. He thinks I tried to flirt with Tony last night. That sick mind of his imagines that I'm interested in Tony. He actually thinks I'd make a pass at my mother's husband! My God, you can't get more demented than that! Suddenly he admires Tony and thinks he's good for you! He's gotten it into his head that nothing must interfere with your marriage, and he has some wild idea that I'm planning to come between you."

Elizabeth didn't answer. Ann looked at her narrowly.

"It wouldn't be that you believe that, too, would it?"

Elizabeth pulled herself together. "Don't be ridiculous. I was thinking about Quigly. I don't know what to do about him, Ann. I just don't know what's going to happen to him." She tried to smile. "I know you had a schoolgirl crush on Tony once," she said, "but you weren't the only one. Laurel loved him. Only *she* never got over it."

The gentle voice had a reassuring effect on Ann. When she spoke, it was with more control.

"I don't understand any of it. Quigly wasn't even around when I first met Tony. He never even saw him until Charlene's wedding. Why would he think that I'd try to do some terrible thing like this?"

"How can a layman explain a troubled mind like Quigly's? We know he has periods when he's totally out of control, but beyond that I believe he has stored up so much hatred and resentment that he can no longer think straight at any time. He's told me some of the things he feels about you, Ann. He blames you for much of his early unhappiness. He has a warped, distorted backward view. He thinks you manipulated him into distrusting me, which indeed he has for most of his life. Perhaps you've become the only symbol of injustice left. Since he has decided that I do love him and always have, I'm no longer useful as a love-hate object. He has no reason to feel angry at Charlene. And I think he has even realized that Tony's devotion to me is selfless and honest. So maybe you're the only one left for him to suspect and try to frighten."

"It's a nightmare," Ann said. "Maybe I did affect his thinking when we were children. I was a pretty bitter kid myself in those days. But to carry a grudge to this extreme, for all these years!"

"It isn't just you," Elizabeth said. "A lot of other situations and people have been responsible for the end result that is Quigly." She told Ann about the disaster in San Diego and the ill-fated affair with Terry Isherwood. "Nothing has had any reality for Quigly for a long, long time. There's been no permanence, no sense of belonging. And then, of course, he's been drinking heavily for years. To forget all the rest, I suppose. In any case, I'm sure he's more than an alcoholic. If it were only that, there might be hope, through A.A. or psychiatry. But I fear it's too late. I think there's permanent brain damage from liquor. That's why I'm so terribly worried about him. I can't keep him here and I dare not let him go. And something must be decided soon."

Ann looked at her curiously. "This isn't like you. You're not a doctor. You must be very sure of how seriously ill Quigly is if you haven't even had him examined."

"You forget, Ann, that I lived with this kind of erratic behavior once before. I recognize the symptoms. I know that there comes a point of no return."

"Still, it only makes sense to have it confirmed by a doctor," Ann persisted.

"Yes it does. Tony and I have already discussed it. We're going to have a talk with Quigly right after the holidays are over." She got to her feet. "Try to get some rest. Peter and the children should be home soon. We'll make it an early evening tonight, because tomorrow will be a full, long day."

"Where's Quigly?"

"I don't know, dear. Somewhere around, I suppose."

"Keep him away from me, Mother. I'm afraid of him."

"Oh, Ann, please don't let Quigly's ravings disturb you that much. He wouldn't physically hurt you. I'm sure of that."

Ann sank back on the pillows. "You didn't see or hear him this morning," she said. "I'll never be alone with him again, ever. And I want you to promise to keep him away from my children."

Elizabeth sighed. "You'll only make him worse, you know. He likes children. He's very gentle and sweet with them. Wait till you see him with Antoinette. He adores her."

Ann turned her face to the wall again. Of course he does, she said. "Antoinette is Charlene's child."

The memory of this conversation with Ann lay heavily on Elizabeth's mind as she woke the next morning. She had not even told Tony about it. Her unaccustomed reticence came from a strange kind of embarrassment about accusations that even indirectly involved him. She had decided that the rest of the visit would be enough of a strain without Tony feeling self-conscious and uneasy every time he exchanged a pleasant word with his stepdaughter. She closed her eyes and silently prayed. "Let us just get through the next few days," she begged, "and I promise you I'll face whatever has to be done about Quigly, no matter what it is."

Reluctantly, she got up and dressed. By the time she reached the kitchen, only two places at the table were still unoccupied. She kissed Tony and each of the others in turn.

"Where's Ann?"

"My lazy wife is still sleeping," Peter said. "It's such a rare opportunity that I didn't have the heart to disturb her. Most mornings she's up at seven, getting all of us out of the apartment."

"The rare opportunity must be catching," Tony said, looking affectionately at Elizabeth.

She laughed. "Apparently! I can't remember when I slept this late. Everybody get fed? Good. Then out of my way! Charlene and Jim will be here by lunchtime and the office crowd is due at eight. I have a million last-minute chores, so I'd appreciate it if you'd all make yourselves scarce this morning."

"I'll take the kids for a walk down the beach, if they'd like to go," Quigly said.

Elizabeth started so violently that her coffee cup fell out of her hand and crashed to the brick floor.

Tony bent down to pick up the pieces. "You're clumsy, Beautiful," he said. "Good thing it was the breakfast china."

"Well, what about it?" Quigly began to sound surly. Or, Elizabeth thought, am I starting to imagine things?

"The walk?" Peter asked. "Great idea. The kids would love it, wouldn't you, troops?"

Three heads nodded in unison.

"Okay," Quigly said. "Let's go. The stairs to the beach are right out in the back, but you hold on to the bannister, Jo. Those rickety old wooden steps are tricky."

"Why don't you go with them, Peter?" Elizabeth said quickly. "The walk is glorious. And if I know Ann, she may not be up for hours."

"Good idea. Mind if I join you, Quigly?"

Quigly looked at Elizabeth and she thought that a faint trace of suspicion crossed his face. But he shrugged his shoulders indifferently.

"Sure. Glad to have you. You want to come too, Tony?"

"No thanks. I think I'll stick around and get in the way of the hard-working hostess."

"Yeah," Quigly said. "Do that. Princess Ann will need somebody to entertain her when she finally wakes up."

"Now what did that mean?" Tony asked when the group had left. "That was a funny crack about Ann. I hate to say it, honey, but I think Quigly's about to lose his gold star for good behavior. He's been acting stranger than ever since the Richardses arrived. And he's on the booze again. I smelled it this morning."

"So did I, when I kissed him." She nearly told him about her talk with Ann, but something held her back. Instead, she reached up and put her arms around Tony's neck. "I love you," she said.

"Terrific. Let's go back to bed."

"Seriously, Tony, I can't ask you to put up with all this much longer. Quigly, I mean. I must convince him to go to a doctor. If there's nothing wrong with his head, then he must get out and get a job and lead his own life, away from us."

"And if there is something wrong?"

"Then he'll have to be hospitalized. I'll just have to live with it. I can't live with this suspense."

Tony gave her a searching look. "Something happened here yesterday, didn't it? You're holding out on me, Elizabeth. It's not like you. What's going on?"

"Ann and Quigly had an argument. I wasn't there, but Ann really believes that he wants to kill her."

Tony's astonishment was real. "My God! Why?"

For the first and last time in her life, Elizabeth told him a half truth. "It was that old childhood thing again. Plus a few other late developments, like the stupid way she didn't prepare the children for Jim and Antoinette." She said nothing about Quigly's conviction that Ann was still after Tony. "Evidently they got into an enormous row and Ann thinks that he might hurt her or her children. That's why I wanted Peter to go with them this morning."

"Elizabeth, you can't believe that hogwash! I know Quigly's sick, and I also know that he's capable of violence. But I don't believe he'd hurt his sister, and I know damned well that he'd never do anything to innocent children."

"I know it, too," she said. "But I promised Ann I'd never let Quigly be alone with them. This is what I mean, darling. We can't live like this. Not really being sure what my son might do in some unbalanced moment."

"Do you think he really threatened Ann? She's always had a flair for the dramatic."

"I don't know whether he really threatened her or not.

But I do know that there's a possibility that he *could* have. And that's one fact I have to face."

"There's another fact you have to face as well," a voice from the doorway said. Ann stood looking at them. "I couldn't make up such an evil story. I'm not a pathological liar or a psychopath, even if you think I'm an accomplished actress."

"No, my dear, but you are a bit of an eavesdropper," Tony said. "Just how much of this presumably private conversation did you hear?"

"Enough to know that you think I'm not telling the truth, Tony. That's too bad. I'd rather be thought of as a homewrecker than a storyteller."

Tony looked baffled. "A homewrecker?"

Ann seemed almost amused. "I gather you didn't tell him that part of the story, Mother."

Tony looked at Elizabeth. "Will somebody please tell me what this is all about?"

"It's all about nothing," Elizabeth said angrily. "It's so unpleasant and stupid that I didn't think it bore repeating. Ann claims that Quigly thinks she's flirting with you, Tony. More than that, according to her, he believes she's trying to break up our marriage. Now, do you really blame me for not even going into that? Even Ann knows it's insane. She told me so yesterday."

"Of course it's insane," Ann agreed. "Isn't that the whole point? Quigly is mad. And whether or not you believe that I'm telling it exactly as it happened, both of you know that he's unpredictable and dangerous. You have no right to let him wander loose, not knowing what terrible thing he'll do next. You wait. He really will murder somebody one of these days and you'll never forgive yourselves for it!"

"I don't want to talk about it any more," Elizabeth said. "We know what we have to do, Ann. Leave it at that, will you, please?"

Ann subsided. "Where are the kids?"

"Walking on the beach with Quigly *and* Peter," Tony said. "That's a nice guy you have. I'm glad you didn't lose him."

Ann poured herself a cup of coffee. "Lose Peter? No chance. I can't believe the way I panicked a few months ago. It was all a big grandstand play—that business about wanting a divorce. Not that I ever would have given him one. Anyway, all's quiet again. As you can see, Peter is happy as a clam. He thinks he asserted himself and won. That's all he needed. Just one teeny little victory. I don't know why I took it so seriously. He'll never try it again."

Elizabeth busied herself at the sink. "How nice to be so confident," she said wryly. "You're always in complete control, aren't you?"

"Of course, Mother. I learned it from you."

Tony stood up. "What a shame you didn't learn a few other things," he said.

"Such as?"

"Oh, nothing big. Just some unimportant traits like loyalty and tenderness and the ability to make a man feel like a man." He looked at her with pity. "Poor Quigly. He really is in a bad way if he thinks you're sexy. You're not woman enough to break up this marriage or any other." He opened the back door. "Sorry," he said, "that was a low blow, wasn't it? I need some fresh air."

Ann watched him go. She was beet-red. Then she turned furiously to Elizabeth.

"How can you live with a man like that? What incredible gall—Tony Alexander accusing me of not being womanly! Implying I don't know how to satisfy a man! Well, *he* should know. He satisfied Robert Gale long enough! I'm surprised he can do anything for you, Mother. Or does he?"

Elizabeth did not raise her voice, but the look in her eyes was as close to hatred as Ann had ever seen.

"I don't want to believe that I heard what you just said, Ann. You'd better get out of my sight before I forget you're my daughter."

The younger woman backed down. "I'm sorry, Mother. I spoke without thinking. I didn't really mean—"

"Get out!" Suddenly it was a scream.

Frightened, Ann ran from the kitchen. In her room she sank trembling to the bed. Then she got up and began to pack. As soon as Peter and the children get back, we'll leave, she told herself. I won't stay in this house another day. Quigly, Tony, Mother—they're all against me. Maybe we can get an afternoon flight to New York. Peter wouldn't understand this precipitous departure, but it didn't matter. She'd just tell him she wanted to go home. He'd do what she wanted. He always did.

She was throwing their clothes feverishly into the bags when her husband came back from his walk. He stood stock still, not able to comprehend what he saw.

"What the hell are you doing?"

"Peter, I want to leave today. We're going back to New York on the first plane we can get. I won't stay here another minute. Please call the airport while I pack our things and get the children ready. You can order a cab, too."

He was dumbfounded. "Ann, what's this all about? Are you crazy? We can't just pick up and leave like this! What's happened?"

"I don't have time to talk about it, Peter. I'm going home."

"Then you can damned well go alone," he said. "You're behaving like a lunatic! What brought this on? Two hours ago we were all having a quiet breakfast and looking forward to tonight. Then I get back from a little walk and find you acting like a madwoman." He pushed her roughly into a chair. "Now you tell me exactly what happened and then I'll decide whether or not we're going home."

She began to cry. "You don't know what it's been like for me. They all despise me. Quigly tried to kill me yesterday, and Mother can't stand the sight of me, and Tony thinks I'm a cold woman, and Charlene's coming here with her black husband and her half-breed child, and all of you think I've set our children's minds against them. I haven't had a moment's kindness or understanding since I set foot in this house. Nothing but hatred and resentment and even threats against my life." She was weeping bitterly now. "I'm going home, Peter. You can't stop me. I won't stay here another hour!"

He tried to piece together her incoherent rambling, to make some sense out of the hysterical accusations. Gently he lifted her to her feet and put his arms around her.

"Take it easy, darling," he said. "Calm down. Let's take this one step at a time. I don't understand what you're saying. Let's go back over it slowly."

"No! I don't want to go back over it! I want to go home and it's your duty to take me!"

"I will take you if you'll explain to me why I should. So far, all I've heard is a lot of emotional raving about everybody despising you. I can't believe that, Ann. I've got to know why we are running out of here like people whose lives are in danger. This is your family, sweetheart. Not a bunch of evil strangers. Now simmer down and try to tell me everything that's happened."

In her wildly upset state, it was not easy to give him an account which excluded—as she knew it must—all references to herself as a threat to her mother's marriage. Peter would be curious as to why Quigly would think such a thing possible, and Ann did not intend to go into any of her feelings about her mother and her young stepfather. There was a great deal she'd always kept from Peter, including the way she'd felt about her life before she'd met him. She could fall into a trap if she made Tony an important part of her current distress.

Trying to be calm, she gave her husband a carefully edited version of the events of the past two days. She explained the argument with Quigly by saying that he was paranoid and had tried to make her fall down the cliff because he became so angry over his imagined childhood injustices. With that as a base, it was easy to make Elizabeth's hostility seem like a maternal defense of Quigly and Tony's accusations appear to be only a reproach for a lack of love and understanding between one woman and the other. As one lie led easily to the next, she became not only more confident but more relaxed. She almost made herself believe that Tony really had no part in all this, that it was simply the outcropping of old resentments and long hidden jealousies between siblings. By the time she finished, she emerged as the misunderstood older sister, hurt and bewildered by the suddenly exposed hatred of a maladjusted brother who was defended by his doting mother and her fatuous husband.

Peter listened carefully. He had lived with Ann for fourteen years and he knew when she was lying. More than that, he knew that she could perform a kind of self-hypnosis in which she actually believed the fabrications. There was much more to this story than she was telling him, but not enough, he decided, to warrant an awkward, unexpected departure from Elizabeth's house.

When she finished her story she was dry-eyed and composed, but still determined to leave that afternoon.

"So you see, darling," she said, "I just can't take any more. Mother knows that Quigly's gone off the deep end, but she feels obliged to defend him, and Tony has to go along. I don't want to start a new year in this atmosphere. It hurts too much. You do understand, don't you?"

"Yes, I understand, but I think we have an obligation to your mother not to spoil this evening for her and everybody else. We'll leave tomorrow, assuming I can get plane reservations. I'll make up some face-saving lie about having to get back to the office two days earlier than I'd planned. But we can't walk out of here on New Year's Eve, Ann. It would be too obvious. Even the children would know something was wrong. If we leave a couple of days earlier than expected, at least we can put some kind of good face on it."

"I don't know why I should worry about everybody else's feelings. Nobody has worried about mine."

"But you can be bigger than they are," Peter said. "You

can have that satisfaction. Besides, dear, as I said, I think we'd upset the children terribly if we took flight today."

The idea of being more magnanimous than her mother appealed to Ann. And Peter was right about the children. They would be full of questions and uneasiness about this sudden change of plan. She supposed she could stand it for twenty-four hours. Maybe she'd get a little drunk tonight so it wouldn't seem so bad. Ann wasn't much of a drinker, but she'd need something to help her through the rest of this horrible visit.

"All right," she said finally. "But you will call and see what time we can get out tomorrow?"

He nodded. "I'll call. Now you'd better get dressed. Your sister and her family are due any minute and you're still in your robe."

She gave him a provocative look. "Yes, I am." She drew him close to her. "Why don't you lock the door for a little while, darling?"

This astonishing change of mood excited him. Later, Ann lay on her back as Peter rested beside her. So Tony Alexander doesn't think I'm enough of a woman to make a man feel like a man, she thought complacently, listening to her husband's heavy breathing. "He should know what a real woman can be like."

The arrival of Charlene and her little family provided welcome distraction for the group already assembled at the Alexanders'. The exotic quality of their new-found relatives fascinated Peter and his children. Antoinette was every bit as appealing as Elizabeth had told them, and even the dubious Elizabeth Joanne was captivated by this doll-child, taking her off almost immediately to show her the library bed they'd share, as protective as though she were a little mother to the smiling, big-eyed Antoinette.

Jim was an equally big success with the male members of the Richards family. He and Peter liked each other instantly, and the boys, hearing that their new uncle was employed by Douglas, immediately bombarded him with questions about new airplanes, listening raptly as he described the technical operations of the very plane they'd come to California on. Tony and even Quigly joined in this male-oriented discussion, which occupied a good part of the afternoon and lasted through an early, amiable family dinner.

By the time she and Tony went to their room to dress for the party, Elizabeth was almost back to her cheerful self. The immediate rapport between the families of her two girls had come as a relief. There'd been no overt display of awkwardness on either side, and the unnatural politeness of Ann's children that Elizabeth had feared had not materialized. She and her daughters had had a comfortable, easy day together while the men talked aviation and Jo and Antoinette played contentedly. Ann miraculously had acted as though nothing untoward had happened since her arrival. In fact, she was more charming than ever, and Elizabeth saw the familiar "little sister adoration" in Charlene's eyes as Ann chatted amusingly about her new life in New York and exchanged young-mother conversation with an enraptured Charlene, who still looked upon her older sister as some kind of sophisticated, beautiful, remote princess.

"It turned out to be a pleasant day after all," Elizabeth said as she began to run her tub. Tony, who, with a bath towel as a sarong, was shaving in front of the bathroom mirror, turned and grinned at her.

"Never underestimate good basic instincts," he said. "It took Peter and his kids about two minutes flat to forget that their new relatives were anything but nice people."

Elizabeth returned his smile. "Even Ann was on her best behavior. Maybe this whole thing will blow over." She sobered. "But of course it won't," she contradicted herself. "There'll always be Quigly and the things he said to Ann."

"How about the things *I* said to Ann?"

"Darling, you only told the truth. About her loyalty and tenderness, I mean. She doesn't have them. She never has had."

He came toward her. "You really are wonderful," he said. "The ability to be objective about your children is only one of the things that constantly amaze me. Like the way you continue to be so eminently desirable." He let the towel slip to the floor. "And, of course, the way you've planned this house, with a fireplace in our bathroom and a very comfortable and inviting fur rug right in front of it." He touched her breasts gently. "Turn off that goddamn tub, will you? This is the last time I'll be able to make love to you in 1959."

I'll never forget this moment for the rest of my life, Elizabeth thought before the beautiful, heedless, all-enveloping waves of passion drove everything else from her mind.

In their room, Charlene turned eagerly to Jim. "How do you like them?"

"Peter and the kids? Terrific. He's a helluva guy, and the boys are bright, nice youngsters."

"I'm so glad that Jo and Antoinette hit it off well."

Jim looked at her tenderly. "Poor baby, you were really worried, weren't you? Well, so was I. I was afraid there'd be a big strain. It can't be easy coming face to face with an uncle and a cousin who are right out of *Uncle Tom's Cabin.*"

"Idiot!" Charlene laughed. "This is nineteen fifty-nine, not eighteen forty-nine!"

"Don't make jokes, baby. Things haven't changed that much for people like the Richardses. In fact, they haven't changed that much for most people. There's a 'thou shalt not' line called mixed marriage, and even the most rabid self-proclaimed liberals usually aren't willing to step over it. Ann may pretend to have forgiven you for choosing a black husband, but let's face it, inside she's still recoiling. To tell you the truth, I was sure she would have brainwashed those kids into some kind of bend-over-backward niceness to Antoinette and me. Maybe I sold her short. Or maybe her husband and kids are decent in spite of her."

"You don't like Ann, do you?" Charlene asked sadly.

"Sweetheart, when you're my color you learn to trust your gut feeling about people. It's like you know right away how they really feel about you, no matter how hard they try to pretend that there's nothing unusual. I don't dislike Ann. I feel sorry for her. She's the most tied-up-in-knots lady I've ever seen. But I can't really say I feel any affection for her, even if she is your sister."

Charlene was reluctant to accept her husband's calm appraisal. She knew, without ever having had to be told outright, how Ann felt about the marriage to Jim. Long years of silence were more revealing than words. But Charlene continued to love her, to even retain some of the awe she'd always felt in Ann's competent, haughty presence. Her sister has been more outgoing today than Charlene had seen her in a long while, and yet the younger woman sensed an undercurrent in both Ann and Elizabeth. There had been nothing said, not even a hint of trouble between them. If anything, it had been an unusually compatible few hours between lunch and now. And still something was terribly wrong in this house. Charlene shivered suddenly.

"Cold, sweetie? Want me to light one of your mother's famous fireplaces to take the chill off?"

Charlene shook her head. "No, I'm not really cold. It was just something spooky for a second. Like somebody walked over my grave."

Jim laughed. "Good lawd, chile, you talkin' like a superstitious ole mammy! You sure you ain't really black, honey? Maybe just a little bit, somewhere 'way back?"

She smiled at his ridiculous parody. Then with a flash of unaccustomed bawdiness, she put her hands on her slim hips and tilted her head wickedly. "If Ah'm black, Jim Jenkins, you can be sure it's only by injection!"

The two of them roared with laughter.

In their room, Ann heard the gales of mirth from the guest quarters where Charlene and Jim were dressing. She frowned with annoyance. How could they be so absolutely sophomoric? Giggling in their bedroom like a couple of adolescents! The word "bedroom" made her think of the thing that had been troubling her all day.

"Peter," she said without preamble, "I hate the idea of Jo sharing a bed with Antoinette."

He looked at her with annoyance. "For God's sake, what kind of trouble are you going to start now? You know that's all arranged and everybody's pleased with it, including the two kids."

"That doesn't mean I have to like the idea."

"Well, what don't you like about it? Are you afraid that Antoinette's color is going to run off on Jo?"

"I don't exactly adore the idea of my daughter sharing a bed with a half-Negro child."

"That half-Negro child," Peter said pointedly, "is your niece. Added to which, she happens to be one of the cutest little things that ever happened. Jo's crazy about her. I swear you're going to drive me out of my mind, Ann! Now forget it! The arrangements are all set, and you're not about to change them because you don't want your fair-haired daughter sleeping with her cousin."

"It isn't just that," Ann said slowly.

"What else, then?"

"They're way off in the other side of the house. And Quigly will be sleeping near them on the living-room sofa."

Peter looked at her in disbelief. "Oh, no," he said. "You aren't going to tell me that you're afraid Quigly will do some harm to Jo! I think you're sicker than he is! Jesus Christ, Ann, what are you saying? Are you trying to tell me that Quigly would molest his eleven-year-old niece?"

"I don't know what that maniac might do!" Ann almost shouted. "He might kill her. He might do anything to get even with me! I'm her mother. Is it so unnatural that I worry about her safety?"

"And I'm her father," Peter said, "and I tell you that you're getting an obsession about this whole damned thing! I don't want to hear another word about this, Ann, and I'm giving you orders not to open your trap about it to Elizabeth."

She looked at him angrily. "I won't close my eyes all night."

"Big deal. You can sleep all the way back to New York tomorrow."

Her expression changed in a flash. "You got reservations? Thank God! What time do we leave?"

"Two o'clock tomorrow afternoon."

"Have you told Mother and Tony that we're going early?"

"No, my dear, I'll leave it up to you to make the lie convincing. I don't think I could pull it off."

"I know," Ann said thoughtfully. "There's no doubt that they'll be upset."

"Maybe," Peter answered. "But in their shoes I think I might be relieved."

Chapter 34

Later, when she went back over that New Year's Eve, Elizabeth saw it as a series of evolving pictures which began with a still life and grew into a blinding eruption of distorted color, light, and shapes. She continually examined the night through the microscope of her mind, peering at every detail, dissecting the creatures who appeared magnified until they were larger than life.

It had started on a note of affectionate humor. In California style, Elizabeth and Charlene wore long dresses while their husbands acknowledged the specialness of the occasion by putting on dark blazers with colorful scarfs at the throat, rather than affecting their usual jacketless, open-collar-shirt look. Only Peter appeared in a black dinner jacket, looking the very essence of the proper New Yorker. The minute he walked into the living room, he recognized his mistake and was embarrassed.

"See what a provincial I am?" he said self-consciously. "Why didn't one of you guys clue me in on what to wear? I'll go change. It'll just take a second."

"Nonsense," Elizabeth reassured him. "You're beautiful. There's nothing more becoming to a man than black tie."

561

"I feel out of place," Peter said. "Your guests will think I'm a funeral director."

"Don't be silly," Jim said kindly. "You give the joint class! Right, Charlene?"

She nodded. "I love the way you look, Peter. Please don't change. You make it seem more festive."

"Well, okay," he agreed reluctantly. "Since Ann made me drag this damned monkey suit all the way out here, I guess I might as well wear it." He smiled. "Maybe the others will think you've hired a butler, Tony."

"You put the rest of us to shame," Tony said, "but to tell you the truth, Peter, I don't envy you. I spent too many years being strangled by tight collars to ever want to wear one again."

Ann remained silent through this whole exchange. She, too, was overdressed in a long black velvet gown with a deeply plunging neckline, the kind of thing she would have worn to a party on Park Avenue. Damn them, she thought. I hate Californians. They're so relentlessly casual. It's the worst kind of reverse snob appeal. Peter probably thinks I did this on purpose.

Her feeling increased as the other guests arrived. They were dressed like the rest of her family—the women in simple, long dresses or wide-legged patio pajamas, the men in easy jackets and slacks. I don't belong in this world, Ann thought. I don't look like them and I don't think like them. Even Quigly seems more a part of this scene than Peter and I do.

She glanced at her brother, who stood at one side of the room with the children. He'd been drinking quietly and steadily, declining the proffered champagne in favor of scotch and water and confining his conversation to the youngsters, who were being allowed to stay up for the early part of the evening.

At eight-thirty, Charlene announced that it was long past Antoinette's bedtime and prepared to carry her into the library.

"Just let her stay one more minute," Elizabeth begged. "I'd love to have a picture of all the family together. It's our very first reunion." She indicated one of the young men from the office. "George brought his camera. I'll have copies made for all of you."

George posed them all in front of the big living room fireplace while the office crew stood back offering suggestions and lighthearted comments. George squinted carefully through the view-finder.

"I feel like I'm photographing the royal family," he said. "You're a very handsome bunch."

Years later when Elizabeth looked at that portrait, she realized that it was a still life—a moment in time when he had captured the essence of all of them on film. She and Tony were in the center of the group, hands entwined. To her right stood Ann and Peter, rigidly self-conscious in their formal dress. To her left, Jim had his arm around Charlene, who laughed up at him. And next to Charlene, Quigly scowled into the camera. The children were in front of their parents: Ditto and Alan sitting cross-legged on the floor with Jo standing just behind them, Antoinette shyly holding the edge of Jim's jacket as she grinned into the camera.

At that moment, a phrase she'd used before crossed Elizabeth's mind: "The past sits for its portrait." She smiled. So does the present, she'd thought. And the future.

One by one the children were trundled off to bed by their mothers. Only Ditto was allowed to stay until midnight, by which time the party had become hilarious. They danced to Tony's records, drank endless bottles of champagne, and, relaxed, laughed and teased each other, all the while assuring Elizabeth that it was the best New Year's Eve party any of them had ever been to.

On the stroke of twelve, Tony banged a spoon against a glass to quiet them. "To friends and family," he said, raising his glass. "To those we rejoice in today and recall from yesterday. Peace, health, joy, love, and—Happy new year!"

"Happy new year!" they echoed.

Amid the hugging and kissing going on all around them, Tony took Elizabeth in his arms. "My love doesn't go by the pages of the calender," he said. "It will be with you always. Not just this night. Every day, every night. Neither of us can ever be alone again. Happy new year, darling."

"And to you, my dearest," she answered. "The focus of every waking, sleeping, loving moment forever."

Jim suddenly came between them. "Hey, lovebirds, break it up! I want to kiss the greatest mother-in-law in the world!"

They separated and began to circulate then, embracing everyone in the room. When Elizabeth came to Quigly, she took his face in her hands and kissed him gently. "Happy new year, Quigly, dear," she said. "It's a new decade. Almost like a new life."

He returned her kiss with surprising tenderness. "You're one of a kind, Mother. I'm glad you're safe and happy." The sadness in his voice wrenched at Elizabeth, but she smiled confidently. "I am," she said, "and you will be, too."

Charlene came up with joyful kisses for them both, but Ann hung back, almost as though she was reluctant to approach her mother. Elizabeth went to her. "Happy new year, darling. I'm so glad we're together."

Ann's kiss was cool, tentative. "Happy new year, Mother. I hope I haven't spoiled your family party."

Elizabeth looked at her with surprise. Ann was quite drunk. It was a shock. She'd never seen Ann take more than one or two cocktails. But then she realized that she'd not been at a party with Ann since her daughter's wedding reception. Her habits could well have changed in fourteen years. Besides, this was New Year's Eve. She laughed at her own foolish dismay.

"Ann, dear, you'd never spoil a party! You're so beautiful you only add to it! Every man in the room has his eyes on you."

Ann's laugh was harsh. "Every man but one," she said. Quite deliberately she turned her back and walked away. In an instant, almost as though he'd been watching the brief little scene, Peter was at Elizabeth's side.

"Talk to you a minute?"

Stunned and confused by Ann's rudeness, Elizabeth nodded.

"I'm probably picking a lousy moment," Peter said, "but I was wondering whether Ann told you that we're leaving tomorrow."

"Tomorrow? I thought you were staying till the third."

"Ann wants to go back," he said. "I told her she'd have to explain it to you, make up some lie about my having to get to the office, but maybe *in vino veritas*, Elizabeth, I'm a little loaded, but I think you ought to know the truth. Your daughter is an emotional, self-centered, willful lady. If things don't go exactly the way she wants them—which means everybody falling at her feet—she picks up her dolls and dishes and goes home. I guess the reason I'm saying this is because I'm tired of taking the rap for everything Ann does. I like you a lot, mother-in-law, and I'm just drunk enough to want you to know the leaving early isn't my idea." He laughed. "Now what the hell did I prove by telling you that? You'd think I was only trying to widen the gap between you and Ann. Well, maybe I am. Maybe misery loves company."

She took his hand. "It's all right, Peter. I understand. In fact, I've rather been expecting Ann to leave. I'm sure she wouldn't have stayed tonight if you hadn't insisted."

"You know," he said, "it's crazy, but I still love her. I

think she's the most selfish, conniving bitch in the world and I still love her."

"I'm glad," Elizabeth said. "She needs love, Peter." They watched Ann weaving slowly across the room in Tony's direction. When she reached him, they seemed, to Elizabeth's relief, to be having an almost affectionate conversation. Tony was smiling gently. Elizabeth turned away. She was neglecting her guests. Peter went back to the bar. Only Quigly continued to watch Ann. Only Quigly saw her take Tony's arm and walk with him into the deserted kitchen.

Tony had made up his mind to be pleasant to his stepdaughter that evening. He'd been rough on her and he was sorry about it, and when she approached him he was glad of the chance to tell her so.

"Ann, I really want to apologize for flying off the handle this morning," he said, smiling. "I don't often get angry, and when I do I hate myself. Please forgive me."

"It's okay. We're going home tomorrow, Tony. I'd like to talk to you privately for a few minutes. There are a few things I'd feel better about if we got straightened out."

"Sure. Go ahead."

"Not here," she said. "Too damned noisy. Let's go in the kitchen where it's quiet. I can't hear myself think."

She took his arm and walked out of the room with him. In the kitchen Ann went over and stood looking into the low-burning fireplace.

"Mother and her damned fireplaces," she said. "I remember even as a child she had a thing about wood burning. She used to say she could see her whole life in the flames. I think I see mine tonight, Tony. It's not a very pretty picture."

He came up beside her and put his arm lightly across her shoulders. "It's not such a bad life, is it, Ann? You have a good husband and nice children and a very comfortable home. You get everything you want, don't you?"

Without warning, she threw her arms around him and kissed him passionately. "No, I don't get what I want," she said when she tore her mouth from his. "That's what I want, Tony. You. I always have. Quigly may be crazy but he's not wrong about that. I'd take you away in a minute if I could. I've always been in love with you, Tony. I only married Peter because you didn't want me. I couldn't stand watching you with Robert Gale. And I can't stand watching you with Mother!"

He tried to disentangle himself from her arms. "Ann, you

don't know what you're saying! This is all a lot of romantic nonsense and you know it! I've never been in love with you."

"Yes you have," she insisted. "You were. You are now! Oh, Tony, let's go away together. I can make you so happy! I'm young, like you are. I'll show you what love is really like." She held on to him tightly, trying to find his mouth with her own. "Touch me, Tony. Kiss me."

Before he could answer, the figure of Quigly exploded into the room and grabbed savagely at Ann.

"You goddamned dirty whore!" he screamed. "I knew it! I heard you, you slut, every stinking, slimy word!" He grabbed the nearest object at hand, the fireplace poker.

Tony lunged for the poker. "No, Quigly!" He pushed Ann away but Quigly's powerful arm already was descending. All his brute strength went into the smashing fatal blow meant for Ann.

Ann's screams brought the others running. Peter and Jim reached the kitchen together and stood looking in horror at the lifeless figure of Tony half sprawled in the fireplace.

"Keep Elizabeth out!" Jim yelled. But it was too late. She stood in the doorway and she didn't say a word. There was a whirling flash of light before her eyes, an unbearable pressure in her head. And then merciful, releasing blackness as she slumped to the floor.

For ten days she slipped in and out of consciousness, never lingering long enough to acknowledge the impersonal faces of the doctors and nurses who bent over her or to give so much as a sign to the familiar figures who hovered nearby, begging her to return.

She knew dimly that the face she saw most often was Charlene's, a haunted face with lips that moved in a plea for recognition. Sometimes it was Jim's face above her. And once she thought she saw Peter. In these brief moments there was no sign of Ann or Quigly. She did not have strength to wonder where they were. She wanted not to wake again. The oblivion was vast and comforting, like a huge black canvas of eternity in which one small, bright speck of light endlessly circulated.

They tore her back to a life she wanted to leave. One morning she awakened aware that there was sunlight in this strange white room. Charlene stood a little way from her bed, talking in a low voice to a doctor. Neither of them realized that Elizabeth was conscious. She closed her eyes and listened.

"It will be some time before we know how extensive the

damage is," the professional voice said. "A stroke like this could leave her completely or partially paralyzed, Mrs. Jenkins. And then there's the matter of mental function. We can't be sure until Mrs. Alexander regains full consciousness. But in either case you must be prepared for the fact that your mother will need constant care. She could go on for many years, but she will be physically and perhaps mentally impaired, hopefully not both."

Tentatively, Elizabeth tried to move her legs. Nothing happened. She felt no sensation in the lower part of her body. But her hands moved lightly on top of the bedcovers and with effort she turned her head toward her daughter.

"Charlene," she whispered.

The two figures came running. Charlene bent over her, tears brushing Elizabeth's face as she bent to kiss her mother. Charlene was crying for joy.

"Thank God," she said. "Oh, Mother, thank God you know me!"

Elizabeth managed a smile. No words came, but she nodded slightly.

"Can you speak to us, Mrs. Alexander?"

She opened her mouth but no sound came. She struggled to form sentences but they eluded her. She knew what she wanted to say, but maddeningly she did not know how to put the noises together. It was all very bewildering. Exhausted by the effort, she felt herself drifting back toward the undemanding nothingness, but not before she heard the doctor reassuring Charlene.

"It's a good sign," he said comfortingly. "She did speak your name. Right now, she can't manage any continuity of speech, but that usually comes back slowly. Remember, Mrs. Jenkins, she's had a severe shock. She doesn't want to face reality. She's letting nature shield her from a memory she can't handle right now. But in time she'll be fully aware and I believe she'll regain her speech. As soon as we can, we'll start therapy. We'll teach her how to talk again, even if we can never make her walk."

How funny, Elizabeth thought. My life has been nothing but talk. And now I have to learn all over again. Eager to escape, she welcomed the return to the darkness and most of all the reunion with the spot of light which she knew was Tony.

He was a good doctor and he was right. There were weeks in the hospital. Every day brought a little improvement, but each mental step forward exacted its price in awful realization. Almost from the moment she came out of her semi-coma, she had been able to understand what was being said to her, and bit by bit she regained the ability to put together coherent phrases. Charlene seemed to be there every waking moment, smiling and encouraging and ignoring the unspoken questions in Elizabeth's eyes. Jim came often in the evenings, pretending to be indignant that hospital rules forbade visiting privileges to a child as young as Antoinette.

"She's dying to see her grandmamma," he told Elizabeth, "but this stupid hospital has rules about bringing in small children. Anyway, she sent you a present."

He handed Elizabeth a crayon drawing. It was a crude picture of a Christmas tree beside which were five tall stick-legged figures and one much smaller one. Charlene was apprehensive as Jim put the drawing in front of Elizabeth, but he looked at Elizabeth evenly as she studied it.

"It's Antoinette's memory of the most wonderful day of her life," he said. "Those people are you and Tony and Quigly, and Charlene and me. The little one is herself. She remembers how happy Christmas was. We all do, Elizabeth. That's what sustains us, that happy memory and others. That's what will sustain you, dear."

Charlene interrupted nervously. "Jim, I don't know whether Mother's ready to—"

Elizabeth held up her hand. "No. Jim is right." She formed the words slowly. "I am alive. Have good memories. And Tony is not dead."

Charlene took her hand. "Yes he is, darling," she said compassionately, "but he lives in all our memories—yours, ours, even Antoinette's."

Frustrated by the limitations of speech, Elizabeth tried to make them understand. "Tony can't die," she said. "Spark goes on. Energy. Here with me. Always. He promised."

Charlene and Jim looked at each other, unable to grasp her meaning. Elizabeth tried once more.

"Haven't lost Tony," she said. "Out there somewhere. Waiting for me."

"We'll talk more later, darling," Charlene said. "You're tiring yourself."

Elizabeth didn't want them to leave. She held Charlene's hand tightly. Suddenly she spoke clearly. "Where is Tony's body?"

Frightened, Charlene looked at Jim. He nodded.

"She needs to know," he said.

Charlene shook her head. "I can't."

Jim took Elizabeth's other hand. "You remember the big

old pine tree that Tony loved? The one all by itself at the north corner of the house?"

Elizabeth smiled. "His favorite."

"He's there, Elizabeth. His ashes are buried under the tree."

At the word ashes, Elizabeth winced. Then she looked peaceful. "Thank you. Now I have a reason to go home." She closed her eyes.

"We'll see you tomorrow, dear," Charlene said.

Elizabeth gave a little nod. "Tell Toni I love her drawing." She opened her eyes. "May I call her Toni?"

When Charlene came the next afternoon, Elizabeth was sitting in a chair by the window. She'd been getting up regularly for some time, going daily in a wheelchair for speech and physical therapy. But this was the first day Charlene had found her in the armchair. Toni's drawing was propped up on the table beside her and she was smiling. Another woman sat beside her, her back to the door. As Charlene entered, the woman turned and spoke.

"Hello, Charley. It's been a long time."

"Laurel! I can't believe it!" Charlene ran to hug her. "I'm so glad to see you! When did you arrive? How long can you stay?"

"Got in an hour ago," Laurel said. She looked at Elizabeth. "And I came on a one-way ticket."

"You're going to stay in California? But that's wonderful news, isn't it Mother?"

Elizabeth nodded.

"I've made your mother a proposition, Charlene," Laurel said. "I'd like to come back and run the business for her. More than that, I'd like to share the house with her. We've been talking." She laughed, "That is, *I've* been talking and *she's* been listening." Laurel's voice was natural and warm, without the slightest trace of pity. "I've got her this time, Charlene. She can't beat me down with that irritating, logical flow of words that used to knock all my best arguments sky-high! I know this one. She'll soon be vibrating like a harp, but *meantime* I can hog the mike for the first time in our long and checkered friendship!"

Charlene looked at her mother. Elizabeth was enjoying Laurel's nonsense. It was like the answer to a prayer. She and Jim had been worrying about what would happen when Elizabeth got out of the hospital. Only the night before they had concluded that there were only three possible solutions: They would sell the Pasadena house and move in with Elizabeth; or they would encourage Elizabeth to sell her house and take an apartment near them in Pasadena; or she could go into a private nursing home. None of the solutions was ideal. Living up the coast would be difficult for Jim's work and presented some problems for Antoinette, who would go to school in the fall. Elizabeth could not live alone in her house or in an apartment. She would have to have a full-time paid companion, an idea Charlene knew she would hate. As for a nursing home, Charlene rejected the idea out of hand. Elizabeth labeled an invalid was an unthinkable idea; it would be like putting a beautiful, free, wild bird in a cage with a flock of sad old crows and dreary brown wrens. Charlene also knew that it had never occurred to Elizabeth that she might not be able to return to the house on the cliff, and she knew that it might kill her mother if she could not.

Looking at her, unable to walk and barely able to speak, Charlene wanted to cry. Sometimes in these past weeks she'd wished that Elizabeth had not survived the stroke. She supposed it was wicked of her, but Charlene was sure that her mother, who had lived fully and with such gusto, would despise the role of the helpless invalid. In the first ten days Charlene had been convinced that Elizabeth was actually willing herself to die. Without Tony and without her full capacities, what was there for her? She was only fifty-five years old, but what good was life if all there was to it was merely eating and sleeping? Charlene did not wish such a life for Elizabeth. And she knew that Elizabeth did not wish it for herself.

And yet her strong heart refused to stop beating and the sheer strength of will that had carried her through so much tragedy reasserted itself in this latest and most terrible crisis.

Even now, Elizabeth did not know the full extent of the tragedy. It was as though she dared not ask, even when she understood everything that was said to her and could even manage short, intelligible replies. None of them had mentioned Ann or Quigly. Elizabeth must be wondering what had happened to them, but she waited. Prehaps she instinctively sensed that she was not ready to hear. Every day Charlene expected the questions and every day Elizabeth refrained from asking them.

It was curious. More curious, even, than the fact that she did not seem to mourn Tony. The fact that she had quietly accepted his physical death and had seemed somehow comforted by the knowledge of his burial was possible only because she did not accept the total obliteration of the only man she'd ever really loved. Charlene knew, from brief past conversations, that both Elizabeth and Tony believed that a spark of everything that had ever lived continued to be. This was what her mother meant about the "energy." To her, Tony was always a spark of life that stayed nearby. He had promised never to leave her, and he never would.

It was a blessing that Elizabeth had been totally unaware those first few days. There had been an ugly scene with Tony's mother. A screaming, hysterical woman, she was determined to reclaim her son and bury him with all the terrible trappings which went with her middle-class attitude toward death. Tony and Elizabeth would have hated it—the morbid "viewing of the remains," the waxlike figure of Tony in an ornate coffin, the uncontrolled, emotional self-indulgence of three days in which his mother could use him as a helpless symbol of her bereavement.

Tony must have known exactly how it would be. In his desk at home, they found a letter addressed to Elizabeth, giving full instructions for his cremation and burial. There was to be no funeral. Only a few words spoken at home by Jim. Jim and Peter showed the letter to Mrs. Alexander, who shrieked and stormed and finally, knowing she was defeated, gave in. She did not attend the simple memorial service a week later. Only Tony's friends came to sit silently in the living room of his house and listen while his stepdaughter's husband, a young black man who loved him well, spoke quietly and eloquently of "the purest of them all."

Elizabeth was spared the newspaper headlines, too. The killing of the prominent decorator by his stepson was juicy news, and though the family refused all interviews, reporters and photographers swarmed everywhere while researchers dug back into the newspaper morgues to dredge up every scrap of information about Tony Alexander, his wife, and her children. They even managed to make oblique references to Alan Whitman as "the widow's first husband, whose sudden disappearance from a top government post caused speculation in Washington in the thirties."

It was all sordid and disgusting. Ann and Peter stayed in a hotel for a week, sending their children back to New York to be met by Peter's parents. Ann, heavily sedated most of the time, seemed uncomprehending. She moved like a robot, answering the district attorney's questions quietly, refusing to go near the hospital, declining to attend the memorial service. She roused only when Quigly's name was mentioned.

"I hope they send him to the electric chair," she said in the same tone she might have used to dismiss the fate of some unknown kidnaper or rapist.

They arrested Quigly, of course, and on the strength of Ann's testimony they charged him with second-degree murder. His lawyer pleaded innocent by virtue of insanity, and Quigly did not go to jail. A battery of psychiatrists found him incompetent and recommended indefinite institutionalizing. Those who knew the truth knew that the killing of Tony was a senseless accident. But they knew, at the same time, that Quigly would have had to be committed even if this unspeakable tragedy had not happened. In a strange way, Tony's death was his last favor to Elizabeth; he had spared her the horror of being the one to confine Quigly to an asylum for life. She would not have paid that price to be spared, but Charlene almost felt that it was preordained, as though Tony knew that he was going to give his life to protect the remarkable woman who *was* his life.

She said as much to Laurel later, when they were alone.

"Strange you should say that," Laurel answered. There was a sad, faraway look in her eyes. "I agree with you. Not that Tony didn't want to live. He only found himself with Elizabeth. He loved her so much, and he had such a very little time with her. But Tony didn't fear death, Charlene. He once told me that he believed he'd die at forty." She gave a humorless laugh. "I wouldn't be surprised if he thought of the last three years of his life as a wonderful bonus—as though he was living on borrowed time. And he made the most of every minute. So did Elizabeth. I misjudged them terribly, Charlene. Thank God your mother and I had some kind of reconciliation, even if it was a remote one, before all this happened." She looked wistful for a moment. "I only wish I could have seen Tony once more to tell him how sorry I was, but I know that Elizabeth must have shared the last letter I wrote her. She knew I realized how wrong I'd been."

Charlene looked puzzled.

"It's too long a story for now," Laurel said. "Someday I'll tell it to you, complete with all its idiotic details. I let my own ego ruin my life, Charlene, and I very nearly ruined theirs. I hope I can make some of it up to Elizabeth now."

"Is that why you've come back, Laurel? If you're here out of guilt, it's wrong. Mother wouldn't want it that way."

Laurel shook her head. "I have guilt, Charley dear, and I'll always have it, but that's not what brought me back. I loved Tony and I love that lady who's a long way from beaten. She'll find life again. Even her business could go on with the people she has. No, I came back because the time was right. I didn't come as a business manager or a nurse or a companion in the house, though I'll be all of these. She called out to me because I'm her dearest friend, as she is mine. You see, Charlene, I knew she needed me. And that's what I've wanted all my life—to be needed."

Twelve years, Elizabeth thought, as she sat quietly in her chair, letting her mind wander undisciplined through the ugly alleys and beautiful pathways of her life. Twelve years since the warm, loving creature who was Tony went away. Twelve years since she'd lost Quigly forever. Twelve years since she'd known the simple joy of putting one foot in front of the other, a small delight she'd never know again.

She looked at the great rush of surf that boomed endlessly, but never monotonously, on the beach far below. She looked at the great pine, so like all the others and yet so different because it sheltered and protected a handful of precious dust that was nothing more than a symbol. Tony wasn't there. He was beside her, deeper in her mind than his physical presence had ever been in her body. She gave the pine tree a jaunty mock salute and smiled at the ridiculous idea that it nodded back at her.

Twelve was a recurring number, Elizabeth mused. She'd been twelve years older than Tony. She tried to imagine what he'd be like if he lived today. Tony fifty-five? What nonsense! Tony was always young, virile, beautiful. She couldn't imagine him well into middle age, just as she couldn't imagine herself anything but eager, passionate and aflame with the love of life. This seemingly gentle elderly lady knocking on the door of her sixty-eighth year wasn't Elizabeth Quigly. This white-haired uncomplaining person who lived in the big house on the cliff with her dear friend and business manager was someone they'd brought home from a hospital a dozen years before. The real Elizabeth Quigly had died in the kitchen of her house on the first day of 1960. This one was an impostor. Charlene and Jim didn't know it. Ann and Peter didn't know it. Neither did her grandchildren or their children.

Of the living, only Laurel suspected. Because only Laurel had known Elizabeth Quigly the woman. Not the mother or the grandmother or the great-grandmother. Laurel knew Elizabeth as she really was—lusty, laughing, angry, rebellious, interfering, well-meaning, misguided Elizabeth Quigly.

But no one knew her as Tony had. As he still did. She rubbed the two rings on her left hand as though they were a bottle from which some genie would appear and take her into the next life with him. What would it be? Would they go back in time or forward? How did it all work, this transformation of a pinpoint of energy into its next physical manifestation? The little dot danced invitingly, beckoning her to join. It had not left since the day it appeared. It was her private vision. No one knew. Not Laurel, not Charlene. Even they would not understand the dark-blue bee.

They marveled at her serentiy, but she knew they expected it. She was outwardly the woman they had always seen—strong, durable, accepting whatever life brought in the way of pleasure and pain. Pitying her as a prisoner, they did not know that for the first time she was blissfully free. All the conflicts and contradictions of her life were behind her. No more the necessity to mask uncertainty with the pretense of capability. No more need to disguise petty fears, to wear the cloak of independence and invincibility. The body of Elizabeth Quigly was immobile, but her mind and spirit floated into the future, guided by the tiny, unquenchable glimmer of light that promised immortal joy.

All she had to do now was wait, eagerly and expectantly, for the real adventure. She cherished her restlessness, aware that it was something to examine with confident curiosity until the moment of escape. Meanwhile, she knew peace.

It was her private joke and she laughed aloud at the thought of it. She'd fooled them all until this very moment. She received compassion without demand. She accepted it with consideration for those who cared for her in every way.

They saw a patient woman in a wheelchair, taking quiet pleasure in her view. It was a mirage. She was really a young girl on tiptoes. Arms outstretched. Ready to run.

Everything wonderful waited for Elizabeth Quigly.

NEW FROM POPULAR LIBRARY

THE GREAT SHARK HUNT   04596 $3.50
  —Dr. Hunter S. Thompson

NEVER BEEN KISSED   04598 $2.75
  —Allan Prior

LOVERS MEETING   04600 $2.25
  —Mollie Hardwick

THE LAST CALL OF MOURNING   04602 $2.25
  —Charles L. Grant

SAVAGE JOURNEY   04614 $1.95
  —Allan W. Eckert

LONG GONE   04603 $2.25
  —Paul Hemphill

ELVES CHASM   04606 $1.95
  —Diane Stevens

CURRENT BESTSELLERS
from POPULAR LIBRARY